THE
COMPLETE
BOOK OF SWORDS

THE
COMPLETE
BOOK OF SWORDS

Comprising the First, Second and Third Books

Fred Saberhagen

Nelson Doubleday, Inc.
Garden City, New York

THE FIRST BOOK OF SWORDS   Copyright © 1983 by Fred Saberhagen
ISBN 0-8125-5343-8

THE SECOND BOOK OF SWORDS   Copyright © 1983 by Fred Saberhagen
ISBN 0-8125-1934-5

THE THIRD BOOK OF SWORDS   Copyright © 1984 by Fred Saberhagen
ISBN 0-8125-5345-4

3V. Set ISBN 1-56865-009-4

Published by arrangement with
TOR BOOKS
Tom Doherty Associates, Inc.
8–10 West 36th Street
New York, New York 10018

Printed in the United States of America

Contents

THE SONG OF SWORDS

Who holds Coinspinner knows good odds
Whichever move he make
But the Sword of Chance, to please the gods,
Slips from him like a snake.

The Sword of Justice balances the pans
Of right and wrong, and foul and fair.
Eye for an eye, Doomgiver scans
The fate of all folk everywhere.

Dragonslicer, Dragonslicer, how d'you slay?
Reaching for the heart in behind the scales.
Dragonslicer, Dragonslicer, where do you stay?
In the belly of the giant that my blade impales.

Farslayer howls across the world
For thy heart, for thy heart, who hast wronged me!
Vengeance is his who casts the blade
Yet he will in the end no triumph see.

Whose flesh the Sword of Mercy hurts has drawn no breath;
Whose soul it heals has wandered in the night,
Has paid the summing of all debts in death
Has turned to see returning light.

The Mindsword spun in the dawn's gray light
And men and demons knelt down before.
The Mindsword flashed in the midday bright
Gods joined the dance, and the march to war.
It spun in the twilight dim as well
And gods and men marched off to hell.

I shatter Swords and splinter spears;
None stands to Shieldbreaker.
My point's the fount of orphans' tears
My edge the widowmaker.

The Sword of Stealth is given to
One lowly and despised.
Sightblinder's gifts: his eyes are keen
His nature is disguised.

The Tyrant's Blade no blood hath spilled
But doth the spirit carve
Soulcutter hath no body killed
But many left to starve.

The Sword of Siege struck a hammer's blow
With a crash, and a smash, and a tumbled wall.
Stonecutter laid a castle low
With a groan, and a roar, and a tower's fall.

Long roads the Sword of Fury makes
Hard walls it builds around the soft

The fighter who Townsaver takes
Can bid farewell to home and croft.

Who holds Wayfinder finds good roads
Its master's step is brisk.
The Sword of Wisdom lightens loads
But adds unto their risk.

THE
COMPLETE
BOOK OF SWORDS

THE FIRST
BOOK OF SWORDS

PROLOGUE

In what felt to him like the first cold morning of the world, he groped for fire.

It was a high place where he searched, a lifeless, wind-scoured place, a rough, forbidding shelf of black and splintered rock. Snow, driven by squalls of frigid air, streamed across the black rock in white powder, making shifting veils of white over layers of gray ancient ice that was almost as hard as the rock itself. Dawn was in the sky, but still hundreds of kilometers away, as distant as the tiny sawteeth of the horizon to the northwest. The snowfields and icefields along that far edge of the world were beginning to glow with a reflected pink.

Ignoring cold and wind, and mumbling to himself, the searcher paced in widening circles on his high rugged shelf of land. One of his powerful legs was deformed, enough to make him limp. He was searching for warmth, and for the smell of sulphur in the air, for anything that might lead him to the fire he needed. But his sandalled feet were too leathery and unfeeling to feel warmth directly through the rocks, and the wind whipped away the occasional traces of volcanic fumes.

Presently the searcher concentrated his attention on the places where rock protruded through the rough skin of ice. When he found a notable bare spot, he kicked, stamped with his hard heels, at the ice around its rim, watching critically as the ice shattered. Yes, here was a place where the frost was a trifle less hard, the grip of cold just a little weaker. Somewhere down below was warmth. And warmth meant, ultimately, fire.

Looking for a way down to the mountain's heart, the searcher moved in a swift limp around one of its shoulders. He had guessed right; before him now loomed a great crevice, exhaling a faintly sulphurous atmosphere, descending between guardian rocks. He went straight to that hard-lipped mouth, but just as he entered it he paused, looking up at the sky and once more muttering something to himself. The sky, brightening with the impending dawn, was almost entirely clear, flecked in the distance with scattered clouds. At the moment it conveyed no messages.

The searcher plunged down into the crevice, which quickly narrowed to a few meters wide. Grunting, making up new words to groan with as he squeezed through, he steadily descended. He was sure now that the fire he needed was down here, not very far away. When he had gone down only a little way he could already begin to hear the dragon-roar of its voice, as it came scorching up through some natural chimney nearby to ultimately emerge he knew not where. So he continued to work his way toward the sound, moving among a tumble of house-sized boulders that had been thrown here like children's blocks an age ago when some upper cornice of the mountain had collapsed.

At last the searcher found the roaring chimney, and squeezed himself close enough to reach in a hand and sample the feeling of the fire when it came up in its next surge. It was good stuff this flame, with its origin even deeper in the earth than he had hoped. A better fire than he could reasonably have expected to find, even for such fine work as he had now to do.

Having found his fire, he climbed back to the wind-blasted surface and the dawn. At the rear of the high shelf of rock, right against the face of the next ascending cliff, was a place somewhat sheltered from the wind. Here he now decided to put the forge. The chosen site was a recess, almost a cave, a natural grotto set into the cliff that towered tremendously higher yet. Out of this cave and around it, more fissure-chimneys were splintered into the black basalt of the face, chimneys through which nothing now rose but the cold howling wind, drifting a little snow. The searcher's next task was to bring the earthfire here somehow, in a form both physically and magically workable; the work he had to do with the fire meant going deeply into both those aspects of the world. He could see now that he would have to transport and rebuild the fire in earth-grown wood—that would mean another delay, here on the treeless roof of the world. But minor delays were unimportant, compared with the requirement of doing the job right.

From the corner of his eye, as he stood contemplating his selected forge-site, he caught sight of powers that raced airborne across a far corner of the dawn. He turned his head, to see in the distant sky a flickering of colors, lights that were by turns foul and gentle. Probably, he thought to himself, they are only at some sport that has nothing at all to do with me or my work. Yet he remained standing motionless, watching those sky-colors and muttering to himself, until the flying powers were gone, and he was once again utterly and absolutely alone.

Then he clambered down the surface of the barren mountainside, moving methodically, moving swiftly and nimbly despite one twisted leg. He continued going down for almost a thousand meters, to the level where the highest real trees began to grow. Having reached that level he paused briefly, regarding the sky once more, scanning it in search of messages that did not come. Wind, trapped and funneled here between the peaks, blasted his hair and beard that were as thick and wild as fur, whipped at his scorched garments of fur and leather, rattled the dragon-scales he wore as ornaments.

And now, suddenly, names began to come and go in his awareness. It was as if he saw them flickering like those magical powers that flew across the sky. He thought: I am called Vulcan. I am the Smith. And he realized that descending even this moderate distance from the upper heights had caused him to start thinking in human language.

To get the size and quantity of logs he wanted for his fire, he had to go a little farther down the slope. Still the highest human settlements were considerably below him. The maplike spread of farms and villages, the sight of a distant castle on a hill, all registered in his perception, but only as background scenery with no immediate significance. His mind was on the task of gathering logs. Here, where the true forest started, finding logs was not difficult, but they tended to be from twisted trees, awkwardly shaped. It occurred to the Smith that an ax, some kind of chopping tool, would be a handy thing to have for this part of the job; but the only physical tools he had, besides his hands, were those of his true art, and they were all back at the site he'd chosen for his forge. His hands were all he really needed, though, clumsy though they could sometimes be with wood. If a log was too awkward, he simply broke it until it wasn't. At last, with a huge bundle that even his arms could scarcely clasp, he started back up the mountainside. His limp was a little more noticeable now.

During his absence the anvil and all his other ancient metal-working tools had arrived at the forge-site, and were dumped there in glorious disorder. Vulcan put down his firewood, and arranged everything in an orderly array around the exact place where he had decided that the fire should be. When he had finished, the sun was disappearing behind the east face of the mountain that towered above his head.

Pausing briefly to survey what he had done so far, he puffed his breath a little, as if he might be in need of rest. Now, to go down into the earth and bring up fire. He was beginning to wish he had some slaves on hand, helpers to handle some of these time-consuming details. The hour was approaching when he himself would have to concentrate almost entirely upon his real work. He longed to see the metal glowing in the forge, and feel a hammer in his hand.

Instead, gripping one five-meter log under his arm like a long spear, he descended for the second time into the maze of crevices that ran beneath the upper mountain. Through this maze he worked his way back toward the place where fire and thunder rose sporadically through convoluted chimneys. This time he approached the place by a slightly different route, and could see the reflected red glow of earthfire shining from ahead to meet him. That glow when it encountered daylight seemed to wink, as if in astonishment at having found this place of air so different from the lower hell in which it had been born.

At one neck in this crevice the rocks on either side pinched in too much to let pass the Smith and his log together. He set down the log, and laid hands on the rocks and raged at them. This was another kind of work in which his hands were clumsy. Their enormous hairless fingers, like his sandalled feet, were splayed and leathery. His skin was everywhere gray, the color of old smoke from a million forge-fires. Now, with his effort against the rocks, the sandals on his huge feet pressed down on other rocks, dug into pockets of old drifted snow, crunched and shattered ancient ice. Presently the rocks that had narrowed the crevice gave way to the pressure of his hands, splitting and booming and showering fragments.

With a satisfied grunt, Vulcan the Smith took up his log again. One final time he paused, looking up at what could be seen from here of the day's clear sky—only a narrow tracery of blue. Then he went quickly on his way.

When he pushed one end of his log into the roaring chimney, the earthfire caught promptly and deeply in the wood. The log became a blazing torch when the Smith pulled it back from the inferno-fissure and tossed it spinning in the shadowed air. Its rosin popped and snapped with hot, perfumed combustion. Vulcan laughed, pleased with the forge-fire he had caught; then he tucked the log under his arm and quickly climbed again.

He built up his forge-fire quickly on the spot he had prepared for it. Now his anvil, a tabletop of ancient and enchanted iron, had to be positioned levelly and solidly in just the right spot relative to the fire. This took time. As he worked with the anvil, adjusting its position in small increments, the Smith decided that he'd have to make at least one more trip downslope for fuel before he'd be able to start his real work. After he'd begun that in earnest, he'd want no interruptions.

His eye fell on the waiting bellows. The sight made him frown. Yes, it would be very good, perhaps essential, to have some helpers.

The more he thought about it the more obvious it seemed. Yes, human help would be necessary at some stage, given the peculiar nature of this job. He now had earthfire burning in earth-grown wood, with the clean upper air of earth to lend its spirit to the flame. Opposed to this, in a sense, was the unearthly metal that he was going to work. At one side of the grotto, sky-iron waited, a lump of it the size of a barrow. It was so heavy that the Smith grunted when he took it up into his arms to look it over carefully. He could feel the interior energies of it waiting, poised in their crystalline layers, eager to be shaped by his art. He could feel the ethereal, unearthly magic of the stuff—yes, even crude-looking as it was, slagged and pitted on all sides by the soft fist of air that had caught and eased the madness of its fall, slowing the fall until mere crashing instead of vaporization had resulted when the mass struck earthly rock at last. Yes, the metal itself would bring enough, maybe more than enough, of the unearthly to the project.

Human sweat and human pain were going to be indispensible. The catalyst of human fear would help to refine the magic too. And even human joy might be put to use—if the Smith could devise any means by which that rare essence might be extracted.

And when the twelve blades had been forged at last, when he could raise them straight and glowing from the anvil—why, for their quenching, human blood would doubtless be best . . .

The keening pipe-music and the slow drum were borne to Mala's ears by the cool night breeze, well before the few dim lights of Treefall village came into her view between the trees ahead. The sounds of mourning warned her that at least some part of the horrible tale that had reached her at home was probably true. She murmured one more distracted prayer to Ardneh, and once again impatiently lashed with the ends of the reins at the flanks of the old riding-beast she straddled. Her mount was an elderly creature, unused to such harsh treatment, and to long night journeys in general. When it felt the sting of the reins it skipped a step, then slowed down in irritation. Mala in her impatience thought of leaping from its back and running on ahead, groping her own way along the lightless and unpaved road. But already she had almost reached her destination; now she could hear the cackling of the village fowl ahead as they sensed her approach. And now the first lighted windows were coming into view amid the trees.

Presently, on a main street every bit as small and narrow as the only street of her own town, Mala was dismounting under a million stars, whose light made gray and ghostly giants of the Ludus Mountains looming just a few kilometers to the east. Autumn nights in this high country grew cold, and she was wearing a shawl over her regular garb, a workingwoman's homespun trousers and loose blouse.

The music of mourning was coming from a building that had to be the village hall, for it was the largest structure in sight, and one of the few lighted. Mala tied up her animal at a public hitching rack that was already crowded. Moving lightly, though her joints felt stiff from the long ride, she trotted the few steps to the hall. Her hair was long, dark, and curly, the loveliest thing about her physical appearance. Her face was somewhat too broad to be judged beautiful by most people's standards; her body also was broad and strong, vibrant with youth and exercise.

Her quick step carried her onto the shadowed porch of the hall before she realized that a man was standing there already. He was in shadows, not far from the curtained doorway through which candlelight and music came out, along with the murmur of many voices and the soft thump of dancing feet. His bearded face was unfamiliar to Mala, but he had a certain look of importance; he must, she thought, be one of the elders here.

To simply rush past an elder without acknowledging his presence would have been impolite, and Mala halted, one foot in the shadow cast by the rising moon. "Sir, please, can you tell me where Jord the blacksmith is?" Since courtesy required speech of her, she would not waste the words, but instead try to use them to accomplish her urgent search.

The man did not answer her immediately. Instead, he only looked in her direction as if he had not clearly heard, or understood. As he turned his face more fully toward Mala, she saw that he was stunned by some great pain or grief.

She spoke to him again. "I'm looking for Jord, the smith. We were—we are to be married."

Understanding grew in the tormented face. "Jord? He still breathes, child. Not like my son—but both of them are in there."

Mala put aside the curtain of hides that half-closed the doorway, and went through, to enter the most crowded room that she had ever seen in her seventeen years of life. She guessed wildly that forty people, perhaps even more, were gathered here in one place tonight. Yet the hall was big enough for the crowd, even big enough to have at its center a sizable area free of crowding. In that central area stood five rude biers, each covered with black fabric, expensive candles burning at the head and foot of each. On each bier a dead man lay draped with ritual cloths; on several of the bodies the cloths were not enough to hide the marks of violence.

Near the foot of the central bier was a single chair. Jord was sitting in it. Mala's first glance at him made her gasp, confirming as it did another aspect of the evil story that had reached her in her own village: the right arm of her betrothed now ended a few centimeters below the shoulder. The stump was tightly wrapped, in fresh, well-tended bandages, lightly spotted with the bleeding from beneath. Jord's beard-stubbled face was aged and shrunken, making him look in Mala's eyes like his own father. In his light hair there was a gray streak that she had never noticed before. His blue eyes were downcast, staring almost witlessly at the plank floor, and the dancers' feet that trod it slowly a pace or two away from him. The ring of village women who danced so slowly to the dirge went round the biers and chair, their feet hitting the floor softly in time to the drum, slow-beaten back in the rear of the large hall.

And outside the dancing ring, the other mourners—yes, there might really be forty of them—mingled and socialized, wept, joked, chatted, prayed, ate and drank, meditated or wailed in loss just as their spirits moved them, each in his or her own cycle of behavior. There was a priest of Ardneh, recognizable by his white suit, comforting an old woman who shrieked above all other sounds her agony of grief. Most of the crowd looked like folk of this village, as was only natural—the story had said that all the dead men were from here, as was Jord. Mala could recognize some of the faces in the crowd, from her earlier visits here to meet Jord and his kinfolk. But most of the people were unknown to her, and a few of them were dressed outlandishly, as if they might have come from far away.

Still standing near the doorway, looking over shoulders and between shifting bodies, Mala breathed a prayer of thanksgiving to Ardneh for Jord's survival; and yet, even as she prayed, she felt a new pang of inner anguish. The man she was going to marry had been changed, drastically and terribly, before she had ever had the chance to know him in his full health and strength and youth. Then as if trying to reject that thought she tried to step forward, meaning to hurry to Jord at once. But the thick press of bodies held her back.

At this moment she had the impression of an odd, momentary pause in the room—but it must have been only a seeming in her mind, she was not used to crowds, and when she looked at the faces in the crowd around her they were all doing just what they had been doing a moment earlier. But in that moment of pause, the hide curtain draping the doorway behind Mala had been put aside by someone else's hand. Amid the din of music and grief and conversation there was no way she could have heard that soft movement, but she did feel the suddenly augmented breath of the cold wind that at night here slid down from the mountains.

And then in the next moment a man's hand came to rest on Mala's arm—not insinuatingly, not harshly either, but just as if it had a right to be there, like the hand of a father or an uncle. But he was none of those. His face was entirely concealed by a mask, made of what looked like dark, tooled leather. The mask surprised Mala, but only for a moment. A few times in her life before, at wakes and funerals, she had seen men wearing masks. The explanation was that feuds could be exacerbated, friendships and alliances sometimes strained, if a man whose opinion mattered were seen to be mourning openly for the enemy of a friend or ally; while at the same time, some conflicting rule of conduct might require him to do so. A mask allowed its wearer's identity to be ignored by those who did not wish to know it, even if it were not really kept a secret.

The masked man was somewhat on the short side, and well enough dressed in simple clothing. And Mala thought that he was young. "What has happened, Mala?" His voice, close to her ear, was almost a whisper.

He knew her; so he was most likely some distant relative of Jord's. Or, thought Mala, noting the short sword at his belt, he might even be some minor lord or knight, one who had perhaps at some time been served by Jord as smith or armorer.

And the masked man must have come here from some distance, and must have just arrived, not to know already what had happened. In the face of such ignorance Mala stumbled over words, not so much trying to repeat the story as she had heard it as trying to find some reasonable explanation of the horror. But an explanation was hard to find.

She tried: "They . . . all six of them . . . they were called by a god to go up on the mountain. Then . . ."

"Which god's call did they follow?" The quiet voice was not surprised by talk of gods; it wanted to nail down the facts.

One of the men who had been standing in front of Mala, unintentionally blocking her path to Jord, turned round at that. "They answered Vulcan's call. No doubt about it, the god chose them himself. I heard him—so did half the village—more than half. Vulcan himself came down here from the mountain in the night and called the six men out by name. The rest of us just lay low in our beds, I can tell you. Next day, when none of the six had come back yet, we gathered here in the hall and wondered. The women kept egging us on to find out what had happened, and eventually some of us started climbing . . . it wasn't pretty, what we found there, I can tell you."

"And what," the masked man asked, "if they had chosen not to follow Vulcan's call?" The light in the hall was too uncertain, the shadows too heavy, for Mala to be able to tell if his hands looked like those of a worker or of a man highborn. The hair emerging from his jacket's cowl was dark, with a hint of curl, giving no clue about his station. Perhaps it was this very indeterminateness in his appearance that first raised in Mala's mind a suspicion that seemed to come out of nowhere: *I wonder if this could be the Duke himself.* Mala had never actually seen the Duke, but like thousands of his other subjects who had not seen him either she knew, or thought she knew, certain things about him. One of the most intriguing of these things was that he was supposed to go out in disguise from time to time, adventuring and spying among his people. According to other information, he was still a relatively young man; and it was also said that he was physically rather small.

Jord, Mala thought, might have worked for the Duke at one time. Or some of the dead men on the biers might have. That could explain why the Duke had shown up here tonight . . . she told herself that she was making things up, but still . . . there were some stories told about the Duke's cruelty, on occasion, but then, Mala supposed, such stories were told about almost all powerful folk. Even if they were true, she thought, they didn't preclude the possibility that Duke Fraktin might sometimes take a benevolent interest in these poor outlying villages of his domain.

The solid citizen who had turned round to speak was plainly not entertaining any such exalted idea of the masked man's identity. Instead, he was looking him over as if not much impressed with what he saw, small sword or not. The citizen snorted lightly at the masked man's question, and shook his head. "When a god calls, who's going to stop and argue? If you want to know more about it, better ask Jord."

Jord had not noticed Mala yet. The brawny, young-old man with one arm and one bandaged stump still sat on his chair where ritual had placed him, almost as if he were one of the dead himself.

Mala heard the solid citizen saying: "His arm's still up there on the mountain, but he brought his pay for it back with him." Without trying to understand what this might mean, she pushed her way between the intervening bodies and ran to Jord. Inside the slow ring of dancers, Mala went down on one knee before the man she had pledged to marry, clutching at his one hand and at his knees, trying to explain how sorry she was for what had happened to him, and how she had come to him as quickly as she could when the news of the horror reached her.

At first Jord said nothing in return, but only looked at Mala as if from a great distance. Gradually more life returned to his face and in a little while he spoke. Later, Mala was never able to remember exactly what either of them said in this first exchange, but afterwards Jord could weep for his friends' lives and his own loss, and Mala was able to comfort him. Meanwhile the dancing and feverish festivity went on, punctuated only by outbursts of grief. Looking back toward the entrance from her place near the center of the hall, Mala caught one more glimpse, between bodies, of the man in the tooled leather mask.

"All will be well yet, lass," Jord was able to say at last. "Gods, but it's good to have you here to hug!" And as Mala stood beside him he gripped her fiercely around the hips with a huge, one-armed blacksmith's hug. "I'm not yet destroyed. I've been thinking it out. I'll sell the smithy here and buy a mill elsewhere. There's one in Arin I can get . . . if I hire a helper or two, I can run a mill with one hand."

Mala said things expressing agreement, trying to sound encouraging. Closing her eyes, she hoped devoutly that it would be so. She told herself that when Jord healed he'd be a young man again, and he'd regain some part of his old strength. Being wed to a one-armed man would not be so bad if he were still a man of property . . . and now two small children, widower Jord's by his previous marriage, came out of the crowd to lean possessively against their father's legs, and distract Mala from her other cares by staring at her.

The hands of the small boy, Kenn, began to play absently with the rough cloth wrapping a long, thin object that stood leaning against his father's chair. Mala, without really giving it thought, had assumed this object was some kind of aid provided for the crippled man, a crutch or possibly a stretcher. Now that she really looked at the bundle she could see that it was certainly not long enough for either. Nor was there any obvious reason for a crutch or a stretcher to be wrapped up; nor, for that matter, did it appear that Jord would be likely to benefit from either one.

Jord saw what she was looking at. "My pay," he said. Gently he eased his son's small hands from the wrapped thing. "Not yours yet, Kenn. In time, in time. Not yours to have to worry about, Marian." And with a huge finger he brushed his tiny daughter's cheek. Then he grabbed the upper end of the bundle firmly in his large fist, and raised it in the air and shook it, so that the rough wrappings fell free except where his grip had caught them. People on all sides were turning to look. The blade was a full meter long, and straight as an arrow, with lightly fluted sides. Both edges keened down to perfect lines, invisibly sharp.

"What? Who? . . ." Mala could only stumble helplessly.

"Vulcan's own handiwork." Jord's voice was rough and bitter. "This is for me, and for my son after me. This is my pay."

Mala marveled silently. In the version of the story that she had heard in her own village, an obviously incomplete version, there had been nothing about a sword . . . Jord's pay? Even in the comparatively dim candlelight the steel had a polished look. Mala's keen eyes could pick out a fine, faint mottled patterning along the flat of the blade, a pattern that seemed to lead deep into the metal though the surface was flawlessly smooth.

The chain of dancers had slowed almost to a stop. Their faces wore a variety of expressions, but all were turned, like many in the crowd beyond, to look at the blade.

"My pay," said Jord again, in the same harsh voice, that carried through the sudden relative quiet. "So Vulcan told me, when he had taken off my arm." He shook the sword in his inexpert hand. "My arm, for this. So the god said. He called this 'Townsaver.' " The bitterness in Jord's voice was great, but still impersonal, the kind of anger a man might express against a thunderstorm that had destroyed his crops. His hand was beginning to quiver with his weakness now, and he lowered the sword and started trying to wrap it up again, a job in which he needed Mala's help.

"I must get something finer than this cloth to keep it in," he muttered.

Mala still didn't know what to say or think. The sword bewildered her, she couldn't guess what it might mean. Jord's pay, from Vulcan? Pay for what? Why should the god have wanted a man's right arm? And why a sword? What would a blacksmith, or any commoner, have to do with such a weapon?

She would have to discuss it all with Jord later, in detail. Now was not the time or place. Now the dance and the noise around them had picked up again, though at a lesser level of energy.

"Mala?" Jord's voice held a new and different note.

"Yes?"

"The dance will be ending soon. I must stay here, they're going to do some more healing spells and ritual. But maybe you'd better be going along now." Jord was lying back weakly in his chair, letting his eyes close.

Mala understood. When a wake-dance like this one ended, there usually followed a final phase of the evening's community action: those mourners who were free to do so would pair off, man with woman, youth with girl, and go out into the fertile fields around the house or village, there to lie coupled in the soil from which the harvests came. Death would be, if not mocked, in some sense negated by that other power, just as old, of life-creation. Mala was still an unmarried woman, still free, in a strict interpretation of the rules, to join in the night's last ritual. But as her wedding was only two days off, it would be unseemly for her to do so with anyone but her betrothed. And Jord was still oozing blood, barely able to sit up in his chair.

She said: "Yes, I'll be going. Tomorrow, Jord, I'll see you then." Now she would have a long ride back to her own village, or else she would have to try to find some place in this village to stay the night. She didn't feel confident about Jord's kinfolk here, how well they liked her, how welcome she'd be made to feel in their houses. Perhaps, except for the two small children, they didn't even know yet that she'd arrived. In accordance with custom, the marriage had been arranged by family elders on both sides, and there had been no long acquaintance between families.

Mala had liked Jord himself well enough from their first meeting. She had raised no objection when the match was made, and had no real objection to going on with it now; in fact his maiming had roused in her a fiercely increased attachment. But at the same time . . .

The center of the hall, with its burden of dead and wounded, seemed to her to stink of death and suffering and defeat. Mala gripped Jord once more, by his hand and his good shoulder, and turned away from him. Other people who like Mala were unable or unwilling to stay, were also leaving now. She went out through the hide-hung doorway with a small group of these. The group thinned rapidly, and somehow by the time she reached the hitching rack she was alone in the dark street. She took hold of her beast's reins to untie them.

"It is not over," said the calm, soft voice of the masked man, quite near at hand.

Mala turned slowly. There were only the massed stars to see him by, with the moon behind a cloud. He was alone, too, holding one hand outstretched to Mala if she wished to take it. Around them other couples passed in the dark street, moving anonymously out toward the fields.

Almost nine months had passed before Mala saw the dark leather mask and its wearer again, and then only among the other images of a drugged dream. She was traveling with her husband Jord to another funeral (this for a man who'd undoubtedly been her most eminent kinsman, a minor priest in the Blue Temple), and she'd got as far as a large Temple of Ardneh, almost two hundred kilometers from the mill and home, before the first unmistakable labor pains had started.

This being her firstborn, Mala hadn't been able to interpret the advance signs properly. Still, she could hardly have arranged to be in a better location no matter how carefully she'd planned. The Temples of Ardneh were in general the best hospitals available on the entire continent—for most folk they were actually the only ones. Many of Ardneh's priests and priestesses were concerned with healing, accustomed to dealing with childbirth and its complications. They knew drugs, and some healing magic, and in some cases they even had access to certain surviving technology of the Old World, enough of it to make possible the arcane art of effective surgery.

It was near sunset when Mala's labor began in earnest. And at sunset music began to be heard in that Temple, music that as it happened was not greatly different from what had been played at that village funeral eight and a half months earlier. It may have been the similar drumbeat that helped to bring that masked face back in dreams. The drumbeat, and of course Mala's fervent but so far utterly secret suspicion that the father of her firstborn was not Jord but rather that man whose face she'd never seen without its mask. Over the past few months she'd tried to find out what she could about Duke Fraktin, but apart from confirming his reputation for occasional cruelty, for occasional excursions among the common people in disguise, for wealth, and for magical power, she knew very little more now than she had before.

Tonight, lying in an accouchement chamber halfway up the high pyramidal Temple, Mala was questioned, in her lucid intervals between pain and druggings, about her dreams. Jord had been sent dashing out on some make-work errand by the midwife-priestess, who now asked Mala with brisk professional interest—and some evident kindness, too —exactly what she had dreamed about when the last contractions came. The drugs and spells reacted with pain directly, turning it into dreams, some happy and some not.

Mala described the masked man to the priestess as well as she could, his stature, hair, dress, short sword, and mask, all without saying when or where or how she had encountered him in real life. She added: "I think . . . I'm not sure why, but I think it may be Duke Fraktin. He rules all the region where we live." And there was a secret pride in Mala's heart, a pride that perhaps became no longer secret in her voice.

"Ah, I suppose the dream is a good omen, then." But the priestess sounded faintly amused.

"You don't think it was the Duke?" Mala was suddenly anxious.

"You know more about it than I do, dear. It was your dream. It might have been the Emperor, for all I know."

"Oh, no, he didn't look like that. Don't joke." Mala paused there, her drugged mind working slowly. Everyone had heard of the Emperor, in jokes and anecdotes and sayings; Mala had never seen him, to her knowledge, but she knew that he was supposed to wear a clown's mask and not a gentleman's. When the priestess had mentioned that relic-title there had sprung into Mala's mind all of the town-louts, all the loafing practical jokers, that she had ever seen or known in any village. And next she thought of a certain real clown who for years had been appearing at fairs and festivals with a sad, grotesque face painted over his own features. Not that it had ever occurred to her that any of those men might really be the Emperor. In the anecdotes and jokes the Emperor was a very old man who was forever arguing an absurd claim to rule a vast domain, claiming tribute from barons and dukes, grand dukes and tyrants, even kings and queens. In some of the stories the Emperor was fond of pointless riddles. *(And what if they had chosen not to follow Vulcan's call?* echoed here, unpleasantly, in Mala's spinning head.) And in some of the stories he played practical jokes, some of which were appreciated as clever, by those who liked such things. There was also a proverbial sense, in which an illegitimate child of an unknown father, or anyone whose luck had run out, was spoken of as a child of the Emperor.

Mala had never had reason to consider the possibility of a real man still going about in the real world bearing that title, let alone that he might conceivably have . . . no, she was drugged, not thinking clearly. The Duke—or whoever it had been—had been young, and he had certainly not worn the Emperor's clown mask.

Through the hallucinatory haze that washed over her with the beginning of her next contractions, Mala could hear Jord coming back. Maybe, she thought, hopefully now, Jord was after all the baby's father. She couldn't see Jord very clearly, but she could hear him, panting from his quick climb up the many Temple steps, and sounding almost childishly proud of having successfully located whatever it was that the priestess had sent him after. And now Mala could feel his huge hand, holding both of hers, while he started talking worriedly to the priestess about how his first wife had died trying to give birth to their third child. What would Jord think now if he knew that it might have been the Duke . . .

And then the dream, into which this latest set of labor pangs had been transformed, took over firmly. There was a shrill magical chanting in new voices, the voices of invisible beings who were marching round Mala's bed. Jord and the priestess and all other human beings were gone, but Mala had no time to be concerned about that, because there were too many purely delightful things to claim all of her attention, here in the flower garden where she was lying now . . .

The chanting rose, but other voices, in unmusical dispute, were intruding upon it, too loudly for any music to have covered them up. They sounded angry, as if the dispute was starting to get serious . . .

There were flowers heaped and scattered around Mala on all sides, great masses of blooms, including kinds that she had never seen or even imagined before, prodigally disposed. She lay on her back on a—what was it? a bed? a bier? a table?—and around her, beyond the banks of flowers, the gods themselves were furiously debating.

She was able to understand just enough of what they said to grasp the fact that some of the gods and goddesses were angry, unhappy with some of the things that Ardneh had been doing to help her—whatever those things were. From where Mala lay, she could see no more of Ardneh than his head and shoulders, but she could tell from even this partial view that he was bigger than any of the other deities. The face of Ardneh, Demon-Slayer, Hospitaller, bearer of a thousand other names besides, was inhumanly broad and huge, and something about it made Mala think of mill-machinery, the largest and most complex mechanism with which she was at all familiar.

She thought that she could recognize some of the others in the debate also. Notably the Smith, by the great forge-hammer in his hand, and his singed leather clothes, and above all by his twisted leg. For Jord's sake, Mala feared and hated Vulcan. Of course at the moment she was too drugged to feel very much about anyone or anything. And anyway the Smith never bothered to look at her, though he was bitterly opposing Ardneh. The argument between the two factions of the gods went on, but to Mala's perception its details gradually grew even less clear.

And now it seemed to Mala that her babe had already been born, and that he lay before her already cleaned and diapered, his raw belly bound with a proper bandage. Ardneh's faction had prevailed, at least for the time being. The baby's blue eyes were open, his small perfect hands were reaching for Mala's breast. The masked figure of his father stood in the background, and said proudly: "My son, Mark." It was one of the names Mala had discussed with Jord, one that appeared already in both their families.

"When the time comes," said the voice of Ardneh now, blotting out all other sounds (and the tones of this voice reminded Mala somehow of the voice of her dead father), "When the time comes, your first-born son will take the sword. And you must let him go with it where he will."

"His name is Mark," said the figure of the masked man in the dream. "My mark is on him, and he is mine."

And Mala cried aloud, and awoke slowly from her drugged and enchanted dream, to be told that her first-born son was doing just fine.

CHAPTER 1

One day in the middle of his thirteenth summer, Mark came home from a morning's rabbit-hunting with his older brother Kenn to discover that visitors were in their village. To judge from their mounts, the visitors were unlike any that Mark had ever seen before.

Kenn, five years the older of the two, stopped so suddenly in the narrow riverside path that Mark, following lost in thought, almost ran into him. This was just at the place where the path came out of the wild growth on the steep riverbank, and turned into the beginning of the village's single street. From this point it was possible to see the four strange riding-beasts, two of them armored in chainmail like cavalry steeds, the other two caparisoned in rich cloth. All four were hitched to the community rack that stood in front of the house of the chief elder of the village. That hitching rack was still an arrowshot away; the street of Arin-on-Aldan was longer than streets usually were in small villages, because here the town was strung out narrowly along one bank of a river.

"Look," said Mark, unnecessarily.

"I wonder who they are," said Kenn, and caught his lower lip between his teeth. That was a thing he did when he was nervous. Today had not been a good day for Kenn, so far. There were no arrows left in the quiver on his back, and only one middle-sized rabbit in the gamebag at his side. And now, this discovery of highborn visitors. The last time the brothers had come home from hunting to find the mount of an important personage tied up at the elder's rack, it had been Sir Sharfa who was visiting. The knight had come down from the manor to investigate a report that Kenn and Mark had been seen poaching, or trying to poach, in his game preserves. There were treasures living in there, hybrid beasts, meant perhaps as someday presents for the Duke, exotic creatures whose death could well mean death for any commoner who'd killed them. In the end, Sir Sharfa hadn't believed the false, anonymous charges, but it had been a scare.

Mark at twelve was somewhat taller than the average for his age, though as yet he'd attained nothing like Kenn's gangling height. If Mark bore no striking resemblance to Jord, the man he called his father, still there was—to his mother's secret and intense relief—no notable dissimilarity either. Mark's face was still child-round, his body form still childishly indeterminate. His eyes were bluish gray, his hair straight and fair, though it had begun a gradual darkening, into what promised to be dark brown by the time that he was fully grown.

"Not anyone from the manor this time," said Kenn, looking more carefully at the accoutrements of the four animals. Somewhat reassured, he moved forward into the open village street, taking an increasing interest in the novelty.

"Sir Sharfa's elsewhere anyway," put in Mark, tagging along. "They say he's traveling on some business for the Duke." The villagers might not see their manorlord Sir Sharfa more than once or twice a year, or the Duke in a lifetime. But still for the most part they kept up with current events, at least those in which their lives and fortunes were likely to be put at risk.

The first house in the village, here at the western end of the street, was that of Falkener the leather-worker. Falkener had no liking for Jord the miller or any of his family—some old dispute had turned almost into a feud—and Mark suspected him of being the one who'd gone to Sir Sharfa with a false charge of poaching. Falkener was now at work inside his half-open front door, and glanced up as the two boys passed; if he had yet learned anything of what the visitors' presence meant, his expression offered no information on the subject. Mark looked away.

As the boys slowly approached the hitching rack, they came into full view of the Elder Kyril's house. Flanking its front door like a pair of sentries stood two armed men, strangers to the village. The guards, looking back at the young rabbit-hunters, wore wooden expressions, tinged faintly with disdain. They were hard, tough-looking men, both mustached, and with their hair tied up in an alien style. Both wore shirts of light chain mail, and emblems of the Duke's colors of blue and white. The two were very similar, though one was tall and the other short, the skin of one almost tar black and that of the other fair.

As Mark and Kenn were still approaching, the Elder's door opened, and three more men came out, engaged in quiet but urgent talk among themselves. One of the men was Kyril. The two with him were expensively and exotically dressed, and they radiated an importance the like of which Mark in his young life had never seen before.

"Ibn Gauthier." Kenn whispered the name very softly. The two brothers were walking very slowly now, their soft-booted feet dragging in the summer dust as they passed the Elder's house at a distance of some twenty meters. "The Duke's cousin. He's seneschal of the castle, too."

Seneschal was a new word to Mark—he'd never heard it come up in the village current-events gossip—but if Kenn was impressed by it, he was impressed also.

The third man in the little group, a graybeard like the Elder, wore blue robes. "And a wizard," added Kenn, his whisper falling almost to inaudibility.

A real wizard? thought Mark. He wasn't at all sure that Kenn would know a real wizard if he saw one . . . but what actually impressed Mark at the moment was the behavior of the Elder Kyril. The Elder was actually being obsequious to his visitors, acting the same way some poor landless serf might when brought in to stand before the Elder. Mark had never seen the old man behave in such a way before. Even during Sir Sharfa's periodic visits, the knight, who was actually the master, always spoke to the old man with respect, and listened to him carefully whenever village affairs were under discussion. Today's visitors were listening carefully too—Mark could see that though he couldn't hear what was being said—but gave no evidence that they regarded the Elder with respect.

The Elder's eye now happened to fall upon the two boys who were gaping their slow way past his house. He frowned abruptly, and called to Kenn by name, at the same time beckoning him with a brisk little wave; it was a more agitated motion than Mark could remember ever seeing the Elder make before.

When Kenn stood close before him, gaping in wonder, Kyril ordered: "Go, and take down that sword that hangs always on your father's wall, and bring it directly here." When Kenn, still goggling, hesitated momentarily, the old man snapped: "Go! Our visitors are waiting."

To such a command, there could be only one possible response from any village youth. Kenn at once went pelting away down the long village street toward the millhouse at its far end. His legs, long and fast if lacking grace, were a blur of awkward angularity. Mark, poised to run after him, held back, knowing from experience that he wouldn't be able to keep up. And Mark also wanted to stay here, watching, to see what was going to happen next; and, now that he thought about it, he didn't want to have any part in simply taking down the sword, without his father's permission, from where it had always hung . . .

The three men of importance waited, gazing after Kenn, ignoring Mark who still stood twenty meters off and watched them. The blue-robed wizard—if wizard he truly was—fidgeted, glanced once toward Mark with a slight frown, and then away.

Kyril said, in a voice a little louder than before: "It will be quicker this way, Your Honor, than if we were all to go to the mill-house." And he made a humble, nervous little bow to the one Kenn had whispered was the Duke's cousin. It was a stiff motion, one to which the Elder's joints could hardly have been accustomed.

Now Mark began to notice that a few other villagers, Falkener among them, had started coming out of their houses here and there. There was a converging movement, very slight as yet, toward the Elder's house. They all wanted to know what was going on, but still were not quite willing to establish their presence in the street.

The man addressed by Kyril, whoever he might really be, ignored them as he might have sparrows. He stood posing in a way that suggested he was willing to wait a little, willing to be shown that the Elder's way was really the quickest and most satisfactory. He asked Kyril: "You say that this man who has the sword now came here thirteen years ago. Where did he come from?"

"Oh yes, that's right, Your Honor. Thirteen years. It was then that he bought the mill. I'm sure he had permission, all in order, for the move. He brought children with him, and a new bride, and he came from a village up toward the mountains." Kyril pointed to the east. "Yes sir, from up there."

The seneschal, who was about to ask another question, paused. For Kenn was coming back already. He was carrying the sword in its usual corded wrapping, in which it usually hung on the wall of the main living room inside the house. Kenn was walking now, not running. And he was not coming back alone. Jord, his solid frame taller still than that of his slim-bodied elder son, strode with him. Jord's legs kept up in a firm pace with the youth's nervous half-trot.

Jord's work clothes were dusty, as they so often were from his usual routine of maintenance on the huge wooden gears and shafts that formed the central machinery of the mill. He glanced once at Mark—Mark could read no particular message in the look—and then concentrated his attention on the important visitors. Jord seemed reluctant to approach them, but still he came on with determination. At the last moment he put his big hand on Kenn's shoulder and thrust the youth gently into the background, stepping forward to face the important men himself.

Jord bowed to the visitors, as courtesy required. But still it was to Kyril the Elder that he first spoke. "Where's Sir Sharfa? It's to him that we in the village must answer, for whatever we do when other highborn folk come here and—"

He who had been called the seneschal interrupted, effectively though with perfect calm. "Sir Sharfa's not available just now, fellow. Your loyalty to your manorlord is commendable, but in this case misplaced. Sir Sharfa is vassal, as you ought to know, to my cousin the Duke. And it's Duke Fraktin who wants to see the sword that you've kept hanging on the wall."

Jord did not appear tremendously surprised to hear of the Duke's interest. "I have been told, Your Honor, to keep that sword with me. Until the time comes for it to be passed on to my eldest son."

"Oh? Told? And who told you that?"

"Vulcan, Your Honor." The words were plainly and boldly spoken. Jord's calm assurance matched that of the man who was interrogating him.

The seneschal paused; whatever words he'd been intending to fire off next were never said. Still he was not going to let himself appear to be impressed by any answer that a mere miller could return to him. Now Ibn Gauthier extended one arm, hand open, rich sleeve hanging deeply, toward Kenn. The youth was still standing in the background where his father had steered him, and was still holding the wrapped blade.

The seneschal said to him: "We'll see it now."

Kenn glanced nervously toward his father. Jord must have signalled him to obey, for the lad tugged at the wrapping of the sword—a neatly woven but undistinguished blanket—as if he intended to display the treasure to the visitors from a safe distance.

The covering of the sword fell free.

The seneschal stared for a moment, then snapped his fingers. "Give it here!"

What happened in the next moment would recur in Mark's dreams throughout the remainder of his life. And each time the dream came he would experience again this last moment of his childhood, a moment in which he thought: Strange, whatever can be making a sound in the air like flying arrows?

The Elder Kyril went down at once, with the feathered end of a long shaft protruding from his chest. At the same time one of the armed guards fell, arrows in his back and ribs, his sword only a glint of steel half-drawn from its scabbard. The second guard was hit in the thigh; he got his spear raised but could do no more. The wizard went down an instant later, with his blue robes collapsing around him like an unstrung tent. The seneschal, uninjured, whirled around, drawing his own short sword and getting his back against a wall. His face had gone a pasty white.

The volley of arrows had come from Mark's right, the direction where trees and bush grew close and thick along the near bank of the Aldan. The ambushers, whoever they were, had been able to get within easy bowshot without being detected. But they were charging out of cover now, running between and around the houses closest to the river-bank. A half-dozen howling, weapon-waving men were rushing hard toward the Elder's front yard, where the victims of their volley had just fallen. Two large warbeasts sprang out of concealment just after the attacking men, but bounded easily ahead of them. One beast was orange-furred and one brindled, and both of their bodies, like those of fighting men, were partially clothed in mail. They were nearly as graceful as the cats from which half their ancestry derived.

Mark had never seen real warbeasts before, but he recognized them at once, from the descriptions in a hundred stories. He saw his father knocked down by the orange beast in its terrible passage, before Jord had had time to do more than turn toward his elder son as if to cry an order or a warning.

The seneschal was the beasts' real target, and they leaped at him, though not to kill; they must have been well trained for this action.

They forced the Duke's cousin back against the front of fallen Kyril's house, not touching but confronting him, snarling and sparring just outside the tentative arc of his swordarm. When he would have run to reach his tethered riding-beast, they forced him back again. Now all four of the tethered animals at the rack were kicking and bucking, screaming their fear and excitement in their near-human voices.

Kenn, in the first instant of the attack, had turned to run. Then he had seen his father fall, and had turned back. White-faced, he stood over his father now, clumsily holding the unwrapped sword, with the blade above the fallen man as if it could be made into a shield.

Mark, who had run two steps toward home, looked back at his father and his brother and stopped. Now with shaking fingers Mark was pulling the next-to-last small hunting arrow from the quiver on his back. His rabbit-hunting bow was in his left hand. His mind felt totally blank. He comprehended without emotion that a man, the soldier who'd fallen with an arrow in his leg, was being stabbed to death before his eyes. Now the charging men, bandits or whatever they were, had joined their warbeasts in a semicircle round the beleaguered seneschal, and were calling on him to throw down his sword and surrender.

But one of the attackers' number had turned aside from this important business, and was about to deal with the yokel who still stood holding a sword. The bandit grinned, probably at the inept way in which Kenn's hands gripped the weapon; still grinning, he stepped forward with his short spear ready for a thrust.

At that point Mark's shaking fingers fumbled away the arrow that he had just nocked. He knelt, in an uncontrolled movement that was almost a collapse, and with his right hand groped in the dust of the road for the arrow. He was unable to take his eyes from what was about to happen to his brother—

A moaning had for some moments been growing in the air, the sound of some voice that was not human, perhaps not even alive. The sound rose, quickly, into a querulous, unbreathing shriek.

It issued, Mark realized, from the sword held in his brother's hands. And a visual phenomenon had grown in the air around the sword. It was not exactly as if the blade were smoking, but rather as if the air around it had begun to burn, and the steel was drawing threads of smoke out of the air into itself.

The spearthrust came. The sound in the air abruptly swelled as the spear entered the swifter blur made by the sideways parry of the sword. Mark saw the spearhead spinning in midair, along with a handsbreadth of cleanly severed shaft. And before the spearhead fell, Townsaver's backhanded passage from the parry had torn loose the chainmail from the spearman's chest, bursting fine steel links into the air like a handful of summer flowers' fluff. The same sweep of the swordpoint caught the small shield strapped to the man's left arm, and with a bonebreak snap dragged him crying into the air behind its arc. His body was dropped rolling in the dust.

Now Mark's groping fingers found his dropped arrow, and he rose with it in his hand. He could feel his own body moving with what seemed to him terrible slowness.

Townsaver had come smoothly back to guard position, the sound that issued from it subsiding to a mere purring drone. Kenn's face was anguished, his eyes were fixed in astonishment on the blade that grew out of his hands, as if it were something that he had never seen before. There was a vibration in his arms, as if he were holding something that he could not control, but could not or dared not drop.

One of the invaders, who must have been the warbeasts' master, aimed a gesture toward Kenn. Obediently the orange-furred beast turned and sprang. At that moment Mark loosed his arrow. Mark had not yet learned to reckon with the animals' speed, and the streaking furry form was out of the arrow's path before the small missile arrived. As if guided by some profound curse, Mark's arrow flew straight on between two bandits' backs, to strike the embattled seneschal squarely in the throat. Without even a cry, the Duke's cousin let go of his sword and fell.

The sword in Kenn's hands screamed, almost the way a fast-geared millsaw screamed sometimes when biting a tough log. Again it drew its smoking arc, to meet the leaping animal. One orange-furred paw leapt severed in midair, with a fine spray of blood. The same stroke caught the beast's armored torso, heavier than a man's. It went down, as Mark had seen a rabbit fall when hit in mid-leap by a slinger's stone. Mark was fumbling for his last arrow as the furred body rolled on its back with legs in the air, claws in reflex convulsions taloning the air above its belly.

Now three men had Kenn surrounded. Mark, with his last arrow nocked, was at the last moment afraid to shoot at any of them for fear of hitting his brother in their midst. He saw blades flash toward his brother, but Kenn did not fall. Kenn's eyes were still wide with bewilderment, his face a study of fear and horror. Townsaver sang vicious circles in the air around him, smashing aside brandished weapons right and left. The sword seemed to twist Kenn's body after it, so that he had to leap, turning in midair, coming down with feet planted in the reverse direction. The sword pulled him forward, dragging him in wide-stanced, stiff-legged strides to the attack.

The sound of its screaming went up and up.

The swordplay was much too fast for Mark to follow. He saw another of the attacking men go staggering backward from the fight, the man's feet moving in a reflex effort to regain balance until his back struck a house wall and he pitched forward and lay still. Mark heard yet another man cry out, a gurgling yell for help and mercy. Mark did not see the brindled warbeast leap at Kenn, but saw the beast go running back toward the riverbank, in a limping but still terribly fast flight. It howled the agony of its wounds, even above the fretful millsaw shrieking of the sword. And now two of the invading men, weaponless, were also running away, leaving the village on divergent paths. Mark got a close look at the face of one of them, and saw wide eyes, wide mouth, an expression intent on flight as on a problem.

The other invaders were all lying in the street. Four, five—it seemed impossible to count exactly.

Mark looked up and down the street, to west and east. Only himself and his brother were still standing.

A little summer dust hung in the air, played by a quiet breeze. For a long moment, nothing else moved. Then Kenn's quivering arms began to droop, lowering the sword. The machine-whine that still proceeded from the red blade trailed slowly down into silence. And now the atmosphere around the sword no longer smoked.

The swordpoint sagged to the ground. A moment later, the whole weapon fell inertly from Kenn's relaxing fingers. Another moment, and Kenn sat down in the dust. Mark could see, now, how his brother's blood was soaking out into his homespun shirt.

Mechanically replacing his last arrow, unused, in his quiver, Mark hurried forward to his brother. Beyond Kenn, Jord still lay in gory stillness; his head looked badly ruined by the passing blow from a warbeast's paw; Mark did not want to comprehend just what he was seeing there.

Farther in the background, the blue-robed wizard was raising himself, apparently unhurt. In each hand the wizard held a small object, things of magic doubtless. His hands moved round his body, wiping at the air.

Mark crouched beside his brother and held him, not knowing what else to do. He watched helplessly as the blood welled out from under Kenn's slashed clothing. The attackers' swords had reached him after all, and more than once. Kenn's hunting shirt was ghastly now.

"Mark." Kenn's voice was lost, soft, frightened, and frightening too. "I'm hurt."

"Father!" Mark cried, calling for help. It seemed to him impossible that his father would not react, leap up, give him aid, tell him what to do. Maybe he, Mark, should run home, get help from his mother and his sister. But he couldn't just let go of Kenn, whose hand was trying to grip Mark's arm.

In front of Kenn, almost within touching distance, a dead bandit crouched as if in obeisance to his superior foe. Townsaver had taken a part of the bandit's face away, and his hands and his weapons were piled together before him like an offering. It did no good to look away. There was something very similar to be seen in every direction.

The sword itself lay in the street, looking no more dangerous now than a pruning hook, with dust blandly blotting the wet redness all along the blade.

Mark let out an inarticulate cry for help, from anyone, anywhere. He could feel Kenn's life departing, running out almost like water between his fingers.

Women were crying, somewhere in the distance.

Someone, walking slowly, came into Mark's view a little way ahead of him. It was Falkener. "You shot the seneschal," the leather-worker said. "I saw you."

"What?" For a moment Mark could not understand what the man was saying. And now the wizard, who had been bending over the body of Ibn Gauthier, came doddering, as if in fear or weakness (though graybeard, he did not look particularly old) to where Mark was. The small objects he had been handling, whatever they were, had now been put away. With what appeared to Mark to be unnatural calm, he rested a hand on Jord's bloody head and muttered something, then reached to do the same for Elder Kyril and for Kenn. His manner was quite impersonal.

The women's crying voices were now speeding closer, with the sound of their running feet. Mark had not known that his mother could still run so fast. Mala and Marian, both of them dusty with mill-work, threw themselves upon him, hovered over their fallen men, began to examine the terrible damage.

"You shot the seneschal," said Falkener to Mark again.

This time, the hovering wizard took note of the accusation. With an oath, he grabbed the last arrow from Mark's quiver and strode away, to compare it with the shaft that still protruded from the throat of the Duke's cousin.

Other villagers were now appearing in the street, to gather around the fallen. They came out of their houses singly at first, then in twos and threes. Some, with field implements in hand, must have come running in from work nearby. The Elder was dead, the village leaderless. An uproar grew, confusion mounted. There was talk of dashing off to the manor with word of the attack, but no one actually went yet. There was more talk of organizing a militia pursuit of the attackers, whoever they had been, wherever they had gone. Wild talk of war, of raids, of uprisings, flew back and forth.

"Yes, they were trying to kidnap the seneschal. I saw them. I heard them."

"Who? Kidnap who?"

"Kyril's dead too. And Jord."

"But it was the boy's arrow that struck him down."

"Who, his own father? Nonsense!"

". . . no . . ."

". . . all wrong, havoc like this, must have been cavalry . . ."

". . . no doubt that it's his arrow, I've found them on my land, near my woolbeasts . . ."

Mala and Marian had by now stripped off Kenn's shirt and were trying to bind up his wounds. It looked a hopeless task. Kenn's eyes were almost closed, only white slits of eyeball showing. Mala went to Jord's inert form, and with tears streaming from her eyes tried to get her husband to react, to wake up to what was happening around him. "Husband, your oldest son is dying. Husband, wake up . . . Jord . . . ah, Ardneh! Not you too?"

A neighbor woman hovered over Mala, trying to help. Together they put a rolled blanket under Jord's head, as if that might be of benefit.

Mark turned from them, and sat staring at the sword. Something less terrible to look at. It was as if thoughts were coming and going in his head continually, but he could not grasp any of them. Only look at the sword. Only look—

He became aware that his mother was gripping his arm fiercely, shaking him out of his state of shock. In a voice that was low but had a terrible power she was urging him: "Son, listen to me. You must run away. Run fast and far, and don't tell me, don't tell anyone, where you're going. Stay out of sight, tell no one your name, and listen for word of what's happening here in Arin. Don't think about coming home until you know it's safe. That's your arrow in the Duke's cousin's throat, however it got there. If the Duke should get his hands on you, he could have your eyes put out, or worse."

"But . . ." Mark's mind wanted to protest, to scream that none of this could be happening, that the world was not this mad. His body, perhaps, knew better, for he was already standing. His mother's dark eyes probed him. His sister Marian looked up at him from where she still crouched with Kenn's lifeless head cradled in her lap, her blue horrified eyes framed in her loose fair hair. All around, villagers were arguing, quarreling, in greater confusion than ever. Falkener's hoarse voice came and went, and the wizard's unfamiliar one.

Impelled by a sudden sense of urgency, Mark moved swiftly. As if he were watching his own movements from outside his body, he saw himself bend and gather up the sword's wrapping from where Kenn had thrown it down. He threw the blanket over the sword and gathered the blade up into it.

Of all the people in the street, only his mother and his sister seemed to be aware of what he was doing. Mala, weeping, nodded her approval. Marian whispered to him: "Walk as far as our house, then run. Go, we'll be all right!"

Mark muttered something to them both, he never could remember what, and started walking. He knew, everyone in the village knew, what Duke Fraktin had done in the past to men who'd been so unlucky as to injure any of his kinfolk, even by accident. Mark continued to move pace after pace along the once-familiar village street, the street that now could never be the same again, carrying what he hoped was an inconspicuous bundle. He walked without looking back. For whatever reason, there was no outcry after him.

When he reached the millhouse, instead of starting to run he turned inside. The practical thought had occurred to him that if he ran away for very long he was going to need some food. In the pantry he picked up a little dried meat, dried fruit, and a small loaf, unconsciously emptying his game bag of the morning's kill of rabbits in exchange. From near his bed he grabbed up also the few spare arrows that were his. Somehow, he'd remembered, out in the street, to sling his bow across his back again.

A few moments after he had entered the millhouse, Mark was leaving it again, this time by the back door. This was on the eastern, upstream side of the building, and now the mill was between him and the village street. From this point a path climbed the artificial bank beside the millwheel, which was now standing idle, and then followed the wooded riverbank out of town. Mark met no one on the first few meters of this path. If earlier there had been people fishing here, or village children playing along the stream, the excitement in the street had already drawn them away.

Now Mark did begin to run. But as soon as he started running, he could feel fear growing in him, an imagined certainty of pursuit, and to conquer it he had to slow down to a walk again. When he walked, listening carefully, he could hear no sounds of pursuit, no outcry coming after him.

He had followed the familiar path upstream for half a kilometer when he came upon the dead body of the brindled warbeast. It had plainly been trying to crawl into a thicket when it died, caught and held by the ragged fringes of its hacked chainmail snagged on twigs. Mark paused, staring blankly. The animal was a female . . . or had been, before the fight. Now . . . how had the creature managed to get this far? It looked like an example of the vengeance of a god.

CHAPTER 2

From the place where he had come upon the dead warbeast, Mark walked steadily upstream. He traveled the riverbank in that direction for another hour, still without meeting anyone. By that time he was feeling acutely conscious of the blood dried on his clothing and his hands, and he stopped, long enough to wash himself, his garments, and at last the sword as clean as possible. The washing had limited success, for by now spots of his brother's blood had dried into his shirt, and there was no getting them out by simply rubbing at them and rinsing them with water. The sword in contrast rinsed clean at once, dirt and gore sluicing from it easily, leaving the smooth steel gleaming as if it had never been used. Nor, despite all the shredded chainmail and the cloven shields, were its edges nicked or dulled.

Yes, Mark had known all his life that the sword called Townsaver was the work of Vulcan himself. He'd known that fact, but was only now starting to grasp something of its full meaning. But maybe the sword would rust . . .

Dressed again, in wet clothes, Mark hurried on. He had made no conscious decision about where he was going. The path was so familiar that his feet bore him along it automatically. He kept putting more distance between himself and his home without having to plan a route. From hunting and fishing trips he knew the way so well here that he thought he'd be able to keep on going confidently even after dark. At intervals he waded into the shallow stream, crossing and recrossing it, sometimes trudging in the water for long stretches. If the Duke's men were going to come after him with keen-nosed tracking beasts, it might help . . .

He feared pursuit, and listened for it constantly. But when he tried to picture in his mind exactly what form it would take, it looked in his imagination rather like the militia that Kenn had had to join and drill with periodically. That was not a very terrifying picture. But of course the pursuit wouldn't really be like that. It might include tracking beasts, and aerial scouts, and cavalry, and warbeasts too . . . again Mark saw, with the vividness of recent memory, the mangled body of the catlike creature that had tried like some hurt pet to crawl away and hide . . .

His thoughts never could get far from the burden that he was carrying, the awkward bundle tucked at this moment under his right arm, wrapped up in a blanket newly stained. Townsaver, let the gods name it whatever they liked, hadn't really saved the town at all. Because it was not the town that the intruders had been trying to attack. They had been after the eminent visitor, and nothing else. (And here Mark wondered again just what a *seneschal* might be.)

Mark supposed that the intruders had been bandits, planning a kidnapping for ransom—everyone knew that such things happened to the wealthy from time to time. Of course as a rule they didn't happen to members of the Duke's family. But perhaps the bandits hadn't known just who their intended victim was, they'd seen only that he must be rich.

And the victim had come to the village in the first place only because of the sword itself; that was what he had wanted to see and hold, what he would probably have taken away with him if he could. If only he had . . .

The killing of Jord and of Kyril had probably been completely accidental, just because they'd been standing in the bandits' way. And the bandits had attacked Kenn only because he was holding the sword, and had gone on holding it. Mark, struggling now against tears, recalled how his brother had looked like he wanted to throw the weapon down, and couldn't. The sword had taken over, and once that happened there had been nothing that Kenn could do about it.

So, if the sword hadn't entered into it, Mark's brother and father would both be still alive. And the Elder Kyril too. And probably even the Duke's cousin would be alive and well cared for in his abductors' hands, to be sent home as soon as a ransom was paid—or, perhaps more likely, released with abject apologies as soon as the kidnappers found out who he was. Yes, the sword had destroyed warbeasts and bandits. But it had also brought ruin upon the very town and people that its name suggested it might have saved . . .

On top of all the other deeper and more terrible problems that it caused, it was also a damned awkward thing to carry. And the more time that Mark spent carrying it, the more maddening this comparatively minor difficulty became. He continually tried to find a safe and comfortable way to hold the thing while he walked with it. In a way his mind welcomed this challenge, as an escape from the consideration of difficulties infinitely worse.

After he washed the sword he tried for a little while carrying it unwrapped, but that quickly became uncomfortable too. The only halfway reasonable way to carry a naked sword, particularly one as keen-edged as this, was in hand, as if you were ready to fight with it. Mark wasn't ready to fight, and didn't want to pretend he was. More importantly, the weight borne that way soon made his wrist and fingers ache.

Careful testing assured him that the edges were still sharper than those of any other blade, knife or razor that he'd ever held; if he were to try to carry this weapon stuck through his belt, his pants would soon be down around his ankles. And, to Mark's vague, unreasonable disappointment, it was soon obvious that the sword was not going to rust because of its immersion in the river. The brilliant steel dried quickly, and in fact to Mark's fingertip felt very slightly oily. With a mixture of despair and admiration he stared at the finely mottled pattern that seemed to lead on deeper and deeper into the metal, under the shiny surface smoothness.

Before he'd walked very far after the washing, he had paused to rewrap the sword in the still-wet cloth, and tied it up again, leaving a loop of cord for a carrying handle. Mark slogged on, shifting his burden this way and that. If he hung it from one hand, it banged against his legs; if he put it over one shoulder like a shovel, he could feel it threatening to cut him, right through its wrapping and his shirt. Of course, with the sword tied up like this, he wouldn't be able to use it quickly if he had to. That really didn't bother Mark. He didn't want to try to use it anyway.

Mark kept fighting against the memory of how Kenn had used the sword—or how it had used Kenn, who was as innocent as Mark of any training with such a weapon. In the militia exercises, Kenn had always practiced with the lowly infantry weapon, a cheap spear. Swords of even the most ordinary kind, let alone a miraculous blade like this one, were for the folk who lived in manorhouse and castle.

And yet . . . this one had certainly been given to Mark's father. Given deliberately, by a being who was surely of higher rank than any merely human lord.

Gods and goddesses were . . . well, what were they? It struck Mark forcibly now that he'd never met anyone but his own father who'd claimed convincingly to have any such direct contact with any deity.

Nor, it occurred to Mark now, could he remember meeting anyone who had sincerely envied Jord his treasure, considering the price that Mark's father had had to pay for it.

All this and much more kept churning uncontrollably through Mark's mind as he trudged the riverbank and waded in the stream, meanwhile listening for pursuers. From the time of Mark's earliest understanding, the sword, and the way his father had acquired it, had been among the given facts of life for him. Never until today had he been confronted with the full marvel and mystery of those facts. Always the sword, with its story, had simply hung there on the wall, like a candle-sconce or a common dish, until everyone who lived in the house had grown so used to it that it had almost been forgotten. Visitors asking about the odd bundle had received a matter-of-fact answer, one they'd perhaps not always believed. And the visitors' repetitions of the story elsewhere, Mark supposed now, had probably been believed even less often.

And Vulcan had said it was called Townsaver . . . thinking again of the town's saving, Mark had to fight back tears again. Now, as in some evil dream or story, the cursed burden of the sword had revealed itself for the curse it truly was, and now it had come down to him. He was the heir, the only surviving son, now that Kenn was dead . . . he knew that Kenn was dead. The sword was Mark's now, and Mark had to run with it, to at least get the burden of it away from his mother and his sister.

Mark didn't want to let himself think just yet about where he might be running to.

His eyes were blurred with tears again. That was bad, because now it was starting to get dark anyway, and he was very tired, so tired that his feet were dragging and stumbling at best, even when he could see clearly where to put them down.

Mark stopped for a rest in a small clearing, a few steps from the main riverbank path. Here he ate most of the food that he'd brought along, and then went to get a drink from the brisk rapids nearby. Already he'd come far enough upstream to start encountering rapids, a fact that made Mark feel even more tired. He went back to his small clearing and sat down again. He was simply too weary to go on any farther, at least not until he'd had a little rest . . .

Mark woke with a start, to early sunlight mottling its way through leaves to reach his face. At once he started to call Kenn's name, and to look around him for his brother, because he'd wakened with the half-formed idea that he must have come out with Kenn on some kind of hunting or fishing expedition. But reality returned as soon as Mark's eyes fell on the sword, which lay beside him in its evilly stained wrapping. He jumped up then, a stiff-muscled movement that startled nearby birds. When the birds had quieted there was nothing to be heard but the murmur of the rapids. There were no indications of pursuit as yet.

Mark finished off what little food he had left, and took another long drink from the stream. About to push on again, he hesitated, and, without quite knowing why, once more unwrapped the blade. Some part of his mind wanted to look at it again, as if the morning sunlight on the sword might reveal something to negate or at least explain the horror of yesterday.

There was still no trace of rust to be seen, and the sword and its wrappings were now completely dry. How should he try to carry the thing today? When Mark stood the weapon upright on the path, point down, and stood himself beside it, the sword's pommel reached as high as his ribcage. The weapon was just too long for him to carry about handily, and far too sharp . . . Mark was momentarily distracted when he looked at the decorations going round the hilt and handle, white on black. He could remember sleepy evenings at home, in the dwelling-rooms beside the creaking mill, when Jord had sometimes allowed the children to take the sword down from the wall and in his presence look it over. Sometimes the children and their mother, interested also, had speculated on what the pattern of the decorations might mean. Mark's father had never speculated. He'd never spoken much about the sword at all, even at those relaxed times. Nor had Jord ever, not in Mark's hearing anyway, said anything directly about the great trial through which the sword had come to him. Nothing about how Vulcan had taken his right arm off, or with what implement, or what explanation, if any, the god had given for what he did. That was one scene that Mark had always forbidden his own imagination to attempt.

The inlaid decoration, white on black, going round the handle of the sword, had always suggested to Mark a crenelated castle wall seen from the outside. Or perhaps it was the wall of a fortified town. Mark had heard of cities and big towns that boasted defensive walls like that, though he'd never come very close to seeing one. Castles of course were a different matter. Everyone saw at least one of those, at least once in a while.

There was the name, of course: Townsaver. And, in one spot on the handle, just above the depicted wall, there was a small representation of what might very well be intended as a swordblade. It looked as if some unseen hand inside the town or castle were brandishing a sword . . .

Mark came to himself with a small start. How long had he been standing here on the pathway gazing at the thing? Even if this weapon was the magical handiwork of a god, he couldn't afford to spend all day gawping at it. Hurriedly he performed his simple packing-up, and once more got moving upstream.

Several times during the morning's travel that followed, the unhandy burden threatened to unbalance Mark's steps when he was wading. And it kept snagging itself by cloth or cord on bushes beside the path. That morning, for the first time, the idea suggested itself to Mark that he might be able to rid himself of the sword and not have to carry it any farther. He could find a deep pool somewhere in which to drown it, or else hide it in a crevice behind a waterfall—by now he'd come upstream far enough for waterfalls. The idea was tempting, in a way. But Mark soon rejected it. Disposing of this sword would not, could not, be as easy as throwing away a broken knife. He did not know yet, perhaps would not yet allow himself to know, what he meant to do with it finally. But he did know that something more than simply discarding it was required of him. Besides, he'd seen often enough the successful working of finding-spells, the minor enchantments of a local part-time wizard. If that country fellow could locate wedding rings down wells, and pull lost coins out of haystacks, what chance would Mark have of hiding a great sword like this one from the real wizards that the Duke must be able to command.

Toward midday, Mark cautiously moved out of the riverbank thickets, and entered high empty pasture land for long enough to stalk and kill a rabbit. He felt proud of the efficiency of this hunt, for which he needed only one clean shot. But as he released the bowstring he saw for one frightening moment the falling seneschal . . .

The food, familiar hunter's fare cooked on a small fire, helped a great deal. It strengthened Mark against the pointless tricks of his shocked imagination, against struggling in his mind with events over which he now could have no control. He told himself firmly that he should instead be consciously deciding where he was going to go.

But he had still reached no such decision when he finished his meal, put out his little fire, and moved on. He knew that if he continued to follow the river upstream for another full day, he'd be quite close to the village in which his father had grown up . . . the place where Jord had worked as a two-armed blacksmith, and from which he'd been summoned one dark night by a god, to trade his right arm for this cursed weapon. Mark felt sure that village was not where he was really headed now.

All right, he'd wait to think things out. He'd just keep going. When plans were really needed, they'd just have to make themselves.

As the sky began to darken with the second nightfall of Mark's journey, he looked up through the screen of riverbank trees to see the glow of sunset reflected on the slowly approaching mountains. Those mountains were near enough now to let him see how steep and forbidding their slopes were—especially up near the top, up there where gods and goddesses, or some of them anyway, were said to dwell. The darkness of the sky deepened, and the pink glow faded from even the highest peaks. Then Mark saw what he'd seen only a time or two before in all his life: sullen, glowing red spots near the summits, what folk called Vulcan's fires. Those fires as he saw them now were still so far away as to be part of another world.

When it was fully dark, Mark burrowed into a thicket, and contrived for himself a kind of nest to sleep in. For a moment that evening, just as he was dozing off, he thought that he heard his father's voice, calling to him, with some urgent message . . .

Throughout the next day, Mark continued as before to work his way upstream. The way grew steeper, the going slower, the land rockier and rougher, the country wilder, trees scarce and people even more so. On that day, though he peered more boldly than before out of the riverside thickets, Mark only once saw distant workers in a field, and no one else except a single fisherman. He was able to spot the fisherman in time to detour round him without letting the man suspect that anyone else was near.

That afternoon, two full days since he'd fled his home, Mark saw certain landmarks—a distant temple of Bacchus, an isolated tabletop butte—that assured him he was now quite near the village in which his father had been born. Some few of his father's kinfolk still lived there, and it was necessary now for Mark to think about those relatives. The angry riders of the Duke might well have reached them already, might have established a watch over every house in all the land where they thought the fugitive would be likely to turn for help. And now, for the first time, one clear idea about his destination did come to Mark: safety for him could lie only outside the Duke's territory, in that strange outer world he'd never visited.

But there was something else, besides distance and dangers, that still lay between him and that possibility of safety. He had, he discovered now, a sense of terrible obligation, connected of course with the sword. The obligation was unclear to him as yet, but it was certain.

Mark held to his course along the river, and did not approach his father's old village closely enough to see what might be going on there. On what he could see of the nearby roads, there were no swift riders, no signs of military search; and his repeated scanning of the sky discovered no flying beasts that might be looking for him. But Mark kept mainly to the concealing thickets, and traveled quickly on.

When the last sunset glow had died on the third evening of his flight, he raised his eyes again to the mountains ahead of him. Again he saw, more plainly now than ever before, the tiny, fitful sparks of Vulcan's fires.

On this third night the air of the high country grew chill enough to keep Mark from sleeping soundly. He wrapped himself in the sword's covering, but built no fire, for fear of guiding his still hypothetical pursuers to him. The next morning, wet from a light drizzle, he climbed wearily on. The country round him grew ever wilder, more alien to what he knew. He continued to follow the river as it carved its way across a high plain, then up among a series of broken foothills. Mark's head felt light now, and his stomach painfully empty. On top of each shoulder he had a sore red spot, worn by the cord from which the sword was slung.

Near midday, with timberline visible at what appeared to be only a small distance above him, Mark came upon a small shrine to some god he did not recognize. He robbed it of its simple offerings, dried berries and stale bread. As he ate he tried to compose a prayer to the anonymous god of the shrine, explaining what he'd done, pleading his necessity. He might not have bothered with the prayer were he not getting so close to the gods' high abode. Even here, so close, he was not entirely sure that the gods had either the time or the inclination to notice what happened at small shrines, or to hear small prayers.

Maybe tomorrow he'd be high enough on the mountain to get some direct divine attention. At any previous time in Mark's life, such a prospect would have frightened him. But, as it was, the shock that had driven him from his home still insulated him against the theoretical terrors that might appear tomorrow.

Not far above the shrine, the Aldan had its origin in the confluence of two brooks, both of which flowed more or less out of the north. At their junction Mark tried his luck at fishing, and found his luck was bad. He grubbed around for edible roots, and came up with nothing that he could eat. He searched for some fresher berries than the shrine had provided, and found a few that birds had spared. If any human dwelling had been in sight he would have tried his skill at burglary or begging to get food. But there was no such habitation to be seen on any of the vast hills under the enormous sky, and Mark was not going to turn aside now to look for one.

He spent the fourth night of his journey, sleeping little, amid a tumble of huge rocks at timberline. Tonight the lights of Vulcan's forge-fires appeared to Mark to be almost overhead, startlingly near and at the same time dishearteningly far above him. Near midnight some large animal came prowling near, staying not far beyond the glow of a small fire that Mark had built in a sheltering crevice. When he heard the hungry snuffling of the beast he unwrapped Townsaver and gripped the hilt of the weapon in both hands. No sound came from the blade, and the air around it remained clear and quiet. Mark could feel no hint of magical protection in its steel, yet in the circumstances the simple weight and razorsharpness of it were a considerable comfort.

In the morning there were no animals of any kind in sight, nor could Mark even find a significant track. The air at dawn was bitter cold but almost windless. During the night Mark had wrapped himself again in the sword's cloth, but now he swathed the weapon again and tied it for carrying. Then he climbed, heading up between foothills, following a dry ravine, moving now on knees that quivered from his need for food. Once he was moving, he was no longer quite sure just how he'd spent the night just past, whether he'd slept at all or not. It seemed to him quite possible that he'd been walking without a pause since yesterday.

Shortly he came upon a small spring, that gave him good water to drink. He took this discovery as a good omen, drank deeply, and pressed on.

All streams were behind him now, as far as he could tell. He kept following what looked like an ill-defined trail up through the ravine. Often he wasn't sure that he was really following a trail at all. By now he was unarguably on the slopes of the mountain itself, but so far the climbing was not nearly as difficult as he had feared that it might be. There were no sheer cliffs or treacherous rockslides that could not be avoided. Even so, the going soon became murderously hard because of sheer physical exhaustion.

Mark considered ways to lighten the load that he was carrying. But it consisted of only a few things, none of which he felt willing yet to leave behind. The idea that he might be able to discard the sword, somehow, along the way had itself already been discarded. The sword was connected with his goal, and it would go with him to the end. At one point, with his head spinning, he did decide to divest himself of bow and quiver. But he changed his mind and went back for them before he'd gone ten steps.

The climb became a blur of weariness and hunger. At some timeless bright hour near the middle of the day Mark was jarred back to full awareness of his surroundings by the realization that he'd run into a new feature of the mountain. Just ahead was the bottom of a cliff face, very nearly vertical, a surface that he was never going to be able to climb . . . gradually he understood that there was no need for him to try.

He was standing on a high, irregular shelf of black rock, with the wind howling around him. But the day was still clear, and the afternoon sun on his back was comfortably warm. The sun had warmed the black rocks here considerably, even if the deeper shadows still held patches of snow, and there was a chill in the wind that played endlessly in the fantastic chimneys of the cliff. Mark stood still for a time, still holding the sword and bearing his other burdens, slowly getting his breath back after the long climb. In some of the chimneys he could hear a roaring that was deeper than the wind, a noise that he thought was coming up from somewhere far below.

Mark was wondering which of the chimneys might hold fire, when his attention was caught by a place he saw at the rear of the rocky shelf, just at the angle where the cliff face went leaping up again. There were signs of old occupancy back there. Mark's eye was caught by scattered, head-sized lumps of some black and gnarled substance. The lumps were of an unfamiliar, off-round shape. He went to one and prodded it with the soft toe of his hunter's boot. The object was hard, and very massive for its size. Mark slowly understood that the lumps were metal or ore that had been melted and then reformed into rough blobs.

He stood now in the very rear of a shallow half-cave in the face of the rising cliff, in a place where the sun struck now and the wind was baffled. Here there were old, cold ashes, from what must have been a very large wood fire. The ashes looked too old, Mark thought, to have any connection with the fires he'd seen up here during the last few evenings. Anyway, he'd assumed, from the stories he'd heard, that what people called the lights of Vulcan's forge were something to do with earthfire, volcanic, whether or not it was the god in person who raised and tended them. Yet plainly someone had once built a large blaze, deliberately, here in this broad depression in the rock floor against the cliff. The stain of its smoke still marked the natural chimney above. The tone of the old soot was a different darkness from that of the rock itself.

In front of the abandoned fireplace Mark slumped to his knees, then let himself sink back into a sitting position. The air up here was thin, and stank of sulphur. It frosted the lungs and gave them little nourishment. At least his stomach had now ceased its clamoring for food; he had reached an internal balance with his hunger, a state almost of comfort . . . with a mental snap he came back to full alertness, finding himself sitting quietly on stone. Had he just started to fall asleep, or what?

He didn't see what difference it would make if he did doze off for a rest. But no, there was something to do, something to be decided, now that he was here. He ought to see to that first, think about it a little at least. He'd come up here for some vital reason . . . ah yes, the sword. When he had warmed himself a little more, he'd think about it.

Still sitting in the faint sun-warmth of the high, sheltered place, Mark slowly began to notice how much unburned wood was lying about nearby. There were large chips and roughly broken scraps, and the half-burnt ends of logs that must once have been too big for a man to lift. He realized that he needed heat. He wanted a fire, and so he painfully began to gather and arrange wood in the old fireplace.

It should have been an easy matter to build a fire using this available material, but weakness made it hard. Drawing his hunter's knife, Mark tried to shave tinder and fine kindling but his hands were shaky, and the blade slipped from the half-frozen wood. He tried the sword and found the task much easier despite its weight and size. With the sword held motionless, its point resting on the ground and the hilt on his bent knee, Mark could draw any chunk of wood against the edge and take off shavings as thin and fine as he wanted. Then when he had his tinder and his kindling ready, his flint struck a fat spark from the rough flange of the sword's steel hilt.

The fire caught from that first spark. It burned well—almost magically well, Mark thought. Larger fragments soon fed it into respectable size and crackling strength. Then, after he'd rested and warmed himself a little more, he took his hunter's cup and gathered some snow from a shaded crevice, to melt and heat himself some water for a drink. Now, if only he had a little food . . . Mark cut that thought off, afraid the hunger pangs would start again.

He sat on the rocky ground with the unwrapped sword beside him, sipping heated water. And found himself staring at large symbols, markings so faint that he hadn't noticed them at first, painted or somehow outlined on the rock of the shallow cave's rear wall. Several of the symbols had been partially obscured by the old stains of smoke. There were in all about a dozen of the signs, all of them drawn with inhumanly straight, geometrical sides; and the lines of one of them, Mark realized, formed the same design that appeared on the hilt of the sword. He took up the sword again and looked at it carefully to make sure.

After that he continued to stare at the wall-signs, with the feeling that he was on the verge of extracting some important meaning from them, until he was distracted by a sound. It was not the wind, or his own fire, but the deep chimney-roaring, louder than before, rising below the never-quite-ceasing whine of wind. It was too breathlessly prolonged to be the voice of any animal or human. The furnaces of Vulcan, Mark thought. The forge-fires. Whatever they really were, they were burning still, somewhere near to where he was sitting. And this old wood-fire place in front of him was . . . that thought would not complete itself.

Mark's sun-shadow on the face of the cliff before him was reaching higher, and he knew that behind him the sun was going down. He thought: I won't live through this night up here; the cold if nothing else will kill me. But in spite of approaching death—or perhaps because of it —he felt a strong and growing conviction that he was going to see Vulcan soon. And somehow neither death nor the gods were terrible; the shock of watching his father and his brother die still numbed

Mark's capacity for terror. Now he understood that ever since he'd picked up the sword from the village street he'd been meaning to confront Vulcan with it. To confront him, and . . . and maybe that would be the end.

Trying to gain strength, Mark built up his fire again, with larger chunks of wood. Then he curled up in front of it, as if he could absorb its radiant energy like food. Again he had the sword's cloth wrapped round his own body as a blanket.

The next time he awoke, he was cold and stiff, and the world was totally dark around him except for a million stars and the brightly winking embers of his fire. Slowly and painfully Mark turned over on his bed of rock, twisting his aching body to get the nearly-frozen half of it toward the fire. His face and the backs of his hands felt tender, as if they'd been almost scorched when the flames were high. But they began to freeze as soon as they were turned away from the remaining warmth. Mark knew he ought to make himself stand up, move his arms and walk, and then build up the fire again. He knew it, but he couldn't seem to get himself in motion. Deep in the middle of his body he could feel a new kind of shivering, and now he was almost completely sure that he was going to die tonight. Still the fact had very little importance.

Get up and tend the fire, and it will save you.

Startled, Mark raised his head, croaked out a half-formed question. The words had come to him as if in someone else's voice, and with the force of a command. He could not recognize the voice, but it made a powerful impression. Now, once he'd moved his head, the rest was possible. He sat up, rubbing his arms together, preparing himself for further effort. Now his arms were able to move freely. And now he forced himself to rise, swaying on stiffened knees, but driving his legs, torso, everything into activity. Half-paralyzed with cold and stiffness still, he gathered more wood and fed the flames when he had blown them back to life.

Then Mark lay down near the new flames, wrapping himself in the blanket again. He rubbed his face. When he took his hands down from his eyes, a circle of tall, silent figures was standing around him and the fire. They were too tall to be human. Mark, too numb to feel any great shock, looked at what he could see of the faces of the gods. He wondered why he could not recognize Ardneh, to whom his mother prayed so much, among them.

One of the goddesses—Mark couldn't be sure which one she was—

demanded of him: "Why have you brought that sword back up here, mortal? We don't want it here."

"I brought it for my father's sake." Mark answered without fear, without worrying over what he ought to say. "This sword maimed him, years ago. It's killed him now. It's killed my brother, too. It's driven me away from home. It's done enough, I'm getting rid of it."

This caused a stir and a muttering around the circle. The faces of the gods, shadowed and hard for Mark to see, turned to one another in consultation. And now the voice of a different deity chided Mark: "It was time enough, in any case, for you to be leaving home. Do you want to be a mill-hand and a rabbit-hunter all your life?"

"Yes," said Mark immediately. But even as he gave the answer, he wondered if it were really true.

Another god-voice argued at him: "The sword you have there has done hardly anything as yet, as measured by its capabilities. And anyway, who are you to judge such things?"

Another voice chimed in: "Precisely. That sword was given to Jord the smith, later Jord the miller, until you, mortal, or your brother had it from him. It's yours now. But you can't just bring it back here and be rid of it that way. Oh, no. Even leaving aside the question of good manners, we—"

And another: "—can't just take it back, now that it's been used. You can't bring a used gift back."

"*Gift?*" That word brought Mark almost to midday wakefulness. It came near making him jump to his feet. "You say a *gift?* When you took my father's arm in payment for it?"

An arm, long as a tree-limb, pointed. "This one here is responsible for taking the arm. We didn't tell him to do that." And the towering figure standing beside Vulcan (Mark hadn't recognized Vulcan till the instant he was pointed out) clapped the Smith on the back. It was a great rude slap that made Vulcan stagger on his game leg and snarl. Then the speaker, his own identity still obscure, went on: "Do you suppose, young mortal, that we went to all the trouble of having Clubfoot here make the swords, make all twelve of them for our game, never to see them properly used? They were a lot of trouble to have made."

For a game . . . a *game?* In outrage Mark cried out: "I think I'm dreaming all of you!"

None of the gods or goddesses in the circle thought that was worth an answer.

Mark cried again: "What are you going to do about the sword? If I refuse to keep it?"

"None of your business," said one curt voice.

"I suppose we'd give it to someone else."

"And anyway, don't speak in that tone of voice to gods."

"Why shouldn't I speak any way I want to, I'm dreaming you anyway! And it *is* my business what—"

"Do you never dream of real persons, real things?"

Smoke from the fire blew into Mark's face. He choked, and had to close his eyes. When he opened them again the circle of tall beings was still there, surrounding him.

"And, anyway, if we gods wish to play a game, who are you, mortal, to object?" That got a general murmur of approval.

Mark was still outraged, but his energy was failing. His muscles seemed to be relaxing of themselves. He lay weakly back on rock half-warmed by fire. Despite all he could do, his eyelids were sagging shut in utter weariness. He whispered: "A game . . . ?"

A female voice, that of a goddess who had not spoken until now, argued softly: "I say that this Mark, this stubborn son of a stubborn miller, deserves to die tonight for what he's done, for the disrespect he's shown, the irresponsible interference."

"A miller's son? A *miller's* son, you say?" That, for some reason, provoked laughter. "Ah, hahaaa! . . . anyway, he's protected here by the fire that he's kindled, using magical materials and tools. Not that he had the least idea of what he was doing when he did it."

"What is so amusing? I still say that he must die tonight. He must. Otherwise I foresee trouble, in the game and out of it, trouble for us all."

"Trouble for yourself, you mean."

And another new voice: "Hah, if you say he must die, then *I* say he must live. Whatever your position is in this, I must maintain the opposite."

They're just like people, Mark thought. His next thought was: I'm almost gone, I'm dying. Now the idea was not only acceptable, but brought with it a certain feeling of relief.

During the rest of the night—his gentle dying went on for a long, long time—Mark kept revising his opinion of the wrangling gang of gods who surrounded him on his deathbed. Sometimes it seemed to him that they were conducting their debate on a high level, using words of great wisdom. At these times he wanted to make every effort to remember what they said, but somehow he never could. At other times what they were saying struck him as the most foolish babble that he had ever heard. But he could not manage to retain an example of their foolishness either.

Anyway, he completely missed the end of the argument, because instead of dying he finally awoke to behold the whole vast reach of the sky turning light above the great bowl of rock that made the world. The near rim of the bowl was very near in the east, almost overhead, while the northwest portion of the rim was far, far away, no more than a little pinkish sawtooth line on the horizon. And to the southwest the rim was so distant that it could not be seen at all.

Mark was shivering again, or shivering still, when he woke up. Now he was cold on both sides. The fire was nearly out, and he immediately started to rebuild it. Somewhat to his surprise, his body moved easily. For whatever reason, he had awakened with a feeling of achievement, a sense that something important had been accomplished while he lay before the fire. Well, for one thing, his life had been preserved, whether by accident or through the benevolence of certain gods. He was not at all sure of the reality of the presences he'd seen. There was no sign of gods around him now; nothing but the mountain and the sky, and the high, keening wind.

Except for the obscure symbols on the wall of stone, and the remnants of that large and ancient fire.

The need for food had now settled deep in Mark's bones, and he thought, with the beginning of fear, that soon he might be too weak to make his way back down the mountain. He had to implement his final decision about the sword before that happened; so as soon as he had warmed himself enough to stop his shivering, he turned his back on his renewed fire and the old forge-place of the gods. Keeping the blanket wrapped around himself, he slung bow and quiver on his back again, and took up Townsaver. He carried the blade as if he meant to fight with it.

Testing the wind, he tried to follow the smell of sulphur to where it was the strongest. It took him only a few moments to stumble right against what he was looking for, in the form of a chest-high broken column of black rock. The middle of the broad black stump was holed out, as if it were a real treestump rotting, and up out of the central cavity there drifted acrid fumes, along with some faintly visible smoke. At certain moments the smoke was lighted from beneath with a reddish glow, visible here at close range even in broad daylight. A breath of warmth came from the fumarole, along with something that smelled even worse than sulphur, as foul as the breath of some imagined monster.

Somewhere far below, the mountain sighed, and the wave of rising heat momentarily grew great.

Mark lifted the sword. He used both hands on the hilt, just as his brother Kenn had held it with two hands during the fight. But no power flowed from the weapon now, and Mark could do with it as he liked. Without delaying, without giving the gods another moment in which to act, he thrust the sword down into the rising smoke and let it fall.

Father, Kenn, I've done it.

The sword fell at once into invisibility. Mark heard the sharp impact that it made on nearby rock, followed by another clash a little farther down. Holding his breath, he listened a long time for some final impact, perhaps a splash into the molten rock that an Elder had once told Mark lay at the bottom of these holes of fire. But though he listened until he could hold his breath no more, he heard no more of the falling sword.

Mark looked up into the morning sky, clear but for a few small clouds. They were just clouds, with nothing remarkable about them. He realized that he was waiting for a reaction, for lightning, for something to embody what must be the anger of the gods at what he had just done. He was waiting to be struck dead. But no blow came.

What did come instead was, in a sense, even worse. It was just the beginning of a sickening suspicion that his throwing the sword down into the volcano had been a horrible mistake. Now he had made his gesture, of striking back at the gods for what they had done to him. And what harm had his gesture done them? And what good had it done himself?

In thirteen years, Jord had never made this awful trek, had never thrown the gods' payment for his right arm back into their teeth. For whatever reason, Mark's father had kept his arm-price hanging on the wall at home instead. Never trying to use it, never trying to sell it, not bragging about it—but still keeping it. Mark had never really, until this moment, tried to fathom why.

One thing was sure, Mark's father had never tried to rid himself of the sword.

The spell of shock that had been put on Mark in the village street by the evil magic of violence began at last to lift. He realized that he was alone upon a barren mountainside, almost too weak to move, many kilometers from the home to which he dared not return. And that he'd just done something awesome and incomprehensible, completed a mad gesture that would make him the enemy of gods as well as men.

He hung weakly on the edge of the smoking, stinking stone stump, growing sicker and more frightened by the moment, until he began to imagine that the voices of the gods were coming up out of the central hole along with the mind-clouding smoke. Yes, the gods were angry. In Mark the feeling grew of just having made an enormous blunder. The feeling escalated gradually into black terror.

Only his lack of energy saved him from real panic. Doing what he could to flee the wrath of the gods, leaning shakily on the black rocky stump, Mark started round it to reach its far side, from which the mountainside went rather steeply down. As Mark moved onto the descending slope, the stump he leaned on turned into a high crooked column, the way around it into a definite descending path.

Mark had not followed this path for twenty steps before he came upon the sword. It was lying directly in his way, right under a jagged hole in the side of the crooked chimney-column, through which it had obviously dropped out. One bounce on rock, the first impact that he'd heard, then this. Altogether the sword had fallen no farther than if he'd dropped it from the millhouse roof.

Even in that short time it had encountered heat enough to leave it scorching. Mark burned his fingers when he tried to pick it up, and had to let it drop again. He had to wait, shivering in the mountain's morning shadow, and blowing on his fingers, until the unharmed metal had cooled enough for him to handle it.

CHAPTER 3

"I am still amazed at the extent of your recent failure, Wearer-of-Blue," Duke Fraktin said. "Indeed, the more I think about it, the more amazed I grow."

The blue-robed wizard's real name was not the one by which he had just been addressed. But his real name—or, indeed, even his next-to-real name—were not to be casually uttered; not even by the lips of a duke; and the wizard was used to answering to a variety of aliases.

The wizard now bowed, though he remained seated, in controlled acknowledgement of the rebuke; he had a way, carefully cultivated, of not showing fear, a way that made even a very confident master tread a little warily with him.

"I have already said to Your Grace," the blue-robed one responded now, "all that I can say in my own defense."

There was a small gold cage suspended from a stone ceiling arch not far above the wizard's head, and inside that cage a monkbird screamed now, as if in derision at this remark. The hybrid creature's ineffectual wings made a brief iridescent blur on both sides of its thin, furred body.

But its brain was too small to allow it the power of thought, and neither of the men below it paid its comment the least attention.

Except for the slave girl who had just brought wine, the two men were quite alone. They were seated in one of the smaller private chambers of the rather grim and drafty castle that was the Duke's chief residence, and would have been thought of as his family seat if any of the duchesses he had tried out so far had succeeded in giving him some immediate family. The present Duke's great-grandfather had begun the clan's climb to prominence by taking up the profession of robber baron. He had also begun the construction of this castle. Much enlarged since those days, it clung to a modest but strategically located crag overlooking the crossing of two important overland trade routes. Trade on both highways had somewhat diminished since the days of the castle's founding, but by now the family was into other games than simple robbery and the sale of insurance on life, health, and business.

Rich wall hangings, in the family colors of blue and white, rippled silkily as a gentle breeze entered the chamber through the narrow windows let into its thick stone walls. In the Duke's father's day the women of the household had begun to insist upon some degree of interior elegance, and the hangings dated from that time. And today for some reason those rippling drapes gave the Duke a momentarily acute sense of the swiftness of time's passage—all the efforts of his ancestors had enabled him to begin his own life with great advantages, but his own decades had somehow sped past him and out of reach, and today his domain was little larger or stronger than when his father had left it to him—a gift rather unwillingly bestowed. The Duke still wanted very much to be king of the whole continent someday, but it was years since he had said as much aloud to even his closest advisers. He would have expected and feared their silent ridicule, because there was so little hope.

Until very recently, that is.

He made a small gesture of dismissal to the slave girl, who rose swiftly and gracefully from her knees, and departed on silent feet, her gauzy garments swirling. Yes, in the matter of women too he thought himself unlucky—time passed, wives appeared, were found for one reason or another unsatisfactory, and departed again. The duty he felt he owed himself, of providing his own heir for his own dukedom, was still not accomplished.

The Duke poured himself a small cup of the wine. "I think," he said to his wizard, "that if you were to try, you might find a few more words to say to me on the subject." As if in afterthought, he poured a second golden cup of wine, and handed it across; he nodded meanwhile, as if confirming something to himself. His Grace was on the small side, wiry and graying, with a hint of curl still in his forelock. On the subject of beards and mustaches, as on much else, he had never been able to make up his mind with any finality, and he was currently clean-shaven except for a modest set of sideburns. The ducal complexion was on the dark side, particularly around the eyes, which made the sockets look a little hollow and gave him a hungry look sometimes.

He prodded his wizard now: "As you have described the sequence of events to me, this young boy first shot my cousin dead, then simply picked up the sword—the sword you had been sent there to get—and walked away with it. No one has seen him since, as far as we can determine. And you made no attempt to stop his departure. You say you did not notice it."

The wizard, apparently unruffled by all this, again made his small seated bow. "Your Grace, immediately after the fight, a crowd gathered in the street. There was much confusion. People were shouting all manner of absurd things, about cavalry, invasions—the scene was far from orderly, with people coming and going everywhere. My first concern was naturally for your cousin's life, and I did all that I could to save him—alas, my powers proved inadequate. But in those first moments I did not even know whose arrow had struck him down. I assumed, reasonably, I think, that it had come from one of the attackers' bows."

"And of course when the fight was over you thought no more about the sword. Even though you'd just seen what it could do."

"Beg pardon, Your Grace, I really did not see that. When the fighting started I went to earth at once, put my head down and stayed that way. As Your Grace is very well aware, most magic works very poorly once blades are drawn and blood is shed. I was of course aware that some very potent magic was operating nearby; I know now that what I sensed was the sword. But while the fighting lasted there was nothing I could do. As soon as silence fell, I jumped up and—"

"Did what you could, yes. Which, as it turned out, wasn't very much. Well, we'll see what Sharfa has to say about these villagers of his when he gets back."

"And have you now summoned him back, Your Grace?"

"Yes, I've sent word that he should hurry, though I hate for him to cut short his other mission . . . well, he must do what he thinks best when he gets my message. So must we all. Meanwhile, let's have the miller and his wife in."

"By all means, sire. I think it a very wise decision for you to question them yourself."

"I want you to observe."

The wizard nodded silently. Duke Fraktin made another small motion with his hand. Though the two men were to all appearances alone, this gesture somehow sufficed to convey the Duke's will beyond the chamber walls. In the time that might have been needed for a full, slow breath, a spear-carrying guard appeared, ushering in two people in worn commoners' garb.

The man was tall and sturdy, and the Duke would have put his age at between thirty-five and forty. His fair hair hung over neatly bandaged temples. He had only one arm, now round the waist of the woman at his side. She was plump but still attractive for one of her class and age, a few years younger than her husband. The dark-haired woman was more than a little frightened at the moment, the Duke thought, though so far she was controlling it well. The man looked more dazed than frightened. It was only today, according to the medical reports, three days after his injury, that he'd regained his senses fully.

Duke Fraktin signed to the guard to withdraw, and then surprised the couple by rising from his chair and coming to greet them, which meant descending from the low dais upon which he and his wizard had been sitting—the wizard was no longer to be seen anywhere. The smiling Duke took the man briefly by the hand, as if this were some ceremony for the award of honors. Then, with a sort of remote possessiveness, he touched the bowing, flustered woman on the head. "So, you are Jord, and you are Mala. Have you both been well treated? I mean, by my men who brought you here?"

"Very well treated, Your Honor." The man's voice, like the expression on his face, was still a little dazed. "I thank you for the care you've given me. The healing."

The Duke waved gratitude away. Whenever quick medical care was needed, for someone whose life mattered, he had a priestess of Ardneh on retainer, and the priestess had reason to be prompt and attentive in responding to his calls. "I wish we might have saved your elder son. He fell as a true hero," the Duke said and added a delicate sigh. "Actually it is your younger son who most concerns me today."

The parents were alarmed at once. The man asked quickly: "Mark's been found?" Their reactions, the Duke thought, would have been subtly different if they had known where their child was. The Duke allowed himself another sigh.

"Alas, no," replied the Duke. "Mark has not been found. And he seems to have taken away with him a certain very valuable object. An object in which my own interest is very strong."

The woman was looking at the Duke with a strange expression on her face, and he wondered if she was attempting to be seductive. A number of women made that attempt with him, of course, and probably few of them had such beautiful black hair. Fewer still, of course, were thirty-year-old millwives with calloused hands. This one had a high opinion of her own attractiveness. Or else something else was on her mind . . .

"Isn't it possible, sir," she asked now with timid determination, "that someone else took the sword? One of those bandits?"

"I think not, Mala. Where was Mark when you saw him last?"

"In the street, sir. Our village street, right after the fight. My daughter and I came running out from the mill, when people told us that Kenn was fighting out there with the sword. When I got there, Mark was standing off to one side. I didn't think he was hurt, so I ran right to Kenn, and . . ." She gestured toward her husband at her side. "Then, later, when I looked around for Mark again, he wasn't there."

The Duke nodded. The daughter had given his men a similar report; she had been allowed to remain in the village, looking after the mill. "And when you first ran out into the street, Mala, it was Kenn who had the sword?"

"Kenn was already lying on the ground, Your Honor, sir. I don't know about the sword, I never thought about it. All I could think of then was that my husband and my son were hurt." Her dark eyes peered at the Duke from under her fall of curly hair. Maybe not trying to be seductive, but trying to convey some message; well, he'd get it from her later.

The woman went on: "Your Grace has close relatives too. If you knew that they were in peril, I suppose that your first thought too would be for them."

The man glanced at his wife, as if it had struck him, too, that she was acting oddly.

The Duke asked: "And *is* another relative of mine now in peril, as you say?"

"I do not know, sir." Whatever the woman had on her mind, it was not going to come out openly just now.

"Very well," the Duke said patiently. "Now. As for young Mark, I can understand his taking fright, and running away, after such an experience—though I, of course, would not have harmed him, had he stayed. I can understand his flight, I say—but why should he have taken along that sword?"

"I think . . ." the man began, and paused.

"Yes? By the way, Jord, would you care for a little of this wine? It's very good."

"No thank you, sir. Your Grace, Mark must have seen both of us fall. His older brother and myself, I mean. So he probably thinks that I'm dead along with Kenn. That would mean . . . I've always told my sons that one day when I was gone the sword would be theirs. Of course I always thought that Kenn would be the one to have it some day. Now Kenn is . . ."

The Duke waited for the couple to recover themselves. In his own mind he thought he was being as gracious about it as if they were of his own rank. Courtesy and gentleness were important tools in dealing with folk of any station; he sometimes had trouble making his subordinates understand that fact. All attitudes were tools, and the choice of the correct one for each situation made a great deal of difference.

Still, he began to grow impatient. He urged the miller: "Tell me all about the sword."

"It was given me years ago, Your Grace." The miller was managing to pull himself together. "I have already told your men."

"Yes, yes. Nevertheless, tell me again. Given you by Vulcan himself? What did he look like?"

The miller looked surprised, as if he had thought some other question would come next. "Look like? That's a hard thing to describe, Your Honor. As you might expect, he's the only god I've ever seen. If it was a man I had to describe, I'd say: Lame in one leg. Carries a forge-hammer in hand most of the time—a huge forge-hammer. He was dressed in leather, mostly. Wearing a necklace made out of what looked like dragonscales—I know that sounds like foolishness, or it would, but . . . and he was taller than a man might be. And infinitely stronger."

Obviously, thought the Duke, this was not the first time the miller had tried to find words to describe his experience of thirteen years ago. And obviously he still wasn't having much success.

"More than a man," Jord added at last, with the air of being pleased to be able to establish that much at least beyond a doubt. "Your Grace, I hope you don't misunderstand what I'm going to say now."

"I don't suppose I will. Speak on."

"From the day I met Vulcan, until now, no man—no woman either—
has truly been able to frighten me. Oh, if I were to be sentenced to
death, to torture, I'd be frightened, yes. But no human presence . . .
even standing before the Dark King himself, I think, would not be so
bad as what I've already had to do. Your Grace, you must have seen
gods, you'll know what I mean."

His Grace had indeed confronted gods—though very rarely—and on
one occasion the Dark King also. He said: "I take your meaning, miller,
and I think you put it well, that special impact of a god's presence. So,
you stood by Vulcan's forge at his command, and you helped him make
the swords?"

"Then Your Grace already knows, I mean that more than one were
made." The miller appeared more impressed by this than by the Duke
himself or his surrounding wealth and power. "I have never met anyone
else who knew that fact, or even suspected it. Yes, we made more than
one. Twelve, in fact. And I stood by and helped. Smithery was my trade
in those days. Not that any of the skill that made those swords was
mine—no human being has skill to compare with that. And five other
men from my village were called to help also—to work the bellows, and
tend the fire, and so on. We had no choice but to help."

Here the woman surprised the Duke again, this time by interrupting,
with a faint clearing of her throat. "Does Your Grace remember ever
visiting that village? It's called Treefall, and it's almost in the mountains."

Duke Fraktin looked at the woman—yes, definitely, he was going to
have to see her alone, later, without her husband. Something was up.
"Why, I suppose I may have been there," the Duke said. The name
meant nothing to him.

He faced the man again. "No, Jord, I don't suppose you had much
choice when Vulcan ordered you to help him. I understand that unfortunately none of the five other men survived."

"Vulcan used 'em up, sir. He used their bodies and their blood, like so
many tubs of water, to quench the blades."

"Yet you he spared . . . except of course that he took your arm.
Why do you suppose he did that?"

"I don't remember that part at all well, Your Grace . . . might I sit
down? My head . . ."

"Yes, yes. Pull up one of those chairs for him, Mala. Now Jord. Go
on. About when you made the swords."

"Well, sir, I fainted. And when I woke again, my right arm was gone.

A neat wound, with most of the bleeding stopped already. And my left hand was already holding Townsaver's hilt. And Vulcan bent over me, as I was lying there, and he said . . ."

"Yes, yes?"

"That now the sword was mine to keep. Townsaver. The Sword of Fury, he called it too. To keep and to pass on as inheritance. I couldn't understand . . . I hurt like hell . . . and then he laughed, as if it were all nothing but a great joke. A god laughing makes a sound like—like nothing else. But it has never been a joke to me."

"No, I suppose not." The Duke turned and stepped back up onto his dais, and poured himself another small cup of wine. When he looked down at the jeweled hilt of the fine dagger at his belt, his hand itched to toy with it, but he forebore. At this moment he wanted to do nothing, say nothing, in the least threatening. He asked mildly: "How many swords did you say that Vulcan forged that day?"

"I don't think I said, Your Grace, but there were twelve." The miller looked a little better, more in control of himself, since he'd been allowed to sit down. "Would you believe it?" he almost smiled.

"I would believe it, since you say so, and you are an honest man. I would know if you were lying. Now, about these other eleven swords. It is very very important that their existence should be kept very quiet. No one outside this room is to hear of them from you. My good people, what do you suppose I should do to make sure of that?"

The man looked to be at a loss. But the woman stepped forward smoothly. "You should trust us, Your Grace. We won't say a word. Jord's never mentioned those other swords until now, and he won't. And I won't."

The Duke nodded to her slowly, then switched his attention back to the man. "Now, smith, miller, whatever—what happened to those other eleven swords?"

A helpless, one-armed shrug. "Of that, sire, I have no idea."

"Did Vulcan name them, as he named your sword? What were they like? Where did they go?"

Again Jord made a helpless motion. "I know none of those things, Your Grace. I never got a good look at any of those other swords, at least not after the early stages of the forging. I saw twelve white-hot bars of steel, waiting for Vulcan's hammer—that was when I counted 'em. Later I was too busy to think, or care—and later still, I had my bleeding stump to think about. I couldn't . . ."

"Come, come, Jord. You must have seen more than that. You were right there, the whole time, weren't you?"

"I was, sir, but . . . Your Grace, I'd tell you more if I could." Jord sounded desperate.

"Very well, very well. Perhaps you will remember more about those swords. What else did Vulcan say to you?"

"I don't know what all he might have said, Your Grace. He gave me orders, told me what to do, I'm sure. I must have understood what he was saying then, but I never could remember afterwards."

"You do remember seeing those twelve white-hot steel bars, though. Were they all alike?"

"All meant to be straight blades, I think. Probably much like the one that I was given. Weapons never were my specialty."

"Ah." The Duke sipped at his wine again, and paced the room. He took thought, trying to find the cleverest way to go. "The sword that you were given. How was it decorated?"

"The blade, not at all, sir. Oh, there was a very fine pattern right in the steel, such as I've never seen elsewhere. But that was, as I say, in the very metal itself. Then there was a rough steel crossguard, no real decoration there either. And then the handle above was straight and black, of some material I didn't recognize; sometimes I wondered if it was from the Old World. And on it was a fine white pattern of decoration."

"What did this pattern represent?"

"I puzzled often about that, sir. It might have been a crenelated wall, like on a castle or a town." And the woman nodded agreement to what her husband said.

The Duke asked: "Do you suppose that you could sketch it for me?"

"I'll have a try, sir." The man sounded reasonably confident.

"Later. Now, you were a smith yourself. Regardless of whether weapons were ever your specialty, I take it that this sword was of such beauty that you must have realized it would be worth a lot of money, even leaving aside any magical properties it may have had. Did it never enter your head to sell it?"

The man's face hardened at that. "Beg pardon, Your Grace. I didn't think it had been given me to sell."

"No? Didn't Vulcan say that it was yours, to do with as you liked?"

"He said it was mine, sir. But until it came time for me to pass it to my sons. That was said very definitely, too."

"I'm curious, Jord. What did you think your son would do with it, when it came to him? Just keep it on the wall, as you did?"

"I don't know, sir."

The Duke waited a little, but nothing more came. He sighed. "A pity. I'd have given you a very handsome price, if you'd brought the thing to me. I still will, of course, should the blade ever happen to come into your control again. If, for example, your son should bring it back. Or if, perhaps, you should look through the woods and find it where he dropped it. I'll give you a good price and ask no questions."

The man and woman looked at each other, as if they wished they could take advantage of the Duke's generosity.

The Duke sat in his chair, leaning forward. "Just realize that, sooner or later, in one way or another, I'll have that sword." He leaned back, brightening. "And I do want to give your son a substantial reward, for trying his best to defend my cousin—as did your older son, indeed. So before I forget—" And from a pocket the Duke produced a golden coin; it spun brightly toward Jord in a practiced toss.

Dazed or not, Jord caught the reward deftly in his huge workman's hand. He stood up, and he and his wife both bowed in gratitude.

As if it had never occurred to him to ask the question before, the Duke inquired: "Where do you suppose young Mark is now? Have you perhaps some relatives in another village, where he might have gone?"

"We have kin in Treefall, Your Grace." It was the woman who answered. Again she was mentioning that village, again with an odd but subtle emphasis in her voice. Yes, he'd have to see her alone soon.

Jord said: "We've told your men already about all our relatives, sire . . . Your Grace, when can we go home? I'm worried about our daughter, left alone."

"She'll be all right. I have people in the village now, keeping an eye on things . . . you have no other children living, besides that daughter and Mark?"

"None, sir," said the woman. High child mortality was common enough. She added: "Your Grace has been very good to us. To provide healing for my husband, and now money."

"Why, so I have. But why not? You are good people, faithful subjects. And when your young boy is found, I mean to be good to him as well. There's a story being told by a neighbor of yours, as doubtless you're aware, that it was Mark's arrow that felled my cousin. Even if that should be so, Mark would not be punished for it—you understand me? If it were so, the evil hit would have happened by accident—or possibly as the result of an evil spell, worked by some enemy. My wizards will find out who did it." And His Grace glanced at the empty-looking chair beside his on the dais. "But I do hope, I hope most earnestly, that your young one is doing nothing foolish with that sword. It has power far beyond anything that he might hope to control or even to understand. I would protect him from disaster if I could. But of course I cannot protect him if I don't know where he is."

The faces of both parents, the Duke decided, were still those of helpless sufferers, not those of schemers trying to decide whether a secret should be told or not. He sighed once more, inwardly this time, and made a gesture of dismissal. "Jord, go make that drawing for me, of the decorations on the sword. Tell the men in the next room what I want you to do, they'll get you what you need. Mala, stay here, I want to hear your story once again."

The spear-carrying guard had reappeared. And in a moment Jord, having made an awkward bow toward the Duke, was gone.

The woman waited, looking out from under her dark curls.

"Now, my dear, you wanted to tell me something else."

She was not going to pretend otherwise. But still she seemed uncertain as how best to proceed. "I spoke of that village, sire. Treefall. The place my husband comes from."

"Yes?"

"I thought, Your Honor, that I had encountered you there one night. Thirteen years ago. At a funeral. The very night that the five men slain by Vulcan were being waked, and my husband prayed for—though he would not be my husband till two days later—and healing magic worked to help him recover from the awful wound—"

"Ah." The Duke pointed a finger. "You say you *thought* you had encountered me? You did not know? You would not remember?"

"The man I met, my lord, wore a mask. As I know the mighty sometimes do, when they visit a place beneath their station."

"So. But why should you think this masked man was me? Had you ever seen me before?"

"No sir. It was just that I had heard—you know how stories go round among the people—heard that you sometimes appeared among your people wearing a mask of dark leather . . ." Mala evidently realized that her words sounded unconvincing. "I had heard that you were not very tall, and had dark hair." She paused. "It was a *feeling* that I had." Pause again. "There were funeral rites that night. I went with the masked man to the fields. Nine months later, my son Mark was born."

"Ah." The Duke looked Mala over thoughtfully, looked her up and down, squinting a little as if trying to remember something. "Folk out in the villages do say, then, that sometimes I go abroad disguised."

"Yes, Your Grace, many say that. I'm sure they mean no harm, they just—"

"But this time, folk were wrong. You understand?"

Mala's dark eyes fell. "I understand, Your Grace."

"Your husband, does he—?"

"Oh no sir. I've never told him, or anyone, about the masked man."

"Let it remain so," said Duke Fraktin. And again he made a gesture of dismissal.

The woman hesitated marginally. Then she was gone.

The Duke turned toward the wizard's chair, which once again was visibly occupied. He waited for its occupant to comment.

The first thing that the Blue-robed one said was: "You did not consider using torture, Your Grace?"

"Torture at this time would be foolish. I'll stake my lands that at this moment neither of them knows where their brat has gone—or where my sword is, either. The woman, at least, would hand the sword over to me in a moment if she could. I think the man would, too, if it came to an actual decision. And when they find themselves safely home again in a day or two, with my gold in their hands—they'll want more. The word will go out from them that their son should come home. Word spreads swiftly across the countryside, Blue-Robes—I've been out there among them and I know. When their child hears that his parents are home, safe, rewarded by me—there's a good chance that he'll bring home the sword. If he still has it, if we haven't found him already. But on the other hand if we begin with pointless torture, he'll hear about that too. What chance then that he'll come home voluntarily?"

"Your Grace knows best, of course. But that man's a stiff-necked one, underneath his meekness. I have the impression that he was holding something back."

"You are a shrewd observer, Blue-Robes. Yes, I agree, he was. But I don't believe it's anything central to our purpose. More likely something that passed between him and the god, years ago."

"Then, sire—?"

"Then why not get it out of him. Indeed." And Duke Fraktin sighed his delicate sigh. "But—it may not be his to tell. Have you considered that possibility?"

"Your Grace?"

"Are we *sure,* Blue-Robes—are we really sure—that we want to know everything that a god has said should be kept secret?"

"I must confess, sire, that your subtlety is oftentimes beyond me."

"You think I'm wrong. Well, later, perhaps, I'll put the whole family on racks or into boots." The Duke was silent for a few moments, thinking. "Anyway, he's a man of property—he's not going to take to the hills and leave his mill to be confiscated. Not unless we frighten him very clumsily."

"And the woman, sire?"

"What about her?"

"The time she spoke of, thirteen years ago, that was before I came into your service. There was no basis in fact for what she said? I ask because a magical influence may sometimes be established through intimacy."

"You heard what I told her." The Duke was brusque.

The wizard bowed lightly. "And what about the young boy, sire? When he is found?"

The Duke looked at his advisor. "Why, get the sword from him, of course, or learn from him where it is, or at the very least where he last saw it."

"Of course, sire. And then, the boy?"

"And then? What do you mean, and then? He killed my cousin, did he not?"

The wizard bowed his little bow, remaining in his chair. "And the village, my lord—the place where such an atrocity was permitted to happen?"

"Villages, Blue-Robes, are valuable assets. We do not have an infinite supply of them. They provide resources. Vengeance must never be more than a tool, to be taken up or put down as required. One boy can serve as an example, can serve better that way, perhaps, than in any other. But a whole village—" And Duke Fraktin shook his head.

"A tool. Yes, sire."

"And a vastly more powerful tool is knowledge. Find out where that sword is. Even finding out whose men those were who tried to kidnap my cousin would be better than mere vengeance."

CHAPTER 4

Getting down from the high mountains was difficult, when your legs were increasingly weakened by hunger, and your head still felt light from hunger, volcanic fumes, altitude, and confrontation with the gods. Getting down still wasn't as difficult, though, as going up had been.

Even carrying the sword was easier now, as if Mark had somehow got used to it. No, more than that, as if it had in some way become a part of him. He could rest its bundled weight on his shoulder now without feeling that he was going to be cut, or swing it at his side without expecting that its awkward weight would trip him up.

He could even contemplate, more or less calmly, the fact that his father and brother were dead, his mother and sister and home out of his reach, perhaps forever. His old life was gone, the gods had agreed on that much at least. But he still had his own life, and the open road ahead, to carry him away from the Duke's vengeance. And the sword.

To find his way down the mountain, Mark simply chose what looked like the easiest way, and this way kept leading him obligingly farther and farther to the south. South was fine with Mark, because he thought that the shortest route out of Duke Fraktin's territory probably lay in that direction.

He seemed to remember hearing also that the lands of Kind Sir Andrew, as the stories called him, were in that direction too. There were a number of stories told about Sir Andrew, all very different from those told about the Duke. Mark supposed that he would willingly have gone south anyway, but the prospect of entering the realm of a benign ruler made it easier to contemplate leaving home permanently behind.

Anyway, his present problems kept him from worrying a great deal about his future. Survival in the present meant avoiding Duke Fraktin's search parties, which he had to assume were looking for him; and it also meant finding food. In this latter respect, at least, Mark's luck had turned. The first stream he encountered on his way down the mountain, a bright small torrent almost hidden in its own ravine, surprised him by yielding up a fish on his first try with his pocket line and his one steel hook. Dried brush along the watercourse provided enough fuel for a small fire, and Mark caught two more fish while the first was cooking. He ate his catch crudely cleaned and half cooked, and went on his way with his strength somewhat renewed.

By now, most of the daylight hours had passed. Looking back, Mark could see that the whole upper two-thirds of the mountains had been swallowed by clouds. He'd got down just in time, no doubt, to save his life from storm and cold. Darkness was gathering fast, and when he came to a small overhang in the bank of the stream he decided to let it shelter him for the night. He tried fishing again, without success. But he found a few berries, and made himself a small watchfire as darkness fell.

During the night there were rain showers enough to put out his fire, and the bank offered him no real protection against the weather. But the deep, bitter cold of the high altitudes was moderated here; Mark shivered, but survived. Dawn came slowly, an indirect brightening of an overcast sky. For Mark the clouds were reassuring—the Duke's menagerie was said to include flying beasts of some degree of intelligence, that he sent out on spy missions from time to time. Again in the morning Mark fished without catching anything. Then he got moving, picking and eating a few more berries as he went. He continued to follow down the channel of the leaping, roaring stream until the way became too difficult. Then he left the streambed to strike out across a less difficult slope.

His chosen way gradually revealed itself as a real path. The trail was very faint at first, but after he'd followed it for half an hour its existence was undeniable. Switchbacking through a field strewn with great boulders, it led him in another hour to a primitive road, which also tended to the south as well as down.

The road's twin ruts showed that it had once been used by wheeled vehicles. But it was reassuringly empty of all signs of present traffic, and Mark continued to follow its twistings among the foothill outcroppings and rockslides. Within a few kilometers it joined a north-south way, much wider and better defined, upon which some effort at road-building had once been expended.

Mark turned onto this highway, still heading south. Presently he came upon evidence of recent use, freshly worn ruts and beast-droppings no more than a day old. His sense of caution increased sharply. The Duke's men and creatures, if they really were searching for him, were likely to be near.

Trying to make himself inconspicuous, Mark left the road and trudged along parallel with it at some fifty meters' distance. But the rocky terrain not only slowed him down, it threatened to completely destroy his hunter's boots, whose soft soles were already badly worn by climbing on rock. To save his feet he soon had to go back to the comparative smoothness of the road.

For half an hour longer he kept going, alert for anything that looked or smelled like food, and wondering when the newly threatening rain was going to break. He glanced back frequently over his shoulder, worried about the Duke's patrols.

And then suddenly he was indeed being overtaken, by two mounted men. Obviously they had already spotted Mark, but at least they were not soldiers. Their riding-beasts were only trotting, giving no impression of actual pursuit. Still they were quickly catching up. The men were both in commoners' dress, very little different from Mark's own. Both were young, both spare and wiry of build. And both wore long knives sheathed at their belts, a detail that Mark supposed was common enough out here in the great world. He thought, as they drew near, that their faces were reassuringly open and friendly.

"Where to, youngster?" The man who spoke was riding a little in advance of the other. He was also slightly the bigger of the two, and carrying a bigger knife. Both men smiled at Mark, the one in the rear thereby demonstrating that he had lost a fair number of his teeth.

Mark had, while walking, prepared an answer for that question, in case it should be needed. "To Sir Andrew's Green," he said. "I hear there's to be a fair." It was common knowledge that Sir Andrew had one every year, military and economic conditions permitting.

The two men glanced at each other. They'd slowed their mounts now, to just match Mark's steady marching pace. "Fairs are fun," agreed the one who had already spoken. "And at Sir Andrew's gates would be a pleasant place to bide, in these times of unrest." He studied Mark. "You'll have some kin there, I suspect?"

"Aye, I do. My uncle's an armorer in the castle." This answer, too, had been thought out in advance. Mark hoped it would put him in the shadow of the distant Sir Andrew's kind protection—for whatever that might be worth.

It was still the same man who did the talking. "An odd-looking bundle you've got there under your arm, lad. Might you be taking along a sword, for your uncle to do some work on it?"

"Yes, that's it." Was it reasonable that the man had guessed, simply from looking at the bundle, what it contained? Or had a general search been ordered, rewards posted, for a fugitive boy carrying a sword? Mark turned his eyes forward and kept on walking.

The talking man now urged his riding-beast ahead of Mark, then turned it crossways to the road, blocking Mark's path, and reined it to a halt. "I'll take a look at your sword," he said, and his voice was still as easy and as friendly as before.

If ever the time had been when wordplay with these two might have helped Mark's cause, that time was obviously past. He skipped into a run, ignoring their cries for him to stop. Bending low, he ran right under the belly of the leader's mount, making the animal whine and rear. Its master was kept busy for a moment, trying to do no more than retain his seat. Meanwhile, the second man, urging his own steed forward, found his companion in the way. Before the two could get themselves untangled Mark had a good running start and was well off the road.

The idea that he might be able to run faster if he threw away the sword never occurred to him, even though its awkward weight joggled him off balance and slowed him down. He held it under one arm and ran as best he could. Two large boulders loomed up just ahead—if he were to dash between them, the men would never be able to follow him mounted. The trouble was that just on the other side of the boulders, open country stretched away indefinitely. They'd ride around the obstacle easily and catch him in the open, before he'd had a long enough run to make him gasp.

Mark feinted a dart between the rocks, then instead tossed his sword up atop the highest one and scrambled up after it, using hands and feet nimbly on tiny projections from the rock. The boulder was more than two meters high, with a flat top surface where his sword had landed. Up here he'd have good footing, and room to stand and swing the sword, though not much more. As his pursuers came cantering, outraged, up to the rock, Mark was relieved to be able to confirm his first impression that they were carrying no missile weapons, slings or bows. And the side of the boulder where he'd scrambled up, steep as it was, appeared to be the least difficult to climb; it wouldn't be easy for them to come at him from two directions.

The men were both roaring at him angrily. Even mounted as they were, their heads were no higher than the level of Mark's feet. Ignoring their noise, he tugged at the cord that bound the bundle. The sword seemed almost to leap out of its wrappings, as if it were eager to be used. Still no sound came from it, no sense of power flowed; it balanced well in Mark's two-handed grip, but remained heavy and inert.

The men below fell silent as he held up the blade. He was ready to use it if he had to, his stomach clenching now like a fist, with feelings worse than hunger. The men were jockeying their mounts backward now, executing a minor retreat. Their faces as they looked at the sword showed that they were impressed—and also, Mark thought, that they were not surprised.

"Put it down, kid," urged the man who did the talking. The other as if in agreement emitted a braying sound, and Mark understood that this man had somehow lost his tongue. Mark had heard the same kind of an unpleasant sound before, from the mouth of a man who was said to have spread nasty stories about the demise of the father of the present Duke.

"Just toss it down to us, young one," the speaker said, his tone encouraging. "We'll take it and go on our way, and you can go on yours." The speaker smiled. He sounded as if he might even believe what he was saying, at least while he was saying it.

Mark said nothing. He only held the sword, and tried to be ready for what would come. The terror he had known on the mountain, after throwing away the sword, did not return now, though the weapon in his hands still felt devoid of power.

His enemies were two, and they were men full grown. Both of them had now drawn their knives, functional-looking weapons worn with sharpening and use. Yet the two men did not immediately try to swarm up onto the rock. Instead they still watched the sword. They remained at a little distance, still mounted, conferring between themselves with quick signs and whispers.

Then the one who could speak rode right up to the rock again. "Get down here right now, kid." His voice was now hard and tough, utterly changed from what it had been. "If I have to come up there after you, I'll kill you."

Mark waited.

The man, moving with an appearance of great purpose, swung himself lithely out of his saddle and onto the side of the boulder at the place where Mark had climbed. But when Mark standing atop the great rock took a step toward him with lifted sword, he hastily dropped to the ground and backed away.

They know what sword I have here, thought Mark. They know what it can do. The Duke has spread the word, and he's offering a reward. But still the weapon in Mark's hands felt totally dead. Was there some incantation he had to utter, something he had to do to call out the magic? What had Kenn been saying, doing, just before the fight? Mark thought that a less magical person than his brother had probably never lived.

If the two men were not going to leap bravely to the attack, neither were they about to give up. Both mounted again, they rode side by side all around the rocks where Mark had taken his position, scouting out his strongpoint. They took their time about making a complete circle of the boulders, pausing now and then to exchange a whisper and a nod.

Mark watched them. He could think of nothing else to do. He still had his bow slung on his back, and a few arrows left. But, looking at the men's faces, marking how their eyes kept coming back to the sword, he felt it would be a bad mistake to put it down. It was their fear of the sword that held them back.

As if he had been reading Mark's thoughts, the speaker called to him suddenly: "Put it down, boy, and let's talk. We're not meaning to do you any harm."

"If that's so, then put your own blades down and ride away. This one is mine."

Presently the two did sheathe their knives again, and rode away a little distance toward the road, and Mark's heart dared to rise. But as soon as the pair were out of easy earshot they stopped for another conference. This one lasted for several minutes. Mark could see the gestures of the speechless man, but could not read their meaning. And

Mark's heart sank again when the two dismounted, tied their animals to a bush as if preparing for a long stay, and then strolled back in his direction. Now the speechless one, moving with a casualness that would not have fooled a child half Mark's age, ambled on past the high rocks. Soon, with a very casual turn at some meters' distance, he had put himself on the opposite side of the high rocks from his friend and the road.

Meanwhile the talking man was trying to keep Mark's attention engaged. "Youngster, there's a reward offered for that sword you got. We could talk about splitting it between us. You know, half for you and half for us. And you to go on free, of course."

The first rock thrown by the speechless one missed Mark by a wide margin. Actually the speaker on the road side of the rocks had to step out of the way of it himself. Mark could see in the speaker's face how he winced, out of embarrassment at his partner's clumsiness. Mark had to turn halfway round, to make sure that he was able to dodge the second thrown stone. Then he had to face back toward the road again, because the man who talked had once more drawn his knife, and was gamely trying again to scramble up the rock.

As Mark moved forward to counter this frontal attack, a third thrown stone went past his head, a little closer than the previous two. The climber, once more seeing Townsaver right above his head, dropped off the boulder's flank as he had before. Again Mark spun around, in time to dodge another missile.

A sound that had begun some time ago now registered in his attention, growing louder. It was the rumble of wagon wheels, drawing nearer with fair speed. And now the wagon came into sight, moving southbound on the road, pulled by two loadbeasts and approaching at a brisk pace. On the wagon's cloth sides large symbols were rather crudely painted. Mark had seen the wagons of tinkers, priests, and peddlers decorated with signs meant for advertisement and magic, but never signs like these. Dancing on his boulder, he had no time to puzzle about meanings now, but sang out for help as loudly as he could.

An open seat at the front of the wagon held three people, the one in the middle being a young woman. All three faces were turned toward the fight, but for a moment it appeared that the wagon was going to rush straight on past. It did not. Instead the driver, another wiry man somewhat older than Mark's assailants, cried out to his team and reined in sharply on one side. The vehicle had already passed the rocks, but now it swerved sharply and came back, leaving the road in a sharp, tilting turn.

When the man at the foot of the rock saw this, he set up his own cry for aid. "Help! We got us a runaway and a thief treed here. There's a reward, that's a stolen weapon he's got in his hands."

His voiceless associate, running back from the far side of the rocks, grunted and waved his arms, achieving nothing but a short distraction. While Mark, in outrage momentarily greater even than his fear, yelled: "Not so! It's mine!"

The wagon had braked to a halt in a swirl of dust, a pebble's toss from where Mark stood. The wiry man who gripped the reins now had his eyes raised judgmatically toward Mark, thinking things over before he acted. The girl in the middle of the seat had straight black hair, cut short, and a round, button-nosed, somehow impertinent face, looking full of life if not exactly pretty. On the other side of her, the seat sagged under a heavy-set youth who wore a minstrel's plumed cap, and a look of no great intelligence upon his almost childish face. In his thick fingers this youth was nursing a lute, which instrument he now slowly and carefully put back into the covered rear portion of the wagon.

In the momentary silence, a thin whining sound arose from somewhere, to fade out again as abruptly as it had begun. Mark's hopes soared for an instant; but the sound, whatever it had been, had not proceeded from the sword.

His enemy who could speak still urged the wagon-driver: "Help us get him down, and we'll split the reward."

Mark pleaded loudly: "I'm no runaway, they're trying to rob me. This sword is mine."

"Reward?" asked the wiry driver. He squinted from one to another of the two men on foot.

The spokesman nodded. "Split 'er right down the middle."

"Reward from who?"

"Duke Fraktin himself."

The driver nodded slowly, coming to his conclusion. He looked up once more at the anguished Mark, then shook his head. "Fetch out the crossbow, Ben—go on, do it, I say."

The crossbow produced by the large youth from inside the wagon was bigger than any similar weapon in Mark's limited experience. He could feel his inward parts constricting at the very sight of it. Ben cocked it with a direct pull, not using stirrup or crank, and without apparent effort. Then he loaded a bolt into the groove, and handed the weapon to the driver.

"Now," said the driver, in his most reasonable voice yet. And with a faint smile he laid his aim directly on the man who was standing closest to his wagon. "You and your partner, mount up. And ride away."

The man who was looking at the wrong end of the crossbow turned color. He made a tentative motion with his knife, then put it back into its sheath. He stuttered over an argument, then gave it up in curses. Meanwhile his speechless companion stood by looking hangdog.

Ben's hands now held a formidable cudgel, and the look on his childish face was woeful but determined. The young woman, her expressive features all grimness now, had brought out a small hatchet from somewhere.

"Of course," remarked the wagon-driver distantly, "if you two don't want your mounts, we sure could use 'em."

The two he was confronting exchanged a look between them. Then they stalked to where they'd left their animals, and mounted. With a look back, and a muttering of curses, they rode off along the road to the northeast.

The muscular youth called Ben let out a tremulous sigh, a puffing of relief, and tucked his club away. The driver carefully watched his two opponents out of sight; then he handed the crossbow back to Ben, who carefully unloaded it, easing the taut cords.

Mark looked more closely at the driver now, and was reminded vaguely of the militia drillmaster he'd once heard shouting commands at Kenn and a hundred others. But there was kindness in the driver's voice as he said: "You can put the sword down now, boy."

"It's mine."

"Why, surely. We don't dispute that." The driver had blue eyes that tended to squint, a nose once broken, and a thick fall of sandy hair. The muscular youth, looking friendly and overgrown, was regarding Mark with sympathy. As was the pert girl, who had put away her hatchet. Mark carefully set the sword down on the rock at his feet and rubbed his fingers, which were cramped from the ferocity with which he'd gripped the hilt. "Thank you," he said.

The driver nodded almost formally. "You're welcome. My name is Nestor, and I hunt dragons to earn my bread. This is Barbara sitting next to me, and that's my apprentice, Ben. You look like maybe you could use a ride somewhere."

Again the keening, moaning sound rose faintly. Mark thought that he could locate it now inside the wagon; some kind of captive animal, he thought, or a pet.

"My name is Einar," said Mark. It was a real name, that of one of his uncles, and another answer that he'd thought out ahead of time. And now, because his knees had started to tremble, worse than ever before, he sat down on the rock. And only now did he notice how dry his mouth was.

And only after he'd sat down did it sink in: *I hunt dragons . . .*

"We can give you a ride, if you're agreeable," Nestor was saying. "And maybe a little something to munch on as we travel, hey? One advantage of a wagon, you can do other things while you keep moving."

Mark pulled himself together and rewrapped the sword. Then with it in hand he slid down from atop the boulder.

"Can I take that for you?" asked Nestor, reaching down from the elevated seat. Mark had made his decision, and handed up the sword; Nestor put it back inside the wagon. Then one of Ben's thick-fingered hands closed on Mark's arm, and he was lifted aboard as if he were a babe.

Barbara had made room on the seat for Mark by going back into the comparatively dim interior of the wagon. She was fussing about with something there, in a place crowded with containers, bales, and boxes.

Nestor already had the loadbeasts pulling. "Going south all right with you, Einar?"

"I was headed that way." Mark closed his eyes, then opened them again, because of images of knives. He could feel his heart beating. He let things go, and let himself be carried.

CHAPTER 5

Riding the wagon's jouncing seat, Mark was startled out of an incipient daze by the return of the squealing noise. This time it came insistently, from close behind them. He looked back quickly. Barbara, crouching in the back of the wagon, had just removed a cloth cover from a small but sturdy wooden cage. Inside the cage—by Vulcan's hammer and Ardneh's bones!—was a weasel-sized creature that could only be a dragon. Mark had never seen one before, but what else could be as scaly as a snake and at the same time be equipped with wings?

Seeing Mark turn his head, Barbara smiled at him. She delayed whatever she was doing with the dragon long enough to hand Mark a jug of water, and then, when he'd had a drink, a piece of fruit. As he bit into that, she got busy feeding the dragon, handing it something that she fished out of a sizable earthen crock. Mark faced forward again, chewing.

Ben had a different, smaller jug in hand. "Brandy?"

"No thanks." Mark had never tasted strong drink of any kind before, and didn't know what effect it might be likely to have on him. He'd seen a village man or two destroyed by constant heavy drinking. Ben—who was getting a frown from Nestor—stowed away the jug.

"Is that blood on your shirt, Einar?" Barbara called from the rear. "You all right?"

"No ma'am. I mean, yes it is, but it's old. I'm all right."

Ben's curiosity was growing almost visibly. "That's sure some sword you got."

"Yes," agreed Nestor, who was driving now at a brisk pace, mostly concentrating on the road ahead, but frequently looking back. "Real pretty blade there."

"I had it from my father." If his hearers believed that, Mark expected them to draw the wrong conclusion from it. No one would be much surprised to find a nobleman's bastard out on the road, hiking in poverty, carrying along some gift or inheritance that was hard to translate to any practical benefit. Now Mark repeated the story about his armorer-uncle being in the employ of kind Sir Andrew. He couldn't be sure how much his audience believed, though they nodded politely enough.

Ben wagged his large head sympathetically. "I'm an orphan myself. But it don't worry me any more." From behind the seat he pulled out the lute he had been holding earlier, and strummed it. Mark thought that it sounded a little out of tune. Ben went on: "I'm really a minstrel. Just 'prenticing with Nestor here till I can get a good start at what I really want to do. We got an agreement that I can quit any time I'm ready."

Nestor nodded as if to confirm this. "Good worker," he remarked. "Hate to lose you when you go."

Ben strummed again, and began to sing:

The song was . . .
No, this song is
The ballad of gallant young Einar
Who was walking as free as . . .

The singer paused. "Hard to find a rhyme for that name." He thought for a moment and tried again:

Young Einar was walking the roads
As free as a lark one day

Along came two men
Who wanted . . .

"That's not quite how it ought to go," Ben admitted modestly, after a moment's thought.

"Must be hard to play while we're bouncing," said Barbara understandingly. There had in fact been one or two obvious wrong notes.

Mark was thinking that Ben's was not really one of the best singing voices he'd ever heard, either. But no one else had any comment about that, and he sure wasn't going to be the first to mention it.

Throughout the rest of the day Nestor kept the wagon rolling pretty steadily. He showed his wish for concealment by expressing his satisfaction when a belt of fog engulfed the road for a kilometer or so. He was always alertly on watch, and he had Barbara and Mark take turns riding in the rear of the wagon, next to the dragon's cage, keeping an eye out to the rear—for the soldiers of the Duke, Mark assumed, though Nestor never actually said so. From inside the covered, swaying cage, the unseen small dragon squealed intermittently. It reminded Mark of the odd noise that a rabbit would sometimes let out when an arrow hit it. Beside the cage was the earthen crock, with a weighted net for a top, that held live frogs. Mark was told that these were the dragon's food, and he fed it one or two. Its tiny breath, too young to burn, steamed at his hand. Its toy eyes, doll-eyes, glittered darkly.

"When do we leave Duke Fraktin's territory?" Mark asked at one point in the afternoon. By now the foothills had been left behind, and the road was traversing firmly inhabited land under a cloudy sky. Fields almost ready for harvest alternated with woodlands and pastures. Nestor had driven through one small village already.

"Sometime tomorrow," said Nestor shortly. "Maybe sooner." The fog had lifted completely now, and he was busier than ever being sharp-eyed. When Mark asked some more questions about the dragon, he was told that they were taking it to the fair on Sir Andrew's green, where it ought to earn some coin as an exhibit. It would also, Mark gathered, serve to advertise Nestor's skill in the hunt. Sir Andrew was a Fen Marcher, which meant he had territory abutting the Great Swamp. He and some of his tributary towns, Mark was told, had chronic dragon problems.

Mark, thinking about it, had trouble picturing one man, however strong and skilled and brave, just going out and hunting dragons as if they were rabbits. From the stories he'd heard, real dragon hunts were vast enterprises involving numbers of trained beasts and people. And Nestor might be brave and skilled, but he didn't look all that strong. Ben, of course, looked strong enough for two at least.

As the afternoon passed, Nestor drove more slowly, and appeared to be even more anxious about seeing what was on the winding road ahead of him. Passing a pack-toting peddler who was coming from the other direction, he slowed still more to ask the man a question: "Soldiers?"

The wink and faint nod that he got in return were apparently all the answer Nestor needed. He turned off the road at the next feasible place, and jounced across an unfenced field to a side lane.

"Just as soon not meet any of the Duke's soldiers," he muttered, as if someone had asked him for an explanation. "There's a creek down this way somewhere. Maybe the water's low enough to ford. On the other side's Blue Temple land, if I remember right."

There was no problem in finding the creek, which meandered across flat and largely neglected farmland. Locating a place where it could readily be forded was somewhat harder. Nestor sent Ben and Barbara to scout on foot, upstream and down, and eventually succeeded. Once on the other side, he sighed with relief and drove the wagon as deep as possible into a small grove, not stopping till he was out of sight of Duke Fraktin's side of the stream. Then he announced that it was time to set up camp. Ben and Barbara immediately swung into a well-practiced routine, tending the loadbeasts and starting to gather some wood for a fire.

As Mark began to lend a hand, Nestor called him aside. "Einar, you come with me. We need some more frogs for the dragon, and I've a special way of catching them that I want to show you."

"All right. I'll bring my bow, maybe we'll see a rabbit."

"It'll be getting dark for shooting. But fetch it along."

From the back of the wagon Nestor dug out what looked to Mark like a rather ordinary fishnet, of moderately fine mesh. On the wooden rim were symbols that Mark supposed might have some magical significance, though often enough such decorative efforts had no real power behind them. With Nestor carrying the net beside him, Mark trudged into the trees, an arrow nocked on his bow. They followed the general slope of the land back down to the creek bed.

As they walked, Nestor asked: "Einar, what's your uncle's name? The one who's armorer for Sir Andrew. I might know him."

"His name's Mark." At least he said it quickly; this was one answer he hadn't thought out in advance.

"No. I don't know him." A cloudy twilight was oozing up out of the low ground. They had reached the creek-bank without spotting any rabbits or other game, and Mark put away his bow and arrow.

"Anyway," said Nestor, "that sword of yours didn't look like it needed a lot of work." He was studying the stream as he spoke, and it was impossible to tell from his voice what he was thinking. Stepping carefully now from one stone to another, he worked his way out near the middle of the stream, where he positioned his net in a strong flow of water, catching the wooden frame on rocks so it would be held in place. He straightened up, stretching his back, still seeming to study the water's flow. "Didn't you say that your uncle was going to work on it?"

Mark hesitated, finally got out a few lame words.

Nestor did not seem to be paying very close attention to what he said this time. "Or, maybe you've given some thought to selling your sword at the fair. That would be a good time and place, if you mean to sell it. Honest business dealings are more likely under Sir Andrew's eye than elsewhere. There might even be one or two people there who could buy such a thing."

"I wouldn't know how to sell it. And anyway, I wouldn't want to. It was my father's." All of that was the truth, which made it a relief to say.

"A sword like that, I suppose it must have some special powers, as well as being beautiful to look at." Nestor was still gazing at the stream.

Mark was silent.

Nestor at last looked at him directly. "Would you get it now? Bring it here, and let me have a look at it?"

Mark could think of no decent way to refuse. He turned away wordlessly and trudged back to the wagon. He could grab his sword when he got there and run away again; but sooner or later he was going to have to trust someone.

He found Ben and Barbara engaged in what looked like a tricky business. They had removed the dragon's cage from the wagon and were cleaning the cage while its occupant shrilled at them and tried to claw and bite them. They looked at Mark curiously when he climbed into the wagon, and again when he emerged with his wrapped sword in hand. But they said nothing to him.

Darkness was thickening in the grove when Mark brought the sword back to Nestor, who was sitting on a rock beside the stream and appeared to be lost in meditation. But the wiry man roused quickly enough, took the sword on his lap and undid its wrappings carefully. There was still enough light for a fairly close inspection. Nestor sighted along the edge of the blade, and then tried it with a leaf. Brushed lightly along the upright edge, the leaf fell away in two neat halves.

With one finger Nestor traced the subtle patterns on the hilt. Then, acting as if he had reached a decision, he let Mark hold the sword for a moment and got to his feet. Lifting his net from the water, he peered into the mass of small, struggling creatures it had captured. The net held, thought Mark, a surprising weight of swimming and crawling things; perhaps the magical symbols round the rim really were effective.

Nestor plunged his hand into the mass, pulled out one wriggling thing, and let the rest sag back into the water. "Baby dragon," he said, holding up a fistful of feebly squirming gray for Mark's inspection. There were no wings, and the creature was vastly smaller than the one back in the cage. "You find 'em in a lot of the streams hereabouts. There's a million, ten million, hatched for every one that ever grows big enough to need hunting."

Then he surprised Mark by taking Townsaver back again. Nestor held the blade extended horizontally, flat side up, and on that small plain of metal he set the hatchling dragon. Freed of his grip, it hissed an infinitesimal challenge, and lashed a tiny tail. Nestor rotated the blade, slowly turning it edge-side up; somehow the creature continued to cling on. Its scales, though no bigger than a baby's fingernails and paper-thin, could protect it from that cutting edge. It hissed again as the sword completed a half-rotation, once more giving the dragon a flat space to rest upon.

Nestor contemplated this result for a moment, as if it were not at all what he had been expecting. Then with a small flick of his wrist he dashed the tiny creature to the ground; and in the next moment he killed it precisely with the sword, letting the weight of the weapon fall behind the point. Nestor handled the sword, thought Mark, as if it had been in his hand for years.

"One less to grow up," said Nestor, turning his thoughtful gaze toward Mark. With the sword point still down in the soil at his feet, he leaned the hilt back to Mark, giving the sword back. "First dragon this sword has ever killed, do you suppose?"

"I suppose," said Mark, not knowing what the question was supposed to mean. He began wrapping the weapon up again.

"Your father didn't hunt them, then. What did he do with this sword? Use it in battle?"

"I . . ." Suddenly Mark couldn't keep from talking, saying something to someone about it. "My brother did, once. He was killed."

"Ah. Sorry. Not long ago, I guess? Then the sword, when he used it, didn't . . . didn't work very well for him?"

"Oh, it worked." Mark had to struggle against an unexpected new pressure of tears. "It worked, like no other sword has ever worked. It chopped up men and even warbeasts—but it couldn't save my brother from being chopped up too."

Nestor waited a little. Then he said: "You were trying to use it today yourself. But—after I got there at least—nothing much seemed to be happening."

"I couldn't feel any power in it. I don't know why." At some point the thought had occurred to Mark that the limitation on the sword's magic might be connected with its name. But he didn't want to go into that just now. He didn't want to go into anything.

"Never mind," said Nestor. "We can talk about it later. But this design on the handle. Did your father, brother, anyone, ever tell you what it was supposed to mean?"

None of your business, thought Mark. He said: "No sir."

"Just call me Nestor. Einar, when we reach Sir Andrew's . . . well, I don't suppose I have to caution you to keep this sword a secret, until you know just what you want to do with it."

"No sir."

"Good. You carry it, I'll bring the net."

Back at the wagon, they sorted out not only a catch of frogs for dragon-food, but a few fish to augment the dinner of beans, bread, and dried fruit that Barbara was preparing. It turned out that Ben was roasting some large potatoes under the fire as well, and for the first time in days Mark could eat his fill.

After dinner, when the immediate housekeeping chores had been taken care of, Ben got out his lute and sang again. Both Nestor and Barbara, for some reason, chose this time to make their personal trips into the woods.

"Hard day tomorrow," Nestor announced when he returned. And, indeed, everyone was yawning. The captive dragon had already been put back inside the wagon, and the dragon-hunter retired there now. Barbara shortly followed, after looking at Mark's boots and vowing that she would soon mend or replace them for him. After throwing out a quantity of bedding, and emerging once more to make sure that Mark had got his share of it, she went in again and closed the flap.

The rainclouds that had threatened earlier had largely blown away, and now some stars were visible. Ben and Mark bedded down in the open, on long grass at a small distance from the dying fire. Wrapped in the extra blanket Barbara had given him, Mark was more comfortable than he'd been since leaving home. He was better fed, also, and very drowsy. His sword was safe in the wagon, and in a way he enjoyed being free of its constant presence at his side. Yet sleep would not come at once.

He heard Ben stirring wakefully.

"Ben?"

"Yah."

"Your master really hunts dragons? For a living?"

"Oh yes, he's very good at it. That's what our sign painted on the wagon means. Everyone in the parts of the country where there are dragons knows what a sign like this means. This isn't really dragon country here. Just a few little ones in the streams."

"I thought that the only people who hunted dragons were . . ."

"Castle folk? I think Nestor was a knight once, but he don't talk about it. Just the way he acts sometimes. Some highborn people hunt 'em, and others just pretend to. And both kinds hire professionals like Nestor when they have to, to hunt or to help out. There's a lot of tricks to hunting dragons." Ben sounded fairly confident that he knew what the tricks were.

"And you help him," Mark prodded.

"Yeah. In two hunts now. Last hunt, we were able to catch that little one alive, as well as killing the big one we started after. Both times I stood by with the crossbow, but I didn't do much shooting. Nestor killed 'em both. Neither of them were very big dragons, but they were in the legged phase, of course. Bigger than loadbeasts. You know?"

"Yeah, I guess." What Mark knew, or thought he knew, about dragons was all from stories. After hatching, dragons swam or crawled around on rudimentary legs for about a year, like the one Nestor had netted, while large birds, big fish, and small land predators took a heavy toll of them. The ones that survived gradually ceased to spend a lot of time in the water, grew wings of effective size, and started flying. They continued as airborne predators until they were maybe four or five years old, by which time they'd grown considerably bigger than domestic fowl. A little more growth, and they supposedly became too big to fly.

Once their wings were no longer used, they withered away. The dragons resumed an existence as belly-crawling, almost snakelike creatures —so far their legs hadn't kept up with the growth of the rest of their bodies—though of course they too were on a larger scale than before. In this, called the snake phase, they were competitors of the largest true snakes for food and habitat.

When they were ready for the next phase—Mark wasn't sure how many years that took—dragons grew legs, or enlarged their legs, rather in the manner of enormous tadpoles. This legged phase was, from the human point of view, the really dangerous period of a dragon's life. Now, as omnivores of ever-growing size and appetite, they stalked their chosen territory, usually marshland or with marsh nearby. They ravaged crops and cattle, even carrying off an occasional man, woman, or child. Mark could vaguely remember hearing of one more phase after the legged one, in which the beasts after outgrowing any possible strengthening of their legs became what were called great worms, and again led a largely aquatic life. But of this final phase, Mark was even less sure than of the rest.

"Sure," he added, not wanting to seem ignorant.

"Yeah," Ben yawned. "And both times, Nestor followed the dragon into a thicket, and killed it with his sword." Ben sounded as if he were impressed despite himself. "Did your father hunt dragons too?"

"No," said Mark, wondering why everyone should think so. "Why?"

"I dunno," said Ben. "Just that, now that I think about it, your sword looks a whole lot like the one that Nestor uses."

CHAPTER 6

Putting aside an arras of blue and white, and signalling his blue-robed wizard to follow him, Duke Fraktin entered a concealed and windowless chamber of his castle, a room well guarded by strong magic. An eerie Old World light, steadier than any flame, came alive as the men entered, shed by flat panels of a strange material hanging on the walls. The light fell brightly on the rear wall of the chamber, which was almost entirely taken up by a large map. Painstakingly drawn in several colors, and lettered with many names, this map depicted the entire continent of which the Duke's domain was no more than a tenth part. Some areas of the map were largely blank, but most of it was firmly drawn, showing both the lines of physical features and the tints of political control. Behind those trusted contours and colors lay decades of aerial reconnaissance by generations of flying creatures, some reptiles, some birds, others hard to classify by species, but all half-intelligent.

On one of the side walls, near the map, there hung a mask of dark, tooled leather, with a cowled jacket on a peg beside it.

But Duke Fraktin's present concern was not with any of these things.

Instead he stopped in front of a large table, on which rested a carved wooden chest, itself the size of a small coffin. He signalled to his wizard that he wished this chest to be opened.

Accordingly the wizard laid both hands upon its lid, whereupon there rose from the chest a faint humming, buzzing sound, as of innumerable insects. In response to this sound the wizard muttered words. Apparently it was now necessary to wait a little, for the conversation between the two men went on with the chest still unopened, the magician's hands still resting quietly on it.

"Then does Your Grace still believe that these attackers were common bandits? Such do not commonly include warbeasts in their armament."

"No," agreed the Duke gently. He was looking at the map now, without really paying it much attention. "Nor do they commonly attempt to kidnap any of my relatives."

"Then it would seem, sire, that they were not simply bandits."

"That had occurred to me."

"Agents, perhaps, of the Grand Duke?"

"Basil bears me no love, I'm sure of that. And of course he too may have learned of the existence of the swords, and he may be trying now to gather them all into his own hands, even as I would have them all in mine . . . hah, Blue-Robes, how I wish I knew how many all across the continent are playing the same game. I presume your latest divinations still indicate that the magic blades at least are not scattered all around the earth?"

"The swords are all still on this continent, Your Grace. I am quite positive of that. But as to exactly where, in whose possession . . ."

The Duke's darkening mood sounded in his voice. "Yes, exactly. And there's no telling how many know of them by now. Bah. Kings and princes, queens and bandits, priests, scoundrels and adventurers of every stripe . . . bah, what a fine mess."

"At least Your Grace has had a chance to get in on the game. You were not left in ignorance that it is taking place."

"Game, is it?" The Duke snorted. "You know I have small tolerance for games. But I must play, or be swallowed up, when others gain the power of the swords. And you need not remind me any more that I have your skill at divination to thank for my awareness of the game, late as it comes; I've thanked you for that already. Gods, I wonder whose men those were. The Margrave's, you suppose? They didn't even seem to know or care about the sword, at least according to the descriptions of events we have."

The wizard, his hands stroking the carven lid of the wooden chest, coughed. It was a sound as delicate and diplomatic as the Duke's habitual sigh. "I think not the Margrave's, sire. Perhaps they could have been agents of the Queen of Yambu?"

The Duke, nagged by irritation on top of worry, flared up sullenly, then recovered. "Have I not told you never to speak of that . . . but never mind. You are right, we must consider Yambu also, I suppose. But I do not think it was her . . . no, I do not think so."

"Perhaps not . . . then we must face the possibility, Your Grace, that they were agents of the Dark King himself. I did find it odd that a mere miller should have mentioned that august name."

"I would say that this one-armed Jord is not your ordinary miller. But then, the commons in general are not nearly so ignorant of their rulers and their rulers' affairs as those rulers generally suppose."

"Just so, sire." The wizard nodded soothingly. "We have then primarily to consider Grand Duke Basil, Queen Yambu—and Vilkata himself. While remembering, as Your Grace so wisely points out, that there are still other possibilities."

"Yes." But now the Duke's attention was straying, drawn by a thought connected with the huge map. His gaze had lifted to the map, and had come to rest at an unmarked spot near the eastern limit of his own domain and of the continent itself, right at the inland foot of the coastal range that was labeled as the Ludus Mountains. Right about there, somewhere, ought to be the high village—what had the woman named it? Treefall, that was it—from which the god had conscripted his human helpers, keeping them for a night and a day of labor, death, and mutilation. It now struck Duke Fraktin as absurd that the village where such an enigmatic and almost incredible event had taken place should not even be marked on his map.

The woman had asked him . . . no, she had as much as told him that he, the Duke, had been there, and had fathered a bastard on her there, the night after Jord's maiming, in one of those hill country funeral rites. The Duke knew something about those.

A bold story indeed for any woman to make up out of nothing. Still, the fact was that the Duke could remember nothing like that happening, and he had, as a rule, a good memory. A better memory, he thought, for women than for most things. Of course he couldn't recall everything from thirteen years ago. Exactly what had he been doing at that time—?

The insect-buzzing sound had died away. The wizard pushed up the lid of the huge box. Both men stared at the fine sword that was revealed inside, nesting in a lining of rare and fantastically beautiful blue fur. The sword had not been brought to the Duke in any such sumptuous container as this; in fact it had arrived, wrapped for concealment, in the second-best cloak of a Red Temple courtesan.

The clear light from the Old World wall panels glinted softly on mirror steel. Beneath the surface of the blade, the Duke's eye seemed to be able to trace a beautiful, finely mottled pattern that went centimeters deep into the metal, though the blade was nowhere a full centimeter thick.

Putting both hands on the hilt, the Duke lifted the sword gently from the magical protection of the chest. "Are they ready out on the terrace?" he asked, without taking his eyes from the blade itself.

"They have so indicated, Your Grace."

Now the Duke, holding the sword raised before him as if in ritual, led the way out of the blind room behind the arras, across a larger chamber, and through another doorway, whose curtains were stirred by an outdoor breeze. The terrace on which he emerged was open to the air, and yet it was a secret place. The view was cut off on all sides by stone walls, and by high hedges planted near at hand. On the stone pavement under the gray sky, several soldiers in blue and white were waiting, and with them one other man, a prisoner. The prisoner, a middle-aged, well-muscled man, wore only a loincloth and was not bound in any way. Yet he was sweating profusely and kept looking about him in all directions, as if he expected his doom to spring out at him at any moment.

The Duke trusted his wizard to hold the sword briefly, while he himself quickly slipped a mail shirt on over his head, and put on a light helm. Then he took back the sword, and stood holding it like the experienced swordsman that he was.

The Duke gestured toward the prisoner. "Arm him, and step back."

Most of the soldiers, weapons ready, retreated a step or two. One tossed a long knife, unsheathed, at the prisoner's feet.

"What is this?" the man demanded, his voice cracking.

"Come fight me," said the Duke. "Or refuse, and die more slowly. It is all one to me."

The man hesitated a moment longer, then picked up the knife.

The Duke walked forward to the attack. The prisoner did what he could to defend himself, which, given the disparity in arms and armor, was not much.

When it was over, a minute later, the Duke wiped the long blade clean himself, and with a gesture dismissed his troops, who bore away with them the prisoner's body.

"I felt no power in it, Blue-Robes. It killed, but any sharp blade would have killed as well. If its power is not activated by being carried into a fight, then how can it be ordered, how controlled? And what does it do?"

The wizard signed humbly that he did not know.

The Duke bore the cleaned blade back into the concealed room behind the arras, and replaced it in the magically protective chest. Still his hand lingered on the black hilt, tracing with one finger the thin white lines of decoration. "Something like a castle wall on his sword, the fellow said."

"So he did, Your Grace."

"But here I see no castle wall. Here there's nothing more or less than what we've seen in the pattern since that woman brought me the sword a month ago. This shows a pair of dice."

"Indeed it does, Your Grace."

"Dice. And she who brought it to me from the Red Temple said that the soldier who left it with her had been wont to play, and win, at dice." Annoyingly, that soldier himself was dead. Stabbed, according to the woman's story, within a few breaths of the moment when he'd let the sword out of his hands. The killers who'd lain in wait for him had evidently been some of his fellow gamblers, who were convinced he'd cheated them. Duke Fraktin had sent Sir Sharfa, one of his more trusted knights, out on a secret mission of investigation.

"Am I to cast dice for the world, Blue-Robes?"

The wizard let the question pass as rhetoric, without an answer. "No common solider, Your Grace, could have carried a sword like this about with him for long. It would certainly have come to the attention of his officers, and then . . ."

"It would be taken from him, yes. Though quite likely not brought here to me. Ah well, it's here now." And the Duke, sighing, removed his finger from the hilt. "Tell me, Blue-Robes, is it perhaps something like our lamps, some bit of wizardry left over from the Old World? And is the miller's tale of how he came by it only a feverish dream that he once had, perhaps when his arm was amputated, perhaps after he'd caught it clumsily in his own saw or his own millstones?"

"I am sure Your Grace understands that none of those suggestions are really possible. Much of the miller's tale is independently confirmed. And we know that the Old World technologists made no swords; they had more marvelous ways to kill, ways still forbidden us by Ardneh's Change. They had in truth the gun, the bomb . . ."

"Oh, I know that, I know that . . . but stick to what is real and practical, not what may have happened in the days of legend . . . Blue-Robes, do you think the Old World really had to endure gods as well as their nonsense of technology? Ardneh, I suppose, was really there."

"It would seem certain that they did, Your Grace. Many gods, not only Ardneh. There are innumerable references in the old records. I have seen Vulcan and many others named."

The Duke heaved a sigh, a great sincere one this time, and shook his head again. As if perhaps he would have liked to say, even now, that there were no gods, or ought to be none, his own experience notwithstanding.

But here was the sword before him, an artifact of metal and magic vastly beyond the capabilities of the humans of the present age. And it had not been made in the Old World either. According to the best information he had available, it had been made no more than thirteen years ago, in the almost unpeopled mountains on the eastern edge of his own domain. If not by Vulcan, then by whom?

Gods were rarely seen or heard from. But even a powerful noble hardly dared say that they did not exist. Not, certainly, when his domain adjoined the Ludus Mountains.

CHAPTER 7

Mark awoke lying on damp ground, under a sky much like that of the day before, gray and threatening rain. Still, blanketed and fed, he was in such relative comfort that for a moment he could believe that he was dreaming, back in his own bedroom at the mill, and that in a moment he might hear his father's voice. The illusion vanished before it could become too painful. There was Ben, a snoring mound just on the other side of the dead fire, and there was the wagon. From inside it the little dragon had begun a nagging squall, sounding almost like a baby. No doubt it was hungry again.

And now the wagon shook faintly with human stirrings inside its cover; and now Ben sat up and yawned. Shortly everyone was up and moving. For breakfast Barbara handed out stale bread and dried fruit. People munched as they moved about, getting things packed up and ready for the road. Preparations were made quickly, but fog was closing in by the time everything was ready to travel. With the fog, visibility became so poor that Nestor entrusted the reins to Ben, while he himself walked on ahead to scout the way.

"We're near the frontier," Nestor cautioned them all before he moved out. "Everybody keep their eyes open."

Walking thirty meters or so ahead, about at the limit of dependable visibility, Nestor led the wagon along back lanes and across fields. Before they had gone far, they passed a gang of someone's field workers, serfs to judge by their tattered clothes, heading out with tools in hand for the day's labor. When these folk were greeted, they answered only with small waves and nods, some refusing to respond at all.

Shortly after this encounter Nestor called a halt and held a conference. He now admitted freely that he was lost. He thought it possible that they might not have crossed the frontier last night after all—or that they might even have recrossed it to Duke Fraktin's side this morning. Mark gathered that the border hereabouts was a zig-zag affair, poorly marked at best, and in places disputed or uncertain. However that might be, all they could do now was keep trying to press on to the south.

The four people in and around the wagon squinted up through fog that appeared to be growing thicker, if anything. They did their best to locate the sun, and at last came to a consensus of sorts on its position.

"That way's east, then. We'll be all right now."

With Nestor again walking a little ahead of the wagon, and Ben driving, they crossed a field and jolted into the wheel-ruts of another lane. Time passed. The murky countryside flowed by, with a visibility now of no more than about twenty meters. Nestor was a ghostly figure, pacing at about that distance ahead of the wagon.

More time passed. Suddenly, seeming to come from close overhead, there was a soft sound, quickly passing, as of enormous wings. Everyone looked up. If there had been a shadow, it had already come and gone, and no shape was revealed in the bright grayness. Mark exchanged looks with Barbara and Ben, both of whom looked just as puzzled as he felt. No one said anything. Mark's impression had been of something very large in flight. He had certainly never heard anything like it before.

Nestor, who had heard it too, called another halt and another conference. He didn't know, either, what the flying thing might have been, and now he was ready to curse the fog, which earlier he had welcomed. "It's not right for this part of the country, this time of the year. But we'll come out of it all right it we just keep going."

This time Nestor stayed with the wagon and took over the driving himself. The others remained steadily on lookout, keeping watch in all directions as well as possible in the fog.

The lane on which they were traveling dipped down to a small river, shallow but swiftly flowing, and crossed it in a gravel ford. Nestor drove across without pausing. Mark supposed that this was probably another bend of the same stream that they'd just camped beside, and that this crossing might mean a new change of territory. But no one said anything, and he suspected they were all still confused about whose lands they were in.

Slowly they groped their way ahead, through soupy mists. The team, and the dragon as well, were nervous now. As if, thought Mark, something more than mere fog were bothering them.

There was the river again, off to the right. The road itself moved here in meandering curves, like a flatland stream.

Suddenly, from behind the wagon and to the left, there came the thudding, scraping, distinctive sound of riding-beasts' hard footpads on a hard road. It sounded like at least half a dozen animals, traveling together. It had to be a cavalry patrol.

The dragon keened loudly.

"Halt, there, the wagon!"

From somewhere a whip had come into Nestor's hand, and he cracked it now above the loadbeasts' backs, making a sound like an ice-split tree. The team started forward with a great leap, and came down from the leap in a full run. So far today they had not been driven hard, and their panic had plenty of nervous energy for fuel.

"Halt!"

The order was ignored. Only a moment later, the first arrows flew, aimed quite well considering conditions. One shaft pierced the cloth cover of the wagon above Mark's head, and another split one of the wooden uprights that supported the cloth.

"Fight 'em!" roared Nestor. He had no more than that to say to his human companions, but turned his energy and his words, in a torrent of exhortation and abuse, toward his team. The loadbeasts were running already as Mark had never known a team to run before. Meanwhile inside the wagon a mad scramble was in progress, with Ben going for the crossbow and Mark for his own bow and quiver. Mark saw Barbara slipping the thong of a leather sling around one finger of her right hand, and taking up an egg-shaped leaden missile.

Looking out from the left front of the wagon with bow in hand, Mark saw a mounted man swiftly materializing out of the mist. He wore a helmet and a mail shirt, under a jerkin of white and blue, and he rode beside the racing team, raising his sword to strike at its nearest animal. Mark quickly aimed and loosed an arrow; in the bounding confusion he couldn't be sure of the result of his own shot, but the crossbow thrummed beside him and the rider tumbled from his saddle.

The caged dragon, bounced unmercifully, screamed. The terrified loadbeasts bounded at top speed through the fog, as if to escape the curses that Nestor volleyed at them from the driver's seat. It seemed to Mark that missiles were sighing in from every direction, with most of them tearing through the wagon's cloth. Someone outside the wagon kept shouting for it to halt. Ben, in the midst of recocking his crossbow, was almost pitched out of the wagon by a horrendous bounce.

Mark saw Barbara leaning out. Her right arm blurred, releasing a missile from her sling in an underhand arc. One of the cavalry mounts pursuing stumbled and went down.

The patrol had first sighted the wagon across a bight of the meandering road, and in taking a short cut to head it off had encountered some difficult terrain. This had provided the wagon with a good flying start on a fairly level stretch of road. But now the faster riders were catching up.

"Border's near!" yelled Nestor to his crew. "Hang on!"

We know it's near, thought Mark, but which direction is it? Maybe now Nestor really did know. Mark loosed another arrow, and again he could not see where it went. But a moment later one of the pursuing riders pulled up, as if his animal had gone lame.

Another bounce, another tilt of the wagon, bigger than any bounce and tilt before. This one was too big. Mark felt the tipping and the spinning, the wagon hitting the earth broadside, with one crash upon another. He thought he saw the dragon's cage, still intact, fly past above his spinning head, all jumbled with a stream of bedding, and a frog-crock streaming frogs. He hit the ground, expecting to be killed or stunned, but soft earth eased the impact.

Aware of no serious injury, he rolled over in grass and sand, the ground beneath him squelching wetly. Nearby, the wagon was on one side now, with one set of wheels spinning in the air, and the team still struggling hopelessly to pull it. Meanwhile what was left of the cavalry thundered past, rounding the wagon on both sides, charging on into thickets along the roadside just ahead. Mark could catch just a glimpse of people there, who looked like Ben and Barbara, fleeing on foot.

The dragon was still keening, inside its upended but unbroken crate beside the wagon.

On all fours, Mark scrambled back into the thick of the spilled contents at the wagon's rear. He went groping, fumbling, looking for the sword. He let out a small cry of triumph when he recognized Townsaver's blade, and thrust a hand beneath a pile of spilled potatoes for the hilt. He had just started to lift the weapon when he heard a multitude of feet come pounding closer just behind him. Mark turned his head to see men in half-armor, wearing the Duke's colors, leaping from their mounts to surround him. A spearman held his weapon at Mark's throat. Mark's hand was still on the sword, but he could feel no power in it.

"Drop it, varlet!" a soldier ordered.

—*and overhead, out of the mist, great wings were sighing down. And the caged dragon's continuous keening was answered from up there by a creak that might have issued from a breaking windmill blade*—

Another inhuman voice interrupted. This one was a basso roar, projecting itself at ground level through the mists. Mark's knees were still on the ground, and through them he could feel the stamp of giant feet, pounding closer. A shape moving on two treetrunk legs, tall as an elder's house, swayed out of the fog, two forelimbs raised like pitchforks. Striding forward faster than a riding-beast could run, the dragon closed in on a mounted man. Flame jetted from a beautiful red cavern of a mouth, the glow of fire reflecting, resonating, through cubic meters of the surrounding fog. The man atop his steed, five meters from the dragon, exploded like a firework, lance flying from his hand, his armor curling like paper in the blast. Mark felt the heat at thirty meters' distance.

Without pausing, the dragon altered the direction of its charge. It snorted, making an odd sound, almost musical, like metal bells. Once more it projected fire from nose and upper mouth. This time the target, another man on beastback, somehow dodged the full effect. The riding-beast screamed at the light brush of fire, and veered the wrong way. One pitchfork-forelimb caught it by one leg, and sent it and its rider twirling through the air to break their bodies against a tree.

All around Mark, men were screaming. He saw the Duke's men and their riding-beasts in desperate retreat.

The dragon changed the direction of its charge again. Now it was coming straight at Mark.

Nestor, at the moment when the wagon tipped, had tried to save himself by leaping as far as he could out from the seat, to one side and forward. He did get clear of the crash, landed on one leg and one arm, and managed to turn the flying fall into an acrobat's tumbling roll, thanking all the gods even as he struck that here the earth was soft.

Soft or not, something struck him on the side of the head, hard enough to daze him for a moment. He fought grimly to stay free of the descending curtain of internal darkness, and collapsed no farther than his hands and knees. He was dimly aware of someone—Ben, he thought it was—bounding past him, into nearby thickets promising concealment. And there went a pair of lighter, swifter feet, Barbara's perhaps.

In the thick fog, cavalry came pounding near. Beside Nestor in the muck, partially buried in it even as he was, there was a log. He let himself sink closer to it, trying to blend shapes.

The cavalry swept past with a lot of noise, then was, for the moment, gone. Nestor scrambled his way back toward the tipped wagon. He had to have the sword. Whatever else happened, he wasn't going to leave that for the Duke.

When he reached the spill, he found the sword at once, as if, even half-dazed, he had known where Dragonslicer must be. With the familiar shape of the hilt tightly in his grip, and the sound of the returning cavalry in his ears, Nestor moved in a crouching run back toward the thickets. He hoped the others were getting away somehow.

Once among the bushes, Nestor crouched down motionless. Once more, in the fog, cavalry went pounding blindly past him, towards the wagon. He jumped up and ran on again. A moment later, a hideous, monstrous bellowing filled the air behind him. It sounded like the grandfather of all dragons, and the noise it made was followed by human screams.

Nestor ran on. He had his dragon-killing sword in hand, but he wasn't about to turn back and risk his neck to use it to save his enemies. Now, with the dragon providing such great distraction, he could calculate that his chances of getting away were quite good. Behind him the sounds of panic and fighting persisted. Possibly the Duke's patrol could be strong and determined enough to fight a dragon off. Nestor kept going, angling away from the direction he thought he'd seen Ben and Barbara take—time enough, later, to get his crew back together if they'd all survived.

In the fog, the bank of the creek appeared so suddenly in front of Nestor that he almost plunged into the water before he saw it. He hadn't been expecting to encounter the stream right here, but here it was, across his path, and maybe he was getting turned around again— small wonder, in this pea soup.

Now Nestor deliberately stepped into the thigh-deep water and started wading. He wanted to put some more distance between himself and the fighting. If the soldiers drove the dragon off or killed it, they might still come this way looking. The uproar slowly faded with distance. It was peculiar, because this wasn't the country where you'd normally expect to find big dragons . . . any more than you'd expect a fog like this . . .

—*wings translucently thin, but broad as a boat's sails, were coming down at him from above, breaking through puffs of low pearly mist— what in the name of all the gods?*—

For a moment Nestor, still knee-deep in water and gazing upward, literally could not move. He thought that no one had ever seen the like of the thing descending on him now. Those impossible wings had to be reptilian, which meant to Nestor that the creature they supported had to be some subspecies of dragon. The reptilian head was small, and obviously small of brain, grotesquely tiny for such large wings. The mouth and teeth were outsized for the head, and looked large enough to do fatal damage to a human with one bite. The body between the wings was wizened, covered with tough-looking scales, the two dangling legs all scales and sinew, with taloned feet unfolding from them now.

It was coming at Nestor in a direct attack. He stood his ground— stood his muck and water rather—and thrust up at the lowering shape. With any other weapon in hand he would have thought his chances doubtful at best, but with Dragonslicer he could hardly lose.

Only at the last moment, when it was too late to try to do anything else, did he realize that the sound he always heard when he used this sword was not sounding now, that this time the sensation of power with which it always stung his arm was absent.

Even shorn of magic, the blade was very sharp, and Nestor's arm was strong and steady. The thrust slid off one scale, but then sank in between two others, right at the joint of leg and body. Only in that moment did Nestor grasp how big the flying creature really was. In the next instant one of the dragon's feet, its leathery digits sprouting talons, as flexible as human fingers, stronger than rope, came to scoop Nestor up by the left arm and shoulder. The embrace of its other leg caught his right arm and pinned it to his body, forcing the sword-hilt out of his grasp, leaving the sword still embedded in the creature's flesh between its armored scales. The violence with which it grabbed and lifted him banged his head against its scaly breast, a blow hard enough to daze him again.

He knew, before he slid into unconsciousness, that his feet had been pulled out of the water, that nothing was in contact with his body now but air and dragon scales. He felt the rhythm of the great wings working, and then he knew no more.

Even as the enormous landwalker charged at Mark, a shrill sound burst from the sword in his right hand. The sound from the sword was almost lost in the roar that erupted from the dragon's fiery throat, and the pulsed thunder of its feet. But the sword's power could be felt as well as heard. Mark was holding the hilt in both hands now, and energy rushed from it up into his hands and arms, energy that aligned the blade to meet the dragon's rush.

The sword held up Mark's arms, and it would not let him fall, or cower down, or even try to step aside. He thought, fleetingly: *This is the same terror that Kenn felt.* And helplessly he watched the great head bending near. From those lips, that looked as hard and rough as chainmail, and from those flaring nostrils, specks of fire drooled. The glowing poison spurted feebly, from a reservoir that must have been exhausted on the cavalry. Mark could feel the bounce and quiver of the soft earth with each approaching thud of the huge dragon's feet. And he saw the pitchfork forelimbs once more raised, to swipe and rend.

The head came lowering at Mark. It was almost as if those forge-fire eyes were compelled to challenge the light-sparks that now flecked the sword, springing as if struck from the metal by invisible flint. The sword jerked in a sideways stroke, driven by some awesome power that Mark's arms could only follow, as if they were bound to the blade by puppet-strings.

The one stroke took off the front quarter of the dragon's lower jaw. The dragon lurched backward one heavy step, even as a splash of iridescent blood shot from its wound. Mark felt small droplets strike, an agony of pinhead burning, on his left arm below his sleeve, and one on his left cheek. And the noise that burst from the dragon's throat behind its blood was like no other noise that Mark had ever heard, in waking life or nightmare.

In the next instant, the dragon lurched forward again to the attack. Even as Mark willed to twist his body out of the way of the crushing mass the sword in his hands maintained a level thrust, holding his hands clamped upon its hilt, preventing an escape.

Mark went down backward before that falling charge. He fell embedded in cushioning mud, beneath the scaly mass. In mud, he slid from under the worst of the weight; he could still breathe, at least. Finally the sword released his hands, and he felt a monstrous shudder go through the whole mass of the dragon's body, which then fell motionless.

The pain had faded from the pinprick burns along his arm, but in his left cheek a point of agony still glowed. He tried to quench it in mud as he writhed his way toward freedom. Only gradually did he realize that he had not been totally mangled, indeed that he was scarcely injured at all. The falling torso had almost missed him. One of the dragon's upper limbs made a still arch above his body, like the twisted trunk of an old tree.

He was still alive, and still marveled at the fact. Some deep part of his mind had been convinced that a magic sword must always kill its user, even if at the same time it gave him victory.

The scaly treetrunk above Mark's body began to twitch. Timing his efforts as best he could to its irregular pulsation, he worked himself a few centimeters at a time out from under the dead or dying mass. He was quivering in every limb himself, and now he began to feel his bruises, in addition to the slowly fading pain of the small burn. Still he was unable to detect any really serious injury, as he crawled and then hobbled away from the corpse of the dragon into some bushes. The only clear thought in his mind was that he must continue either to try to hide or to run away, and at the moment he was still too shaken to try to run.

Sitting on the muddy ground behind a bush, he realized gradually that, for the moment at least, no danger threatened. The dragon had chased the cavalry away, and now the sword had killed the dragon. He had to go back to the dragon and get the sword.

Standing beside the slain monster he couldn't see the sword. It must still be buried where his hands had last let go of it. It must still be hilt down in mud, under the full weight of more than a thousand kilograms of armored flesh.

Going belly down in mud again, Mark reached as far as possible in under the dead mass. He could just touch the sword's hilt, and feel through it a faint, persistent thrum of power. The blade was hilt-deep in the dragon; though Mark could touch the weapon, it seemed impossible without moving the dragon to pull it out.

Mark was still tugging hopelessly at the handle when he heard Ben's voice, quiet but shaken, just behind him.

"Bigger'n any dragon I ever saw . . . where's Nestor?"

Mark turned his head halfway. "I don't know. Help me get the sword out, it's stuck in, way down here."

"You see what happened? I didn't." Without waiting for an answer, Ben planted his columnar legs close beside the plated belly of the beast, then raised both hands to get leverage on one of the dragon's upper limbs, which appeared to be already stiffening. Grunting, he heaved upward on the leg.

Mark tugged simultaneously at the sword's handle, and felt it slide a few centimeters toward him. "Once more."

Another combined effort moved the hilt enough to bring it out into full view. When Ben saw it, he bent down and took hold—there was room on that hilt for only one of his hands. One was enough. With a savage twist he brought the blade right out, cutting its own way through flesh and scale, bringing another flow of blood. The colors of the blood were dulling quickly now.

As soon as Ben had the sword free, he dropped it in the mud, and stood there rubbing the fingers of the hand with which he'd pulled it out. "I felt it," he muttered, sounding somewhat alarmed. He didn't specify just what it was he'd felt.

"It's all right," said Mark. He picked up the weapon and wiped it with some handy leaves. His hands were and remained black with mud, but, as before, the sword was clean again with almost no effort at all.

Mark became motionless, staring at the hilt. It showed no castle wall, but the white outline of a stylized dragon.

Ben wasn't looking at the sword, but staring at Mark's face. "You got burned," Ben said softly. "You must have been close. Where's Nestor?"

"I haven't seen him. Yes, I was close. I was the one who held the sword. This sword. But this isn't mine. Where's mine?" As he spoke, Mark rose slowly to his feet. His voice that had been calm was on the verge of breaking.

Ben stared at him. There was a sound nearby, and they both turned quickly to see Barbara. She was as muddy and bedraggled as they were, carrying her hatchet in one hand, sling in the other.

"Where's Nestor?" she asked, predictably.

Haltingly, his mind still numbed by the fact that his sword was gone, Mark recounted his version of events since the wagon had tipped over. They looked at him, and at the sword; then Barbara took the weapon from his hands, and pressed gently with the point right on the middle of one of the dragon's thickest scales. There was a spark from the steel. With a faint, shrill sound, the blade sank in as into butter.

Mark said: "That looks almost exactly like my sword, but it must be Nestor's. Where's mine?" The feeling of shock that had paralyzed him was suddenly gone, and he ran to search amid the jumbled contents of the wagon. He couldn't find the sword there, or anywhere nearby. The others followed him, looking for Nestor, but he was not to be found either, alive or dead. They called his name, at first softly, then with increasing boldness. The only bodies to be found were those of soldiers, mangled by the landwalker before it had been killed.

"If he's gone," said Mark, "I wonder if he took my sword?"

He might have, by mistake, they decided—no one thought it would make sense for Nestor to take Mark's weapon and deliberately leave his own behind.

"But where'd he go?"

"Maybe the soldiers got him. And the other sword."

"They were in a blind panic, just getting out of here. The ones who're still alive are running yet."

Dead riding-beasts were lying about too, and some severely injured. Ben dispatched these with his club. The team of loadbeasts was still attached to the spilled wagon, and fortunately did not appear to be seriously hurt. The human survivors, pushing together, tipped the wagon back on its wheels again, and saw that all four wheels still would roll.

While Mark continued a fruitless search for his sword, the others reloaded cargo, throwing essentials, valuables, and junk all back into the wagon. They reloaded the now empty frog-crock, and at last the tumbled dragon-cage.

Barbara paused with her hand on the cage, whose forlorn occupant still keened. "Do you suppose the big ones came after this? They must have heard it yelping."

Ben shook his head decisively. "Never knew dragons to act that way. Big ones don't care about a small one, except maybe to eat it if they're hungry, which they usually are." Ben was worried, but not about dragons. "If Nestor's gone, what're we going to do?"

Barbara said: "We've looked everywhere around here. Either he's still running, or else he got hurt or killed and washed down the river. I can't think of anything else."

"Or," said Mark, coming back toward the others in his vain seeking, "the soldiers got him after all. And my sword with him."

They all looked once more for Nestor and the sword. They even followed the river downstream for a little distance. It seemed plain that a body drifting in this stream would catch in shallows or on a rock before it had gone very far.

Still there was no sign of man or weapon.

At last Barbara was the decisive one. "If the soldiers did get him, he's gone, and if he's dead he's dead. If he's still running, well, we can't catch him when we've got no idea which way he went. We'd better get ourselves out of here. More soliders could come back. Einar, your sword's just not here either. If Nestor's got it, and he catches up with us, you'll get it back."

"Where'll we go?" Ben sounded almost like a child.

She answered firmly: "On to Sir Andrew's. If Nestor is going to come looking for us anywhere, it'll be there."

"But what'll we say when we get there? What'll we do? Sir Andrew's expecting Nestor."

"We'll say he's delayed." Barbara patted Ben's arm hard, encouragingly. "Anyway, we've still got Nestor's sword. You can kill dragons with it if you have to, can't you? If little Einar here can do it."

Ben looked, if not frightened, at least doubtful. "I guess we can talk about that on the way."

CHAPTER 8

Two men were sitting in Kind Sir Andrew's dungeon. One, who was young, perched on a painted stool just inside the bars of a commodious whitewashed cell. The other man was older, better dressed, and occupied a similar seat not very far outside the bars. He was reading aloud to the prisoner out of an ancient book. To right and left were half a dozen other cells, all apparently unoccupied, all clean and whitewashed, all surprisingly light and airy for apartments in a dungeon. Though this level of the castle was half underground, there were windows set high in the end wall of the large untenanted cell at the far end of the row.

At a somewhat greater distance, down a branching, stone-vaulted, cross corridor, were other cells that gave evidence of habitation, though not by human beings. Sir Andrew had caused that more remote portion of his dungeon to be converted into a kind of bestiary, now housing birds and beasts of varied types, whose confinement had required the weaving of cord nets across the original heavy gratings of the cell doors and windows.

Yes, there were more windows in that wing. You could tell by the amount of light along the corridor that way. The young man on the stool inside the cell, who was currently the only human inmate in the whole dungeon, and who was supposed to be listening to the reading, kept looking about him with a kind of chronic wonder, at windows and certain other surprises. The young man's name was Kaparu—at least that was the only name he could remember for himself. He was thin-faced and thin-boned, and had lank, dark, thinning hair. His clothes were ragged, and his weathered complexion showed that he had not been an indoor prisoner for any length of recent time. He had quick eyes—quick nervous hands as well, hands that now and then rubbed at his wrists as if he were still in need of reassurance that they were not bound. Every now and then he would raise his head and turn it, distracted by the small cheerful cries that came from his fellow prisoners down the corridor.

Kaparu was no stranger to the inside of jails and dungeons, but never in all his wanderings had he previously encountered or even imagined a jail like this. To begin with, light and air were present in quite astonishing quantities. Yes, the large cell at the end of the row had real windows, man-sized slits extending through the whole thickness of the lower castle wall, like tunnels open to the bright late summer afternoon. The way it looked, the last prisoner put in there might just have walked out through the window. In through those embrasures came not only air and light, but additional cheerful sounds. Outside on Sir Andrew's green the fair was getting under way.

There was also a sound, coming from somewhere else in the dungeon, of water dripping. But somehow, in this clean, white interior, the sound suggested not dankness and slow time, but rather the outdoor gurgle of a brook. Or, more aptly, the lapping of a lake. The castle stood on a modest rise of ground, the highest in the immediate neighborhood, but its back was to a sizable lake, whose surface level was only a little lower than this dungeon floor.

Resting on the floor of the prisoner's cell, not far from the feet of his stool, was a metal dish that held a sizable fragment of bread, bread fresh from the oven today and without insects. Beside the plate, a small pottery jug held clean drinking water. At intervals the prisoner involuntarily darted a glance toward the bread, and each time he did so his left foot as if in reflex lifted a trifle from the stool-rung it was on—but in this peculiar dungeon there were evidently no rats to be continually kicked and shooed away.

And each time the prisoner turned his head to look at the plate, his gaze was likely to linger, in sheer disbelief, upon the small vase filled with fresh cut flowers, that stood beside his water jug.

The man who sat outside the cell, so patiently reading aloud from the old book, had not been young for some indeterminate time. He was broadly built, and quite firmly and positively established in middle age, as if he had no intention at all of ever growing really old. His clothing was rich in fabric and in workmanship, but simple in cut, and more than ordinarily untidy. Like his garments, his beard and mustache of sandy gray were marked with traces of his recently concluded lunch, which had obviously comprised some richer stuff than bread and water.

At more or less regular intervals, he turned the pages of the old book with powerful though ungraceful fingers, and he continued to read aloud from the book in his slow, strong voice. It was a knowledgeable voice, and never stumbled, though its owner was translating an old language to a new one as he read. Still there were hesitations, as if the reader wanted to make very sure of every word before he gave it irrevocable pronunciation. He read:

" 'And the god Ardneh said to the men and women of the Old World, once only will I stretch forth the power of my hand to save you from the end of your own folly, once only and no more. Once only will I change the world, that the world may not be destroyed by the hellbomb creatures that you in your pride and carelessness have called up out of the depths of matter. And once only will I hold my Change upon the world, and the number of the years of Change will be forty-nine thousand, nine hundred, and forty-nine.

" 'And the men and women of the Old World said to the god Ardneh, we hear thee and agree. And with thy Change let the world no longer be called Old, but New. And we do swear and covenant with thee, that never more shall we kill and rape and rob one another in hope of profit, of revenge, or sport. And never again shall we bomb and level one another's cities, never again . . .' "

Here the reader paused, regarding his prisoner sternly. "Is something bothering you, sirrah? You seem distracted."

The man inside the cell started visibly. "I, Sir Andrew? No, not I. Nothing is bothering me. Unless . . . well, unless, I mean, it is only that a man tends to feel happier when he's outside a cell than when he's in one." And the prisoner's face, which was an expressive countenance when he wished it to be, brought forth a tentative smile.

Sir Andrew's incipient frown deepened in response. "If you think you would be happier outside, then pray do not let your attention wander when I am reading to you. Your chance of rejoining that happy, sunlit world beyond yon windows depends directly upon your behavior here. Your willingness to admit past errors, to seek improvement, take instruction, and reform."

Kaparu said quickly: "Oh, I admit my errors, sir. I do indeed. And I can take instruction."

"Fine. Understand that I am never going to set you free, never, as long as I think you are likely to return to your old habits of robbing innocent travelers."

The prisoner, like a child reprimanded in some strict school, now sat up straight. He became all attention. "I am trying, Sir Andrew, to behave well." And he gave another quick glance around his cell, this time as if to make sure that no evidence to the contrary might be showing.

"You are, are you? Then listen carefully." Sir Andrew cleared his throat, and returned his gaze to the yellowed page before him. As he resumed reading, his frown gradually disappeared, and his right hand rose unconsciously from the book, to emphasize key words with vague and clumsy gestures.

" '—and when the full years of the Change had been accomplished, Orcus, the Prince of Demons, had grown to his full strength. And Orcus saw that the god Draffut, the Lord of Beasts and of all human mercy, who sat at the right hand of Ardneh in the councils of the gods, was healing men and women in Ardneh's name, of all manner of evil wounds and sickness. And when Orcus beheld this he was very wroth. And he—' "

"Beg pardon, sir?"

"Eh?"

"That word, sir. 'Wroth.' It's not one that I'm especially familiar with."

"Ah. 'Wroth' simply means angry. Wrathful." Sir Andrew spoke now in a milder tone than before, milder in fact than the voice in which he generally read. And at the same time his expression grew benign.

Once more he returned to his text. "Where was I? Yes, here . . . 'In all the Changed world, only Ardneh himself was strong enough to oppose Orcus. Under the banner of Prince Duncan of the Offshore Islands, men and women of good will from around the earth rallied to the cause of good, aiding and supporting Ardneh. And under the banner of the evil Emperor, John Ominor, all men and women who loved evil rallied from all the lands of the earth to—' "

"Sir?"

"Yes, what?"

"There's one more thing in there I don't understand, sir. Did you say this John Ominor was an emperor?"

"Hm, hah, yes. Listening now, are you? Yes. The Emperor in those days—we are speaking now, remember, of a time roughly two thousand years in the past, at the end of what is called Ardneh's Change, and when the great battle was fought out between Orcus and Ardneh, and both of them perished—at that time, I say, no man was called emperor unless he was a real power in the world. Perhaps even its greatest power. It might be possible to trace a very interesting connection from that to the figure of mockery and fun, which today—"

"Sir?"

"Yes?"

"If you don't mind, sir. Did you say just a moment ago that Ardneh perished?"

Sir Andrew nodded slowly. "You *are* listening. But I don't want to get into all that now. The main thrust of this passage, what you should try to grasp today . . . but just let me finish reading it. Where was I? Ha. 'In all the Changed world, only Ardneh himself—' and so forth, we had that. Hah. 'In most dreadful combat the two strove together. And Orcus spake to Ardneh, saying—' Ah, drat, why must we be interrupted?"

The prisoner frowned thoughtfully at this, before he realized at just what point the text had been broken off. Sir Andrew had been perturbed by certain new sounds in the middle distance, sounds steadily drawing near. A shuffling of feet, a sequential banging open of doors, announced the approach of other human beings. Presently, at the highest observable turn of the nearby ascending stair, there appeared the bowed legs of an ancient jailer, legs cut off at the knees by a stone arch. The jailer came on down the stairs, until his full figure was in view; in one arm, quivering with age, he held aloft a torch (which surely had been of more use on the dark stair above than it was here) to light the way for the person following him, a woman—no, a lady, thought the prisoner.

She was garbed in Sir Andrew's colors of orange and black, and she brought with her an indefinable but almost palpable sense of the presence of magical power. She must have been a great beauty not long hence, and was attractive still, not less so for the touch of gray in her black hair, the hint of a line or two appearing at certain angles of her face.

As soon as this lady had become fully visible at the top of the stairs, she paused in her descent. "Sir Andrew," she called, in a voice as rich and lovely as her visual appearance, "I would like a little of your time, immediately. A matter of importance has come up."

Grunting faintly, Sir Andrew rose from his stool, turning as he did so to address the visitor. "It's really important, Yoldi?" he grumbled. And, a moment later, answered his own question. "Well, of course, it must be." He had long ago impressed upon everyone in the castle his dislike of being interrupted when he was at his favorite work of uplifting prisoners.

Sir Andrew went to the stair, and took the torch from the hand of the aged jailer, making a shooing motion at the man to signify that he was dismissed. Then, holding the flame high with one arm, bearing his precious book under the other, the knight escorted his favorite enchantress back up the stairs, to where they might be able to hold a private conference.

Once they had climbed round the first turn, Dame Yoldi glanced meaningfully at the old book. "Were you obtaining a good result?" she asked.

"Oh, I think perhaps a good beginning. Yes, I know you're convinced that my reading to them does no good. But don't you see, it means they have at least some exposure to goodness in their lives. To the history, if you like, of goodness in the world."

"I doubt that they appreciate it much."

There were windows ahead now, tall narrow slits in the outer wall where it curved around a landing, and Sir Andrew doused his torch in a sandbucket kept nearby. Trudging on to where the windows let in light, he shook his head to deny the validity of Dame Yoldi's comment. "It's really dreadful, you know, listening to their stories. I think many of them are unaware that such a thing as virtue can exist. Take the poor lad who's down there now, he's a good example. He has been telling me how he was raised by demon worshippers."

"And you believed him?" Good Dame Yoldi sounded vexed, both by the probability that the true answer to her question would be yes, and the near certainty that she was never going to hear it from Sir Andrew.

The knight, stumping on ahead, did not seem to hear her now. He paused when he reached the first narrow window, set where the stair made its first above-ground turn. Through the aperture it was possible to look out past the stone flank of the south guard-tower, and see something of the small permanent village that huddled just in front of the castle, and a slice of the great common green beyond. On that sward, where woolbeasts grazed most of the year, the annual fair had been for the past day or so taking shape.

"I should have ordered him some better food, perhaps. Some gruel at least, maybe a little meat." Sir Andrew was obviously musing aloud about his prisoner, but his distracted tone made it equally obvious that his thoughts were ready to stray elsewhere. "Crops were so poor this year, all round the edge of the Swamp, that I didn't know if we'd have much of a fair at all. But there it is. It appears to be turning out all right."

Dame Yoldi joined him at the window, though it was so narrow that two people had trouble looking out at once. "Your granaries have taken a lot of the shock out of poor years, ever since you built them. If only we don't have two bad years in a row."

"That could be disastrous, yes. Is that what you wanted to see me about? Another village delegation? Is it crops, dragons, or both?"

"It's a delegation. But not from any of the villages this time."

Sir Andrew turned from the window. "What then?"

"They've come from the Duke, and I've already cast a sortilege, and the omens are not particularly good for you today. I thought you'd like to know that before you meet these people."

"And meet them I must, I suppose. Yoldi, in matters of magic, as in so much else, your efforts are constantly appreciated." Sir Andrew leaned toward his enchantress and kissed her gently on the forehead. "All right, I am warned."

He moved to the ascending stair, and again led the way up. He had rounded the next turn before he turned his head back to ask: "What do they say they want?"

"They don't. They refuse to discuss their business with anyone else before they've seen you."

"And they exhibit damned bad manners, I suppose, as usual."

"Andrew?"

On his way up, the knight paused. "Yes?"

"Last night that vision of swords came to me again. Stacked in a pyramid like soldiers' spears in the guardroom, points up. I don't know what it means yet. But as I said, today's omens are not good."

"All right." When the stair had brought him to a higher window, Sir Andrew paused again, to catch his breath and to look out once more and with a better view over the hectares of fairground that had sprung up before his castle almost as if by magic. Jumbled together were neat pavilions, cheap makeshift shelters, professional entertainers' tents of divers colors, all set up already or still in the process of erection. The present good weather, after some days of rain, was bringing out a bigger crowd than usual, mostly people from the nearby villages and towns. The lowering sun shone upon banners and signs advertising merchants of many kinds and of all degrees of honesty, all of them getting ready to do business now or already engaged in it. Sir Andrew's towers dominated a crossroad of highways leading to four important towns, and a considerable population was tributary to him. On fine evenings, such as this promised to be, the fair would likely run on by torchlight into the small hours. The harvest, such as it was, was mostly already in, and most of those who worked the land would be able to take time out for a holiday.

The master of the castle frowned from his window, noting the booths and tables of the operators of several games of chance. Their honesty, unlike that of the other merchants, tended to be of only one degree.

"Hoy, these gamblers, gamesters." The knight's face expressed his disapproval. "Remind me, Yoldi. I ought to warn them that if any of them are caught cheating again this year, they can expect severe treatment from me."

"I'll remind you tomorrow. Though they will undoubtedly cheat anyway, as you ought to realize by this time. Now, may we get on with the important business?"

"All right, we'll get it over with." And the knight looked almost sternly at his enchantress, as if it were her fault that the meeting with the Duke's people was being delayed. He motioned briskly toward the stair, and this time she led the way up. He asked: "Who has the Duke sent to bully me this time?"

"He's sent two, one of which you'll probably remember. Hugh of Semur. He's one of the stewards of the Duke's territories adjoining—"

"Yes, yes, I do remember him, you don't have to tell me. Blustery little man. Fraktin always likes to send two, so they can spy and report on each other, I suppose. Who's the other this time?"

"Another one of the Duke's cousins. Lady Marat."

"For a man without direct heirs, he has more cousins than—anyway, I don't know her. What's she like?"

"Good-looking. Otherwise I'm not sure yet what she's like, except that she means you no good."

The pair of them were leaving the stair now, on a high level of the castle that held Sir Andrew's favorite general-purpose meeting room.

He caught up with Dame Yoldi and took her arm. "I hardly supposed she would. Well, let's have them in here. Grapes of Bacchus, do you suppose there's any of that good ale left? No, don't call for it now, I didn't mean that. Later, after the Duke's dear emissaries have departed."

The emissaries were shortly being ushered in. The Lady Marat was tall and willowy and dark of hair and skin. Again, as in Dame Yoldi's case, what must once have been breathtaking beauty was still considerable—in the case of Lady Marat, thought Sir Andrew, nature had almost certainly been fortified in recent years by a touch of enchantment here and there.

Hugh of Semur, a step lower than Her Ladyship in the formal social scale, was chunkily built and much more mundane-looking, though, as his clothes testified, he was something of a dandy too. Sir Andrew recalled Hugh as having more than a touch of self-importance, but he was probably trying to suppress this characteristic at the moment.

Formal greetings were quickly got out of the way, and refreshment perfunctorily offered and declined. Lady Marat wasted no time in beginning the real discussion, for which she adopted a somewhat patronizing tone: "As you will have heard, cousin, the Duke's beloved kinsman, the Seneschal Ibn Gauthier, was assassinated some days ago."

"Some word of that has reached us, yes," Sir Andrew admitted. Having got that far he hesitated, trying to find some truthful comment that would not sound too impolite. He preferred not to be impolite without deliberate purpose and good cause.

Her Ladyship continued: "We have good reason to believe that the assassin is here in your domain, or at least on his way. He is a commoner, his name is Mark, the son of Jord the miller of the village of Arin-on-Aldan. This Mark is twelve years old, and he is described as large for his age. His hair and general coloring are fair, his face round, his behavior treacherous in the extreme. He has with him a very valuable sword, stolen from the Duke. A reward of a hundred gold pieces is offered for the sword, and an equal amount for the assassin-thief."

"A boy of twelve, you say?" The furrow of unhappiness that had marked Sir Andrew's brow since the commencement of the interview now deepened. "How sad. Well, we'll do what we must. If this lad should appear before me for any reason, I'll certainly question him closely."

The Lady Marat was somehow managing to look down her nose at Sir Andrew, though the chair in which he sat as host and ruler here was somewhat higher than her own. "Good Cousin Andrew, I think that His Grace expects a rather more active co-operation on your part than that. It will be necessary for you to conduct an all-out search for this killer, throughout your territory. And when the assassin is found, to deliver him speedily to the Duke's justice. And, to find and return the stolen sword as well."

Sir Andrew was frowning at her fixedly. "Twice now you've called me that. Are we really cousins?" he wondered aloud. And his bass voice warbled over the suggestion in a way that implied he found it profoundly disturbing.

Dame Yoldi, seated at Sir Andrew's right hand, looked disturbed too, but also half amused. While Hugh of Semur, showing no signs but those of nervousness, hastened to offer an explanation. "Sir Andrew, Her Ladyship meant only to speak in informal friendship."

"Did she, hah? Had m'hopes up high there for a minute. Thought I was about to become a member of the Duke's extended family. Could count on his fierce vengeance to track down anyone, any child at least, who did me any harm. Tell me, will you two be staying to enjoy the fair?"

The Lady Marat's visage had turned to dark ice, and she was on the verge of rising from her chair. But Dame Yoldi had already risen; perhaps some faint noise from outside that had made no impression on the others had still caught her attention, for she had gone to the window and was looking out into the approaching sunset.

Now she turned back. "Good news, Sir Andrew," she announced in an almost formal voice. "I believe that your dragon-hunters have arrived."

Yoldi's eyes, Sir Andrew thought, had seen more than she had announced.

CHAPTER 9

Nestor, struck on the head with stunning force for the second time in as many minutes, lost consciousness. But not for long. When he regained his senses he found himself being carried only a meter or two above the surface of a fogbound marsh, his body still helplessly clutched to the breast of a flying dragon of enormous wingspan. His left shoulder and upper arm were still in agony, though the animal had shifted its powerful grip and was no longer holding him directly by the damaged limb.

He thought that the dragon was going to drop him at any moment. He knew that a grown man must be a very heavy load—five minutes ago he would have said an impossible load—for any creature that flew on wings and not by magic. And obviously his captor was having a slow and difficult struggle to gain altitude with Nestor aboard. Now the mists below were thick enough to conceal flat ground and water, but the tops of trees kept looming out of the mists ahead, and the flyer kept swerving between the trees. No matter how its great wings labored, it was unable as yet to rise above them.

From being sure that the creature was going to drop him, Nestor quickly moved to being afraid that it was not. Then, as it gained more altitude despite the evident odds, he progressed to being fearful that it would. Either way there appeared to be nothing he could do. Both of his arms were now pinned between his own body and the scaly toughness of the dragon's. He could turn his head, and when he turned it to the right he saw the hilt of the sword, along with half the blade, still protruding from between tough scales near the joining of the animal's left leg and body. The wound was lightly oozing iridescent blood. If Nestor had been able to move his arm, he might have tried to grab the hilt. But then, at this increasing altitude, he might not.

The great wings beat majestically on, slowly winning the fight for flight. Despite the color of the creature's blood, its scales, and everything else about it, Nestor began lightheadedly to wonder if it was truly a dragon after all. He had thought that by now, after years of hunting them, he knew every subspecies that existed . . . and Dragonslicer had never failed to kill before, not when he had raised it against the real thing. Could this be some hybrid creature, raised for a special purpose in some potentate's private zoo?

But there was something he ought to have remembered about the sword . . . dazed as Nestor was, his mind filled with his shoulder's pain and the terror of his fantastic situation, he couldn't put together any clear and useful chain of thought. This thing can't really carry me, he kept thinking to himself, and kept expecting to be dropped at any moment. No flying creature ought to be able to scoop up a full-grown man and just bear him away. Nestor realized that he was far from being the heaviest of full-grown men, but still . . .

Now, for a time, terror threatened to overcome his mind. Nestor clutched with his fingernails at the scales of the beast that bore him. Now he could visualize it planning to drop him when it had reached a sufficient height, like a seabird cracking shells on rocks below. In panic he tried to free his arms, but it ignored his feeble efforts.

Once more Nestor's consciousness faded and came back. On opening his eyes this time he saw that he and his captor were about to be engulfed by a billow of fog thicker than any previously encountered. When they broke out of the fog again, he could see that at last they had gained real altitude. Below, no treetops at all could now be seen, nothing but fog or cloud of an unguessable depth. Overhead, a dazzling white radiance was trying to eat through whatever layers of fog remained. The damned ugly wounded thing has done it, Nestor thought, and despite himself he had to feel a kind of admiration . . .

When he again came fully to himself, his abductor was still carrying him in the same position. They were in fairly smooth flight between two horizontal layers of cloud. The layer below was continuous enough to hide the earth effectively, while that above was torn by patches of blue sky. It was a dream-like experience, and the only thing in Nestor's memory remotely like it was being on a high mountain and looking down at the surface of a cloud that brimmed a valley far below.

The much greater altitude somehow worked to lessen the terror of being dropped. Once more the sword caught at Nestor's eye and thought. Turning his head he observed how, with each wingstroke, the hilt of the embedded weapon moved slightly up and down. A very little blood was still dripping. Nestor knew the incredible toughness of dragons, their resistance to injury by any ordinary weapon. But this . . .

He kept coming back to it: A dragon can't carry a man, nothing that flies is big enough to do that. Of course there were stories out of the remote past, of demon-griffins bearing their magician-masters on their backs. And stories of the Old World, vastly older still, telling of some supposed flying horse . . .

The flight between the layers of cloud went on, for a time that seemed to Nestor an eternity, and must in fact have been several hours. Gradually the cloud-layers thinned, and he could see that he was being carried over what must be part of the Great Swamp, at a height almost too great to be frightening at all. The cloud layer above had now thinned sufficiently to let him see from the position of the sun that his flight was to the southwest.

Eventually there appeared in the swamp below an irregular small island, bearing a stand of stark trees and marked at its edges by low cliffs of clay or marl. At this point the dragon turned suddenly into a gentle downward spiral. Nestor could see nothing below but the island itself which might prompt a descent. And it was atop one of those low, wilderness cliffs of clay that the creature landed.

Nestor was dropped rudely onto the rough ground, but he was not released. Before his stiffened limbs could react to the possibilities of freedom, he was grabbed again. One of the dragon's feet clamped round his right leg, lifted him, and hung him up like meat to dry, with his right ankle wedged painfully in the crotch of a tree some five meters above the ground. He hung there upside down and yelled.

His screams of new pain and fresh outrage were loud, but they had no effect. Ignoring Nestor's noise, his tormentor spread its wings and flapped heavily off the cliff. It descended in a glide to land at the edge of the swamp, some fifteen or twenty meters below. There, moving in a cautious waddle, it positioned itself at the edge of a pool. Placid as a woolbeast, it extended its neck and lapped up a drink. It continued to ignore the sword which still stuck out of its hip.

When it had satisfied its thirst, would it wish to dine? That thought brought desperation. Nestor contracted his body, trying to pull himself up within grabbing distance of the branches imprisoning his leg. But his right arm, like his whole body, was stiff and sore, and his left arm could hardly be made to work at all. The fingers of his right hand brushed the branch above, but he could do no more, and fell back groaning. Even if by some all-out contortion he were to succeed in getting his foot free, it might well be at the price of a breakbone fall onto the hard ground at the top of the cliff.

Sounds of splashing drew Nestor's attention back to the swamp. Down there the dragon had plunged one taloned foot into the swamp. Shortly the foot was brought out again, holding a large snake. Nestor, squinting into his upside-down view of the situation, estimated that the striped serpent was as thick as a man's leg. It coiled and thrashed and hissed, its fangs stabbing uselessly against the dragon's scales. The head kept on striking even after the dragon had snapped a large bite out of the snake's midsection, allowing its tail half to fall free.

Nestor drew some small encouragement from the fact that the dragon seemed to prefer snake to human flesh. He tried again, more methodically this time, to work himself free. But in this case method had no more success than frenzy.

He must have fainted again, for his next awareness was of being picked up once more by his captor. He was being held against the dragon's breast in the same way as before, and his arms were already firmly pinned. This time the takeoff was easier, though hardly any less terrifying—it consisted in the dragon's launching itself headlong from the brink of the small cliff, and gaining flying speed in a long, swamp-skimming dive that took Nestor within centimeters of the scummy water. Moss-hung trees flitted past him to right and left, with birds scattering from the trees in noisy alarm. A monkbird screamed, and then was left below.

Again Nestor faded in and out of consciousness. Again he was unsure of how much time was passing. If the damnable thing had not hauled him all this way to eat him, then what was its purpose? He was not being taken home to some gargantuan nest to feed its little ones—no, by all the gods and the Treasure of Benambra, it could not be that. For such an idea to occur to him meant that he was starting to go mad. Everyone knew that dragons built no nests and fed no young . . . and that no flying dragon was big enough to carry a grown man . . .

The clouds in the west were definitely reddening toward sunset before the flight was over. At last the creature ceased its steady southwestern flight and began to circle over another, larger, island of firm ground in the swamp. Most of the trees and lesser growth had been cleared away from a sizable area around the approximate center of the island. In the midst of this clearing stood a gigantic structure that Nestor, observing under difficult conditions, perceived as some kind of temple. It had been built either of stone, brought into the swamp from the gods knew where, or else of some kind of wood, probably magically hardened and preserved against decay. The circles of the dragon's flight fell lower, but Nestor still could not guess to which goddess or god the temple—if such it truly was—had been dedicated; there were so many that hardly anyone knew them all. He could tell that the building was now largely fallen into ruin, and that the ruins were now largely overgrown by vines and flowers.

The largest area remaining cleared was a courtyard, its stone paving still mostly intact, directly in front of what had probably been the main entrance of the temple. The flyer appeared to be heading for a landing in this space, but was for some reason approaching very cautiously. While it was still circling at a few meters' altitude, one possible reason for caution appeared, in the form of a giant landwalker that stalked out into the courtyard from under some nearby trees, bellowing its stupidity and excitement. While the flyer continued to circle just above its reach, the landwalker roared and reared, making motions with its treetrunk forelimbs as if it meant to leap at Nestor's dangling legs when they passed above. Once he thought that he felt its hot breath, but fortunately it had no hope of getting its own bulk clear of the ground.

Then a prolonged cry, uttered in a new and different voice, penetrated the dragon's noise. The new voice was as deep as the landwalker's roar, but still for a moment Nestor thought that it was human. Then he felt sure that it was not. And, when the sound of it had faded, he was not sure that it had borne intelligence of any kind, human or non-human. The basic tone of it had been commanding, and the modulation had seemed to Nestor to hover along the very verge of speech—just as a high-pitched sound might have wavered along the verge of human hearing.

Perhaps to the landwalker dragon some meaning had been clear, for the enormous beast broke off its own uproar almost in mid-bellow. It turned, with a lash of its great tail, and stamped back into the surrounding forest, kicking small trees aside.

Now the way was clear for the flying dragon, and it lowered quickly into the clearing. Then, summoning up one more effort, it hovered with its burden, as from underneath vast trees a being who was neither dragon nor human strode out on two legs—

Nestor looked, then looked again. And still he was not sure that his sufferings had not finally brought him to hallucinations.

The being that stood below him on two legs was clothed from head to toe in long fur, a covering subtly radiant with its own energies. The suggestion was of light on the edge of vision, its colors indefinable. The figure was easily six meters tall, not counting the upraised arm of human shape that reached for Nestor now. The face was not human— certainly it was not—but neither was it merely bestial.

Despite its subtly glowing fur, the giant hand that closed with unexpected gentleness round Nestor's torso was five-fingered, and of human shape. So was the other hand that reached to pluck out delicately the sword still embedded in the hovering dragon's hip. At that, the flyer flapped exhaustedly away. As it departed, it uttered again that creaking-windmill cry that Nestor remembered hearing once before, a lifetime in the past when he had still been driving his wagon through the fog.

The enormous two-legged creature had put the sword down on the paving at its feet, and both furred hands were cradling Nestor now. And he was about to faint again . . .

But he did not faint. An accession of strength, of healing, flowed into his maltreated body from those hands. A touch upon his wounded shoulder, followed by a squeeze that should have brought agony, served instead to drain away the existing pain. A tingling warmth spread gratefully, infiltrating Nestor's entire body. A moment later, when he was set down gently on the ground, he found that he could stand and move easily. He felt alert and capable, indeed almost rested. His pains and injuries had entirely vanished. Even the thirst that had started to torment his mouth and throat was gone.

"Thank you," he said quietly, and looked up, pondering his rescuer. Although the day was almost gone, the sky was still light. The glow of daylight tinged with sunset surrounded the subtler radiance of fur, on the head of the treetall being who stood like a huge man with his arms folded, looking down at Nestor.

"I am sorry that you were hurt." The enormous voice sounded almost human now. "I did not mean you any harm."

Nestor spread his arms. He asked impulsively: "Are you a god?"

"I am not." The answer was immediate, and decisive. "What do you know of gods?"

"Little enough, in truth." Nestor rubbed at his shoulder, which did not hurt; then he dropped his gaze to the sword, which was now lying on the courtyard's pavement at his feet. "But I have met one, once before. It was less than a year ago, though by all the gods it seems at least a lifetime. Until that day, I don't suppose I ever really believed that gods existed."

"And which god did you meet that day, and how?" The huge voice was patient and interested, willing to gossip about gods if that was what Nestor wanted. Above the folded arms, the immense face was—inhuman. It was impossible for Nestor to read expression in it.

Nestor hesitated, thought, and then answered as clearly as he could, and not as he would have responded to questions put by any human interrogator. Instead, he felt himself to be speaking as simply as a child, without trying to calculate where his answers might be going to lead him.

"It was Hermes Messenger that I encountered. He came complete with his staff and his winged boots. I was living alone then, in a small hut, away from people—and Hermes came to my door and woke me one morning at dawn. Just like that. He was carrying in one hand a sword, the like of which I'd never seen before, and he handed it over to me—just like that. Because, as he said, I would know how to use it. I was already in the dragon-hunting trade. He told me that the sword had been for far too long in the possession of people who were never going to use it, who were too afraid of it to try, though they had some idea of its powers. Therefore had Hermes taken it from them, and brought it to me instead. It was called the Sword of Heroes, he told me, and also known as Dragonslicer. He said that it would kill any dragon handily.

"Well, I soon had the opportunity to put Dragonslicer to the test, and I found that what Hermes had told me was the truth. The blade pierced the scales of any dragon that I met like so much cloth. It chopped up their bones like twigs, it found their hearts unerringly. Hermes had told me that it had been forged by Vulcan, and when I saw what it could do I at last believed him on that point also."

"And what else did Hermes say to you?"

Trying to meet his questioner's eyes was giving Nestor trouble. Staring at the giant's legs, he marked how their fur still glowed on the border of vision, even now when direct sunlight was completely gone. Night's shadows, rising from the swamp, had by now crept completely across the cleared courtyard and were climbing the front of the enormous, ruined temple.

"What else did he say? Well, when I thought he was about to turn away and leave me with the sword, I asked him again: 'Why are you giving this to me?' And Hermes answered: 'The gods grow impatient, for their great game to begin.' "

" 'Great game'?" The giant's voice rumbled down to Nestor from above. "Do you know what he meant by that?"

"No, though I have thought about it often." Nestor forced himself to raise his head and look the other in the eye. "Do you know what he meant?"

"To guess what the gods mean by what they say is more than I can manage, most of the time. And is this sword here at our feet the same that Hermes gave to you?"

"I thought so, when I tried to kill the flying dragon with it. But, now that I think back . . ." Nestor bent quickly and picked up the sword, examining its hilt closely in the fading light. "No, it is not, though this one is very like it. A boy I met, traveling, was carrying this one. There was a fight. There was confusion. And Duke Fraktin's soldiers probably have my sword by now." Nestor uttered a small, fierce sound.

"Explain yourself." The huge dark eyes of his questioner were still unreadable, above titanic folded arms.

"All right." Nestor's sudden bitter anger over the loss of his own sword helped suppress timidity. And the longer he spoke with the giant, the less afraid of him he felt. Briefly considering his own reactions, Nestor decided that his childlike forthrightness resulted from knowing himself, like a child, completely dependent on some benevolent other. "I'll explain what I can. But is there any reason why you cannot answer a question or two for me as well?"

"I may answer them, or not. What are these questions?"

The mildness of this reply, as Nestor considered it, encouraged his boldness; and anyway, with him boldness was a lifelong habit, now beginning to reassert itself. "Will you tell me your name, to begin with? You have not spoken it yet. Or asked for mine."

There was a brief pause before the bass rumble of the answer drifted down. "Your name I know already, slayer of dragons. And if I tell you my name now, you are almost certain to misunderstand. Perhaps later."

Nestor nodded. "Next, some questions about the creature that brought me here. I have never seen anything like it before, and I have some experience. It flew straight here to you as if it were acting on your orders, under your control. Is it truly a dragon, or some thing of magic? Did you create it? Did you send it after me?"

"It is a dragon, and I did send it. I am sorry that you were injured, for I meant you no harm. But I took the risk of harming you, for the sake of certain information I felt I had to have. Rumors had reached me, through the dragons, of a man who killed their kind with a new magical power that was embodied in a sword. And other word had reached me, through other means, of other swords that were said to have been made by the gods . . . I have good reason to want to know about these things."

Nestor thought that possibly he was becoming used to the burden of that dark gaze. Now he could meet it once again. "You are a friend of dragons, then, and talk to them."

The giant hesitated. " 'Friend' is perhaps not the right word for it. But in some sense I talk to them, and they to me. I talk with everything that lives. Now, I would ask you to answer a few more questions for me, in turn."

"I'll try."

"Good. There is an old prophecy . . . what do you know of the Gray Horde?"

Nestor looked back blankly. "What should I know? I have never heard the words before. What do they mean?"

His interrogator considered. "Come with me and I will show you a little of their meaning." With that, the towering figure turned and paced away toward the temple. Nestor followed, sword in hand. He smiled briefly, faintly, at the enormous furred back moving before him; the other had not thought twice about turning his back on a strange man with a drawn sword. Not that Nestor was going to think even once about making a treacherous attack. Even if he'd had something to gain by it, he would as soon have contemplated taking a volcano by surprise.

The front entrance of the temple was high enough for the giant to walk into it without stooping. Now, once inside, Nestor observed that the building had indeed been constructed of some hardened and pre-served wood—traces of the grain pattern were still visible. He thought that it must be very old. Much of the roof had fallen in, but the ceiling was still intact in some of the rooms. So it was in the high chamber where Nestor's guide now stopped. Here it was already quite dark inside. As Nestor's eyes adapted to the gloom, the fantastic carvings that filled the walls seemed to materialize out of the darkness like ghosts.

The giant, his body outlined in the night by his own faintly luminous fur, had halted beside a large open tank that was built into the center of the floor. The reservoir was surrounded by a low rim of the same preserved wood from which the floor and walls were made, and Nestor thought that it was probably some kind of ritual vat or bath.

Moving a little closer, he saw that the vat was nearly filled with liquid. Perhaps it was only water, but in the poor light it looked black.

From a shelf his guide took a device that Nestor, having seen its like once or twice before, recognized as a flameless Old World lantern, powered by some force of ancient technology. The giant focussed its cold, piercing beam down into the black vat. Something stirred beneath that inky surface, and in another moment the shallowness of the tank was demonstrated. The liquid it contained was no more than knee-deep on the smallish, man-shaped figure that now rose awkwardly to its feet inside. Dark water, bright-gleaming in the beam of light, ran in rivulets from the gray naked surface of the figure. Its hairless, sexless body reminded Nestor at once of the curved exoskeleton of some giant insect. He did not for a moment take it as truly human, though it was approximately of human shape.

"What is it?" Nestor demanded. He had backed up a step and was gripping his sword.

"Call it a larva." His guide's vast voice was almost hushed. "That is an old word, which may mean a ghost, or a mask, or an unfinished insect form. None of those are exact names for this. But I think that all of them in different ways come close."

"Larva," Nestor repeated. The sound of the word at least seemed to him somehow appropriate. He observed the larva carefully. Once it had got itself fully erect, it stood in the tank without moving, arms hanging at its sides. When Nestor leaned closer, peering at it, he thought that the dark eyes under the smooth gray brow fixed themselves on him, but the eyes were in heavy shadow and he could not be sure. The mouth and ears were tiny, puckered openings, the nose almost non-existent and lacking nostrils. Apparently the thing did not need to breathe. Nestor thought it looked like a mummy. "Is it dead?" he asked.

"It has never been alive. But all across the Great Swamp the life energies of the earth are being perverted to produce others like it. Out there under the surface of the swamp thousands of them are being formed, grown, raised by magical powers that I do not understand. But

I fear that they are connected somehow with the god-game, and the swords. And I know that they are meant for evil."

The god-game again. Nestor had no idea what he ought to say, and so he held his peace. He thought he could tell just from looking at the figure that it was meant for no good purpose. It did not really look like a mummy, he decided, but more like some witch's mannikin, fabricated only to facilitate a curse. Except that, in Nestor's limited experience at least, such mannikins were no bigger than small dolls, and this was nearly as big as Nestor himself. Looking at the thing more closely now, he began to notice the crudity of detail with which it had been formed. Surely it would limp if it tried to walk. He could see the poor, mismatched fit of the lifeless joints, how clumsily they bulked under the smooth covering that was not skin, or scale, or even vegetable bark.

The giant's hand reached out to pluck the figure from the tank. He stood it on the temple floor of hardened wood, directly in front of Nestor. As the hand released it, the figure made a slight independent movement, enough to correct its standing balance. Then it was perfectly still again. Now Nestor could see that its eyes under the gray brows were also gray, the color of old weathered wood, but still inanimate as no wood ever could have been. The eyes were certainly locked onto Nestor now, and they made him feel uncomfortable.

And only now, with an inward shock, did Nestor see that the figure's arms did not end in hands but instead grew into weapons; the right arm terminated in an ugly blade that seemed designed as an instrument of torture, and the left in a crude, barbed hook. There were no real wrists, and the weapons were of one piece with the chitinous-looking material of the forearms. And the bald head was curved and angled like a helm.

With a faint inward shudder Nestor moved back another step. Had he not been carrying the sword, he might have retreated farther from the figure. Now he made his voice come out with an easy boldness that he was far from feeling: "I give up, oh giant who wishes to be nameless. What is this thing? You said 'a larva,' but that name answers nothing. I swear by the Great Worm Yilgarn that I have never seen the like of it before."

"It is one cell of the Gray Horde, which, as I said, is spoken of in an old prophecy. If you are not familiar with that prophecy, believe me that I cannot very well explain it to you now."

"But thousands of these, you say, are being grown in the swamp. By whom? And to what end?"

The giant picked up the two-legged thing like a toy and laid it back into the tank again. He pressed it down beneath the surface of the liquid, which looked to Nestor like swamp-water. No breath-bubbles rose when the larva was submerged. The vast figure in glowing fur turned off the bright light and replaced the lantern on the shelf. He watched the tank until its surface was almost a dark mirror again. Then once more he said to Nestor: "Come with me."

Nestor followed his huge guide out of the temple. This time he was led several hundred paces across the wooded island and into the true swamp at its far edge. A gibbous moon was rising. By its light Nestor watching the furred giant wade waist deep into the still water, seeking, groping with his legs for something on the bottom. He motioned unnecessarily that Nestor should remain on solid ground.

For a full minute the giant searched. Then he suddenly bent and plunged in an arm, big enough to have strangled a landwalker, to its fullest reach. With a huge splash he pulled out another larva. It looked very much like the one in the tank inside the temple, except that the two forearms of this one were connected, grown into one piece with a transverse straight gray shaft that went on past the left arm to end in a spearhead.

The larva let out a strange thin cry when it was torn up from the muck, and spat a jet of bright water from its tiny mouth. Then it lay as limp as a broken puppet in the huge furry hand.

The giant shook it once in Nestor's direction, as if to emphasize to the man the fact of its existence. The larva made no response to the shaking. "This mouth cannot breathe," the giant said. "Or even eat or drink, much less speak, or sing. It can only whine as you have just heard, or howl. It can only make noises that I think are intended to inspire human terror."

Nestor gestured helplessly with the sword that he still carried. "I do not understand."

"Nor do I, as yet. I had feared for a time that the gods themselves, or some among them, were for their own reasons causing these things to come into existence. Just as, for their own reasons, some of the gods decided that you should be given great power to kill dragons. But so far I can discover no connection between the two gifts. So I do not know if it is the gods who are raising these larvae, or some magician of great power. Whoever is doing it, I must find a way to stop it. The life energies of the land about the swamp will be exhausted to no good purpose. Already the crops in nearby fields are failing, human beings are sickening with hunger."

Nestor, looking at the larva, tried to think. "I believe I can tell you one thing. I doubt that the gods had any hand in making these. Because the swords made by the gods are beautiful things in themselves, whatever the purpose behind them may be." And Nestor raised the weapon in his right hand.

The giant, looking at the sword, rumbled out what might have been a quotation:

> *"Long roads the Sword of Fury makes*
> *Hard walls it builds around the soft . . ."*

Nestor waited for more that did not come. Then he lowered the sword, and suddenly demanded: "Why do you deny that you are a god yourself?"

The enormous furred fist tightened. The gray carapace of the larva resisted that pressure only for a moment, then broke with an ugly noise. Gray foulness in a variety of indistinct shapes gushed from the broken torso. What Nestor could see of the spill in the moonlight reminded him more of dung than of anything else. The gray limbs twitched. Wildly, the spear waved once and was still.

The giant cast the wreckage from him with a splash, then washed his hands of it in the black water of the swamp. He said: "I am too small and weak by far, to be a proper god for humankind."

Nestor was almost angry. "You are larger than Hermes was, and I did not doubt the divinity of Hermes for a moment once I had seen him. Nor have I any doubts about you. Is this some riddle with which you are testing me? If so, I am too tired and worn right now to deal with riddles." And too much in need of help. Indeed, the feeling of strength and well-being that Nestor had experienced when the giant first touched him was rapidly declining into weariness again.

The other gazed at him for a moment in silence, and then in silence waded out of the swamp. The mud of the swamp would not stick to his fur, which still glimmered faintly, radiant on the edge of vision. He paced back in the direction of the center of the island, where stood the temple.

Nestor, following, had to trot in his effort to keep up. He cried to the giant's back: "You are no demon, surely?"

The other answered without turning, maintaining his fast pace. "I surely am not."

Nestor surprised himself, and ran. Almost staggering with the effort, he got ahead of the giant and confronted him face to face. With his path thus blocked, the giant halted. Nestor was breathing hard, as if from a long run, or as if he had been fighting. Leaning on his sword, he said: "Before I saw Hermes face to face, I did not believe in the gods at all. But I have seen him, and I believe. And now when I see—well, slay me for it if you will—"

Surprising himself again, he went down on one knee before the other. He had the feeling that his heart, or something else vital inside him, was about to burst, overloaded by feelings he did not, could not, understand.

The giant rumbled: "I will not slay you. I will not knowingly kill any human being."

"—but whether you admit you are a god or not, I know you. I recognize you from a hundred prayers and stories. You are the Beastlord, God of Healing, Draffut."

CHAPTER 10

The high gray walls of Kind Sir Andrew's castle were growing higher still, and darkening into black against the sunset. Mark watched their slow approach from his place in the middle of the wagon's seat. Barbara, slumping tiredly for once, was at his right, and Ben at his left with driver's reins in hand.

Now that their road had emerged from the forest and brought the castle into view, Barbara stirred, and broke a silence that had lasted for some little time. "I guess we're as ready as can be. Let's go right on in."

No one else said anything immediately. From its battered cage back in the wagon's covered rear, the battered dragon chirped. Ben looked unhappy about their imminent arrival, but he twitched the reins without argument and clucked to the team, trying to rouse the limping, weary loadbeasts to an enthusiasm he obviously did not feel himself. Earlier in the day Ben had suggested that they ought to travel more slowly though they were late already, delaying their arrival at Sir Andrew's fair for one more day, giving Nestor one more chance to catch up with them before they got there. But Ben hadn't argued this idea very strongly. Mark thought now that neither Ben nor Barbara really believed any longer that Nestor was going to catch up with them at all.

As for Mark himself, he pretty well had to believe that Nestor was going to meet them somewhere, with Townsaver in hand. Otherwise Mark's sword was truly lost.

It had been pretty well established, in the few days that the three of them had been traveling without Nestor, that Barbara was now the one in charge. She was little if any older than Ben was—Mark guessed she was about seventeen—and probably not half Ben's weight. But such details seemed to have little to do with determining who was in charge. Barbara had stepped in and made decisions when they had to be made, and had held the little group and the enterprise together.

Before they'd left the place where the wagon had tipped, she'd had them cut off the ears of the freshly dead landwalker, and nail them to the front of the wagon as trophies to show their hunting prowess. Later she'd got Ben and Mark to tighten up all the loosened wagon parts as well as possible, and then to help her wash and mend the cloth cover. All their clothes had been washed and mended too, since the great struggle in the mud. Mark thought that the outfit looked better now than it had when he'd joined up.

After the fight they'd traveled as fast as they could for some hours. Then, when they'd reached a secluded spot along a riverbank, Barbara had decreed a layover for a whole night and a day. The animals had been given a chance to eat and drink and rest, and their hurts had been tended. Medicine of supposed magical power had been applied to Mark's burned face, and it had seemed to help, a little. That night Ben had made his one real effort to assert himself, deciding that he wanted to sleep in the wagon too. But it had been quickly established who was now in command. Ben had wound up snoring on the ground again.

A small hidden compartment directly under the wagon's seat held a secret hoard of coin, tightly wrapped in cloth to keep it from jingling when the wagon moved. Ben and Barbara knew already of the existence of this cache, and during that day of rest they'd brought out the money in Mark's presence and counted it up. It amounted to no fortune, in fact to less than Mark had sometimes seen in his father's hands back at the mill. Nestor's success in hunting dragons evidently hadn't paid him all that well in terms of money—or else Nestor had already squandered the bulk of his payment somehow, or had contrived to hide it or invest it somewhere else. He had been paying both Ben and Barbara small wages, amounts agreed upon in advance. They said that beyond that he had never discussed money with either of them.

As soon as the coins were counted, Barbara wrapped them tightly up again and stuffed them back into their hiding place and closed it carefully. "We'll use this only as needed," she said, looking at the others solemnly. "If Nestor comes back, he'll understand."

Ben nodded, looking very serious. All in all it was a solemn moment, a pledging of mutual trust amid shared dangers; at least that was how it impressed Mark. Before he had really thought out what he was going to do, he found himself telling Ben and Barbara his own truthful story, even including his killing of the seneschal, and his own right name.

"Those soldiers of the Duke's were really after me," he added. "And my sword. Maybe they got the sword; I still keep hoping that Nestor has it, and that he's going to meet us somewhere. Anyway, even if we're over the border now the Duke will probably still be after me. You two have a right to know about it if I'm going to go on traveling with you. And I don't know where else I'd go."

The other two exchanged looks, but neither of them showed great surprise at Mark's revelation. Mark thought that Ben actually looked somewhat relieved.

Barbara said: "We were talking about you—Mark—and we kind of thought that something like that was going on. Anyway, your leaving us now wouldn't help us any. We're going to need you, or someone, when we get to the fair, to help us run the show. And if we still manage to get a hunting contract we're going to need all kinds of help."

Ben cleared his throat. "I know for a fact that the Duke wanted to get his hands on Nestor, too. I don't know exactly why, but Nestor was worried about it. It made him nervous to cut through the Duke's territory, but we didn't have much choice about that if we were going to get down to Sir Andrew's from where we were up north."

And here they were at Sir Andrew's now, or very nearly so. Just ahead, vague in the twilight, was the important intersection that the castle had been built to overlook. And just beyond that intersection, which at the moment was empty of traffic, a side road wound up to the castle, and to the broad green where the fair sprawled like something raised by enchantment in the beginning twilight. The fairgrounds were coming alive with torches against the dusk. They stirred with a multitude of distant voices, and the sounds of competing musicians.

As the wagon creaked its way toward the crossroads, Mark left his seat and went back under the cover. He had agreed with the others that it would be wise for him to stay out of sight as much as feasible until they knew whether or not the Duke was actively seeking him this far south. He felt the change in the wheels' progress when Ben turned off the main road. Then, looking forward through a small opening in the cover, Mark saw that people were already trotting or riding out from the fairgrounds to meet the wagon when it was still a couple of hundred meters down the side road that wound up from the intersection.

One of those riding in the lead was the marshal of the fair, a well-dressed man identifiable by the colors of his jerkin, Sir Andrew's orange and black. The marshal silently motioned for the wagon to follow him, and rode ahead, guiding it through the busy fairgrounds to a reserved spot near the center. Mark, staying in the wagon out of sight, watched the blurred bright spots of torches move past, glowing through the wagon cover on both sides. Sounds surrounded the wagon too—of voices, music, animals, applause. Barbara had thought that the end of daylight would signal the fair's closing for the day, but obviously she had been wrong.

When the marshal had led them to their assigned site, he rode close to the wagon and leaned from his saddle to peer inside. Mark went on with what he was doing, feeding the captive dragon from the replenished frog-crock—if the authorities here were really going to search for him, he would have no hope of hiding. But the marshal only stared at Mark blankly for a moment, then withdrew his head.

Mark heard the official's voice asking: "Where's Nestor?"

Ben gave the answer they had planned: "If he's not here somewhere already, he'll be along in a day or two. He was dickering over some new animals. A team, I mean."

"Looks like you could use one. Well, Sir Andrew wants to see him, mind you tell him as soon as he gets here. There's a hunting contract to be discussed."

Barbara: "Yessir, we'll remind him soon as we see him. It shouldn't be long now."

The marshal rode away, shouting at someone else about garbage to be cleaned up. The three who had just arrived in the wagon immediately got busy, unpacking, tending to the animals, and setting up the tent in which they meant to exhibit the dragon. Their assigned space was a square of trodden grass about ten meters on a side, and the wagon had to be maneuvered into the rear of this space in order to make room for the big tent at the front. Their neighbor on one side was the pavilion of a belly-dancer, with a crowd-drawing preliminary show that went on every few minutes out front—Ben's attention kept wandering from his tasks, and once he tried to feed a frog to a loadbeast. In the exhibitor's space on the far side, a painted lean-to advertised and presumably housed a supposedly magical fire-eater. The two remaining sides of the square were open, bordering grassy lanes along which traffic could pass and customers, if any, could approach. Along these lanes a few interested spectators were already gathering, to watch the dragon-folk get settled. They had hoped to be able to set up after dark, unwatched, but there was no hope of that now. Nor of Mark's remaining unobserved, so he did not try.

The tent in which the dragon was to be shown was made of some fabric lighter and tougher than any that Mark had ever seen before, and gaudily decorated with painted dragons and mysterious symbols. Ben told Mark that the cloth had come from Karmirblur, somewhere five thousand kilometers away at the other end of the world.

As soon as the tent had been put up and secured, and a small torch mounted on a stand inside for light, the three exhibitors carried the caged dragon into it without uncovering the cage; the bystanders were going to have to pay something if they wanted to catch even the merest glimpse. The three proprietors were also planning to keep at least one of their number in or beside the wagon as much as possible. All obvious valuables were removed from the wagon, some to be carried in purses, others to be buried right under the dragon's cage inside the tent. But Nestor's sword remained within the vehicle, concealed under false floorboards that in turn were covered with a scattering of junk. Barbara, at least, still nursed hopes of being able to put the sword to use eventually, even if Nestor never rejoined the crew. Several times during the last few days Ben had argued the subject with her.

He would be silent for a while, then turn to her with a lost, small-boy look. "Barb, I don't see how we're going to hunt dragons without Nestor. It was hard enough with him."

Barbara's mobile face would show that she was giving the objection serious consideration, even if she had answered it before, not many hours ago. "You know best about that, Ben, the actual hunting. Maybe we could hire some other hunters to help us?"

"Wouldn't be safe. If we do that they'll find out about the magic in the sword. Then they'll try to steal it." Despite the fact that it had taken Ben himself more than long enough to notice. But Mark didn't think that Ben was really slow-witted, as he appeared to be at first. It was just that he spent so much of his mental time away somewhere, maybe thinking about things like minstrelsy and verse.

At last, after several arguments, or debates, Barbara had given in about the hunting, at least temporarily. "Well then, if we can't, we can't. If Nestor never shows up at Sir Andrew's, we'll just act more surprised than anyone else, and wonder aloud what could have happened to him. Then we'll wait around at Sir Andrew's for a little while after the fair's over, and if Nestor still isn't there we'll pack up and head south and look for another fair. At least it'll be warmer down south in the winter. Anyway, I don't suppose Sir Andrew would be eager to hire us as hunters without Nestor."

"I don't suppose," Ben agreed with some relief. Then he added, as if in afterthought: "Anyway, if Sir Andrew takes me on as a minstrel, you'll be going south without me."

He looked disappointed when Barbara agreed to that without any comment or hesitation.

Mark didn't have any comment to make either. He suspected that if Nestor didn't appear, Barbara meant to sell the sword if she couldn't find a way to use it. He, Mark, would just have to decide for himself when the time came what he wanted to try to do about that. This sword wasn't his. But he felt it was a link, of sorts, to his own blade, about the only link that he still had. If Nestor came back at all, it would be with the idea of recovering his own sword, whatever other plans he might have.

Of course, he might not have Mark's sword with him when he showed up. And if he did have it, he might not be of a mind to give it back.

Any way Mark looked at the current situation, his chances of recovering his sword, his inheritance, looked pretty poor.

Three hours after the dragon-people had arrived, the carnival was showing some signs of winding down for the night, though the grounds were by no means completely quiet as yet. Barbara still had the dragon-exhibit open, though business had slowed down to the point where Ben was able to put on his plumed hat, collect his lute, and announce to his partners that he was going out to try his hand at minstrelsy.

Mark's help was not needed at the showtent for the moment either, and he had retired to the wagon, where he meant to get something to eat, meanwhile casually sitting guard over the concealed sword.

The inside of the wagon looked about twice as big now, with almost everything moved out of it. From where Mark was sitting he could just see the entrance to the tent, which had been erected at right angles to the wagon. Barbara had just finished conducting one small group of paying customers into the tent to see the dragon and out again, and she was presently chatting with a prospective first member of the next group. This potential customer was a chunkily-built little man, evidently of some importance, for he was dressed in fancier clothes than any Mark had seen since the seneschal, the Duke's cousin, went down.

Mark was chewing on a piece of boiled fowl—Ben had laid in some food from a nearby concession before he left—and thinking gloomy thoughts about his missing sword, when he heard a faint sound just behind him, right inside the wagon. He turned to see a man whom he had never seen before, who was standing on the ground outside with his head and shoulders in the rear opening of the wagon. Knotted on the man's sleeve was what looked like the orange-and-black insignia of an assistant marshal of the fair. He was looking straight at Mark, and there was that in his eyes that made Mark drop his drumstick and dive right out of the front of the wagon without a moment's hesitation. Only as Mark cleared the seat did it fully register in his mind that the man had been holding a large knife unsheathed in his right hand.

Mark landed on hands and knees on the worn turf just outside the wagon. He somersaulted once, and came up on his feet already running. As he reached the doorway of the tent he was drawing in a deep breath to yell for help. Inside the tent, the small dragon was already yowling continuously, and this perhaps served as a subliminal warning; Mark did not yell. When he looked into the tent he saw by the light of the guttering single torch how Barbara lay limp in the grasp of a second man in marshal's insignia, how the dragon's cage had been tipped over backwards, and how the well-dressed stranger, who a moment ago had been chatting innocently with Barbara, was now frantically digging with his dagger into the ground where the cage had been, uncovering and scattering fine valuable crossbow bolts and bits of armor.

Mark did not yell. But the men inside the tent both yelled when they saw him, and turned and rushed in his direction. He was just barely too quick for them, as he darted away and then rolled under the flimsily paneled side of the fire-eater's construction on the adjoining lot.

The inside of that shelter was as dark as the toe of a boot; no flames were being ingested at the moment. But there came a quick stir in the blackness, an alarmed fumbling as of bedclothes, an urgent muttering of voices. Mark somehow stumbled and crashed his way through the darkness, once tripping over something and falling at full length. When he had come to the opposite wall he went out under it, in the same manner he had come in. There was no one waiting in the grass outside to seize him; for the moment he had foiled his pursuers. But for the moment only; he could hear them somewhere behind him, yelling, raising an alarm.

He made an effort to get in under the wall of the next shelter, which was a tent, found his way blocked, and slid around the tent instead. Now a deep ditch offered some hope of concealment, and he slid down into the ditch to scramble in knee-deep water at the bottom. When he had his feet more or less solidly under him he followed the ditch around a turn, where he paused to look and listen for pursuit. He heard none, but realized that he'd already lost his bearings. This fairground was certainly the biggest of the two or three that Mark had ever seen. There, the dark bulk of the castle loomed, enormous on its small rise, with lights visible in a few windows. But to Mark in his bewildered state the castle was just where it ought not to have been, and at the moment it gave him no help in getting his bearings.

Now people were yelling something in the distance. But he couldn't tell whether or not the cries had anything to do with him. What was he going to do now? If only, he thought, Kind Sir Andrew himself could be made to hear the truth . . .

Mark followed the ditch for a few more splashing strides, then climbed from it into the deeper darkness behind another row of tents and shelters. He was moving toward lights and the sounds of cheerful music. It was in fact better music than Ben was ever going to be able to make, if he practiced for a hundred years. If only he could at least find Ben, and warn him . . .

With this vague purpose of locating Ben, Mark looked out into the lighted carnival lanes while keeping himself as much as possible in the shadows. He crawled under someone's wagon, then behind a booth, seeking different vantage points. In another open way were clowns and jugglers, drawing a small crowd, laughter and applause. Mark tried to see if Ben was in the group somewhere, but was unable to tell. He moved briefly into the open again, until orange and black tied on a sleeve ahead sent him crawling back into hiding, through the partly open back door of a deserted-looking hut. Once more his entry roused an unseen sleeper; a man's voice muttered alarm, and half-drunken, half-coherent threats.

Mark darted out of the hut again, and went trotting away from people, along a half-darkened traffic lane. Brighter torchlight shone round the castle's lowered drawbridge, now not far ahead of him. More suits of orange and black were there, gathered as if in conference. To avoid them, Mark turned a corner, toward more music. This time there were drums, and roistering voices. Maybe this crowd would be big enough to hide him for a while. And there, a few meters ahead, stood Ben, plumed hat tipped on the back of his head, his lute temporarily forgotten under one arm. His stocky figure was part of the small crowd gawking at the belly-dancer's outside-the-tent performance. Mark realized that he had unconsciously fled in a circle, and was now back near the place where he had started running.

He took another step forward, intending to warn Ben. And at that same moment, the chunky dandy reappeared, approaching from the direction of the dragon-tent beyond. He saw Mark, and at once raised a fresh outcry. Mark yelped and turned and sped away. He didn't know whether Ben had even noticed him or not.

Now, several more of the marshal's men were blocking the lane ahead of Mark. He turned on one toe, to dash in at right angles under the broad banner advertising the Maze the Mirth, past a startled clown-face and into a dim interior. The stuffed figure of a demon, crudely constructed, lurched at him out of the gloom, and a mad peal of laughter went up from somewhere behind it. The inside of this place was a maze, furnished with crude mirrors and dark lanterns flashing suddenly, constructed of confusingly painted walls all odd shapes and angles. The head of a real dragon, long since stuffed and varnished, popped out at Mark from behind a suddenly open panel.

Mark could feel the burn on his face throbbing. Now another panel opened unexpectedly when he leaned on it, and he spun in confusion through a dark opening. A mirror showed him a distorted image of the chunky dandy, coming after him, perhaps still two mirrors away. The man's mouth was opening for a yell.

An arm, banded in orange and black, came out of somewhere else to flail at Mark, and then was left behind when yet another panel closed. The very walls were shouting as they moved, roaring with mad laughter . . .

A new figure loomed before Mark, that of a tall, powerful clown in jester's motley. The clown was holding something out to Mark in one hand, while at the same time another hand, invisible, pushed at the jester's painted face. The face moved. It became a mask that slid back, revealing—

The mask slid back from the face of the one-armed clown. The face revealed was fair and large and smiling. It was lightly bearded, as Mark had never seen it before, but he had not an instant's doubt of just whose face it was.

"Father!"

Jord nodded, smiling. The shape he was holding out was half-familiar to Mark. It was the shape of a sword's hilt. But this time the weapon was sheathed in ornate leather, looped with a leather belt. As Mark's two hands closed on the offered hilt, and drew the weapon from its sheath, his father's face fell into darkness and away.

"Father?"

Now someone's hands were moving round Mark's waist, deftly buckling a swordbelt on him. "Mark, take this to Sir Andrew. If you can." It was half the voice of Jord as Mark remembered it, half no more than an anonymous whisper.

"Father . . ."

Mark turned, with the drawn blade still in his hands, trying to follow dim images that chased each other away from him through mirrors. He saw the form of a lean carnival clown, two-armed and totally unfamiliar, backing away. Mark tried to follow the figure through the dim mad illumination, the light of torchflames beyond mirrors, glowing through mirrors and cloth. This time Mark could feel power emanating from the blade he held. But the flavor of the power was different, somehow, from what he had expected. *Another* sword? It fed Mark's hands with a secret, inward thrumming—

With a terrific shock, something came smashing through thin partitions near at hand. It was an axe, no, yet another sword, this one quite mundane though amply powerful. Enchantment seemed to vanish, as it was supposed to do when swords were out. A nearby mirror fell from the wall, shattering with itself the last image of the retreating clown.

And now hard reality reappeared, in the form of the chunky little man in dandy's clothes. He was all disarranged and rumpled with triumphant effort. His face, as he closed in on Mark, displayed his triumph. His mouth opened, awry, ready to bawl out something. The dandy lifted a torch toward Mark—and then recoiled like one stabbed. Still staring at Mark, he made an awkward, half-kneeling gesture that was aborted by the narrowness of the passage. The orange-and-black armbands who now appeared behind him also stared at Mark, in obvious stupefaction.

Mark could see now, without knowing quite how he saw it, that they were not what their armbands proclaimed them.

The stocky leader said to Mark: "Your Grace . . . I am sorry . . . I never suspected that you would be . . . which way did he go?"

Mark stood still, clutching the naked sword, feeling the weight of its unfamiliar belt around his waist. He felt unable to do anything but wait stupidly for whatever might happen next. He echoed: "He?"

"That boy, Your Grace. It was the one that we are after, I am sure. He was right here."

"Let him go, for now." Magic's mad logic had taken hold of Mark, and he knew, as he would have known in a dream, that he was speaking of himself.

"I . . . yes, sire." The man in front of Mark was utterly bewildered by the order he had just heard, but never dreamt of disobedience. "The flying courier should have the other sword at any moment now, and will then depart at once. Unless Your Grace, now that you are here, wishes to change plans—?"

"The other sword?"

"The sword called Dragonslicer, sire. They must have hidden it there somewhere, in their wagon or their tent. Our men will have it any moment now. The courier is ready." The stocky man was sweating, and not only with exertion; it bothered him that it should be necessary to explain these things.

Mark turned away from him. A great anger at this gang of thieves was building in him. Holding his newly acquired sword before him like a torch, he burst his way out through the hacked opening that made a new solution to the Maze of Mirth. Feeling the rich throb of the weapon's power steady in his wrists, he ran along the grassy lane outside, past men in orange and black who stumbled over each other to get out of his way. He heard their muttered exclamations.

"His Grace himself!"

"The Duke!"

Mark ran in the direction of the dragon-hunters' tent and wagon. The wagon had been tipped on one side now, and men were prying at its wreckage, while a large gray shape with spread wings squatted near them on the ground. Before Mark was able to get much closer, the large winged dragon rose into the air. Mark heard the windmill-creaking of its voice, and he saw that it was now carrying a sword, clutched close against its body in one taloned foot.

Once again a sword was being taken from him. Mark, incapable at the moment of feeling anything but rage, ran under the creature as it soared, screaming at it to come down, to bring the stolen weapon back to him. In the upward glow of the fairgrounds' varied lights, Mark saw to his amazement how the dragon's fanged head lowered in midflight. Its long neck bent, its eyes searched half-intelligently for the source of the voice that cried at it. It located Mark. And then, to his greater amazement still, it started down.

The people who were standing near Mark scattered, allowing him and the dragon ample room to meet. At the last moment Mark realized that the creature was not attacking him. Instead it was coming down as if in genuine obedience to his shouted order.

Feeling the sword surging in his hands, he stepped to meet the dragon. In rage grown all the greater because of his previous helpless fear, he stabbed at the winged dragon blindly as it hovered just above the grass. The attack took it by surprise, and Mark felt his thrust go home. The dragon dropped the sword that it was carrying, and Mark without thought bent to pick it up.

For just an instant he touched both hilts at the same time, right hand still following through his thrust, left fingers touching the hilt that had fallen to the ground.

For an instant, he thought that a great wind had arisen, and was about to blow him off his feet. For that heartbeat's duration of double contact, he had a sense that the world was altering around him, or else that he was being extracted from it . . .

The rising movement of the flyer pulled from Mark's extended hand the hilt of the sword with which he'd stabbed it. The dragon was taking off with the blade still embedded in its side. Mark, on his knees now, squinting upward as if into dazzling light, lost sight of the sword that went up with the dragon. But before his eyes the dragon's whole shape was changing, melting and reforming. He saw first a giant barnyard fowl in flight, then an enormous hawk, at last a winged woman garbed in white. Then the shape vanished, climbing beyond the effective range of the fairgrounds' lights.

Slowly Mark stood up straight, still holding the sword that the dragon had dropped in front of him. It was Dragonslicer—by now, he found, he was able to tell one from another by the feeling, needing no look at the hilt.

The world that had been trying to alter around him was now trying to come back. But its swift shifting had been too violent for that to be accomplished in an instant.

The stocky man who had attacked Barbara and had been chasing Mark had now caught up with him once more. But the man only stood in front of Mark in absolute consternation, gazing first at Mark and then up into the night sky after the vanished courier.

From somewhere in the gathering crowd, Barbara came stumbling, staggering, screaming incoherent accusations. The dandy, bemused and rumpled, turned on her with his dagger drawn. Before Mark could react, a huge hand reached from behind the man to grab him by one shoulder and turn him, spinning him into the impact of a fist that seemed to break him like a toy.

Men in orange and black had Ben surrounded. But now, from the direction of the drawbridge, another small group of men in black and orange came charging. These were half-armored with helms and shields, and held drawn swords. Led by a graybeard nobleman, they hurled themselves with a warcry at the first group.

Mark knew that his own hand still held a sword. He told himself that he should be doing something. But the sense that his place in the world had changed still held him. It was not like anything he had ever felt before. He thought that he could still feel the two hilts, one in each hand.

And then he could feel nothing at all.

CHAPTER 11

"Yes, I am Draffut, once called by humans the Lord of Beasts. And now they call me a god." In the deep voice were tired tones that mocked the foolishness of humans. "Stand up, man. No human being should kneel to me."

All around Nestor and the giant the night creatures of the swamp were awakening, from whatever daytime dreams they had to noisy life. Nestor stood up. His emotional outburst, whether or not it had been based on some misconception, had relieved something in him and he felt calmer. "Very well," he said. "What shall I call you, then?"

"I am Draffut. It is enough. And you are Nestor, who kills dragons. Now come with me, you will need food and rest."

"Rest, first, I think." Nestor rubbed at his eyes; exhaustion was rapidly overtaking him. The sword dragged down whichever hand he held it in.

Draffut led the way back to the ancient temple. Standing beside the building, he raised a shaggy arm to indicate a place where, he said, Nestor should be able to rest in safety. This was a half-ruined room on an upper level, in a portion of the structure that once had had a second floor. The stairway nearby had almost entirely disappeared, but Nestor was agile and he found a way to scramble up. His assigned resting place was open to the sky, but at least it should offer him some degree of isolation from creeping things. When Nestor turned from a quick inspection of the place to speak to Draffut again, he saw to his surprise that the giant had disappeared.

Neither the hard floor of his high chamber, nor the possibility of danger, kept Nestor from falling quickly into a deep sleep, that turned almost at once into a vivid dream.

In this dream he beheld a fantastic procession, that was made up partly of human beings, and partly of others who were only vaguely visualized. The procession was marching through brilliant sunlight to the temple, at some time in the days of that building's wholeness and glory. At first the dream was quite a pleasant experience. Then came the point when Nestor realized that in the midst of the procession was being borne a maiden meant for sacrifice—and that the prospective victim was Barbara.

In the dream Barbara was straining at the bonds that held her, and crying out to him for help. But in terror Nestor turned away from her. Clasping the hilt of his precious sword, which he knew he must not lose no matter what, he ran with it into the jungle surrounding the temple closely. This was a dream-growth of spectacular colors, very different from the scrubby woods that his waking eyes had beheld covering most of the island. But as soon as Nestor had reached the jungle, the sword-hilt in his hand turned into something else—and before he could understand what it had become, he was waking up, gasping with his fear.

Night-creatures were being noisy at a little distance, yet the darkness round him was peaceful enough, though he was breathing as hard as if he had been fighting. The gibbous moon was by now almost directly overhead, in a sky patched with clouds; it was some time near the middle of the night.

The image of Barbara remained vividly with Nestor for some time after he had awakened. Ought he to have stood by the spilled wagon, sword in hand, to fight for her and for the others?

Nonsense. Before he'd managed to get his hand on a sword, they'd all run away, scattering and hiding as best they could. He would have been killed, and it would have done no one any good at all.

Maybe he knew that he would have run away, even if the others hadn't. But it was nonsense, dredging up such theoretical things to worry about.

Though the unpleasantness of the dream lingered, Nestor soon fell asleep again. He woke with the feeling that no time at all had passed, though the sun was now fully up in a bright sky, and monkbirds were exchanging loud cries in branches not far above his head.

Nestor sat up, reflecting on how well he felt, how rested. He rubbed the shoulder that yesterday had been—he was sure of it—broken. It felt as good as the other shoulder now.

He vaguely remembered having some disagreeable dream, but he no longer remembered what it had been about.

The sword was at his side, just where he had put it down. What had Draffut said, that sounded like quoted verse? *Long roads the Sword of Fury makes, Hard walls it builds around the soft* . . . Nestor would have given something to hear the rest.

Beside the sword now was a pile of fresh fruit, that certainly had not been there when he last fell asleep. Nestor sniffed at something yellow and round, then nibbled cautiously. Then, suddenly ravenous, he fell to. The sword made a convenient tool to slice and peel.

Before Nestor had fully satisfied his appetite, Draffut appeared, walking tree-tall from among the trees. The giant exchanged rather casual greetings with Nestor, and claimed credit for the provision of the man's breakfast, for which Nestor thanked him. In the bright morning Draffut's fur glowed delicately, just as it had in twilight and after dark, holding its own light. As Draffut stood on the ground outside the temple his face was approximately on a level with Nestor's, who was standing on what had once been a second floor.

This morning Nestor felt no impulse to kneel. He realized that his awe of Draffut was already fading into something that approached familiarity, and in an obscure way the man partially regretted the fact. As soon as a few conversational preliminaries had been gone through, he asked: "Draffut, will you tell me about the gods? And about yourself. If you maintain you are not one of them, I don't intend to argue with you. But perhaps you can understand why I thought you were."

Draffut answered thoughtfully. "I understand that humans often show a need for beings greater than themselves. But I repeat that I can tell you very little about the gods. Their ways are often beyond my understanding. As for my own story, it is very long and I think that now is not the time for me to begin to tell it. Right now it is more important that I learn more about your sword."

"Very well." Nestor looked down at the blade with which he had been halving fruit, that was not really his. He sighed, and shook his head, thinking of the one he'd lost. Then he explained as briefly as he could how the wagon he had been driving had been pursued, and had tipped over, and what had happened to him after that, and what he surmised might have happened to his companions. "So, the landwalker, which I suppose was your creature too, attacked Duke Fraktin's men in the vicinity of the wagon—or at least that's what it sounded like. I could not stay to see who won the fight, for your messenger came to invite me to be your guest. So, that boy may have my sword now. Or the Duke might have it, or some of his soldiers. As for this blade here, the boy told me that it can kill fighting men with great efficiency. I've never put it to the test."

Draffut stared as if he thought a particularly interesting point had been raised. Then the giant asked: "You have fought against other men at some time in the past, though? And killed them sometimes?"

Nestor paused warily before he answered. "Yes, when it seemed to me there was no way of avoiding such a fight. Soldiering is not a profession that I'd choose to follow."

"It is no more dangerous than hunting dragons, surely."

"Less so, perhaps, most of the time. Still I'd not choose it." And at the same time, Nestor could not help wondering again what might have happened back at the wagon if he had turned with this sword in hand to fight the Duke's patrol. Probably if he'd survived that by some magic, he would have had to fight the dragon too. Almost certainly he'd now be dead, magic swords or not, just like the brother that young Einar—if that was his real name—had spoken of. Well, he was sure he was going to die in some kind of a fight, sometime, somewhere. But there was an inescapable fascination about the particulars.

Meanwhile Draffut stood in thoughtful silence, considering Nestor's answer. Once the giant reached with two fingers to the pile of fruit, and popped several pieces into his mouth at once, chewing with huge fangs that appeared much better suited to a carnivorous diet. To Nestor, this mere fact of eating somehow added force to Draffut's disclaimer of divinity—though if he thought about it, he recalled that the deities were often described as feasting.

Nestor as last broke the silence with a question: "What do you plan to do with me?"

Draffut roused himself from thought with a shake of his head. "I am sorry now that I sent dragons to bring you here, at risk of your being killed or injured. For it seems that you can tell me little that is useful."

"I would if I could."

"I believe it. I could arrange for the flying dragon to carry you out of the swamp again."

"Thank you, no. I think I would rather remain here as your guest for the next twenty years or so. Is there some other alternative?"

"The number of alternatives is quite limited. Still, I can probably arrange something to get you out of the swamp. In which direction would you prefer to go?"

"I was headed with my companions toward the domain of Kind Sir Andrew, with whom I had a hunting contract to discuss. If my friends somehow managed to survive both the dragons and the Duke's men, they are probably there now, looking for me."

"And if they should still have with them your own sword . . ."

"Dragonslicer. Or, the Sword of Heroes, so Hermes told me. Yes, it may be there too."

Draffut took a little time to consider before he spoke again. "Would you be willing to make the trip on the back of a large landwalker? I can influence them, as you have already seen. But they are somewhat less docile and dependable than the flying dragons. Also I fear that the journey would probably take longer that way, several days at least."

"Are there no boats to be had here in the swamp? No people living here at all?" Nestor was sure that there were at least a few, grubbing around in savage conditions. "If it comes down to the choice, I'll try to carve my own boat out of a log and paddle it out, rather than depend again on the whim of any dragon. Regardless of what spells you may be able to put on them."

"I put no spells on dragons," said Draffut almost absently. "I am no magician."

"You spoke of influencing them . . ."

"As for making your own boat, I do not think that you would live for many hours in the swamp, traveling alone in any boat you could build for yourself under these conditions. And unfortunately I cannot spare the time it would take to escort you to safe land myself. But I will see what I can do to help you."

You cannot spare the time from what? Nestor wondered. But he kept the question to himself; the giant had already turned and was walking purposefully away. In a few moments Draffut had vanished from Nestor's view behind a screen of trees. His head briefly reappeared, topping a screen of shorter trees in the middle distance. Then it sank abruptly below the treetops' level, as if he had stepped into the swamp.

Left to himself, Nestor out of curiosity soon undertook a more or less complete exploration of the temple. In several of the rooms he examined the carvings on the walls fairly closely. These reliefs depicted men, women, and unidentifiable other beings engaged in what Nestor took to be a variety of ritual activities; it was difficult to make out any details of what they were about.

In the room where Draffut had shown him the odd thing he called a larva, Nestor peered again into the tank. The surface of the water was once more mirror-quiet. On the shelf nearby waited the Old World lamp, but Nestor made no move to take it down. He had no wish to raise the larva again.

He continued his explorations. He was in another large chamber, pondering what appeared to be a row of empty closets, when his thoughts were interrupted by a noise. This was a sudden outburst of shrill cries, delivered in an inhuman voice that sounded as if it were somewhere close outside the temple. Nestor went to a doorway, sword in hand, and cautiously peered out.

A flying dragon was hovering nearby, above the courtyard. Somewhat smaller than the one that had earlier kidnapped Nestor, it looked at him but kept its distance. It circled a few more times, hovered some more, and shrilled at him. It was almost as if, he thought fancifully, the beast had something it was trying to communicate.

It kept on making noise until Nestor at last spoke to it, as a man alone speaks to a thing or an animal, not expecting understanding. "If it's Draffut you're looking for, he's not here. He stalked off into the swamp, to the southwest, more than an hour ago. No telling when he'll be back."

To Nestor's considerable surprise—after years of dealing with dragons, he considered their intelligence to be about on a par with that of barnyard fowl—the creature reacted as if it had in fact understood him. These flying creatures must indeed be a subspecies he had never heard of. At least it ceased its noise and flew away at once. Whether it really headed southwest Nestor could not tell, but it flapped its way around the bulk of the temple and might have gone in that direction.

Nestor, shaking his head, went slowly back inside the building, intending to explore some more. Looking around the place gave him something to do while he waited for Draffut, and the more he knew about his immediate environment the more secure he felt. On the ground level he discovered one large chamber whose floor was padded with heaps of fronds and springy vines; he wondered if this was the place where Draffut rested. Everyone agreed that gods could eat, but did they have to rest?

Pondering, or trying to ponder, the mysteries of Draffut, and of the multiple swords of magic, and of what the god-game might be, Nestor made his way outside again. This time he exited through the place where a wall had tumbled, to emerge on a slope leading to an upper level of the temple. He climbed across a high ruined section, that was littered with tilted slabs of fallen roof. From here it was possible to see above the island's treetops, or most of them, but there was apparently nothing but more swamp and trees beyond.

The morning sun had climbed, but it was not yet too hot to make it uncomfortable to stretch out on a fallen slab of roof and bask. Relaxation sometimes helped a man to think.

But soon, instead of concentrating on the intriguing questions that had arisen, Nestor was almost dozing. In his thoughts images came and went, pictures of Draffut and the swords. Then Barbara and the imagined gods. Somehow, thought Nestor, the world ought to fit together, and basically make sense. People always hoped it would. But, as far as he knew, the human race had never been given any such guarantee . . .

He was almost asleep when a faint sound caught at his attention. A light tap first, like a cautious footfall, and then a small scraping or sliding sound. It was repeated, tap and slide, tap and slide. Nestor listened, heard the sound no more, and went briefly back to his dozing thoughts.

Then it came again: tap-slide. Tap-slide. Almost like footsteps. But limping footsteps. Almost like—

He leaped up, just as a shadow fell across him. And he snatched up the sword barely in time to parry the first blow of the crude barbed hook.

CHAPTER 12

First Mark was moving through a world of dreams, then he was not. The vision of many swords was gone, but now he was not at all sure at just what point the transition from sleep to waking life had taken place.

His eyes opened to a view of a ceiling of vaulted stone. Quickly raising himself on one elbow, he could see that he was for the first time in his life inside a real castle. This large and richly furnished room could be part of nothing else. And he was lying in a real bed, with sunlight that had a morning feeling to it coming in through the room's single narrow window.

On a table in the center of the room, the Sword of Heroes rested— Mark could make out the small white dragon in the decoration on the black hilt. Lying on the bare wood beside the weapon were the belt and the scabbard that had been given to Mark—last night?—along with a different sword.

Sharp as a dagger's stroke, the memory returned now of his father's face, bearded as Mark had never seen it before, but unmistakable. The smiling kindness, the look of recognition in the eyes. That face in the Maze of Mirth had been so real—

On a small lounge beside the single bed, Barbara was sleeping. She appeared to be wearing her ordinary clothes, but a rich shawl had been thrown over her. It was as if she had been watching over Mark and had fallen asleep, and then perhaps some other watcher had covered her for warmth. And now Mark saw where his own clothes were draped over another chair, with a set of much handsomer garments beside them. Was the finery meant for him? He'd never worn such things.

A familiar snore disturbed the air, making Mark turn his head. In a far corner of the room, almost lost behind more furniture, Ben lay snoring on a heap of fancy pillows. He too was covered with a rich, unfamiliar robe.

As soon as Mark sat up straight in bed, Barbara stirred too. She opened dark eyes and looked at him for a moment without comprehension. Then, wide awake in another instant, she smiled at him. Then she had thrown the shawl aside and was standing beside the bed to feel Mark's head for fever. She asked: "Are you all right?"

"I think so. What happened? Who brought us into the castle? I remember there was a fight . . ."

"And you fell over. Then Sir Andrew had us all brought in. Ben and I have told him just about everything. We were all worried about you, but the enchantress said she thought you'd just sleep it off. Dame Yoldi's her name, and I'm supposed to call her as soon as you wake up. Just stay there and I'll go get her."

Barbara went out of the room quickly. Mark, disregarding her orders, got up and began to dress, choosing his own old clothes though the elegant new ones beside them appeared to be of a suitable size. Meanwhile Ben snored on peacefully in the corner.

When Mark was dressed he looked out the window briefly at distant fields and forests beneath the rising sun. Then he stood over the table that held the sword, looking at the weapon but not touching it. He was trying to remember, to reconstruct the experience that must have made him lose consciousness the night before, evidently many hours ago. He could not remember suffering any blow to the head or other injury. Only touching, for a moment, two swords at the same time, and then feeling strange. He didn't seem to be wounded now, or hurt in any way, except for the old, half-healed mark of dragon's fire on his left cheek.

The voice came from the doorway behind him: "You are Mark. Son of Jord, who is a miller in Arin-on-Aldan."

Mark whirled at the first word. He found himself confronted by the man who last night had led the charge of men armed with swords from the drawbridge, and who could only be Sir Andrew himself. Beside the knight was an elegantly dressed woman who must be his enchantress. Mark stuttered something and started to go down on one knee.

"No, stand up." Sir Andrew's voice was powerful, but so far not threatening. He was frowning as he stood with hands clasped behind him. "Duke Fraktin sends me word that he considers you a thief and a murderer."

"I am not, sir." The tone in which the accusation had been passed along had seemed to encourage a bold denial. In the far corner of the room, Ben was now waking up, trying to remain inconspicuous even as he lumbered to his feet.

"I hardly thought that you were," Sir Andrew agreed. "I know Duke Fraktin is guilty of both charges himself, and perhaps worse . . . and last night the agents he sent here showed they were no better. They've committed what amount to acts of war against me. They—"

The beautiful woman who was standing beside Sir Andrew put a hand on the knight's arm, gently interrupting him. When he had let himself be silenced, she spoke urgently to Mark: "What do you remember of last night?"

Haltingly at first, then gaining confidence as he was granted a patient hearing by both the highborn folk,˙Mark recounted his experiences at the fair as he remembered them. He began with his arrival in the wagon with Ben and Barbara, and went on to the moment when the dragon-courier of Duke Fraktin had soared away, the sword Mark had stabbed it with still wedged into its scales.

"As the dragon went up, it looked—changed. It looked unreal to me. Like it was one different creature after another. And then I lost sight of it, and people were fighting all around me. As you must know, sir, ma'm. And then I think that something must have struck me down. But just before that I was feeling—strange."

The enchantress came toward Mark, and stood in front of him looking at him very closely. At first he was frightened, but something soon drained away the fear. She said to him: "You were not wounded, were you?"

"No ma'm, I wasn't wounded. But . . . I just had the feeling that something was . . . happening to me."

"I don't doubt you did." Dame Yoldi finished her long look at Mark, and sighed. She looked around at each of the other people in the room. "I was watching from a castle window, while most of the rest of you were out in the fairgrounds. There was a magic in that stolen sword, that made the creature carrying it seem to change. We each of us saw it as something different when it rose up through the air—but each of us saw it as something harmless, or as a being that ought to be defended. Just as everyone saw you, Mark, as someone to be obeyed, protected, served—as long as you were carrying that sword."

Mark nodded solemnly. "Once I had it, the man who had been chasing me called me 'Your Grace'—what became of him?"

Sir Andrew grunted. "Hugh of Semur was among last night's dead." The knight glanced momentarily toward Ben, who was continuing to stand in his corner, still wrapped in his blanket and trying to look small. "And my own men fought well, once we understood that we were required to fight. Some of those who were pretending to be my marshals got away from us, I fear. But some are dead, and one or two are in my dungeon now. I fear they'll be a bad influence on my one honest criminal." To Mark's further bewilderment, the knight here shook his head, apparently over some private worry.

Dame Yoldi asked: "Mark, who gave you that other sword, the one that's now flown away? You've just told us that the man who did so appeared to be your father, as long as he had the sword. But what did he look like afterward, when he'd passed Sightblinder over to you?"

"When I had the sword, I saw him only as a masked clown. Lady, I do not understand these things of magic."

There was a pause before the enchantress answered. "Nor do I, all too often." As she turned quickly away from Mark, he thought he caught a glimpse of some new inner excitement in her eye. Again she took the lord of the castle by the arm. "Andrew, send out men to search for the carnival clowns. They're scattered now, I'm sure, after last night, along with all the merchants and the visitors. But if we could only find him . . ." For the moment Dame Yoldi appeared to be lost in some wild private speculation.

Sir Andrew stared at her, then went to the door where he barked out orders. In a moment he was back. "They must be scattered like chaff, as you say. But we can try."

"Good." The enchantress was contemplating Mark again, now with something enough like awe to make him feel uncomfortable. "I do not know much yet, lad, about these magic swords. But I am learning. I do know the names of some of them, at least. It was Sightblinder that you stabbed the dragon with, last night. It is also known as the Sword of Stealth. He who carries it is disguised from all potential enemies—and

perhaps from his friends as well. And the man who gave it to you . . .
did he say anything?"

"Yes." Mark blushed for his forgetfulness. "He said that I was to give
it to Sir Andrew. If I could."

"Did he, hah?"

"And I meant to, sir. But then they told me that the other sword was
being stolen. And—and I had to do something."

"And so you did something. Yes, yes, I like having folk about me
who sometimes feel that something must be done. I do wish, though,
that we still had Sightblinder here. I suppose it's in the Duke's hands
now, and I don't like to think what he might do with it." The knight
looked at Dame Yoldi, and his worried frown was deeper than before.
"My own flyers have all come back now, Yoldi. They couldn't catch his
courier in the air, or even see it. Luck is with Fraktin at present."

"In the form of Coinspinner, yes," Dame Yoldi said. She nodded
tiredly, and spoke to Mark again. "Is it possible, boy, that for one
moment last night you had your hands on two swords at the same
time?"

"Yes ma'm, it's more than possible. It happened that way. And that
was when the—the world started to go strange."

"I thought as much. And now the Duke, with his luck augmented by
Coinspinner, is going to have the Sword of Stealth in hand as well. No
one else in the world has ever owned two of those swords since they
were made . . . Mark, I have learned that the smith who helped Vulcan forge them was your father."

Mark could feel himself standing, a small figure, alone, beside the
table that held the sword called Townsaver. "I knew that he helped
make this one. But, until I left home, I never heard that Vulcan had
forged other swords at the same time. My father never liked to speak of
it at all. And now he's dead. I saw him die, the same day my brother
died, and Duke Fraktin's cousin in our village.

"Last night when I thought it was my father—" Mark covered his
eyes briefly with his hands. "But I know it was only some piece of
magic."

Two sentries, armed and alert, had arrived at the room's door, and
now one of them entered to whisper something to Sir Andrew.

"Bring her in," the knight ordered grimly.

Before whoever it was could be brought in, Dame Yoldi moved to the
table near Mark's side. With a small piece of black cloth that might
have been a handkerchief she draped the hilt of the sword that lay on

the table, so that the little white design of decoration could not be seen. Then she stepped away from the table and nodded to the guards.

A moment later, a dark lady appeared in the doorway, of elegant appearance and malevolent expression. Her air of arrogance made the soldiers at her sides appear to be a guard of honor.

She glared at each person in the room in turn. Her gaze lingered longest on Mark, and he had the sensation that something invisible, but palpable and evil, had passed near him. Then, with her lifted chin turned to Sir Andrew, the lady said: "I demand to be released."

"Most likely you soon will be." The knight's voice had turned cold, much changed from what it had been. "My investigation of what your agents did at the fairgrounds last night is almost complete. If you were not here on business of diplomacy, woman, you'd likely be down in my dungeon now."

The lady chose not to hear this. She tossed back dark hair imperiously. "And where is Hugh of Semur?"

"That dog is dead. Diplomat or not, he succeeded in earning himself a broken neck last night."

The dark lady demonstrated shock. "Dead! Then his killers must be placed in my custody, that I may take them to face the Duke's justice. As I must take him." She pointed a long fingernail at Mark. "And that sword on the table. It belongs to His Grace too."

"I think, m'lady, that you'll take precious little out of my territory but yourself."

The lady started to pretend surprise at this refusal, then shrugged lightly and gave it up. "It will go ill for you, Sir Andrew, if you refuse the Duke his property, and his just vengeance. Who will guarantee the security of your frontiers if he does not?"

"Oh, ah? Speaking of property, there's the matter of the damage done to some of mine last night, and to some of my people, too. That fine coach that brought you here, my fine Lady Marat, should fetch something on the market. Enough, perhaps, to pay some of the bills that you've run up in damages. I'll see if I can find a farm wagon somewhere, and a loadbeast or two, to furnish you and your servants transportation home. A somewhat bumpy ride, perhaps, but—"

Now indeed she flared. "Beast yourself! How dare you treat me, the Duke's emissary, in such a way? How dare you?"

"—but, as I say, it would be a long way for you to walk."

The lady now had a hard struggle to restrain her tongue, but she managed it at last. After delivering one last glare at each person in the room, she turned between her guards with a fine swirl of glittery fabrics, and with her guards was gone.

Dame Yoldi reached to brush her fingers through Mark's hair; it was as if she were only petting him, but Mark had the sense that something, a cobweb maybe, that he had not known was there, was brushed away. The enchantress smiled at him faintly, then closed her eyes. She held Mark by the hand, as if she were learning something from the feel of his hand.

"The son of Jord," she said, her eyes still closed. "Of Jord who was a miller—and before that, a smith."

"Aye, ma'm."

"Aye, and aye. But I wonder what else your father was?" Dame Yoldi's eyes opened, large and gray and luminous. "Mark, in all the world, your father Jord is, or was, the only human being ever to have handled more than one of the swords. And only you yourself have ever handled as many as three of them, since their steel was infused with the gods' magic. And a question that has nagged at me was answered here, last night, in part: what would happen if a person, a being of any nature, were to touch and use more than one of the swords at the same time?"

Dame Yoldi paused, looking around at all the people in the room. "And what if two or more of the gods' swords were to touch each other? What if they should be used directly against each other in battle?"

No one could answer her.

All were thinking that Duke Fraktin soon would have two swords, unless his courier were somehow stopped.

Mark met Barbara's expressive eyes, and knew what she was thinking: In our old wagon we had two swords at once, and never tried . . .

CHAPTER 13

Nestor, after making that first parry in time to save his life, got quickly to his feet and stepped back from the attacking larva. As it came after him he backed away. It continued to advance, limping even as he had imagined it must move. Nestor was backing up with cautious steps that took him along the jagged edge of a broken roof. On his left was the paved courtyard, seven meters below; sloping upward on his right was the jumble of tilted, fallen slabs, which would be sure to offer abominable footing.

The thing that limped after Nestor blew little moaning cries at him out of its absence of a face, as if it might be in agony, or perhaps in love. On the almost featureless front of its head only the dark eyes moved a little, staying locked on Nestor. The larva was advancing with its bent arms raised, both its weapons held up near its head, ready to parry a swordstroke or to swing at him again. Not only were those forearms armed with barbed hook and torture-knife, but they were in themselves as hard as bronze. Nestor had a good gauge now of that metallic hardness; his first edged parry had nicked and dented the thing's right wrist, but no more than dented it. A human arm would almost certainly have been completely severed.

After backing up only a few steps along the rim of the roof, Nestor decided retreating was more dangerous than standing his ground would be. He was a competent swordsman, and the blade in his hand a superb weapon, even when, as now, whatever magic it might possess was in abeyance. Why then had he automatically retreated, and why did deep terror still lie in his stomach like a lump of ice? The terror must come, he realized, only from the peculiar nature of his enemy, and not from any powers that it had so far demonstrated. The movements of his foe showed speed and strength—but no more speed or strength than many human opponents might have shown. And the larva was fighting with one considerable, obvious disadvantage—though its weapons were two in number, they were no longer than its arms. If Nestor could keep his nerve and his footing, and use his own magnificent weapon as it deserved to be used, such an attacker ought not to be able to defeat him.

On the other hand, it was already plain that the larva had certain advantages as well: devilish persistence, and a horrible durability. When Nestor stood his ground and struck back, landing a hard chop on its torso, he had the sensation of having hewn into frozen mud. The gray shell cracked at the spot where the blow landed, and substance of a deeper gray began oozing out. But the larva was not disabled, and it seemed to feel nothing. It still came after Nestor, nor was it minded to seek its own safety after what the sword had begun to do to it.

Nestor feinted a high blow, and then hit his opponent in the leg. And now the limp that he had so accurately forecast became more pronounced. When Nestor experimentally retreated a step again to see what the thing would do, it followed. Its gait was now a trifle slower.

Of course it might be keeping speed in reserve, something to surprise the man with at a critical moment. But somehow Nestor doubted that. He had trouble imagining that there could be much in the way of cleverness behind that lack of face. The larva blew its whistling, forlorn whine at him, and advanced on him implacably.

He hit it again, this time in the arm, stopping its advance. This was a harder blow, with much of the swordsman's weight and strength behind the driving edge, and now one of the larva's wrists and weapons dangled from a forearm that had been almost severed for all its hardness. The cut was leaking slow gray slime instead of blood.

Nestor, gaining confidence now, made up his mind and charged the larva suddenly. He caught it with its weight on what seemed to be its weaker leg, and it went back and over the edge of the roof under the impact of a hard swordthrust that only started to pierce its tough breastplate. As it went back and over, the larva made grabbing motions, trying to seize the blade, but it lacked the hands with which to grab anything, and anyway one of its arms was almost severed, its weapon flapping like some deadly glove. Still, Nestor had one horrible moment, in which he feared that the sword was stuck so firmly into the chitinous armor that it might be pulled from his hands or else pull him after the larva as it fell. But the point tugged free when the weight of the gray body came on it fully.

No skill or magic broke that fall, and the paved court was a full seven meters down. Looking over the edge of the roof at the inert, sprawled figure after it had bounced, Nestor could see that the whole gray torso was now networked with fine cracks. More of the varied grayness that must serve the thing as life was oozing from inside.

Nestor had no more than started his first easy breath when the thing stirred. Slowly it flexed its limbs, then got back to its feet. It tilted its head back to let its eyes find its human enemy again. Then, moving deliberately, it limped back into the temple on the level below Nestor. He felt sure that it was coming after him again.

He was sweating as he stood there on the broken roof, though heavy clouds were coming over the sun. He had the feeling that he had entered the realm of nightmare. But the urgency of combat was still pumping in his veins, and before it could dissipate back into fear he made himself start looking for the stairway where the thing would logically come up if it was coming. He was going to have to finish it off.

They faced each other, Nestor at the top of a flight of half-ruined, vine-grown stairs, the larva at the bottom. A monkbird screamed somewhere, still mocking the noise that they had made. With scarcely a pause, the larva started up, dragging one foot after it in its methodical limp, dripping spots of grayness from its cracked carapace. It raised the twisted little knife that was its one remaining weapon.

Nestor, watching with great alertness, saw a tiny tip of something appear like a pointed tongue just inside the larva's small round mouth. He ducked, swiftly and deeply, and heard the small hiss of the spat dart going past his head. Then Nestor leaped forward to meet his enemy halfway on the stair. He piled one swordstroke upon another, driving the thing backwards down the stairs again, and then into a stone corner where it collapsed at last.

Though it went down, Nestor kept on hacking at his foe. When both of the larva's arms had been disabled, and one leg taken off completely, he went for the torso, which at last burst like a gray boil. Nestor had to fight down the urge to retch; the smell that arose was of swamp mud and putridity.

"And no heart, by all the demons," he muttered to himself. "No heart to stop in the damned thing anywhere." Indeed, nothing that he could recognize as an internal organ of any kind was visible, only thicker and thinner grayness that varied in its consistency and hue.

Still, the broken arms of the thing kept trying to hit at Nestor's feet, or grab his legs. The attached gray leg still wanted to get the body up. Nestor, reciting all the demons' names he knew, swore that he was going to finish the horror off, and he went at it like a woodchopper, or rather a madman, abandoning skill. Some of his strokes now were so ill-aimed that the sword rang off the flagstones of the paved yard.

Taking the head completely off settled the thing at last. With that, whatever spells had given the larva the semblance of life were undone. The gray chitin of its outer surfaces immediately started to turn friable. It crumbled at a poke, and the inner grayness that ran out of it thinned out now and spread like mud and water.

Which, as Nestor could now see, was all it was.

Some huge raindrops had already begun to fall. These now multiplied in a white rush. Parts of what had been the larva were already dissolving, washing away into the ground between the paving stones.

Nestor deliberately remained for a time standing in the rain, letting it cool him. He raised his face to the leaking skies, wanting to be cleansed. The downpour grew fiercer, yet still he remained, letting it wash the sword as well. From his experience with Dragonslicer, he did not think that this blade was going to rust.

When Nestor felt tolerably clean again he went back into the temple. Just inside the doorway he leaned against the wall, dripping rainwater from his hair and clothing, watching the continuing rain and listening to it. The thing he had just destroyed with his sword was already no more than a heap of wet muck, rapidly losing all shape as it was washed back into the earth.

"Draffut—god or not, Beastlord, healer, whatever you may or may not be—I am sorry to have destroyed your pet. No, that's doubly wrong. It wasn't your pet, of course. Your experiment in magic, or whatever. And naturally I'm not really sorry, it was a hideous thing. When something comes sneaking up and attacks a man with a hook and a peeling knife, he really has no choice—what's that?"

What it had sounded like was human voices, a small burst of excited conversation. Nestor waited in silence, listening, and presently the voices came again. They were in the middle distance somewhere. He couldn't make out words, but they sounded like the voices of panicked people who were trying to be quiet.

What now?

The sounds came again. Nestor still could not make out any of the words. Some language that he did not know. Most likely that meant some of the savages of the swamp.

Muttering a brief prayer that he might have to do no more fighting, to gods whose existence he still partly doubted, Nestor took a good grip on his sword and went to see what he could see, through a ruined room and out into the slackening rain again. He would move, then wait until he heard the voices and move again.

Climbing a tumbled corner of the temple, past a tilted deity with rain dripping from his nose, Nestor had a good view out to the northeast. In that direction an arm of the swamp came in closer to the center of the island than in any other. This inlet was visible from the high place where Nestor crouched, and he could see that a handful of dugout canoes had just arrived there. The last of them was still being pulled up on the muddy shore. There were about a dozen people, with straight black hair and nearly naked coppery skins, already landed or still disembarking. It wasn't a war party. Among them they were armed with no more than a couple of small bows and a few clubs—not that they were carrying much of anything else. There were women and children among them, in fact making up a majority of the group. Everything they had looked poor—the Emperor's children, these were, born losers if Nestor had ever seen any.

One of the women pointed back into the swamp, away from Nestor and the temple, and made some statement to the others in the language that Nestor did not know. Then the whole small mob, now gathered on shore, turned inland and began hurrying through low bush toward the temple. They were certainly not aware of Nestor yet, and he crouched a little lower, concealing himself until he could decide what he ought to do next.

Before he could make a plan, something that looked like a large, low-slung lizard came scrambling up out of the swamp behind the people. Though it was mostly obscured by bushes, Nestor could tell it was moving with an awkward run in the same general direction as the humans—but it was not pursuing them. It passed them up and they ig-nored it. A general migration of some kind? A general flight . . . ?

Farther back to the northeast, in the depths of the swamp, another shape was approaching, with Nestor's view of it still dimmed by rain. Presently he made it out to be another canoe, paddled by two more copper-skinned men. Two women crouched amidships, slashing at the water with their cupped hands as if determined to do everything possi-ble to add speed. The people on shore ceased their progress inland to turn and watch.

When the craft was just a little nearer, Nestor could see a horizontal gray shape coming after it. For a moment he thought this new form was some kind of peculiar wave troubling the water of the swamp, bearing dead logs on its crest. But then he realized that what he had first taken for a wave was really an almost solid rank of larvae like the one he had just destroyed, marching, swimming, clambering forward through the swamp. Beyond this first jumbled rank there appeared a second; Nestor, looking to right and left, could not see the end of either. Scores of the things at least were coming toward the island, and more probably hun-dreds. He could hear them now, what sounded like a thousand whistling utterances that could not be called voices; he could hear the multitudinous splash of their advance, and the forest of their dead limbs, knocking together softly like tumbled logs in a flood.

Now more animals and birds, large and small together, came fleeing the swamp, as if before a line of beaters in a hunt. The approaching terror came closer, and Nestor's view of it grew less blurred by rain. Now he could see, all along the advancing lines of larvae, how arms ended in spears, in flails, in maces, clubs, and blades. No two pair of raised arms appeared quite alike, but all of them were weapons.

A hundred meters to Nestor's right, he saw a man-sized dragon climb from the muck onto a hummock and turn at bay before the advancing horde, snarling defiance. In an instant the dragon was surrounded by half a dozen of the dead-wood figures. It hurled one back, another and another, but more kept crowding in, their deadly arms rising and fall-ing. Somewhere farther in the distance, a great landwalker bellowed, and Nestor wondered briefly whether it too would choose to stand and fight, and what success it might have if it did.

The people who had already reached the island were waving their arms and calling now, trying to cheer on the last canoe. Its paddlers appeared to Nestor to be gaining on the pursuing horror. But then the bottom of their craft scraped on some large object, log or mud-hump, under water. The next moment, despite all their frantic paddling, they were stuck fast.

Nestor could see now that both of the women in the canoe were carrying, or wearing, infants strapped to their bodies. All four of the adults in the canoe were working frantically to free it, and they seemed on the point of success when the gray wave overtook them, and the first handless arms reached out. To the accompaniment of human screams the canoe tipped over, and its passengers vanished.

Those who had already gained the shore turned from the scene in renewed panic. Crying to one another in a fear that needed no translation, they ran for the temple.

Nestor hesitated no longer over whether to show himself, but jumped up into their full view. He was not going to be able to outrun the oncoming threat, particularly not on a small island; nor were the refugees from the boats. In union lay their only possible chance of making a successful stand against it; and that possible of course only if Townsaver's latent powers could somehow be called into action, and if they were as great as Nestor had been led to expect. The mental map that he had formed during his exploration of the temple showed him another key factor in his hope: a certain high room, open only on one side, that would perhaps be defensible by three or four determined fighters.

The people Nestor was calling to now, who paused in their frightened flight at the sight of his figure in their path with a sword, probably did not understand his language any more than he knew theirs. But they were ready to follow shouts and gestures, to grasp at any straw of hope. In obedience to Nestor's energetic waves, they came running to him now, and past him. Then they let him get ahead and lead them, at a run over piled rubble and up tilted slabs and collapsing stairs, to reach the place he had in mind.

This was one of the highest surviving rooms of what had once been a towering structure. The only way to approach it now was up a long, rough slope of rubble. When Nestor had led the whole group toiling up this ascent, and had them gathered in the high room, they came to a reluctant stop, looking about them in bewilderment.

He gestured with sword and empty hand. "I'm afraid this is it, my friends. This is the best that we can do."

He could see the understanding growing in the adults' faces, and the renewed terror and despair that came with it.

Nestor turned away from those looks, facing downslope and to the north as he looked out of the room's open side. Not a very large width to defend, hardly more than a wide doorway; but it was a little more space than any one man with any one sword could cover. From this high place he could see now that which made his heart sink: the ranks of the larvae, that had come sweeping across the swamp from the north, extended to both east and west across and beyond the entire width of the island, and farther, for some indeterminate but great distance out into the swamp. There must certainly be thousands of them, and perhaps tens of thousands.

There was movement among the people behind Nestor, and he turned around. Slowly the four or five males of fighting age among the group of refugees were taking their places on his right and left, their bows and clubs as ready as they were ever going to be. Nestor looked at them, and they at him. Fortunately there seemed to be no need to discuss strategy or tactics.

The wave of the enemy had some time ago reached the island, and was now sweeping across it. The gray ones had swarmed into the temple, perhaps in extra numbers because of fleeing prey in sight; the ranks looked thicker than ever when they came into Nestor's view at the foot of the long slope of rubble. They paused there, continuing to thicken with reinforcements behind the steady upward stare of a hundred faceless heads, that gazed upslope as if already aware of determined resistance waiting at the top. What sounded like a thousand larval voices were whistling, whining, mocking, making a drone as of discordant bagpipes that seemed to fill the world.

The ranks of the Gray Horde paused briefly to strengthen themselves at the foot of the long hill of rubble. Then they began to mount.

The women behind Nestor, brought to bay now with their young, were arming themselves too. He glanced back and saw them picking up sharp fragments from the rubble, ready to throw and strike. Something flashed across Nestor's mind about all the concern that warriors, himself included, had for their own coming deaths, all the wondering and worrying and fretting that they gave the subject whether they talked about it or not. And these women, now, had never had a thought in their lives about image and honor and courage, and they were doing as well as any . . .

As for Nestor himself, the thousand voices of the larvae assured him that his time was now, that he was never going to have to worry about it again.

Just behind Nestor, a baby cried.

And at the same moment something thrummed faintly in Nestor's right hand. The swordhilt. His own imagination? Wishful thinking? No . . .

The gray wave was coming up on limping, ill-made legs, brandishing its dead forest of handless arms, aiming its mad variety of weapons, shrieking its song of terror.

Nestor opened his mouth and shouted something back at them, some warcry bursting from he knew not what almost-buried memory. And now around him the bowmen loosed their first pitiful volley of arrows, that stuck in their targets without effect. Other men murmured and swung their clubs. Nestor realized that he was holding the sword two-handed now, and he could feel the power of it flowing into his arms, as natural as his own blood. Now the blade moved up into guard position, in a movement so smooth that Nestor could not really tell if it had been accomplished by his own volition or by the forces that drove the sword itself. And now with the blade high he could see the threaded vapor coming out of the air around it, seeming to flow into the metal.

He had not a moment in which to marvel at any of these things, or to try to estimate his chances, for now a dart sang past his shoulder, and now the awkwardly clambering gray mass of the enemy was almost in reach.

He yelled at them again, something from the wars of years ago, he knew not what. *Townsaver,* pronounced a secret voice within his mind, and he knew that it had named the sword for him.

Townsaver screamed exultantly, and drew the line of its blade through a gray rank as neatly as it had sliced the fruit. It mowed the weapon-sprouting limbs like grass.

CHAPTER 14

"This is it, Your Grace," said the lieutenant in blue and white. "This is the place where the dragon-pack attacked us."

Duke Fraktin halted his riding-beast under a tree still dripping from the morning's rain, and with an easy motion dismounted from the saddle. He made a great gesture with both arms to stretch the muscles in his back, stiffening somewhat after hours of riding. He looked about him.

He did not ask his lieutenant if he were sure about the place; there was no need. From where the Duke now stood, surrounded by a strong force of his mounted men, he could see and smell the carcass of a giant landwalker. The dead beast lay forty meters or so away among some more trees, and now that the Duke looked carefully in that direction he could see a dead man lying close to the dead dragon, and a little farther on one of his own cavalry mounts stiffened with its four feet in the air.

The pestilential aftermath of war, thought the Duke, and stretched again, and started walking unhurriedly closer to the scene of carnage. With a war coming, indeed at hand already, he decided it would be wise to reaccustom his senses as soon as possible to what they were going to be required to experience.

As he walked, with his right hand he loosened Coinspinner in its fine scabbard at his side. "And where," he asked his lieutenant, "is the wagon you were chasing? Did you not tell me that it tipped over in the chase, and then the dragons sprang out and attacked you before you could gather up the people who were in it?"

"That's how it was, Your Grace." And the pair of survivors of that ill-fated patrol who were now accompanying the Duke began a low, urgent debate between themselves as to just where that cursed wagon had been and ought to be. The Duke listened with impatient attention, meanwhile using his eyes for himself though without result. According to the best magical advice he had been able to obtain, that wagon might well have had another of the swords hidden in it somewhere—possibly even two of them.

Before his subordinates' argument was settled, the Duke's attention was drawn away from it by a rider who came cantering up with the report that another kind of wagon was arriving on the road that led from the southwest. This, when it presently came into sight, proved to be a humble, battered vehicle, a limping farm-cart in fact, pulled by a pair of loadbeasts even more decrepit than itself. The Duke at first was mystified as to why some of his advance guard should have doubled back to escort this apparition into his presence.

And then he saw who was riding in the middle of the one sagging seat, and he understood, or began to understand.

"Gentle kinsman," said the Lady Marat, as she held out her hand for the Duke's aid in dismounting. His voice and gesture were as casual as if her humiliation did not concern her in the slightest. But her words indicated otherwise. "I want you to promise me certain specific opportunities of vengeance, on the day that the castle that I left yesterday lies open to your power."

Fraktin bowed his head slightly. "Consider the promise made, dear lady. So long as its fulfillment does not conflict with my own needs, with the necessities of war. And now, I suppose it likely that you have something to report?"

But before he could begin to hear what it might be, a trumpet sounded, causing the Duke to turn away from the lady momentarily. He saw that the head of the long column of his main body of infantry, approaching at route step along the road from the northeast, had now come abreast of the place where they were talking. Duke Fraktin returned the salute of the mounted officer who led the column, then faced back to his discussion with the Lady Marat. And all the while that they were talking there, the ragged, heavy tramp of the infantry kept moving past them.

The Duke offered the lady refreshment. But she preferred to wait until, as she said, she had made her preliminary report, and thus a beginning toward obtaining her revenge. She had plans for everyone in that castle, but particularly for the knight who had stolen her coach and treated her with such total disrespect.

Duke Fraktin listened with close attention to her report, learning among other things that the dragon-hunters' wagon had indeed gone on to Sir Andrew's rather than being destroyed by dragons here.

He asked: "My courier did get away from Sir Andrew's castle with one sword, though? You are sure of that?"

"Yes, good cousin. Of that fact I am very sure. Though I cannot be sure which sword it was."

The Duke, not for the first time, was beginning to find this lady attractive. But he put such thoughts aside, knowing that right now he had better concentrate on other matters. "Then where is this flying courier now? It has never reached me."

The lady could offer no explanation. The Master of the Beasts, when summoned from his place among the Duke's staff officers, gave his opinion that such a dragon ought to be able to fly easily and far, even after being stabbed once or twice with an ordinary sword. The Master of the Beasts had no explanation for the absence of the courier either, except that, as everyone knew, dragons could be unreliable.

Now the Duke turned to consult with yet another figure, who had just dismounted. "What have you to say about my luck now, Blue-Robes? What of the supposed power of this sword I wear?"

The magician spread his hands in a placating gesture. "Only this, Your Grace; that we do not know what your luck might be now, if you did not have Coinspinner there at your side."

"I find that answer something less than adequate, Blue-Robes. I find it . . . what are you gawping at, you fish?" This last was directed aside, at one of the retainers of the Lady Marat. This man had been driving the farm wagon when it arrived. Having been somewhat battered in the lady's service over the past few days, he was now receiving treatment for his wounds from the Duke's surgeon.

The surgeon looked up at the Duke's voice, and stilled his hands. The man who had been addressed started to say something, took a second look at the Duke's face, and threw himself prostrate, bandages trailing unsecured. "A thousand pardons, Your Grace. I was remembering that I . . . that I thought I had seen you at the fair."

"What? At . . ." And even as the Duke spoke, there came in his brain the remembered echo of the voice of someone else, telling him that he had been seen in some other place where he had never been. "Explain yourself, fellow."

The man began a confused relation of what had happened at Sir Andrew's fair, on the night when he and the Duke's other secret agents had got their hands on Dragonslicer. He told some details of that sword's subsequent loss, and of the uncanny, magically changing appearance of the courier dragon as it had soared away.

The Duke nodded thoughtfully. "But me? Where did you think that you saw me?"

"Right there in the fairgrounds, sire. As surely as I see you now. I understand now that what I saw must have been only an image created by magic. But I saw you running toward the courier when it first flew up, and I heard your voice calling it down. And then I saw you stab it."

The Duke turned to look at the Lady Marat, who nodded in confirmation. She said: "Those are essentially the details that I was about to add in my own report."

Next the Duke looked at his wizard, whose eyes were closed. The blue-robed one muttered, as if to himself: "We knew there was another of the swords involved, located at Sir Andrew's castle. And now we know which one it was. That called Sightblinder, or the Sword of Stealth. It is—"

The Duke jogged his arm, commanding silence. "Wait."

Something was going on, up in the vaguely dripping sky. The Master of the Beasts, with head tilted back, was calling and gesturing. Now a reptilian messenger of some kind—the Duke was unable to distinguish the finer gradations of hybrid dragons and other flying life—could be seen in a descending spiral. Alas, thought Duke Fraktin, watching, but this creature was too small to be the courier that had disappeared with one of the swords. This was some smaller flying scout reporting.

In fact it was small enough to perch upon the Master's wrist when it came down. He carried it to some little distance from the gathering of other humans, that the Duke might be able to receive its news, whatever it might be, with some degree of privacy.

In a hoarse whisper the Master translated the report for the Duke a few words at a time, first listening to the dragon's painfully accomplished, almost unintelligible half-speech, then turning his head to speak in human words. "Your Grace, this concerns the dragon-hunter, the man whose human name is Nestor."

"Aye, aye, I know of him. He wronged me once. But what has he to do with our present situation?" Passing this query on to the dragon was a slow and difficult process also. Sometimes the Duke thought that his Beast-Master, indispensably skilled though the man was, had grown half-witted through decades of conversation with his charges.

At length a reply came back. "It is that this Nestor has been carried off into the Great Swamp, sire. By a great flying dragon, not one of ours."

"A grown man, carried off by a flyer? Preposterous. And yet . . . but what else is it trying to say?"

Another guttural exchange took place between trainer and beast. "It says, the Gray Horde, sire. It tells me that the Gray Horde is raised, and marches toward Sir Andrew's lands."

There was silence, except for the drip of water from the trees, and the eternal background tramp of marching soldiery. At last the Duke breathed: "Someone has taken a great gamble, then. Raised by whom?" Although he thought that he could guess.

There was another exchange of bestial noises. Then the Beast-Master said: "By humans who follow a woman, sire. A woman mounted on a warbeast, and leading a human army through the swamp."

Duke Fraktin nodded slowly, and made a gesture of dismissal. The Master rewarded his charge with a small dried lizard, laced with a drug that would give the flyer a sleep of delightful dreams.

Meanwhile the Duke, walking the short distance back to where his staff and the Lady Marat were waiting for him, prepared to call a major conference. Things had changed. What confronted him now was no longer the simple conquest of a smaller power that he had planned.

It appeared to him that the gods were once more actively entering the affairs of humankind.

CHAPTER 15

The screaming of the sword had seemed to Nestor to go on at its full voice for centuries. But then at last it had declined to a low whine, and now it was dying down to silence. And the life, the power, that still flowed from the hilt into Nestor's shaking hands was gradually dying too.

Gasping with exhaustion, his skin slippery everywhere with sweat and in places with his own blood, he took one staggering step forward. The long, sloping hill of rubble was still before him, and he still stood at the top of it alive. He looked round him for something, some deadwood figure, to strike at with the sword. But none of those that were still in sight were still erect.

He could still hear, starting to fade with distance now, the myriad whining voices of the larvae-army. Those gray ranks had split around the temple and gone on. But not all of them. Over a broad, fan-shaped area of the slope immediately in front of Nestor, the hill had gained a new layer of rubble. It was the debris of a hundred gray bodies, hewn by Townsaver into chunks of melting mud.

Those fallen bodies were all quiet now. Nothing but the returning rain moved on the whole slope.

Stray drops of rain touched Nestor's face. And he turned round slowly in his tracks, looking dazedly at the equally dazed people who had been fighting beside him, and covering his back. He saw that two of the men had gone down, their clubs still in hand. And one of the women had been butchered, along with her small child. But all of the other people were still alive. They were mostly cowering in corners now, and some of them were hurt. Townsaver's shrieking blur had covered almost the whole wide doorway.

—hard walls it builds around the soft—

Only now did Nestor become fully aware of the small wounds he himself had sustained, here and there. He had tried when he could to use the sword to parry, to protect his own skin as much as possible. But the magic power that drove the sword in combat had been in ultimate control, and it had been less interested in saving him than in hacking down the foe.

A dart was still stuck loosely in Nestor's shirt, scratching him when he moved, and drawing blood. As he pulled the small shaft loose and threw it away he wondered whether it might be poisoned. Too late now to worry about it if it was.

At least he could still move; in the circumstances, he could hardly ask for more. He looked once more at the stunned survivors, who remained where they were, numbly looking back at him. Then he scrambled down across the slope that was littered with the bodies of his foes, and up another hill of ruins. He was heading for the highest remaining point of the temple's roof. From up there he should be able to see a maximum distance across the swamp in every direction.

Clinging to that precarious remnant of a roof, Nestor could see in the distance the waves of the larvae-army that had broken on his strongpoint and then rolled on, rejoining like waves of water when they were past the temple. The sight gave him a strange feeling. The hundred larvae that he had destroyed were suddenly as nothing.

From this high place Nestor could see something else as well. It was a sight that made him hurry down, passing as quickly as he could the people he and the sword had saved, and who had now decided that they wanted to prostrate themselves before him as before a god. His body shaking now with fatigue, relief, and perhaps with poison, Nestor made his way down to the ground level of the temple, and then out of the building to the south.

In another moment, Draffut, who in Nestor's view from the roof had been only a distant, toylike figure, was coming around a corner of the temple from the southwest. The giant moved in vast strides, his two-legged walk covering ground faster than any human run. A flying dragon of moderate size, perhaps the very one that Nestor had earlier spoken to, was flitting along near Draffut's head, almost as if it were planning to attack him. But Draffut ignored the flying thing, and it did him no harm.

The small mob of refugees had followed Nestor down to ground level. Draffut was obviously known to them, and a very welcome sight; Nestor supposed it was hope of the giant's protection that had brought them fleeing to the island in the first place. Now they offered Draffut worship, and clamored to him at length. The giant answered them in their own language. With his huge hands he raised them from their knees, and touched their wounds and healed them.

Then one of his enormous hands reached out for Nestor, who once more felt its restoring power. As his touch healed, Draffut said to him: "You have fought well here. And with the use of more than ordinary powers, if what these people tell me is correct."

"It probably is. Thank you again, Healer-who-is-not-a-god." The shaking was gone from Nestor's body, and the places where his small wounds had been were whole. He felt healthy, to a degree that made the long fight just past seem as unreal as a dream. He was surprised at a passing feeling that, along with the fear and pain, something valuable had been wiped away.

"Yes," Nestor went on, "there were very many of them. Very many, including your pet that rose up in advance of the others and tried to kill me. The sword gave me no more than ordinary service against that one."

Abstractedly Draffut lifted one of his huge wrists, and the flying dragon perched on it like a falcon. "My airborne scouts," the giant rumbled, "tell me that the Great Swamp is being invaded from the west by a large human army. Its soldiers wear the black and silver of Yambu, and it may be that the queen herself is leading them."

"Ah." Nestor felt shaken by the news; he bent to take up again the sword he had cast down when Draffut reached out to him. Nestor like everyone else had heard of that queen and of her power. "I suppose that her objective is not the conqest of the swamp."

"And I suppose that it is probably the domain of Kind Sir Andrew. The sorcerers of her army chant their spells as they march, and all across the swamp the larvae that they have cultivated from afar rise up and form in ranks to follow them."

"So," said Nestor. "We know now who is responsible for the larvae. And why is this army being led against Sir Andrew in particular? And why just now?"

Draffut made a motion of his arm, so that the dragon flew up from his wrist; it had rested, and now with vigorous wing-strokes went off on its own business. Draffut said: "Two of the god-swords, at least, are there now. A tempting booty to be taken, would you not agree?"

Nestor looked at the refugees, who were following the talk with reverence if little understanding. He said to Draffut: "One sword at least is there, and that one mine. I suppose if the Queen of Yambu knew where it was, and its importance, she might risk much to take it. As would Duke Fraktin, or a hundred others, I am sure. So what are we to do? I'd risk much myself to get it back."

Draffut said: "You should go to Sir Andrew, and warn him. And do what you can, with that you have there in your hand, to help him. Now that we know who is raising the Gray Horde, and where it is being led, I no longer feel that I must remain in the swamp. In fact, there is somewhere else I want to go now, and we can go part of the way together."

Again Draffut held brief conversation with the surviving swamp-folk. Then he explained to Nestor: "I have told them that they can return to their village now, on another island not far from here. They will be safer there than here, if powers should come seeking here for followers of mine."

"What powers might those be?"

"I mean to go," said Draffut, "and start an argument with the gods. Or with some of them at least. Are you ready to depart?"

Nestor had no baggage to bring with him except the sword. Which was, he now observed, an awkward thing to have to carry in one's hand for any length of time. This difficulty loomed larger when he realized that he was going to have to ride a long way on Draffut's shoulders, and that he might at times want both hands free to hang on with. Draffut, suggesting a solution, sent Nestor to rummage in a certain room of the temple that he had not found in his own explorations, a long-abandoned guardhouse or arsenal. Much of the weaponry stored therein had rusted and rotted away, but Nestor turned up a copper scabbard that fit Townsaver tolerably well. To make the necessary belt, he used the sword itself to cut a length of tough vine from the temple wall.

The surviving swamp-people and their canoes had already disappeared back into their native habitat when Draffut, with Nestor clinging to his back, left solid land behind and strode into the morass, heading to the northeast. Draffut's long wading strides soon overtook the paddlers; the people in the canoes made way for him, waving as they pulled aside.

For half an hour or so, Draffut made steady and uneventful progress. If any of the multitude of life-forms large and small that inhabited the marsh ever considered molesting the Beast-Lord in his passage, Nestor at least was not aware of it. Draffut never went more than waist-deep in the water and mud, and Nestor was easily able to keep himself dry. Now and then he had to dodge a tree-branch, but that was his most serious immediate problem. He clung with both hands to his mount's glowing fur, and was actually beginning to enjoy himself. It seemed to Nestor that sometimes even the thorntrees bent aside before the giant reached them.

This pleasant interval ended abruptly just as Draffut was mounting a ridge of dry, comparatively high ground. At that point a large warbeast, armored and collared in the colors of Yambu, sprang in ambush at the Beast-Lord from a brake of reeds. The giant's reaction was practically instantaneous; before Nestor could draw his sword, Draffut had caught the attacker in midair, as if he were playing with a kitten. But then the giant threw the warbeast violently, so that the flying, screaming body broke tree branches and vanished behind a screen of trees some thirty meters distant before it splashed into the swamp.

Almost as if in response, there came a distant, whistling call, that sounded like some hunter's cry. Nestor had heard similar signals used to control warbeasts. Draffut paused for a moment, turning to gaze over the treetops to his left; then he moved swiftly off to his right, walking at a greater speed than ever. Now Nestor had to clap his half-drawn sword back into its scabbard and once more hold tight with both hands.

"The advance guard of Yambu," said Draffut over his shoulder, in what he used for a low voice. "We will outspeed them if we can."

Looking back, Nestor saw more warbeasts already in pursuit. He counted three, and there might well be more. Hundreds of meters farther back, beyond the great catlike creatures, he could see the first advancing elements of a human army, some of them mounted and some in boats. He announced this to Draffut's ear, but the giant did not bother to answer. Draffut was almost, but not quite, running now. Maybe, thought Nestor, his size and build made a real run an impossibility for him. Nestor had considerable confidence in Draffut's powers;

but at the same time the man could almost feel those huge warbeast talons fastening on him from behind . . .

The chase went on. From time to time Nestor reported, in a voice he strove to keep calm, that their pursuers were catching up. Then abruptly Draffut stopped, and calmly turned to stand his ground.

"It is no use," he said. "They are too fast. And they are maddened with the lust to fight, and will not listen to me." With one hand he lifted Nestor from his shoulders, and placed the man in a high crotch of a dead tree. "Defend yourself," the Beast-Lord laconically advised him, and turned to do the same.

A moment later, half a dozen warbeasts, hot on the trail, came bounding out of the brush nearby. Draffut cuffed the first one to come in reach, grabbed and threw another by its tail, and had to pick a third one from his fur when it was actually brave enough to leap on him. He hurled it into the remaining three. With that all of the warbeasts that were still able to move scattered in flight, emitting uncharacteristic yelps. Nestor, his sword drawn and ready though showing no special powers, had nothing to do. Which, under the circumstances, was quite all right with him.

Draffut had just retrieved Nestor from his high perch when a new figure appeared. It was the form of a woman with long black hair, her body clothed in light armor of ebony and silver, on another ridge or island of dry land about a hundred meters distant to the west. She was mounted on a gray warbeast of such a size that Nestor for an instant thought it was a dragon.

Beneath the cloudy sky, the woman's armor flashed as if it were catching desert sunshine. She brandished a silver needle of a sword, and she was shouting something in their direction.

The words came clearly in her penetrating voice: "Remove yourself from my army's path, great beast, or I will set men to fight against you! I know your weakness; they'll kill you soon enough. And who is that you carry?"

Nestor had heard of people who rode on warbeasts, but never before had he seen it done. As he resumed his seat on Draffut's shoulders, the giant roared back: "Rather remove your blood-mad warbeasts from my path! Or else I will send you dragons enough to make your march through the swamp much more interesting." Without waiting to see what effect his words might have, he turned and stalked away, resuming his passage to the north.

There was no observable pursuit.

"That was the Silver Queen herself. Yambu," said Nestor to Draffut's ear a little later. The comment was undoubtedly unnecessary, but the man was unable to let the encounter pass without saying something about it.

"Indeed." The huge voice came rumbling up through Draffut's neck and head. "There are elements of humanity that I sometimes wish I were able to fight against."

Once more they were traversing bog and thicket at what would have been a good speed for a riding-beast on flat, cleared ground. Some time passed in silence, except for the quick plash and thud of Draffut's feet, while Nestor pondered many things. Then he asked: "You said that you are planning to go and start an argument with the gods?"

"I must," said Draffut. And that was all the answer to his question that Nestor ever got.

But little further conversation was exchanged. Nestor welcomed the comfort of his ride, and watched the sun move in and out of clouds in the western sky. By the time Draffut stopped again, some hours had passed and the reddening sun was almost down. Imperceptibly the land had changed, continuous marsh giving way to intermittent bogs bridged by dry land. Once Nestor saw herdsmen watching from a distance.

The giant set Nestor down carefully on dry ground, and said to him: "Go north from here, and you will find Sir Andrew. From here on north the land is solid enough for you to walk, and savage beasts are fewer. My own way from here lies to the east."

"I wish you good luck," said Nestor. And then, when he had looked to the east, he would have said something more, for never until now had he known the sunset fires of Vulcan's forge to be so bright that they could be seen from this far west.

But Draffut was already gone.

CHAPTER 16

When Dame Yoldi took Mark for the first time to her workroom, he discovered it not to be the dismal, forbidding chamber that he had for some reason expected. Rather it was open, cleanly decorated with things of nature, and as light as the dying, cloudy day outside could make it, entering narrow windows.

The enchantress lighted tapers, from a small oil lamp that was already burning. She distributed a few of these in the otherwise dark corners of the room, and placed two more on the central table where Dragonslicer now rested on a white linen cloth. Most of the floor space in the room was open, while shelves round all the walls contained an armament of magic, arrayed in books and bottles, boxes, jars, and bags. One set of open dishes held grain and dried fruit, another set what looked like plain water and dry earth.

Yoldi made Mark sit down at the table near the sword, where she made him comfortable, and gave him a delicious drink, not quite like anything he had ever tasted before. Then she began to question him closely about his family, and about the several god-swords he had seen, and about what he thought he would do with his own sword if he could ever get it back. Her questions suggested new ideas to Mark, and made him see his own situation in what seemed like a new light, so that when he looked at the sword before him on the table now he saw it as something different from the weapon he had once held in his own two hands and used to kill a dragon. The more he talked with Yoldi the more fearfully impressive the whole business grew. But somehow he was not more frightened.

Their chat was interrupted by an urgent tapping at the door. Yoldi went to open it, and listened briefly to someone just outside. A moment later, with a solemn face, she was beckoning to Mark to follow her out of the room. She led him up many stairs, and finally up a ladder, which brought them out onto what proved to be the highest rooftop of the castle. This was a flat area only a few meters square, copper-sheeted against weather and attack by fire, and bounded by a chest-high parapet of stone. Sir Andrew's Master of the Beasts, a dour young man who gave the impression of wanting to be old, was on the roof already, doing something to one of a row of man-sized cages that stood under a shelter along the northern parapet. In these cages were kept the flyers, the inhuman messengers and scouts, temporarily before launching and when they had returned from flights.

When Dame Yoldi and Mark appeared on the roof, the Beast-Master silently pointed to the east, into the approaching night. In that direction a large arc of the horizon was sullenly aglow, with what looked like an untimely dawn, or distant flames.

"The mountains," Mark said, understanding the origin of the glow. And then: "My home."

Dame Yoldi, standing behind him, held him by the shoulders. "In which direction exactly is your village, boy?" Her voice at first sounded almost eager. "Can you point toward it? But no, I don't suppose that's possible. It's somewhere near those mountains, though."

"Yes." And Mark, continuing to stare at the distant fires, lapsed into silence.

"Don't be afraid." Yoldi's tone turned reassuring, while remaining brisk, refusing to treat volcanoes as a disaster. Her grip was comforting. "Your folk are probably all right. I know these foothill people, ready to take care of themselves. It might actually be a good thing for them, make them get out of Duke Fraktin's territory if they haven't done so already." The enchantress turned away to the dour man, asking: "When is your next scout due back from the east?"

Mark did not understand whatever it was that the man answered. He was intent on wondering what might be happening to his home, on picturing his mother and his sister as stumbling refugees.

"I wonder," Dame Yoldi was musing to herself, "if anyone's told Andrew about this yet. He ought to be told, but he's down there talking to the fellow from Yambu—probably wouldn't do to interrupt him now."

And now Mark saw that one of the airborne scouts was indeed coming in against the fading sky; coming from the south and not the east, but approaching with weary, urgent speed.

Baron Amintor, who was Queen Yambu's emissary to Sir Andrew, was a large man, the size of Sir Andrew himself but younger. The Baron with his muscles and his scars looked more the warrior than the diplomat. He had the diplomat's smooth tongue, though, and Sir Andrew had to admit to himself that the man's manners were courteous enough. It was only the substance of what the visitor had to say that Sir Andrew found totally objectionable.

The two men were conversing alone in a small room, not far above the ground level of the castle, and within earshot of Sir Andrew's armory, where the clang of many hammers upon metal signalled the process of full mobilization that the knight had already put into effect. It was a sound he did not want his visitor to miss.

Not that the Baron appeared to be taking the least notice of it. "Sir Andrew, if you will only hand over to me now, for delivery to the Queen, whichever of these swords you now possess, and grant the Queen's armies the right of free passage through your territory—which passage you will not be able to deny her in any case—you will then be under her protection as regards these threats you have lately been receiving from Duke Fraktin. And, I may add, from any similar threats that may arise from any quarter. *Any* quarter," Amintor repeated, with a sly, meaningful look, almost a wink. At that point he paused.

Sir Andrew wondered what particular fear or suspicion that nearwink had been calculated to arouse in him; but no matter, he was worrying to capacity already, though he trusted that it did not show.

Baron Amintor went on: "But, of course, Her Majesty cannot be expected to guarantee the frontiers or the safety of any state that is unfriendly to her. And if for some misguided reason you should withhold from her these swords, these tools so necessary to Her Majesty's ambitions for a just peace, then Her Majesty cannot do otherwise than consider you unfriendly." At this point the Baron's voice dropped just a little. It seemed that, bluff soldier that he was, it rather shocked him to think of anyone's being unfriendly to Yambu.

"Ah," Sir Andrew remarked. "The tools necessary for a just peace. I rather like that. Yes, that's quite good."

"Sir Andrew, believe me, Her Majesty has every intention of respecting your independence, as much as possible. But, to be unfriendly and small at the same time—that is really not the policy of wisdom."

"Wisdom, is it? Small, are we?" Bards would never repeat such words of defiance; but Sir Andrew felt that the man standing before him did not deserve anything in the way of fine or even thoughtful speech. And anyway he felt too angry to try to produce it.

"Good sir, the fact is that your domain *is* comparatively small. Comparatively weak. Duke Fraktin is of course as well aware of these facts as you and I are, and the Duke is not your friend. The people of your lands—well, they are brave, I am sure. And loyal to you—most of them at least. But they are not all that numerous. And they are widely scattered. This castle—" and here the Baron, being bluff and military, thumped his strong hand on the wall "—is a fine fortress. The noise from your armory is entertaining. But, how many fighting men have you actually mobilized so far, here on the spot and ready to fight? Two hundred? Fewer, perhaps? No, of course you need not tell me. But think upon the number in your own mind. Compare it to the numbers that are ready to cross your borders now, from two directions, east and west. You can prevent neither the Queen's army crossing, nor the Duke's. And then think upon the people in your outlying villages that you are never going to be able to defend. At least not without Her Majesty's gracious help."

Sir Andrew stood up abruptly. He was so angry that he did not trust himself. "Leave me now."

The Baron was already standing. He turned, without argument, without either delay or evidence of fear, and took a couple of steps toward the door. Then he paused. "And have you any further message for the Queen?"

"I say leave me for now. You will be shown where to wait. I will let you know presently about the message."

As soon as Sir Andrew was alone, he left the small chamber where he had been talking with Baron Amintor, and walked into another, larger room, where most of his old books were kept. There by lamplight he picked up a volume, fingered it, opened it, closed it, and put it down again. When was he ever going to have time to read again? Or would he die in battle soon, and never have time again to read another book?

After that, he took himself in a thoughtful, silent, solitary walk down into the dungeon. There he stood in front of the one cell that held a human being, gazing thoughtfully at the prisoner. Kaparu his captive looked back at him nervously. Down the side corridor, workers were busy opening the cells where birds and animals were confined, preparing to set the small inmates free. War was coming, and luxuries had to go, including the dream of a vivarium in the castle grounds.

At length the knight spoke. "You, Kaparu, are my only human prisoner. Have you meditated upon the meaning of my last reading to you? I do not know when, if ever, it will be possible to read to you again, and try to teach you to be good."

"Oh, yes, indeed I have meditated, sire." Kaparu's hands slipped sweatily on the bars to which he would have clung. "And—and I have learned this much at least, that you are a good man. And I was quite sure already that those who are planning to invade your lands are not good people. So, I—I would give much, sire, not to be in this cell when . . . that is, if . . ."

"When my castle is overrun by them, you mean. A natural and intelligent reaction."

"Oh, if you would release me, sire, if you would let me out, I would be grateful. I would do anything."

"Would you go free, and rob no more?"

"Gladly, sire, I swear it."

Sir Andrew, hesitating in inward conflict, asked him: "Is your oath to be trusted, Kaparu? Have you learned that it is no light thing to break an oath?"

"I will not break mine, sire. Your readings to me . . . they have opened my eyes. I can see now that all my earlier life was wrong, one great mistake from start to finish."

Sir Andrew looked long at Kaparu. Then, with a gentle nod, he reached for the key ring at his own belt.

A little later, when the knight had heard the latest message from the flying scouts, and had begun to ponder the terrible news of the raising of the Gray Horde, he sent away Yambu's ambassador with a final message of defiance. There seemed to him to be nothing else that he could do.

After that, Sir Andrew went up to the highest parapets of his castle, which at the moment were otherwise unoccupied, there to lean out over his battlement and brood. Everywhere he looked, preparations for war and siege were being made, and he had much to ponder.

Presently he was aware that someone else had joined him on the roof, and he looked up from his thoughts and saw Dame Yoldi standing near. From her expression he judged that she had no urgent news or question for him, she had simply come in his hour of need to see what else she might be able to do to help.

"Andrew."

"Yoldi . . . Yoldi, if the power in these god-forged swords is indeed so great, that these evildoers around us are ready to risk war with each other, as well as with us, to obtain even one of them—if it is so great, I say, then how can I in good conscience surrender to them even one source of such power?"

Dame Yoldi nodded her understanding, gently and sadly. "It would seem that you cannot. So you have already decided. Unless the consequences of refusing to surrender strike you as more terrible still?"

"They do not! By all the demons that Ardneh ever slew or paralyzed, we must all die at some time, but we are not all doomed to surrender! But the people in the villages haunt me, Yoldi. I can do nothing to protect them from Fraktin or Yambu."

"It would give those village people at least some hope for the future —those among them who survive invasion—if you could stand fast, here in your strong place, and eventually reclaim your lands."

"If I try to stand fast, here or anywhere, then I must say to my people: 'March to war.' We know, you and I, what war is like. Some of the young ones do not know . . . but it appears that the evil and the horror of war are coming upon them anyway, whatever I decide. No surrender will turn back such enemies as these, once they are mobilized upon my borders, or moderate what they do to my people. Regardless of what they might promise now. Not that I have asked them for any promises, or terms. Why ask for what I would never believe from them anyway?"

A silence fell between the knight and the enchantress, the world around them quiet too except for the distant chinking from the armorers. "I must go back to my own work," Yoldi said at last, and kissed the lord of the castle once, and went away.

"And I must go down," said Sir Andrew aloud to himself, "and inspect the defenses."

A little later when he was walking upon the castle's outer wall, near one of the strong guard-towers that defended the main gate, Sir Andrew encountered one of his old comrades in arms, and fell into conversation with him.

"A long time, Sir Andrew, since we've had to draw our swords atop these walls."

"Yes, a long time."

At some point the comrade had turned into quite an old man, white-haired and wrinkled, and Sir Andrew, not remembering him as such, could not quite shake the feeling that this aged appearance was some kind of a disguise, which the other would presently take off. The talk they had sounded cheerful enough, though most of the matters they talked about were horrible, siege and stratagem, raid and counterattack and sally.

"That kept 'em off our backs a good long time, hey sir?"

"Not long enough." Sir Andrew sighed.

And presently he was once more left alone, still standing on the wall near the main gate. This was a good vantage point from which to over-look the thin, intermittent stream of provision carts, fighting men, and refugees that came trickling up the winding road that led from the intersection of the highways to the castle.

Here came some priests and priestesses of Ardneh, white-robed and hurried, who had just passed an inspection at the checkpoint down the way. They were driving two carts, that Sir Andrew could at least hope were filled with medical supplies. Sometimes, in time of war, Temples of Ardneh stood unscathed in the midst of contending armies. Each leader and each fighter hoped that if he were wounded, he would be cared for if there were room. But evidently it would not be that way this time. Ardneh, in a sense, was coming to Sir Andrew's side; and, medical supplies aside, the troops were sure to take that as a good omen.

Sir Andrew closed his eyes, and gripped the parapet in front of him. He thought of praying to Ardneh for more direct help—although with part of his mind he knew, knew better than almost anyone else in the world, that though Ardneh had once lived, he had now been dead for almost two thousand years. Sir Andrew knew it well. And yet . . .

And this mystery regarding Ardneh called to mind another, that had long troubled Sir Andrew and that none of his studies had ever been able to solve: If Ardneh was dead, why were all the world's other gods and goddesses alive? The common opinion was that all of them had been living since the creation of the world, or thereabouts, and that of course Ardneh was still alive with all the others. But Sir Andrew had the gravest doubts that the common opinion was correct.

He tended instead to trust certain historical writings, that spoke in matter-of-fact terms of Ardneh's existence and his death, but did not so much as mention Vulcan, Hermes, Aphrodite, Mars, or any of the rest —with the sole exception of the Beast-Lord Draffut. And Draffut was not assigned the importance of Ardneh, or of their evil opponent Orcus, Lord of Demons.

And whatever Sir Andrew might think of gods, he had no doubts at all about the reality of demons.

At some time in his long years of study and deep thought, a horrible suspicion had been born, deep in his mind: That the entities that who now called themselves gods, were recognized by humanity as gods, and who claimed to rule the world—whenever they bothered to take an interest in it—that these beings were in fact demons who had survived from the era of Ardneh and of Orcus. But there were, comfortingly, important difficulties with that theory too.

After all Sir Andrew's study of the gods, all he could say about them with absolute certainty was very little: That most of them were real, here and now, and very powerful. The swords were testimony enough to the real power of Vulcan.

Yoldi was a fine magician, and a brave one. But there were limits to the ability of any magician to reach and control the ultimate powers of reality.

Why in the names of all the gods and demons did the universe have to be such a complicated, confused, and contrary place? Sir Andrew thought now, not for the first time, that if he had been put in charge of the design, he would have done things differently.

Sir Andrew had opened his eyes for a while, closed them again, and was trying to decide whether he was really praying to Ardneh now or not, when he heard his name called from below. Looking down, he saw that one man had stepped aside from the continued trickle of traffic approaching the castle, and was now standing just below Sir Andrew on the shoulder of the road. The man was in his late youth or early middle age, rather slight of build, and with a traveled look about him. He wore a large sword, belted on with what looked like rope or twine, that immediately drew Sir Andrew's attention.

The man had to speak again before Sir Andrew recognized the dragon-hunter, Nestor. "Sir Andrew? I bring you greetings from the Beast-Lord, Draffut."

CHAPTER 17

Even traveling almost without pause, at the best speed made possible by his enormous strides, it had taken Draffut a day and a half to get from the temple island near the middle of the Great Swamp east as far as the high plains. And night was falling again before he reached the region in Duke Fraktin's domain where the upward slope of land began to grow pronounced. The volcanic fires that had lighted the eastern sky when seen from hundreds of kilometers away were at this close range truly spectacular.

Almost immediately upon leaving the swamp behind, Draffut had begun to encounter refugees from the eruption. These were mainly folk from Duke Fraktin's high villages, where a mass evacuation had obviously started. The villagers were fleeing their homes and land in groups, as families, as individuals, moving anywhere downslope, most of them lost now in unfamiliar territory. Some of these people, passing Draffut at a little distance, shouted to him word of what they considered Vulcan's wrath—as if Draffut should not be able to see for himself the flaming sky ahead.

Draffut was not sure whether these folk were trying to warn him, to plead for his intercession with the gods, or both. "I will speak to Vulcan about it," he said, when he said anything at all in answer. Carefully he avoided stepping on any of the people. For the most part of course they said nothing to him. They were astonished and terrified to see him, and in their panic would sometimes have run right under his feet, or would have driven their livestock or their farm-carts into him. Draffut made his way considerately around them all, and went on east, and up.

He had no such need to be careful with the small units of Duke Fraktin's army that he encountered along the way, some of them even before he had entered the Duke's domain. Whether mounted or afoot, these always scattered in flight before Draffut's advance, as if they took it for granted that he would be their deadly enemy. Draffut could not help thinking back to the time when soldiers had cheered him and looked to him for help. But that had been many ages and wars ago, and halfway around the world from here.

In a lifetime that had spanned more than fifty thousand years, Draffut had often enough seen swarms of human refugees, and even burning skies like these. But seldom before had he felt the earth quiver beneath his feet as it was quivering now.

When he got in among the barren foothills he continued climbing without pause. Now the rumbling towers of fire loomed almost above his head, and fine ash drifted continuously down around him. He thought that there were forces here that could destroy him, that he was no longer immune to death, as he might once have been. His own powers, absorbed over ages, were fading as slowly as they had been gained, but they were fading. Yet he could feel little personal fear. By his nature, Draffut could not help but be absorbed in larger things than that.

The shuddering, burning agony of the mountains against the darkening sky brought back more old memories to Draffut. One of these recollections was very old indeed, of another mountain, upon another continent, that once had split to spill the Lake of Life . . . that had been in the days of Ardneh's greatest power. Ardneh, whom Draffut had never really known at all, despite the current human version of the history of the world. It hardly mattered now, for now Ardneh was long dead . . .

The question to be answered now was, where had these new creatures of power sprung from, these upstart entities calling themselves gods? Ardneh in his days of greatest strength had never claimed to be a god, nor had the evil Orcus. Indeed, it seemed to Draffut looking back that for thousands of years the very word *god* had been almost forgotten among humanity.

If he tried to peer back too far into his own past, he reached an epoch where all memory faded, blurring into disconnected scenes and meaningless impressions. He knew that these were remnant of a time when his intelligence, brain, and body had been very different from what they were now. But certainly Draffut's memory of the past few thousand years was sharp and clear. He could recall very well the days when Ardneh and Orcus had fought each other. And in those days, not one of these currently boasting, sword-making upstarts who called themselves gods and goddesses had walked the earth. They bore names from the remote past of human myth, but who were they? By what right did they plan for themselves games that involved for humanity the horror of wars? Draffut could no longer delay finding out.

He had climbed only a little way up the first slopes of the real mountain when he found his way blocked by a slow stream of lava, three or four meters wide. The air above the lava writhed with heat. And in the night and the hellglow on the far side of the molten stream, visible amid swirling fumes and boiling air, there stood a two-legged figure far too large to be human, even if a human could have stood there and lived. The figure was roughly the same size as Draffut himself, and it was regarding Draffut, and waiting silently.

In the raging heat he could see nothing of the figure clearly but its presence. He stopped, and called a salutation to it, using an ancient tongue that either Ardneh or Orcus would have understood at once. There was no reply.

Now Draffut summoned up what he could of his old powers, concentrating them in his right hand. Then he bent down and thrust that hand into the sluggish, crusting, seething stream of lava. Without allowing himself to be burned, he scooped up a dripping handful of the molten rock. With another exertion of his will he gave the handful of magma temporary life, so that what had been dead rock quickened and soared aloft in the hot, rising air, making a small silent explosion of living things exquisite as butterflies.

Still the figure that waited beyond the lava-stream would not move or speak. But now another like itself had joined it, and as Draffut watched yet another and another one appeared. The gods were assembling to watch what he was doing, to judge him silently.

He wanted more than that from them. He stood erect and brushed his hands clean of smoking rock. It was impossible to tell from the silent observation whether the onlookers were impressed by what he had done.

In a carrying roar he challenged them: "Why do you not tell humanity the truth? Are you afraid of it?"

There was a stir among the group, images wavering in the heat. With the noise of the earth itself pervading all, Draffut could not tell what they might be saying among themselves. At last a voice, larger than human, boomed back at him: "Tell them yourself, you shaggy dog."

Another voice followed, high clear tones that must be those of a goddess: "We know well what you used to be, Beast-Lord, when first you followed your human masters into the cave of the Lake of Life, fifty thousand years ago and more. Do not pretend to grandeur now."

And yet another voice, belligerent and male: "Yes, tell them yourself —but will they believe what they are told by a dog, the son of a bitch? Never mind that some of them now think you are a god. We can fix that!"

Draffut could feel the fervor of his anger growing, growing, till it was hotter than the lava that made the earth burn just in front of him. He roared back: "I have as much right to be a god as any of you do. More! Tell the human world what you really are!"

Beyond the wavering heat, their numbers were still increasing. Another voice mocked him: *"You* tell them what we really are. Ha, haaa!"

"I would tell them. I will tell them, when I know."

"Ha, haaa! We are the gods, and that is all ye need to know. It is no business of a son of a bitch to challenge gods."

In a single stride Draffut moved forward across the stream of lava. And now he could see the last speaker plainly enough to be able to recognize him. "You are Vulcan. And now you are going to give me some answers, about the swords."

Vulcan answered boldly enough, with an obscene insult. But at the same time he appeared to shrink back a little within the group. There was wrangling and shoving among the deities, amid a cloud of smoke and dust. Then another figure, pushing Vulcan aside, stepped forward from behind him. Now the shape of a gigantic and muscular man, carrying a great spear, his head covered with a helm, stood limned against a fresh flow of red-hot lava spilling down a slope.

"I am traveling west from here," said Mars. His voice was one that Draffut had not heard before, all drums and trumpets and clashing metal. "War draws me there. I see a besieged castle, and one in the attacking army who offers me sacrifice with skilful magic. I think it is time for me to answer the prayers of one of my devoted worshippers."

From the group behind the speaker there came a discordant chorus of varied comments on this announcement. Draffut noted that they ranged from applause to enthusiastic scorn.

Mars ignored them all. He did not turn his terrible gaze from Draffut, who stood right in his way. Mars said: "I am going to that castle, there to spend some time in killing humans for amusement."

Draffut said simply: "No, that you will not do."

At this point someone in the rear rank of the gods threw a burning boulder straight at Draffut. It seemed to come with awesome slowness through the air, and it was accurately aimed. Catching it strained his great strength, but from some reserve he drew the power to hurl it back —not at its unseen thrower. Instead Draffut aimed it straight for Mars, just as the long spear leveled for a throw. Rock and spear met in mid-air, to explode in a million screaming fragments.

Another spear already in his hand, the God of War strode forward to do battle.

CHAPTER 18

Dame Yoldi herself had told Mark several times that she considered his survival vitally important, and that she meant for that reason to keep him in comparative safety at her side as much as possible when the fighting started. Thus it happened that they were together on the high roof of Sir Andrew's castle, in early morning light, when the first attack of the Gray Horde broke like a dirty wave against the walls.

The defenders were as ready as they could be for the assault, for there had been no way for the attackers to achieve surprise. On the previous day, Sir Andrew's enchantress had announced that the speed and direction of the larvae's advance could be only approximately controlled by the magicians of Yambu. For the past few days, Yoldi and several of her assistants had attempted to interfere with the enemy magic, and turn the larvae against those who had raised them. But that effort had failed, and Dame Yoldi was necessarily concentrating upon other matters now. She said that in any case the larvae would not be able to remain active for more than a few days. Once raised from the swamp, they drew no nourishment, no energy of any kind, from their environment. This made them difficult to interfere with, and almost impossible to poison, but also awkward for their masters to control. However, for the few days that their pseudo-life endured they were an almost invincible army, immune to weariness and fear.

Their massed howling, like distant wind, could be heard in the castle for more than an hour before their first charge at the walls. Therefore the defenders were alerted and in place when the hundred scaling ladders of the Horde were raised.

As the light grew full, Mark could see from his high vantage point how Ben was taking part in the fighting atop the eastern wall, using his great strength behind a pole to topple scaling ladders back as fast as the handless, clumsy larvae below could prop them up; there were no humans to be seen at all in the first wave of attackers.

And Barbara was on the wall west of the guard towers and the main gate, one of a company of men and women armed with bows and slings. Their missiles went hailing thickly down into the sea of the attackers, but Mark could not see that they did much damage. An arrow might penetrate a larva's shell, but the thing kept advancing anyway, pushing up another ladder and then climbing to the attack. A slung stone might crack a carapace, but the hit figure came on anyway, until a leg joint was broken too badly to let it walk, or its arms disabled to the point where it could no longer climb a ladder.

The hundred ladders carried forward to the walls in that first attack, Mark decided, must have been made for the larvae by their human masters and allies. Last night he had heard Nestor talking in the castle, describing in detail what he had seen of the larvae at close range, and what kind of fighting might be expected when their horde swept to the assault on the castle walls.

Sir Andrew had listened very carefully to the same account. The knight had then sat alone for a while, the picture of grim thought, and then had issued orders, disposing of his defense forces as best he might. Mark had got the impression, listening, that all the experts on hand knew that the walls were going to be undermanned.

Then Sir Andrew had had Nestor speak to the defenders also of Draffut, of how the Lord of Beasts had seemed to favor their cause, and to hint of active intervention on their side. This raised the hopes of everyone somewhat, though Nestor was careful not to claim that any such promise had been made by Draffut.

Nestor, as he had explained to a smaller gathering of his old companions of the wagon, had decided he had no real choice but to take part in the fighting, once he had decided to come to Sir Andrew's castle with the sword.

"Besides, where would I have gone to get away? From here all roads lead ultimately to Fraktin or Yambu, except those that go back into the swamp, or to the northwest; and I expect that even those are closed by now."

Armed with the Sword of Fury, and wearing the best armor that Sir Andrew had been able to fit him with at short notice, Nestor was somewhere in one of the central guard-towers when the first attack began. The strategy was for him to wait there until close combat provided a suitable chance to bring the sword's powers into use. But though the sword whined restlessly when the attack began, and drew its threads of vapor from the air into itself, that chance did not come with the first assault.

Not that there was much of a break between the first and second. The Gray Horde did not retreat from the foot of the walls to reform, as a human army would certainly have done. Instead its thousands milled around, indifferent to slung stone and arrow.

And then surged forward behind the ladders once again.

By now it had been discovered that large stones dropped on the attacking larvae below the walls were somewhat more effective than slings and arrows, but that fire was disappointingly inefficient. The dead-wood figures were not really dry, and they would have to be burnt into ashes to be stopped.

"A breach! A breach!"

Mark heard the cry go up some minutes after the second surge with ladders against the walls began. Looking down at the top of the west wall, to his right, he saw that gray mannikins were on it, their arms windmilling as they fought.

"The sword comes!"

"Townsaver!"

Through the defenders' thin reserves the figure of Nestor, recognizable in his new armor, was moving into action. Above and through the banshee-howling of the enemy sounded the high shriek of the blade. The sound called up for Mark his last day in his home village, and he felt a surge of sickness.

The hand of Dame Yoldi pressed his arm. "It comes awake, and timely too. We have a holding here, and unarmed folk in it to be defended. The gods cannot be wholly evil, to have forged a weapon of this nature."

Mark could not think beyond that screaming sound. Nestor had reached the foe now, and the blade in his hands blurred back and forth, faster than sight could follow it, and the first gray rank went down.

This was Duke Fraktin's first chance to hear Townsaver scream, and he was greatly interested. He watched from a distance as the small blur in one man's hands cleared the west wall of larvae. The Duke was impressed, but not particularly surprised.

He watched also, with fascination, how gracefully and angrily Queen Yambu rode her prancing warbeast in front of her own ranked army of human men, even as he himself paced near the center of his own. The bulk of the Duke's forces were now disposed in a semicircular formation, with its right wing on the lake almost behind the castle, left wing anchored just about where the winding road came up the hill to find Sir Andrew's fortified main gate. Upon that gate a hundred larvae were now battering with a ram fashioned from the trunk of a huge tree. Their feet slipped and slid in mud that had been their predecessors' bodies, while stones and fire decimated their ranks from above. Meanwhile, along the road, rough battalions of replacements jostled forward, howling dully, ready without fear or hope to take their turn beneath the walls.

From the winding road around west to the lake again, the human forces of Yambu held the field. They were arrayed, like the Duke's army, in a rough half-circle. The Duke like everyone else was well aware that the two armies of attackers were watching each other closely and uneasily, even as both watched the progress of the swarming preliminary attack on the castle by Yambu's auxiliaries.

The Duke turned to his blue-garbed wizard, who was waiting nearby clad in incongruous-looking armor. "At least," His Grace remarked, "a good part of the Horde is going to be used up against those walls, and particularly by that sword. We can hope that most of those dead-wood monsters will be out of the way before it comes our turn to fight Yambu, for the spoils."

"Indeed, sire."

"I'm convinced now, Blue-Robes, that it was *she* who tried to kidnap my cousin. Obviously she's got word of the swords somehow . . . what word is there from the east?"

This last was spoken to the Duke's staff at large. None of them had any real news to report from that direction. At night there were the reddened eastern skies for all to see, and by day the distant plumes of smoke. When the Duke had dispatched a flying scout with a message for the small garrison at Arin-on-Aldan, the scout had come back with a report of being unable to find the village or its garrison, in the altered landscape and foul air. (The message had been an order for the family of Jord the Miller to be brought into the Duke's presence for some serious interrogation, milder methods having failed.) Indeed it appeared now that communications with the foothill region had broken down completely. Reports, scattered and uncertain, indicated that the whole civilian population of that area was now in flight, and military patrols were at best disrupted. The Duke sighed, for his vanished family of subjects for interrogation. But he had a battle to fight here, and could spare no extra manpower for search operations of doubtful utility over there.

Still, the blue-robed wizard did not appear entirely unhappy when this subject came up for discussion. He had the air of holding good news in reserve, and, sure enough, at his earliest good chance he announced it.

"Sire, I am pleased to be able to report that my private project has achieved a measure of success."

"What other project?" The ducal brow creased with a slight frown. "Oh. You are speaking now of . . . of what you spoke to me about last night in secret."

"Exactly so, sire." The wizard bowed, a small dip with an air of triumph. "We now have reason to hope that Mars himself is soon going to come directly to our aid. Then, what will our rivals have gained from their paltry success in raising the Horde?"

"By the Great Worm Yilgarn." Duke Fraktin was indubitably impressed. But he was suddenly somewhat worried as well. "Do you think, Blue-Robes, that such a raising is . . . the *god? Mars?* Are you sure you're serious?"

"Oh, entirely serious, sire."

A hundred people or more might be watching, even if probably none of them were close enough at the moment to hear. The Duke made himself smile. "Do you think it entirely wise?"

At this the wizard began to look downcast; he had surely been expecting more enthusiasm from his master. He was somewhat relieved when their talk was interrupted. A close-ranked body of men had surrounded, and were now bringing into the Duke's presence a man who (it was reported) insisted on speaking to the Duke himself, who swore that he had been within the past day inside the besieged castle, and who claimed to know a way by which it would be possible to enter secretly with a body of armed men.

Presently, after the man was thoroughly searched, and tested for magical powers, the Duke confronted him. "Well? Spit it out, fellow." The fellow before him was poorly garbed, and young, with a lean, hunted look. "My name is Kaparu, Your Grace. I have worked as an agent of Queen Yambu in the past, but I'll be pleased to work for a prince as well-known for generosity as yourself instead."

Throughout the whole morning the fighting continued with scarcely an interruption. What small pauses there were resulted not from any weariness or unwillingness on the part of the inhuman mob that tried to swarm upon the walls, but from their need for new ladders, as numbers of the old ones burned or broke under the impact of rock or fire or molten lead. And even when the fighting ebbed for a time, the howling of the Horde went on without pause. The volume of sound did not seem to diminish much with their necessarily diminishing numbers.

As Mark came down from the roof to the level of the top of the outer walls, he heard a stalwart swordsman mutter: "We have cut down thousands of them, and yet still they come." The man was not exaggerating.

Presently Mark was making his way across the crowded main courtyard of the castle, passing hastily arranged stockpiles of supplies, tethered animals, a row of moaning wounded being cared for. He had come down from the roof with Dame Yoldi's permission, in response to a wave from Barbara. A longer break in the fighting than any previous had set in, and the magicians of Yambu had even summoned the Horde back from the walls, out of reach of fire and hurled rock, till more ladders could be got ready. Inside the castle, those who had borne the burden of the battle were being relieved now, wherever possible, for food and rest. Still it seemed to Mark that the yard was crowded mostly with noncombatant refugees, all of whom seemed to be muttering complaints that too many others had been let in. Mark heard several people assuring others that whatever food supplies Sir Andrew had available could not possibly be enough to see this crowd through a long siege.

Mark repeated this saying to his old companions, when he came to the place against a damp-stoned wall where Barbara, and now Ben as well, were waiting for him.

Barbara sat leaning against the wall, but Ben was standing, as if his nerves and muscles were still on alert, tuned to too high a pitch to let him rest. He was not tall, but neither was he as short as his thick build sometimes made him look. The mismatched breastplate and helmet he had scrounged somewhere now gave him an almost clownish look.

Looking at Barbara, Ben laughed tiredly. "I only hope we have the chance to try out a long siege. I think we'd like it better than . . ." He didn't finish, but let himself slump back against the wall, and then slide down till he was sitting beside her.

Now Mark could see Nestor, swordless at the moment but still wearing most of his new armor, picking his way wearily across the crowded court toward them.

Nestor said nothing until he had come up to where they were, and had let himself down with a great sigh, that seemed to have in it all the exhaustion of war. He tipped his head back and kept it that way, gazing up into the gray sky which dropped a little rain from time to time. Only occasionally did he lower his gaze to look at any of his companions.

"The fighting . . ." Nestor began to say at last. And then it appeared that he did not mean to finish either.

For some time there was a silence among them all. Mark knew, or at least felt, that there were things that needed saying, but he had no feeling for how to begin.

He kept expecting at any moment to hear the call to arms, but it did not come. The respite in the fighting was growing unexpectedly prolonged. From the distance came the repetitive, soothing chants of the lesser magicians of Yambu—it was said that the Queen there was her own best wizard. The chanting was being used to keep the Horde treading in place or marching in a circle until a greater number of ladders could be made and distributed for the next assault.

. . . Mark roused with a start, and realized he had been dozing, his back against a wall. Dame Yoldi had appeared in the midst of their resting group. It was early afternoon now, and she was bending over Nestor, talking to him. "Are you hurt?"

"No, lady. Not much. But tired. And stiffening now. I've had a fair rest, though. I'll be ready to take back the Sword and use it when the fighting starts again."

Yoldi, straightening up, nodded abstractedly. She said: "Whoever has Townsaver in hand, fighting to protect unarmed folk in a held place, cannot die so long as he keeps on fighting, no matter how severe his wounds. But if he is badly hurt, he will fall as soon as the fighting slackens."

Nestor said nothing, but continued gazing at the sky. After a time he nodded, to show that he had heard.

Mark, happening to look toward a far part of the courtyard where vehicles were gathered, saw something that made him speak without thinking.

"Look," he said. "Our old wagon."

The others looked. "My lute is there," Ben said.

"I wonder," asked Barbara, of no one in particular, "if the money's still under the front seat."

Mark had nodded into sleep again, only to waken to a heart-pounding shock. It was late in the day, very late now, and long afternoon shadows had come over them all.

"Listen!" Nestor ordered, urgently.

Mark sat bolt upright.

The distant chanting of the sorcerers of Yambu had fallen into silence.

There was no time for farewells or good wishes. Mark rushed to rejoin Dame Yoldi on the roof, as she had bidden him do if an alert sounded. On his way to the first ascending stair, Mark ran past Sir Andrew. The knight's armor was dented here and there from the earlier fighting. He was exhorting his troops, in a huge voice, to make another winning effort.

It was a long climb back to the roof. When he emerged on it at last, Mark found Dame Yoldi already there, her arms raised to a darkening sky and her eyes closed. A pair of her helpers, a man and a woman, arranged things on the parapet before her, things of magic in bottles and baskets between two burning candles.

Looking down, Mark saw the next surging attack of the larvae strike against the walls on a broad front, and wash up like a wave upon a hundred scaling ladders. He could draw some encouragement from the fact that the creatures' reserve force, that in the morning had stretched endlessly across the fairgrounds, was much compacted now. Their legions had been hacked and broken into a vast mud-flat that stained the ground for meters in front of every wall they had assaulted.

But, beyond those thinning deadwood ranks, the human armies of Fraktin and Yambu were both readying themselves for an attack. Mark realized that the human onslaught would be timed to fall upon an exhausted and weakened defense, just as the last of the larvae were cut down—if indeed the last of the larvae could be defeated. Already the defenders' ranks, thin to begin with, had suffered painful losses.

Sir Andrew's voice, now distant from Mark's ears, roared out from a wall-top: "Save your missiles! We'll need them to hit men!"

And the slingers and the archers on the battlements held their fire. Mark supposed that Barbara had rejoined her group there, though he could not pick her out.

The sun was setting now, beams lancing between dark masses of cloud, red-rimmed like some reflection of the renewed red glow in the east. Torches were being lighted on the walls, for illumination and weapons both, and they shone down on the advancing, climbing Horde. Darts and arrows flew up at the defenders from below the walls, but in no great numbers. The Horde was not well supplied with missile weapons.

Dame Yoldi still stood like a statue on the high roof, her arms raised, her eyes closed, a rising wind moving her garments. She appeared to be oblivious to what was happening below. She would be trying to strike back at the enemy somehow, or else to ward off some new harm from them—Mark was unable to tell which.

The attack this time was on a broader front than before, along almost the entire accessible rim of wall, and just as savage as the previous attacks had been. It prospered quickly. Two calls for Townsaver went up at the same time, from opposite directions on the walls.

Was it Nestor again, the helmed figure Mark saw now, running out from a guard-tower with the sword? Mark could not be sure. Whoever it was, he could fight in only one place at a time.

Again the screaming of the Sword of Fury rose above the eternal whistle-howling of the foe. Again Mark watched Townsaver's blade carve a dead-wood legion into chunks of mud and flying dust. Again the sword built a blurred wall through which the invaders could not force their way, press forward as they might.

But, again, Townsaver prevailed only where it could be brought to bear.

Now, Mark could hear despairing cries go up, from the defenders on the wall where the sword was not. The enemy had gained a foothold there, at last, and was now pouring in reinforcements. Dame Yoldi, rousing herself from what had seemed a trance, abruptly abandoned her work, snapping orders to her assistants. Then she grabbed Mark by one arm and began to tow him to the trapdoor that led down. In his last glance from the high roof at the fighting, he could see warbeasts starting to mount some of the scaling ladders far below.

And, across what had once been the fairgrounds, the human troops of Fraktin and Yambu were answering to trumpets, marshalling for their own move to attack.

The enchantress, still clutching Mark tightly by the wrist, left the stair at the level of the castle where her own workroom was. Already there was panic in the corridors, folk running this way and that bearing weapons, children, treasures great and small that they had hopes of saving somehow. Yoldi ignored all this, moving almost at a run to her own chambers. There, without ceremony, she lifted Dragonslicer from the table, and grabbed a belt and scabbard from a shelf.

She began to buckle the sword on her own body—then, with a rare display of hesitation, paused. In an instant she had changed her mind and was fastening it round Mark's waist instead.

"It will be best this way," she murmured to herself. "Yes, best. Now let us get on down."

Once more they hurried through hallways, then down flight after flight of stairs.

"If anything should happen to me on the way, lad, you keep going. Down as far as you can, to the bottom of the keep, to where the dungeons are."

"Why?"

"Because we can't hold the castle now, and the last way out is down there. And you are the one, of all of us, who must get out."

Mark wasn't going to argue about it. Still he couldn't help wondering why.

When they reached ground level inside the castle, uproar and confusion swept in at them from a courtyard, where the sounds of fighting were very near. Voices were crying that Sir Andrew had been wounded.

Dame Yoldi halted abruptly, and when she spoke again her voice had changed. "I must go to him, Mark. You go on. Down to the dungeons and out. Our people down there will show you the way."

She hurried out. Mark turned toward the doorway she had indicated. He had almost reached it when a mass of struggling soldiers knocked him down.

Duke Fraktin and his handpicked force of fifteen men were following their volunteer guide, Kaparu, toward the castle. It had been a quick decision on the Duke's part, made when the larvae had won success atop the walls, and it looked as if the citadel might after all fall quickly.

The Duke would not have trusted any of his subordinates to lead a mission like this one, not when he wanted to be sure that the prize gained reached his own hands. He had faced war at close range many times before, when the prizes at stake were far less than these Swords. And now, secret but most powerful encouragement, Coinspinner was giving signs that he took to mean its powers were fully active. Just as the small force had started out toward the beleaguered castle, the Sword of Chance had begun a whispering thrumming in its scabbard, so soft a sound that the Duke was sure no one but he could hear it. He could hear it himself only when he put a hand upon the hilt. Even then the thrum was more to be felt than heard; but it was steady, and it promised power. The Duke kept one hand on the hilt as he walked.

The small body of men, seventeen in all, had moved out from the lines of the ducal army about an hour after dark, just as soon as the Duke had convinced himself that Kaparu's offer represented a worthwhile gamble. The gamble had to be taken soon if it was to be taken at all, for it was impossible to count on the defenders of the castle being able to hold out much longer, and at any moment the human army of Yambu might move as well.

Moving toward the castle, the Duke's small force traversed a slope of worn grass, cut by ditches, that Kaparu said had been a fairground only a few days ago. The ditches afforded a certain amount of cover—not that the castle's defenders had any attention to spare right now for this little group of men. Torches still burning on the walls ahead showed that parts of them were still held by Sir Andrew's troops, but new assaults against those sections were being readied to left and right, where now the regular troops of Fraktin and Yambu alike were moving forward, following the larvae.

But, just ahead, where the keep itself almost became a part of the outer wall, that wall rose to a forbidding height. Until now, no direct attack had been attempted at this point.

When his party was halfway across what had been the fairgrounds, the Duke stopped. He warned Kaparu yet once again, with Coinspinner's edge against his throat: "You will be first to die, if there is any treachery here."

The fellow took the threat calmly and bravely enough. "There'll be no treachery from me, Your Grace. I look forward too eagerly to receiving the generous reward that you have promised."

Silently the Duke pushed him forward.

When he and his men had topped the outer lip of the almost waterless moat, they could see rectangular patches of faint light in the castle wall, now just a few meters in front of them.

"The windows," breathed Kaparu. "As I promised. I tell you the old man is a soft-brained fool; I only wonder that his defenses held out as long as they did."

The Duke had to admit that the rectangles certainly looked like windows, open and undefended. Any castle lord who came to be known as Kind could hardly expect to keep his castle . . .

The group easily forded the muddy moat, and easily climbed its inward wall, which was badly eroded and had obviously been neglected for years. As they came at last in reach of the castle wall itself, Kaparu leaned a hand upon the giant stones, and paused for a final whisper: "As I have already warned you, there will be ponderous iron bars inside. Once through the wall, we'll be inside a large dungeon cell, whether locked or unlocked I do not know."

The Duke nodded grimly. "Bars we can deal with," he said, and glanced at some of his men who carried tools, and at Blue-Robes in his incongruous armor. They silently nodded back. The wizard had volunteered half-willingly to accompany this expedition, as a sort of penance; Mars had not, after all, made his appearance as predicted.

In a voice barely audible, the Duke hissed at Kaparu: "Just so there are no tricks."

The guide Kaparu was made to be the second man in through one of the tunnel-like windows, with Duke Fraktin right behind him. The Sword of Chance, throbbing faintly with the risks its master was taking, was touching its needle point to the guide's back.

Once inside, through the five or six meters of the wall's thickness, the Duke dropped down from windowsill to stone floor, following closely the men ahead of him and moving to make room for those who followed closely after. Yes, they were in a cell, all right. The bars were visible as dark outlines against some illumination of ghostly faintness that came through an archway atop some stairs.

As the Duke motioned his tool-workers and wizard forward, to grope in silence for the door, he found himself starting to sweat. As the last of his party dropped in through the window, and his men milled around him, he found uneasiness, queasiness, growing in the center of his belly. Fear, he reminded himself, was quite natural when a man was engaged in an enterprise as dangerous as this. Even fear enough to make him feel sick . . . but this . . . this sickness had been only in his gut at first, but now it felt as if it were centered somewhere even more central than that, if such were possible . . .

Beside the Duke, one of his hand-picked men cried out in a low voice, then seemed to be struggling with himself, trying to muffle yet another cry. Another's weapon fell clashing on the stone floor. A third sobbed loudly. The Duke would have struck out at them all, in anger at their noise, but something was turning like poison in the core of his own being, and he could hardly move his limbs . . .

Not poison, no.

The wizard was perhaps the first to understand what was happening to them all, and he choked out the first words of a phrase of power. But it was too late to be an effective counter, or perhaps too weak—something strangled the next words in his throat.

The sensation of deadly illness had now fastened upon all the men who were crowded into the large cell. Blue force, no longer completely invisible, hung in the black air around the windows, preventing any effort at retreat. Some of the men had groped and pushed their way to the cell bars, and hung on the bars now, rattling them. Now blue fiery tongues, constructions almost more of darkness than of light, were playing in the air all around the men, tongues of force that became more clearly visible as the wakefulness and the hunger of their possessor grew.

With Coinspinner drawn and throbbing strongly in his hand, the Duke managed to tear himself free of momentarily faltering blue tongues of light. He threw himself down on the stone floor of the cell, rolling violently from right to left and back again. He was trying, and managing successfully so far, to avoid that groping, subtle touch, that was so wholly horrible . . .

Two men were hurriedly carrying Sir Andrew downstairs on a stretcher. They had shoved their way somehow through a melee on the first floor of the castle, and then had slammed a door on a charging Yambu warbeast to get down to ground level. Their intention was to carry their master through the dungeons and then on out through the secret passage that here, as in so many other castles, offered one final hope when defenses and defenders failed.

The bearers entered the long dungeon stair. The warbeast had been evidence enough that human attackers, coming in their own hordes on the heels of the remnants of the Horde itself, were now battering at the doors of the keep above. Above were screams and murder, fire and panic; down here there was still almost silence.

At any other time, the sight of the faint blue horror that hazed the air inside the large end cell might well have stopped the stretcher-bearers and sent them running back. But now they knew there could be no going back. They set their burden down in the narrow corridor that ran between the cells, and one of them ran on ahead, through a false cell whose secret they knew. He meant to scout the secret way ahead and make sure that it was still undiscovered by the enemy. The other bearer meanwhile crouched down by the stretcher, watching and resting with his knife drawn. He was willing to die to protect Sir Andrew; but at the moment the man's bloodied face showed only terror as he gazed in between the bars of the end cell.

Sir Andrew, who was still wearing portions of his armor under the rough blanket that covered him, winced, and stirred restlessly on his pallet. When his eyes opened he was facing the end cell. In there, behind the bars, the silent blue terror wavered and grew and faded and came back, like flickering cool flames. All of the seventeen men in that cell were like candle wicks, being slowly consumed, as from the inside out.

One shape among them was clinging to the bars, and the mouth of it was open in a soundless yell.

Sir Andrew recognized that face. His own voice was a weakened whisper now. "Ah, Kaparu. I'm sorry . . . I am sorry . . . but there's nothing I can do for you now."

The tortured mouth of the blue-lit figure strained again, but still no sound came out of it.

The knight's weak voice was sad but clear. "I told you you were my only *human* prisoner, Kaparu. I had one other captive, as you now see . . . no stone or steel could have held him in that cell, but Dame Yoldi's good work could . . . he had been half-paralyzed, you see, long before we encountered him. Some skirmish against Ardneh, two thousand years ago."

Kaparu looked as if he might be listening. His fingers were being slowly shredded from the bars.

"He's a demon, of course." Sir Andrew was having some trouble with his breathing. "We've never learned his name . . . no possible way we could kill him, you see, not knowing where his life is kept. And it would have been an atrocity against humanity to let him go. So . . . in there. And I had the windows of the cell made bigger, thinking . . . hopeless pride on my part, to think that I might someday teach a demon to be good. That if I let him contemplate the sunlit earth, and the people on it who were sometimes happy when I ruled them . . . well, it was a foolish thought. I've never had to worry, though, about anyone coming in those windows."

The soldier who had gone scouting ahead now came scrambling back and said a quick word to his companion. The man who had been waiting sheathed his knife and between them they lifted Sir Andrew again on his stretcher. Not heeding the knight's weak, only half-coherent protests, they bore him away in the direction of possible safety. The entrance to the secret tunnel, which was hidden in a cell wall, closed after them.

For a few moments then the dungeon was almost silent, and untenanted, save for what moved in blue light in the large cell at the end of the passage. Then suddenly the door of that cell clanged open. One man came rolling, crawling out, the grip of almost invisible blue tongues slipping from his body. The man lay on the floor gasping, a drawn sword in his hand. Blue tongues strained after him, slapped at him, recoiled from his sword, and at last withdrew in disappointment.

The door of the cell had not been locked.

Summoning what appeared to be his last strength, the man on the floor put out an arm and slammed the cell door shut behind him, which had the effect of confining the blue tongues. Then he rolled over on the floor, still lacking the strength to rise.

"Luck . . ." he muttered. "Luck . . ."

He fainted completely, and the sword that had been in his grasp slipped from his fingers. There was a pause after the first slip and then the sword moved, as if of itself, a few more centimeters from the inert hand that had let it go.

Moments later, a half-grown boy in torn clothing, with a burn-scar half healed on his face and fresher scratches on his arms and legs, came bounding down the stairs and into the dungeon. He had a swordbelt strapped round his waist, and a sword, considerably too big for him, in his right hand.

He stopped in his tracks at the sight of the blue glow, and of the man that it illuminated, sprawled on the floor. Then he darted forward and picked up in his left hand the sword that had eluded the man's grasp. The boy stood with a heavy sword in each hand now, looking from one to the other. An expression of wonder grew on his face.

Meanwhile, the man had roused himself. And now he saw what had happened to his sword. With a strangled cry, that sounded like some words about a snake, he lunged with his drawn dagger at the boy.

In a startled reaction the boy jerked back. With the movement the sword in his left hand snapped up awkwardly, almost involuntarily. The point of it found the hairsbreadth gap in the armor of the lunging man, sliding between gorget and the lower flange of helm.

Life jetted forth, blood black in the blue light. "Luck . . ." said Duke Fraktin once again. Then he fell backward and said no more.

Mark looked down at the body. He could tell only that it was the carcass of some invader, clothed like five hundred others in the Fraktin white and blue.

Now, on the stairs, not far above, there was the sound of fighting. Quickly the clash was over, and a man's voice asked: "Do we go down and search?"

Another voice said: "No, look around up here first. I think the old fox's escape hatch, if he has one, will be up here."

There was the sound of departing feet. Then silence in the dungeon again, except for the distant drip of water. And now the faint *tink* that a sword's tip made, touching iron jail bars as its holder turned. Mark had sheathed Dragonslicer now, and was holding Coinspinner in both hands. From the moment he had picked it up he had been able to feel some kind of power flowing from its hilt into his hand. The thrumming he could feel in the sword grew stronger, he discovered, when he aimed the point in a certain direction.

By what was left of the blue glow from the end cell, he looked inside the other unlocked cell at which the Sword of Chance was pointing. Then he looked carefully at the cell's rear wall. In a moment he had discovered the escape tunnel's secret door.

With that door open, he delayed. He turned back, and with his eyes half-closed swung Coinspinner's tip like a compass needle through wide slow arcs. Up, down, right, left, up again.

There. In that direction, he could feel the power somehow beginning to work, drawing an invisible line for him up into the castle above. Now slowly it swung again, by itself this time, toward the head of the stair.

In another moment it had brought him Ben, in bloodied armor, carrying an unconscious Barbara.

The secret passageway was narrow, and twisting, and very dark. Neither Ben nor Mark had anything with them to give light. Once they had closed the door on the dungeon and its fading demon-glow, the way ahead was inky black. Ben continued to carry Barbara, as before, without apparent effort, while Mark moved ahead, groping with hands and feet for obstacles or branchings of the tunnel. In the blackness he used

Coinspinner like a blind man's cane, though the sensation of power emanating from it was gone now. As they moved, Mark related in terse phrases how he had picked up the new sword from the dungeon floor. If Ben was impressed, he hadn't breath enough to show it.

Once Mark stumbled over the body of a man in partial armor, who must also have entered the tunnel in flight and got this far before dying of wounds. After making sure that the man was dead, Mark led the way on past him, his feet in slipperiness that presently turned to stickiness on his bootsoles. Horror had already become a commonplace; he thought only that he must not slip and fall.

The sound of dripping water was plainer now, and more than once drops struck Mark on the face. The general trend of the passageway was down, though nowhere was the descent steep. Twice more Mark stumbled, on discarded objects that clanged away on rock with startling metallic noise. And once the sides of the tunnel pinched in so narrowly that Ben had to shift his grip on Barbara, and push her limp form on ahead of him, into the grasp of Mark waiting on the other side of the bottleneck. Mark when he held her was relieved to hear her groaning, muttering something; he had been worried that they might be rescuing a corpse.

This blind groping went on for a long time, that began to seem endless. Mark developed a new worry, that they were somehow lost in a cave, trapped in some endless labyrinth or circle. He knew that others must have taken the secret passage ahead of them; but, except for one dead man and a few discarded objects, those others might as well be somewhere on the other side of the world by now. At least no pursuers could be heard coming after them.

Mark continued tapping his way forward with the sword he had picked up in the dungeon; he had had to put it down when he helped to get Barbara through the narrow place in the tunnel, and then in pitch darkness grope past its razor edges to pick it up again.

At last the fear of being in a circular trap bothered Mark to the point where he had to stop. "Where are we, Ben, where're we going to come out?"

Ben had necessarily stopped suddenly also, and Mark could hear the scraping of his armor as he leaned against the wall—as if he were more tired or more badly hurt than Mark had realized.

"We got to go on," Ben grunted. Mark for some reason was surprised to hear that his voice still had in it the almost fearful reluctance as when he and Barbara had used to argue about hunting dragons.

"I don't know, Ben, if we're getting any—"

"What else can we do, go back? Come on. What does your lucky sword tell you?"

"Nothing." But Ben was plainly right. Mark turned and led the way again.

They progressed in silence for a time. Then Ben surprised with a remark. "I think we're going west."

Mark saw immediately what that would mean. "We can't be. This far west from the castle? That'd be . . ." He didn't finish it aloud. Under the lake. Around him the water dripped. The passage floor underfoot now felt level, but there was never a puddle.

They had come to another tight place, and were manhandling Barbara through it when she groaned more loudly than before. This time she managed to produce some plain words: "Put me down."

She still couldn't walk too steadily, but her escort were vastly relieved to have her standing, asking questions about Nestor and Townsaver, trying to find out the situation as if getting ready to give orders. They couldn't answer most of her questions, and she was still too weak to take command.

But from that moment on the journey changed.

Their passageway, as if to signal that some important transformation was close ahead, twisted sharply, first left then right, then dipped to a lower level than ever. And then it rose steeply. And now the first true light they had seen since leaving the dungeon was ahead. At first it was so faint it would have been invisible to any eyes less starved for light, but as they advanced it strengthened steadily.

The light was the dim glow of a cloudy, moonless night sky, and it came down a twisted, narrow shaft. Mark, thinnest and most agile, climbed ahead, and was first to poke his head out of the earth among jagged rocks, to the sound of waves lapping, almost within reach. In the gloom he could make out that the rocks surrounding him made a sort of islet in the lake, an islet not more than five meters across, one of a scattered number rising from the water. By the lights of both common torch and arson Mark could see Sir Andrew's castle and its reflection in the water, a good kilometer away. Flames gusted from the high tower windows even as he watched.

He didn't gaze long at that sight, but scrambled down into the earth again, between the cloven rocks that must sometimes fail to keep waves from washing into the passage. "Ben? It's all right, bring her up." And

Mark extended a hand for Barbara to grasp, while Ben pushed her from below.

They crowded together on the surface, peering between sharp rocks at the surrounding lake.

"We'll have to make for shore before morning—but which direction?"

Mark held up the Sword of Chance. When he pointed it almost straight away from the castle, he could feel something in the hilt. It was impossible to see how far away the shore was in that direction.

"I can't swim," Barbara admitted.

"And I can't swim carrying two swords," Mark added.

Ben said: "Maybe I can, if I have to. Let's see, maybe it isn't deep."

The lake was only waist deep on Ben where he first entered it. He shed bits of armor, letting them sink. From that point, following the indication of the blade Mark held ahead of him, the three fugitives waded into indeterminate gloom.

The sword worked just as well under the surface of the water as above it. At one point Mark had to go in to his armpits, but no deeper. From there on the bottom rose, and already a vague shoreline of trees was visible ahead. The strip of beach, when they reached it, was only two meters wide, and waves lapped it, ready to efface whatever footprints they might leave.

The sheltering trees were close to shore, and just inland from their first ranks a small clearing offered grass to rest on.

For a moment. Then, just beyond the nearest thicket, something stirred, making vague crackling sounds of movement. Mark let Ben grab up Coinspinner from the grass, while he himself drew Dragonslicer from its sheath.

They moved forward cautiously, around a clump of bushes. An obscure shape, big as a landwalker but not as tall, moved in the night. There was a faint squeal from it, a muffled rumble . . . the squeal of ungreased axles, the rumble of an empty wagon-body draped with a torn scrap of cover.

The two loadbeasts harnessed to the empty wagon were skittish, and behaved in general as if they had been untended for some time. This wagon was smaller than the one the dragon-hunters had once owned. This one too had some symbols or a design painted on its sides, but the night was too dark for reading symbols. Barbara murmured that this must be the vehicle of some other fairgrounds performer, whose team must have bolted during the recent speedy evacuation.

There were reins, quite functional once they were untangled. With Barbara resting in the back, Ben drove forth from thickets looking for a road. Dragonslicer was at his feet, and Mark on the seat at his side with Coinspinner in hand. The Sword of Chance was coming alive again, telling him which way to go.

THE END

THE SECOND
BOOK OF SWORDS

CHAPTER 1

Fire from the sky came thrusting down, a dazzling crooked spear of white light that lived for an instant only, long enough to splinter a lone tree at the jutting edge of the seaside cliff. The impact beneath the howling darkness of the sky stunned eyes and ears alike. Ben winced away from the blinding flash—too late, of course, to do his shocked eyes any good—and turned his gaze downward, trying to see the path again, to find secure places to put down his sandaled feet. In night and wind and rain it was hard to judge how far away the stroke had fallen, but he could hope that the next one would be farther off.

Ben's thick and powerful right arm was stretched forward across the rump of one heavily burdened loadbeast, his hand grasping the rope that bound the panniers on the animal's back. Meanwhile his left hand, extended backward, tugged hard on the reins of the loadbeast reluctantly following.

The little packtrain was composed of six loadbeasts, along with the six men who drove and led and cursed the animals forward. A seventh animal, considerably more sleek and graceful than the six that carried cargo, came a few meters behind the train. It bore a seventh man, a cloaked and hooded figure who rode with a cold, flameless Old World torch raised in his right hand. The torch shed an unflickering light through wind and rain, projecting some of its rays far enough ahead to give the train's drivers some hope of seeing where they were going.

Like some odd crawling compound creature possessing three dozen unsynchronized feet, the packtrain groped and struggled its way forward, following a mere sketch of a path across the wild landscape. Ben was pushing the first animal forward, more or less dragging the second after him, and trying to soothe them both. Hours ago, at the beginning of the trip, the drivers had been warned that tonight the usually phlegmatic animals were likely to become skittish.

There would be dragon-scent about, the officer had said.

Another flash of lightning now, fortunately not quite as close as the last one. For just an instant the rocky and forsaken wilderness surrounding the small train was plain to see, including the next few meters of the path ahead. Then darkness closed in deeper than ever, bringing with it harder rain. Its parts linked by the push and pull of human arms, the beast with three dozen feet advanced, making slow progress over the treacherous footing of rain-slicked rocks and yielding sand. Meanwhile the wind howled continuously and the rain assaulted everything.

Ahead of Ben, the soldier leading the first loadbeast was wrapped and plastered like Ben himself in a soggy blue-gold uniform cloak, with a useless helmet drizzling rain into his eyes. Now Ben could hear him loudly calling down the doom of demons and the wrath of gods upon this whole situation—including the high functionaries whose idea it must have been, and who were no doubt somewhere warm and dry themselves this moment. The man was almost shouting, having no fear that the priest-officer, Radulescu, who rode behind the train, might be able to hear him above the wind.

The cold torchlight from behind suggested, and the next flash of lightning proved, that the scanty path the train was following was now about to veer sharply to the left. At the same time, a large indentation in the line of the nearby cliffs brought their potentially fatal edge sweeping in sharply toward the path from that direction. Ben, not liking this sudden proximity of the brink, leaned harder against the animal whose rump his right arm was embracing. Using his great strength and his considerable weight, he forced the beast a little farther to the right. Now the packtrain was moving so close to the cliff's edge that when the lightning flashed again it was possible to look down and glimpse the pounding sea. Ben thought those rock-torn waves might be a hundred meters below.

He supposed that a common soldier's life in any army was not a happy one. More than one old proverb, repeated mostly among soldiers themselves, testified to that, and Ben had been given plenty of chance to learn the truth of the proverbs for himself. But what worried him tonight was not the usual soldier's concerns of dull abuse and passing danger. Not the storm. Not really the danger of falling off this cliff—that risk was obvious and could be avoided. Nor was it even fear of the guardian dragon up ahead, whose presence the drivers had been warned of because it might make the loadbeasts nervous.

What bothered Ben was a certain realization that had been growing upon him. If it was correct, then he had more than dragons to worry about. So, for that matter, did the other drivers who were here tonight; but Ben had no reason to think that any of them had yet realized the fact.

He wondered if he was going to have a chance to talk to them about it without the officer overhearing. He decided that he probably was not. . . .

By Ardneh, how could any man, even one afraid for his life, manage to think straight about anything in the middle of a storm like this? Ben couldn't even spare a hand to try to wipe the rain out of his eyes, or hold his cloak together. Now, sodden as the garment was, it had blown loose from its lower clasp, and streamed out uselessly in the wind. Even in the brilliance of the lightning the cloak no longer looked gold and blue. It was so wet and matted that it might have been woven out of the gray of the night itself.

More lightning, more wind, more rain. Through it all the twelve linked bodies of angry men and burdened animals kept struggling forward. Under ordinary conditions, one or two men could have managed six loadbeasts easily. But Ben had to admit that whoever had assigned six drivers to this job tonight had known what he was doing. Certainly two or three men would not have been enough to manage it tonight, when lightning and the scent of dragon rode the air together.

Radulescu had earlier reassured the drivers, telling them that he had at his command powerful spells, sure to keep the dragon at a distance. Ben believed that. Blue Temple officers, he had observed in his year's stint as an enlisted man, were generally competent in matters that they considered to be important. And this trip tonight had to be important . . . and that led Ben back to his new private worry. He wanted to be able to argue himself out of that dreadful idea, but instead the more he thought of it the more real it became.

And the less time was left to try to deal with it.

They had been told nothing about the nature of the cargo, so well-wrapped, so compact and heavy, that they were transporting through the night. Other hands than theirs had wrapped it, and loaded it into the animals' panniers. From the way it weighed, and felt, it could hardly be anything but heavy stone or metal.

Ben couldn't really believe that it was stone. He could tell from the way the animals moved that it must weigh like lead. But of course Blue Temple, the proverbial worshippers and hoarders of wealth, were unlikely to be trafficking in lead.

That narrowed the possibilities down considerably. But there was more.

When the packtrain had left the local Temple, some hours before dark, it had been accompanied by an escort of some three dozen heavily armed cavalry. These were mercenary troops, speaking only some bizarre dialect of their own; Ben thought that they must have been recruited from halfway around the world.

Progress had at first been easy; the sky was threatening but the storm had not yet broken. The armed escort had surrounded the packtrain most of the slow way, the loadbeasts had been docile, and the six drivers had been able to take it easy, riding themselves on six spare mounts. Their journey, along back roads and then increasingly slender trails leading into the back country, had been entirely on Temple lands—or so Ben thought; he could not be completely sure. Such a heavy escort, on Temple lands, seemed to be overdoing it a bit—unless of course the cargo was very, very valuable.

And to think that didn't help the new worry at all. . . .

Just before nightfall, the train had halted in a small clearing amid the scrubby growth and boulders of the wasteland. In a smooth and evidently prearranged fashion, the laden animals with their six drivers had been detached at this point from their escort, and under the command of Radulescu had continued forward over this rugged thread of trail.

According to the announced plan, their escort was to wait in the clearing for their return. As the separation was taking place, and almost as an afterthought, the six drivers had been ordered to leave their own weapons behind in the escort's care. Swords and daggers, Ben and the five others had been told, would not be needed up ahead, and would just get in their way when they went to work on the unloading.

Radulescu had been the officer who told them that, raising his crisp professional voice above the rising wind, while behind him the cavalry sat their own mounts, waiting silently. And when the weapons of the six drivers had been collected under a waterproof, and the spare cavalry mounts returned, Radulescu had ordered the train forward along this unknown thread of a trail. Then he had followed it on his own steed.

Ben had never set eyes on the priest-officer before today, and as far as he could tell the man was unknown to the other drivers as well—even as they were to each other. Certainly Radulescu was not one of the regular cavalry or infantry officers assigned to the local Temple's garrison. Ben suspected that he came from somewhere very high up in the loftier strata of Blue Temple power—perhaps he even had some connection with the Inner Council that ruled the Temple in all its branches. All of the regular officers had deferred to him, even though his uniform of plain gold and blue was devoid of any of the usual insignia of rank. That, thought Ben, had to mean he was a priest. Still, Radulescu seemed perfectly at home astride his cavalry mount, and also quite at home with giving orders in the field.

And now through the night the men and animals continued to struggle on, to move their heavy cargo forward. Ben thought it might not be all gold that they were carrying. He could imagine, inside the heavily padded, shapeless bundles that filled the wicker baskets, a certain proportion of jewelry, for example. Precious stones, and maybe some things of art . . .

With every minute the worry that had fastened upon him grew and grew. And the wind continued to blast the little procession, as did the rain, until even the four-footed creatures were slipping and sliding on the wet and rounded rocks that made up so much of this poor excuse for a path.

Again Ben shoved against the beast whose hindquarters were under his right arm. He shifted the animal bodily a small distance to the right, farther away from that dreadful brink that now again came curving in from the left to run close beside the path.

And now, to Ben's mild surprise, the officer came cantering forward on the right side of the small train. Radulescu was urging his mount to a greater fraction of its speed, so that it quickly got ahead of the slow loadbeasts. Lights and shadows shifted with the change in position of the cold torch still held in the officer's hand. That torch was a thick rod whose rounded, glassy tip glowed steadily and brightly white, impervious to wind and rain. Ben had seen similar lights in use a time or two before, though certainly they were not common. In that steady light, Radulescu's officer's cloak shone, glistened as if it might be waterproof, and his head was neatly dry under a hood instead of wet in a damned dripping helmet. From under his cloak on the left side a sheathed sword protruded like some kind of stiffened tail.

As soon as Radulescu had gotten ahead of the train, he turned back into its path and reined in his swifter mount. And now, with a motion of his light, he signaled to the drivers that here they were going to leave the precarious path. He was waving them inland, across utterly track-less country.

The driver just ahead of Ben cursed again.

With the officer now riding slowly on ahead of the train, his cold light held high for guidance, the first driver got the first animal turned off the trail and headed inland, to the west. Ben followed, leaning on the first animal's hindquarters as before. The animal behind had to agree, with Ben's grip still on its reins. The others followed.

Now, moving across country on footing even worse than before, they were traveling even more slowly. From what Ben could see of the sur-rounding land, it was absolutely trackless and abandoned. All six of the drivers were cursing now; Ben was sure of it, though he could hear no maledictions other than his own.

The edge of the cliff was now safely distant. But now men and ani-mals had to pick their way over uneven slopes of sand, push through prickly growth, negotiate more rocks whose surfaces were slicked by rain. This land, thought Ben, was in fact good for nothing but raising demons, as the old folksaying had it of the deserts. If indeed a large dragon was nearby—and he did not doubt that it was—then it was hard to imagine what it found to eat.

He thought that the dragon was making its presence known. The farther west and south the loadbeasts were made to struggle, the more restive they became. And now Ben, who had more experience than most in locating dragons, thought that he could detect the unique tang di-rectly in the wet air, coming and going with variations in the wind. In that scent there was something swinish, and something metallic too, and something else that Ben could not relate to anything outside itself.

And now, unexpectedly, the packtrain was jouncing and stumbling to a halt. A few meters ahead, the priest-officer Radulescu had already reined in his animal and was dismounting. Reins held firmly in one hand, Radulescu lifted his torch high in the other, and began to chant a spell. Ben could not hear him chanting, but could see in profile a regular movement of the officer's short beard, chewing words boldly out into the wind.

And now something else came into view, above and beyond the cowled head of Radulescu, who now turned fully away from Ben to face the apparition. First the two eyes of the dragon were born in the midst of darkness, greenly reflecting the Old World light. The height of those eyes above the ground, and the distance between them, were enough to impress even an experienced dragon hunter. In the next moment, as the monster drew in a slow breath, there appeared below and between the eyes a red suggestion, glowing through flesh and scale, of the inner fires of nose and mouth, an almost subliminal red that would have been invisible by day. The purring snort that followed was a nearly musical sound, the rolling of hollow metal spheres in some vast brazen bowl.

Ben's sense of magic in operation was not particularly strong, but now even he could feel the flow, the working of the chant. The spell had already held the dragon back, and now was turning it away. With blinking eyes the great landwalker snorted again, and then melted back out of the train's path, disappearing into storm and darkness.

With the going of the dragon, Ben's real worry only sharpened. He had no trouble now in concentrating on it. In fact, as he waited for Radulescu to conclude his spell, demonstrating how firmly the powers of the Blue Temple were in control, it was impossible for him to think of anything else.

The worry that deviled Ben was not rooted in any single warning, any one thing that he had seen or heard. Rather it had sprung into existence like some kind of elemental power, out of a great number of details.

One detail was that all six of the drivers here tonight, including Ben himself, were newcomers to this particular Temple garrison. That meant, Ben supposed, that none of them were likely to have friends around. All six had been transferred in from local Temples elsewhere, within the past few days. Ben had managed to discover that much from a few words casually exchanged while they were waiting for the train to start. He had not been given any particular reason for his own transfer, and he wondered if the others had, for theirs. So far he had had no chance to ask them.

At the time, the transfer orders had seemed to Ben only one more incomprehensible military quirk; in a year's service with Blue Temple he had gotten used to such unexplained twitches of the organism. But now . . .

In Ben's memory, repository of a thousand old songs, one in particular had now come alive and was dancing an accompaniment to his thoughts. He couldn't remember where or when he had heard it first. He probably hadn't heard it at all for years. But it had popped up now, as an ironic background for his fear.

If only, he thought, he was able to talk to the other drivers. They might be able to shout a few words back and forth now through the wind, but Ben needed more than that, he needed time to ask them things and make them think . . . he suspected he wasn't going to get the chance.

He had only a very little time in which to decide whether to act, or not to act, alone. And if he decided wrong, either way, then very soon he would be dead. . . .

The priest-officer, in the act of concluding his spell, used his wand of light to make one long, slow gesture after the departing dragon. Then Radulescu held the wand upright again, looking after the retreating beast and perhaps trying to listen after it through the storm. Then he remounted, turned to the waiting drivers, and once more motioned the train forward.

The drivers moved reluctantly. The loadbeasts were more easily convinced than their masters that the dragon had in fact departed. With dragon-scent now vanishing quickly in the wind, the animals moved forward again with more willingness than they had shown for several hours. And now, as if to suit the improvement in the atmosphere, the rain began to lessen too.

There followed a hundred meters more of stumbling along their trackless way, now and then tearing clothes and skin on thorns. Then the officer reined in again, and again motioned the packtrain to a halt. Another dragon? Ben wondered. He could perceive no other reason for stopping at this point. Radulescu was indicating with his light the exact place where he wanted them to halt the animals, close beside a rocky hillock that looked no different than a hundred other rocky hillocks that surrounded it. There's nothing here, thought Ben . . . and then he understood that that was just what he was supposed to think.

Radulescu had dismounted again. With torch still in hand he moved to stand beside the lower end of a great slab of stone that in itself made up a large portion of the hillock's flank. Putting one hand on this huge stone, he raised his voice above the wind: "You men, secure the animals. Then gather here and lift this rock. Yes, here, lift, I say."

The boulder he was indicating looked too heavy for a score of men to budge. But orders were orders. The drivers hobbled their beasts, and

crowded round. Some of them were brawny men and some were not—
but anyway, the priest was proven not to be mad. As soon as they lifted,
the enormous stone went tilting and tipping up with surprising ease, to
come to rest balanced in a new position. Now where its lower end had
been, the dark triangle of a cave opening was revealed. The black hole
in the hillside looked to Ben a little too regular in shape to be entirely
natural, and was about big enough for a single man to be able to pass
through it readily.

First in was the officer, moving confidently, holding his cold torch
before him to light the way. The utter interior darkness melted before
that light, to reveal a single-chambered cave, with its flat floor sunken
three or four meters below the land outside. There was room on that
floor for perhaps a dozen people to stand without crowding. From
where Ben stood at the triangular entrance, a narrow stairway crudely
carved from rock twisted down to the floor, and now in the center of
that floor Ben noticed, between two lips of stone, another man-sized
aperture, this one leading into deeper blackness.

When he reached that lower opening, Radulescu stopped. He leaned
his torch against a wall, and from some inner pocket, evidently waterproof, brought out two stubby candles. He produced a flame—so
quickly that Ben did not see just how it was done—and in a moment
had placed a lighted candle on either side of the hole in the floor.

And now he looked up to where the drivers' faces were crowding the
small entrance. "Begin unloading," Radulescu ordered briskly. "You
are to carry the sacks of cargo down here, carefully—carefully! And
drop them here, into this aperture." With a light stamp of his foot he
indicated the opening in the floor. He had given the last order with
special clarity and emphasis, as if wishing to avoid having to repeat it
for those who thought they had not heard it properly the first time. On
either side of Radulescu the candles burned, blue wax and golden
flames; and on the flat rocks where they stood, Ben could see drippings,
encrustations of old wax. It was evidently not the first time, nor the
second or third, that a cargo had been delivered here.

The six drivers, as they drew back from the upper entrance, getting
ready to obey orders, all looked at one another for a moment. But there
was really no time for Ben to talk to them. He could see surprise in
some of their faces, but nothing like his own fear mirrored.

Will it be here, he thought to himself, as soon as the unloading's
finished? And if so, how? Or do I have a little more time, until we get
back to where the cavalry's waiting . . .

"Move! Quick! Unload!" Radulescu was climbing the stair with his bright torch in hand. He was not going to give them time to think about anything except getting the job done.

The men had been trained, in a hard school, to obedience. They sprang into action. Ben moved with them, as automatically as any of the others. Only now, as he lifted his first bundle from a pannier on a loadbeast's back, did he realize how effective the Blue Temple training had been.

The bundle he had taken was small but very heavy, like all the others. It was wrapped against weather in some kind of waterproof oilskin that had been sewn shut. Inside the outer covering Ben could feel thick padding, that made it hard to tell what the true shape of the contents might be. To Ben the loading felt like several metal objects, all of them heavy, hard, and comparatively small.

Despite the weight, Ben could have carried two of the bundles at once easily enough. He did not do so, wanting to prolong the unloading. He might have only the time it took to do that job in which to try to think, to nerve himself, to act. . . .

As he passed through the upper doorway of the cave for the first time, bearing his first load down, he looked carefully at the great stone as it rested in its raised position. Ben was stuck by how close it must be to its point of balance. What six men had heaved to open, it appeared, could be easily tilted shut again by one.

Going down the crooked stairs for the first time, watching carefully by candlelight where he put down his feet, he noticed that the stairs were beginning to be worn. As if many processions of laborers had borne their burdens here. . . .

Think, he ordered himself. Think! But, to his silent, inward horror, his mind seemed paralyzed.

Down in the cave, putting his first bundle obediently down into the dark hole in the floor, Ben noticed something else. The heavy bundle made no noise of fall or landing when he released it into darkness. Either it was still falling—or it had somehow been caught.

Moving in slow procession with the other drivers, now emerging from the cave to get his second load, Ben saw that Radulescu had again set his Old World torch leaning against a rock, this time just outside the entrance. The officer had gone back to his tethered riding beast and was taking something from the saddle, untying a light, long bundle that Ben had not really noticed until now. The bundle was just about the same size and shape as the sword that Radulescu wore, and heavily wrapped like all the other cargo.

Ben kept moving as he watched. He shouldered his second load, lightening another animal's burden. Again the weight of the package he picked up was startling for its size. No, it wouldn't be lead that the Blue Temple was putting down into the earth so secretly.

The location of their main hoard had been a subject of stories and speculation for generations. At least one song had that hoard as its subject—the same tune that was still running, very unhelpfully, in Ben's mind.

The other five men in the line of treasure-bearers gave no indication that they had guessed what they were about. The implications of their situation, as far as Ben could tell, had simply not dawned on them at all. Their faces were dull, and set against the rain; set against knowledge, too, as it now seemed to Ben. He saw no possibility that he would be able to talk to them meaningfully before he had to act.

Both the stairway and the upper entrance to the cave were so narrow that the process of carrying in the cargo was necessarily slow and inefficient; men moving down always had to stop and wait for men moving up to pass them, and vice versa. Even so, with six steadily at work, the unloading wasn't really going to take very long.

Six men, Ben kept thinking, who now know where Benambra's Gold is really buried. Were there six other workmen still living in the world who had managed to learn so much?

The unloading proceeded, and it seemed to Ben that the process was going very fast. Outside the cave there was the light of the Old World torch to work by, and inside the warm smoky flicker of the two blue candles.

"Move along there!"

Ben had just dropped another bundle into the dark hole in the cave floor. He was in the act of straightening up and backing away when he brushed lightly against the officer who came moving forward just behind him. As the two men grazed past each other, the tip of the bundle that Radulescu carried brushed Ben's arm. Even through his sleeve and the object's wrappings, Ben could feel the passing presence of some power of magic. It tugged at his memory as some old perfume might have done, some fragrance lost since childhood and suddenly known again. And the incident made his fear suddenly more powerful than ever.

Ben had climbed the stair and was outside again, getting yet another bundle to carry down, when Radulescu also emerged from the cave. When the officer looked sharply at Ben, Ben looked dully back.

In his twenty-three years of life, Ben had learned that there were only two things about his own appearance that were at all likely to impress others. One, that never failed, was his squat bulk; he was really not shorter than average, but so heavily built that he appeared that way. The second thing was his apparent dullness. Something about his round slab of a face tended to make people think he was slow-witted, at least until they knew him. For some reason this effect was intensified by the fact that his body was so broad and strong. It was as if no one wanted intelligence and unhandsome strength to coexist in the same man. Ben had convinced himself that he was not particularly slow of mind, but he had learned also that there were times when it was helpful to be thought that way. He let his jaw sag just a little now, and returned the impatient officer's gaze blankly.

Radulescu stepped closer to him. "Move along, I say. Are you taking root there? Do you want to stand out in this storm all night?"

Ben, who would have been delighted to settle for just that, shook his head slightly and let himself be spurred again into obedient motion. Mechanically he rejoined the slowly shuffling line of the other drivers.

Burdened again with what he thought must certainly be gold, heading down once more into the cave, he observed again how precariously the great sealing rock was poised near its point of balance. One man standing outside the cave ought to be able to close that doorway quickly, with one hand. Whereas six men caught inside would never be able to crowd themselves into position to reach the rock and lift it open. Of course, if given time, they ought to be able to manage some way of getting out. If given time.

The rock was not going to come crashing shut behind him this trip. Not all of the treasure had been unloaded yet.

As he let this weighty bundle slide down into the hole in the cave floor, Ben started back reflexively. Half a meter or so below the level of the floor, a pair of hands, inhumanly large and white, had come momentarily into view to catch the package. As quickly as they had appeared, the hands were gone again, all in utter silence.

Ben turned away again, saying nothing. As he moved past a line of burdened men all waiting to drop more cargo into the pit, he realized with a pang of fear that the unloading must now be almost finished. He took quick strides toward the stair, wanting to make sure that he got out of the cave again before the job was done.

At the upper entrance, the officer had just delayed the last driver, who was just about to start down with what must be the last bundle on his shoulder. "Wait for me below, out of the rain," Radulescu was telling him. "I want to speak to all of you."

And the last man, burdened, entered the cave. Just inside the entrance Ben shouldered past him. Ben got out, leaving behind him a voice that muttered obscene protests at almost being forced off the stairs.

The officer, with his Old World light once more in hand, greeted Ben's emergence with another look of disgust; this time there was perhaps something more dangerous in the glance as well. And Radulescu cursed Ben wearily. No real curse fortunately, but one of the hollow forms used automatically to relieve feelings and abuse subordinates: something about an Emperor's child, lacking in both wit and luck.

"Sir?" Ben responded numbly. Now, he was thinking to himself, I must move now, before it is too late, before . . .

"The unloading is finished," the officer informed him, speaking slowly and plainly now, as to the company dullard. "I want all of you to assemble in the cave. Go down there and wait for me."

Behind Radulescu the six unburdened loadbeasts were waiting patiently. And down in the cave the five other drivers waited, displaying the same kind of patience. Ben felt unable to move. He had the sensation that he was about to be forced to jump from a high tower into unknown darkness.

Something must have altered in his face, for the officer's own expression suddenly grew dangerous. "Inside!" Radulescu shouted, and in the same instant cast down his torch and began to draw his sword.

Ben could feel the dead weight of training on him, and also the weight of fear. Terrified at his own obedience, he took a step toward the cave. But when he looked down through the entrance at the burning candles, the old wax congealed on rocks, and the five loadbeast faces of his fellow drivers, he saw with sudden and dreadful clarity that he was about to step into his grave.

Instead he shot out his right hand, seizing the officer by the upper part of his left arm. The man howled and tried to draw his sword, but the action was difficult for Radulescu to complete with Ben's strength pulling him forward, bending him off balance. Suddenly pushing with all his power, Ben sent Radulescu stumbling and reeling into the cave. The force of the thrust propelled the officer right on down the stairs, and if he had managed to draw his sword by now it was not going to do him any good.

Before Radulescu could draw breath for a second outraged yell, Ben pivoted and threw his weight on the great sealing stone. For one heart-stopping instant the sheer inertia of the huge boulder resisted him. Then the mass moved, slowly for the first fraction of a second, faster in the next, then falling with a doomlike thud to close the cave. Ben pulled a foot back just in time to save it from being crushed.

Candlelight had been sealed down into the earth now, along with yells and wrath, but the cold torch lay as brilliant as ever on the ground. Ben, who wanted to pull darkness round him like a cloak, left it where it was. He turned and ran into the night. He had already considered taking Radulescu's riding beast, and had rejected the idea. Where he planned to go his own feet would serve him better.

That mode of travel had its drawbacks too. Almost at once Ben banged his feet on rocks concealed in darkness, and tore his legs on thorns. He had to slow down to a quick walk, to keep from breaking a shin or toe. If he crippled himself now, the damage would very soon become permanent. He was moving, he hoped, south and a little east, trying to angle toward the coastline with its irregular brink of cliffs somewhere not far ahead. Ben had in mind a plan of sorts. It was not an elaborate plan, having necessarily been made on very short notice. That might be just as well.

What he had feared was going to happen next now happened, and almost immediately. Once more the dragon's chiming snort came clearly through the night, this time from right behind Ben, and disconcertingly close. The officer Radulescu, though sealed into the cave and probably injured, had been able to release the binding magic. Now Ben could hear the monster coming after him, the sounds audible through the unceasing wind and his own heavy breathing as he trotted. He heard the crunch and roll of stones beneath the dragon's feet, the breaking of thorny bushes as it trod them down.

Very little of Ben's bulk was fat. And he had been known to dash for short distances at a speed that others found surprising. But running was not really his strong point, and he knew that he was not going to outrun a landwalker; nobody was, not even on a fast and level track, which this certainly was not. Running all out, gambling against the chance of broken toes and shins, he angled more sharply toward the east and the invisible clifftop.

Now those huge feet behind him, terrible in the slow length of stride that gained on him, had settled into what was certainly direct pursuit. The ground-shaking rhythm of that walk grew perilously near, and nearer still. Ben, the experienced dragon hunter, made himself wait until the last possible moment before he tore his trailing cloak free of its last clasp and flung it up into the wind behind him. He dared not break stride or turn his head to find out what effect the action had.

Two of his own strides later, his ears told him that the effort at distraction had been at least a momentary success. There was a thunder-roar behind him that came from a little closer than the sky, and the earth-quivering pursuit faltered.

Ben managed to get in twenty more gasping strides before he could hear the dragon coming after him again. And then he came near running clean off the cliff's edge before he saw it in the night. Just in time he managed to throw himself down, clinging to the very brink. He clambered over it as carefully as possible, groping with his feet and legs for some kind of solidity below. At last his sandals scraped on rock, found purchase of a kind. As he had hoped, the steepness of the cliffside here was not quite too much for human hands and feet. Ben let go of his grip on the edge and found places lower down where he could hang on with his hands. Then he tried to extend his feet downward once more.

Now, when he could have used some lightning to see by, it had ceased almost entirely. Ben clung to one rock after another that he could barely see, working his way slowly down the cliff. And even more slowly he made some progress to the south along its face. For the present he could no longer hear the dragon. It might have given up on chasing him. Or it might not. They were like that, unpredictable.

With no lightning in the sky, the ocean a hundred meters down was completely invisible. Just as well, no doubt. But Ben could still hear its waves, rending themselves on rock. Breathing devout prayers to Ardneh and to Draffut, those two most merciful of gods, groping for one handhold and foothold below another, half expecting each moment to be his last, Ben fumbled his way down the face of the cliff toward the absolute darkness of the sea.

CHAPTER 2

The tall young man stood on the bank of a small, muddy stream, looking around him uncertainly in bright sunlight. Even in broad day, and even with the distant mountains in the east to give a landmark, he could not be sure that the village he was looking for had ever existed on this spot.

Still, he was almost sure.

He could remember that most of the surrounding territory had once been prosperous farming and grazing land. No more. It was largely abandoned now. And here, where the Aldan had once run clean and fair, this mucky and unrecognizable stream now followed a strangely altered course through a sadly altered countryside. Even the distant mountains bore new scars. So much had everything changed that the young man remained uncertain of precisely where he was until his eye discovered a portion of a remembered millwheel sticking up out of a bank of earth amid the dried stalks of last year's weeds.

Only one corner of one broad wooden blade was visible, but the young man knew what it was at once. Staring at that cracked and splitting wood, he let himself sink down on the ground beside it. This sitting was the heavy movement of an old man, though the youth could hardly have been more than twenty at the most. His tanned face under its ragged growth of beard was still unlined, though from the expression in which it was set it seemed that lines ought to be there; and already the blue-gray eyes were old.

The bow and quiver that rode on the young man's broad back looked well-used, as did the long knife sheathed at his side. He might have been a hunter or a ranger, perhaps a military scout. Parts of his clothing and equipment were of leather, and some of these might once have been components of a more formal soldier's outfit. If so, their identifying colors had long since been cut or bleached away. The young man's hair was moderately short, as if it might be in the process of growing out from a close military or priestly cut.

He now put out a hand, large and tanned deeply like his face, and as rough-worn as his clothing. With it he touched the visible corner of the decaying millwheel blade. He let his hand rest there briefly on the old wood, as if he were trying to feel something in it. Meanwhile he raised his eyes toward the eastern mountains.

There was a faint sound behind the young man, as of someone or something moving through the thicket there to the west. He turned quickly, without getting up, then sat still, watching the thicket carefully. In his position he was half hidden by the rise of the earthen bank.

Presently a half-grown boy dressed in ragged homespun emerged from the scrubby growth of bushes. The boy was carrying a pail crudely fashioned out of bark, and was obviously coming to the stream for water. He was almost at the water's edge before he caught sight of the motionless young man watching him, and came to a vaguely alarmed halt.

An Emperor's child for sure, the young man thought, surveying that small dirty figure in wretched clothing. "Hello, young one," he said aloud.

The boy did not answer. He stood there holding the empty pail, shifting his weight from one bare foot to the other as if uncertain whether he ought to run away or try to go on about his business.

"Hello, I say. Have you been living around here very long?"

Still no answer.

"My name's Mark. I mean you no harm. I used to live near here myself."

Now the boy moved again. Still keeping a wary eye on Mark, he waded into the stream. He bent his head to fill the pail, then looked up, tossing back long greasy hair. He said: "We been here a year now."

Mark nodded encouragingly. "Five years ago," he said, "there was a whole village here. A big sawmill stood right about where I'm sitting now." And he moved a hand in a vague gesture that ought to have included the village street. Only five years ago, he marveled silently. It seemed impossible. He tried without success to visualize this boy as one of the smaller children in the village then.

"That's as may be," the boy said. "We came here later. After the mountains burst and the gods fought."

"The mountains burst, all right," Mark agreed. "And I don't doubt that the gods fought too . . . what's your name?"

"Virgil."

"A good name. You know, when I was your size, I played here along this stream. It was a lot different then." Mark felt a sudden need to make someone understand just how totally different it had been. "I swam here, I caught fish . . ."

He broke off. Someone else was coming down through the thicket.

A woman emerged, as ragged and dirty as the boy. Her walk was the walk of age, and much gray showed in her disordered hair. A dirty bandage covered both her eyes. Mark could see the ends of scars showing past the edges of the cloth.

Just at the edge of the thicket the blind woman halted, one hand touching a bush as if by that means she could assure herself of her position. "Virgil?" she called out. It was a surprisingly young voice, and it carried fear. "Who's there?"

"One lone traveler, ma'm," Mark called in answer. At the same time the boy replied with something reassuring, and came out of the water with his filled pail.

The woman turned her face in Mark's direction. There were indications in that face that she was still young, even evidence that a few years ago she might have been called pretty. She called toward Mark harshly: "We don't have much."

"I don't want anything you have. I was just telling the young man that I used to live nearby."

Virgil put in: "He says he was here five years ago. Before the mountains burst."

Mark was on his feet now, and approached a little closer to the woman. "I'll be going right along, ma'm. But could you tell me one thing first, maybe? Did you ever hear any word of the family of Jord the

Miller? He was a big man with only one arm. Had a wife named Mala and a daughter, Marian, real blue-eyed and fair. Daughter'd be in her twenties now. They lived right here on this spot, five years ago, when Duke Fraktin was alive and claimed this land."

"Never heard of any of 'em," the woman said at once in her hard young voice. "Five years ago we weren't here."

"None of the old villagers were here when you arrived?"

"No one. There was no village."

And the boy Virgil said, as if repeating a lesson learned: "The Silver Queen now holds dominion over this land."

"Aye," said Mark. "I know she claims that. But I suppose you don't see her soldiers way out here very often?"

"I don't see them at all." The woman's harsh voice was no harsher than before. "The last time I saw them was when they blinded me. We ceased our wandering, then."

"I'm sorry," Mark said. In his heart he cursed all soldiers; at the moment he did not feel like one himself.

"Are you one of her army too? Or a deserter?"

"Neither, ma'm."

Virgil asked Mark unexpectedly: "Were you here when the gods were fighting among themselves? Did you see them?"

Mark didn't answer. He was trying to discern in the bandaged face of the blind woman the countenance of any of the village girls he could remember. But it was useless.

Young Virgil, evidently feeling braver now, persisted. "Did you ever see the gods?"

Mark looked at him. "My father did. But I have only seen them in—visions, and that only once or twice." He made himself smile. "In dreams, no more than that." Then, seeing that the woman had turned her back on him and was about to retreat into the thicket again, he called to her: "Let me walk with you, back up the hill, if that's the way you're going. I won't be any bother to you. A manor house stood up there once, and I want to see if anything is left of it."

The woman made no reply, but moved on, groping her way from bush to bush along what must be a familiar path. The boy came after her, carrying the pail of water in silence. Then Mark. The three of them climbed more or less together along the path worn through the hillside thicket.

When they reached the top of the little hill Mark could see how little was left of Sir Sharfa's manor house. The great stone hearth and chimney remained, and almost nothing else. Against the chimney a crude lean-to shelter had been built from scraps of wood. From inside the shelter came a snoring sound, and a man's bony hand and wrist were visible in the muddy doorway, their owner evidently lying on the floor inside. The snore sounded unhealthy, as if the man emitting it were drunk or dying. Maybe he was both, thought Mark.

The boy, who had put his pail down now, was not ready to abandon the subject of the gods. "Mars and Draffut had their fight right over on those mountains," he resumed suddenly, pointing to the east. "And the twelve magic Swords were forged right up there. Vulcan kidnapped a smith and six men from a village, to help him make 'em. Afterwards he killed the six men, and he took off the smith's arm . . ." Virgil stopped rather suddenly. He was looking at Mark, with the expression of a boy who has suddenly remembered something.

"How do you know how many Swords there were?" Mark asked him. It amazed Mark how knowledge spread—or how, sometimes, it seemed determined on remaining secret. It was almost twenty years now, he knew, since the twelve Swords had been forged, and half a dozen years ago still only a few people in the whole world had known about them. And now it seemed that the whole world knew.

The boy looked at him, as if Mark had asked how it was known that a woolbeast had four legs. "Twelve Swords, that's how many there were. Everyone knows that."

"Oh."

Virgil's eyes were intense, his voice hurried. "But Hermes played a joke on all the other gods. He gave the Swords only to mortals, and he scattered them all across the world. Each Sword went to a different man or woman to start with, and none of the gods got any themselves. And each Sword gave whoever got it a different kind of power."

"Oh." It was true, for the most part anyway. He didn't want to appear to possess superior knowledge, and he didn't know quite what to say. "Why would Hermes have done a thing like that?"

"Part of the game that the gods play with each other. Aye, he scattered them and gave them all to people. I wish I could have got one."

Mark was looking at the woman, who stood leaning with one hand on the shelter, blindly listening. The man inside snored on. Suddenly Mark felt a great necessity to do something for these people; maybe he could at least shoot them a rabbit or two before he left. And then—yes, he had decided now. There was something much more important that he was going to do for them, and thousands like them.

Virgil asked him: "Did you say that the miller only had one arm? Was—he your father?"

Mark studied him a moment, then put another question in return. "If you had one of those Swords, what would you do with it? Hide it away somewhere?"

The boy's expression showed he thought that question was insane. "Whoever gets all those Swords into his hands will rule the world."

"Aye," said Mark. "But if you had one? Coinspinner, maybe. What then? What would you do with it? Try to rule a twelfth of the world, or what?"

Neither of his listeners answered him. Maybe he had scared them now. But now that he'd started he couldn't stop. "What would you say about a man who knew where one of those Swords was hidden? Maybe Dragonslicer . . . a man who could go and get it, but he just let it stay hidden. When there's so many wrong things in the world, like . . . when there's so much that needs to be set right."

The woman's scarred and blinded face turned slowly back and forth. She was shaking her head. "You'll straighten out the wrongs of the world, young man? You might as well set out to serve the Emperor."

CHAPTER 3

In darkness Ben continued his methodical struggle to work his way down the face of the cliff. Whenever he could he made a little headway south along its face as well. The plan he had in mind required that he go south. It was a simple plan, basically. It was also madly dangerous—or he would have thought it so, had he not found himself in a situation where every other course seemed suicidal.

Anyway, he had now acted on his plan. He had rebelled, assaulted an officer, deserted, and there was nothing to do now but go on. From handhold to foothold he moved down, and slowly south.

At least he was able to see a little more clearly now, by the light of a horned moon that had recently come up over the eastern sea. The sky was gradually clearing after the storm, but low fog still shrouded the ocean and its shoreline, which were still at a frightening and discouraging distance below him. The sound of breakers still came drifting up, weaker now, almost indistinguishable from the weakening wind. And Ben had certain bad moments, in which he thought he was able to hear another sound as well—the voices of six men trapped and howling in a cave. One of the six was armed with a sword. But would that do him any good, when the great white hands came reaching out for him?

Ben fought down the images springing from his imagination. Then another kind of sound reached his ears, and was enough to drive imaginary terrors away. He heard the steps of the dragon. It was coming back for him, walking the flatland now some uncertain number of meters above his head. Ben continued to descend, a few centimeters at a time. There was nothing else for him to do.

The dragon must have been able to sense his presence, for it came to the clifftop immediately above him. Looking up, Ben caught one glimpse of its head, a lovely silver in the moonlight, and saw the red glow of its breath. After that he kept his own head down.

The dragon bellowed at Ben. Or, for all he knew, it might be the horned moon that drew its wrath. Stamping with table-sized feet along the brink, it shook down stones and clods of earth. Ben's helmet saved him once from being stunned. The dragon projected fire out into the night. Ben saw the glow on the rocks around him, and he felt the backwash of the heat, as if a door had opened briefly to some tremendous oven. But either the creature could not bend over the cliff far enough to breathe at him directly, or it did not care to try. Ben was confident that it lacked the intelligence to try to trickle fire on him along the rocks.

Presently, as he continued moving down, the hail of dirt and stones abated. Then the stamping moved away, until he could no longer feel it in the earth. Ben heard the chiming snort again, this time from some considerable distance, and almost drowned in wind.

As if he had never had any other goal in life, and could imagine none, he kept on moving. Mechanically he went down, and south. And presently he found to his relief that the slope was no longer quite so steep. He began to make real progress.

His way now took him round a large convexity of cliff, and out of most of the remaining wind. Looking to seaward now, from a level only a little above the tendrils of the fog, he saw that he was confronting a long but possibly narrow inlet of the sea, a fjord that stretched inland to the west for some indeterminable distance. Ben could just discern high land across the water, but in fog and intermittent moonlight he could only guess at that land's distance and its nature.

According to the mental map that he relied on for guidance, he had to continue south if he was to have any hope of leaving Blue Temple land behind him before daylight. But now continuing south meant somehow crossing this arm of the sea. There was no choice. Unless he stumbled on a boat when he got down to the shore—and he had no reason to think he would—he was going to have to trust his fate to the powers of the deep, and swim across.

As he worked his way lower and lower, getting into patchy fog, he kept trying to estimate the height and distance of those opposing cliffs. But under the conditions he could not. He was not even certain he was not looking at an island. All he could really be sure of was that if he stayed where he was until morning, he would be discovered by Blue Temple searchers who would be out in force. He had to assume that they would have flying creatures out looking for him at sunrise. And if they found him on this cliff he would do well then to hurl himself to speedy death. . . .

The land flattened briefly at the cliff's foot. Ben moved among fallen boulders, able to feel the spray now from invisible waves. He moved onto a shingle of coarse rounded stones, and was granted a dim vision of the sea at last. There was no boat, of course, nor any sign of one. Not even a scrap of log.

Uttering silent prayers to Neptune, he crept forward onto a jutting rock, with sea-foam bubbling at his feet. He stripped off a few more garments, and threw his helmet out as offering to the sea. Then, not giving himself time to think, he entered the water in a bold leap.

He surfaced gasping with the salt chill, and struck out boldly. How the tides and currents might run here he had no idea. His fate was in the hands of the sea gods, but drowning was hardly the worst fate that might overtake him in the next few hours.

Ben was a strong swimmer, and all but impervious to cold. The water was not warm, but he doubted that it was cold enough to kill him. Glimpsing the horned moon through ragged clouds as he swam, he tried to keep it on his left. The waves were strong and regular. Once he got out a little from the shore, it was hard to tell if they were helping or hindering his progress. Patches of fog closed in at times, obscuring the moon and making him doubt whether he was swimming in the right direction. But always the moon came back, and he was never very far off his chosen course.

Eventually he thought that the moon was higher. Had he been swimming for an hour now? For two? It couldn't have been for very long, he told himself, or there'd be signs in the sky of the coming daylight. . . .

He tried to hold his thought on how difficult it was going to be for the Blue Temple searchers when they came looking for him. They'd find his cloak right away, up on the cliff, if the dragon hadn't swallowed it whole. They'd think that it had swallowed him . . . they'd never find him in this kind of fog.

He was wondering seriously whether he was going to make it, when a mass of land loomed vaguely ahead, and from the same direction he heard the sound of waves on rocks again.

The dawn rising grayly out of the sea seemed to carry Ben up with it, lifting him onto land.

On a small strip of sandy beach he lay quietly for a few minutes, breathing heavily, having a little difficulty realizing that he was still alive. He was nearer exhaustion than he had realized. But he did not forget a prayer of thanks to Neptune.

A few meters inland, the foot of an unfamiliar cliff confronted him. As soon as he felt able, he got to his feet and began to climb it. The mist from the sea seemed to rise with him as he climbed, like some demonic substance seeking to escape the depths. Even though he still moved through fog, the movement dried and warmed him.

When he'd gained what he thought was a considerable height he paused to catch his breath and look back. Across the fjord, the headland that he'd fled was hard to make out. Clouds shrouded it from the first direct rays of the morning sun. The search for him had probably already started over there, but he couldn't see it. He trusted that so far they hadn't been able to see him, either.

What he had to do now was get himself off this exposed cliff, get inland as rapidly as possible. Climbing now at the fastest pace he could sustain, Ben saw with alarm that his tough hands were starting to bleed from their prolonged struggle with sharp rock. If the Blue Temple's flying scouts should come to visit this cliff as well, would they be able to trail him by those tiny flecks of blood?

If so, there was no point in worrying about it. He was doing all he could do to survive, he told himself. If he'd gone meekly down into the cave that last time as he'd been ordered, he'd be quite meekly dead by now. That much he was sure of. He was convinced that the five other drivers were dead by now . . . unless, he thought suddenly, they had somehow been kept alive for questioning about the plot. The higher-ups were sure to think that there had been some kind of plot. Probably even Radulescu, if *he* was still alive, was being questioned.

Excuse me, sir, there wasn't no plot, sir. Just Big Ben, Slow Ben, doing his best to stay alive.

He thought about that as he climbed. Certainly, last night when he'd started running, there'd been nothing more on his mind than keeping himself alive. And even now, climbing rapidly, he was willing to settle for that.

But now . . .

Now, with the possibility of escape looking more real with each passing moment, other ideas were inviting themselves into Ben's mind. True, he hadn't been *trying* to carry away any important secrets. But, since they were going to hunt him anyway . . . well, he'd be a fool not to try to get some chance to benefit out of this, as well as the chance of getting killed.

Twenty-three years' experience had taught Ben that the life of a poor man was not much of a life. It was too bad the world was like that, but so it was. He wanted money, enough at least to promise some kind of minimal security. Once a man had a little gold in his pocket, he could be somebody, could have some kind of chance for a decent life. Ben had joined the Blue Temple service a year ago only because he saw in it the possibility at least of modest success, security—in a word, of getting a little money. A man had to have a certain minimum of that. At least he did if he was ever going to attract and keep a woman whose own yearnings were for prosperous stability.

Once Ben had enlisted, given his size and strength and lack of other education, there was little doubt about which branch of the Temple service he'd be assigned to. Not for him one of the easy desk jobs, tallying and re-tallying the Temple's wealth in all its categories, figuring up the interest on all the loans they had outstanding. He'd seen the rows of busy clerks, scribbling at the long desks. That looked like an easy life. But he himself had been sent into the Guards.

For Ben, already accustomed to a hard, poor existence, and not expecting much from his new career right at the start, the life of a military recruit had not seemed too unpleasant. He had already taken part in more actual fighting than he had ever wanted to see, but he had managed to live through it; in the peaceful Blue Temple garrison where he was first assigned, he really did not expect to be called upon for more. Adequate food and clothing were regularly provided, and a man who did what he was told could usually keep himself out of trouble.

It had turned out, though, somewhat to Ben's own surprise, that he was not the kind of man to always do what he was told.

He might have enlisted in other organizations than Blue Temple, sought jobs under other conditions of service, in other places, that would have offered him just as good a chance of security. It was easy to realize that now. Now, he saw that he had picked Blue Temple really because the idea of its great wealth had attracted him. He hadn't been quite naive enough to imagine that he was going to become personally rich as soon as he signed up—as the recruiter had somehow managed to suggest. No. But still Ben had known that all the money, the wealth, the gold of the Blue Temple, was going to be around, and the idea of it had attracted him. At the time he'd told himself that he'd chosen to join Blue Temple because it lacked the reputation for gratuitous oppression and cruelty that was shared by so many of the world's other powers. The Dark King, for example, or the Silver Queen of Yambu, or the late Duke Fraktin.

Blue Temple were the worshippers of wealth, the harvesters and heapers-up of gold. Somehow they usually contrived to extract the stuff from everyone who came in reach, from rich and poor, devotees and scoffers, friends and deadly foes alike. In the process they also somehow financed and indirectly controlled much of the world's trade. Ben's bunk in the guardhouse had been remote from the inner chambers where financial matters were seriously discussed, but information, as always, had a way of seeping through walls. In the morning the Temple accepted a rich man's offering, in return insuring him against some feared disaster; in the afternoon it levied a tax on a poor widow—making sure to leave her enough to sustain life, that next year she would be able to pay some tax again.

And incessantly the Temple complained about how inappropriately poor it was, how much help and protection and shelter it needed against the financial dangers of the world. Always the Guardsmen were exhorted to be ready to lay down their lives in defense of the last shreds of assets remaining. It was never actually stated that the wealth was almost gone—any more than the location of the main hoard was revealed—but the general implication was that it had to be dwindling fast. Always the soldiers were reminded how much their meagre pay, their weapons and clothes and food, all cost their poor masters. And how essential it was, therefore, for the soldiers—especially those who hoped someday to be promoted, and those too who wanted to eventually draw a pension—how essential it was that they return some generous fraction of their pay as a Temple offering.

If a man were to serve in the ranks for twenty years, investing a substantial part of his pay as such an offering each year, he would be able to retire at that point with a pension. Exactly how much of a pension was a little vague.

The recruiter had mentioned generous pensions to Ben, but had somehow neglected to explain just what a soldier had to do to qualify for one.

So, there were financial as well as other reasons why the enlistment hadn't been working out for Ben as well as he had hoped. Even before last night's crisis he had been ready to get out. Of course he could have bought out his enlistment at any time, if he'd had the money to do so—but then, if he'd had that much money he never would have joined up in the first place. Barbara would have been willing to marry him, or live with him permanently anyway. The two of them could have stopped their precarious wandering about with shows and carnivals, a life that kept them usually very little better off than beggars. They could have bought themselves a little shop somewhere, in some prosperous strong city with high walls. . . .

It was a year now since he'd seen Barbara, and he had missed her even more than he'd expected to. He didn't want to go back, though, until he'd accomplished something at last, got a start in some kind of life that she'd want to share. He'd sent her letters from his garrison station once or twice, when the opportunity to do so had arisen, but he hadn't heard from her at all. For all Ben knew, she'd taken up with someone else by now. There had been no promise from her that she would not.

Ben's reason for enlisting had, of course, been to get himself established in some kind of secure Blue Temple post, something that would pay well enough to let him send for her . . . looking back at it now, it seemed a very foolish hope. But then, at the time he'd enlisted, every other hope had seemed more foolish still.

Now, in the gradually brightening daylight, Ben continued his climb. This cliff was not quite so steep, he thought, as the one he'd had to come down in the dark. Or it might just be that having some daylight made things that much easier. Anyway, he was making good progress, and quite soon reached a place from which it was possible to look up and feel sure he'd be able to make it all the way to the top. He had not the slightest idea of what he was going to find up there, except he expected and hoped that he'd no longer be on Blue Temple land. He might, of course, be wrong. . . .

When he had climbed a little farther still, Ben paused to look upward again. Yes, from here on the slope was definitely gentler, and he had no doubt that he could climb it. He could even see a short stretch of what looked like a genuine trail, up there near the top.

Ben climbed another hundred steps and stopped to scan the way ahead again. This time he received something of a shock. Right beside that upper trail, in a spot where no one had been a few moments ago, a man was now sitting on a squarish stone, gazing out to sea.

The man appeared to be taking no notice of Ben, and as far as Ben could tell he was not armed. His body was wrapped in a plain gray cloak that effectively concealed whatever else he might be wearing. The cloak at least didn't look like part of any soldier's or priest's uniform that Ben was familiar with. Maybe the watcher was not a sentry, but he was in a place that a sentry might well choose. And, should he be minded for some reason to dispute Ben's passage up the steep slope, his position would give him a definite advantage.

There was nothing for Ben to do but climb on, meanwhile thinking what he ought to say to the man when he came near. It occured to Ben that he might represent himself as a shipwrecked mariner, just cast ashore at the foot of these cliffs after clinging for days to a bit of wreckage. No notion of where he was—yes, that was the idea. A story like that might well be accepted; the gods knew that Ben was wet and weary enough for it to fit him.

The man who sat alone on the rock did not look down at Ben until Ben was only a few meters below him. But when he did look it was without surprise, as if he'd known all along that Ben was there.

"Hello!" the watcher called down then. He was a nondescript sort of fellow in appearance, smiling and openly cheerful. At close range his gray cloak looked old and worn.

"Hello!" Ben called back. Something in him had wanted to respond at once to the lightheartedness of the other's greeting, and as his voice came out he thought it sounded too cheerful for the tale of woe he had to tell—though on second thought he supposed that any shipwrecked sailor who came to shore alive might have good reason to sound happy.

Ben climbed closer. The man continued to regard him with a smile. Not quite, thought Ben, like an idiot.

Drawing even with the man at last, and no longer at the disadvantage of the steep slope, Ben felt confident enough to pause to regain his breath. Between slow gasps he asked: "Whose lands have I arrived at, sir?" He was ready now with some details of his shipwreck, should they be required.

The man's smile faded to friendly seriousness. "The Emperor's," he said.

Ben stood there looking at him. If the answer had been seriously meant, Ben could derive no sense from it at all. The Emperor was a proverbial figure of fun and ridicule, and hardly anything more. Of course, if Ben thought about it, he supposed that a real man afflicted with that title might still exist somewhere in the world. But . . . a landowner? The Emperor was a clown-masked caperer through jests and stories, a player of practical jokes, the proverbial father of the wretched and the unlucky. He was just not someone that you thought of as owning land.

With a small shake of his head, Ben climbed on a few more steps, just high enough to let him see inland over the final sharp brink of the cliff. He warily kept half an eye on his companion as he did so.

He didn't know quite what he had expected, but the view inland surprised him. Beginning from the barren cliff-face's very edge, a lush meadow sloped inland, knee-deep with dewy grass and wildflowers, to end in an abrupt semicircle where a stately grove or forest began, about a hundred meters inland. Neither meadow nor forest showed any signs of human use.

Ben said: "Well, the cliff here is certainly poor enough to be the Emperor's wall. But someone else must lay claim to this meadow, and to the wood yonder."

The fellow sitting on the rock looked quite grave when he heard this. He gazed back at Ben but did not answer. Ben, deciding that he did not need the complications of a debate with some stray madman, climbed the last three steps to stand gratefully in soft grass. He saw now that the meadow formed a rough triangle, and he was standing very near its seaward point. Not enjoying this exposed position on the cliff's edge, he at once walked inland, heading for the baseline of the woods.

After the long struggling climb, it was a joy to take swift steps through soft grass on almost level land. Patches of mist were rolling up over the edge of the cliff, as if determined to accompany Ben inland. Field-nesting birds, clamoring as if they were unused to disturbance, flew up from almost under his feet.

He reached the trackless grove, and entered it. There was little undergrowth and he moved swiftly. And now, almost before he'd had time to wonder how far the wood extended, he was confronted by a high wall, constructed roughly of gray fieldstone.

The wall stretched left to right as far as Ben could see, losing itself among the trees. But it was so rough-surfaced that climbing it proved easy. Raising his eyes cautiously above the top, Ben observed that on the far side of the wall the woods soon petered out, and innocent-looking countryside began, with a narrow, rutted road winding across it from left to right. In the distance Ben could just discern the top of a tall white pyramid. That was the only building in sight, apart from a couple of distant cottages.

Ben observed that pyramid with relief, taking it as proof that he'd put Blue Temple lands behind him—or, at the worst, that he was just about to do so. In another moment he was over the wall and trotting toward that winding road. As he passed through the last of the trees, with patches of mist still hanging about them to lend an air of mystery, it struck Ben for the first time that the grove had the look of some kind of shrine. For what god it was meant he couldn't guess. He didn't think it was associated with the Temple of Ardneh—that looked too far away.

He should really stop at Ardneh's temple, he told himself, and make some thanks-offering for prayers very recently answered. He certainly would do that, if he had anything left to offer, but he was practically naked as he was. On second thought he would stop, and try to beg some clothes. Also, now that he thought about it, a little food. Yes, definitely, food.

Less than an hour later, a white-robed acolyte of Ardneh was ushering Ben up a long flight of white steps.

When Ben emerged from Ardneh's temple a short time later, he was dressed in warmer garmets. They were third- or fourth-hand pilgrim's garb, and patched, but they were clean and dry. And he was no longer ravenously hungry. But he was very tired, and frowning thoughtfully.

Again he strode along the road, still heading south. He'd have to stop somewhere soon and get some sleep, but right now he wanted to make distance, to get as far from the Blue Temple as he could. He had a better knowledge now of where he was, and he'd known all along where he was heading for.

Sometime this month the carnival that he and Barbara had been with ought to be making a spring move to Purkinje Town, if it kept to the old schedule. If she was still with it, he would find her there.

Ben made the long journey almost entirely on foot. It took him approximately a month, so spring in these parts was well advanced when he arrived. And the journey was not without adventure, though if Blue Temple were on his trail, as he thought they must be by this time, he saw no signs of them. Gradually his fears receded, and he began to believe that they thought him dead.

By the time Ben reached Purkinje Town, or rather the place outside the town's crumbling walls where the small carnival was encamped, he'd worn out and replaced his sandals, and had had to replace some of his pilgrim's garb as well. He had also begun a beard, which was coming in a dull, bleached brown to match his hair. He had acquired as well one of the packs and something of the appearance of an itinerant peddler he'd fallen in with early in his journey. The peddler, once convinced that Ben meant him no harm, had been glad to have the strong man as an escort, had cut a sturdy quarterstaff for him to carry, and had rewarded his companionship with food and clothing.

But their paths had diverged, many kilometers back. Ben was alone when he arrived outside Purkinje's half-tumbled walls toward evening on a clear, late spring day. Those walls were no longer a very impressive defense. The city, though, was still flying its own flag of orange and green, evidently still managing to maintain a measure of independence from the brawling warlords whose armies endlessly came and went across the land.

The carnival still looked independent too, though in the past year it had grown even shabbier than Ben remembered it. The tents and wagons that Ben could recognize had endured another year of wear and tear, and he found it difficult to discover among them any traces of repair, new paint, or fresh decoration. And there were now a couple of wagons that he did not recognize.

The crude painting on the cloth side of one of these vehicles caught Ben's eye, and he paused to look at it. Large, somewhat uneven lettering proclaimed Tanakir the Mighty. Tanakir's painted portrait showed him expanding biceps and chest to break great iron chains that might have held a drawbridge.

Ben delayed only for a moment to look at this. Then, with a strange feeling inside his own chest, he went on to Barbara's recognizable small tent. As usual she had the tent set up beside her wagon. If she was keeping a small caged dragon inside her conveyance as usual, it was hidden by cloth coverings, and made no sound at Ben's approach.

The flap of her tent was closed, but Ben could see that it was not tied shut. Ben threw down the wooden staff that the peddler had given him. Then, obeying the traditional rules of courtesy, he cleared his throat and scratched on the tent wall near the flap—there was of course no way to knock. He waited a few decent seconds then, and when there was no response he lifted the fabric gently and stepped in.

At a small table near the center of the tent sat Barbara, wrapped in the shabby familiar robe that she often wore around camp. Despite the poor light in the tent she was trying to do something to prettify her fingernails. She looked up sharply at the intrusion, her small, spare body coiled like a spring. Between the two black sheaves of her hair, her round, expressive face showed anger, even before she had time to recognize Ben and be surprised—she had been keeping her anger ready, he thought, for someone else.

"You've got a look in your eye, Ben." That was how she greeted him after a year's absence, uncoiling the spring of her body slightly. Barbara was very nearly the same age as Ben, though not much more than a third his weight. They had known each other for a number of years. He saw now that her straight black hair had been allowed to grow a little longer since he'd left. Otherwise she looked just about the same. She went on: "Fuzz on your chin and a look in your eye. What are you up to now? I don't suppose you rode back here in a golden coach pulled by six white showbeasts?"

"Thinking," he replied, choosing to answer the one halfway sensible question in her speech, letting the rest of it go by. It was a way he had. He thought it was one of the things that she did like about him.

"Thinking about what?"

"About certain things that I've found out." Ben slid off his peddler's pack, looked about for a place to put it, then dropped it on the floor and kicked it under the small table, conserving floor space.

"It sounds like you've managed to addle your mind somehow, whatever else you've done. I suppose you're hungry?" Barbara gave up the pretense of continuing to fuss with her nails. She turned to give him her full attention and frank interest.

Ben crouched and reached under the table to get something from his pack. His hand rejected a half-loaf of bread that was going stale, and pulled out some good sausage. "Not really. I have this, if you'd like some."

"Maybe later, thanks. Did you go to the Blue Temple and enlist, as you were saying you'd do?"

"Didn't you get either of my letters?"

"No."

That was hardly surprising, Ben supposed. "Well, I wrote twice. And

I did enlist." He took a bite off the end of the sausage himself, and offered it again. "Ever hear from Mark?"

"Not since he left." This time Barbara was not so reluctant. Chewing, she regarded Ben for a little while in silence, while he stood there unable to keep himself from smiling at her. He could, as always, see thoughts coming and going in her face, though he was hardly ever sure of what they were. It sounded simple, but it was one of the things about her that gave Ben a sensation of enchantment.

At last Barbara said to him: "There's more on your mind than Mark, or bringing me sausage. I suppose you've deserted. Is that the big secret I can see in the back of your eyes? A Blue Temple enlistment should run for four or five years, shouldn't it?"

Ben's eye had caught sight of his old lute. It was hanging in a prominent place, tied high up on the tent's central pole. Seeing the instrument so honored gave him a good feeling, and seeing it also brought back memories. Ben reached up and took it down.

"I've kept it as a decoration, like."

He strummed the instrument, but only briefly and softly. He could see at once that the strings were in bad shape. It seemed too that his hands were well on the way to losing entirely whatever poor skill they'd once possessed. For years, for most of his life, Ben had nursed deep, fervent dreams of being a musician. His broad mouth twisted now, under his new beard, remembering that.

Now that he had some form of music in his hands, the tune that had been haunting him ever since that night of treasure and terror and flight came back irresistibly. In his mind the music ran sweet and clear—all tunes ran that way for him, in his mind. It was only when he tried to get them to come out properly through his fingers or his voice that his difficulties started.

He sang the old tune now, very softly and almost to himself, in a voice that sounded as inadequate as he had feared it would:

> Benambra's gold
> Doth glitter coldly . . .

"Gods and demons, what a noise!" judged the harsh bass voice of someone standing just outside the tent. A moment later the entrance flap was whipped aside, this time by no gentle hand. The man who had to bow his head to enter seemed to fill up what little space Ben's presence had left in the small interior.

The newcomer could be no one but Tanakir the Mighty, though perhaps he did not quite do justice to his portrait on the wagon's side. Well, thought Ben, no human figure could do that. Tanakir was almost a head taller than Ben, and his upper body proportionately broad. His shirt, a garment undoubtedly once expensive though now badly faded, was worn halfway open to reveal the carven plates of muscle on his chest. His biceps were more than simply large, and as he came into the tent his movements were ponderous, as if slowed down by equal weights of muscle and of vanity. At second glance he was a considerably older man than Ben. There were a few gray hairs showing in his long dark braids.

Once inside, Tanakir paused, fists on hips in a pose that might well be some part of his act. He glared at the two other people in the tent as if he were demanding an explanation from them.

"We have a strongman now," said Barbara in conversational tones to Ben. "You never wanted that job while you were here."

Tanakir from his greater height glowered down at Ben, who stood with lute in hand, blinking back at him. "So, this is Ben," the strongman rumbled. "He didn't *want* the job? Him? This chubby minstrel?"

Ben turned a little away, to hang up the lute again carefully, high up on the central pole, out of head-knocking range. It was one of the few times in his life that anyone had ever called him a minstrel, and he felt unreasonably pleased.

Tanakir told him: "You're leaving very soon."

Ben blinked at him again, then backed up carefully and sat down on a small chest, which creaked a little with the burden. He sat in a position that left his hands and feet ready if they should be needed. "I haven't decided about that yet."

"I'm deciding for you."

"All right," said Ben mildly. He allowed the other just a beat in which to begin triumphant relaxation, before he added, "One of us leaves tonight, if you feel that way. Well, maybe in the morning. No one wants to start out on the road at night."

Ben paused briefly, then suggested: "Arm-wrestle for it?" It was impossible not to notice how the other's god-like arms had been circled with bands and bracelets to make them look still thicker, and what pains had been taken with short, tattered sleeves, that they might be best revealed. Ben's own arms, if they had not been hidden in his long pilgrim's sleeves, would by comparison have looked almost as chubby as they did strong.

Tanakir, after having been kept mentally off-balance for a few moments, now looked pleased. All strongmen, thought Ben, are certainly not bright. And this particular one must be a chronic pain to have around.

"Arm-wrestle," Tanakir repeated, nodding. "All right, we'll do that. Yeah."

Barbara, who knew them both, must also have been pleased by Ben's suggestion, for she made no objection to it. When Ben saw this his heart dared to rise again. He smiled at Barbara as she moved quickly to clear the little table for their contest, and he got the briefest of smiles from her in return.

Before the contest could get started there was an outburst of whispering from outside the tent. First, it sounded like some conspiratorial meeting getting too loud; and then, suddenly, like they were greeting someone in surprise.

Then imperturbable old Viktor, who by consent and diplomacy ran the carnival, put his head into the tent. There was an uncommon smile on his face. Ben understood the smile when, a moment later, the head of a much taller and younger man appeared above Viktor's, grinning.

Still it took Ben a moment to make the recognition. He jumped to his feet then, and cried out: "Mark!" It had been two years. Ben would have moved forward, but Barbara was in his way. She had already darted to the doorway to give the tall young man a great hug and kiss.

Tanakir was upset all over again. "What is this?" he roared at them. "Come on, arm-wrestle, or just get out."

Barbara turned to him. "Don't be so eager; you've never managed to out-wrestle *me*." She turned back to Mark. "Look at you, you're taller than Ben."

"I was that when I left. Or very nearly."

"And just as strong—"

Mark had to grin at that.

"Come on!" This was Tanakir again. "Whoever that clown is, he can wait his turn."

So the rest of the reunion had to be postponed. Old Viktor, as usual, kept things moving with a few diplomatic words and gestures. Mark remained in the background, smiling. Viktor, having greeted Ben, nodded sagely when he saw what was developing in Barbara's tent. Then he sent one of his wives on an errand, while he himself stood by, authoritatively twirling his gray mustache.

The wife was back promptly, bringing two stubs of candles into the darkening tent, along with a burning twig to light them. Ben noticed with irrational relief that the candles were not blue beneath their golden tongues of flame. They were set burning on the small table to the right and left of the two contestants.

Barbara gave up her single folding chair to Tanakir. It creaked impressively when he sat down. Ben hitched the little chest around and sat on it, so that he faced his opponent across the table. He noted that Barbara and Mark together were now finishing off his sausage. Fortunately he, Ben, had not arrived weak with hunger. Mark looked good—but there was something that had to be taken care of first, before he could enjoy the company of friends.

The two big men sat facing each other, their noses a meter apart. The carnival strongman made a show of getting ready, rolling up his right sleeve a trifle more. He managed to ripple the muscles of his arm impressively as he did so.

"Don't fear the flame," said Tanakir, leaning forward to put his elbow on the table. Ben's elbow was already there. The strongman's fierce scowl emanated onions. "I'll not burn you very much. Cry out once and I'll let you go."

"Don't fear the flame," returned Ben, "for I'll not burn you at all." And he reached forward, ready to meet the all-out surge of strength that the other was certain to apply as soon as he could grab Ben's hand.

"Get him, Ben!" called Mark.

Their grips locked in the surge, the table quaked beneath their elbows.

And Barbara, with a greater urgency in her voice than merely friendship: "Win, Ben! Win!"

Tanakir cried out, but not with victory, nor yet with candle-burn. The back of his hand descending had snuffed the flame before the heat could even scorch the hairs. Snuffed out the flame, and thudded on to squash the wax below.

CHAPTER 4

The small man rode the once-paved road upon a fine but almost starving riding beast, and wore at his side a poor scabbard that had the hilt of a fine sword protruding from it. Some things about this man, including his long, carefully trained black mustache, suggested that he might be castle-born. But most of his clothing, and certain other indications, argued for a more humble origin. He was bareheaded, and under the shock of wild black hair his lean, elegant face was grim. He was mumbling to himself as he rode slowly through the warm spring sunshine.

Two more men, on foot, were following the mumbling rider across the grimly peaceful countryside, past abandoned farmsteads and untilled fields. And several paces behind those two shuffled along a lad not quite full grown, though already tall. On the right shoulder of this youth there rode a hooded shape, that under its covering of green cloth had to be that of some trained flying creature, bird or reptile perhaps.

Taken as a group, the four men looked like the token representation on a stage of some defeated army. But the only thing their various costumes had in common was the look of wear and poverty; if this was truly an army, it had no other uniform.

Of the two who were walking together, one carried a battle-hatchet in a kind of holster at his belt, and had a bow slung on his back. His taller companion wore a sword on one side of his own belt, with a sling and stone-pouch on the other. The visible hilt of this man's sword, in contrast to their leader's, was dull and cracked.

The surface of the road they traveled had once been paved and cared for, though like most of its users it was now experiencing hard times. And the land through which the road passed looked as if it might once have been well tended. A feral milkbeast, lean and scarred, stared at the procession as if it might never have seen men before, then leaped a broken fence to bolt into a thicket. The man with the bow, hunger starting in his eyes, made the start of a motion to get the weapon off his back, but gave up before completing it. The beast was already out of sight.

The leader appeared to be paying very little heed to any of this. He continued to mouth words to himself as he rode on, eyes fixed ahead. One of the two men following, he who had the bow, was more concerned than the other by this circumstance. He now nudged his taller companion, and signaled that they should lag back a few more steps behind their leader.

As soon as the gap between the two men and the rider had widened enough to give them good prospects for some privacy, the shorter man whispered: "Why does he mutter so?"

The taller man who wore the battered sword had a long face with an habitually grave expression, that made him look like a solemn servant dressed up as a soldier. And he answered gravely: "I think his woes have driven him half mad."

"Ha. Woes? If that would do it, we'd all be jabbering and snarling as we moved about. I wonder now . . ."

"What?"

"I wonder if I decided wisely, yesterday, when I chose to follow him." The shorter man, whose name was Hubert, paused at that point, as if expecting to receive some comment from his companion. When none was immediately forthcoming, he went on. "He spoke me fair enough—well, you were there, you heard. I've yet to hear, though, just what enterprise he plans to use us in. And you say he's not told you, either. Well, at first I thought there was no need to ask. There's little business of any kind to be transacted on these roads, except for robbery.

I've not done that before, but I was hungry enough to try anything . . . and there *you* were, looking sane and tolerably well fed, following him already. You looked as if you might know where you were going. And now you tell me he's half mad."

"Sh!"

"You said it first."

"But not so loud." The taller, grave-faced man, whose name was Pu Chou, appeared for a moment to be annoyed. Then he answered thoughtfully: "I followed him because, as you say, he spoke fair. He's fed me, so far. Not a lot, but better than nothing. And he did promise when I joined him that we were going to find wealth."

Hubert said, flatly: "Wealth. And you believed him."

"You said you believed him, when he spoke to you. He can speak convincingly."

"Aye. Well, we've passed travelers who I thought looked like easy game, and not tried to rob them. He must have some other means of gaining wealth in mind. Well, that sword he's got is certainly worth a coin or two, even if the sheath is poor."

Pu Chou was quietly alarmed. "Don't even think of taking it from him. I've seen him use it once."

"Once? He hauls it out at every crossroad. There's some fine charm of magic in it, or at least he thinks there is, for he consults it to choose his way. Whether it works or not—"

"I meant I've seen him use it as a sword. When I was his only follower, and still unarmed myself. Three bandits thought they wanted it. One of them got away. It's one of the others' sword I'm wearing now."

"Oh."

And for some time after that the little procession trudged on in silence. Hubert glanced back once at the lad who was still bringing up the rear, probably too far back to have overheard the whispered conversation. The name of this youth was Golok, and Hubert had rarely heard him speak at all. Instead he appeared to spend most of his life staring straight ahead as if in abstract thought. Whatever the creature was on his shoulder—Hubert had not yet gotten a good look at it without its cover—it was as quiet as if it were asleep, or perhaps dead and stuffed. Hubert had learned from Pu Chou yesterday that Golok had once been apprentice to the Master of the Beasts at some important castle; some kind of a problem had arisen, and he had had to leave. Whether he was the true owner of the thing that perched on his shoulder now was a question that had not been raised. Hubert had no urge to press for details in the lives of these his new companions, even as he was content for his own history to remain unknown to them.

Now Hubert turned his eyes ahead again. The sky in that direction was darkening, he observed, as if a storm were coming. Especially ahead and off there to the right.

Of more immediate interest was something that now lay only a few strides ahead, namely yet another crossroads. Here the disintegrating pavement of what had once been a king's way intersected another and more common road. This was of hard-packed earth and gravel, and it wound away to left and right amidst the gentle rolling of the land. Like most roads in this time of failing commerce, it was beginning to be overgrown by weeds and grass.

To the left, this intersecting thoroughfare led off into a near-monotony of gradually improving fields. It was possible to see for several kilometers in that direction, and in the distance intact houses and barns were visible, as well as small groups of laborers in those far fields. Maybe, thought Hubert, they had now come to the edge of the Margrave's well-protected lands. That suggested to Hubert that they might expect to encounter some of the Margrave's soldiers shortly, and that in turn suggested to him that perhaps this would be a good point to turn back. But then, he was not the leader.

To the right conditions were different. In that direction the simple crossroad soon became a dismal, muddy, heavily rutted way, almost a sunken road. It lost its way among leafless thickets, and clumps of inordinately tall thistles, that seemed to have grown where they were for no other purpose than to provide some ideal sites for ambush. A chill wind drifted down on the travelers from that direction, where, as Hubert had noted earlier, the sky was growing dark. On the horizon to the right the clouds were really ominous.

The leader had reined in his steed at the very center of the crossroads. Hubert had expected him to draw his fine sword, as usual, as soon as the intersection was reached. But the horseman had not done so yet. He was looking from right to left, and back again, as if considering. At last his mumbled monologue had ceased.

Tall Pu Chou, shading his eyes from local sunshine, was squinting off into forbidding shadows to the right. "What's that, I wonder? I can make out a certain tall structure, almost half a kilometer off. Just at the edge of those trees, beside the road."

The youth Golok had come up close to the others now, and it was his surprisingly deep voice that next broke the silence. "That's a gallows," he intoned.

The mounted leader looked at him, and made a brisk gesture with one hand. Obediently Golok reached up and whisked off the cloth covering the creature that rode his shoulder. It's a monkbird, thought Hubert, moderately surprised. He himself was no expert at handling beasts, but it was his understanding that the small flying mammals were notoriously hard to train, and that few beast-handlers would attempt it. Golok crooned low orders to the beast, as its eyes blinked yellow against dark brown fur. Hubert noticed suddenly how handlike the tiny feet of the creature were, at the ends of its hind limbs.

"Go, Dart, fly," Golok whispered. His voice when he spoke to the animal was much changed.

In a moment the monkbird had risen into the air from its master's shoulder. It flew in a low circle on membranous wings, as if orienting itself. Then it flapped softly off to the right, following a course above the road that led to darkness.

The mounted leader sat motionless in his saddle, gazing after the winged scout, long after distance and shadows had taken the monkbird out of Hubert's effective range of vision. The leader's hand was resting on the black hilt of his fine sword. As if, Hubert thought, he knew that he was going to have to draw it soon, but wished to postpone that act as long as possible.

And now the leader spoke again. He was still talking to himself, but this time Hubert was close enough to hear some of the words. ". . . cursed poverty . . . more real than many another curse. Whether some wizard has fastened it upon me, or . . ."

The monkbird's reconnaissance did not take very long. It reappeared in the shadowy distance and drew closer, until with a final flourish of the forelimbs that unfurled its wings it sat again on Golok's shoulder. Then it shivered slightly, as if it might have experienced a chill under that dark portion of the sky.

"Man on tree?" Golok asked it, evidently confident that it would understand the question.

"Two-leg fruit," the monkbird answered, the first intelligible sounds that Hubert had heard from it. Its voice was tiny but piercing in tone.

"Two-leg is living?" Golok questioned.

"No." It was the single, sharp note of a birdcall.

At this, the mounted leader, with one final muttered comment to himself, drew out his sword, wrenching it from the scabbard with a violent motion and holding it aloft. As Hubert had observed before, when that sword cleared its sheath it negated all the poverty in the appearance of the man who held it. The blade, a full, perfect meter in length, was moderately wide, incredibly straight and sharp. A mottled pattern on the flat side seemed to exist just beneath the perfect polish of the surface, and appeared to extend into the metal, to a depth greater than the blade was thick. The hilt was rich and rough in texture, of lustrous black, with some small design worked on it in white. Earlier Hubert had been able to read this design as the symbol of a small white arrow, point aimed upward toward the pommel.

The lean right arm of the mounted man held out the weighty sword without a quiver. The blade was extended in turn to each of the four roads leading from the intersection. When the point was aimed along the rutty road in the direction of the gallows, Hubert thought that he could see the blade-tip quivering, as if after all there might be a trace of weakness in that determined arm.

"This way," the leader ordered. And his voice was no more unsteady than was the single ringing snap with which he sheathed his blade.

He rode along the rutted way toward that darkened sky, no faster and no slower than before. This time, the two soldiers and the youth all followed closely. And in silence. Their surroundings, once they had turned at the crossroads, were not conducive to unnecessary talk.

A daylight owl fled through a roadside thicket, as if it were horrified at something it had found within. The road here took a winding course among the ugly thickets, making it impossible for the traveler to see more than a few meters ahead at any point. The gallows—if that was what it was—had disappeared from sight for the time being. But it was waiting for them, thought Hubert, up ahead.

When at last the tall skeletal structure came into view again, there was no doubt of what it was. The rude scaffolding had room for three or four victims, but there was only one in residence, though the frayed ends of other ropes indicated that once he had enjoyed company.

One lone, attenuated human shape hung from the weathered cross-tree. From the half-face that remained, a single empty eyesocket looked down upon the travelers, and seemed sardonically to mark their progress. Hubert could not keep from looking up at it several times, though their march did not pause as it went by. At last the windings of the road took the gallows out of sight behind a screen of barren trees. All the plants here were oddly leafless, Hubert suddenly realized, though spring was well advanced.

Still the mounted leader rode on in silence, concentrating his attention on the road ahead and the surrounding woods and thickets. Even leafless as it was, the growth beside the road still seemed to promise ambush. No birds sang. A hush held, as if some enemy already lay in wait, and had only a moment ago fallen silent in anticipation. At intervals the leader, as he rode, put hand to sword once more. But he did not draw. His fingers rested carefully, almost caressingly on that black hilt, then slid away again.

When they were a few hundred meters past the gallows, he sighed gently, and appeared to come to the conclusion that any immediate challenge from the roadside was unlikely. He relaxed a trifle in the saddle, and, while still keeping an alert eye on his surroundings, rode forward a trifle faster and more boldly.

Hubert, reassured by this sight, and growing ever more conscious of his rumbling stomach, speeded up the pace of his own feet somewhat until he drew close to the rider's stirrup. Then, when the way ahead appeared to be clear for a little way at least, Hubert dared to speak. "Sir? Will the blade show us where we can find some food? I'm empty, pack and belly both."

There was no immediate response. At least there had not been, as Hubert had half-feared there would, a flash of rage.

Encouraged, Hubert tried again. "Baron Doon? Sir?"

The rider did not turn his head by so much as a centimeter, but this time he answered. "If food were what I wanted," grated the low voice from between his teeth, "what I, the owner and master of this Sword, desired more than anything else in the sweet universe, then Wayfinder would guide us to as great a feast as I desired. But since food is not what I crave at this moment, it does not. Now keep quiet, and follow me alertly. Safety is not what I am looking for either."

Wayfinder, thought Hubert to himself. Wayfinder. I've heard some story about that, some tale of magic Swords. . . . But, having been ordered to keep quiet, he kept quiet.

The four men continued to move forward—again, more slowly, for now the riding beast, well-trained though it was, was giving signs of reluctance to proceed any farther along this road. At a sign from Baron Doon, Golok unhooded his monkbird again, though for the time being he kept it on his shoulder.

The road continued a progressive deterioration, till now it was doubtful whether it deserved that name at all. And now, as if capriciously, it branched again. Again it was the right-hand fork that bore the most unfavorable aspect, even though the left appeared to lead into nothing better than another nasty thicket, this one so overgrown as to almost swallow up the track entirely.

Still there was no doubt that the right-hand way looked worse. Even though—and here Hubert rubbed at his eyes, blinked, and looked again —even though it did appear to lead to a house. Yes, there was an abandoned dwelling down there, right on the edge of an encroaching swamp. It was a large house, or rather it looked as if it might have been large before portions of it had suffered a collapse. The swamp, thought Hubert, had probably begun to undermine it from the rear.

The surviving portion had been sturdily built of timber and of stone, the masonry discolored and weakened now. There might be, Hubert supposed, three or four rooms still standing roofed and usable, counting the fragment of an upper story that remained. Usable, that is, if the whole thing did not collapse the first time someone walked into it.

The road to the right did not go past the house, but terminated at it, or, more precisely, at a narrow bridge a few meters from the wooden door. The rickety, unsafe-looking bridge spanned a noisome ditch formed by an advanced arm of the swamp. The bridge was fashioned of two thin, round logs, slippery-looking with damp and moss. There was a sketch of a railing on one side, and crosswise between the logs a scattering of short boards for footing. Some of these floorboards already hung down broken.

Again Baron Doon had recourse to his Sword. This time, Hubert observed with a fatalistic lack of surprise, the blade quivered only when its owner pointed it in the direction of the house.

This time Doon did not sheath the blade, using it instead to gesture to Golok. Then he went back to watching the house intently.

Again the flying mammal, after a low-crooning conference with its master, took to its dark, membranous wings. It circled the house first. Then it hovered briefly in front of one shadowed window, but balked at entering that dark, blank space. In another moment it had returned to its master's shoulder, where it sat shivering. When Golok spoke to it this time, it would not answer.

Doon, drawn blade still in hand, dismounted. Then silently, leading his mount behind him, he approached the bridge. The riding beast allowed itself to be led, though unwillingly, its hide quivering with its high-strung nerves. Hubert saw how its feet curved, the hard footpads trying to grip the slippery logs of the bridge where the crossboards were missing.

The others were all hesitating. Hubert swallowed, and crossed second. Once he made up his mind to follow and serve a leader, he'd serve and follow him. Until the time came when he decided to quit altogether. Provided, of course, that when the time came he was still able. . . .

Firmly he banished thoughts like that. Become a coward, and the world was through with you for good. The bridge under his feet felt more solid than it looked.

Once across the bridge, Hubert shot one glance behind him, and saw that the other two were starting over. He could not help seeing, also, that the world back there, the distant parts of it at least, looked infinitely inviting. Yonder in the background a clear sky spanned fair, green hills, and happy fields. . . .

Such pleasant things were not for the highwayman-adventurer. Hubert turned his back on them. Now the frowning, vacant windows of the house were scant meters in front of him. They reminded him uncomfortably of the empty eyesocket that had seemed to watch him, only a little while ago.

As soon as Golok, the last man, was across the bridge, Doon gestured to him again. In obedience Golok again sent the monkbird forward. But again it refused to enter any of those dark apertures, darker than windows ought to be even on such a gloomy day.

The Sword in Doon's hand quivered, lightly and insistently. It was guiding them toward the single broad door that was set in the front of the building at ground level. Doon led his mount right up to the door, and rapped on the panels with Wayfinder's hilt. Then he tugged to open it. It proved not to be locked, but only stuck; noisily it yielded at last.

The interior revealed was not as dark as the upstairs behind those windows. Hubert, looking past his leader, could make out a passageway, surprisingly deep and broad. And at the end of the passage—could that be some kind of an interior courtyard? Somehow, the closer Hubert approached to the building, the larger it became to his eyes. Yet he was never at any point conscious of observing any unnatural change.

Hubert would have liked to delay the others, to talk over with them in whispers this fact and its implications. But Doon was already leading them forward, into the house. The passage was too low for a mounted man to ride through it comfortably, and he continued to tug his animal after him.

Once Hubert had gotten well inside, he blinked his eyes again. Why, he thought, again it's grown bigger. The passageway, its sides doorless and windowless, went straight on for six or eight meters; and the interior court when they reached it was ten meters square, surrounded by two-story building on all sides. Four doors, one in each wall, were at ground level. Only the door by which they were entering the courtyard stood open. More dark windows showed in the walls.

"Magic," breathed Golok in the rear. He was following Hubert and Pu Chou closely now, as if he feared to get very far from the armed men. His word said no more than they had all already realized. This courtyard, now that they were standing in it, was certainly bigger than the whole house had looked when they had first seen it from the road. There were cloisters cracking into disrepair, and a dry, cracked fountain. There were a couple of long-dead trees, and in the tile paving blank clay places that might once have been meant for flowerbeds. Most of the paving was covered with years of blown-in dead leaves and dirt.

Golok drew in his breath with a sharp sound. The door just opposite that they had entered by was slowly creaking open. In a moment a huge, black-furred, two-legged shape had appeared in the doorway. The figure slouched there, almost of human shape, though it looked inhumanly broad and strong. Bright eyes, of a different blackness than its fur, glittered at the intruders, and white teeth showed sharp in a black mouth.

It was—at least, perhaps it was—no more than a beast, and they were four men armed and ready. Yet three of the four men started back.

Doon had already swung himself back up into his saddle, from which vantage point he now confronted the creature with drawn sword. His mount, as if it were relieved to at last face something in the way of concrete danger, snorted but held steady.

Doon cried, to the ebon beast: "Be warned, if ye have power of understanding! I am not here to be entertained by bogey-games. Nor will I be sent hence without that which I need. Be warned also, that this blade when in my hand is doubly magic!"

The monstrous ape retreated. Hubert could not tell quite how it managed the maneuver, only that one moment the midnight bulk still filled the doorway, and the next moment it was gone.

There was a faint sound from the closed door to the right. As one, the men spun in that direction, to watch that broad door creaking open . . .

. . . pushed by a skeletal hand. The hanged man from the gallows was standing just inside it. Hubert could not be mistaken about that face.

Pu Chou uttered a sound that could not be described as speech. But

Doon, wheeling his mount, faced this apparition as coolly as he had the other. As if addressing the same entity, he went on speaking. "I tell you, trickery will not move me, nor will threats. Now do you mean to fight me, or listen to me?"

Again, the thing that he confronted disappeared.

All four men were now turning about, twisting their necks, trying to keep all four doorways under observation at the same time. None of them were taken by surprise by the next appearance, in the doorway that had so far remained unoccupied. The tall, richly robed figure that stood there now was that of an old man, gray but sturdy. His massive bald crown was surrounded by a long gray fringe that matched his beard. Great blue eyes, with something in them as innocent as infancy, looked out from under white bushy brows.

Facing Doon, this man asked in a low, impressive voice: "What seek you here?"

Doon lowered his Sword slowly. He started to speak, then looked down at his mount. The riding beast had suddenly relaxed.

And now the Baron heaved a great sigh, as if he too felt finally able to allow himself the luxury of weariness. When he spoke, his voice was no longer as taut as a drawn bowstring. "What I seek is simply wealth. No, not yours; I suppose your treasure might be considerable, but even so it won't be enough for me, and I don't purpose to take it. I believe that the treasure I want is elsewhere. But for some reason the pathway to it leads through your door."

Now Doon's riding beast had suddenly turned its long, gaunt neck aside, and was beginning to graze on something near the ground. Hubert, with a sensation of blurred eyes, saw that the flowerbeds were still active after all, indeed that they were richly grown with leaves and blossoms. There was a splash from the fountain, where moments ago he had seen a cracked and dusty basin. Doon turned his head in mild bewilderment at this new sound, then shrugged and dismounted, letting his animal graze. But he retained his Sword in his right hand.

When a shadow wavered across Hubert's vision, he looked up to see that a bright sun in a clear sky had been intercepted by a full-leaved branch of a tree that was after all not dead.

The tall old man in the doorway was asking: "What is your name?"

"I am the Baron Doon." The words were a quiet distillation of pride.

The old man nodded. "And I am known, for the present, as Indosuaros. Do you need to ask my profession?"

"No, I think not."

"Nor I yours. Well." A songbird twittered in one of the trees, and the monkbird, Dart, on Golok's shoulder replied in happy mockery. Indosuaros added: "I am pleased to offer you and your men my hospitality. Though, as you have doubtless deduced by now, my usual habit is to discourage visitors."

Doon needed only a moment to think about it. "And we are pleased to accept, with thanks." He sheathed his Sword.

Now Hubert was aware that the house around them was altering even more swiftly than before. Dust and dead leaves had disappeared from the courtyard, as had the cracks from the cloisters and the walls. Beside the burbling fountain a table had materialized, flanked by benches and chairs and covered in snowy linen. Hubert could half-see moving forms, whether human or not he could not tell, moving through the air around the table, juggling plates, setting and arranging. The air held a sudden and delicious smell of food, subtle, yet almost staggering to the hungry senses. And, for one breath-catching moment, Hubert was sure that he beheld the delicate shape of a young servant girl, seductively clad. A moment later, only immaterial powers swirled the air where she had been.

An elderly serving man, whose drab shape seemed real and solid enough, had emerged from the house to stand with bowed head at the side of Indosuaros. The tall wizard conferred with him in whispers, then made a gesture of dismissal. Now the benches that had been placed beside the table were whisked away, to be replaced presently by carven chairs. Dishes and platters of substantial food began to appear, and flagons of wine. The settings were enhanced by cutlery and goblets of precious stone.

"Pray be seated," said Indosuaros courteously. "All of you."

"One moment, if you please," said Doon, equally polite. With a nod to the wizard—it was a gesture, Hubert thought, that did not quite ask permission—the Baron drew his magic blade and consulted it again. It pointed him directly to a chair. He took it. At his gesture, the other men moved to seat themselves, with little ceremony.

Indosuaros took his place at the table's head, in a chair whose carven serpents, Hubert thought, could be seen from time to time to move. The wizard lounged there, nibbling at a few grapes from the banquet, watching indolently while his guests satisfied their thirst and hunger. Delightful soft music could now be heard, from somewhere in the background. The courtyard was now certainly a pleasant place, with the trees placed just right to shade the table.

Doon scarcely relaxed. In businesslike fashion he polished off a plate of food, and a single cup of wine, then signified politely that he had finished eating. Again the form of the serving girl was suggested in the air, and plates began to vanish selectively. Doon scarcely glanced at her. He was watching his host carefully.

Indosuaros helped himself to one more grape. Then he leaned toward his principal guest, and in a low and pleasant voice began what amounted to a blunt interrogation.

"We all want gold, don't we? But what makes you think that, as you put it, your road to wealth leads through my door? Speak plainly, please —as I believe you have, so far."

"Why, I intend to do so," Doon answered calmly. "But first, my thanks again for this excellent refreshment."

"You are welcome. By the way, I am curious, Baron. You ate and drank with no sign of hesitancy or suspicion. Did it never cross your mind, even as a possibility, that . . . ?"

Hubert, who had just mopped up some delicious gravy with a morsel of soft white bread, experienced a momentary difficulty in swallowing.

But the Baron only laughed. It seemed almost too big a sound to come out of his small frame. "Sir Wizard, ordinarily, of course, if some-one of your obvious skill were minded to do me harm with poison, I'd have little hope of avoiding it. But my Sword has led me to your table, and I trust it to lead me well."

"Your sword, you say." The old man sounded skeptical.

"Indosuaros, if you can read the page of magic a tenth as well as I believe you can, you already know which Sword it is I wear. Wayfinder. The Sword of Wisdom. Forged, along with its eleven fellows, by none less than the god Vulcan himself."

Hubert forgot about swallowing altogether.

Doon had pushed his chair back a few centimeters. He had both hands resting on the table's edge, and looked ready to push himself back farther and leap up. "God-forged, it is. And not even your powers, Sir Wizard, I think, are able to turn it away from true service to its owner. No magic that mere humans can control can do so."

"And it leads you where you command it?"

"Where my wishes command it. Aye. On to wealth."

"And it makes you immune to death?"

"No. Oh no. I have not commanded it to seek my safety. But, you see, if you had been trying to poison me, that would have been certain death, and certainly not wealth. No, the Sword of Wisdom would not have led me into that."

The old wizard appeared to be giving all of this the deepest thought. "I admit," he said at last, softly, "that I recognized Wayfinder very quickly. But I was not sure at first that you knew what you were carrying. . . . However, Sir Baron, toward what sort of wealth do you think the Sword of Wisdom is leading you?"

"Why, no less wealth," said Doon, "than the greatest in the world. I speak of the main hoard of the Blue Temple itself. And you may be sure, Sir Wizard, that I know what sort of an idea I am carrying when I speak of that."

Hubert could behold his own amazement mirrored in Pu Chou's face, and in Golok's. *Rob the Blue Temple? Impossible!* was his own first reaction, held in silence. On second thought he had to admit that to a master who could hold his own amid all this enchantment, and sit bargaining calmly with its creator, anything in the world might well be possible.

". . . so you," Doon was saying to the wizard, "ought to have no objection to my plan. If you'll provide me with whatever it is the Sword has brought me here to find, why then I'll be pleased to share the treasure with you. Or help you in whatever other way I can."

"And if I do not," asked the wizard softly, "choose to provide you with this help?"

Doon considered this, drumming his fingers on the table, as if such an idea had never crossed his mind before. "Then, by all the gods," he said at last, "I'll find some way to hinder you."

Hubert, listening to the steady voice, thought that he had never heard a more truly impressive threat.

The old man at the head of the table was silent for a little time, as if he too might have been impressed. Then he gestured with one large, gnarled hand, its fingers heavy with ornate rings, and Hubert watching felt a pang of apprehension. But the gesture evoked nothing stranger than the old manservant, to hold another whispered conversation with his master. And now the clearing of the table proceeded more rapidly.

Hitching his chair a little closer to the table, the wizard said to the baron: "Let us talk. When you say you mean to rob the Blue Temple, I gather that you mean to despoil it in no trivial way."

"I have spoken plainly, as you wished."

"Indeed . . . you don't mean, I suppose, one of those little vaults, that all local Blue Temples have, for the day-to-day business—"

"I've told you what I mean, wizard, as plainly as I know how. And I understand what I am talking about."

"Indeed." Still looking doubtful, Indosuaros lounged back in his chair again. "Well, I can only say that, coming from anyone less well-equipped and less determined than yourself, such an announcement would deserve derision."

"But coming from me," Doon answered calmly, "the announcement is to be taken very seriously. I am glad you have been so quick to grasp that essential point."

"I think I have. But let me restate it just once more, so there can be no ambiguity. You intend to carry off some substantial portion of Benambra's Gold."

"A substantial portion," Doon agreed, nodding affably. "Yes, that's well put. I'd try to take it all, you see, if I thought there was any chance that my men and I could carry it."

"And do you know," asked Indosuaros, "where Benambra's Gold is kept?"

"Wayfinder is going to lead me to it," Doon answered simply. "And now you know the bare bones of my plan. Before I go into any greater detail, let me know whether you object to it."

The grizzled manservant was still standing close by his master's chair, and the two of them now exchanged a glance. In a moment the old wizard began to make a peculiar noise, and perform little lurching motions in his chair. It took Hubert a little while to realize that their host was laughing.

At last Indosuaros said: "I? Object to the Blue Temple's being robbed?" And he laughed again, and waved a hand about him in a gesture that seemed to take in his whole establishment. "I have secluded myself like this from the world for one reason only: that I may devise the most terrible vengeance possible upon the Blue Temple and all its leaders. For the past . . . for never mind how many years, I have devoted all my energies to that one object. And what worse vengeance could there be, upon *them,* than to rob them of what they hold dearer than life itself . . . hey, Mitspieler? Are we going to throw open those vaults of theirs or not?" And with a gesture that looked somehow out of character, he thumped his manservant awkwardly on the arm.

The servant called Mitspieler looked, if not quite as old as his master, somewhat more worn. His was a workman's face, beardless and lined. His stature was fairly small, his build sturdy, his arms emerging wiry and corded from short sleeves. His hair, short, curly, and dark, was richly mixed with gray.

His dark eyes gazed off into the distance as he answered. "In those vaults lies treasure, truly beyond price and beyond compare . . . aye, we can open them. When we are ready. We have been waiting for the help we need."

"And I have woven spells," said Indosuaros, "that the needed help might be brought to me, for until it was, a robbery on the requisite scale seemed well-nigh impossible." He smiled at Doon. "And you still think that your coming here was a matter of your own choosing?"

"I have told you what it was—the Sword's guidance. But come, I'm interested. Just why are you devoting your life to getting back at the moneybags? Vengeance for what?"

"It is a long story."

"I'll hear one, if necessary."

"Later," said Indosuaros, vaguely. "Baron, will you draw your Sword once more if I request it? And hold it up for me to see?"

Doon pushed his chair back farther, and stood up, to make the motion easier. And yet once more he brought Wayfinder bright out of its sheath. The wizard now appeared to focus his full attention for the first time on the blade; and the servant standing beside his chair gazed at it too.

All the others were quietly intent, watching Indosuaros.

At last the old magician looked away, frowning lightly. "I will admit," he said, "that your Sword is genuine. Considerable power rests there in your hand."

"*Considerable?*" Doon came near to being outraged. "Is that the best word that you can find for it?"

Indosuaros was unruffled. "My own powers are also . . . considerable. And I tell you that they have been at work for a long time to solve the problems of attacking the Blue Temple. I have set them to bring— someone well qualified—perhaps you—here to help me. So, whether your presence here is actually due to the Sword, or—"

Doon brandished Wayfinder once, then clapped it back into its sheath, as if to save it from the gaze of disrespectful eyes. The Baron cried: "Forged by a god! By Vulcan himself!" It appeared that he could not credit the other's attitude. He seated himself again, banging his chair on the pavement.

"I have admitted that your Sword has worth." Indosuaros was looking at his guest more sternly now. "My chief question now is, what do you, yourself, bring to this enterprise? Apart, that is, from your indisputable greed, and courage—or perhaps foolhardiness. Are you the man whose help I need? I must seek an answer to this question in practical terms."

"Then seek it."

It was probably Hubert himself who unwittingly gave warning. Doon must have seen, mirrored in Hubert's face, that something untoward was developing behind the Baron's chair.

The door leading into that wall of the courtyard had swung open, to show blackness gathered behind it, an interior as dark as ever. And the ebony ape was there again, as silent as before. As soon as its eyes fell upon Doon, it came hurtling toward him from behind. The rush was swift and noiseless, and made with log-sized arms uplifted to seize the man or deal him a crushing blow.

Hubert was on his feet. But he knew he was too late, too slow, knew it even as he stood there with his own weapon but half-drawn, his chair still in the act of toppling behind him. Doon had meanwhile rolled sideways from his own chair, coming out of the movement somehow on his feet even as the great ape's fists crashed down to splinter his chair's back. Hubert had not seen Wayfinder drawn again, but now it flickered in its master's hand, the silver tongue of some swift serpent.

The ape turned with a roar, but not in time. Black fur gushing red that was not wine upon white linen, it sprawled forward among the remaining winecups. Gurgling its death, it slid off the table slowly, dragging cloth and cups to crash down with it.

Four men stood around the table armed, ready for the next threat—but there was none. One man sat smiling at the table's head. Nothing but approval glinted in the eye of Indosuaros.

Once more Doon waved the Sword. "I told you, wizard!" he roared in triumph. "I told you! In *my* hand, doubly magic!"

CHAPTER 5

The three of them, Mark, Ben, and Barbara, had been awake most of the night. They had been busy packing, swapping histories and stories, trading off to the other carnival people things that they weren't going to need. Then they had left the carnival at sunrise, driving in Barbara's wagon, one item she hadn't wanted to trade just yet. Tanakir had bartered them some food and a little coin for Barbara's little dragon and its cage, which he meant to incorporate into his own act. He was staying on with the carnival, seeing that she and her friends were leaving. Viktor waved goodbye to the three of them at dawn, and shouted his hope that they'd come back next season.

Mark doubted that very much. One way or another, he thought, they were sure to be somewhere else.

Purkinje Town and the carnival encampment were a couple of hours behind them now. The road ahead had already straightened out, entering a long rise of nearly flat and mostly empty country that mounted slowly toward distant mountains that were now only just visible. An hour ago they had paused for breakfast, and Mark, as in the old days, had used his bow to hunt down a couple of rabbits.

Now they were well under way again, heading south by mutual though still largely unspoken agreement. The decision had been arrived at in the camp, surrounded by eavesdroppers, and the reasons for going south had not been discussed as yet.

Ben was driving the wagon at the moment, and Barbara talking.

"Ben, you haven't told us what you're up to. You say you joined the Blue Temple, but you're not with 'em any more. All right, so you deserted. But you've got a look about you. What're you planning now?"

Ben smiled faintly. "I'm planning to marry you."

Barbara looked exasperated. "We went through all that before you left. Nothing's changed. When I marry somebody, it's going to have to mean that I can live like a real person somewhere. No more—" She waved a hand, vaguely indicating the wagon and the road.

"Fine with me," said Ben.

Her curiosity obviously aroused, Barbara looked at him closely. "Have you got any money in your pockets?"

"Not in my pockets. Not with me."

"Hidden somewhere, then?"

"I haven't got it yet. But . . ."

With a loud sigh, Barbara sat back between the men, folding her arms. One more dream-possibility demolished.

Mark enjoyed listening to the two of them. He was curious about Ben's plans too, but he didn't want to interrupt. Now Ben appeared to be content, for the time being, to look mysterious as he gazed into the distance along the road ahead.

They drove for a while without conversation. Then Barbara said to Ben: "I know what it is. You want to get your Sword back, you're ready to try to sell it."

"I want to get it back, yes. Sell it, no. We got rid of the idea of selling them even before we hid the two Swords. We'd get cheated or murdered for sure. No, I've got a use for Dragonslicer."

Mark asked him: "A dragon hunt somewhere? Even Nestor never made much money doing that, remember?"

They all remembered. Ben said: "Nestor wasn't at it long enough. Anyway, it's a special hunt that I have in mind. There's just one dragon that needs to be got rid of."

"Everyone who's plagued with dragons on his land says that," Barbara advised him. "Get your pay in advance." Now she swiveled her head to look at the two men in quick succession. "Both of you, coming back at the same time like this—I wonder if there's some connection?"

"I want my Sword back too," said Mark. "But I'm not going dragon hunting. And I had no idea Ben had gone off to enlist, or that he'd be looking for Dragonslicer now."

"What do you need Coinspinner for?" Barbara asked him. "Not that I have to know. I'll get it back for you anyway."

"No secret about it. I'm going back to Sir Andrew's army."

"Why do you want to do that?" Ben shot at him.

"I don't know if I want to. I just feel like I've got to. I told you I was with him for a while, and then things got to seeming hopeless, and I left. And then . . ."

"They probably are hopeless," said Ben.

"Then I went back to my old village, Arin-on-Aldan, to see if I could locate my mother and my sister. There . . . wasn't any village any more. Five years since I've been there. Maybe I'll never know what happened to them." Mark paused. "But I'm going back to Sir Andrew now. With Coinspinner, if I can."

"Why?" pursued Ben.

Mark leaned forward to talk past Barbara. "Look, he's trying to help his people. The people who were his, before he lost his lands. Don't you think they want him back? It isn't just the lands, the wealth, that he's trying to recover." Feelings, ideas, were struggling in Mark but he couldn't find the words to let them out. "He keeps on fighting the Dark King," he concluded, feeling even as he spoke how inadequate the words were.

"Sounds hopeless," said Ben, remorselessly practical.

"Everything's hopeless, as long as people don't try." And Mark added suddenly: "I wish that you and Barbara would come with me."

"To join an army?" Barbara laughed, though not unkindly.

Ben just shook his head in silence.

Mark hadn't really expected any other answer, but still the refusals, Ben's in particular, irritated him. "So, you're going to hunt dragons instead? That's as hard as fighting in a war, even if you do have Dragonslicer."

Ben turned. Enthusiasm entered his voice again. "I told you, the hunting's only a small part of it. The dragon is just in the way of something else. I wish that both of *you* would come with *me.*"

"I'm no good at riddles," Barbara said.

"What would we do?" Mark asked.

"Gain some money. More than just that. Wealth."

"I'm not out to get wealthy," Mark told him.

"All right. You're out to help Sir Andrew fight for his land and get it back—"

"And for his people."

"All right, for his people. Now you could help Sir Andrew a lot more by taking him a share of treasure, couldn't you? Imagine yourself showing up in his camp with jewels and gold enough to feed his army for a year."

"An army, for a year?"

"Ten years, maybe."

Barbara had turned to look at the huge man with concern. "Are you sick?" she asked him. The question sounded uncomfortably serious.

And Mark asked: "Where's anyone going to find wealth like that?"

Ben was calm. "I'll tell you both if you say you're with me."

This wasn't like Ben, and Mark couldn't figure it out. "Look, Sir Andrew needs real help. Not some scheme that. . . . I'm going to get Coinspinner and take it to him. If it's still wherever Barbara hid it."

Ben was looking stubborn now, maybe offended. Mark added: "I think now that we were wrong to hide them the way we did."

Barbara said: "Then you've forgotten how tired the three of us were of Swords. Remember? We'd worry that they'd be stolen. Or that somebody powerful would find out that we had them, and an army would come after us, or a demon, or some magician that we'd have no way to cope with. Then we'd think of trying to sell them to someone, and we'd realize that we'd be cheated when we did, and murdered afterwards. Then we'd worry that Coinspinner would get lost of itself . . . remember how it'd move around? We'd hide it underneath something on one side of the wagon, and find it on the other. Or just outside. I'm not sure it's going to be there when we look for it."

"We'll look, though," said Mark. He paused. "Neither of you has ever heard anything of Townsaver, I guess?"

As he had expected, the others signed that they had not. Mark's father, Jord the blacksmith, had been the only survivor among the half dozen men conscripted by Vulcan to forge the Swords. And when the job was done, the god had taken Jord's right arm—and given him, in payment he had said, the Sword of Fury, Townsaver. All this before Mark had been born.

Then Jord, and Mark's older brother Kenn, had died in the fight when Townsaver saved their village—a hollow victory indeed, as Mark had seen for himself. . . .

". . . recovered from his wounds?" Barbara was asking him something.

With an effort Mark recalled his thoughts, and figured out what she was talking about. "Sir Andrew? You mean his wounds from when his castle fell? That was five years ago. He's had more wounds since then, and overcome them—he does right well for a man his age. Or of any age, for that matter. Keeps his own small army in the field, most of the year. Supports Princess Rimac, and her General Rostov. Harasses the Dark King. And fights Queen Yambu, of course; she now holds Sir Andrew's old lands."

"Dame Yoldi's still with him?"

"Sir Andrew'd not trust any other seer, I think. Nor she, I suppose, any other lord."

Now again for a time there was silence, except for the plodding of the loadbeasts' feet and the creaking of the wagon. All three people riding in it were examining different but related memories. Ben reached up, unconsciously, to rub a scar that crossed his left shoulder and the upper part of his arm. It was from a wound received in the fierce defense of Sir Andrew's castle, five years ago. . . .

And Mark returned to that day now, as he sometimes did in nightmares. Seeing the scaling ladders nosing up over the walls, the Gray Horde ready to swarm up. And massed behind its hideous ranks were the black and silver of Yambu, the blue and white of the army of Duke Fraktin who was now no more. That had been Mark's first real battle, and very nearly his last.

Barbara said: "Every time I think of that day, I think of Nestor."

"Aye," said Ben. And then again all three were silent. On the subject of Nestor there was no more to be said. Dragonslicer had been Nestor's, as had this very wagon; and Nestor must have fallen at some point in the defense, perhaps with Townsaver still in hand. By inheritance, or at least by unspoken agreement among Nestor's friends, Dragonslicer had come to Ben.

"How large is Sir Andrew's army now?" Barbara asked Mark.

"Even if I knew the numbers, I'd be wrong to tell them. Even to you two . . . anyway the numbers change, with fortune and the seasons. But he needs help." Raw urgency was in Mark's voice as he repeated: "I wish you'd come with me. Both of you."

Barbara laughed again. It was not a mocking sound, but quick and unhesitating. "I'm fed up with armies and with fighting. I'd like to try the opposite side of life for a while. Live in some peaceful town, and be a stodgy citizen with my own house and my own bed. A solid bed with four legs, one that doesn't roll. Let the world do its fighting outside the city walls." Again she looked quickly to her companions on left and right. "The last time that the three of us were in a fight, you two had to carry me out of it—that should have been warning enough for all of us."

"And I," said Ben, "have had enough of armies too. March back and forth to no purpose, take stupid orders and sweat and freeze and starve. That's what you do on the good days. And once in a while bad days come along. As both of you know." He faced Mark. "I admire Sir Andrew, but I have to say that I think his brains are addled. He's never going to win his lands and people back."

"So instead," said Mark, "you are going back to something safe and pleasant, like hunting dragons—all right, just one dragon. And that's going to make you fabulously rich. Is that what you said?"

"I didn't say that. But it will."

Barbara made a derisive sound. "The dragon guards a treasure?" That was a situation arising only in old fantastic tales.

"In a manner of speaking, yes, it does." Her mockery had stung Ben. "And I'll tell you something of the treasure. It has at least one more of the Swords in it. I know. I saw it put there myself, down into the earth."

Mark blinked, and suddenly found himself listening to Ben seriously. "One more Sword? Which one?"

"That I don't know," said Ben calmly. "The Sword was well wrapped when I saw it put away, along with six loadbeasts' burden of some other treasure. But I brushed against the Sword once, and even through the wrappings I could feel the power. After living with two of 'em here in the wagon for a couple of years, I know what I felt."

Barbara's face had altered. And her voice, too, when she spoke again. Now it came out in a whisper, almost awed. "You were in Blue Temple service."

"Of course. That's what I've been telling you."

But plainly the implications, the possibilities, hadn't really dawned on her till now.

At sunset they made camp. As so often in the old days, Ben and Mark slept under the wagon, with Barbara inside. In the morning they moved on, steadily and without hurry.

Several days passed in a southward journey. Spring would have shaded into summer around them, except that the country was growing higher. Modest mountains rose up ahead, apparently barring their progress. Mark had never learned the right name for this range, though he had passed this way at least once before.

Next day the road started to wind upward. It remained a comparatively easy way, for a route that traversed a mountain pass. Here at higher altitude the end of winter lingered still, in wasted fragments of snowbanks that survived among the bold spring flowers. The scenery began to tend toward the tremendous.

"I remember this place now. This was where we turned."

There was a small side canyon, that went curving up from the main road that traversed the pass. The wagon could get up the side canyon for a couple of hundred meters, and that was far enough. Suddenly the three who rode in it came in sight of a ruined shrine or temple, built on a small rise. It was a beautiful setting, prettiness nearby in the grass and wildflowers, and grandeur in the distant vistas. What god or goddess the temple might have been raised to honor seemed impossible to determine now. Certainly it was very old.

It was midday when they stood before the ruin. They had left the wagon standing just a few meters downslope, where the drivable surface petered out completely.

"You hid them in here? In the ruins?"

Barbara nodded.

"Why in here?"

"Coinspinner itself directed me to the place. I thought I told you that it had guided me."

The wind sighed through the walls of the canyon, rocks splintered with some ancient heaving of the earth. In the distance, far down the pass, the gentler slopes were beautiful with spring. Mark could see a group of white-robed pilgrims there in the distance, approaching slowly through the pass. If they were chanting a song to Ardneh, as seemed likely, he couldn't hear it at this range.

"Is this one of Ardneh's shrines, I wonder?"

"I suppose the local people would know," said Barbara. "If there were any local people."

But when they went inside the roofless walls and looked about, they found strong evidence that there were. Dried flowers, and freeze-dried fruit, were arranged on a low, flat stone, that might or might not originally have been part of an altar.

Two years ago, Barbara had climbed up to this place alone one night, from their camp a couple of hundred meters down the hill. She had climbed by night, with moonlight to show her the way picked out by the Sword that quivered in her hands.

Once the three had decided among themselves to hide the Swords, Coinspinner itself, in their troubled juggling with it, had shown them how to proceed.

Every time Mark or Ben had taken that weapon in hand, and tried to think of where it and its fellow should be hidden, the point had indicated Barbara.

And then, when they gave her Coinspinner to hold, she could feel no power in it at all. Then she had picked up Dragonslicer too—Mark had been apprehensive lest the two Swords come into contact, and something awkward, or worse than awkward, happen as a result. Then Coinspinner had vibrated almost angrily in Barbara's grasp, pointing out for her a path to follow. But it had ceased its indications whenever the men had tried to follow her.

So they had let her proceed alone. The moon had been the only witness of her climb up to this temple. The ruined structure was not visible from the main road through the pass, and she had not suspected its existence until the Sword of Chance had led her to it.

When the final place was indicated to her, she had hidden Coinspinner and Dragonslicer with a feeling of great relief. After years of hiding them and carrying them about, the nerves of all three people were worn with the strain. At that time their friend Sir Andrew had been a hunted fugitive, hiding they knew not where, and none of them had yet heard of Princess Rimac or her General Rostov, Sir Andrew's potential allies.

Swordless, Barbara had returned to camp. Mark and Ben, both obviously relieved to see her, had started to ask questions.

She had declined to answer. "It's done," she told them shortly. "We can stop worrying. And now I'm going to get some sleep."

And now, almost two years later, they were back.

It was hard to tell, by looking at the temple, what style of building it had been originally. Time and ruin moved all things toward simplicity. If any of the stones had ever been painted, they were now all white again, matching the surface of some nearby cliffs. If there had been carving, it was crumbled now. Architecture had all but vanished, leaving rubbly walls that in places were little more than outlines.

As soon as Ben saw the modern offerings on the flat altar stone, he dug into his pockets until he found a few fragments of bread. These he tossed beside the desiccated fruit and flowers. When he saw the others looking at him, he explained. "Some gods may not amount to much, but it pays to keep on the good side of Ardneh. I've found that out."

Mark was shaking his head. "We don't know it's his temple anyway."

"It might be."

"All right. But Sir Andrew says that Ardneh's dead. And out of all the gods we know are living, there's none whose attention I'd like to attract."

Ben stared at him for a moment, then shrugged and tossed a few more crumbs. "If Ardneh's dead—then this is for the unknown god who means us well, whoever he may be. Or she, if it's a goddess. Can't do any harm, certainly."

"I suppose not," Mark admitted. And, because he could tell that Ben would feel better if he did, Mark dug into his own pockets for some scraps of food, and tossed them on the stone.

Barbara was ignoring them, and had already moved on to more practical matters. "It was dark, before," she was murmuring, more to herself than to the men. "Moonlight, but . . ." And she moved from one angle of wall to another, pausing to look at the ancient stonework thoughtfully. Most of the blocks that were still in place were finely fitted together, without mortar. Few of them were large.

At last she bent, and, with wiry strength, moved aside what looked like a portion of a windowsill. "Come help me. This is the place."

In the men's hands the stones moved rapidly. Presently the old sill had disappeared. The low wall here proved to be hollow. Between the larger stones that made its base, a sizable cavity appeared.

Barbara stepped back, making room for them to reclaim their property. "Reach in," she directed.

Ben pulled up his right sleeve, revealing an arm that looked almost stubby in its thickness. He thrust it into the hole up to his shoulder, and at once pulled out a sword-shaped bundle. The wrapping on it at once started to fall free, exposing portions of the fabric that had been folded under. Now Mark could recognize the cloth's pattern as that of an old blanket that Barbara had once had in the wagon.

Ben, murmuring something about the feel of power, shook the bundle, and the dusty wrappings fell away entirely. Dragonslicer, unchanged from when they'd seen it last, gleamed forth in meter-long straightness and sharpness. There was the mottled pattern, inside the flat of the bright steel, undimmed by rust. As Ben held the Sword up, cradled in two hands, Mark could see on the jet-black hilt the tiny white outline of a stylized dragon.

Ben made room beside the wall, and Mark knelt and groped into the cavity. He could feel stones and dust, but no wrappings and no blade. He reached farther, extending his fingers slowly and cautiously, in case Coinspinner's blade might be exposed—well he knew the extreme sharpness of the Swords. But still his hand found nothing—no, here was something. An object small and hard and round.

Wonderingly Mark brought out the coin, and held it up and saw that it was gold. The symbols on it were in some language that he could not recognize. The face on the obverse looked to him like that of Hermes, depicted as usual in his cap.

"It ought to be right in there," Barbara was saying to him. "Unless . . ." Her voice died when she saw what Mark held in his hand.

Mark gave her the coin to look at. Then he and Ben removed more stones, and looked into the wall more deeply. The whole cavity was now exposed, but Coinspinner was gone.

No one sang Coinspinner's verse aloud. But it was running in their minds.

When they were satisfied that the Sword of Chance was no longer there, they restored the half-ruined wall, to a condition at least a little better than it had been on their arrival.

Then Mark sat down on the reconstructed sill, staring at the gold coin that was now in his hand again, while Ben and Barbara stood nearby regarding him.

"The coin is yours to keep," said Barbara.

"Of course," added Ben.

"Worth a good deal," said Mark, flipping it. "But not a Sword. I want to take a Sword back to Sir Andrew."

"Mine does not go there," said Ben. He paused, then added: "But I know where there's at least one more."

Mark, who had forgotten about other treasure for a time, turned Ben's offer over in his mind. He looked up, about to speak, and then was distracted by the oddity of a certain small shadow in the sky. He jumped to his feet, hushing Barbara with a raised hand just as she was about to say something.

High above their heads a creature flew, a small dark shape against the sky. Mark could see that it was a monkbird—that peculiar twisting of the wings in flight was a hard thing to mistake. It was surprising to see a monkbird up here in the highlands, far from its usual habitat.

The creature's flight path was curving in a circle around the zenith, as if it were deliberately observing the ruined temple and the three people who were inside it.

Barbara had scrambled up atop one of the ruined walls, to get a better view downslope. "Some men are coming up the canyon," she announced. "Six of them, I think."

Ben and Mark got into position to see for themselves. On the trail that ascended from the main road, two mounted men led four who moved on foot. Some of them at least were heavily armed.

"Following our wagon tracks?"

"No—maybe not—see the rider's drawn sword? I think he's using it for guidance."

"Coinspinner, then!"

"It could be Wayfinder."

As they watched, the monkbird left off circling and flew down to the approaching procession. It landed on the shoulder of the man walking in the rear, and presumably it could be reporting what it had seen.

Barbara hopped down from the wall. "What do we do? We can't retreat uphill with the wagon."

Ben spat. "I don't feel like just giving them a team and wagon. Six aren't that many, even assuming that they do mean harm." So the three, with good rocks at their back and some advantage in high ground, stood to face those who were approaching.

The leader of the six, he who rode holding a drawn sword in front of him, drew up his mount when he saw the three of them waiting. He was a small man with a large mustache. His gestures at once suggested an imperious manner. And, certainly, it was one of the Twelve Swords that he gripped, though it was impossible to see at the moment which white symbol marked its hilt.

The second rider was a tall, graybearded man—a wizard, thought Mark, if he had ever seen one. Four more men came tagging along on foot, none of them looking particularly impressive.

When the leader drew up his riding beast some twenty meters or so away, Ben—in response to that brandished Sword—let the wrapping fall free from Dragonslicer. Mark had an arrow already nocked, and Barbara had drawn the sling from her belt and slipped a smooth stone into it from her small pouch. Now she was holding the weapon in expert readiness, letting the weight of the stone swing gently on the thongs.

The armed men in the other group began to draw their weapons also, but without any great appearance of eagerness. He who was so obviously a wizard, however, was frowning and shaking his head. "Peace!" he cried out, in a huge voice, and held up an open palm toward each side.

Ben made no move to put down Dragonslicer, nor Mark to lower his bow. Having weapons out and ready was probably the best move that non-magicians could make to ward off spells.

"Oh, aye, I'll have peace, if I can." The voice of the mustached man was easily loud enough for those confronting him to hear, as he replied to the wizard. Then, when Ben brandished his own Sword again, the man rounded on him and added: "But peace or war, I'll have my treasure. Unless it's Shieldbreaker that you're mishandling there so awkwardly, young man, I'll be able to take it from you if I try."

Mark chose to answer that. "And if that's Coinspinner in your dainty hand, you'd better know that it belongs to me, and that I mean to have it back. If it's Townsaver, the same. That's mine by inheritance."

The rider controlled his mount. "Ha, we've met an owner of two Swords, by Hades! Neither of which he happens to have with him at the moment, unfortunately . . . since you appear to be so well-versed in the lore of Swords, I'll tell you that I hold Wayfinder here. It's guided me to this place, and now I must determine why." Again the rider had to struggle briefly with his high-spirited mount. He added then: "I am the Baron Doon, and this at my right hand the wizard Indosuaros. And who are you?"

"Mark," said Mark, touching his chest with his free right hand. Then he gestured to his side: "Ben, and Barbara."

"Ha, a notable economy of names. And a lack of pretension in the way of titles. But why not?" And now the mustached one heeded his wizard, who had jockeyed his own mount, a pale loadbeast trained for riding, closer to speak to him in a low voice.

After a short whispered conference, the man who had called himself Baron Doon looked up again. "So. What you have there is Dragonslicer. Doubtless the very implement I need, to break the second sealing." He spoke like a man making his private plans aloud.

There was a moment of ominous silence. Then Ben said in a calm voice: "Why, I have heard of a dragon-sealing, in a song. An old song, about treasure, where the sealings are numbered up to seven."

The Baron—Mark was beginning to believe that he might be such, for he looked proud enough to be a king—the Baron studied calmly the three who faced him. "It may be," Doon said at last, "that I will have use in my enterprise for some of you, as well as for that Sword. We had better talk."

Barbara spoke up, as bold as he. "Use for us in what enterprise? And at what rates of pay?"

The Baron looked at her appreciatively for a moment. Then he said: "I mean to have Benambra's Gold. You say that you know the old song; then you may know as well that it is more than a song, much more than a story. It's real, and those I choose to help me are going to share in it generously."

There was a silence, broken only by the wind feeling its way down the pass to mourn in the stones of the ruined temple. And now the wind brought with it the faint voices of the distant pilgrims, chanting to Ardneh as they drew slowly closer.

Mark exchanged glances with Ben. Then he called to Doon: "We might be willing to join you. We'll have to hear more, first."

And Ben, to Doon: "Whether we agree or not, this is my Sword, and it stays with me."

The Baron called back to them: "I want to consult Wayfinder on which of you, if any, I ought to enlist. You'll pardon me if I come nearer to you with it drawn."

And Barbara: "As long as you'll pardon us for holding our own weapons ready."

Doon now rode slowly forward, while the rest of his group stayed where they were. At a distance of no more than three or four meters he halted again, and now he pointed with the blade in his hand at Mark, Ben, and Barbara in turn. Mark could see the tip quivering, lightly and rapidly, when it was aimed at himself and at Ben. But it remained steady, he thought, when Doon leveled it at Barbara.

Doon told the two young men: "Your young piece there is not going to come with us. Can you trust your lives to her ability to hold her tongue?"

And Ben again: "Speak of the lady gently, or you might get Dragon-slicer where you don't want it."

Doon raised an eyebrow, a signal more elegant by far than his attire. "Your pardon, I'm sure, your ladyship. I meant only that I decline to invite you to take part in this enterprise. And I most strongly advise that you say nothing to anyone about it."

She flared back at him fearlessly, "It's well that you decline to invite me, for I'd decline to go. And if my two friends are going, my tongue'll not put them in danger." Her manner softened just a little. "You don't know me, or you'd spare yourself the worry."

Doon slid his Sword back into its poor sheath. Suddenly he appeared somewhat diminished, though still vital and flamboyant. He sat his mount in silence for a few moments, looking over the three people who faced him. Apparently he was satisfied by what he saw, for he smiled suddenly; it was a better smile than any of the three confronting him expected.

"If there are any farewells to be said among you," he told the three, "say them now. My men and I will be waiting for two of you a little down the slope." With that he turned his back and slowly rode away, signing to his men to put their weapons up. They fell in behind him, and without looking back proceeded down the canyon.

The three who were left behind looked at one another.

Ben drew a deep breath, and addressed Mark. "Well, then. I take it we are going?"

"Benambra's Gold," Mark marveled softly, shaking his head.

"And Swords," said Ben, "for Sir Andrew."

"Aye, you tell me there's a Sword."

"Or maybe more than one."

"I'll have to go," said Mark. "I'll have to risk it then."

"And I know you're going too," said Barbara to Ben.

Mark went to her, and put his golden coin into her hand. "What do you have to say," he asked, "about our leaving you? I see no way around it."

"Nor do I, I suppose." If Barbara had any strong feelings in the matter she was keeping them well concealed. "There are some pilgrims moving through the pass, and I expect they'll be glad to have someone with a wagon join them, for a time at least." She tossed the coin once, then put it away inside her garments. "I'll keep this for you. It's less likely that I'll lose it than you will, where you seem to be going."

"Spend it if need be—you know that. It won't buy you a shop in a walled city, but—when Ben comes back, perhaps you can." Mark paused, aware of Ben waiting his turn to say goodbye. "Are you going back to the carnival, then?"

"I didn't think so when I left it. But now—what else? First, though, I'm going to watch from a hilltop, to see if that gang tries to murder you both right off."

"We'll scream for help," said Ben. He took her in his arms and kissed her roughly, swinging her off her feet. "I'll find you with the carnival, then, when I come back with a fortune. And listen. Tell that strongman, if he's still there, that—that—"

"I can manage him. I have so far."

And Mark heard no more, for he walked apart a little, to let the two of them say goodbye alone. Presently, looking back, he saw Ben lifting Barbara into the wagon. She waved her arm once more to Mark, and then drove off.

There had evidently been an old scabbard in the wagon, for Ben was fitting Dragonslicer into it, and belting it round his waist, when Mark caught up to him.

"Let's go get our treasure, comrade."

Following the swiftly driven wagon down the hill, they saw Barbara drive past the place where Doon and his men were loitering, waiting for their two recruits. Moments later they saw her pause, looking back, watching from a small hilltop as she had promised.

CHAPTER 6

Doon welcomed the two of them briskly when they came striding downhill to him, and the combined descent to the main road got under way without delay. Introductions went round among the men while they were moving.

When they reached the place where the trail from the side canyon rejoined the main road through the pass, Doon drew and consulted his Sword again. Barbara's wagon was now out of sight, around the curve of the main road; and the pilgrims' chant was faintly audible from that direction.

Doon's Sword pointed back to the north, in the direction from which Ben and Barbara and Mark had come. Dismounted now, leading his animal, the Baron set the pace in that direction, and motioned for Mark and Ben to walk close beside him.

Now Doon began a conversation by posing them a few cautious questions about their background. He seemed glad to hear that they claimed some minor experience as dragon hunters. Their claim was more readily accepted, thought Mark, because they made it modest.

"And what about yourself, sir?" Mark countered.

"What about myself?"

"How do you come to be leading this expedition?" Mark asked bluntly. "It seems to me that qualifications beyond the ordinary are required."

Doon did not appear to object to being questioned in such a way, but smiled at them graciously. "True," he agreed, "and my qualifications have already been tested, in more ways than one. But it is chiefly a matter of will."

"How's that?" Ben wanted to know.

Doon smiled again. "You see before you, gentlemen," he began, "a man almost devoid of what the world calls wealth. The powers that rule the universe have determined, for what reason I do not know, that pauperism is to be my lot. Whereas I, on my own behalf, have made a different determination. I will have wealth." He said it with majestic sincerity.

"I am impressed," said Mark.

"You should be, young man. If I am willing to defy gods, demons, and unguessed-at powers, think how little likely I am to be turned aside by any merely human obstacles."

"The gods must favor you somewhat," said Ben, "or you would not have a Sword."

"They can never all agree on anything, can they? Tell me—"

"Yes."

"Why were both of you disposed to believe me so quickly, when I mentioned Benambra's Gold? Most folk of any wit would be more skeptical."

"I was a minstrel once," said Ben. "I knew the old song."

"More than that."

"Yes." He looked at Doon steadily as they trudged along. "A couple of months ago, I helped to bury part of it. I've seen it with my own eyes."

"Ah. What have you seen, exactly?" The Baron's question was calm, reserving judgement.

"The gold of the Blue Temple, I'm telling you. Six loadbeasts' burden of it. It was wrapped up in bundles, but there was no mistaking what it was."

"You helped to bury it, you say."

"To put it into a cave, and I know where that cave is."

"What I have heard," said Doon, "is that men who do that work are always slain, immediately afterward."

"There were six of us, and I think five were killed. I didn't wait to make sure."

"Ah."

The wizard was riding close behind the three of them and doubtless listening. The four other men were keeping close as well, taking in every word.

Doon said: "Wayfinder of course can lead me to the site. But it will be good to learn the location from you in advance, so we can begin to plan more carefully."

Ben squinted up at the sun and got his directions. "I'll tell you this much now. Your Sword is taking you in the right general direction."

"Ah. But you see, for the past month it has been leading me on a zigzag path. I wondered about this when I first realized it, but the reason quickly became clear. When I began I was alone, and I have been gathering the necessary tools and helpers. The Sword has led me to different people—as to you—and to other necessities. But it has been up to me to gain them for my cause, by one means or another."

"I see," said Mark. "And when will your expedition be finally complete and ready?"

"It may be so now, for all I know. Your friend says that we are now heading toward the gold."

"There are a few more things," the wizard put in suddenly, "that I could wish we had, before we reach the hiding place and try to breach it."

Mark turned to look at him. "Such as?"

"You—or your friend—spoke of the sealings, back there. Do you truly know what all six of them are?"

"The song says seven—doesn't it, Ben? And they must be the various protections of the treasure."

Doon meanwhile was looking round, and appeared to be considering the extent of the train of men and beasts he now had following him. In an aside to himself, he muttered: "A few more, and I'll have to form them into companies, and start making out duty rosters . . . well, there's good as well as bad in numbers. The more of us there are, the more treasure we'll be able to carry out. When I know the location, I'll be able to make some better plans on that as well. The gods know there'll be enough for all of us. No need for greedy squabbling."

"No need at all," agreed Ben. And Mark murmured something similar. Then again he looked back at the tall gray man who rode behind him. "Sir Wizard, what are the other things you wish we had?"

"D'ye know the song?" the wizard asked.

In answer, Ben sang it lightly:

> Benambra's gold
> Hath seven sealings . . .

He let it die there.

Doon chuckled. "I already know what the next lines are, I'll not be frightened if you sing them." He pressed on, though, without pausing for any such performance. "Indosuaros and I have pooled our knowledge, and we make it but six sealings that guard the gold, the number seven being merely a poetic convention." He glanced back at the gray man.

Indosuaros nodded confirmation. "The song does not name seven individual barriers."

"No, it doesn't," Ben agreed.

"All right, then," asked Mark, "what are the six?"

"The first," said Doon, "is the location of the place—pretty well impossible to rob it if you don't know that. The secret of the location has been kept for a long time, and with incredible success. But since your friend knows where it is, and we have Wayfinder, that should present no problem." If he had any doubts about the veracity of Ben's claim to knowledge, he was not expressing them.

Mark said: "I suppose the second barrier is some kind of fence or patrol, or both, around the area where the cave is."

"The fence," said Indosuaros, "is made of dragon's teeth."

"A landwalker," said Doon. "I suppose that you, my big friend, may have seen it—?"

Ben only nodded. "With Dragonslicer I think we can get by. Though it still won't be easy."

"We have another trick or two that we can try as well," Doon assured him.

Ben said: "And the third sealing, I suppose, is something that I saw inside the cave. Just a glimpse, in darkness, of giant white hands. They were grabbing the sacks of treasure as we put them down into the floor, and they looked—well, dead—but at the same time very strong and active. The song doesn't mention anything like them, but—"

The tall wizard, his frame bobbing with the motion of his loadbeast's walk, was signing disagreement. "No, I think not, I think not. Those huge pale creatures are no more than laborers and clerks. They can be trusted by their Blue Temple masters, because they never emerge into the light of day, and have their only contact with the upper world through the Blue Temple priests themselves."

"They're very large and strong," Ben repeated doubtfully. "What are they called?"

"I have knowledge of them from other sources." And the wizard glanced back suddenly over his shoulder, as if someone or something of importance could be following him. " 'Whitehands' is as good a name as any," he concluded.

Ben repeated, stubbornly: "Whatever they are, their hands are very large."

"Well, so are yours," said Doon. "And my hands are well-armed, as are your friend's, who walks beside you. And we have sturdy company."

"I am only trying to be clear about what we face."

"An admirable plan. No, the third sealing is something else. The researches of my learned friend here"—and he nodded toward the wizard, rather formally—"confirm some small investigations of my own. The third sealing is in fact a subterranean maze, and, as might be expected, one of no little danger and difficulty. But I have a long key here at my side to open it." And again he fondled Wayfinder's hilt.

The eight men trudged on in silence for a while. In the distance, past the mouth of the pass, flatlands stretched for many kilometers, greening here and there with crops or only with onrushing summer. Beyond, more mountains, very far away and barely visible.

"And the fourth sealing?" Mark finally prodded.

"A kind of maze again," said Indosuaros. "But this one of pure magic. I have been preparing for more than a century to breach it, and you may depend upon it that the key to it is also with us."

"And then, the fifth?" asked Ben.

"There is an underground garrison," answered the magician, "who guard Benambra's wealth. They are human soldiers, yet not human as you and I."

"What does that mean?"

"We will have to discover exactly what it means. But I am confident that we can pass."

Mark put in a question: "Who's Benambra, anyway?"

Ben, who had undergone some indoctrination in the history of the institution he had once joined, could answer that one. "He was the first

High Priest of the Blue Temple. From him, all who worship wealth still draw their inspiration."

Doon was closely studying the huge man who walked beside him, no doubt revising a first impression of his recruit.

"So," said Mark, "let's try to complete this inventory that we've begun." It came to him as he spoke that his own attitude had already been revised. He had entered this conversation to learn what Doon's plans were, but now he found himself taking part in the planning, as for an enterprise he had already joined. "Whoever these guardian soldiers of the fifth sealing may be, they appear to stand in our way. What means do we have of getting past them?"

Doon said briskly: "Wayfinder will point one out to us, when the time comes. Of course we are going to face risks; but what prize could be worth greater risks than this one?"

"So we come to the sixth sealing," Ben urged. "You said that there were six."

Indosuaros answered shortly. "The sixth—and last—is apparently some kind of demon. You need not be too much concerned, young man, only do your part to get us through the others. I've dealt before with demons, as you and your friend have with landwalkers."

Ben did not appear entirely satisfied. "I don't suppose you have this particular demon's life in hand? No? Then you have words of magic certain to command him?"

The ghost of a fearful murmur could be heard among the listening men. The wizard appeared to be making an effort to restrain his temper. "I have not his life in my hand, no. His name, yes, though I should not speak it now. I have said that there are things I wish we had. But what we do have is sufficient. Else I should not be here now."

"Whatever we may truly need," Doon said firmly, "Wayfinder will bring us to it."

Wherever it might be bringing them now, they passed four more days in the process, entering lands that none of the men knew very well.

Ben warned them all, first Mark in private and then the others, that Wayfinder's last few crossroad choices were in fact taking them farther and farther from the place where he knew the gold to be. Doon did not argue the point, calmly insisting that there might well be something else they had to obtain first. Nor did he press Ben to reveal the location of the hoard.

Ben had already given that information to Mark, privately. The two of them continued to meet frequently, apart from the others, to assess their situation. They were doing this late one afternoon, on a hillside covered with a wild orchard of tall, almost tree-like bushes, covered at this season with fine pink and white blossoms that had drawn innumerable bees.

The two sat on a patch of grass, in conference, and Mark was asking: "Doesn't it come down to this: How long can we trust Doon?"

"As long as he needs us. Which ought to be till we've got past the dragon, at least."

"Of course after that, he's still going to need all the help that he can get, to get past the other sealings. . . ."

"And after *that,* if we win through, there'll be more treasure in our hands than we can carry, if we were eighty men instead of eight. No reason for us to fight over it then, that I can see."

Mark still marveled, silently, every time he thought about it. If he could bring Sir Andrew two Swords, possibly, or even three. . . . "Blue Temple won't be watching the area, you think? I have trouble believing that."

"If they are watching, we should discover the fact when we get near. Then . . . I don't know. But I don't think they're watching. They probably think I'm dead, as I've told you. Even if they doubt that, they won't believe that I could be coming back so soon, with a band as well-organized as this one is."

"I suppose. You know, Ben, about Doon . . ."

"Yes?"

"Indosuaros wouldn't have joined up with him, would he, if Doon didn't know what he was doing? I get the feeling that the wizard definitely knows what *he's* doing."

"Me too. Good point." Ben stretched his arms, then lay back on the grass, staring at the sky. "I hope Barb made it back to the carnival safely."

"We could ask the magician to send one of his powers to find out."

Ben shook his head. "I don't want to draw his attention to her."

"Hm. Yes. I wonder why he hates Blue Temple so?"

"Hah, why not?" Ben reared himself up on an elbow. "If ever I meet someone who doesn't hate them, then I'll be puzzled and ask why."

Their talk was interrupted by a small black shadow, that darted toward them among roseate blossoms. The monkbird had plainly not come spying on them, but had been sent to summon them to rejoin the others. It clung for a moment to a nearby branch with its handlike feet, whistling at them with soft urgency. Then next moment it was gone, back in the direction it had come from, keeping its flight below the tops of the bushes.

Wordlessly Mark and Ben grabbed up their weapons. As silently as possible they scrambled after the messenger.

Doon and the others were gathered at the edge of a slope, peering downhill between branches toward a road not much more than a hundred meters away. The Baron pointed. "Look."

A slave caravan was passing on the road, from right to left. It consisted mainly of short columns of people chained together, men, women, and children in separate groups. They were being watched over and prodded along by mounted spearmen wearing the red and black of the Red Temple. There were a few litters in the procession too, some of these borne by male slaves and some by animals.

Mark, hearing a drawn-in breath from the Baron, turned his head. Wayfinder, in Doon's hands, was pointing straight downslope at the caravan. There was a fierce vibration in the blade's tip.

Suddenly the monkbird flew among the men at head height, yammering. Then it sought shelter on its master's shoulder, just as a new sound arose from a little distance uphill among the trees and bush.

The men had their weapons drawn, but little time to accomplish more in the way of readiness, when the mounted Red Temple patrol burst shouting out of the bush and onto them, sabers leveled and scarlet-lined cloaks flying in the charge.

CHAPTER 7

The charge was clumsily planned, coming as it did through the awkward bushes where it had to be both slow and noisy. The men who were its target had plenty of time and plenty of places in which to step aside. Still the long cavalry swords were formidable weapons. Mark saw Pu Chou go down before that first rush, amid a blizzard of pink and white blossoms. Golok also had been struck down, or had thrown himself flat, while his creature Dart howled, and managed to hover like a hummingbird in the air above its fallen master. Indosuaros and Mitspieler were crouching under showers of blossoms, presumably doing as much as they could with their magic given the conditions. Ben, like Mark himself, had taken shelter behind a bush. Then Ben had stepped out at the right moment to use Dragonslicer to good effect on a trooper thundering by. Doon and Hubert had adopted the same tactic, and both had done damage to the foe.

Mark nocked an arrow to his bow while he avoided that first rush. Stepping into the open again to shoot, he got his first clear look at the face of the Red Temple officer who had led the attack. The man's countenance was flushed and glassy-eyed, as he fought to wheel his mount around between constricting bushes, presumably with the idea of making another charge. That charge was never ordered, never made, for Mark's arrow took the officer in the throat an instant later.

The other riders of the patrol were circling in the bushes, milling around in what looked like complete confusion. Mark saw one man scraped from his mount by projecting branches; a stroke from Hubert's battle hatchet finished him off in an instant. Many of the mounts were already riderless, thrashing and crashing in panic through the wild orchard, and the snowstorm of delicate petals did not slacken.

Doon, back in his own saddle now, parried a saber-slash and killed a rider in his saddle. Dragonslicer hewed at human flesh. Red-and-black capes lay crumpled and twisted on the ground, amid the blossoms and the blood. Hubert's bow twanged. The last survivor of the patrol had dropped his saber and turned his mount to flee, when Mark's second arrow of the skirmish struck him in the back. The rider screamed and fell.

Even more quickly than it had begun, the crash of combat ceased. Mark turned to look for Ben. The big man was on his feet and apparently unhurt, and gave Mark a salute with bloodied Dragonslicer.

Now there was almost silence. Mark could hear the blood in his own head, his own panting, gasping breath, the loud thrashing of a downed and wounded riding beast. Doon, prevented by the noise from listening, set his foot on the animal's neck and cut its throat.

Golok had risen to his hands and knees and was crawling toward the animal, evidently with the intention of giving it some kind of help. The youth paused, transfixed in horror and disbelief with his eyes on Doon.

His leader was paying him no attention. But now Doon started to relax. There were no sounds of any more enemies approaching, or of any who might have gotten away to alarm the other troopers with the caravan.

Indosuaros and Mitspieler were both on their feet again, apparently unhurt, their four arms spread, their two mouths chanting softly.

A quick look at Pu Chou was enough to show that he was beyond help; a heavy saber-stroke had caught him full in the forehead. Of all the fallen men, only the enemy commander still breathed, with Mark's arrowhead protruding from the side of his neck. A good arrow, that one, Mark found himself thinking distantly. If the shaft's not cracked, I'll have to retrieve it before we go on.

The officer's lips were moving. Doon bent over him, trying to hear whatever the man was trying to say, then sniffed and straightened up, frowning with contempt.

"Stoned blind," Doon muttered scornfully. "You can smell it on him." He looked round at the human wreckage of what had been this officer's command. "Probably his whole patrol was in the same shape. Typical Red Temple."

Hubert looked up from his self-assigned task of going through Pu Chou's pockets. "But usually they're not this hot to get into a fight."

"Usually," said Doon, and bent to wipe his Sword before putting it away. The fallen officer was not going to mind this misuse of his cloak, for he had now stopped breathing altogether.

Wayfinder, thought Mark, heightens risks. One more flower petal drifted down past his eyes, and sideslipped, just missing a landing on another dead man's face.

And now Wayfinder, already gleaming clean again, was pointing in the direction of the passed caravan.

"Well, we must overtake it," said Doon, moving on quickly to the next order of business. Briskly he climbed a tree, trying to see more of the hillside and the road below. "This slope is all ravines below us—we could hardly have jumped on their caravan from here. Very poor operation on their part. Well, Golok, get your little monk up in the air, bring us some news of the caravan—I can't see it from here now. Indosuaros, now that swords are put away again, see what you can do to calm these riding beasts and bring them to us. We'll need six new mounts—no, Pu Chou's gone, five will be enough."

The magician and his aide began a process of soft soothing magic, summoning the hurt and frightened animals to submit to strange human hands. Golok, as the riding beasts came within his reach, touched and spoke to them, using beast-master's lore to soothe their hurts and make them tractable.

Doon watched this process impatiently, and meanwhile issued orders to his other men. "We're going to dress ourselves in these Red Temple uniforms—in parts of them, anyway. It's all right if we look sloppy, half out of uniform, that's typical Red Temple too. If we look totally like swine, they'll take us for some of their mercenaries. Or maybe even regulars. I want to be able to get close to that caravan without another fight."

Golok and Mitspieler had to physically treat the hurts of a couple of the animals before five mounts were ready. By then, all the men had replaced some of their garments with those of the dead enemy, and helped themselves to choice weapons here and there. Very shortly afterward, what now indeed looked much like a Red Temple mercenary patrol was on its way.

The caravan had had no very great start on them, nor was it moving any faster than a weary slave could be compelled to walk. But Doon's men had to master their new mounts and nurse them along. And there was the difficult hillside, that had to be negotiated before they even got down to the road. By the time they had managed that, the caravan was long out of sight; but Dart brought back word to Golok that it was still on the road, proceeding no faster than before.

Still, dusk was falling before the mounted men caught sight of it again. If Doon had been seeking an opportunity to attack it in isolation on the road, that chance had now slipped away. The caravan was traversing a busy crossroads now. And, only a couple of hundred meters farther on, the gates of a large Red Temple complex were standing open to receive it.

Doon gestured, slowing his troop's progress, that they might have a chance to look over the Temple complex as they approached it. It was, as the first glimpse of it had suggested, of considerable size. The walls surrounding it were not much more than head high, but armed with jagged projections along the top that would make a climbing entry difficult. Within the walls were several large but low-built buildings. Buildings and walls alike appeared to be constructed mainly of earthen bricks. The colors of red and black were prominently displayed.

The main gate remained standing open after the caravan had entered it. The entry was flanked by torches, that at dusk were just now being lighted. A brief period of observation was enough to show that the flow of traffic in and out the gate was fairly high, as might be expected of a Red Temple near the intersection of two well-traveled roads.

"A lot of customers," Golok commented. He had evidently got over his outrage now. "There must be a busy town or two nearby. Maybe a large castle, too."

"Aye." Hubert chuckled. "Red Temple always does good business."

"I think," said Doon, "we're going to be able to ride right on in without being challenged."

"And if we are challenged?" asked Indosuaros. He had contrived a black-and-red cap for himself, suggesting a minor wizard working in Red Temple pay.

"We'll see," said Doon. "Be ready to take your cue from me—get that, everyone? Let's go."

The guard post at the main gate was manned by a single sentry. He was sitting with his head slumped, half asleep or perhaps entranced by drugs. He paid little or no attention to the passage of what might well have been a mercenary patrol.

The compound seen from inside was as large and busy as its appearance at a distance had suggested. This main portion of it, generally open to the public, was well lit by torches. Spaces and hitching racks were provided to accommodate customers' vehicles and animals. On three sides of this broad open courtyard were the several houses of pleasure that made up the usual Red Temple layout. To the right, as Doon and his men rode in, were the Houses of Dancing and of Joy. Gaming was on the left, and Drink and Food were straight ahead—music, like the smell of drugs, seemed to be everywhere once the main gate had been passed.

Passages led between buildings, to what would be the non-public parts of the compound. Mark was able to catch just a glimpse of one of the caravan's litters, disappearing down one of these alleyways, before a closing gate cut off the sight. The gangs of slaves who had been driven in on foot were probably already back there, in some kind of pens.

Doon drew his Sword briefly, and found that it guided him to the right. A couple of passing customers looked at him curiously before he put the blade away again.

He turned right, then signed to his men to halt their animals and dismount. They tied their riding beasts at one of the hitching racks nearest the entrance of the House of Dancing. So far, no one else in the compound appeared to be paying them much attention.

"Golok," the Baron ordered quietly, "stay here and keep the animals quiet. Be ready for a quick start when we come back." Golok nodded; the hooded monkbird was resting behind his saddle now.

Doon left his Sword sheathed, but unbuckled the whole apparatus from his waist, and carried it in his hand, pausing now and then to feel his way forward with it, almost like a blind man with a cane. It still looked odd behavior, thought Mark, but it was not going to draw as much attention as the Baron would have by waving a meter of bare blade.

The entrance to the House of Dance was watched inside by fee-collectors, who, as Mark had expected, let the red uniforms pass in free. Red Temple mercenaries were probably not paid very much in coin, but there appeared to be certain compensations. Inside the House of Dance, drum music throbbed in thick, warm air. Most of the interior was a single vast, low room. Scantily clad girls and young women, with a few boys and young men mixed among them, sat round the edges of the room. These were slaves of the Temple, waiting for the personal attentions of some customer. Some couples were dancing, and in the center of the large floor a professional group performed, dancers and musicians mingling.

Doon moved at first as if to cross the floor directly, then evidently thought better of interfering with the dance, and led his men around the edge. Now, in the distant corners of the hall, Mark could recognize the traditional four Red Temple statues: Aphrodite, Bacchus, Dionysus, Eros. Here at one side was a broad stairway, going up, probably communicating on an upper level with the House of Joy next door. A painted young man was just ascending, giggling, supported on either side by two customers, man and woman. Meanwhile on the far side of the dance floor, four men were just emerging from some back room. They were all uniformed in blue and gold, and though they paid attention to the dancers as they strolled, Mark thought that probably they were here on business rather than on pleasure only. It was no secret that connections existed between the Blue Temple and the Red, particularly on the upper levels of organization.

In the corner of the dancehall farthest from the entrance, broad open steps led down. As Doon led them down the steps, following the discreet guidance of the Sword, Mark began to realize that some large part of the whole Red Temple complex was probably underground. Different musicians were playing down here, from somewhere out of view; and the sound they made was different, having a disconnected anguish in it. The air was thicker too, with more torch-smoke in it, as well as heavier fumes of incense and of drugs.

For a few moments Doon and his followers tramped an empty corridor in silence. Suddenly Mark thought that he knew where the Sword was taking them. It was a part of the usual Red Temple installation that he'd heard about, but had never seen on the few occasions when he'd visited other branches of the Temple as a customer.

The corridor branched. And still the Sword of Wisdom led the way unhesitatingly.

"Are we going to the worm-pit?" Hubert grumbled quietly. "What's in *there*, or who, that we could need?"

No one had an answer for him. Soon the Sword would tell.

Still the path chosen by Wayfinder led through the public precincts of the Temple, and they were not challenged. It guided them at last through a heavily curtained doorway, into another large, low room, this one much darker and worse-smelling than the dancehall above.

Here only a few candles were burning, to illuminate what looked at first glance like some barracks or dormitory. Or perhaps a ward in some hospital-dungeon, if such a combination could be imagined. The place was almost too long to be called a room, too wide for a corridor. It was lined on both sides with bunks and couches, about half of which were occupied. A few bent figures, those of male and female attendants, were moving about in the gloom. As one of these passed before a candle, Mark could see that she was carrying a small saucer-shaped tray of earth, and tools that looked like a pair of tweezers and a large, fine-toothed comb.

The light was a little better near the curtained doorway where Doon and his men had entered. Here some of the customers were conversing from couch to couch, and sipping at winecups. Men and women alike could be seen to be for the most part naked under their beds' sheets. One or two were currently in the phase of ecstasy that the pleasure-worms induced. These sobbed or groaned on their cots, executing jerky motions, kicking aside coverings, scratching at their skin with combs, now slowly and now in rapid frenzy.

As Doon, still trying to hold his sheathed Sword unobtrusively, led the way slowly forward between rows of beds, Mark saw the attendant with the tray of earth stop at the side of a recumbent customer. From the saucer of earth the attendant lifted, in the tweezers, a tiny pale gray worm—weight for weight, Mark knew, worth more than gold. The creature was inconspicuous, and would have been unnoticeable except for the attention that was focused on it. The client, a stoutish woman with an obviously well cared for body, turned beneath her sheet, exposing her wide back in the candle's light. The attendant applied the tweezers near the customer's shoulder with one hand, and quickly brought a candle closer with the other. The small worm, released by the tweezers, promptly disappeared. Mark knew, though he had not seen, that it was gone into the skin, driven by its burrowing instincts and the painful light. Worm-pits were always underground, because the creatures had to be cultivated away from daylight.

An attendant approached Doon as he led the way forward, but the Baron shook his head in silence and pressed on, his men following him closely. The attendant appeared momentarily puzzled, Mark thought, but then went on about his tasks. Like the others working here he looked thin and vaguely unhealthy.

Here was another client, a man, recently infected with one worm, or several, and now crying out with the full sensation. His trembling hands went scratching back and forth, all ten fingernails working on the skin over his left ribs. The worms followed the paths of nerve-tissue in their hosts, inducing pleasure in exchange for food and shelter inside a mammalian body. Sometimes the pleasure shaded into unendurable tickling, hence the work for fingernails and combs. Mark had even heard once that the worms were used in Red Temple dungeons as tools of torture, with the victims simply infected and kept from scratching.

On succeeding couches, people tossed and scratched and moaned. Attendants were at work on some of them with combs. As he got farther toward the rear of the room, Mark decided that it was probably arranged by classes of addicts, with beginners or occasional users near the front, those more enslaved by the habit near the middle. In the dimmer reaches of the rear, where Mark and his companions now walked among them, were people who by appearances never left their cots at all. The bodies back here tended to look starved and wasted, marked with old scars and not-so-old dried blood. Here attendants gave less attention. Sometimes—inevitably, Mark had heard—the worms turned inward from the skin toward the spinal column and the brain.

In the room's farthest recess was an inconspicuous door. It would be the way out, thought Mark, for customers who could either not continue paying or not walk. The Sword led Doon directly to this door. It was not locked, and swung open at a touch, revealing a dim passage. In a side room off this passage, another attendant moving amid trays and racks of earth looked up in dim candlelight as six armed men came tramping through. But he made no protest or even comment.

The service corridor soon branched. Wayfinder chose the left-hand way, which quickly ran into a strong grill-work door, tightly closed and probably locked. Beyond the door, a red-helmeted soldier was on guard, and beyond the guard Mark could see what looked like the doors of individual cells lining the corridor.

"Open up," commanded Doon, rattling briskly at the grill.

But the soldier was not in a mood to be intimidated. "No passage through here without a written order. What do you want in here, anyway? You field troops think you can come in here and have fun any time, without any—"

Wayfinder, still sheathed and belted, hit the floor stones with a muffled thud. It had been replaced in Doon's right hand with a dagger, handier tool for such close work. Meanwhile Doon's thin left arm had snaked through the grill to seize the guard by the front of his garments and snatch him sharply forward. Instantly the Baron's right hand shoved the dagger home, up beneath the breastbone. The soldier's eyes bulged, then glazed. If he made a sound at all, it was too faint to be heard over the now-distant music.

"Keys," said Doon laconically, supporting his victim against the grill. The man was wearing a ring of them on his belt.

Mark reached in through the bars, detached the keys and brought them out. One part of his mind was protesting that this had been cold murder, while another part exulted in the triumph, the demonstration of Doon's proficiency. War required capable leaders, and this was war, a part of Sir Andrew's fight against the Dark King and the cruel Silver Queen. This robbery was meant as a stroke of war against the allies of Sir Andrew's foes, the Temples Red and Blue.

The grill-door was opened, and the dead man propped sitting in a corner, his presence made as inconspicuous as possible in the restricted space. Apparently none of the other Temple people had noticed anything wrong as yet. The music went on as before, behind doors in the distance. Somewhere nearby, around a corner, the clashing of pots and the slosh of water told of a kitchen of some kind functioning.

Bundled Wayfinder in hand again, the Baron led his small troop of armed men down the corridor lined with cells. All of the doors were closed.

The Sword paused. "This one, here. Try the keys."

The ring held six of them. Mark fumbled past one key that did not look meant to fit this crude lock, tried another that looked as if it might but didn't. The third try was lucky, and the brass-bound oaken door swung back. The space behind it was very dark, as one might expect the interior of a cell to be.

Quick reflexes ducked Mark safely under an onrushing metal blur. He recognized the missile as a brass chamber pot, as it clanged and spattered on the opposite wall of the narrow corridor.

"Keep away from me!" The voice coming out of the dark cell was certainly a woman's, but forceful enough to have served an infantry sergeant. "You putrid collection of loadbeast droppings, do you know who I am? Do you know what'll happen to you if you touch me?"

Doon, who had started in at the open door, recoiled now, swearing by several demons, as another missile of some kind flew past his head.

The cell's sole occupant was now visible in the light from the open door. She was a tall young woman, sturdily built, her pale skin streaked with dirt and her red hair matted. Her clothing was rich, or had been once, long ago before it approached its present state of wear and dirtiness. Her height overtopped Doon, who now moved into the cell again, by a good measure, and indeed came within a few centimeters of matching Mark's, who was tallest of the men present.

Doon, murmuring something no doubt meant either to frighten or reassure, took her by the arm and tried to tug her from the cell. She would have none of it, but cursed at him again. Her white hands and arms, emerging from torn sleeves, grabbed at him and fought him off.

The little man, unwilling to use deadly force, struggled ineffectually in the grip of the big young woman—the big girl, really, Mark realized, for she was very young. The Baron's momentary predicament would perhaps have been comic, at some other time. It was not, now.

"I am Ariane!" the girl was shouting at them all, as Mark moved forward to try to help his leader. Her cries had awakened an echoing clamor from some of the other cells, so that the corridor reverberated with unintelligible noise. The girl was yelling: "I am the . . ."

Her voice faltered, at the first instant when she looked Mark full in the face. And when it came back, it was vastly changed, a dreamer's whisper to match the sudden wonder in her eyes. "My brother," she breathed. And in the next instant Mark saw her eyes roll up. He stepped forward just in time to help Doon catch her slumping body. She apparently had fainted.

Doon was supporting her, but turning his head, looking for his wizard. "Indosuaros, what—?"

"Not my doing," said the magician, incongruous figure of power against the shabby background.

Doon was not going to puzzle over it now. Leaving the girl to Mark to hold, he had his Sword in hand again. "It points us back the way we came . . . bring her, and let's get out."

Mark, impeded by the longbow still on his back, had to struggle in the narrow corridor to carry the heavy girl along. Ben stopped him and wordlessly relieved him of the burden. Without effort Ben hoisted her body over one shoulder and strode on. Long red hair, even matted as it was, still fell nearly to the floor, and strong white forearms dangled.

As they tramped past the dead guard, his fixed eyes seemed to gaze at Mark.

CHAPTER 8

The Blue Temple furnished itself elegantly here on the upper levels of the central office, especially in the chambers where the members of the Inner Council met to talk business, among themselves and with other folk of comparable importance in the world. The clerks and administrators who worked on the lower floors might have to make do with worn furniture and blank paneled walls, but up here there was no stinting on slaves and fountains, marble and gold, tapestries and entertainment.

Not that Radulescu had been provided with any entertainers to keep him company as he cooled his heels in the High Priest's outer office, actually an anteroom of one of a suite of offices. But he could hear string music in the distance somewhere. He could distract himself, if he liked, by getting up from the luxuriously padded couch from time to time to pace the floor, and gaze out of the curtained window. That window overlooked walls, and parapets, and some lesser towers belonging to folk of somewhat less importance, affording a clear view above rooftops all the way to the inner side of the city walls themselves. Those walls were even higher—designedly so. They were famed for their height and strength, and this city for its impregnability—indeed, many people believed that the central hoard of the Blue Temple was concealed in some subterranean vault beneath this very building.

Radulescu of course knew better. But he, the High Priest, and two or three members of the Inner Council—Radulescu was not sure which ones—were the only people on the surface of the earth who knew with certainty where Benambra's Gold was kept, and how to reach it.

It was generally understood, among those who knew anything of the world, that the present High Priest was the *de facto* ruler of this city and of much other territory besides, to which he laid no formal claim. But cities, no matter how strongly defended, always drew the attention of money-hungry kings and other potentates; and no, the Blue Temple was not going to put its treasure, the main reason for its existence, in any such obvious place as that.

The whole organization appeared so straightforward to the uninitiated, and it was really so devious. Radulescu's thoughts were on that fact, as it related to his own career, when there was a stir at a curtained doorway, and a bald-headed, gold-garbed secretary appeared.

"The Chairman will see you now."

And Radulescu, as he hurried to follow the aide through one elaborate office after another, allowed himself a small sigh of relief. When the chief functionary of the Blue Temple chose to use that title, the business at hand was more likely to be business than some ecclesiastical ritual—as, for example, the unfrocking of some priest-officer who had been found derelict in his duty.

The final door opened by the secretary disclosed a large room. Among its other luxurious appointments was a conference table large enough for twenty potentates to have gathered at it. There was, however, only one other person in the room, a rather small man with a rubicund face and a head as bald as that of the secretary who served him. This man was seated at the far end of the table, with a bundle of papers spread out before him on the polished wood.

The High Priest—or Chairman—raised his round, red face at Radulescu's entrance. The chief executive looked quite jovial—but then, he always did, at least in Radulescu's limited experience.

"Colonel Radulescu, come in, be seated." The Chairman motioned to a place near his own. "How are you getting along on detached duty? Have you been finding enough work to keep you busy?"

Radulescu, in the months since the ill-fated delivery of treasure, had been reassigned under several formal classifications while his case was being considered and reconsidered by the Inner Council and the High

Priest. In the last ten days or so Radulescu had begun to sense a moderation in the official attitude toward him, and had seized on this as a favorable sign.

"I have worked diligently on the problem of finding ways to contribute to the Temple, Chairman, and I hope that I have had some success." Fortunately he had anticipated some such question, and he counted the composition of a good answer for it as part of the work that he had found.

"Fine, fine," said the Chairman vaguely, looking down at his spread papers once again. They looked to Radulescu like reports having to do with his own case. The windows behind the Chairman were windows such as few eyes ever saw, with real and almost perfect glass in them, and round the edges semiprecious stones set to transmit the light like bits of glass. The thought crossed Radulescu's mind that the Chairman was really only a man, and that he had a name, Hyrcanus; but rarely would anyone speak or even think of such an exalted personage by a mere human name. Only a few scurrilous and regrettably popular songs did that.

"Fine . . . good. Now, I see here that more than two months have already passed since you had that—misadventure. Would you say that is a good term to describe what happened?" And the Chairman looked up with sudden sharpness at Radulescu, treating him to eyes of jovial blue ice.

Radulescu had no trouble managing to look properly solemn as he considered the question. "My own understanding of that event has not really improved in two months, Chairman, I confess." He almost sighed. "I will be very pleased if you will enlighen me with yours." Be weary, be puzzled, be not *too* repentant, he cautioned himself; Radulescu had never admitted any culpability in the events of that strange night, beyond the minimum that the officer in charge and on the scene could not escape.

The icy eyes considered him; the red face nodded lightly, and bent again to a consideration of the many papers. "The man is really still unaccounted for," the Chairman mused. There was no need for him to specify which man he meant. "The dragon has now been replaced . . . very expensive, that, in itself. We had the dragon that was involved in the incident killed soon after, so the stomach contents could be examined. The results, I regret to say, were inconclusive. A few shreds of cloth found in the stomach were identifiable as having come from the rascal's cloak—or at any rate from one of our general issue infantry cloaks. As you may remember, his cloak was found between the cave entrance and the cliffs, looking somewhat chewed."

"I remember, sir. I of course released the spells binding the dragon as soon as I fully recovered my wits inside the cave, and realized what must have happened."

"Yes . . . yes." Papers shuffled. "So you stated here in your deposition. And at the, ah, debriefing sessions."

"Yes sir." Those interrogations had been hardly less frightening than that first shock of realization in the dark cave, where the physical pain of the enforced tumble down the stairs had soon been swallowed up in the fear of what was going to happen next.

The five drivers, knowing only that they were all blocked in, had set up a despairing noise. Responding as usual to this signal, the Whitehands had started to come up into the upper cave on their usual post-delivery mission, and Radulescu had had to use his sword by flickering candlelight to fight them off. Fortunately he hadn't forgotten to release the spells that bound the dragon. After giving it a little time in which to destroy the villain outside, he had called it with another spell to tilt the great rock open from outside.

Briefly Radulescu had been tempted to try to keep the whole fiasco a secret from his superiors. But when he got outside again and saw no trace of the missing man except a cloak, he knew he'd be on shaky ground in trying to do that.

The animals, terrified by the great dragon raging near them, had broken their tethers and run off. Radulescu pledged his surviving drivers to silence on the journey back to the Temple, by the most terrifying oaths, and then marched them back, sword in hand, to where the cavalry was still waiting, getting restless. No use disposing of the five drivers now, he knew. They'd certainly be wanted for questioning.

The Chairman was moving on, at least for the time being, to another aspect of the situation. ". . . underwater search along that portion of the coastline has turned up one battered helmet, the type of standard issue for our garrisons . . . regrettably, it is not certain whether this is the helmet issued to the missing man."

Radulescu raised his eyebrows. "I would presume, sir, that a magical investigation of the helmet has been attempted?"

"Oh yes. Certainly."

"And—even after that—we still don't know if it belonged to this Ben or not?"

Once again the Chairman gave him his full attention. "Regrettably not. Certain pernicious influences have been at work."

"Sir?" All of a sudden Radulescu found himself totally lost—a feeling that, in the circumstances, would lead almost at once to desperation.

The Chairman looked at him, and appeared to undergo a moment of uncertainty himself. Then he came to a decision. He rose from his chair at the head of the table and went to one of the long walls of the conference room, whereon a large map was displayed. The site of the treasure trove had of course not been marked on this or any other map, but Radulescu's eyes automatically went to that coastline spot anyway.

The Chairman raised a pointer, not to that vital point, but to another place very near it. "Here, this headland, across the fjord—do you see the ownership indicated for this small piece of land right on the promontory?"

It was only a tiny dot of color, that meant nothing to Radulescu until he had consulted the key at the bottom of the map. "Imperial lands," he said then, softly. He hesitated, then added: "Yes sir, I think I begin to understand."

Even that much was a daring claim, and the Chairman kept on looking at him. Radulescu was evidently expected to say more. He began to flounder. "The Emperor is—is then—an opposing force?"

The Chairman carefully laid down his pointer, and posed in front of the map with hands clasped behind his back. "I doubt you truly do begin to understand. Not your fault, really, you couldn't be expected to . . . you ought to soon, though. A man in your position, presumably ready for advancement to the Council itself at the next vacancy . . . yes, we must have you in soon for a briefing session with our top magicians, on the subject of the Emperor. That is, of course, provided your status is not downgraded at some point in the near future, for some reason." Thus Radulescu's spirits, that had shot up at the mention of promotion, were carefully cut down again to the proper size. "You do know at least that the Emperor is not a myth, that he's still a real factor to be considered?"

Obviously there was only one answer that could be returned to that.

"I'll try to arrange that briefing soon. If nothing arises to prevent it." The Chairman returned to his chair, and his voice to its usual somewhat dusty joviality. "I think we may say that all the direct evidence we have at this time, Colonel, points to the conclusion that this man Ben, Ben of—what was it? Purkinje, it says here—that this Ben of Purkinje leaped or fell to his death in the sea, *if* indeed he did manage to escape the dragon. By all reports he was somewhat slow on his feet, so the probability that he escaped the dragon is perhaps not very great.

"What I would like to ask you now is this. Do you, yourself, see any reason why this office should not consider the incident closed? Take some routine precautions of course, such as changing the spells for the guardian dragon—that's already been done—but then go on, by and large, as we were?"

Radulescu cleared his throat carefully. He did not need to exert much cleverness to sense that the bland question might well contain some kind of trap. "Have the drivers been questioned, sir?" he asked. "I would assume they have."

"Oh, indeed. No indications of any plot emerged during questioning."

Radulescu tried to think. "I suppose, sir, that an actual inventory of the treasure has been taken by now?"

The Chairman nodded. "By myself, personally. It is secure."

There was a pause. "Well, sir," Radulescu said at last. "There are still a couple of things that bother me."

"Ah. Such as?"

"A clever man, pursued by a dragon, might well think of throwing away his cloak to distract the beast. And from what I've heard about dragons, such a ploy might well succeed, at least momentarily."

"This Ben of Purkinje was far from being a clever man, according to the officers who knew him. You know that clever men are not commonly selected for these jobs."

"That's true, sir, of course. But . . ."

"But what?"

"I supervised, as you know, three previous deliveries to the cave, before this ill-starred one. Out of more than twenty drivers involved in the four deliveries I supervised, *he* was the only one to suspect that anything was amiss. Amiss from his own point of view, I mean. At least he was the only one who took any steps to save his own miserable life."

The Chairman was silent for a little while, pondering. He surprised Radulescu somewhat when he spoke at last. "Wretched life those fellows must lead. I really don't know why they would object too much to having it ended for them—ever think of it that way?"

"No sir, I can't say that I have."

After meditating a moment longer, the Chairman said: "However that may be—I daresay you were warned, before you started making deliveries, that other officers have had to deal with recalcitrant drivers in the past?"

"I was told about the possibility of some such trouble, yes sir. I got the impression that all actual instances had been in the fairly remote past."

"And did they tell you that the officer in charge had always, in the past, managed to deal with it successfully? That's why we see to it that you are armed, you know, and they are not."

Radulescu could feel his ears burning. "Yes, Chairman, I certainly got that impression too."

"What do you think we ought to do now, Radulescu? You've had a couple of months to think about it. What would you order if you were in my position? It may, but it shouldn't, surprise you to hear that I have enemies on the Council, people who would love to see me make a grave mistake and have a chance to bring me down."

Radulescu had thought about it indeed, but his thinking had been of doubtful benefit, as far as he could tell. "Well, sir, we might patrol the area more or less regularly for a time. I know that ordinarily we don't do that because—"

"—because of the excellent reason that if the area were patrolled regularly, its importance would soon no longer be a secret. Of course, if we were *sure* that your man had got away, then, yes, we might patrol. At least until we could arrange to relocate the whole depository somewhere else. And how much chance would we have then of keeping the new location secret? And how much would the move cost us, just the move alone, have you any idea? No, of course you haven't. Just be glad I don't propose to take it out of your pay."

A pleasantry, by all the gods.

CHAPTER 9

The little ship looked old, at least to Mark's admittedly non-expert eyes. But despite this appearance of age, and a thick-bodied shape, she had a certain grace of movement. Whether this was due to her construction, to sheer magic, or to the fact that she was steered and driven by a djinn, was more than Mark could tell.

The ship had two masts, and two cabins, and it belonged to Indosuaros, who had summoned it to meet Doon's party at the coastline, three days' hard ride after their rescue of Ariane from the Red Temple. Unmanned by any visible power, the vessel had come sailing into shallow water to meet them, almost grounding itself. And when its eight human passengers had climbed aboard with their slight luggage, it had needed only a word from the wizard to put out to sea again. And all this without the touch of a human hand on line or sail or rudder. The djinn was harmless to people, or at least to Indosuaros' friends, so Mitspieler assured them all. It was visible only desultorily, as a small cloud or vague disturbance in the air, usually above the masts; and sometimes there was audible an echoing voice, that seemed to come from some great distance, exchanging a few words with Indosuaros.

Right now, in the broad daylight of late morning, the djinn could not be seen. What could be seen was fog, not far ahead. There usually was fog close ahead, except when it lay just behind the ship, or between the ship and the coastline, or enveloped the little craft entirely. Except for fog, the coastline had not been out of sight for the three days of the voyage.

The weather occupied a good deal of the attention of everyone on board. It had been good, except for the patchy fog, and Mark suspected that the weather too was at least partially under the control of In-dosuaros. Mark and Ben, both landlubbers, had been seasick at the start of the voyage, but Mitspieler had dosed them with some minor potion that effected an instant cure.

Mark and Ben were sitting on the foredeck now. Doon and In-dosuaros were closeted in one of the small cabins below, and Ariane was in the other. Golok and Hubert were looking over the stern, en-gaged in their own conversation; and Mitspieler was coming abovedecks and going below again, engaged in an endless series of observations and reports on the weather, the ship's position, and perhaps other factors that Mark was not magically sensitive enough to appreciate. Meanwhile the monkbird, Dart, was moving about in the rigging. It spent most of its time up there now, having reached a not entirely easy truce with the djinn who ran the ship.

Ben, for approximately the tenth time since they had left the Red Temple, was asking Mark: "Why did she call you brother, do you sup-pose?"

Mark gave virtually the same answer that he had given nine times before. "I still have no idea. She looks nothing at all like the sister I do have. Marian's blond, and smaller than this girl, and older than I am. This one says she's eighteen, but I'll bet that she's three years younger than that, even if she is large."

"And I'll bet that she's a little mad," said Ben. "Probably more than a little."

Mark pondered that theory. "She says they gave her drugs, in the caravan, to keep her quiet. She was still drugged when we got to her, and that's why she behaved strangely at the start. Fainted, and so on."

Ariane had started to regain her senses as soon as they reached fresh air, before they were out of the Red Temple compound, and Ben had set her on her feet and let her walk the last steps to where their mounts were waiting. She'd regained her wits enough by then to grasp that the men had not come simply to attack her, and she had cooperated with them. Golok had promptly and neatly stolen another riding beast for her to ride. With the men clustered around her, they'd ridden unchallenged out through the main gate.

"Fainting and confusion I can understand," said Ben. "But—the daughter of a queen? And she still holds to that."

"Well—kings and queens must have daughters sometimes, I suppose, like other people. And she looks like—well, there's something special in the way she looks, apart from being well-shaped, and comely."

"And red-haired. And big. Aye." Ben did not appear to be convinced.

"And being a queen's daughter might not be a bad claim to make to brigands like us, to try to get good treatment for herself. You know, sometimes I get the feeling that she's laughing at the rest of us."

"If that's not madness, in her situation, then I don't know what is."

Mitspieler had gone below, just a moment ago, with one of his many reports. And now Doon stepped up on deck, his Sword in his hands, looking as if he wanted to try an observation for himself. When the girl had first told him her story, he had heard it patiently, and nodded as if he might accept it, mad as it sounded. Mark thought that princess, beggar-girl, or queen would be all one to the Baron, provided only that she served in some way to advance his schemes.

From the hour when Ariane had first come into their hands, Doon had grimly warned his men that she was under his personal protection. One of the ship's two small cabins was inviolately hers. Doon himself slept in the passage athwart her door, leaving the other cabin to the magicians.

Now, as Doon was sighting carefully along his Sword, trying to frown his vision through the fog ahead, Ariane herself came up on deck, and talk ceased momentarily among the men. She was dressed now in man's clothing, a clean and sturdy shirt and trousers from the rich store of resources that Indosuaros had provided for the expedition, and a large-size pair of sandals on her feet.

At once she sprang up into the bow, and poised there, gripping a line for balance. She looked for a moment like a model for some extravagant figurehead as she tried to peer into the fog ahead. Since she had been away from litters and cells her fair skin was growing sunburnt. Her hair, washed in her cabin's privacy, blew free in a soft red cloud.

"Cliffs ahead now," she called out gaily. Her voice was almost that of a child, very unlike that in which she had called out abuse to the men entering her cell. And she turned now, ignoring Doon for the moment, to drop to the deck beside Mark and Ben. She was smiling at them as if this were all some pleasant picnic outing. As far as Mark knew, she had never yet asked where they were going.

Neither Ben nor the Baron seemed to know quite what to say. So it was Mark who spoke to her first. "Who is your mother—really?"

Ariane sat back cross-legged on the deck, and became abruptly serious. "I suppose it is hard to believe. But I really am the daughter of the Silver Queen. I must have been still dazed when I first told you that, but it's the truth." She shot a glance at Doon. "If you have any ideas of getting ransom from her, though, you may as well forget it. She is my deadly enemy."

Doon made a gesture of indifference. "Well, girl—Princess, if you'd rather—I care very little if your story be true or not. Just out of curiosity, though, who's your father? Yambu reigns without any regular male consort, as far as I'm aware. I think she always has."

Ariane tossed a magnificence of red hair. "I wouldn't count on getting any ransom from my father, either."

Doon repeated his gesture. "I tell you that I don't count on any ransom . . . you'd better bind up that hair, or braid it, or get it out of the way somehow. It might be a problem where we're going . . . and why is your mother so bitterly your enemy? Was it she who sold you into slavery?"

"Indeed it was." Ariane seemed to accept the dictum about her hair without argument, for her fingers began working at it as if testing which mode of treatment would be best. "Certain people in the palace, I am told, had the idea of disposing of my mother and putting me on the throne instead. The heads of those people are now prominently in view above the battlements. Maybe they were even guilty, I don't know. They never consulted me. And I've seen very little of my mother in my lifetime. I don't know . . ."

"You don't know what?" asked Mark, fascinated.

"It doesn't matter. Also, I sometimes have powers—"

"I know you do," Doon cut in. "I count on them, in fact."

She looked at him again. "Do you? I wish I could count on them to help me, but as I say I only sometimes have them, and they are unreliable. I am told, again, that they depend somewhat on the fact that no man has ever known me. The Red Temple set great store on my virginity, when their magicians were satisfied that it was intact. They would have sold me for a fortune, I suppose to someone who had other than magical concerns about it. And where are we going, anyway, that I must bind up my hair?"

But Doon had another question of his own to put. "And why did not your mother simply have you killed, instead of selling you?"

"Perhaps she thought that going into slavery would be worse. Perhaps some seer or oracle warned her against it. Who knows why great queens do the things they do?" Mark had heard the same tone of bitterness, exactly, in the voice of the peasant woman whose eyes had been put out by soldiers.

The Baron had sheathed his Sword now, and was standing with arms folded, eyes probing at his captive—if that was really the right word, Mark thought, for her status. "You say your mother is your enemy," Doon demanded. "Then you are hers?"

Ariane's blue eyes were suddenly those of an angry child. "Give me the chance to prove it and I will."

"I intend to do just that. Now, the Silver Queen has a deep interest in the Blue Temple, does she not?"

As if she had been expecting to hear something else, the girl had to pause for thought. But then she agreed. "Aye, I am sure she must have. Why?"

"Because we are going to enter the central storehouse of the Blue Temple, and rob it of its wealth. My Sword here informs me that you— your powers—are going to be very useful in the execution of this plan. Cooperate with me willingly, and I promise you that when the time comes for sharing out the treasure, you will not be forgotten. And I promise also that in the meantime you'll take no harm from any man." And he cast a meaningful look at the two members of his crew who were immediately present.

And she is so beautiful, Mark was thinking, that there are a lot of men who'd fight to have her. But there was something almost too impressive in her beauty, so that it served as a warning as well as an invitation. And Mark could not forget that moment in which Ariane had hailed him as her brother. Whenever he had asked her about it later, she had said that she could not remember, that she had been drugged when she called him that. He told himself that there was no way he could actually be her brother. Still . . .

Doon was speaking to the girl again. ". . . and how would you like to find yourself, when we part company, with a purse full of Blue Temple jewels and gold as dowry? Or for any other purpose. You need be dependent upon no prince or potentate then, if you don't want to be."

Ariane mused. *"Her* gold and jewels, in my hands—I think I would like that." She seemed to be accepting without difficulty the prospect of getting into the Blue Temple vaults and robbing them. Mark and Ben exchanged a glance, and Ben nodded slightly; the girl must be at least a little out of touch with reality.

Mitspieler had come up on deck again, and was hovering in the background trying to get Doon's attention. As soon as he had done so, Doon went below again, to consult with the magicians.

The moment the Baron was out of sight, Hubert, with Golok trailing behind him, came forward from the stern. Mark had noticed before now that Hubert was fascinated by Ariane, and could not keep from approaching her when he had the opportunity.

But something that the soldier saw in the sea or fog ahead of the ship appeared to distract him, and when he came up to the others he was frowning. The first thing he said was: "I hope we'll not go near those cliffs."

Ben, still sitting on the deck, leaning back against the rail, looked up at him curiously. "Why not?"

" 'Why not?' the big man asks. Because of who might be up there, that's why not. I've heard our masters talking—all right, if you don't like to call 'em that, our leaders, then. And I know a thing or two about this part of the world myself, without asking them."

"And who is so important, up on the cliffs?" asked Ariane. Suddenly she appeared to be intensely interested, though she usually cared nothing for Hubert's talk.

Hubert chuckled, pleased at having made an impression for once. "That's the Emperor's land up there, young lady. Those cliffs ahead of us, beyond the fog."

Ariane almost gasped to hear this. "No, not really!" Though Mark was observing her as keenly as he could, he still could not tell if she was really impressed, frightened, or subtly mocking Hubert.

The short man, at least, had no doubt about what kind of an impression he was making. He seemed to swell a little. "Oh aye . . . did you think that the Emperor was only a story? That's what most people think. A few bright ones know better. I've heard about this place. Down below those cliffs there's a grotto, and in that grotto the Emperor keeps a horde of his pet demons. Oh, he owns other lands too, scattered about the world, but this place is special. I've heard about it from those who've seen it.

"Maybe you thought he was only a story, or only a joke? Ah no, lass, he's real, and no joke. He likes to sit up there on a rock, wearing a gray cloak, and looking like an ordinary man, waiting for shipwrecked folk or anyone else to land and come up to him out of the sea. And when they do, he likes to whistle up his demons. And the victims are dragged by demons down into the grotto, where for the rest of time and eternity they wish that they could die—why, what's the matter, big man, seasickness come back on you?—that's the Emperor's idea of a joke . . . oh, you don't believe me, lass?"

Mark glanced curiously at Ben, who did indeed appear to be upset about something. But Ariane certainly did not. Far from being upset or even impressed by Hubert's tale, she had burst out laughing.

It made Hubert angry to be laughed at, and his ears reddened. "Funny, is it? And if anyone resists, or tries to run away, all the Emperor has to do is throw open his gray cloak. Underneath it, his body's so twisted away from human shape that anyone who sees it will go mad. . . ."

The girl's laughter did not sound to Mark as if it sprang from madness, but from a healthy sense of the ridiculous. Hubert was glaring at her, and his fingers worked. But Mark and Ben were one on each side of her, and watching him; and Doon had spoken his warning. The short man turned and retreated quickly to the stern. And Golok still hovered nearby, watching.

Presently Doon was back on deck, Indosuaros with him. Shortly afterwards the ship changed course, and was bearing in toward land, though not toward the cliffs where the Emperor was said to lie in wait. The wizard was now muttering almost continuous instructions to the djinn. The other humans stood out of the way as much as possible, as the vessel was maneuvered by the invisible power, in through breakers to a small scrap of sandy beach. The ship was brought to a stop just before it ran aground, in water so shallow that it was possible to disembark with no worse effect than a wetting.

Ariane, with her hair already tied up neatly, took part as one of the crew in passing packs and weapons safe to shore.

In a few moments they all stood on the beach, dripping—all but Indosuaros, whose robes had refused to absorb any water even when immersed. The wizard stood conferring cryptically with his djinn, which was visible only as a small cloud of troubled air above the ship.

Meanwhile Doon, gazing up at the towering cliffs, asked Ben: "This is where you climbed down?"

Ben had not yet told anyone, even Mark, the details of his escape after getting away from the dragon and starting down the cliff. And, with Hubert's lurid story still fresh in his mind, he felt reluctant to start talking about them now. He looked at the cliffs uncertainly, and then to right and left. "A little farther south, I think it was. It's hard for me to tell; it was night then, of course. All this cliff looks much the same."

"Aye." Doon studied the face of it to north and south. "Then you worked your way south along the shoreline, I suppose . . . how'd you get across the fjord?"

"Swam. Where it was narrower."

Doon nodded his acceptance. And now, like some infantry commander about to set out on a dangerous patrol, he ordered all packs opened and the contents spread out. In addition he checked the water bottles and skins, making sure all were full and fresh. There was a coil of rope for each member of the expedition. Food supplies were in order —Ben had heard the tale of the feast magically provided by Indosuaros at his headquarters, but there had been no indication of any such service being available on the road. There were weapons, climbing and stonecutting tools. Hubert appropriated a crossbow from Indosuaros' armory. Ariane was given a pack as a matter of course, and, when she spoke to Doon, a knife and a sling to wear at her belt. The magician and his aide had their own inventory to take, and Indosuaros certified that they were ready.

The ship, relieved of its passengers and their modest cargo, bobbed in the water a few score meters offshore, remaining in one spot just as if it had been anchored.

Doon waded out a few steps, to question his magician, who was standing in calf-deep water, gesturing. "What about the djinn?"

"It must stay with the ship, to protect it, move it about as needed, and bring it back to us here when we call."

At another gesture from Indosuaros, the sails emptied, flapped, then bellied as they refilled themselves. The vessel turned away from shore and toward the open sea.

"Wait!" called Doon sharply. When the ship's progress had been stayed by another gesture from the wizard, the Baron added: "I want to know something first, magician. Suppose that when we return to this shore, loaded with treasure, neither you nor your worthy assistant happen to be with us. How do we get the boat to come to us then? And where will it be in the meantime? We may well be gone for days."

"It will be at sea," said Indosuaros, looking down with dignity at the smaller man. "But close enough to be brought back here quickly. And the djinn will maintain enough fog in the area to keep the ship from being very easily observed."

"That's fine. And how do we get it back? There is some small chance, you know, that you will not be here. The place we are going to visit is not without its dangers."

Tension held in the air for a long moment. Then Indosuaros said, mildly enough: "I will give you some words to use for a summoning. And your men should hear them too, just in case *you* are not here, when *they* come back."

If Doon had any objection, he bit it back. The wizard devised a four-word command, and let them all repeat it aloud to be sure they had it memorized. After a trial, in which Ariane successfully summoned the vessel back toward shore, it was dispatched at last, and disappeared into a looming patch of fog.

Doon drew Wayfinder. To no one's surprise, it pointed the way for them straight up the cliff.

The climb began. Doon led the way, as usual, with the monkbird fluttering on ahead and coming back frequently to Golok to report.

Once Doon turned to Ben, who was climbing just behind him. "This cliffside is more irregular than I thought, looking up at it from below. There might be a dozen cave-mouths concealed around here. Do you suppose there could be one, a side entrance to the cave we seek? That would save us from having to face the dragon on the top."

"There might indeed be a dozen such openings, for all I know. It was night when I came down. Your Sword should point out such an entrance if there is one."

"I don't know . . . sometimes I think that there are two ways, and it picks the way of higher risk deliberately."

And they climbed on.

At the brink they paused, peering cautiously over, while once more the monkbird was sent ahead to scout. Wayfinder now pointed directly inland.

Across the rocky headland, a hundred stony hillocks rose, looking like choppy waves frozen in a sea of lava. The thorny vegetation looked even sparser now to Ben than it had on the night of his great escape, when it had seemed to him that he stepped on thorns with almost every stride. Indeed the whole scene, before his eyes now for the first time in daylight, looked unfamiliar. His confidence declined in his ability to find the cave again without the aid of magic.

The monkbird came back to report the way was clear, and was

promptly sent out again. The humans climbed over the brink and moved cautiously inland, Doon in the lead.

The black flutterer returned almost at once. Perching on Golok's shoulder, it gave him what sounded like a report of a landwalker inland, almost exactly in the same direction that they were heading.

"How far?"

It jabbered something to its master, something unintelligible to the others.

Golok explained. "Almost a kilometer, I think. Horizontal distances are hard for it to estimate. Dart seems to be telling me that the dragon's eating something."

The Sword was pointing in the same direction still.

Doon chewed at his mustache, a sign of nervousness that Ben had not observed in him before. "You tell me, big man, that it should not be nearly a kilometer from here to the cave."

"Nothing like that far, no."

"Then likely we'll be able to get in, before . . . we'll chance it." Again Doon led the way inland, advancing quickly.

Golok relaunched his airborne scout, and Dart flew inland at low altitude. And returned in a few moments, this time chattering urgently.

"The dragon's moving toward us," Golok translated. "Coming straight this way." Then the youth ran ahead of Doon, who had paused to listen to the warning. "Let me get out in front of you," Golok urged, "and try to manage it. It's accustomed to being managed, from what you tell me."

"Manage a dragon?" But Doon let Golok get out ahead, then led the others in a quick advance.

Ben, even as he trotted forward, drew Dragonslicer from its sheath. Beside him he saw Mark pulling his longbow off his back and reaching for an arrow. Hubert paused for a moment, to throw his weight on the crossbow, cock it, and set the trigger.

You had to hit a big landwalker right in the open mouth, Ben was thinking, or in the tiny target of its eye, to do yourself any good even with a crossbow bolt . . . and now already he could hear the first chiming of the dragon. It was out of sight behind hillocks, but no longer very far ahead. It had to be coming on to meet them.

Ben scrambled up the nearest hillock to get a better look. Golok had climbed another mound, some twenty-five or thirty meters ahead, and from its top he was already talking and crooning and gesturing to the monster.

Not the same dragon I saw that night, thought Ben, this one's a little smaller. Some twenty meters beyond Golok it had paused, leaning with one of its forearms on a mound three meters high, so that for a moment it made a parody of some irate proprietor behind a counter. It was angry at Golok for being where he was; it was probably angered by his mere existence. Ben could hear the anger in the near-musical chiming of its voice. So far it did not appear to have noticed Ben, or any of the others. It bowed its head once toward Golok, as if in some kind of formal acknowledgement of his existence, and then without further warning it came after him in a clumsy-looking charge. Fire sighed and whistled in its nostrils.

People near Ben were scrambling wildly to and fro among the rocks. Golok abandoned the useless position of his mound in a surprisingly graceful leap. A few long strides and he had scrambled up atop another, farther from the people and the dragon and a little closer to the cliffs. He was still gesturing and singing, and something in his method took effect. The dragon's movements slowed abruptly, the charge declining into a mere advance. The monkbird was flying like a sparrow round the dragon's head, as if trying to distract it, but Dart received no attention.

Doon, near Ben's elbow, whispered fiercely: "Indosuaros?"

The wizard's whispered answer was just as taut. "We must use no magic here, if we can possibly avoid it. There will be traces of our passage, if we do."

Ben could sense Doon's indecision. The Baron wanted to get his party into the cave as quickly as possible, and if possible without an open combat against the dragon. Yet at the same time he did not want to lose Golok, or even to separate from him.

Golok made yet another sideways withdrawal, leading the dragon still farther out of their indicated path. And again it lurched and lunged toward him, this time punctuating its advance with the sideways sweep of a clawed forelimb against a mound. Rocks scattered, flying as if cast by some giant's sling.

That movement was enough for Mark. His longbow twanged at a range of no more than twenty meters. The straight shaft, driven, Ben knew, by a thirty-kilo pull, struck within a handsbreadth of the moving dragon's right eye. The arrowhead broke on one of the small scales there, the shaft rebounded like a twig. The dragon paid it not the least attention.

Doon was whispering again. "I don't want to lose my beast-master before we even get below. We'll need him there. We've got to save him, kill the dragon if we must."

And if we can, thought Ben. Still the creature was advancing, in fits and starts, toward Golok. The youth with his best efforts was managing to blunt the edge of its wrath for seconds at a time, but not to turn it away. He dodged, retreated, tried to stand his ground, and was forced back again.

Golok was gradually being driven back toward the edge of the cliffs, now only a few meters behind him. Seven other people, working from one rock-shelter to the next, were following as closely as they dared.

"Go over the edge," Ben called to him, trying to make his voice no louder than was necessary for the youth to hear, fearing to startle the beast into another forward rush. "Over the brink, and hang on. It won't see you then. Maybe it—"

Again, abruptly, the dragon charged at Golok, this time with a thundering full roar. The subtle nets of control, woven of beast-master's lore, had given way totally at last.

Both Mark and Hubert, meanwhile, had maneuvered away from Ben, so that the dragon was charging more or less in their direction and they had a good shot at the roof of the open mouth. Ben, scrambling forward as fast as he could toward the dragon's flank with Dragonslicer gripped in both hands, thought that even so the chance was small that the bowmen could hit the brain, and that even if you hit the brain your problems with a landwalker were not over necessarily. . . . Already Dragonslicer's powers had awakened, and Ben could feel the Sword, hear it, shrilling as he ran.

Golok had fallen, scrambling, near the brink. Longbow shaft and crossbow bolt, simultaneously, entered the open mouth that loomed above him. There was an explosion of fire that gutted the dragon's left cheek outwards; the jolt of liquid hell that was to have been projected at Golok went spewing and sizzling away instead, some of it over the cliff's edge, some to spill upon the nearby rocks. One of the missiles had burst a fireland in the cheek.

Ariane was yelling bravely, and slinging stones at the dragon, whether accurately or not made no difference in the least. The two wizards were sensibly lying low.

Drooling flame, and certainly now aware of pain, the monster turned toward the other people who beset it. Doon, scrambling desperately over and around rocks, behind the enemy now, struck with Wayfinder at one of its hind legs, aiming for a spot where there should be a tendon beneath the scales. The heavy, razor-edged blade rebounded like a toy sword from an anvil. The dragon did not see or feel him.

It saw Ben though, and it heard him. The Sword of Heroes was in his hands, making its shrill sound, and now he felt the more-than-human power of the weapon flow into his arms.

As always, the great damned beasts were unpredictable. At the last moment the dragon turned again away from Ben, and bent to pick up the screaming Golok in its left forelimb. Ben could see the youth's legs, still living, kicking wildly. Ben yielded himself to Dragonslicer, letting the force of it in his hands pull him forward to the attack. The blow struck by the Sword was almost too swift for his own thought to follow it, and it took off cleanly the dragon's right paw as it swiped at him. The severed forelimb thudded like an armored body falling to the ground, the iridescent blood gushing out.

The Sword of Heroes shrieked.

Ben got one more close look at Golok's living face.

Dragonslicer thrust home for the heart, parting hand-thick scales as if they had been tender leaves. The landwalker stumbled backward, leaving the Sword still keening in Ben's hands. The treetrunk legs kicked out in reflex, hurling stones and dust. With a last roar that ended in eruptive bubbling, the beast went backward over the cliff, Golok still clutched to its scaly breast.

Ben had time to scramble forward to the brink and watch the ending of the fall. The two bodies did not separate until they hit the water and the rocks.

CHAPTER 10

The monkbird screamed, on and on. To Ben it seemed to have been screaming for days. With the Sword of Heroes still dripping dragon's blood in his right hand, he clung to the cliff-edge rocks, looking down a hundred meters at the sullen surge and smash of waves below. It was a fine day, and the sea wore delicate shadings of blue and green over most of its vast surface. The fall on rocks had pulped the huge beast's body like a dropped fruit, but the waves were already sorting and sifting and dispersing the organic wreckage, on the way to accomplishing a tidy disposal of it. And Golok's body had already disappeared completely.

Mark had come to Ben's side, had taken him by the left arm, was pulling him back from the brink:

Doon was frothing angry. "The bird, the demon-damned bird!" He looked up at Dart's small, frantic shape flying not far above his head, as if he were about to strike at it with his Sword. Dart's voiceless keening mingled with the racket of a cloud of seabirds that had been startled up from the shoreline rocks. "How are we going to be able to use it now?"

As if intentionally answering his question, it came down suddenly, down in an abrupt swoop to Ariane standing nearby. Her left arm was extended in the traditional gesture of beast masters to their flying pets. Now, with its fur dark brown against the coils of her red hair, the monkbird huddled on her shoulder, mourning almost silently for its dead master, clinging there with feet and wings like some half-human orphan. Ariane whispered to it and stroked it. When Mitspieler came to her to see if he could help, she sent him away with a gentle headshake, and continued to soothe the creature.

Doon observed this with visible relief. "Good job, Princess. We may not have lost much here after all." He took a quick glance at the sky. "They may think they've lost their dragon over the cliff by accident, chasing a rabbit or some such. Anyway we'll have come and gone, if we do the job right, before the dragon's missed. Let's move."

And he moved ahead himself, Wayfinder drawn. Ben, having cleaned Dragonslicer as well as he could on prickly leaves, followed closely. Mark was near Ben, and the others only a few steps behind.

Ben could still recognize no details of his surroundings, though it looked in general like the same landscape from which he had fled by night. Now, in broad day, it held no sign anywhere of humanity or of human works, apart from the adventurers themselves. The wasteland stretched away to north, west, and south, kilometer after kilometer, empty and grimly beautiful.

"Where's your local Blue Temple?" asked Mark, sticking his head up over a hillock beside Ben's, to scan the way ahead.

"Somewhere inland, over there. Kilometers away. It took us half a day and half a night to get here from there, even riding part of the way."

And on impulse Ben turned his head to look back across the water. On the other side of the fjord rose the opposite headland, emerging belatedly from the last of the morning's mists to warm itself in early summer's sun. The meadow and the forest on its top were indistinguishable at this distance and in this light. The cliffs, with this side of them just coming into sunshine now, were vaguely blue.

Did I really swim all that way, and climb those cliffs? Ben asked himself. Swimming through the tides at night, with no idea of where I was really going? Someday, he thought, I'll tell my grandchildren all about it. My grandchildren and Barbara's, in our fine house. I saw the Emperor sitting there in his gray cloak, and he looked just like a man. . . . Ben had been on the way to forgetting the incident completely until Hubert had startled him with his tale. But no use worrying now about the real truth of it—there had been no demons in evidence, anyway.

He looked inland again, and moved on, following the others who were getting ahead of him.

Doon, with his Sword in his hands, led them steadily on across the trackless waste. Ben several times murmured to the others that now the proper hillock could not be much farther. In trying to pick it out, he became aware for the first time of how much alike were all these stony knobs. It even seemed that each hillock had on one side an enormous stone, and that each such stone was of a size and shape to possibly form the balance-door protecting the hidden cave. This fact was not immediately obvious, for no two of the huge stones were exactly alike in appearance, nor were they on the same sides of their respective hills. But any of at least a hundred, as far as Ben could tell, might possibly be the one they sought. He wondered silently if this might have been arranged by magic; it seemed impossible that chance alone would be responsible.

Wayfinder was immune to these as to all other distracting elements. Following Doon, who held to an almost straight course, Ben tried to recall in which direction the cave opening had faced. Indelibly he remembered that moment in which he'd turned from the entrance, and, with Radulescu's yell still hanging in the air, had grabbed and pulled the great stone down to bang the doorway shut. Then, himself on the edge of panic, running off into the night, almost blind in darkness, banging his legs on rocks . . . he had run, that night, with the ocean on his left . . .

"Here," said Doon abruptly. He had come to a halt standing in front of a hillock that looked to Ben no more familiar than any of the others standing round it. Facing the side of the mound, Doon stretched forth his arm until the tip of the Sword in his hand touched rock. Now Ben could plainly see the strong vibration in the blade.

"Here?" Ben echoed, questioning; the hillock was still unrecognizable to him among its fellows. There was one way to make sure, and he slipped off his backpack. "All right. Lend a hand at this end of the rock and help me lift it." And he bent to grip the base of the enormous stone himself. Suddenly, with the feel of it, he was sure that this was the right spot.

But Indosuaros touched his shoulder. "Wait." The magician raised both hands, and rested ten fingertips upon the rock. He stood there for a moment, his eyes closed, then stepped back, glancing at his assistant. "I sense no guardian magic. Lift away."

With Ben exerting himself, Mark and Hubert gave enough help to tilt the great stone back. Ben's remaining doubts vanished; there was the dark triangular opening, just the same.

Doon, his weapon ready, glared into the doorway for a moment, then stepped back, nodding with satisfaction. "Lights," he pronounced.

These, seven Old World devices, were taken out of one of the packs and passed around. They were somewhat different in shape and style from the torch that Ben had seen Radulescu using, but functionally the same. And these had modern, handmade leather straps attached.

Doon demonstrated quickly how the straps could be used to put the light on like a helmet, leaving the wearer's hands free. "For these, again, we have our wizard to thank. We'll see to it, Indosuaros, that your years of preparation were not wasted." He took the helmet off to demonstrate its function. "Press here, and it gives light. Press again and it goes dark. Turn this to make it brighter or dimmer. Twist and push like this, and you can focus the light into a beam. Twist and draw back again, and the glow spreads out to light a room."

"How long will they keep burning?" asked Hubert, who was obviously fascinated. He had probably, Ben thought, never seen the like before.

Doon shrugged. "They're already nearly as old as the world itself. I suppose they may keep burning until its end, so don't fear to use them."

The actual entry into the cave seemed to Ben almost an anticlimax. With the new light shining from his forehead, he noted the old wax candle drippings still on the floor. There was no visible trace of the six men he had shut in here with his own hands. But now the memory of that night came back more sharply than ever, for the cave looked no different now than it had looked then in the beam of the Old World light carried by Radulescu.

Indosuaros, standing by the large opening in the floor, again reported that he could detect no guardian magic. "Not here . . . but far down, yes. There's magic moiling in the earth, well below us. Magic, and . . ."

"And what?" Doon asked him sharply.

The magician sighed. "I think . . . there is something down there of the Old World, also. Something large."

"Is that all you can tell us?"

"Old World technology." Indosuaros curled his lip. "Who can tell about technology?"

"The magic that you sense, then—are you going to be able to deal with it, when we reach it?"

The wizard appeared for a moment to be taking some kind of inward inventory. He stared hard at his assistant. Then he answered, firmly enough: "I can."

"Then," said Doon briskly, "the next order of business is to make sure we can open the outer door here, when we come back." And he trotted back up the crooked stair to scrutinize the great rock carefully. Ben had already explained to everyone how he had used that door to get away.

Now Doon sighed, dissatisfied. He scowled at the rock as if it offended him. "Ben, tell me this. The priests must come here on inspection tours from time to time, to see that their treasure's safe. Don't they?"

"I suppose they must," Ben answered, climbing the stairs too. "But I never heard anything about it."

"Well, you say it can't be opened from the inside. That officer would have opened it if he could, and pursued you. Right?"

"I don't think," said Ben, "that I could lift it alone, from inside, if my life depended on it. And only one person can get at it from inside, there's room only for one."

"I doubt that the priests leave this open behind them when they come. And I doubt they come with half a dozen slaves each time, to wait outside and lift this for them when they want to leave." Again Doon sighed. "Once we are well down and in, of course, we may discover some alternate way out. Or we may not. Now I have stonecutting tools, but . . . ." Just looking at the rock, Doon shook his head. Then he made a gesture of giving up. "Indosuaros? I know our plan was not to leave any magic traces of our passage, so near the surface anyway. But to seal ourselves into this cave without a known way out would be even worse."

The wizard had to agree, gloomily. "I fear that you are right." Then Indosuaros held a hurried, whispered conference with Mitspieler, after which the two of them drew objects from a pack. Soon they were standing just outside the upper doorway, rubbing at the huge rock with what looked to Ben like raw slices of some kind of vegetable.

All this time Ariane was content to remain in the lower cave, occupying her time by petting the monkbird and whispering to it soothingly. She showed little or no sign of fear.

When the magicians had finished their treatment of the rock, Doon summoned Ben to pull it down and close the door. It felt to Ben as if the mass of the stone were now greatly diminished; when he tried, he was able to catch it falling, halfway closed, and push it up again very easily. One after another, all the members of the party now tried lifting it open from inside, and all could manage it.

With everyone inside the cave at last, and the outer door closed, Doon gathered his party around the large slot in the lower floor.

"This is where we put the treasure down," said Ben. "And where I saw the Whitehands reach for it."

The wizard Indosuaros smiled, as if he were now determined to be reassuring. "They come this close to the surface only to receive treasure, as they did on the night when you were here."

"How do you know?"

Ben's answer was an arrogant look, that said the sources of the wizard's knowledge were doubtless beyond Ben's grasp, and were not really any of his business anyway.

"It would be a neat trick," offered Hubert, "if we could capture one of those to serve us as a guide. They must know a quick way to the treasure. Trust those who have to carry it to know the shortest way."

"If we meet one of them," muttered Doon abstractedly, "we'll ask him." The Baron had braced his body directly above the aperture, and was looking intently down into it with the aid of a beam from his headlamp. "There are steps carved into the side here," he announced. "And it doesn't look far down. I don't think I'll need a rope—but let me have one, just in case. Two of you hold it up here."

Mark and Ben gripped one of the thin, supple coils, and paid out an end. Doon sheathed Wayfinder and in a moment had vanished, sliding down.

The line went slack in their hands almost at once. "I'm down," the Baron's voice called up to them softly. "Come ahead." Ben, looking down through the aperture, could see the Baron's headlamp moving about just a short distance below. In the augmented light, the series of niches for steps and grips, carved in the side of the short shaft, stood out plainly. One side of the shaft joined with a wall of the chamber below, and the steps went down nearly to that lower floor.

Ben followed his leader, and soon the whole party was down. The chamber in which they now found themselves was about the same size and shape as the one they had just descended from, and again there was a single lower exit. This time, though, the exit was a tunnel mouth, cut in the side of the cave approximately opposite the entrance shaft. The tunnel was narrow, and just about high enough for a moderately tall man to walk into it erect. Ben expected that Mark would have to watch his head.

Again Doon led the way, the others following necessarily in single file. After first twisting to the right, the tunnel bent back to the left, while continuously and ever more steeply descending. As the steepness increased, carved grips and steps appeared again in sides and floor.

They had followed this passage for no more than a few score meters, when Doon stopped, calling softly back to the others that the tunnel ahead turned into a perfectly vertical shaft.

The Baron refused the suggestion of a rope, and simply continued to work his way lower, by means of the plentiful niches provided in the shaft's sides. Ben followed cautiously. Above and behind him, Indosuaros looked down and ahead with eyes half-closed, as if he were groping his way along by the use of senses beyond the normal. After Indosuaros was Ariane, the monkbird riding unhooded on her shoulder, clinging tightly to her shirt. Hubert was next, then Mark, with Mitspieler bringing up the rear.

Again there was an easy egress from the lower end of the shaft. It ended a little more than a meter above a circular dais that was two or three meters wide, and raised perhaps a meter above the floor of the surrounding room.

The lower end of the shaft was finished in what looked like ancient masonry, with hairline gaps showing between blocks, so that Ben marveled as he let go of the last grip that it had not all come crashing down with his weight on it.

But soon all seven members of the expedition were safely down out of the shaft, and standing round the dais. They were in a squat cylinder of a room, perhaps ten meters across, larger than either of the two rooms above. Here the stone wall, floor, and ceiling were all carved quite smoothly into a regular shape. Twelve dark doorways were more or less regularly spaced round the circumference of the circular wall. From near the center of the room it was not possible to throw a beam of light very far into any of the twelve apertures, as the passages beyond all curved sharply after a few meters, turning down or sideways or both. Each tunnel, at the start at least, was wide enough for only one person to enter it comfortably at a time.

"We have reached the third sealing," said Doon. And he raised his Sword in a salute, as if to a worthy foe.

CHAPTER 11

Doon was standing near the round wheel-hub of the dais, turning his body slowly, aiming Wayfinder to determine which of the dark tunnels they ought to follow. Mark, watching the Baron's face, saw him for once frowning at what his guide told him.

Indosuaros, gazing over Doon's shoulder, prodded. "There seems no doubt about it, does there? The Sword says that's the one to take." And the magician pointed with a long, gnarled forefinger at a tunnel.

All the more irritated by this advice, Doon moved the Sword. "But first, a moment ago, it indicated this other passage, over here. I'm sure of it. And now it doesn't."

"It certainly does not," Indosuaros agreed. He paused, then added: "Your hand may have been shaking, man. Or perhaps the light was unsteady for a moment."

"My hand did not shake! And I really don't need any light to feel the vibration in the blade."

Ben chimed in: "There could be a smaller amount of treasure at the end of the passage where it first pointed, and a larger at the end of this one. Anyway, I'd read the augury so."

"Or," suggested Ariane, "one treasure that's being moved about, even as you attempt to get a bearing on it?" There was something like enjoyment in her voice, that did not fade even when Doon glared at her.

"I doubt we're very near to any treasure yet," the Baron growled.

And the magician again: "Either trust your Sword or not, is all I can advise you. If you're going to trust it no longer, then I'll start to try to find our way by other means." Why, he's jealous of the Sword, thought Mark.

The Baron evidently thought the same. "You'll start to try? Why no, I think we'll trust this god-forged metal yet awhile. And we'll take the way it showed me first." The two men stared at each other for a moment.

"Some of us could try one way and some another," Hubert offered, though not as if he really thought it was a good idea.

Doon gave him a brief glare too. "No, I'll not divide my forces. Not yet anyway. We'll take the way Wayfinder showed me first."

Mark, having some experience of using Coinspinner for guidance, thought that the point called for more discussion. But that too would have its dangers, and he kept quiet, and read agreement in Ben's eyes. Mark met Ariane's gaze too, and thought he saw the beginning there of a realistic concern. And in her eyes as well were other things less easy to interpret.

The party entered the tunnel that Doon had chosen. They were moving in single file as before, and once more Mark found himself next to last, just in front of the silent Mitspieler, and behind Hubert. Mark had to stoop his back or bend his neck almost continuously to keep his headlamp from scraping on the roof of the passage as he moved. If this goes on for very long, he thought, I'll have to take the lamp off and carry it in my hand. Or depend on others' lights while we're in here—this passage was at least a little wider than the last one, though it still lacked room for two to go comfortably abreast.

The tunnel curved sharply from left to right and back again, while constantly descending. But here the slope of the descent never became as steep as it had in the previous tunnel, and the rough floor here was enough to provide secure footing. It occurred to Mark to look at the ceiling for torch-smoke stains as he scraped his way along beneath it. Surely not all of the Blue Temple people who had come through this maze to reach the treasure would have used Old World lights, and generations of traffic ought to have left stains along the proper route.

Indeed Mark thought that he could see some blackening, though on the dark rock it was difficult to be sure.

"Look at that," said Ben's voice, quietly, from a few meters ahead. The procession did not stop. A few more steps and Mark saw what Ben had meant. They were passing what had once been the mouth of an intersecting passage, its opening now completely blocked by a cave-in, filled with jumbled slabs and fragments fallen from overhead. From this mass, down near the floor, there protruded a pair of dead skeletal hands —Mark found himself taking note that they were of no more than normal human size. Somehow the mute warning seemed all the more impressive because it had no look of having been planned as a deterrent to intruders.

Mark saw Ariane look down at the bones as she walked past. The girl showed no sign of shock or fright. What kind of a growing-up must she have had? Mark wondered to himself. Could it have been as strange as my own, or even stranger? Maybe her powers, if she truly has any, knew me as her brother in that much at least.

There were no more branching passages. Having no real choice now of which way to go, Doon was not consulting Wayfinder. Now they had reached a comparatively straight stretch of the tunnel, where Mark could see Doon's light bobbing at the head of the procession, revealing the tunnel walls—

Which now ended, not far ahead, in a simple circle of darkness. It was as if the passage here debouched into some vast cave. As they grew closer with their lights, vague distant forms as of jagged rock appeared in the opening.

"What's this, by all the demons?"

The tunnel widened somewhat at its mouth, and the intruders crowded together there as best they could to see what kind of a place they had reached. There was indeed a large cave in front of them now, and it looked virtually impassable. The floor of it, if it could be called a floor, was at some distance below the one on which they stood, and it bristled with spiny projections of rock, that gleamed here and there with flecks of brightness but were also heavily stained and coated with what looked in the lamps' beams like some kind of fungus.

And again, behind a sharp outcropping, Mark saw the startling white of human bone. Some kind of bones, at least; these were jumbled and broken, and Mark could not be sure that they were human.

This deadly looking chamber was some twenty or thirty meters deep, and without any other visible entrance or exit. On right and left it extended for only a few meters before its side walls closed in to come close to the wall from which the tunnel emerged; on each side the space between was far too small to admit a hope that people might be able to squeeze themselves through it. Mark, looking upward as best he could out of the tunnel's mouth, could see only the smooth slight bulge of the rounded wall from which the tunnel emerged, and above that, a jagged rocky roof some meters out of reach. Looking down, the prospect was even more discouraging; upjutting corners of stone waited amid shadows at an intimidating distance below. In no direction could he see anything that looked like a practical continuation of their path.

At Doon's urging, Ariane now prevailed upon the monkbird to try a short scouting flight into the cave ahead. The beams of headlamps lit its way, but still it fluttered about uncertainly and had to be encouraged. At last it flew out for some distance, and was near a far unpromising shelf of rock when there came a sudden popping noise from the fungi near it, and a cloud of dust burst up around the flying creature. The monkbird came speeding back to Ariane's shoulder, where once more it clung tight in fear. It brought with it a taste of choking dust, and at the same time an acrid, poisonous odor drifted to the humans' nostrils from the far reaches of the cave.

Doon, muttering demon-oaths between sudden fits of coughing, had his Sword out and was aiming it at various portions of the cave. But he obtained no response until he pointed it back into the tunnel, in the direction from which the expedition had just come. He looked so black at this that even Indosuaros thought it wise to make no comment at the moment.

Meanwhile Mark was looking back into the cave, and something he saw there kindled an idea. He pulled off his headlamp, and, bending down, placed it on the floor, focusing a tight beam of light upon some rocks in the cave that were twenty or thirty meters distant.

"Turn off all the lights but this one," he told the others. "I'm trying to see something."

The Baron, on the verge of issuing new orders, hesitated and then did as he had been told. The other people muttered questions and protests, mingled with their sneezes and coughs. But in a moment Mark's was the only lamp alight.

He straightened up again. "Look. My lamp isn't moving at all, it's resting on the floor. Watch the light."

From a few bright facets of the distant rock, spots of brilliance were being reflected back into the tunnel, glowing dimly on walls and ceiling and on the faces of the people.

"Look."

The spots of light were all in motion. It was a slow movement, steady and concerted. It appeared that the fixed rock, the whole cave out there, was turning past the tunnel's mouth, in a gradual unvarying rotation. Looking closely at the cave, it was obvious that the perspective of it had changed in the short time the party had been standing in front of it.

People coughed in the fading traces of the poison-spores, and marveled.

"That can't be right."

"But it is moving."

"I think," said Mark, "that I know what's happening. Let's get out of this dust, back through the tunnel. I'll tell you there."

The others were ready enough to go, and Doon to lead the way. In a short time they had climbed back through the twisting tunnel and re-entered the large cylindrical room.

There Mark offered his explanation. "It isn't the cave down there that's moving, it's us. I mean all twelve of these tunnels, and the room we're standing in. What looks like the hub of a wheel here"—and he thumped his hand upon the circular dais—"really is just that. And look up here, around the end of the shaft where we came down. You see what look like loose masonry joints. The two parts are free to turn past each other. Indosuaros, when we were still up there in daylight you said that you could sense something huge down here, something of the Old World."

"I did feel that." The wizard tilted back his head and closed his eyes. "And I feel it now. Technology." And as before, he curled his lip contemptuously at the word.

Doon was incredulous. "A whole section of this cliff, with the twelve tunnels running through it like the spokes of a wheel? It would have to be big enough to build a village on."

Hubert chimed in: "A slab of that size, rotating all the time? Without even making noise, or—nobody could build such a thing. Nobody could . . ." But he let it die away there. He knew, like the Baron and everyone else, that the Old World had made a thousand wonders just as great.

Mark said to Doon: "But it means that the Sword must have been right, both times. If we'd been quick enough to follow the first tunnel that it chose, we'd have come out in the right place . . . don't you see, the rotating tunnels must match up with a fixed one, or some exit, cut in the solid rock somewhere around the wheel. The twelve tunnel mouths probably turn past it, one after another. At least some of them must."

"Actually," put in Ben, "there could be more than twelve tunnel-mouths, depending on how the tunnels branch inside the wheel."

Doon shook his head, as if to clear it. "Let's try what Wayfinder can tell us now."

This time the Sword indicated a completely different tunnel, not the next one in order around the wall.

"I see," said Ben. "They bend and twist, as we've seen, and probably some of them cross over and under each other, within the thickness of the wheel."

"I wonder, then," asked Hubert. "How do the priests who come here ever manage to find their way in and out? Have they some spell to stop the wheel?"

"Technology won't stop and start on spells. They might know, from the time of day when they enter from outside, which tunnel will be properly aligned when they get down here."

"We've not proven this mad idea yet," growled the Baron. "This time we go with Wayfinder in front of us. Come on!"

"Aye, we'd better use Wayfinder," muttered Mark. "I just thought—there may be other tunnel exits in the fixed rock around the wheel, that could lead to something even worse than that cave we just came from."

Again the group filed single into a chosen tunnel. This time Hubert, anxious now to stay close to Doon in this uncertainty, managed to get right behind him.

Again the tunnel twisted and went down. Again its explorers came to one cross passage, but this time the alternate way was not blocked. The Sword made its choice, pointing to the right. Again, after they had followed it a little farther, the tunnel they were in straightened—but this time something different was visible beyond its ending.

Its mouth, as Mark had predicted, was nearly aligned with a matching opening beyond a modest gap. Here, with the stator and rotor of the great system only a couple of meters apart at the farthest, the slow-creeping rotation of the central wheel was much easier to see.

The tunnel in which they had arrived widened out considerably just at the end. The aperture opposite closely matched it in both size and shape; each was equipped with a stone step just at the lip, as if to facilitate the easy leap, no more than a long stride, between them. The intervening space was deep enough to almost swallow up their light beams, but less than two meters wide. The other opening was also equipped with handgrips, elementary metal studs, set into masonry sockets on both sides of it.

The Sword urged them straight ahead, across the slowly misaligning gap. Doon leaped out first, and landed lightly on the step. He at once moved up another step, into the other tunnel, which appeared to slope downward sharply from just inside its entrance. With his hand that did not hold the Sword, he motioned imperiously for the others to lose no time in following.

Ben took a step forward, that would have been followed by a jump, but for the sudden drag of Ariane's hand upon his sleeve. He halted his movement and turned to meet her eyes, saw them for a moment looking entranced and almost sightless.

In the moment when Ben delayed, Hubert, with the crossbow jouncing lightly on his back leaped out and landed—

Under Hubert's feet the first step of stone fell free at one end like a trapdoor, slamming back against the wall. His hands, grabbing in reflex for the iron studs, for anything to hold, clutched at flat slippery stone. The metal projections, moving in concert with the falling stone, had slid back into their sockets. Hubert's fingers banged helplessly at the smooth surface and were gone, as he fell with a maddened scream into the gap between the walls.

Doon had spun around and tried to grab him, but no human being could have moved quickly enough. Nor could any of the people who were still on the inner, slow-turning wall react in time. Mark, looking down into the narrow chasm, could see Hubert's Old World headlamp turning and bouncing, bouncing and turning again, receding with the body that still wore it. The man's screams had already ceased. The light flashed and flickered in its spinning fall, at one instant revealing fantastic rock formations that in the next instant were again plunged into darkness.

The light bounced once more and was still. The beam, as bright as ever, shone steadily now on more sharp rocks, and also on what looked like a boneyard of the fallen, a scattering of white distant splinters and what might have been round skulls.

The survivors had not a moment to spend in pondering Hubert's fate, not with the relentless rotation of the inner wall steadily carrying the tunnel mouths apart. Some internal mechanism had already brought the trapdoor shelf back up into its innocent-looking raised position. Doon, on the far side of the gap, caught one end of a rope thrown him by Ben, and braced himself well back in the descending tunnel. With Ben holding the other end of the rope, Mitspieler was the first to cross with its insurance, gripping a loop as he jumped and landed on the step, which this time held its load solidly. Mitspieler scrambled on to where Doon stood, and helped him to hold the far end of the rope.

"The Sword didn't warn us!" Ariane complained, as if surprised at some friend's treachery. Meanwhile she landed safely in her turn.

"That is not its function!" the Baron snapped at her, as she appeared beside him to help him hold the rope. And in the next instant Mark was safely over.

Indosuaros was next. And Ben, holding his own end of the rope, and with the monkbird fluttering dumbly round his head, was last to cross. The hinged step supported his bulk solidly, as it had done for everyone but Hubert.

The six survivors, gathered now on the side of the gap that they hoped was toward the treasure, looked back to watch the mouth of the tunnel they had just quitted turn slowly out of sight behind a flange of rock.

"We'll not have long to wait for a passage to open when we come back," said Doon. There was great confidence in his voice, as if Mark's idea of the turning tunnels had been his all along; more, as if he, Doon, had proven that it was right, beyond all possibility of doubt. "There are twelve or more of those rotating tunnels, we calculated. So if yon great wheel turns only twice a day, there should never be need to wait more than an hour for an alignment. We can be sure of that."

Whether they were all sure of it or not, no one said anything. At the moment there was only one thing in Ben's mind: with the vanishing of the last crescent of the other tunnel, there was no immediate possibility of turning back.

The Baron added: "When we come back, we might be in a hurry. So before we go on we'd better figure out just how this damned trap-step works." He spoke in a businesslike tone. And he began cautious experimentation, which soon revealed that the step remained rock-solid as long as no one was standing on the step just above it—where Doon himself had been standing when Hubert made his fatal jump. A substantial weight upon the second step evidently released some kind of hidden latch that let the first step swing down the instant it was burdened.

"I suppose the priests and the Whitehands have that little game memorized—or they don't forget it more than once, when they come this way two at a time. Well, we know it now. Let's move on."

Although there seemed to be only one possible way to go from here, Doon used the Sword. It pointed them forward, through the descending tunnel, and they followed it. After that short, steep descent they were plunged into a maze of tunnels, passages interconnecting sometimes by holes in floor and overhead as well as ordinary doorways. There were doors, some closed, some standing open. On doors and walls alike strange symbols had been carved and painted.

Wayfinder ignored the symbols and the doors alike, and chose an open way. Again, as always, Doon led the others with his Sword in hand. He looked more carefully now at the stone floor before he trod on it, and those behind him looked at it again in turn.

Once or twice in the maze the Baron paused, and ordered Ariane to send the monkbird on ahead. Each time it came back soon, and said little. She had trouble interpreting what it said, and presently they gave up trying to use it altogether.

Now suddenly there was only one tunnel again. It curved sharply, first to the right, then back to the left again. From beyond that final bend a light appeared, that looked to Ben like cheerful daylight. Moving forward, he could hear running water, and then the songs of birds.

CHAPTER 12

In the last meters of its length, the curving tunnel's smooth interior gave way to rough rock, so that the passage appeared to be turning into a natural cave. Mark, emerging behind Doon from the cave's mouth, blinked in what appeared to be sunlight, filtered through the foliage of majestic treetops some meters overhead. The air was warm, and a fresh breeze stirred the high branches. Birds flitted among them, and along the face of the red rock cliff from which the cave emerged. The sound of rushing water, as from a small waterfall or tumbling stream, came from somewhere near at hand but out of sight.

The forest grew up close to the cliff. Its grassy, open floor was some meters below the rocky shelf on which the six intruders gathered in front of the cave's mouth. From that shelf a barely discernible path wound down, among boulders of the reddish rock, to disappear as soon as it got in among the trees. The highest portion of the cliff was masked by branches of the towering trees, which also effectively concealed most of the sky; but so bright was that seeming sky that the effect was not gloom, but welcome shade. Mark raised a hand to turn off his head-lamp, and saw that everyone else was doing likewise.

"We have reached the sealing of magic," Mitspieler announced, in a deep solemn voice. He spoke so rarely that everyone tended to look at him when he did. "Given the correct password, we could walk through it as easily as the Blue Temple priests must do. Master, do you think it is worthwhile for us to try again to divine what that word is?"

Indosuaros glanced at him, sighed, and shook his head. "We have tried that often enough, and learned nothing."

Doon said impatiently: "The Sword will guide us through."

Indosuaros agreed. "But, as we have seen, it cannot warn of traps. In this sealing, that task will be up to me. It will not be easy, and I want to rest before we start."

The Baron considered. "Agreed. We can·all use a rest at this point, if we can find a suitable place."

The two wizards looked out over the scene and conferred together in low voices for a few moments. Then Indosuaros announced: "We can at least go down to the foot of the cliff safely. I suppose no one needs warning that not everything you will see here conforms to reality. I can tell you already that the grass and trees *are* real, at least for the most part, though I suppose they must be magically maintained. We are of course still inside a cave. This is a very large room—just how large I cannot tell as yet—and naturally lightless. What you perceive as sun and sky and wind are all artifacts of wizardry, and just what reality they may conceal I cannot yet be certain. But we can go forward in safety for a little way at least."

"What about the stream?" Ariane asked shortly. They had started down the path, moving again in single file, and already the twisting path had brought them into sight of a small waterfall, which broke out tumbling from the jagged cliff at no great distance from the cave's mouth. The small stream danced down over the lower rocks, then plunged into a flatter bed that led it away among the trees.

"The water is real enough," Indosuaros answered her after a moment. "Whether it will be safe to drink, or even to touch, I cannot tell until we reach it."

That was soon enough. As soon as the party had reached the grass, growing from what looked and felt like rich forest soil, the two wizards moved forward to the bank of the stream and knelt beside it. There they busied themselves briefly with the art, and presently they rose to give assurance that the water was safe.

"I'm not surprised," said Doon. "There are living humans—well, in some sense living—in the garrison, down below. And the visiting priests must have need of water, not to mention the Whitehands. So this comes from some natural spring. We'll rest here, then, wizard, if you can mark out some safe boundary for us."

Again the two magicians went to work. They paced back and forth, mumbling, gesturing, watching things which common human eyes saw not. They walked apart and then came back to the others. Indosuaros warned the group: "Stay within this first loop of the stream, between it and the foot of the cliffs."

The territory so defined was comfortably large, giving six people plenty of area in which to relax. It even contained enough in the way of trees and rocks and bushes to offer a minimum of privacy. People slipped off their packs and laid their weapons down—within handy reach.

Mark bent to drink from the stream, conserving his carried water, and found it clear and cold. Then with a weary sigh he lay back in the comfortable grass, letting his eyes close. Around him he could hear the others seeking ease in various ways.

He meant to get up in a moment, and find Ben and confer with him on the question that now loomed large in Mark's own mind: Was it time to give up and turn back, or try to do so? Already three were dead out of the small group that Doon had started with. The thought of Sir Andrew's struggling army drove Mark on; but going on to certain death was hardly going to help Sir Andrew or himself.

The first question was of course whether it was less dangerous, or even possible, to turn back now. Doon and the wizard would have to be persuaded, and that might be hopeless. Or else Doon, at least, would probably have to be fought—and it was hard for Mark to imagine any course very much more dangerous than that. . . .

Lying in the grass with his eyes slitted open, Mark was aware of the dappling deceptive sunlight far above. If he turned his head slightly he could still see the place where they had come out of the cliff. The boundary of cliff and sky was still obscured, as if designedly, by the massed intervening foliage of the trees. He wondered if it would be summer here all year round.

When he closed his eyes completely, even his dull ability to perceive magic could sense the magic all around him, as steady as the sound of running water in the stream. It was there, but what it was doing he did not know.

It was hard to relax, to rest. He was afraid. He was almost ready to quit, and he would have quit before now, if Ben had not been here, or if the imagined images of Sir Andrew's suffering people did not move before him, hopelessly fighting the Dark King, clamoring for the help that another Sword or even two might give their cause. . . .

Someone was moving near Mark, very near, and his eyes flew open and he started up. Mitspieler was almost within reach, on hands and knees, with his right hand extended toward Mark's bow and quiver that lay nearby in the grass.

The graying, compact man recoiled sharply at Mark's sudden movement.

"What do you want?" Mark demanded.

"O—only a touch, young sir, I bring you only a little touch of something from my master! To anoint your weapons with, that is. See? This!" And Mitspieler held up what looked like a small bundle of dried herbs. "So if you should have need to use your weapons here in the realm of magic, they will not betray you. I fear that before we are through it we may encounter some creatures that are bigger than songbirds."

"All right. Next time say something, don't come sneaking up on me like that." And Mark sat and watched Mitspieler minister briefly to his bow and arrows, then handed over his knife to be given a similar treatment. Meanwhile Mark observed that Ben and Ariane were now seated together, a few meters off, with their heads close together in conversation.

In a little while he was approaching to join them, wiping another drink of fresh water from his lips as he approached. But there was a distraction. Just beyond a nearby bush, Doon was arguing with Mitspieler that *his* Sword needed no extra magical treatment of any kind, and by all the gods it was not going to be given any.

The junior wizard's voice argued with this claim, but took care to do so diplomatically. "Of course that may be so, sir—may I test it to make sure?"

Mark delayed, watching and listening to the confrontation as well as he could.

"What kind of test are you talking about?" Doon demanded.

"If you would just let me hold the Sword for a moment, sir. You need not worry that it will be damaged—ah, thank you." Mark saw that in one hand Mitspieler was now holding a bundle of fresh-cut twigs or withes, tied up with an ornate cord that Mark remembered seeing among the contents of Indosuaros' pack.

Mitspieler went on. "If truly your Sword needs no further treatment to function well inside this realm of magic, then it should repel the twigs when I strike it with them—thus—"

There was a bright flash that startled even Mark, who had been more or less expecting some spectacular effect. Mitspieler yelled, and dropped the sheathed Sword to the grass. He threw away the twig bundle, which on contact with Wayfinder had burst violently into flame. Then he went after the twigs, and kicked the bundle angrily, to the accompaniment of Doon's loud laughter, until it plunged into the quenching stream.

Mark did not wait to see if Indosuaros might be angry about the burning of his fancy cord, but instead went on to talk to Ariane and Ben. He told them what he had seen and heard of the incident, and it made them smile. But presently they went back to looking grim, as they had when Mark first approached.

Ariane was still taking care of the monkbird, and it sat either on her shoulder, or on a low branch nearby, while she talked.

"It doesn't like this realm of magic any more than I do," Ben observed about the animal.

The girl said: "I wish that I could let it go—I feel that I'm holding it a prisoner, and I know what it is like to be one of those."

"But it has nowhere else to go," said Ben. Then, with a glance at Mark, he asked her: "Why did you delay me at the leap? You put your hand on my arm just as I was about to jump, and I think you saved my life."

"If I did that—I really don't remember why. I'm very glad, of course, if I saved your life, but . . . my powers just work like that. When they work at all."

Mark said: "I'm sure that Doon is counting on them, to help us somehow later on. But I don't know how, or when."

"I wish I could count on them," the girl answered in a sad whisper. "I wanted to come here and look for treasure. I thought it would be . . . I don't know what I thought. Something easy and swift, I suppose, like breaking into a beehive and getting away with the honey."

Mark's face cracked in a smile, as if reluctantly. He asked her: "Have you done that?"

Ariane almost smiled in turn. "I was not raised in a palace. Or even in a house, really. The people who had me in their charge were rough, in many ways. But . . . maybe someday I'll tell you the story. I knew I was a queen's daughter, but mine was not the kind of life that I suppose most queen's daughters have."

They rummaged in their packs and began to share some food. They talked of inconsequential things, until presently they heard the Baron's voice, warning everyone that it was time to get ready and move on.

Doon, in good spirits again, took Sword in hand and determined which direction to go next. Wayfinder directed them promptly into the forest, at an angle to their right, away from the uneven line of the cliffs. There was no path at all to be seen along their route, and Mark routinely began to store up minor landmarks in his memory, to provide a means of finding his way back, as he would have done on entering any unknown wood. They walked through grass and wildflowers, past widely scattered bushes and an occasional upstanding red-rock boulder. The land sloped downward, very gradually, in the same direction they were walking. The stream had sought its own slope, curving away behind them, and was now out of sight. Now there was only the forest, the look of it somehow already monotonous; and now they had put enough of the forest behind them to cover up the last sight of the cliffs.

Presently a sunlit glade appeared, some fifty or sixty meters ahead and directly in their path. Mark looked forward in a minor way to reaching it and being able to take at least a squinting look more or less directly at the sun of the realm of magic. But in approaching the place minor detours were necessary, first around a large stump and its fallen log, then around some trees, and then around a solitary bush. And when they reached the place where he had seen the open glade, there was only the same thick-topped forest around them as before, lit only by small dancing spots of sunlight too small to show you anything but shattered brilliance when you sighted back upward along the ray. Now Mark could see other sunny glades, all of them somewhat in the distance. The Sword led on indifferently.

He was vaguely alarmed by this minor experience, and looked back when they had walked on a few strides past the place. The last landmark he had noted was a large stump with its broken, fallen tree, and already that was nowhere to be seen. Abruptly Mark lost his automatic outdoorsman's confidence in being able to retrace his steps.

Presently they came to the stream again. Of course it might have been another stream of about the same size, but it looked and sounded like the first one, and it came winding its way back across their path from the same general direction in which the first stream had flowed away. The Sword pointed them straight across it, an easy wading.

Ben, walking now behind Ariane, found his attention continually being distracted by the rhythm of her moving body. He had to warn himself repeatedly to concentrate on being alert for possible danger. Though if he thought about it he was not sure there was any point in doing so, because whatever he saw or heard here was likely to be some magical deception. . . .

Somewhere above the trees and the seeming sky there was, he knew, the maze, containing among its other parts the huge turning mass of the Old World wheel and all its nested tunnels. If Mark was right about that, and it seemed he was . . . abruptly, frighteningly, there came into Ben's imagination a picture of Hubert's battered body, bouncing and falling out of this magic sky. There'd be a riffle through the treetops and then instantly a heavy thud—might they be going to come upon it here at any moment, the shattered head still wearing a glowing lamp?

Or would a mangled corpse, here in the realm of magic, look like something else entirely—?

Whatever a man looked at here, or whatever he tried to think about, it seemed that it had to be done in fear.

Doon kept them moving, maintaining a good pace over the almost-level ground. The forest flowed past them, and flowed past them some more. Ben wondered if he should have started counting steps. The sameness of it, he thought, was already starting to make it seem endless.

Once more they approached and crossed the stream. It looked and sounded the same as ever. The ground, Ben thought, was now rising very slightly beneath their feet as they walked on. The sun, as nearly as he could tell from sighting distant clearings, was somewhere near the zenith, making it hard to tell directions that way. But he could have sworn that they were traveling in a straight line, or very nearly so, ignoring the small necessary detours around minor obstacles.

They passed another sunlit glade, off to their right. Birds sang in it, apparently enjoying the vertical sunshine.

Mark called forward to the leaders: "How big is this cave that we're in, anyway? Are we even still absolutely sure that we're in a cave?"

Indosuaros, next to the head of the line, turned his head with an indulgent smile. "Of course we are. But you are not moving through it as fast as you think."

"I'm having doubts that I'm moving through it at all. Can you see the far end yet?"

The magician turned his eyes forward again, and seemed to be gazing off into the distance as he walked. "Even for me," he began confidently, "it is . . ."

His voice trailed off there. In a moment he had stopped abruptly, and in another moment the whole procession had stumbled to a halt. The two wizards went through a session of whispering together, after which both of them continued to stare off in the same direction.

Looking in the same direction himself, Ben could see—or might it be only his imagination—a faint cloud above the trees, or at least a dimming of the sunshine there. The darkening, whatever might be its cause, deepened swiftly and mysteriously. It was passing like a slow wave, from the left of the observers to their right.

All six of the humans could see it now. The monkbird appeared indifferent, but now the people all gave evidence of being able to feel it, too. It was as if the temperature in the forest had dropped, though where they stood the sun appeared to shine through leaves as brightly as before. But leaves hung quiet in motionless air; whatever was passing was not wind. Ben had not the least doubt now that he was underground; the tricks of light and sky seemed poor and obvious shams.

Over there, something . . . some power . . . was passing. Passing, yes, thank all the gods! And it was gone.

The first to break the silence was Doon, and his voice was now constrained to a whisper: "What was *that?*"

Indosuaros turned to him slowly. The wizard's face looked disturbingly pale, and sweat was beaded on his brow. "I had not expected this. That was a god."

A murmur went up, as if involuntarily. Most people, including Ben, had never seen a god or goddess in their lives, and had no real expectation of ever doing so. In human society the presence of a deity was somewhat rarer even than that of a king or queen. "Which god?" several voices asked.

The magician answered thoughtfully. "I believe that it was Hades—or Pluto, as most people call him. No one sees him at close range, or face to face, and lives."

"But what is he doing here?"

The magicians could come up with no real answer for that. "Gods go where they will. And Hades' domain after all comprises everything that is under the earth. But he is not worshipped by the Blue Temple, so we can hope that he is here somehow as their antagonist—that he will favor our enterprise, if he takes notice of it at all."

Ben was worried. "Then we should make sacrifice to him right away, shouldn't we?"

He had realized for a long time that magicians in general held a low opinion of the efficacy of routine sacrifice and prayer offered to any god; and these two magicians now proved to be no exception. Indosuaros only gave him a look and turned away. Mitspieler did the same, but then turned back to say: "Do something of the kind quietly, for yourself, if it will make you feel any better. I will not. If it had any effect at all, it would only be to draw to myself the attention of a being whose attention I do not want."

Doon was consulting his Sword, which pointed him in the same direction as before, very close to the area in which they had seen the shadow passing. For the first time he hesitated visibly to follow Wayfinder's guidance. Instead he turned to Ariane. "Girl, is that creature ready and willing to fly? If so, send it out ahead."

Ariane whispered to Dart, and in a moment the monkbird was in flight. Its flight path curved slightly to the left, and in a moment it had disappeared among the trees in the very area where the shade of the presence of the god had seemed to linger longest. A few moments later a small cry, faint and mournful, drifted back. It seemed to Ben more a cry of exhaustion than one of pain or shock.

The six people waited, but they heard no more, nor did the monkbird reappear.

"Come, we'll move on," said Doon at last. He looked at Ariane. "It can catch up with us on the way, if nothing's happened to it."

She protested. "But shouldn't we look for it?"

"It has not proved as useful as I had hoped," said Doon. And the tall wizard shook his head. "Not there, not now. If it can come to us it will."

Ariane looked off into the woods on the left for a moment more, but made no further protest. They tramped on, for what seemed to Ben a long time, without further conversation. It was hopeless to try to measure the day by the featureless light that filtered down through the high branches. Ben now had no idea in which part of the sky the sun was, if there was really something like a sun up there at all. It was still full daylight, as it had been ever since they had entered the realm of magic. And it seemed to Ben that they had been moving all that time in a straight line.

At last Doon called another halt for rest. This time he did not sheathe his Sword at all, but sat in the grass holding it and looking at it, and his doubt was plain to read upon his face.

Meanwhile the two wizards had gone a little apart, for what appeared to be one of their regular periodic conferences. But when Indosuaros returned it was to say that he had sent Mitspieler on ahead to scout.

Doon exploded at the news. He scrambled past the other man, looking wildly off in the direction in which the assistant magician had evidently vanished. Then he rounded on Indosuaros. "What's the idea? *I am in command here.* How dare you do such a thing without telling me?"

Indosuaros, instead of lashing back, suddenly looked somewhat ill. He leaned his back against a tree, and then slowly slid down it, until he was sitting in the grass.

"What's wrong with you?"

The graybeard looked up. "It will pass. I advise you to wait for Mitspieler to come back, before you take any action."

"*If* he comes back, you mean. Gods and demons, man! What possessed you to send him off like that without asking me?"

This time Doon received no answer. Indosuaros' eyes were closed, and Ben saw with alarm that the wizard—now the only wizard that the party had available—was slumping down even more, looking as if he were in pain.

Doon gazed round at the other people, as if he were minded to order them to do something, but could not think of what. In a moment he went back to staring after the vanished Mitspieler.

Ariane had sat down too, and her eyes were closed. But she appeared to be only resting or thinking, and not sick. Presently she said softly: "I think it is the magic all around us that makes the old man sick."

"What can we do about it?" Mark asked her the question as if he really thought she might have a useful answer.

"We should get him out of here. But then we can't travel here without guidance."

Doon was looking at his Sword again. Now he swore, and jammed it violently into the ground, instead of putting it back into its scabbard.

Mark and Ben conferred together, but were unable to decide upon a course of action. As they talked, they became gradually aware that the forest around them was growing darker. This was a different kind of phenomenon from the previous darkening. Now the whole sky was slowly dimming, very much as it would at dusk outdoors on a cloudy day.

Indosuaros roused himself a little, enough to assure the others that this was indeed analogous to the natural fall of night outside, and harmless in itself. Then he lay back, putting his head on his pack and muffling himself in his robes as if preparing to go to sleep. Doon approached him as if intending another confrontation, but shrugged and seemed to give the matter up for the time being when he had taken a close look at the wizard's face.

The four people who were still active drank from the nearby stream, and again ate sparingly from their supplies. As darkness thickened under the trees they turned their headlamps on again. In the soft-focused beams the forest around them looked almost reassuringly normal.

Mark wondered aloud if their lights were going to be noticed.

Doon sniffed. "No need to worry about that, I'd say. Anything that's here already knows that we're here too."

They examined Indosuaros again, and as far as any of them could tell, the wizard was sleeping almost normally, though he looked ill. By general agreement it was decided to let him sleep until morning—no one voiced any doubt that morning was going to come.

Night in the forest deepened further, to an utter blackness that would have been unnatural in the world above. The headlamps were adjusted to throw a diffuse illumination and set on the ground spaced around the party, so that they provided light on the surrounding woods while leaving their owners in partial shadow. The circle included Indosuaros, as well as the four wakeful people who took turns talking and dozing through the night.

It was a long night, and for a long time in the middle of it Ben found himself awake, with Ariane's hand closed tightly in his. The two of them were lying chastely side by side, and her eyes would watch his for a while and then close in rest or slumber. Doon and Mark both dozed, on either side of them, and Indosuaros nearby faintly snored. Ben's right hand kept the girl's right hand enfolded. Her hand was large and strong, and he could feel the calluses here and there on it that testified she had not been brought up in a palace. Most of the time he was not thinking consciously of anything, but was only conscious of her hand, and all the strange miracle of life that flowed inside it. He was glad that she could sleep, and after a long time he slept himself.

When he woke, the air felt a little cooler, and Mark was crawling here and there and turning off the lights. Dawn, or some analogue of it, was once more brightening the sky above the trees.

Presently Doon was sitting up too, and Ariane. In the morning light, swiftly brightening now, they all looked haggard, the men's beards growing untrimmed and unkempt. Indosuaros looked catastrophic. The others took turns trying to rouse him, first gently and then vigorously, but he could not be made to open his eyes or utter anything but moans.

Doon shook him brutally, and slapped his face. "What's the trouble with you, man? What can we do?"

There was only an incoherent mumble in reply.

Doon, more to himself than to the others, muttered: "I don't know whether to leave him here or not."

Ariane protested. "You can't do that."

"We may have to. Do you think we can carry him?"

"And what about Mitspieler?"

"If he's not back by now, I don't think he's coming back."

"The next question," said Mark, "is which way are we going when we do move? Are we still trying to find the treasure, or are we going to turn around and try—"

Doon cut him off. "We are going to find the treasure. We are going to help ourselves to it, and then we are going to find the way out again. I say so, and the Sword is mine, and in my hands. Anyone who says otherwise is going to have to fight me." He glared at them each in turn, and Wayfinder had come into his hands, so quickly and naturally that it seemed to have been there all along.

Ben asked: "And will you fight all of us at once?"

The Baron looked at them, one after another, a long moment for each. "I will fight none of you unless I have to," he said then, in a reasoning voice. "Look here, lads, and you, girl, it's madness for us to talk of fighting each other now. But I think it would be equal madness to split up, or to try to turn back now that we've come this far. For all we know, there may be some easier exit up ahead."

He paused for a few moments, taking counsel with the Sword again, and with himself. Then he said: "The three of you wait here a little longer, with Indosuaros. I'll go alone and scout ahead a little—I have a hunch we may be almost at the end of this damned woods."

"You just said that we should not split up."

"The separation will be very brief. I'll not go more than a hundred paces before I turn back—see, the Sword now directs me right along the bed of the stream, it hasn't done that before. So, wait for me—unless you prefer to leave the wizard where he lies, and come along."

The others looked at one another. "We'll wait, then," said Mark.

Ben added: "At least for a reasonable time."

"Wait. I'll not go far, and I'll be back." And Doon splashed away downstream, the Sword evidently guiding him, as he had claimed, right along the current's curving course. When he had gone about forty meters the density of the intervening forest hid him from their eyes, and the endless murmur of the stream drowned the sound made by his splashing feet.

The others gathered once more around Indosuaros. "We've got to wake him," Ariane declared. "Or else we really will be forced to leave him here."

The magician's frame inside his robes now looked incredibly wasted, but when they tried to move him he felt abnormally heavy. His breathing was now barely perceptible; his face was wizened and shrunken, and his eyelids as well as his lips had the look of being pinched together by invisible clamps.

Ben turned round suddenly, crouching, motioning the others to be silent. "Someone's coming . . . or something," he whispered. "From upstream. Look out."

They grasped their weapons and waited motionless, concealed in such cover as was immediately available. In another moment, Doon's unmistakable figure had come into view, Sword held out before him like a challenge to the world, splashing toward them from upstream.

The Baron was if anything more surprised than they were. "What is this? What made you come here?"

"We've not moved a centimeter, Doon. Look—the wizard is resting under the same tree as before."

At first, Doon could not believe it. "But—I've kept going downstream ever since I left you." And for a moment Ben thought that the little man might fling his Sword away.

Before any further debate could begin, another approaching figure was sighted. Everyone seemed to discover it at almost the same time. When first seen, in the distance, it appeared to flit and jump among the trees, as if it were part of a mirage. As it drew closer, it could be seen first to be human, and then to be a man; and next to bear in one hand some kind of sword, with which it groped about as if for guidance. And lastly, as it came near, it could be recognized as Mitspieler, walking simply and normally.

Before any one else could say anything, Indosuaros had roused himself, and propped himself up on one elbow. With a faint, glad cry he turned toward the approaching man. "Master!"

Mitspieler's wiry, graying form was unchanged, except that now he wore something that Ben had never seen before, an ornate belted scabbard. At close range it was easy to see that the weapon in Mitspieler's hand was one of the Twelve Swords, but with his grip upon the hilt there was no way to tell which one it was.

As he approached he ignored the first burst of questions directed at him, and at once bent down over Indosuaros, who had fallen back again and was flat on the ground.

A long moment later Mitspieler straightened up again. "I fear there is nothing I can do for you now," he told the supine man, who did not react and might not have heard.

"What Sword is that you carry?" demanded Doon. His voice was suddenly suspicious. An instant later the Baron's hand grabbed for the weapon at his own side; but that vanished even as he grasped the hilt, turned to nothingness right before Ben's watching eyes.

For a moment Doon stared blankly at the empty claw of his right hand. Then he would have sprung to the attack, with his dagger or barehanded, but for the fact that the Sword, in Mitspieler's suddenly capable-looking fist, was pointing straight at him.

"Do not lunge upon the point, Baron. I may not be able to heal you if you do. Hear me!" And the voice of the graying man boomed out with a sudden authority. "Yes, I have the Sword of Wisdom here. I hope that it will be back in your hand before we leave this sealing, so you can use it when we reach the next—but before I give it back, I require that you hear me."

Doon mastered himself. "Then speak on, and quickly."

"I borrowed Wayfinder a short time ago, under the pretext of testing it. To replace it in your scabbard I left a phantom sword of my own creation—of course the phantom could not really guide you anywhere. But I needed the real Sword to go ahead on my own reconnaissance, and I foresaw that you would not lend it to me willingly."

Doon nodded grim agreement. "In that you read the future well . . . what is your real name?"

"Mitspieler will still do. And his name"—the speaker threw a moment's glance to one side and down—"is really Indosuaros . . . now listen to me, all of you. The god whose presence brushed us yesterday was really Hades. I have just been trying to look for him, to see where he has gone, but I was unsuccessful. I think that he has left the caves completely now. In any case, the way ahead now seems clear for us to go on . . . I take it you are all still ready to go on?"

"We are ready," the Baron told him. "Give me the Sword."

"There is one thing more."

"I thought there might be. Well, speak."

"The treasure *I* seek," Mitspieler said, "is not gold or jewels, and it is not with the gold in the vaults below the demon-sealing, but only on the next level down from this one. I want you to swear, Baron, on your honor and on your hope of wealth, that you will help me get it. I, in my turn, swear now most solemnly and on my oaths of magic, that if you help me I will then go with you and help you however I can, to reach the last level and to prosper there." He swung his gaze away from Doon, to let it rest on Mark and Ben and Ariane in turn. "I swear the same to each of you, if you will help me first."

Doon was shaking his head in doubt. He squinted at Mitspieler as if the man were hard to see. The Baron said: "You and I are now to trust each other's pledges? Now, after you've stolen my Sword? After you've lied to us all along, about—" and he gestured sharply toward the fallen form of Indosuaros.

"I borrowed your Sword, no more than that. Because I had to have it, nothing less would serve. And yes, I'll trust your pledge, if you will swear it as I've said. You are a man of honor, Baron Doon. Swear now, and your blade comes back to you at once. I'll even swear over to you now my share of whatever treasure there may be on the bottom level."

Doon appeared to be impressed in spite of himself by this last offer. "No need to talk of sharing that treasure, man. There's so much—"

"Don't say that until you've seen it . . . as I have, though only in tranced visions. There are certain morsels choicer than the rest. . . . Well?"

Doon made up his mind—perhaps, thought Ben, a shade too quickly. "Very well, you have my word to help you on the level below this one, as long as it does not prevent my reaching my own goal."

"Have I your solemn oath, just as I said it should be given?"

There was a pause. "You have."

And Wayfinder, tossed hilt upward, came leaping toward Doon, so that his right hand had no trouble to pluck if safely from the air.

"Master . . ." The cry was an almost vanishingly faint moan, and it came from the fallen husk of Indosuaros. Ariane was squatting beside him again; she was holding a much shriveled hand, from whose fingers some of the ornate rings had already fallen off.

"There's nothing to be done for him now, girl." Mitspieler, looking down, appeared saddened, but not greatly; he might perhaps have been watching the death of his second favorite pet animal. "Could he have finished this journey, it would have served as his—what is the word that other guilds and professions sometimes use?—his masterpiece. His passport to the upper ranks of magic . . . but he will never be a master now. He simply was not strong enough."

"But what's wrong with him? What is he . . . dying of?"

"You who are not magicians can pass through this sealing freely—provided you can find the way to pass through it at all. But we of the profession, from the moment that we enter, are engaged by the local powers in a continuous struggle. We undergo a ceaseless assault upon our specially developed senses. I am strong enough to bear it. Regrettably, my faithful helper here was not—not without me at his side to aid him."

Doon demanded: "Why did you let him play the leader until now?"

"Oh yes, that. As you must know, Baron, being a leader has its problems as well as its advantages. It elevates one, but often as a target. I could not be sure at first about you and your men, whether or not you were really just the simple adventurers that you appeared to be. There was a whiff of something subtle and dangerous about you—I think now that it was the Sword, no more. . . . Well, Baron, you have it in your hand again. Are we going on, or not? I am ready to follow, if you will lead the way."

Doon, looking half entranced himself, inspected the weapon in his hand. He felt of it, and tried it once or twice in and out of the scabbard. Then like a sleepwalker he raised it ahead of him, moved it to right and left and back again.

"But what about—" Ben, looking down upon the crumpled robes of Indosuaros, began a protest. Then he realized that those garments were no longer tenanted by any human form.

Ariane, reluctant to believe that, lifted the robes and shook them. A giant spider leaped out and went running away into the grass.

The Sword—the real Sword, for the first time here in the sealing of magic—directed Doon at an angle away from the curving stream. With haggard confidence he followed its guidance again. Mitspieler, having picked up Indosuaros' rings, and taken what he wanted from the contents of his pack, marched second in the shortened line. Ariane was in the middle, with Mark just behind her and Ben to guard the rear.

The real Sword neither followed the stream nor kept to what looked like a straight line among the trees. Instead it subjected its users to sudden and apparently purposeless shifts of course. They walked fifty meters in a straight line, then turned a sharp corner and walked straight in a new direction for forty meters more. This was followed by another turn, after which it seemed to Mark that they moved in the arc of a great lefthanded circle; and yet another change, after which they walked a circle curving to the right. Mark was just beginning to wonder if even the genuine Sword were now malfunctioning, when through the treetops ahead he caught sight of what looked like a familiar line of cliffs.

The rock formation was no more than about fifty meters away when it first became visible; they had hiked no more than a hundred and fifty meters or so from the place where they had seen the last of Indosuaros. Now the Sword guided them rapidly toward the rocks, though their course was still not quite a straight line. Once more the inescapable stream appeared, curving toward the explorers, flowing in the direction of the cliffs. In a few moments they were close enough for Mark to see where the current tumbled precipitously into a cave that opened just at the cliffs' base.

Looking higher on the rocky wall, he tried to locate the entrance through which they had come into this realm of magic, at what now seemed like some time in the remote past. The cliffs looked very much the same, but if the entrance cave was actually here he could not see it.

Doon now led them wading into the shallow water. They followed the course of the stream bed almost to the cave, before stepping out onto a dry path, that switchbacked its way down into the earth beside the stream. The water disappeared now into a jumble of rocks, though the tumbling roar of it stayed with them.

The stream reappeared near the bottom of the dark cliff, its channel now become a complex of artificial basins and waterfalls, followed by a paved ditch at the bottom.

As the false sunlight faded out completely behind the expedition, another kind of light came into view ahead of them. It took them some time to get down near its source.

CHAPTER 13

The reddish light ahead emanated from fierce torchlike flames, flames that sprang from many vents high on the sides of another great cave. These torch-flames appeared to consume invisible fuel, as if they fed on jets of gas flowing somehow from inside the earth. So large was this cave that only parts of it were effectively illuminated by this strange light; its size was therefore hard to estimate, but certainly it was enormous.

Here again the stream vanished. This time its disappearance had an air of permanence, as it dove into a broad pipe or conduit of what looked like ancient masonry, with its intake covered by a heavy, rusted grill; and from this point on even the sound of the stream faded, until soon it was altogether gone.

And here the path completed its descent into this new cave, across a fan of fallen rubble. Mark could make out sections of high wall still standing on either side of the path. It appeared that some defensive works had once stood here, had been breached by some powerful attack, and then had never been repaired. And indeed the dark hillside that the party was now descending looked in the headlamps' beams like some dream of an old battlefield, with fragments of old bones and rusted weapons mingled with the earth and the fallen stones of the wall.

Now, from somewhere ahead, a new sound was suddenly audible. It was dull and thick, heavy and rhythmic, loud as a great slow drum, ominous as a troubled heart.

"Our presence has been noted, I'm afraid," Mitspieler commented on hearing it. "I will do what I can, but I advise you to be ready to fight."

At a distance of twenty meters or so ahead, the cave's illumination was somewhat brighter. There the walls narrowed in, bringing the towering gas-flames a little closer on either hand. At about the same place, the slope of the rubbled hillside gentled, until there ceased to be a slope at all. The drum, if such it was, continued sounding somewhere in the distance. It was accompanied now by other dull, booming sounds, that made Mark think of the stone lids of sarcophagi falling back. He wished that image had not come to him, for now in the middle distance, beyond the narrowing of the cave, he could see long rows of what might be couches, or, in the poor light, elevated coffins. He saw, or imagined that he saw, draped human forms recumbent upon some of these, or perhaps in them. And he thought or imagined that some of these forms were stirring into action as the great war drum quickened its beat slightly . . .

. . . but there were two drums, Mark realized now, and probably no sarcophagi-lids at all. He thought of focusing his lamp's beam into the distance to make sure, but decided not to risk disturbing whoever might be there with a bright light.

Doon and his four followers continued their advance. But now, directly in their path, just at the place where the cave narrowed and the flames were brighter, a limping human form appeared to bar their way. This figure, armed with shield and spear and helmet, was quickly joined by another and another. More appeared, until there were ten in all, all in motley clothing and irregularly armed and armored. Unmatching uniforms, faded or shredded, hung upon unhealthy-looking bodies, some scrawny and some bloated. The thin men were so thin that for a moment Mark feared that he and his companions were about to encounter skeletons animated by some new power of magic; but this impression passed as they drew closer.

The force assembled to oppose them acted more effectively than their first appearance had suggested. When their leader barked a short command it was vigorously executed. Their weapons, drawn and presented now, were in some cases little more than bars of rust, but they were held in firm readiness.

He who acted the part of their officer now slouched a step forward from the center of the patchwork line. "The password!" he demanded, facing toward Doon's advancing group. His voice was a dry croak, as if the throat that formed it might not have been used for a long time. "Give me the password!"

"In a moment," Doon called back, quite calmly. "I have it here in hand." He brandished Wayfinder. In the near-darkness at Mark's right, Ariane's sling had begun whining its dull song of warning, and the hope passed briefly through his mind that she might be as good as Barbara with that weapon. Mark had his bow in hand already, and had dropped his pack. Now he reached back to draw an arrow from his quiver. He saw Ben's Sword come out. And from the corner of his eye he saw Mitspieler start to raise one hand, and disappear.

The opposing leader snapped out another command, and his ragged rank of followers charged to the attack. They made their move with evident good discipline and determination, though not with overwhelming energy or speed. Mark was able to get off two shots, scoring hits with both, before he had to drop his bow and defend himself at close quarters with his long knife. A moment later the spearman who was menacing him had his thin legs cut out from under him by Ben's Dragonslicer.

Two more of the enemy had already been chopped down by the Baron, and the two struck by Mark's arrows were out of action. From the hands of one of these Ariane had seized a mace, and she was making the air perilous around her with inexpert swings.

The first clash was over, and Doon's party had managed to get through it without injury. Six or eight of the enemy were still on their feet—they must, thought Mark, have received some reinforcement that he had not noticed during the skirmish—and they had retreated now to some little distance, dragging wounded with them. Even as they were trying to re-form their rank, some invisible force began to strike at them. One after another were felled, as by blows from an unseen hand. As the third man went down, the rest scattered in fear and confusion. They cried out alarms as they dispersed back into the shadowed depths of the enormous cave, among the rows of couches.

In the area that they had just quitted, a human form now seemed to materialize out of the air. It was Mitspieler; the wizard was holding a bloodied dagger in one hand as he came strolling back to his companions.

"I think," he called to them, "that the help they cry for may be some little time in arriving. But it will come in great numbers when it does, so we should waste no time. Baron—and the rest of you as well—I now hold you to your pledge. Loan me the Sword again, or else bend your own will upon it, to help me find what I am looking for."

The Baron, like his followers, was picking up the backpack he had dropped to fight. He hesitated only briefly before answering. "And what is that?"

"I am trying to locate a certain member of the garrison, who came here as a robber like ourselves, but more than a century ago. Most likely he is in one of these barracks-beds, but the rows of them look endless, and it could take a long time to find him without the Sword."

"Very well," said Doon resignedly, and gripped Wayfinder with both hands, as if preparing to deal some mighty blow. He stared at the Sword. "Let Wayfinder lead us to him, whoever and wherever he is— and then on to the gold." And he swung the blade's point in an arc, until the power in it signaled to him.

Headlamps probing ahead, the five raced in the indicated direction, between long rows of coffin-couches, and into dim regions that were farther from the torch-flames on the receding walls. Gradually the enormous size of this cavern was becoming more apparent. The bed-pedestals, some of which bore the dead or sleeping forms of warriors, when seen close at hand were not quite like normal beds and not like biers— Mark was suddenly reminded of the worm-addicts' couches in the basement of the Red Temple.

"The garrison is enormous," he commented as they trotted through it. "Where did they all come from?"

Mitspieler, panting as he kept pace, answered. "From parties like our own. Some large, some small, all coming, like us, to pillage the Blue Temple."

"So many?"

"It's been going on for centuries, since before any of us were born. . . . They are bound by strong magic in this portion of the cave, till death releases them. Or until someone brings a stronger magic to their rescue—as I mean to do for one of them today."

"A garrison of enormous numbers," agreed Doon. "But the ones we fought just now did not seem all that tough."

"Some will be tougher." Mitspieler, trotting, panting, shook his head.

"Those were only the first pickets. There may well be shock troops here somewhere, an elite cadre . . . though when folk are kept here for centuries, their bodies and minds both must at least begin to deteriorate. That's why I fear what we may find . . . ah, this row now."

They were approaching another angle of the cave wall, where torch flames flared closer and as a result the light was better. Somewhere in the distance the long drum-alarm continued, and Mark could faintly hear the warning cries of the survivors of the first skirmish.

"Too bad," said Ariane, "that our wizard can't make us all invisible." She had discarded her captured mace, and was easily keeping up with the pace set by the trotting men.

"I can do that only for myself," said Mitspieler, "and not for very long." Mark did not think that the strain in the wizard's voice and face was only a result of running. "And it is doubly hard to do when Swords are out. Today I am squandering the saved capital of a hundred years of sorcery. . . . Do not expect more of me in the way of tricks, for I am near the limit of my powers now."

Still the somewhat irregular ranks and files of the couches of the garrison flowed past. The rows seemed to stretch out into a dream-like infinity of gloom, the individual units spaced on the average only two or three meters apart. The pattern of occupation was even more irregular, with whole ranks of unoccupied beds followed by areas wherein most were tenanted. How far could it go on? Mark, tuning his headlamp's beam to a sharp focus, projected it as far as possible into the distance. But it was muffled there by what appeared to be rolling clouds of mist, leaving the far wall still undiscovered.

Doon ordered: "Turn off your lamps! There's some firelight here, we can see well enough without them. No use showing everyone just where we are."

Lamps went off. And then, just as it seemed to Mark that the search might be going to last indefinitely, prolonged by magic like the trek through the forest above, Doon came to an abrupt halt.

"Here. This bed. Whoever he is . . ."

A head of curly hair gleamed darkly in the glow of Mitspieler's lamp when the magician briefly switched it on again. The wizard's hand tore back the rough blanket covering the rest of the recumbent form. The face of the man revealed was very young-looking, and handsome as a god's. The youth's uncovered upper body was compact and muscular, clad in worn clothing that did not appear to be a uniform, and in a few fragments of armor as well.

Mitspieler bent over the young man and took him by the hand. "Dmitry," the magician murmured, in a changed and tender voice. In another moment he had dropped the hand, pulled off his own backpack, and was rummaging in it for magical equipment.

The ritual that Mitspieler chanted now was very brief, and it appeared to have been intensely practiced. The power of it was obvious, for at the concluding words even Mark's dull sense of magic could perceive a passing shock. A convulsion ran through the body of the youth, and in a moment he was sitting bolt upright and blinking blue eyes in the soft glow of Mitspieler's dimmed headlamp.

"Father?" the young man murmured, looking at the wizard. "What are you doing here? And who are these?"

"Dmitry, I'm getting you out of here, bringing you back to the world above. These are my friends, they're helping. The bonds that held you here have been broken. Get up quickly, we must leave. . . . Dmitry, it's been so long. Very long. But you haven't changed."

"Leave? Back to the world? But . . ." Half supported by the older man, Dmitry was already on his feet. In another moment he had pushed the support away and stood alone, though swaying a little on his feet. Like his father he was of low-average height and sturdily built, though otherwise they looked little enough alike. "Wait, I can't leave. Not without my friends."

"What friends? Come on, hurry."

Dmitry lurched back, pulling his arm free again from Mitspieler's grasp. From blankness and confusion, the youth's face had settled into a childish scowl. "They're my friends, I said! I'm not going anywhere without them."

The wizard, his own look of tenderness already gone, glared back at him. "If you mean people from that bandit gang you came here with, forget it. I'm not going to waste—"

"Then I'm not leaving. I mean two men in my squad here, Father, Willem and Daghur. They're both great pals of mine and I can't go without . . . well, hello there." His eye had at last fallen upon Ariane.

Doon had had more than enough. In a fierce muted roar he ripped out an oath. "Who doesn't get moving in the next instant, I'll run him through. Now move!"

Dmitry had by now regained his full balance. He used it to vault back over the bed that he had just left. His weapons, sword and dagger, had been stashed on that side of the couch and he grabbed them up. Smiling happily, he told Doon: "Just who in all the hells do you think you are? I'll move on when I am ready."

Mitspieler, with more than a century of experience to draw on, found gesture and speech to quell them both—at least for the moment. "Put down your weapons, the two of you. Put them down, I say! It would be madness to fight here among ourselves. Dmitry, where are these other two? I'll wake them swiftly if I can." He turned to Doon and added: "It'll mean two more men with us. Two more fighters."

"All right then. But be quick, demons blast you!"

Dmitry indicated to his father the two nearby couches. The following rituals were if anything quicker than the first had been, but Mark thought that when Mitspieler straightened up from the last one he looked notably weaker than before. "No more," the magician murmured in a drained whisper. "Come, we must move on."

Two loutish-looking men, the latest fruit of his endeavors, had sprung up stumbling to their feet. They recognized Dmitry grinning at them, and pleaded in loud bawling voices to be let in on what was going on. He thumped their backs, and swore at them joyfully. "We're going on to pillage the treasure after all!"

Willem was tall and black, his face a whitened mass of scars as from some old ill-treated wound or wounds. He roared out now in a jumble of oaths that he was ready to follow Dmitry anywhere. "Best squad leader in the whole damned garrison!"

Daghur concurred with this, expressing himself with an eloquent grunt. He was short and pale, with good muscles burdened under a thick layer of unhealthy-looking fat. A horned helmet with one horn broken off sat slightly sideways on his head. His gross arms were heavily tattooed, and many of his teeth were broken.

"But where'd you get the rest of this scum?" he demanded of Dmitry, meanwhile glaring at Mark and Ben and Doon. "What made you think they could keep up?"

"The best I could find on short notice!" Dmitry shouted, hugging the two around their necks. "Never mind them, come on."

"And who's the old one here?" Willem wanted to know.

"Never mind, he'll keep up too!"

"So, it's a revolt, hey, Dimmy? I'm for it, what the hell, let's go." Then Willem broke off suddenly, staring at Ariane. It was as if he had deliberately kept her the last to notice. "Wow. This's yours already, I suppose?"

Mark had observed some time ago that Doon could control his temper very neatly whenever its unleashing or display would not advance his purpose. So it was now. The Baron spoke very quickly and earnestly to Mitspieler, and the wizard, his brow now even a little paler than before, spoke solemnly to his son. Dmitry, with a look and a nod, managed to convey much information quickly to his otherwise obtuse friends. Immediately the little army of intruders and escapees began to move in the direction that Doon wanted them to go, following the Sword. Mark, close behind the Baron now, could hear him murmuring to it as to a woman: "Bring us to the treasure now, my beauty!"

Doon's band was now eight strong, and it followed him at a quick pace. But before the group had gone a hundred strides, muttered warnings were exchanged among its members. Looking off to the right, Mark could now discern another band of people, some forty or fifty meters distant, trotting at comparable speed along a parallel course. The headlamps of Doon's party were turned off, and they could not make out the other group very clearly, but undoubtedly it was there.

Mark trusted strongly in the Sword, and he tended to trust Doon's leadership as well. Mark ran now, keeping up with the Baron, who had accelerated his own strides. But already Daghur and Willem were panting, starting to lag, swearing away in protests what little wind they had. Dmitry too was falling behind, declaring in gasps that he was bound to stay with his two companions—it sounded like a transparent excuse, meant to hide his own poor condition.

Even so they had gained a little on the party running to their right. But now Mark could see yet another force, at about the same distance to the left and also speeding along a parallel course, with torchlight glinting on its weapons. The garrison appeared to be rousing itself piecemeal to meet the incursion. Now someone in the group to the left called out, and Mark realized that those were women.

"Amazons," a voice beside him panted. "Bandits and warriors just like the rest of the garrison. I'd rather face the men."

Doon was not disposed to loiter for the benefit of stragglers, and Dmitry and his two friends kept falling farther back. Mark looking over his shoulder saw that there was now pursuit to the rear as well; whatever they might encounter up ahead, doubling back did not appear to be an option.

And now, directly ahead, another armed, torch-bearing contingent was assembling, soldiers moving into position to block the way.

Doon halted, his people stopped around him, all gasping with the effort of the futile run. The enemy array blocking their path was already solidly in place behind its leveled spears, and in itself had some advantage in numbers over the intruders. Certainly the other forces on both flanks and in the rear would have time to close in before any breakthrough could be made.

Now for a little time there was silence in the cave, except for the less and less distant shuffle of many feet, a sound that gradually shuffled into silence; and for the faint sizzle and drip of the torches that a number of the enemy were carrying; and for the slowly quieting breathing of hardworked lungs.

Now, from the very center of the opposing front line, a grotesquely squat, thick-bodied figure detached itself, and waddled a few paces forward. This man wore an elongated helmet, as if in some preposterous effort to achieve impressive height. His strange, waddling gait made Mark look at his feet, and these also appeared lengthened, by oddly thick-soled boots. Torches on either side of him cast a flickering red light upon his bulbous, red-nosed face. In a hoarse voice this figure bellowed: "Surrender, you scurvy sons of loadbeasts! We have you surrounded!" The sentences were punctuated with waves of a short sword.

Dmitry for once was quiet; Mark from the corner of his eye observed that the youth appeared sullenly downcast. But Doon was equal to the occasion, and put on his best commander's voice and manner: "Who speaks? Where's your captain?"

The squat one bellowed back at him: "I'm captain here! Commander of the bloody garrison of the Blue Temple Main Depository. Field Marshal d'Albarno—ever hear of me?" He rolled a few paces farther forward, into somewhat brighter light, as if he took pride in his bizarre appearance. His face, now more clearly visible, was bloated and spectacularly ugly.

"There's elfin blood in him, I'll bet." The tense whisper came from Ariane, at Mark's side. He looked at her. Elves were only superstition, or so he thought that all well educated people believed.

Field Marshal d'Albarno—Mark, at least, had never heard of either the rank or the name before—was now roaring at them: "So, are you all going to surrender, you bloody lumps of demon-dung? Or are we going to have to hack you all to bits and get our weapons dirty?"

"Aphrodite's armpits!" Doon's answering blast was equally, hearteningly loud. He too knew how to swear, and with some artistry. "Shut your mouth for a moment, wormcast-brain, and listen to me. What's the most important thing there is in life, to you, to me, to any soldier?"

D'Albarno blinked. His almost bestial visage gave evidence of trying to register surprise. "Oh." The enemy commander's voice had diminished to something like mere thunder. "Oh, we're getting to that soon. It's our due whenever we're called up to active duty here, our pay for beating back your damned attack." Again he raised the level of his voice to an inhuman bawling. "Do you surrender, or—?"

"Vulcan's vomit, man, of course we're going to surrender!" No matter how loud the other got, the Baron so far had been able to measure up. "The only point is this—do we get to keep our weapons, and join you like good comrades in your frolic first? Or do we have to mow down half your company to make you meet our terms? That won't leave you with much strength to enjoy your carousal, will it? And maybe not much time for it either." The last sentence was added in a knowing way, as if to hint at inside knowledge.

The self-proclaimed Field Marshal—he did seem to wear a number of decorations on his chest—planted his ham-sized fists upon his bulbous and unmilitary hips. He turned his head from right to left and back again, as if calling upon witnesses.

"Now," he mumbled, in a voice again reduced almost to human volume, "there's a man who understands what soldiering's about. It ought to be a joy to have him in the garrison. A comrade I can damned well drink with. I might even be able to endure his stories of his wars and battles. I might even—ho there, put down your bloody bow!" This last injunction was directed at a decrepit-looking archer in d'Albarno's own company who, after much effort with trembling fingers, had gotten an arrow nocked and was not disposed to waste the effort but seemed clearly intent upon shooting into the group with Doon.

"Put it down, I say!" the Field Marshal repeated. "And you, you bloody invaders, fall in with us quickly and come along. I'll send a bloody formal announcement of our victory on to the civilians—but not just yet. The damned joyless slugs have gone into hiding, as they do whenever there's an alert, and for all they know, or need to know, we're still locked in bloody combat. As soon as they realize that you've surrendered, they'll come out of their holes and start preaching to us all, and close the party down. We who have faced death to guard their metal will have our fun restricted, and we'll all be stuffed back into our shells until the next excitement starts. Are you with me?"

Doon pressed him to make sure. "We keep our weapons, then? Until the victory party's over?"

"Aye, all right, until the bloody surrender is made official. But try to use them, and we'll chop you into bloody hash!"

Doon signed to his own people to put down their slings and bows, and sheathe their blades. He put Wayfinder back into its sheath himself. D'Albarno gave the same orders, and with a flourish put his own sword away. Ranks melted. Slowly, suspiciously at first, the confrontation turned into an awkward, then a less awkward, march.

What is this? thought Mark. Have we surrendered or not? He caught Ben's eye, but got no help from the big man's expression of bewilderment. Doon was marching beside d'Albarno, the two already conversing as if on terms of old acquaintance. And Mitspieler seemed to have disappeared again.

The hard-faced Amazon warriors rushed to encircle Ariane, and welcome her as a new recruit. Mark caught a last frightened look from her as she was swept away.

At least they were all going in the same direction.

On to the party!

CHAPTER 14

The place of revelry was not completely walled off from the surrounding cave with its gloomy appearance of half barracks and half cemetery. Instead it was only partially separated by head-high partitions, constructed of stacked barracks-beds, and of piled-up barrels, crates, and kegs. These containers, Mark deduced, held the supplies necessary for proper celebration. D'Albarno had evidently already sent ahead this far at least the word of his triumph in the field, for the bar was almost ready to open when his combined force of troops and prisoners, now mingled almost indistinguishably, arrived. The bar itself was a crude three-sided enclosure, built up of barracks-beds, some upside down, stacked lower than the walls. Smaller stacks made tables nearby, and single beds simply uncovered served as benches. The scene was lit by mounted torches.

The only halfway permanent-looking structure in sight was a crude stone fireplace, its sides so low that it was not much more than an open pit. One of the garrison, who was either a minor conjuror or thought he was, was waving his arms to create a spell in hopes of making the smoke rise straight up into the unfathomed darkness overhead. There was a pile of ordinary-looking wood for fuel, brought perhaps from the magic forest on the level above. Over some newly kindled flames a large four-legged beast of some kind was being roasted virtually whole. Turning the spit, and bustling around on various other lowly tasks, were a few of the scroungier and weaker-looking members of the garrison.

Inside the three-sided enclosure of the bar, and setting about more prestigious work, were three beings of a type that Mark recognized at once from Ben's description, though he himself had never seen the like before.

Ben nudged him. "Whitehands," the big man murmured. Indeed the main distinguishing feature of the beings leaped to the eye at once: the huge, pale hands, now at work setting out kegs probably of ale, bottles of wine, crocks of something that might be mead, to judge by the sudden sweetish smell in the air. The strength of those large hands was being demonstrated, yet they looked soft. The rest of the beings' physical appearance also varied from that of common humanity. They had large, staring eyes—the better, Mark supposed, to see in darkness—set in pallid faces. Large ears as well, and worried, thin-lipped mouths. Hair was mostly worn or withered away, and skin was wrinkled. Stature varied, among the three now present, but the average of this small sample was on the short side for humanity. All were in uniform, wearing high-necked blue shirts and smooth short golden capes. Their clothing was immaculate, as compared to the scruffy patchwork garb worn by the military garrison.

The commander of that garrison, the conductor of its most recent successful defense, waddled straight up to the bar. Before he could speak, the tallest of the creatures behind it pounced upon him verbally, asking whether the fighting had been extensive. "It sounded bad, from here. Was there much damage? Costly?"

The Field Marshal roared back at him: "With me and my best people on the job? Not bloody likely! Now bring on the booze, we've earned it. And start the food. And how about some music?"

A shout of approval for this speech went up from d'Albarno's followers, who were already massing just behind him and along the bar. This noise left audible only the last words of the next anxious question from the Whitehand leader: ". . . the prisoners?"

"Of course I've got the prisoners under control! Who's commander of the garrison here, anyway? Not you, you damned white-handed, white-livered blob of money-fat!"

The one who stood behind the bar looked perfectly secure in his own superiority to such behavior, and only distantly offended. "As soon as First Chairman Benambra shows up, I'm going to speak to him about this."

Mark thought that this threat had an effect on d'Albarno. But the Field Marshal was not going to let it show if he could help it. "Speak away," he thundered at the other. "But, until then, you're going to serve us BOOZE!"

Another explosive expression of support burst up behind him. Men and Amazons surged forward to the bar. Those weaker, or perhaps only less desperate for drink, were pushed aside. The Whitehands who had been speaking to d'Albarno nodded fatalistically to his fellows, and he and the others began to pour and serve.

Ben, appearing more bemused than ever, looked over at Mark and asked: "What was that about 'Benambra'?"

Another man answered him before Mark could speak. "Most of the people we get in here recognize that name." This was from one of the garrison, a comparatively healthy-looking specimen, who had been forced close to the prisoners in the increasing crush. (And were we really facing *this* many of them out there? Mark wondered silently. If so, Doon had certainly been wise to do what he did.)

The trooper who had just spoken had by some legerdemain already gotten a filled mug in his hand. He added now: "The first High Priest. You know. There used to be an old song about him, when I was still topside. He's still here, though I bet the cave's changed a lot since he first started hiding Temple treasure in it. You better push your way up there and get a drink while you've still got the chance."

Mark and Ben exchanged another look. Together they began to force their way through the crush, working toward the bar.

The Amazons had come to the party in a group, and this segregation still persisted, though it was beginning to fray out around the edges. Ben kept peering toward their company, trying to catch sight of Ariane. He could obtain occasional glimpses of red hair and a pale face, and from what little he could see of her she appeared to be all right. If she wasn't all right next time he looked, he wasn't sure what he could do about it. Starting a fight would probably be suicidal. So far Doon's strategy, whatever its ultimate goal, was keeping them all from being killed, or enslaved, or even disarmed. But . . .

The talkative garrison man had come along, pushing his way with Mark and Ben toward the bar. He still had his drinking mug in hand, almost full, so he probably had something besides another drink in mind. Standing beside Ben now, he reached out casually for Dragon-slicer's hilt. Ben knocked the reaching hand away.

"Neat sword," the man commented, unperturbed. "You might as well hand it over now, and save trouble later. I'm claiming it as spoils. No use my trying to get that headlight of yours, the priests or the Whitehands will latch onto that for sure."

"They will?" Ben couldn't think of anything more helpful to say.

"Sure. Whatever weapons prisoners are captured with are forfeit. After you go through your basic training for the garrison, you can draw new arms from the armory, anything they have available."

"A pile of rusty crap," complained another man nearby, overhearing at least the tail of the conversation.

The first man shrugged. "Maybe you can get something better from the next batch that comes in to rob and gets captured."

"When'll that be?" Ben had now adopted his stupid look. He figured that he ought to keep on talking, while he waited for a chance to do something. He might even be able to learn something useful.

"Who knows? Who can keep track of time down here? Hey, what's going on topside these days? Is Blue Temple in a war? Wish they'd get into a real one, we'd get a lot of recruits down here, I could get a promotion. A war with the Amazons, maybe. The bunch we have is getting a little old." He licked his lips and looked in that direction.

Ben, who before today had never heard of Amazons outside of an old story or two, looked that way again also. Ariane now appeared to have mastered her fears. She was telling some kind of a story, accompanying the tale with sweeping arm-gestures, and had a small audience of war-rior-women around her more or less interested. Not far from the slowly dissolving group of women sat Willem and Daghur, who did not in the least look as if they thought of themselves as prisoners, recaptured deserters. They were fraternizing with other men who had to be their old buddies from the garrison. And Dmitry, laughing fit to burst at something, was sitting in the lap of one of the larger Amazons while she drank from his mug.

Doon and d'Albarno, now showing an indefinable but strong similar-ity despite the disparity in build and features, were sitting with others at a head table, elevated upon some kind of dais. Mark saw the first plat-ters of food, meat sliced nearly raw, were being served there now by garrison youngsters, mostly frightenable-looking Amazon girls. Musi-cians had now appeared from somewhere, and were at work in their own seats a little below the head table. Whether they played well or badly, or indeed if their instruments made any sound at all, it was impossible to tell amid the general din.

D'Albarno was now obviously telling Doon a story, and from the mammary shapes that the Field Marshal's large hands were sketching in the air, it was easy to guess what kind of a tale it was. Mugs and flagons were passing in profusion everywhere now, and with incredible speed. Kegs and barrels were being appropriated from the Whitehands by main force, and hoisted onto tables to be broached and tapped, as the regular troops impatiently took over the duties of tending bar. Somewhere in the midst of the melee a woman screamed, loud enough to be heard, but more it seemed in delight than in terror.

A man who had been standing on one end of a table fell off, clutching as he went down for the barrel that he and others had been trying to open. The container swayed, wobbled, and fell from the table in its turn, hitting the stone floor with the sound of doom. Liquid and fumes burst forth together in an overpowering flood. People fell and scrambled, and some went down on hands and knees, lapping at the floor. The crush shifted, and the man who had reached for Dragonslicer was borne away in the press of bodies.

Ben had not seen Mitspieler since their capture, and had started to take vague hope from this fact. Now he did see him, seated at the head table, but so inconspicuously slumped among garrison officers that Ben realized his searching eye might well have passed him by before.

Ben fought his way around to the head table, Mark getting slightly separated from him in the process, and approached Mitspieler to try to learn what was going on. At Ben's approach the wizard raised his head, looking exhausted. The small, half-finished drink that sat before him appeared to have knocked him out already.

There was no need to worry about being overheard. Mitspieler had to shout to make himself audible to Ben's ears a matter of centimeters away.

"I went around, invisible . . . tried to wake up everybody . . . thought if we got the whole garrison . . . escape in the confusion." He glared at Ben as if he thought Ben were to blame for the scheme's failure. "Then I lost invisibility."

"You tried your best."

Part of the wizard's reply was lost in the ambient noise. ". . . tried m'best. Tried hard, for a hundred years and more. And there he is. There he stands. So why bother? Never become a father, lad. Never become a parent. It's a great . . . a great sorcery, that's what. Turns your whole life inside out."

Mark, who had managed to get near the leaders at the other end of the head table, now came working his way along to Ben, coming close enough to communicate through the uproar. "We're not yet disarmed. Doon says to bide our time, wait for his signal."

"To do what?"

"That's all he had a chance to say. I'm going back, and stay near him for a little, if I can."

"And I'm going to Ariane." Ben pushed himself away from the dais, into the press.

The Amazons by now were widely dispersed among the general population. They were heavily outnumbered, but even so there was not really that much direct competition for their favor. In truth most of the male garrison seemed more interested in drinking, falling down, and bellowing about their prowess sexual and otherwise, than they did in actually coming to grips with the women. Great bragging songs were going up toward the invisible ceiling, but some of the singers were already flat on their backs.

Between the dais and the place where Ben had last glimpsed Ariane, the floor was even thicker than before with bodies. Mitspieler's tactic might be working, or at least it might help when Doon moved to implement his own plan, whatever that might prove to be. Of course Doon himself might have a hard time getting away from the head table without rousing suspicion. In that regard, one urgency was always possible to plead when a drinking bout was on—there, a few meters past the partitions, away from the center of revelry, floor stones had been taken up to improvise a cesspit, soldiers standing round it in a ring and others waiting for their turn.

A drink was thrust into Ben's hand, and to be a good fellow he sampled it before moving on. The taste was horrible, whatever it was supposed to be, but the potency was certainly above reproach.

Ariane was not really hard to locate. It seemed she had a persistent suitor, a garrison man who was not to be discouraged by smiling appeal, either from her or from Ben, and who went for his dagger when Ben put a hand on his arm a second time. Ben twisted the arm enough to hold the fellow still, then clubbed him on the temple with a fist. Distastefully he lowered the limp body into a sticky mess below a bench; Ben disliked fighting all the more when it had a personal basis.

"I've lost my pack," Ariane told him distractedly, shouting so that he could hear.

"That's all right. Never mind. We're going to try to get out soon. Doon will give us a signal." And somehow she was sheltering in the curve of his arm, though normally she was a centimeter or two taller than he was.

Now she was shouting something else at him. "I'll knife the next one, if he won't listen."

"Not yet. Hold back. Start no blood-fights in here, if you can help it. I'll stay with you. Better yet, you come with me."

With Ariane still muffled part of the time in Ben's protective grip, they struggled back to a place close to the head table. The floor just below the dais was newly awash with booze; maybe, quite likely in fact, at least one more barrel had been dropped and broken. One at least must have been mead. And it was like walking in glue. If they ever did succeed in getting away, thought Ben, it would be impossible for anyone to lose their trail. If there was anyone in shape to try to follow it. . . .

The leaders were sitting pretty much as before. Doon looked up haggardly, but his glance at Ben conveyed nothing of import. At the Baron's side, d'Albarno was at the moment boasting loudly about his capacity for drink, and how he was today going to demonstrate it as never before. In mid-sentence he lost first his train of thought and then his consciousness; few around him paid much attention as he released his grip upon his destiny, and slid already snoring to join a cadre of old comrades who were already nested beneath the table.

Ben, Mark, and Ariane quickly gathered around Doon, who passed the word succinctly: "Leave here, but separately. We'll meet two hundred strides away, in this direction." And inside the cupped fingers of one hand, held close against the table's edge, the Baron pointed with one finger of the other, indicating a direction that Ben assumed he had somehow managed to determine with the Sword.

The small group split up immediately. Doon himself worked his way along the table to speak to Mitspieler. The others pushed themselves away in various directions through the crush. Ben parted from Ariane with a fierce hand-squeeze, and from Mark with an expressive look.

Ben worked his way through a gradually thinning crowd out to the cesspit. From thence he moved on a curve that took him gradually farther from the celebration. Stumbling as if with drink, he lurched along from one barracks-bed to another. A few of these were tenanted by collapsed celebrants, the others empty.

He paused now and then to try to see if anyone was watching him. As far as he could tell, nobody was. He continued moving in his erratic curve, aiming to reach the rendezvous point from a direction at right angles to the party. After a while he dropped to all fours. He was far from being the only one in that condition, and he hoped to progress even less conspicuously in that mode.

Now all the couches that he passed were empty, and still more garrison troops came streaming and straggling in from the outer reaches of the cave toward the uproar near the center. Of course the noise alone, he thought, ought to be enough to wake anyone within a kilometer, be they asleep, dead, or enchanted. No one paid Ben any attention, and he crawled on.

He was beginning to wonder if he might have misjudged the distance, or the direction of Doon's pointing finger, when he came upon Mark and Ariane, sitting huddled under an empty barracks-bed. From underneath the next bed the bearded head of Doon protruded fiercely, and the Baron motioned Ben to take shelter also and lie low.

He did so and waited. Presently Mitspieler came into view, not crawling but stumbling along in a way that gave an even more convincing portrait of defeat. Approaching together, some meters behind Mitspieler, were Dmitry, Willem, and Daghur. The wizard of course had not been able to leave without telling his son. The son and his two friends were proceeding with exaggerated gestures of caution, preserving a silence that now and then erupted with half-smothered drunken giggles.

Doon's face, as he emerged from his hiding place to survey them, was a study. But, Ben realized, there was not much that the Baron could do. He was still determined on going on—he would not have come this far without a truly fanatical determination—and he had to have the wizard, some kind of wizard, with him on the next level down when it would be necessary to confront at least one demon. And Ben was ready to go on. Now, when he was directly faced with the prospect of unending slavery in the garrison, he himself could not find any distant and still unseen demon all that terrifying. He was not only ready, he was eager.

Almost no words were exchanged. The reunited party slunk off in the direction indicated by Doon, moving directly away from the noise and the crowd, and into regions empty of waking people. Some of the party had lost their packs during their captivity—Mitspieler, Ben noted, had somehow retained his—but all were still armed. And all had their headlamps, though Doon ordered that they not be used for the present.

Little by little, as the scene of celebration fell farther behind them, they stood up straighter in their march, and became more an advancing group, less a collection of individuals sneaking along in the same direction. Still there was little said among them.

Presently Doon paused, evidently intending to have out his difficulties with Mitspieler; but the wizard urged him on.

"Not here, not now. I know what you want to say, and I am sorry for it. But we must reach the next level before we can pause to talk or argue. And then I must rest, before we can go on."

Doon, after a brief silent struggle with himself, had to agree. The small procession went on quietly. Even Dmitry and his friends were quiet, for the time being. Perhaps, thought Ben, they were all sick with drink.

Now Ben became aware that the cave was narrowing in around them as they progressed. The change was gradual at first, then swift. Doon continued to forbid the use of headlamps, but still it became possible to see that they were headed straight toward a wall, a wall formed not far ahead by the ceiling of the cave coming down in a great curve. Now the side walls closed in even more drastically, and at the same time the floor of the cave tilted into a downward slope. And suddenly they were no longer in the vast and seemingly unbounded room of the garrison-sealing, but had been funneled into a passage only three or four meters wide.

Wall-flames in the cave behind the travelers still cast enough light here to let them see their way. Now the ceiling was only a few meters overhead, curving sharply down over the high rock shelves that topped the walls on either side.

Doon led them quickly on. The light from behind them was fading rapidly with distance, and soon they would need their headlamps.

"We've done it," Ben said aloud. And just as if the words had been a signal, rock-weighted nets of rope and cord, cast by concealed hands, sprang out simultaneously from the high shelves on both sides of the passage. One of the falling rocks struck Ben on the shoulder with almost numbing force. He had just time enough to reach for Dragonslicer before his arms were tangled completely in the net, but not time enough to draw clear of the scabbard. More cordage tripped him, and he fell.

Someone else's headlamp shot forth a beam, perhaps in an attempt to dazzle the attackers. It might have been a good idea before the net was thrown, but now it was too late. As Ben thrashed and rolled on the rock floor, struggling to get free, he had a good look at Ariane, and a look at Mark. They were both floundering in the grip of some of the attacking Whitehands, a number of whom now came leaping down like clumsy monkeys from the high shelves where they had set their ambush. Clumsy, perhaps, but also strong; and not nearly as clumsy now as were their victims, tangled in the clever weaving of the cords.

Four more Whitehands, large for their kind, now came trotting up out of the passageway ahead. They wore, strapped to their heads, little golden glow-lamps of a kind that Ben had never seen before, and they bore a litter on their shoulders. It was more like a stretcher, really, a mean, penurious-looking equipage.

Ben didn't wait to see what this arrival meant, but continued to roll from side to side, in a furious but so far futile effort to bring his full strength to bear on any of the strands of the net that wrapped him round and bound him down. If he just seized one of the thin cords and pulled as hard as he could, he'd cut his hands to the bone and disable himself from further effort. Maybe he could get hold of one of the thicker ropes properly—

The litter was set down, a few meters away, and a Whitehands, obviously ancient, got himself out of it with some help, and then came to look at Ben and the other captives at close range. He wore a uniform all of gold, the like of which Ben had never seen before.

"Careful, my Founder! Not too close. This one still thrashes."

"You reported that they were already your prisoners, ha hum?" The voice of the ancient one matched his ghastly appearance. He was so pale that the others with him looked almost tanned by comparison.

"Yes, First Chairman, they are." This was another subordinate, who glanced jealously at the first.

"Ha, hum. I think I shall be First High Priest today. Yes, some function in that capacity may be necessary." He was bent, smaller than the other Whitehands and more wizened. Ben was being distracted, despite himself, from his hopeless efforts to burst free.

"Yes," the old man repeated. He was obviously talking more to himself than to his subordinates—though they were certainly expected not to miss anything. "Yes, that fool Hyrcanus has never run things properly topside." And the old man—he was of course an altered human like the others—with his grotesquely large and withered white hands hanging all but useless at his sides, kicked at one of the fallen prisoners. Too feebly, Ben was sure, to hurt. "Well, down *here,* thank Croesus, the man in charge is still Benambra." And one of the impotent huge hands came up with a gesture to flap at its owner's chest.

Now the Founder, First Chairman, First High Priest, bent closely over another captive. "Ah, a fine weapon here, a treasure in itself." A slow straightening of the curved old spine. "And our famous Field Marshal I suppose is drunk as usual after one of these affairs, making ready his report of a dazzling victory. I'm going to have to replace him, I think, after this debacle. Are you sure we've caught them all?

"And we must send word to Hyrcanus to change the passwords everywhere again. . . . I wonder if they have any conception of duty left at all, up there. Prepare these captives for induction processing and then basic training. Let me see the inventory of their possessions when you have it."

There was more, but Ben heard almost none of it. He heard Doon shouting something, and then another Whitehands, capering before Ben with a wizard's gestures, bent down to blow a dusty powder into his face. With his first sneeze, the world was gone.

He was being awakened, for what must be the first watch of the morning. He was going to have to drag his body out of this uncomfortable but oh-so-welcome bed. . . .

No, it wasn't first watch that he had to get up for. He had just signed up for Blue Temple service, and he was still in basic training, and he faced another day of that . . . at least his shoulder didn't hurt him so much any more, time had healed it. Ben moaned and grumbled to himself. Today he'd try to get another letter off to Barbara, if there was a caravan going that way, and he hoped that this time she might answer. . . .

"Still sleeping, hah?" *Thud.* The sergeant had come back.

Kicked off his wooden barracks-bed, Ben managed to extend one leg and one arm toward the stone floor, enough to partially break his fall. Picking himself up, feeling bruised, he noticed an odd thing: his bed was a different kind from the one he seemed to remember rolling into the night before. Odd. And, wasn't the sun up yet at all?

Then, with a jolt like that of falling into nightmare, much became clear. Ben realized that he was still in the cave. The horror and fear of the recapture returned. And he understood dimly that this was far from being the first time that he'd been awakened in this way, in this dark place. But whatever had happened to him after those earlier awakenings had already been lost again in the mists of dark magic that fogged and clogged the workings of his memory.

Get dressed . . . no, he was dressed already. It was his own clothing, but now all sadly soiled and worn and tattered. Too much damage, he thought, to be accounted for even by all the things that he could remember happening to him since that unlucky hour when he had followed Doon into the upper cave. . . .

Doon, yes. And Mark, and Ariane. And all the others. Where were they, what had happened to them? The other figures stumbling and cursing around Ben in the darkness now were all strangers to him. His fellow trainees, or fellow prisoners, but he remembered none of them at all. None of them spoke to each other as they formed a crude queue and groped their way through the darkness, on their way to . . . all that Ben could remember, and that dimly, was that to please the sergeant they were expected to go somewhere and line up in a formation.

Dragonslicer was of course no longer at Ben's side. Sheath and belt were gone too, as were his headlamp, and his pack, and the simple little dagger that had been his only other weapon.

The dead weights of training and of fear were back now, hanging on him as a compelling burden. Ben stumbled into the formation with the group of unfamiliar men. Somehow he knew which place in which line was his. In a flash of something like clarity he realized that all of these could hardly be newly taken prisoners. Perhaps this was some kind of a punishment company . . . but it hardly mattered.

Their drill-ground was quite small, a space lighted by torches at its four corners and cleared of barracks-beds and other obstacles. Here in their small formation they practiced marching, and drilled with clumsy wooden spears.

The sergeant wore no badge of rank, but there was no doubt of who he was. He acted like a sergeant, striding through the ranks, barking commands, inspiring terror, yelling and kicking at anyone who displeased him. The drill went on unendingly. It had always been going on, thought Ben, and it always would be, and even that last sleep from which he could remember being awakened was really only one more illusion born of magic. Nowhere could Ben find the foothold of hope that he would have to have to be able to rebel against the sergeant's orders.

He didn't know where he was, except that he was still inside the cave. Which way was out? And where were the other people who had been captured with him? Were Ariane, Mark, Doon all dead? He tried once to ask a question of the sergeant, and got a curse and a kick for answer.

The drilling and the marching went on and on. There was a mindlessness about it that precluded even sadism as a motive. It was, like most basic training, utterly pointless except that it instilled the habit of instant obedience to command, and it filled the time.

At last there came an end, or at least an interruption. Ben was allowed to return to his barracks-bed and rest. But it seemed to him that as soon as he had closed his eyes, he was aroused again, and made to stagger back to drill some more, this time for an even longer period than before. He felt beyond exhaustion, as if his body and mind alike were struggling through thick cotton padding. He was caught in some mesh of magic, so that he hardly knew any longer who he was, or had been, or whether this existence constituted suffering or was only the standard of the universe, with nothing else left in the universe to judge it by.

March and rest. Drill and rest. Then march again. The real merged with the unreal. Ben told himself that he was dreaming this horror, he had to be. Or else all the rest of his life, before his entrance with Doon into the cave, had been a wonderful but lying dream.

Voices, some real and some fantastic (and no way of telling which was which) taunted him with the thought that never again would he see Ariane. Never . . . except, perhaps, just once a century or so, he'd be able to catch a glimpse of her across the battlefield during some brawl, and would see how the long decades as an Amazon had changed her. He would still know her, by her hair if nothing else. And then after the battle he might be able to see her across the hall of celebration, with foulness unspeakable and impassable filling all the space between them . . .

. . . and from time to time he was allowed to tumble back into his barracks-bed to rest. When his eyes closed, he feared to dream, and dreaming he feared even more to wake.

He knew that somewhere, in the real world, whatever that might really be, many days at least were passing.

Benambra, the First High Priest, came in a litter and looked at him once, and said something through withered lips, and smiled and went away. . . .

From time to time Ben was allowed, or perhaps compelled, to sit at a table in a dimly lit space called a messhall, where stuff was put before him on a plate. He really couldn't think of it as food. Slop, worse than anything that the Blue Temple had ever tried to feed him as a recruit topside, his first hitch. This was the second time that he'd been taken into Blue Temple service, and if they ever found out, ever realized who he was and how that first hitch of his had ended . . .

But usually Ben was too stupefied to even worry about that.

Just as he was allowed or perhaps compelled to eat, so it was with his dreams. Sometimes the dreams that were permitted or inflicted were not ordinary nightmares, but instead strange yearning visions in which Ben walked again the sweet fair earth above, and never thought of gold, and saw the face of Ariane. She was free too, and smiled at him. Once or twice there appeared a short man with a clown's painted face, wearing a gray cloak, who laughed and pointed as if it were all some happy joke. Then the next thing Ben knew, *she* was with him, holding his hand and smiling, asking him where he wanted to go next.

. . . and next he would wake up to darkness, and the groans of someone else bound down in magical punishment nearby.

Oh yes, he would be allowed to see her again someday. On the battle-field, as the tormenting voices told him. And after the battle if he still lived (maybe after he'd watched her die) he'd be allowed his drink, allowed to joke and bellow with his comrades, to fall down drunk, gradually to forget that once he had been someone else.

While he was actually drilling or marching, lucid moments were al-lowed to him more often. And in these moments Ben was able to swear solemnly to himself that he would never fight for the Blue Temple. But even as he swore he feared the compulsions that were being put upon him, that would leave him no real choice when the time came. He might once have sworn that he would never endure the kind of existence that he was enduring now. *When the time comes, you'll fight all right. Or die, and you won't want to die.* Who had said that to him, the sergeant? And truthfully life was precious, even now.

Then without warning there arrived a day and an hour when the mists of magical compulsion were wiped away. Ben was sleeping, then he was awake, and in a moment it was as if those mists had never been, even though when he opened his eyes the cave and the barracks area of the punishment company were still as hideously real as ever.

Ben was allowed to stand up from his bed as his own man again. Two sober Whitehands were standing nearby, holding torches, so that he had to squint in unaccustomed light. Also nearby there crouched a large, gray warbeast, a catlike creature bigger than a man, who hummed an intelligent warning growl at Ben.

Another figure, human, stood beside the beast. It was real also, some-one Ben had never seen in dreams.

Not Ariane who had come for him this time.

Radulescu.

"Ben of Purkinje, we meet again. Keep quiet!"

The command at the end was really unnecessary. Seeing this, and smiling faintly, the officer made a gesture. One of the Whitehands moved off obediently with his torch, showing Ben which way to go. Ben followed automatically, thinking as he moved that Radulescu looked good, looked fit and healthy, his small beard neatly trimmed, his clothes and his body clean. Before Radulescu fell into step just behind him, Ben had time to see that there was a sword—the same sword he had once tried to draw, just outside the cave?—at the officer's belt. And he was wearing what looked like the same officer's cloak of gold and blue, though it was dry now and the hood was lowered. Despite all greater considerations, Ben instantly felt the contrast with the way that he himself felt and smelled and must appear.

He was quite clearheaded now, in control of his own body and his own thoughts. But with the warbeast sniffing at his heels as he walked, he was really no freer than before. Unless he wanted to decide to end things quickly now, before Radulescu's interrogation and revenge could start—but no, it was unlikely that the beast would kill him quickly, unless it were ordered to do so. Warbeasts were intelligent enough to handle fine gradations of command.

They had walked for only a hundred meters when, to Ben's faint surprise, they came upon Mitspieler and Doon, looking as shabby as Ben felt, also under guard and apparently waiting for the arrival of Ben and Radulescu. Here another warbeast and two more Whitehands were in attendance. There was enough torchlight now for Ben to see, at some distance ahead, the great curve of the cave's ceiling coming down to make a wall. It looked like the same place where they had been cap-tured—but then, the different sides of this cave might look much alike.

Ben came up to where the others were and obeyed an order to halt. Now he saw with a shock of mixed feelings that Mark and Ariane were waiting nearby also, sitting in what had been the shadow of an empty bed and was now torchlight. They looked up as if they were glad to see him, but said nothing. Ben saw in Mark's familiar eye that there was some news—something important, but not to be told now. For right now, only a warning to play dumb.

And there, sitting in another shadow, were Dmitry, yes, and Daghur and Willem too. Ben thought that he understood now. All the members of Doon's party were being transferred to some special lock-up. Their break-in had been relatively successful, and he, Ben, was involved in it, and now the priests were going to conduct an investigation into the whole mess.

Right now, he couldn't help welcoming as a relief anything that took him out of basic training.

What was happening now? Ben looked round, and realized that Radulescu was in the process of dismissing the Whitehands, all four of them evidently.

"I can manage well enough from here on. I have the beasts."

One of the pale attendants looked worried. "But sir—"

"You heard my order."

"Yes sir."

The warbeasts no longer looked ready to pounce on Ben immediately. He risked a cautious step, that brought him close enough to Ariane to whisper to her. "Are you all right?"

"Right enough," she whispered back. He thought her tone was somewhat sprightlier than it had a right to be, as if she possessed some encouraging secret. Or, he supposed, she might still be drugged.

She added: "How are you?" The way she asked the question indicated that she cared about the answer.

Ben thought about how he was. He felt of his unkempt beard, brushed back his filthy hair. He was a mess, hungry and weary, but basically he still felt able to function. "By Ardneh, how long have we been here?"

"Many days." Still her voice was lively.

"How many?"

She picked up the real meaning of his question. "No, it's been days only, not months or years. It could have been that. It would have been, except . . ."

Ariane let it trail away there, but not unhappily. Smiling faintly, she looked up past Ben. Radulescu, a torch in one hand, was approaching, while behind him the four Whitehands and their other torches were receding into darkness, going back toward the central cave.

Radulescu with a gesture made his two warbeasts lie down and relax. Grinning crookedly at Ariane, he pointed at Ben and said: "Here he is."

"Thank you," she answered calmly, and got to her feet, brushing mechanically at her filthy trousers as if to dust them off. "Now I am ready to go on."

For Ben, the last to be set free, there were still some moments of confusion. He didn't really understand what was happening until Doon, after a quick talk with Radulescu, had begun to harangue the others again in his old fiery way:

"You all look so astonished! Why? Did you think I was dim enough to come seeking treasure in a place like this without being able to expect help along the way? I'd have had to be as stupid as the rest of you to take a chance like that. The colonel here's been planning with me for more than a year now on how to rob the treasury. He's able to get in by himself, of course, but not to get away again with a proper load."

As Doon spoke, he squatted down and began to unwrap a large bundle that Ben only now took notice of. It had been lying at Radulescu's feet. There were weapons in it, Ben observed dully, and backpacks, and headlamps too. People began to crowd around to help themselves.

Ben took a step forward, and Radulescu was standing just in front of him with a Sword . . . unbelievably, the officer was handing Dragonslicer back to him.

Radulescu said: "I'd not part from this so readily, you understand, if I didn't know there's even better down below. And you and I are comrades, partners now." It almost sounded as if Radulescu himself believed the words. "We are in this enterprise together."

"Aye." Ben swallowed. "It seems we are. I had no wish to hurt you, that time, throwing you into the cave and down the stairs. It was just that I had to get away."

The officer nodded. "I must concede that, the necessity of it from your viewpoint, I mean. Well, I hold no grudge." But it was still an officer speaking to an enlisted man, thought Ben; there had been no offer to shake hands.

Doon, looking large and whole again with Wayfinder back in his grip, was trying out its powers. He conferred briefly with Mitspieler—getting, Ben supposed, confirmation that this was the genuine article that he now held, and not another phantom.

Then the Baron approached Radulescu, and with something of his old testiness wanted to know why Radulescu hadn't warned him about the step-trap in the maze. "I lost a man there, and it came near pitching me into the underworld, in more ways than one. I can understand about the password for the magic-sealing; it would have been changed, and you had no chance to give me the new one. But that step—"

Radulescu waved an authoritative hand. "I would have cautioned you on all the traps, of course, could we have held our final meeting as we planned. But I've spent most of the last three months in what amounted to house arrest. I had no hope of getting word out to you. It would have been suicide to try."

Doon nodded. "That's what I hoped. I mean, that nothing worse had happened to you. When the big man here told me the name of the officer he'd thrown down into the upper cave, well . . . but even then I couldn't think of giving the attempt up. Not really."

"I didn't suppose you would. I wasn't really terribly surprised to find you where you were just now."

Suddenly Doon was looking more sharply at Radulescu. "What're you supposed to be doing down here now?"

The other chuckled. "Why, I'm thinking up new ways to protect the treasure, naturally. The Chairman told me to spend some time down here and study the problem thoroughly. He has proven to his own satisfaction, after lengthy investigation, that Ben of Purkinje here and I are not involved in any robbery plot together—ergo, I am not involved in any robbery plot at all, and am therefore the most freshly proven innocent of all his trusted lieutenants. Ergo again, I am the one to be trusted with this job. Hyrcanus wants results; he has virtually put me on probation until I can think up some real improvements for the security system. Maybe I'll leave a list for him when we depart." Now it was Radulescu's turn to ask a sudden pointed question. "Do you have some means of hauling away the treasure? Did you bring a ship?"

"There's a vessel, magically concealed, standing by for us—I hope." Doon glanced toward Mitspieler. "Nay, I'm sure it will be there. But if we have to haul the gold on our backs all the way up from the lowest level, back through the six sealings, I don't know how much . . ."

Radulescu smiled mysteriously. "As to that, we may be able to find some better way, when we get down below."

Ben, wondering what that might mean, exchanged a look with Mark. But they could hear no more of the dialogue. The co-leaders had turned away, to conduct the next part in muffled privacy.

Ben sighed. He noted how Dmitry and his father were glaring at each other. And how Willem and Daghur, giggling together about something, sat waiting to be told what to do next so they could try to make a joke of it.

CHAPTER 15

Armed again, with headlamps glowing and the two warbeasts loping peacefully alongside, the party pushed on. Mark was sure now that they were retracing the path that had previously led to capture. They were moving quickly. Divided into small groups, they were united at least in the wish to leave this level of the cave before Benambra or someone else awoke to the fact that they were again escaping. Radulescu had said that there was a good place to rest not far past the entrance to the next lower level; they would reach it soon, and before entering the area where the demon was usually encountered.

Mark, in hurried conversation with Ben and Ariane, soon learned that their experience in captivity had been much like his own: drug- and sorcery-induced drill and marching. Looking back on their capture, they discussed what they might have done to avoid it, but could come up with no really good ideas.

"At least we have an experienced guide this time," Mark murmured to Ben, who walked beside him.

"Aye. And trustworthy—at least until he gets the use he wants out of us." Ben paused. "He would rather have left me where I was, just now."

He looked at Ariane, walking on his other side. "I thank you, for refusing to go on until I was released. That's what happened, isn't it?"

"She did the same for me," said Mark. "And I'll thank her again now. Ben, neither of us was really wanted on this part of the trip— unless Doon's Sword pointed to us again, before he lost it . . . anyway they must have decided that we'd be useful to carry treasure, and use weapons when needed. But they definitely wanted the young lady here, so much so that they brought us along just to please her. They'll take great pains to get her to cooperate. And they seemed much relieved when Mitspieler's magic gave assurance that her virginity had not been lost."

Ariane observed, "They still think that I have powers that are going to help them somehow." She looked to her right and left. "I may require more in the way of thanks, from both of you, before we're done."

"You'll have it." And Ben took her briefly by the hand.

They were passing now under the high shelves, from which, this time, no ambush sprang. The sides of the passage narrowed in on them and the floor turned down. Now they were entering territory that was unfamiliar to all of them save Radulescu. Doon, as if he had some reservations about blindly following the priest's guidance, had now drawn Wayfinder and was using it to make sure he was on the right path, even though the chance of going wrong here seemed remote.

The descent of the passage steepened, and its floor became a stair. The tunnel was fairly well lighted here, by small gas flames set at intervals along the neatly finished stonework of its walls. They might, Mark thought, almost have been inside some fort or military guardhouse on the surface. The walls here showed a different workmanship than that of the maze or the other, upper regions of the cave complex. Of course there was no reason to assume that the whole place had been dug out or finished at one time, or under the direction of a single planner.

The stair was forty or fifty meters long, with most of its length in one smooth descending curve. At its bottom the passage leveled out, and then ran for another forty or fifty meters before branching into two. Here Radulescu with a small gesture directed them to the right.

Doon's Sword must have indicated otherwise, for instead of turning at once he paused, looking at the other questioningly.

"The place of rest," said Radulescu patiently. "Looking at you, I can well believe that you all need it."

The right-hand way led through a constricted doorway into a rough cave chamber, perhaps fifteen meters broad and twenty deep. Large rocks made an irregular litter around the sides; there was a clear area of sandy floor in the center, and a sloping ceiling. Mark could hear water running, and when he turned the beam of his headlamp toward the rear of the room he saw the pool. It was fed by a small stream that leapt from a crevice in the upper rocks, then gurgled away on the other side of the cave to provide drainage. Probably it was the same stream, here somewhat diminished, that they had encountered earlier on the higher levels of the complex.

The warbeasts went immediately to the pool, and began lapping at it thirstily. Most of the human members of the party hung back a little, watching without comment as Mitspieler went to the water. First he touched it, then tasted it, and at last drank some of it himself. Soon the whole party except Radulescu were drinking, filling water bottles, and making an effort to wash up. Mark, able at last to rinse what he hoped was the last taste of messhall garbage from his mouth, began to feel more like the person he had been when he first followed Doon into the upper cave.

After drinking, Mitspieler washed himself minimally. A few seconds later he was stretched out sound asleep, his head pillowed on his pack. His face in repose wore a look of total exhaustion, that brought to it a resemblance to the countenance of Indosuaros in that wizard's last hours. Mark's imagination worked briefly on the question of what kind of basic training a captured wizard might be given in the garrison; but he got nowhere with it and soon gave up.

Everywhere people were opening their packs, in search of real food. Nothing seemed to have been stolen from the packs, or spoiled. To people who had subsisted on prisoners' fare for many days, the field rations seemed like a banquet. Dmitry, who had never had a pack, rifled his father's, taking deft care not to disturb its owner. He shared his loot with Daghur and Willem, but only on demand, and somewhat petulantly.

Mark, sitting on a rock and chewing on some dried fruit from his own supply, found himself gazing into the eyes of Radulescu. The officer, sitting nearby, was wearing an air of patience—rather, thought Mark, like a man allowing his herd of beasts to drink and graze a while before he whipped them on.

Obeying an impulse, Mark asked the officer suddenly: "What made you decide to rob what you were guarding, and join forces with the Baron?"

Probably Radulescu was surprised by what must have struck him as impertinence. But he made no objection, and answered promptly enough. "Have you seen Benambra?"

"Aye. It was he who led the Whitehands who took us prisoners."

"Well, I have seen him too. And it was my first look at him, about a year ago, that made me decide to rob what I was guarding, as you put it. Seeing just what I had to look forward to, if I worked diligently as a good officer, and was clever, devoted, fanatical, and lucky enough to rise to the very top of the Blue Temple hierarchy."

The rest stop went on longer than the leaders really wanted. Doon and Radulescu were soon sighing and fidgeting, walking about nervously. But Mitspieler continued in a deep sleep, and Doon when he looked at the wizard's face decided not to wake him, despite what were evidently the Colonel's whispered urgings that he do so. The others meanwhile were ready to take advantage of whatever time for rest they were allowed.

When Mitspieler did awaken, it was suddenly. And perhaps of himself; Mark, who happened to be watching, thought it was as if some unseen power had whispered into the wizard's ear. The man sat up, alert from the start. His first look, a grim one, was aimed at his son. Then he cast a speculative glance toward Ariane.

Getting to his feet, Mitspieler asked Radulescu: "Have you the password that we'll need to get past the demon?"

"I have, of course. I would not have come down into the caves without it."

"And you're sure it's not been changed since you came down? Hyrcanus on the surface can change it at any time, can't he?"

Radulescu frowned at this. "Of course he can. But he won't, he knows I'm down here. If he had wanted to get rid of me, he wouldn't have done it that way."

"I'm not so sure." Mitspieler looked at the officer meditatively. "The Whitehands don't need a password, naturally."

"Naturally not. The demon is magically compelled to ignore their comings and goings. The only ones who need a password are normal human visitors." Radulescu smiled. "Like us."

Mitspieler sighed, and seemed to discard his misgivings, whatever they had been. "Well and good then. Let's get on."

In a matter of moments everyone had packed up, and the party was moving on, with headlamps lighted against the darkness that Radulescu warned was just ahead. Mark felt uneasy at the thought of his first encounter with a demon, now soon to come, even though he was basically confident of Radulescu's magical protection.

They had only just left the cave of rest, and were passing the place where the tunnel branched, when a faint sound like a distant yell came drifting down the tunnel that led to the level above.

The leaders muttered briefly to each other, then ignored the sound and moved right on.

Ben asked Mark: "What was that? An alarm?"

"If it was, we're past it now. We might as well move on."

"If they're looking for us up there, we'll run into trouble coming back."

Radulescu had heard this, and turned his head long enough to be reassuring. "There will be ways. I know the caves, backward and forward and inside out."

"But maybe someone besides you has discovered that the dragon's missing. And the entrance stone's been enchanted, so it can be lifted from the inside."

The Colonel frowned. He dropped back a little to walk with them. "Of course, I discovered those things. That's why I felt sure I'd find you all down here somewhere. But I was alone. There are no regular patrols on the surface; Hyrcanus is dozing, as usual, in blissful ignorance. And Benambra, if he's been given any report at all on my taking you away, thinks I'm marching you off to interrogation somewhere. He's fairly bright, but he'll be kept busy for a while yet, disciplining the Field Marshal and his merry men, or trying to do so. Trust me, I know the workings of this place."

The party advanced, but more slowly now, the leaders proceeding with caution. The tunnel they were following soon opened up on the top and one side, to become a mere ledge that clung to the face of an underground cliff. The cliff's smooth face rose vertically here for about ten meters, and grew higher as the path continued its gradual descent.

The outer edge of the winding path was protected by a knee-high stone wall, and beyond this wall a slope went steeply down into the dismal darkness of a dry ravine. A few meters beyond the ravine, another cliff went up to meet the roof. The slopes were littered with fallen rocks. Mark expected to see more bones among them, but discovered something else. When he turned his light fully on one strange object he realized that it was either a grotesque doll, or a human body, clothes and all shrunken to the size of a withered child. But once it had been bearded like a man.

"One of Dactylartha's victims," said Ariane, walking beside him. Her voice was more dreamy than afraid.

"Dactylartha?"

"That is the demon's name."

"How do you know?"

She didn't answer. The two warbeasts were uncomfortable now, prowling first ahead of the human party, then hanging back. Radulescu had to call them frequently to keep them close to his side.

The air in here smelled strange, thought Mark. No, it was not so much a smell as it was a feeling, as if the temperature were uncomfortably high. Or perhaps low. . . .

"He leaves his victims so?"

"Some demons do. Others . . . do other things, perhaps even uglier." Her abstracted voice perturbed him.

"What do you know of demons? Where have you ever met one?" This was from Ben.

Again Ariane did not answer. She walked on, moving steadily and smoothly enough, yet almost as if entranced. Mark and Ben exchanged a momentarily helpless look behind her back.

The . . . wrongness . . . in the air increased. Mark had heard that demons sometimes advertised their proximity so, but he had not felt the effect before. Looking at the others, he thought that now it was bothering them all. Except for Radulescu, who might be used to it, and perhaps Doon, whose pride probably refused to let a feeling of illness show. Even Mitspieler, who presumably could defend himself to some extent, looked paler than before.

Now the officer stopped and turned. With a gesture he stopped the others, who were now all following him at a distance of a few paces. "Wizard, you come forward with me, if you will—just in case, as you suggested, there is some difficulty about the password."

"Why should there be?" demanded Doon.

Radulescu doubtless would have liked to ignore him, but knew better than to try. "I don't know. But just in case. The rest of you wait here. Imp, come with me, lad." This last was addressed to the grayer and larger of the warbeasts, which whined at the command but reluctantly obeyed.

Seven humans and one warbeast waited, while Radulescu, Mitspieler, and Imp went on, following the ledge around the next bulge of the cliff. Mark did not know exactly what he was expecting to happen next, but what did happen surprised him. It began with a show of multicolored lights, playing on the far wall of the cave, thirty meters beyond the ravine.

For a moment there was little to hear. Then some words, indistinguishable, cried out in Radulescu's voice. Then a frightening bass tremor, and screams in animal and human voices.

The animal did not reappear, but the two men came into sight, reeling and staggering back along the path. Mitspieler turned once, gesturing behind him, as if he might be hurling invisible weapons from his fingertips.

Those who had been waiting needed no urgings, no spoken warning, to turn and run. Ben dragged Ariane, who was screaming something and seemed for a moment hesitant, along with him. Mark, taking one final look over his shoulder as he fled, saw Mitspieler with gestures erecting a haze of magic on the path, then turning to run also, with Radulescu. Beyond the two running men Mark saw the figure of the demon, looking itself like a tall man clad in dark armor. And the strangest thing of all about the sight was that the very rock of the path seemed to be stretching and sagging beneath the demon's feet.

Doon, running unabashedly in the lead as ever, had his Sword out, held in front of him. And Mark was sure that he was not willing it to find him treasure now, but refuge.

"The cave!" someone shouted. Mark saw Doon turn hard to his left, and leap into the room in which they had just been resting. The others went pounding after him, in headlong flight. Mark, running right after Ben and Ariane, was the last one in before the wizards. Just before he entered, he was almost knocked off his feet by the remaining warbeast, which was running about insanely, across the path and up and down the slope.

The two wizards, sobbing for breath, made it somehow, and threw themselves down just inside the narrow doorway. They grabbed implements of magic from their sleeves and pockets, and from Mitspieler's pack. Gripping these, their four hands wove across the opening a fine net of magic, whose substance seemed to be drawn into being right out of the air itself. They completed it none too soon. There sounded heavy footfalls, right outside the door, and the feeling of sickness and wrongness that heralded the demon reached in insidiously to grip them all.

But the pressure remained bearable. "We are safe, but only for the moment," Mitspieler gasped.

"The password," Radulescu panted, "must have been changed." And he dug yet one more object from his pocket, and used it as if in afterthought to strengthen the defenses of the doorway. What filled the doorway now had the look of translucent paper, or thin cloth; but it was evidently stronger than it looked. Dactylartha was trying to do something to it from the outside, but so far it gave no sign of yielding.

"Of course it has," said Doon coldly. "So Hyrcanus must be out to kill you after all. That means he's aware of the whole plot, now."

Radulescu stared at him. "Even so, we can still get away, if that ship you promised is truly waiting for us."

"And if we can get out of this room without being devoured. Tell me, you who know the caves forward and backward, how do we do that?"

The Colonel was saved from having to answer, at least for the moment. For now the demon's voice boomed forth from beyond the door, smothering all other sounds. "Come out, humans, come out. A pair of warbeasts make but a small meal, and I am starved. My hunger cries for human minds and bodies."

Inside the cave all was silence for a few moments. Then Ariane in her little girl's voice offered: "I was taught a charm of old white magic, once, when I was small." No one bothered to reply to her. All eyes were on the wizard, and the priest of the Blue Temple.

Mitspieler let out a small sigh. "We have done all we can to seal the door. It will not be enough, for very long." Then he turned to Doon and spoke deliberately: "I think it is time now."

"Time for what?" Mark wanted to know.

But Doon understood, and he was ready to explain. His manner, as much as his words, served at first to calm the others.

"The failure of the password need not be fatal. Mitspieler and I—and Indosuaros—considered the possibility of something of the kind happening, before we ever came near the cave. We knew we needed some other method of getting past the demon, to fall back on. And Wayfinder found us what we needed."

The Baron's eyes turned now toward Ariane. But it was to Mitspieler that he spoke. "Wizard, are you ready? Can we do it?"

Mitspieler's answer came in a changed voice, tones harder and more powerful. "Yes, I'm reasonably sure we can. Not only is she a virgin, but the daughter of a queen as well. I've now made sure of that. But we must waste no time. Our defenses are not going to hold this doorway for long."

As if to underscore this point, a raging though muffled demonstration by the demon now took place outside. The light filtering in from the passage changed, and rage and hatred and choked noise oozed in as well.

Inside the cave a silent pause stretched on. It was long enough for a multiple exchange of looks, for calculation, for a sudden tightening of muscles, and shifting of weapons.

Then Ariane leaped to her feet with a sudden shriek. "They mean to kill me!" The terror in her voice now, like the wistfulness of a moment ago, was that of a young girl. And, recoiling from the reaching arm of Doon, she scrambled across the cave, and got herself into a position between Ben and Mark.

"What is this?" Ben was on his feet and roaring. And his Sword, like Doon's, was out already.

Doon was smiling at him from across a few paces of sandy floor. Now that blades were drawn in anger, the Baron looked vastly more cheerful, and even at his ease.

But he was in no hurry to attack. "I don't want to kill you, lad," he said to Ben, his voice quite calm and reasonable. "Look you—and you too, Mark, if you stand with him. We all of us now have only two choices. First, we can stay here, and wait for the demon to break in upon us. That'll happen soon, and we'll all perish—nay, perish is too good a word. You saw, out there, what Dactylartha likes to do to those he takes. We'll face what's worse than dying—unless we kill each other first, or kill ourselves.

"But there's a second choice, and that's the one I'm going to take. So are the rest of us. To sacrifice one now—" At these words the shouting of the three across the cave rose up in opposition, but Doon only raised his own voice and went on, "—the daughter of a queen, a virgin girl. Her death properly offered will bind any demon for a time—at least it will bind this one, and for long enough.

"And then the rest of us can go on freely. On to the gold. Have you forgotten?"

Here the Baron paused again, long enough to make sure that the silence from across the cave still represented stubborn refusal, and not a sullen wavering toward assent. "Ben, your own girl on the outside, have you forgotten her? What will you choose, your little shop somewhere with her, or withering for a century in Dactylartha's gut?

"And Mark. Those Swords Sir Andrew needs so badly are down below, waiting for us. How many lives of his people can they save? You've already killed to get them. Now one more small life stands in the way. That of someone you hardly know . . . hey?"

Again Doon halted briefly. When he went on, his voice was still calm. "I'll say one thing more, before we come to kill you. This demon is the last sealing that we'll have to face . . . six is the true number, and the old song lies. Am I right, Radulescu?"

But the Colonel clumsily chose this moment to attempt to assert an officer's authority. "You three, lay down your arms, at once!"

He was ignored, of course. Mark had an arrow already nocked; to draw and loose it would take an eyeblink only. I must get Doon with my first shot, he told himself. Get him, get him certainly, before he can come within a blade's length of any of us. We none of us can match him with a blade, and none of the others over there are likely to be half so dangerous.

Mitspieler, standing with hands half-raised in front of him, made an incoherent sound. He looked almost ready to collapse. A physical fight within this chamber would only weaken the barrier at the doorway, and bring the demon ravening in upon them all; so it seemed he might have pleaded, if he could have found clear speech.

Again the demon stirred outside. Mark could hear and feel it passing the doorway, like a bad wind, like a vicious dog, like the hunter who is coming back.

At last Mitspieler managed to find words. "Mark, lay down your bow. Make your friend see sense!"

Mark had noticed meanwhile that Dmitry, having no regular missile weapon, had picked up a small rock, as if he were getting ready to throw it. Mitspieler's son was looking across the cave at Mark. He was perhaps clever enough to follow Mark's thought on the coming fight, and take the plan one step farther. If the rebellious three were to be pacified without too much damage to the stronger side, then Mark must be prevented from shooting Doon in the first moments of the brawl. Dmitry, while ready to attack with a small rock, was also prudently sheltering most of his own body behind one of the larger ones. . . .

And Willem and Daghur had disappeared altogether; but Mark doubted that they were attempting any kind of a flanking movement, and doubted even more that the configuration of this cave would lend itself to such a try.

Afterwards, Mark was never able to say just whose sudden movement had triggered the outbreak of the fight. One moment, all were statues, limned in the different headlamps' light. Next moment all were blurring in violent motion.

Mark loosed his arrow, aimed at Doon, but missed. Dmitry's rock, flung with unexpected speed and skill, missed Mark but at the last instant just grazed the bow held in Mark's hands. The shaft flew wide, to break against a rock.

Some headlamps went off, others flashed on, beams dancing crazily about the cave, as different people tried different strategies. It was hopeless now to try to use the bow, and Mark dropped it along with his quiver; he had already slipped out of the straps of his backpack. Switching his own headlamp off, he drew his long knife and crouched down waiting.

Darkness was conquering the cave as that strategy became unanimous. Mark thought he could hear Ariane's sling, a short distance to his right, whine softly, one spin, two, and then unload itself at high velocity. Amid the faint staccato of scrambling sounds within the cave the result was impossible to distinguish.

Now the darkness was total, except for the strained glow from the besieged doorway. Outside, the demon still mumbled in his wrath and tried to paw his way in through the spells. Inside the room, rocks continued to click gently, as furtive feet and crawling knees disturbed them. Some people were repositioning themselves, while others waited listening. Those on the other side would be trying to close in on Ariane. She had Ben as one defender to her right, Mark to her left. And she herself, even if her voice did sometimes turn childish, was no timid, helpless . . .

Mark started, as Mitspieler's voice cried out, shouting at full volume into darkness: "Stop it, you fools, all of you!" There was a momentary pause; then the wizard's voice came back, a notch lower: "Ben, Mark, isn't it better for one to die than—"

He cut off there, abruptly. It was as if he had heard or sensed something that stopped him. Now to Mark all was utter silence in the cave, except for the muted rush of the small stream. Whatever Mitspieler had sensed had probably been perceptible to him alone.

Now there were stumbling footsteps in the darkness, those of one person moving, careless of being heard. And now Mitspieler had turned his headlamp on again, deliberately, as if he had decided or divined that the time for fighting was now over, or else that fighting had become irrelevant. The back-reflection of his light revealed his own face, aged, untidily bearded as were the faces of all the men, and slack-jawed now with fear or awe.

The wizard stood in the middle of the cave. He was looking at the sealed doorway, the translucent barrier that he had himself erected. Again he spoke, and yet again his voice was changed.

"Wait. This is no ruse. The demon is gone. Gone somewhere . . . I don't know how far, but . . ."

Suddenly Mitspieler slumped to his knees, still staring at the fragile-looking barrier of magic.

Now Mark could hear a new kind of movement just outside, different from the demon's. And there was a change in the faint light, a brightening out in the tunnel. And now something appeared in the center of the barrier. It was a hand, not armored, and quite human-looking, except that it was larger than the hand of any normal human being. But it had neither the Whitehands' deformity nor the armor of the giant fist of the demon. The hand, whomever it belonged to, brushed Mitspieler's blocking spells out of its way just as a man might have flicked aside a cobweb.

Now the owner of the hand entered the cave behind it, bringing with him his own kind of alteration. A giant human figure, male, youthful-looking and lightly clad, wearing a Phrygian cap and carrying in one hand a staff. Mark understood that for the first time in his life he was looking at a god. And in the next moment he recognized the god as Hermes.

Most of the cave was now—not lighted so much as revealed, by Hermes' presence. The beam of Mitspieler's headlamp had become irrelevant. Mark's own vision was now able to peer into the far recesses of the cave, and it seemed to him that he could almost see behind the rocks. Hermes had come here seeking something, and in the face of that seeking any kind of human concealment seemed to have become impossible.

None of the humans moved or spoke. All of them remained sitting, crouching, kneeling, just as they had been. Casually Hermes looked around. Then, with the matter-of-fact movements of a strong man who had to interrupt some toddlers' squabble in the course of business of his own, Hermes approached Ben.

Ben was down on his backside, the Sword still in his right hand, quaking as the god approached him. At the last moment he was unable to keep his eyes open, and had to raise one hand to hide his face. When Hermes reached out and took Dragonslicer away from him, Ben's huge frame quaked in a spasm that might have been meant as resistance—but it came too late, and in any case would have been hopeless.

The god dropped something small into the sand in front of Ben— Mark caught the flash of gold. Then Hermes turned away, already seating Dragonslicer in one of the empty scabbards at his belt. Only now did Mark notice that Hermes was wearing perhaps a dozen empty sheaths in all, hanging like a fringe around his waist.

And now Mark found himself getting to his feet, he was not sure why. He was standing straight up, even though his knees were shaking with the fear of it.

Hermes observed this movement. The god paused in mid-stride, on his way back across the cave. He turned his head and looked at Mark. It was a brief look but expressive—even though Mark was not quite sure what it expressed. Recognition—*what,* you *here?*—seemed to be at the start of it, with unreadable complexities trailing off from there.

But the pause and the look were only momentary. Hermes had come here on his own business, in pursuit of which he now approached the Baron.

Doon, finding himself in the path of this advance, made a great effort and struggled to his feet. With both hands he raised Wayfinder to guard position.

Hermes halted in front of him, and spoke for the first time. His voice was huge, remote, aloof. "Give it me. That Sword that you are holding."

"Never. It is mine by right." The words were barely understandable, but Doon managed to get them out. He was shaking almost as badly as Ben had been, as Mark's knees still were. Shaking with what must have been fear, compounded by anger and helplessness.

The deity deigned to speak to him once more. "I suppose you're going to argue that you've been using it properly, unlike some of the others. In accordance with the game. Well, perhaps you have. But that no longer matters."

"I am. I have. It's mine, it's mine."

The god reached out impatiently. Doon struck at him. The stroke would have been a killing blow against a human, but appeared now as no more than some child's petulant protest against authority. Then the Sword was in the hand of Hermes Messenger, who with a flick of his staff, more a gesture than anything else, stretched Doon out on the floor of the cave. The man lay there in agony, crying with pain and frustrated rage.

"Unseemly pride," the god remarked, sliding Wayfinder into a sheath. "In one as mortal as yourself."

The only human being standing now was Mark—and why he should be standing was something that he hardly knew himself, though it was costing him a tremendous effort. He could see that the great wizard Mitspieler was down on his face in the sand. Doon sprawled, groaning. Ariane was somewhere out of sight. Ben was sitting up, but with his face still buried in his hands. And Mark was thinking: This is what my father had to face, some small part of what he endured, when Vulcan took him to help create the Swords. Always until now Mark had felt for his father some faint buried touch of shame, for the implied weakness, for Jord's letting himself be used, letting his right arm be taken. But no more. Now Mark had some idea, some appreciation of what Jord must have felt.

Only a moment had passed since Hermes had last spoken. But something else was happening now, a new presence was announcing itself. Just as light had spread throughout the cave upon Hermes' entrance, so now it was with shade. The wizard Mitspieler, sensing the new presence, raised his head, and the beam from his headlamp was engulfed and blotted out by the intensity of shadow gathering inside the unguarded door.

Mark, still on his feet, could see the dim form of the newcomer, roughly human, standing within the pall of blackness. The voice issuing from the shadowed manlike face was strangely reverberant; it seemed to swell up out of the rocks, out of the earth itself.

"The underworld is my domain. What are you doing here, Hermes Messenger? What is there in my world that you seek to change?"

Hermes Messenger did not appear to be disturbed. "I am collecting Swords—as you ought to realize, Hades. I am going about the business of the gods."

"What gods?"

"Why, all of us. You too. All of us who know what's going on, at least. I only carry out the gods' collective will."

"Hah!" The sound was more like a stony impact than a syllable of speech. "Since when have all of us agreed to that extent on anything? Say rather that you are determined to cheat in the game. That's how I interpret your behavior."

Hermes stood up very tall. It seemed to Mark that the ceiling of the cave must be bending a little to make room for his head. "The game has been—suspended. At least for the time being. There are certain dangers in it that at first were not fully appreciated."

"Oh, has it, indeed? By whose decision?"

Now both gods, as if by common agreement, were starting to move toward the low cave exit, as if their argument would be better carried out elsewhere. Hades was already stooping his tall figure to go out.

But Hermes paused, arrested by the sight of Doon still moaning at his feet. He prodded the helpless form with the end of his great staff.

"Well, man, what treatment shall I give your pride before I go? Perhaps I'll give you a loadbeast's head to wear from now on. What say you to that idea? Hey? Answer me!"

Hades at the doorway was bored by this distraction, and stood waiting for it to be over.

"No—no, don't. Spare me . . . please." Doon's voice was almost inaudible, and almost unrecognizable, too.

Hades in his impatience grumbled something, in a bass voice pitched too low for Mark to understand. Hermes on hearing it forgot his human toy, and both gods went on out of the cave. Just as they emerged into the corridor outside, Mark heard the sound of the demon out there again. Hades spoke again, and then did something; and Dactylartha fled, yapping and bounding like a kicked cur.

And with that the gods were gone. Inside the cave the humans were stirring, shakily, as if each and all of them were trying to recover from an illness.

Even as others were getting to their feet, Mark sat down, his knees suddenly shakier than before. Why, he realized, I have just looked upon the face of Pluto himself . . . and here I am. Mitspieler, or Indosuaros, one of them, told us once that no man can do that and live. And here I am. . . . Mechanically he picked up his quiver and slung it on his back. He picked up his bow. What was he going to do with it now?

When Doon sat up, the first thing he did was to look around him suspiciously, to see who might have been a witness to his weakness. Mark noticed this vaguely but his own thoughts were elsewhere. Dmitry had emerged from hiding, and was calling out all demons and gods to witness that Daghur was dead.

"Look at that, a rock got him, it looks like. Who uses a sling?" All Mark could see of Daghur was a limp arm as Dmitry raised it.

Ben was calling out too, calling for help, from where he stood bending over Ariane. Mark rushed to them. The girl was sitting up, but blood from a head injury was streaking down one side of her face. Either a stone from the other side had hit her, or she had fallen during the scrambling in the dark.

And now Mitspieler was on his feet. He pointed, with a shaking arm, to where the doorway of the cave yawned unprotected. "The demon!" he choked out the words. ". . . is stunned. Run! Run for it now!"

Ben scooped up Ariane, disdaining any help from Mark. With Mark running as a rear guard, the big man hurried out of the cave. He moved quickly but the others were already gone ahead of him. Outside, they could see headlamps bobbing on the downward path. Doon's Sword might have been taken from him, but his determination was not yet dead. And if he had had any thought of running back instead toward the upper levels of the cave, it had probably been squelched by the sound of human yells that now came drifting down from that direction. The alarms were louder and closer than before.

The demon had retreated or fallen into the chasm of the ravine. Mark could see multicolored lights flash up from those dark depths, and could feel the waves of hatred, as distinct as spoken curses.

Doon was running in the lead, gaining with every stride. After him came Mitspieler, who looked back to find his son, then increased his pace again as both Dmitry and Willem rushed past him at top speed. Radulescu, who supposedly knew better than anyone else the best place to seek safety, was running in the same direction. Ben with Ariane in his arms pounded in the same direction with surprising fleetness, Mark keeping right behind them.

They passed the curve of the path where the demon had first sent them dashing back. Mark had a quick look at the body of the first warbeast to die. It was draped limply over the low wall beside the path, dropped there like a chewed fruit-rind, shrunken, still steaming or smoking.

Just as animals that were natural enemies might flee together from some disaster, so did the humans overtake and pass each other on the path, taking no more notice than did strangers in a crowded city.

Ariane had partially regained consciousness, and was struggling to get Ben to put her down.

And now the demon had recovered, from whatever the gods had done to it in passing. The lights of it again spun and flickered in the air, the noise and sickness of it came trampling, hurtling in pursuit.

Mitspieler, now fallen to last place among the racing humans, unable to run faster, was now unable to run any more at all. He turned and struck with desperate magic against the flying thing. Mark, looking back with some remnant of a wish to help the man, saw bolts of fire shoot from the wizard's fingertips, to splash into the light that roiled in midair and represented Dactylartha. And then Mark saw the stronger fire strike back, along the pathway of the first, and he saw what happened to Mitspieler when it engulfed him.

The demon now flashed through the air, easily overtaking and passing Mark and Ben, and Ariane, who now moved on her own feet supported between them. It was obviously trying to cut off the leaders of the human rout, who now fled down the last section of the path toward a dark doorway. It failed. The last man of the advanced group vanished into that portal just before it got there.

Balked, it turned back. Three living victims yet remained to it.

It spewed its sickness at them. Blue immaterial flames burst around Ben, and he fell, choking and gasping. Mark felt the pain. . . .

Ariane pushed herself erect against the wall of rock beside the path, and faced the thing directly. Her girlish voice rang out, in what must have been the charm learned in her childhood:

"In the Emperor's name, forsake this game, and let us pass!"

There was a burbling and a shrieking in the air. Dactylartha's substance boiled and spurted. It struck at the three humans but it could no longer reach them. A wall as of glass, invulnerable and invisible, was outlined along the path, imaged in midair by the demon's fire that splashed against it harmlessly. The pathway, just to one side, was clear.

The flames had disappeared from Ben's body, leaving no signs of physical damage. Mark with an effort got the big man back on his feet and shoved him forward. Then Mark took Ariane by the arm and pulled her along; he realized that he was in better shape than either of the others, but at the same time he knew he was half-dazed himself.

Supporting themselves and each other as best they could, the three of them limped and hobbled forward, passing shielded just under the storm of the demon's wrath. It deafened and blinded but could not touch them. Now the dark doorway was close ahead, and now they were entering it, and now, with a shock of sudden silence, the domain of the demon had been left behind.

They stood in a quiet place, of stone and friendly darkness; a little light was coming from somewhere ahead of them and below.

"This looks like a drainpipe," Ben muttered dazedly. "Or a sewer."

Maybe it did, thought Mark. But it was a passage to where they wanted to go, and even reasonably clean. As they moved forward and the descent steepened, there were steps and grips to use.

Ben was starting to come out of his confusion. "What happened back there?" was the next thing he asked. "I thought it had us for a moment. Did Mitspieler fight it off?"

Ariane had nothing to say. She kept moving along, putting down one foot after another, but she looked bad, her face stark white behind the bruise and the dried blood.

Mark made no answer either. Not now. Later, when he had had time to think, he would have questions of his own.

"Look," said Ben, and stopped momentarily, opening his hand, displaying a gold coin.

"Yes," said Mark.

They moved on. The tunnel was bottoming out. Mark could see that just ahead it widened into a level space, wide and open, extending farther than he could see from here. Some Old World lights there appeared to be turning themselves on in welcome. And the light that shone up into the tunnel was yellow with the reflected burden of the gold.

CHAPTER 16

The ugly dazzle of the demon's influence faded quickly from Ben's mind as he moved on. But his mind did not really clear. Instead the more entrancing glamour of the gold came on to absorb his thoughts.

Down here long hallways were lined with shelves displaying gold. Niches and alcoves and entire rooms were filled with the yellow hoard. As far as Ben could see it was all unguarded, open, free to their touch whenever they wished to reach out and touch it. There were neat piles of bars and ingots, heavy baskets filled with ore and nuggets. Wordlessly the three walked past stack after stack of coin, cases of jewelry, shelves crammed with artifacts of gold. Some of these were simple, some were ugly, some were of intricate workmanship whose origin and purpose Ben could not identify.

In the rooms of the treasure cave nearest to the entrance, many of the stacks of coin were toppled, many of the shelves were disarranged, as if intruders' hands had already played and sported with them greedily. Doon and Radulescu, Dmitry and Willem, must have passed this way only a little earlier.

The rock ceiling here was relatively low, only a meter or two above the wooden walls and partitions and stacked shelves that held the treasure. In the ceiling Old World lights were mounted somehow; lights in individual rooms and halls and alcoves came on individually ahead of Mark and Ben and Ariane as they approached, and lights behind them darkened again as soon as they had passed. Ben, looking very far ahead —this cavern like those above it went on for a great distance—could see that there, too, lights in other rooms were going on and off. He assumed that Doon and the three others were probably there, had probably by now ceased marveling and were busy stuffing their pockets and their packs . . . come to think of it, he doubted that anyone still had a pack, after that last chase. Neither he nor Mark nor Ariane had one now, though Mark had somehow retained his bow and quiver.

And there continued ever more piles of bullion to marvel at, more stacks of coin, more shelves of golden ornaments, all yellowing the light. High shelves of stored gold lined the passages between rooms, and made up the partitions between rooms, and covered the walls of the rooms themselves. There had to be, Ben supposed, some overall plan of organization to the hoard, but so far he could not tell what it was.

They walked on and on, saying nothing to each other, discovering more and more. Their wonder at the vastness of the treasure grew, until it blurred into a sense of unreality. This was too much. This must be some enchantment, or some joke. . . .

At an intersection of long aisles, or galleries, Ben looked down a long vista—a hundred meters? two hundred?—to a rock wall at the end. About halfway down, he glimpsed an end to gold, if not to treasure. Another light had just come on there, where someone else must be moving through the hoard, and it illumined a kind of borderline where it seemed that yellow metal might give way to silver. And might that starry detail be the twinkle of distant diamonds?

It was all too much. It somehow carried matters beyond the enjoyment or appreciation even of successful robbers that there should be *this* much.

Then, without warning, turning a corner into a room that had just lighted itself ahead of them, the three of them encountered Doon. The little man, who had probably just entered from the other side, recoiled at first, as startled as they were. He said nothing. Dirty and disheveled as were they all, he appeared somehow shrunken without his Sword. There was a dagger still at his belt, but he made no move to draw it. After staring wildly at the three of them for a moment, he mumbled something, but it was evidently addressed only to himself.

Ben had automatically drawn his own remaining weapon, which was a simple dagger also. But in spite of their recent fight, he felt no urge to strike the man in front of him. At the moment the Baron seemed more pitiful than dangerous.

"Where's Radulescu?" Mark demanded sharply of their former leader. "Where are the Swords—the ones kept here in the treasury?"

At mention of the Swords, a gleam of purpose came into Doon's eyes. He again mumbled indistinguishable words, and stumbling past the three who confronted him, he ran on, searching his own search. They could follow his progress for some little distance, by the lights that went on ahead of him, and winked off again when he had passed. If the irregularity of his path indicated anything, he did not know where he was going.

"Hermes has undone him," Ben said.

Mark asked: "What are the three of us going to do? Separate and search? I assume that the Swords here are kept together in one place."

Ben briefly and silently considered his own plan, the plan that had brought him here, for enriching himself. In the midst of all this it somehow now seemed almost inconsequential, a detail that he could take care of at any time by simply stretching out his arm. But the Swords . . . yes, they were indeed important.

He looked at Ariane, and almost forgot about the Swords. She looked bad, not right yet by a long way, far from being out of the fog from that blow she'd taken on the head. She gave him a weak smile in return for his look, but did not speak.

"No," said Ben. "Let's stick together."

They moved on. Now, just around another corner ahead, lights were on. And now a crash sounded from that direction, and then another, like pieces of pottery being smashed, one at a time. They moved on, Mark with an arrow nocked, Ben with dagger drawn.

Rounding the corner, they beheld a room crammed with small statuary. Dmitry and Willem had located it already. The two of them were standing there, the pockets of their ragged clothing bulging, spilling gold coins. Each had a sword in hand, and they were playing a game of smash among the statues.

Willem and Dmitry looked up with animal wariness as the three appeared, and paused in their game. They smiled vaguely at the bow and dagger, but said nothing. The swords they played with were only their own ordinary blades.

Mark, with a small motion of his head, signaled his two companions. The three of them moved on, watching with a wariness of their own.

Some distance farther, in a room along one of the main aisles, another light was on. When they peered in cautiously through the doorway, they discovered Radulescu, quite alone. This room was filled with statues too. These were all of fine clear crystal, and the Colonel was holding a small example carefully in his hands. As the three came in, he looked up at them almost indifferently, certainly without enmity, and went on fondling his prize; his mind was clearly somewhere else. It was as if the effort to sacrifice Ariane had happened twenty years ago, or in another lifetime.

He looked down at his little statue again, then held it up for their inspection. "This was my first theft," he explained. "Pretty, isn't she?" Then he gazed at his visitors with more awareness. "You can relax now. We can all take our time, rest a little. Gather what treasure you want, and then I'll show you the way out."

"Show us now," said Mark. "Didn't you hear those yells?"

"There's time," said Radulescu. "Enough time now for everything." He gazed again at his little figure. It was of a woman dancing. ". . . my first theft. I took it out of here once before, you know. Smuggled it back to my quarters, wrapped up in my cloak, enfolded against detection in protective spells that I had devised myself. I took it to my quarters guiltily, as if it had been a real woman, and I some kind of acolyte sworn to celibacy. Of course she is more real, more vital, than any woman I have ever seen in flesh. But . . . there was no way for me to keep it, without discovery. I knew even when I took it that I couldn't keep it, that I'd have to bring it back before the next formal inventory."

"Show us the way out now," said Ben.

Radulescu looked up, startled, as if he had forgotten that they were there. "We'll take it shortly. Rest a little first."

Mark demanded: "Where are the Swords kept?"

"Ah." Radulescu thought a moment, then pointed. "You'll find them down that way . . . if you should be planning to kill me when you have them, remember that I haven't shown you the way out yet."

Ben turned away without answering. His two companions followed him, leaving Radulescu to the contemplation of his treasure.

His solitary communion with the crystal dancer did not last for long. Presently he looked up again, to see the two surviving deserters from the garrison standing in the doorway gazing at him. Their eyes were almost blank, and they had their swords in hand.

They didn't look at Radulescu for long; the surrounding roomful of treasure was obviously more to their liking.

"Come in, gentlemen, come in," said the Colonel, stretching a point in the interests of harmony. "Come in and help yourselves. There's plenty here for us all."

Dmitry's eyes came back to Radulescu, then fell to what Radulescu was holding in his hands. "Give me that one," Dmitry said.

"No." The officer backed up a step. And noted, with hardly more than irritation, that the one called Willem was shifting his position as if to come at him from one side. "And if you're thinking of attacking me, remember—"

But before he could get the next word out, Dmitry's drawn sword was thrusting at his chest.

Ben and Ariane and Mark were already a good distance away from the room of crystal statuary when the bubbling scream reached their ears. They turned their heads at the sound, but no one thought of stopping, still less of going back.

Ariane spoke her first words in some time. "The seventh sealing . . . we've reached it now."

The others looked at her.

"The greed of robbers . . . the old song hints at it." Then she clenched her eyes shut, and walked leaning on Ben for guidance and support. "Gods and demons, but my head hurts. It's bad."

"I don't wonder." And Ben kissed her softly as they kept walking, and wished that they could stop to let her rest. But he knew better.

They passed more chambers filled with crystal, and long rooms occupied by one special rack after another, holding tapestries. When they came to rooms of jewels, Ben detoured for a moment to grab up a handful and stuff a pocket with them. Next was a hall lined with shelves filled with glass jars, containing unknown powders and liquids, all brilliantly lighted to allow for easy inspection by someone simply walking past. There were labels on the jars and on the shelves, but written in a language or a code that was unreadable to Ben.

And now there was another lighted room ahead. It was very near to the wall of living rock that formed one end of the treasure-cave.

They peered into the bright room through the partition that made one of its walls, and was composed of racks of glittering weaponry.

Inside the room they gazed upon a mad variety of other weapons still. These were not made, most of them, merely for use; gold again here, silver again, gems in profusion. Ben thought he saw a poinard worked from a single emerald, and arrowheads of diamond.

Toward the far side of the room there stood a great tree-like wooden rack, no thing of art or value in itself, but good to hold display. It had twelve wooden branches, and from each branch there hung a woven belt and sheath, each of the twelve a different color. Nine of the tree's branches—Ben counted quickly—and nine of the sheaths were empty.

And three were weighted down with Swords, heavy fruit with only the black hilts visible.

Baron Doon was standing alone in the middle of the chamber of weapons, and holding one more Sword in his hands. The hilt was concealed in his two-handed grip, but there was no mistaking the perfection of that blade; it could have come from nowhere but Vulcan's forge.

The Baron had his head bent low over the weapon, and seemed to be mumbling something to it. He stood with feet braced wide apart, legs tensed, as if he wanted to be ready to strike instantly some prodigious blow.

Mark's hand had gripped Ben's arm, enjoining silence. Ben's eyes flicked up again to the three Swords that were still hanging on the tree, seeking the white symbols on the hilts. Mark, he thought, probably knew what they all were—Dame Yoldi had taught him years ago—but Ben himself didn't recognize any of these. One looked like a tiny white wedge, splitting a white block; a second was just a simple circle, a rounded line returning upon itself. And the hilt of the third Sword was turned away, making it impossible for Ben to see its symbol; like the hilt itself, the sheath and belt that held that one were black.

Doon's mumbling voice suddenly rose louder, and for a moment Ben thought that the three of them watching through the rack of arms had been discovered. But if Doon was aware of their presence there he did not care about it. He went on mumbling—not to himself, Ben realized. It was some ritual that he was chanting, the same few words over and over:

". . . for thy heart, for thy heart, who hast wronged me! For thy heart . . ."

Standing in the middle of the open floor, Doon bowed toward the one dark doorway of the room, a gesture apparently directed toward no one and nothing. Then he turned, and in the same motion crouched, crouched down and in the same motion continued turning, so that in an instant he had become a spinning dancer. And now it was as if the Sword in his hands had somehow been activated, and it was dragging him around. The blade, held out in his extended arms, turning ever more swiftly, became a blur. Quickly the whine of its passage through the air acquired an unnatural timbre. It swelled and hummed, the noise of some great flying insect.

Above this whine, the last words of Doon's grim chant came through: "—thy heart—who hast—wronged me!" And with that Doon released the Sword—or it, perhaps, let go of him.

He staggered and fell down in his tracks. The great whine vanished abruptly from the air, as did the Sword itself. At the speed with which it had leapt from Doon's hands, it must have struck one of the partitions or solid walls that formed the room, or whirred out through the open doorway. But it had done neither. It was simply gone.

For a long moment there was only silence in the cave. Then—

The cry, when it came, even muffled by great distance and by walls of rock, was truly unlike anything that Ben in his whole life had ever heard before. For a moment he could think only that the earth itself must be in torment. Or that the gods were fighting again among themselves, and some landquake was coming to bring the whole headland crumbling down, carrying all the caves and creatures and treasure inside it into the sea. The cry went on and on, beyond the capacity of any human lungs to have sustained it.

Then silence fell again.

Then Doon was laughing.

He sat there in the center of the floor, just as the Sword had dropped him, with his legs crumpled awkwardly underneath his body, and he laughed. His mirth was loud, and hideous, and to Ben it sounded at least half mad. And yet it was also the most human sound that he had uttered since he had faced Hermes.

Mark moved at last. He was into the weapons room, and past Doon, and standing beside the tree of Swords, before the Baron took notice of the fact that he was no longer alone.

Doon did not appear to care much. "Not many men," he began to say—and then his laughter burst up again, and he had to pause to conquer it before he could continue. "Not many men—have ever slain a god. Hey, am I right?" He looked at Mark, and then at Ben and Ariane, who now stood in the doorway of the room. "But here was Farslayer—here, waiting for me. Even the gods must be subject to the tricks of Fate."

"Farslayer," Mark echoed, in a voice that held wonder, and concern. The Baron got to his feet, his eyes glittering, and turned toward Mark. "The Sword of Vengeance," said Doon. "You who know the Swords will know what has just happened."

It was at that moment that Ariane collapsed, quite softly and without fuss. Ben, who was standing right at her side, was only just in time to catch her. He lowered her gently to the floor, and bent over her in anguish.

A girl's fainting or dying was of no consequence to Doon. "One god is dead," he said. "I'll be my own god now, with these." He took a determined step toward the tree of Swords, and stopped just as suddenly as he had moved. One of the three Swords that hung there had come sighing out of its black sheath into the hands of Mark, and Mark now stood confronting him.

"All three of these are going to Sir Andrew."

"Oh? Ah?"

"Yes . . . if you're willing to come with them, he needs good fighting men, as much or more than he needs any metal."

The Baron squinted at him. Then asked, almost happily: "Which one do you have there in your hands, young man? I took no complete inventory when I came in; not after I had seen the one I needed."

"I have the one that I need now," said Mark. And the Sword in his hands had come to some kind of life, for it was throbbing faintly. Ben could hear it, though it was almost too low to hear: the tap tap tapping as of some distant but determined hammer, working at the hardest metal.

"So?" Doon raised an eyebrow, considering this. "It seems that you do. But we'll see. I've never yet given up on a fight—even against a god —nor lost one, when I had to win."

And with marvelous sudden speed he feinted a movement toward the tree; then, when Mark moved to block him from it, he spun away to reach for another rack of elegant weaponry upon another wall. From this he snatched down a small battle axe and a matching shield, both of beautiful workmanship, embossed with silver and ivory and gold.

"Ben," called Mark, "stay out there. I'm all right. Stay with her."

And in his hands Mark could feel the faint, cold hammering vibration of the Sword he held. This was not Townsaver with its impressive scream, but perhaps equally powerful, perhaps more so . . . in his mind's eye Mark again saw his father dead, his brother too, who had held that other Sword, that had saved nothing. . . .

Doon said to him considerately: "You should first drop your bow and quiver, lad. They'll hinder you. Go ahead, I'll wait."

Mark made a little shrugging motion, meaning: it will make no difference. Doon seeing his shoulders move perhaps thought that Mark had been distracted, that his grip on the hilt was poor, that the ruse had worked. For the Baron brought up his axe and shield, and closed with a rush.

Mark expected the axe to come at him from one direction, and realized too late that it was swinging from another. His arms unaided could never have parried it with any weapon.

But the weapon he was holding was no longer subject to his control. Shieldbreaker only emphasized two notes amid the almost hypnotic streaming rhythm of its sound. Its movement on the two beats drew Mark's arms with it unhurriedly, melding him into its own power and speed. The parry caught the flashing battle axe in midstroke, ripped it from Doon's grasp and hurled it like a missile across the room, where it smashed into a jeweled breastplate and set a whole rack of fancy armor toppling, a crash that seemed to go on endlessly.

The backstroke of the Sword of Force came at Doon himself, but he was able to catch it on his shield. The steel buckler was ripped almost in half, the strips of its precious metal inlays torn loose and sent flying. Doon was knocked down, but he scrambled back to his feet almost at once, ridding his numbed left arm of the useless twisted metal. He darted to another rack of weapons, grabbed up a javelin with a jeweled point, and hurled it with all his strength at Mark. Shieldbreaker flashed to shatter the weapon in midair, the pieces flying like slung stones.

Mark, breathing only a little harder than normal, held the Sword easily in his two hands—rather, he stood there letting it hold him. He could not now have let go the hilt if he had wanted to. "Ben. Move her back a little farther. Out of the way."

But, just then, Ben's wordless, helpless cry went up. Mark understood, without taking his eyes from Doon, that Ariane was dead.

Doon had already rearmed himself from the walls of this mad arsenal. This time with a morningstar. He spun the spiked head rapidly on its chain, and probably meant to try to tangle the blade of the Sword of Force and pull it from Mark's grip. But Shieldbreaker's shining blur this time intercepted the weight itself. With the clang of a split anvil, the spiked iron ball, points tipped with bronze and gold, spun free to give up its momentum in the devastation of another shelf or two, from which inlaid helmets and gilded gauntlets cascaded in metallic thunder.

Doon had a broadsword now; in his hands the silvered blade of it made a blur that looked as swift and bright as the arc drawn by the Sword of Force. But when the two met, only one remained.

Staggering amid the wreckage of the room, marked with blood from minor wounds from metal fragments and splintered wood, the Baron grabbed up a spear. Holding this like a lance under one arm, and swinging a scimitar with the other, he let out a scream of defiance and despair, and ran with all his force at Mark.

"Stop! I—"

Whatever argument Mark might have made, there was no time for it. The Baron closed with him—or came as close to him as will and skill could drive. The Sword hammered briskly, blurred impersonally. How many teeth of the gleaming millsaw bit at Doon, Mark could not count. The spear was in three pieces before it hit the floor, and Doon himself was left in more than one. One of his arms was gone, and when the Sword of Force at last came to rest it had transfixed his body.

Mark watched the life depart from Doon's eyes, which were fixed on him. And Shieldbreaker's rhythm, perhaps keeping time with the heart it pierced, went thudding softly down into silence.

Still the body stood almost upright, glaring as if the Baron's will were not yet dead. But in fact the Baron's flesh was supported by a set of tilted shelves that he had crashed into, and by the thrusting Sword itself. Mark raised a foot and pushed. The dead weight slid from the blade, away from the supporting shelves, and fell amid debris with a last crash.

The Sword was suddenly a dead weight as well. Mark let it sag. He turned to the doorway, where Ben still crouched, oblivious to everything but the dead girl he rocked in his arms.

Just then, a strange voice boomed, from somewhere out in the dark cave: "You four in the weapons room, surrender! We have taken your two friends already, and you are trapped!"

Mark forced himself to move methodically. He turned first to the tree of Swords, and got down the belt that had held Shieldbreaker, and put the weapon bloody as it was into the sheath, and strapped it to his waist. He called: "Ben, come on. You must leave her, for now. Come here, quickly."

Ben came lumbering toward him. "Where's Dmitry, Mark? He threw the rock. He hit her." The big man was obviously in shock. "I've got to get him. But—she's gone. She's gone, Mark. She . . . just . . ."

"I know. Come on, Ben, come on. I know where Dmitry went. No, just leave her there. You've got to leave her." He dragged Ben almost unresisting to the tree of Swords, and there loaded him with Doomgiver and its belt. Then Mark took down the last Sword, Stonecutter, for himself, for the moment carrying it belt and all in one hand. For a moment, touching Stonecutter and the Sword of Force at the same time, he was aware of the old feeling that when he was still half a child had terrified him to the point of fainting—a feeling of being taken out of himself, of what he had imagined death itself to be like.

Now to find a way out. Or make one.

He went to the set of huge shelves that stood at the far end of the room, almost against the rock wall of the cave. "Ben, help me tip these back."

The big man followed the order mechanically. The shelves toppled until they caught leaning against the wall of rock, more treasure spilling and crashing from them unheeded. Now they made a high ladder, or crude steps. Mark led the way, climbing up them.

Again the distant voice called: "Your last chance to surrender!"

Ben had mechanically strapped on the first Sword, Doomgiver, that Mark had handed him; and now, while they balanced awkwardly atop the leaning shelves, Mark gave him Shieldbreaker to hold, saying: "Fight them if they come."

Ben nodded numbly. "What are you doing?"

For answer, Mark turned to press Stonecutter against the wall of stone, feeling the blade come alive in his grip as he did so. Like Shieldbreaker, this Sword generated a hammering vibration, but Stonecutter's was heavier and slower than that of the Sword of Force. When Mark pressed Stonecutter against the wall, the point sank right in, as if the stone it touched had turned to so much butter.

The first piece he cut free, an awkward cone the size of a man's head, came sliding out. It fell heavily between the two men's feet, bounced from the angled, tilted surface of the top shelf, and crashed down to the floor below.

"You're carving steps? To where?"

"It'll have to be more than steps."

The next pieces that Mark cut out were larger. Quickly their crashing fall became an almost continuous sound. Mark was cutting them at an upward angle, so that each block when loosened slid free of its own weight. This meant that the men had to keep their feet out of the way; it also meant that the hole now rapidly deepening in the wall was angled upward. But that was all right, they wanted to go up anyway. Rough-cut pyramids and lopsided cones continued to fall free at an encouraging rate.

Soon Mark had to widen the mouth of his excavation, to be able to step up into it and continue to reach the receding workface, while still keeping his feet and Ben's out of the way of falling blocks.

Ben was coming out of shock a little, belatedly getting the idea. "We can cut a tunnel, and get out!"

"So I hope. If we have time. Watch your feet!"

There were renewed cries for their surrender, coming from somewhere cautiously out of sight. Ben and Mark were now completely inside their ascending mine, and the Old World lights somehow registered their departure, and turned themselves off. One headlamp, tuned to a dim glow, gave enough light to work with.

There was a rush of invisible feet below.

Ben said: "Let me cut for a while. Take your bow and lob an arrow or two at them."

Now, for just a moment, it was Ben who had two Swords in hand at once. Seeing his expression change, Mark said to him: "It'll be all right. Go on."

With Ben's hand driving the heavy Sword, the work of tunneling went even faster. The tunnel grew, wide enough to let them keep clear of the sliced-out pieces as they fell, its surface rough-hewn to give them footing and handgrips where needed. The blocks, hewn out as easily as so many puffs of smoke, still came falling and crashing down like the heavy stone they were. The constant barrage of their falling had already broken down the tilted wooden shelves, splintering them and pounding their load of treasure into twisted metal and debris, beneath the fast-growing pile of the rock itself.

Now the enemy below was lighting torches, trying to get a better look at what was going on; the presence of Whitehands evidently did not trigger the Old World ceiling lights. Mark fired all his remaining arrows but one at torch-lights, and heard cries of pain. Now he could hear the Whitehands climbing on the talus of rock that grew under the strange new opening in the wall, but more rock continued to fall upon them there, crushing them and beating them back.

Ben had begun to bend the tunnel around a corner. Already the whole opening was some five or six meters deep, and still growing fast. Presently the bend began to afford them the protection that Ben had forseen they'd need; when the first flung stones began to fly up from below, they could make themselves safe around its angle. The Whitehands, like the cave's regular garrison of soldiers, were used to fighting in the dark or by poor light when they fought at all, and bows or slings were not in common use among them.

As the work progressed, each loosened piece of rock slid and fell for a greater distance, building up a greater speed, before it struck anything or anyone. The blocks swept the tunnel clean of climbing Whitehands faster than they could be made to enter it. Before long the attempt was abandoned, and the yells of the wounded were heard no more.

The carving and crashing down of rock, the climbing, went on for a long time. Rock dust began to choke the two men's nostrils. The beams of their headlamps were white now with the fog of it.

Pausing to try to breathe, Ben asked: "What if we're below the level of the sea when we come out?"

"I don't think we can be. Or the cave down there would be already flooded." As he spoke, Mark hoped that he was right.

"How do we know where we'll come out?"

"We don't. Keep going up, and we'll come out somewhere. Unless you've got a better idea."

Mark took another turn at digging. Again touching Stonecutter and Shieldbreaker at the same time, he wondered aloud: "Why didn't Blue Temple ever *use* these Swords?"

"You don't know Blue Temple. If it's valuable it's treasure, and if it's treasure you bury it in a hole in the ground so you don't risk losing it. We'll hear Benambra screaming all the way up to the surface when he sees what's gone."

And at last, without warning, the cutting Sword broke through, broke upward into clear space, and what had to be daylight, though it was dim and indirect. The two men muttered and marveled more than they had for jewels and gold. Some fine dirt trickled down.

Mark quickly widened the hole, then climbed up through it. Ben followed. They were standing in a narrow, cavelike fissure that ran horizontally toward the light, and in the opposite direction from it. Walking, climbing toward the light, they soon got a glimpse of misty sky. Now they could smell the ocean, and hear the steady waves.

At a couple of places Mark had to use Stonecutter to carve a secure step, or widen the fissure so they could squeeze through.

They emerged at last upon a narrow ledge, in living sunshine, half-way between the clifftop and the sea.

CHAPTER 17

Blinking and squinting in the mild sunlight that contended with clouds of blowing mist, they emerged from the crevice into full view of the sea. Mark realized that it must be early morning. The air was warm, and summer had evidently not yet departed. Beyond the first reach of water, slate gray and shaded blue, the opposite headland was half in sunshine, half in shadow.

"What's that?" asked Ben, cocking his head. There had been some kind of distant clash and cry.

"It sounded like a fight. But it didn't come from behind us, in the cave."

"No. Maybe from on top of the cliff?"

The sound was not repeated. "Anyway we're going down. Get to the shore, and then try our charm-words to bring in Indosuaros' ship."

They began to work their way down, carefully. Rounding a bulge of the cliff, they came upon a broader ledge, and stopped. A marvel lay before them, half-wreathed in mist.

The giant figure had fallen sprawled out, in a prone position. It was crumpled and broken over rock, and as dead as any corpse that Mark had ever seen. The Phrygian cap had fallen off, the great head was turned to one side, the sightless gaze bored at a surface of rock only centimeters from the face.

"It's Hermes." Ben whispered it.

There was a long pause before Mark whispered: "Yes."

"But—he's dead."

"Yes."

The two living men looked at each other as wildly as if it were a dead friend that they had found, and more fearfully.

"Doon boasted that he had slain a god."

"But—if a god is mortal—what does it mean?"

They looked at each other and could see no answer.

Small wreaths of smoke, or steam, were rising from the figure, as if it might be beginning to dissolve into the sea-mist that had come to lave around it. In the middle of the naked back there was a raw, fresh wound. It was just of a size, thought Mark, to have been made by the thrust of a broadbladed Sword.

He said aloud: "It was Farslayer that Doon threw, with a spell from the old Song of Swords. It must have done this. But where is it now?"

"And where are the other two Swords, Dragonslicer and Wayfinder, that Hermes took from us?"

They counted the empty sheaths that were fringed around the fallen giant's waist. Whatever the number had been before, now there were only ten, and all were empty.

Mark made a violent motion with his hand, rejecting the whole situation. "Let's leave this. The death of gods is not . . . let's move on down, there's nothing for us here."

"Except it seems that Hermes will not be coming after us, to take away the Swords that we have now."

They went on down the cliff. It was, as elsewhere on this face, a difficult climb but not impossible.

They had just gotten down to where the slope began to gentle, when a Blue Temple infantry patrol sprang upon them in ambush, leaping out of shadows and caves and fog. Ben had just time to cry a moment's warning; he had felt Shieldbreaker come suddenly to life in his fist. It thudded loudly, and when the warbeast leaped at him, chopped its life out with the first stroke.

The rush of another of the trained animals had knocked Mark down; Stonecutter in his hands only wounded the beast, and he almost despaired of his life before Shieldbreaker's blur passed over him to kill it.

He lay there, still half-stunned, knowing that men in blue and gold were crowding in. Shieldbreaker raised its voice, in a sound like the hammering of Vulcan's forge, and their shattered ranks went reeling back.

Then more help was arriving, in the form of fighting men in black and orange; the enemy fled scattering, crying out as if they expected help of their own to be at hand. Mark saw the helmeted head of one of his rescuers bending over him, and then the helmet was lifted to reveal a broad, strong, familiar face. The mustache and beard were of sandy gray. The strong, slow voice of Sir Andrew himself was asking Mark how he did.

Helped to sit up, Mark recovered enough to deliver a quick report. He outlined their raid on the Blue Temple treasury, and described how they had just gotten out of it. He concluded: "We've got with us all the Swords that were there—except one. And there'll be no use in your trying to get back into the hoard now—unless you've brought your whole army with you." He paused there, not understanding how Sir Andrew had come to be here at all.

"Hmf, hah, yes. Hyrcanus has done that, it seems." Sir Andrew threw back his head, gazing up the cliff. "Perhaps the Chairman suspected that his great secret was out. Well, let us not fall victim to greed. You have there all that we really hoped to get." The knight turned to a waiting officer. "Sound the horn, call in our ships."

Mark, helped to his feet, was able to move without help, feeling only minor injuries. Another familiar face, that of Dame Yoldi, loomed into sight. Her sturdy frame was dressed in man's clothing, prudently ready for cliff-climbing and combat. Mark began to blurt out to her the tale of slain Hermes. At the first words the enchantress hushed him, then drew him and Ben close to her and Sir Andrew, so that she and the knight could hear the news privately even as they made their way down the remainder of the slope.

As Mark related what had happened to Hermes, he could see the three longships, orange and black at their mastheads, appearing out of the mist. The oarsmen were pulling hard in light surf; and the ships' prows had grated in sand before the shore party reached the water.

Mark was saying: "I knew that Farslayer and the other Swords were powerful, of course. But I never expected . . ." He let it die away.

"Nor would any of us," said Dame Yoldi. She looked shaken, and repeated: "Nor would any of us."

Sir Andrew asked the two men: "And you saw him before? He took Dragonslicer, then it was gone again?"

Ben and Mark both nodded.

There was no time for much discussion now. They waded into light waves with the rest of the patrol that had gone ashore, and reached for gunwales.

Barbara came jumping from a ship into the water to greet them, wrapping her arms round Ben. Quickly she explained how, instead of returning to the carnival, she had taken Mark's goldpiece on to Sir Andrew, together with the story of the treasure-hoard. Ben when saying goodbye to her had told her of its location.

There was sunlight bright upon the opposite headland as the longships pulled out to sea. Ben was gazing in that direction.

"What do you see?" Barbara asked him.

"I . . . nothing."

Mark looked. Someone standing there, perhaps? But the impression faded. It was much too far off to be sure.

Ben was pouring jewels from his pocket, joylessly, into Barbara's outstretched hands, while her eyes questioned him.

Mark stood watching. For the moment he was quite alone.

THE END

THE THIRD
BOOK OF SWORDS

CHAPTER 1

Up at the unpeopled borderland of cloudy heaven, where unending wind drove eternal snow between and over high gray rocks, the gods and goddesses were gathering.

In the grayness just before dawn, their tall forms came like smoke out of the gray and smoking wind, to take on solidity and detail. Unperturbed by wind or weather, their garments flapping in the shrieking howl of air, they stood upon the rooftop of the world and waited as their numbers grew. Steadily more powers streaked across the sky, bringing reinforcement.

The shortest of the standing figures was taller than humanity, but from the shortest to tallest, all were indisputably of human shape. The dress of most members of the assembly displayed a more than mortal elegance, running to crowns and jewels and snow-white furs; the attire of a few was, by human standards, almost ordinary; that of many was bizarre.

By an unspoken agreement amounting to tradition the deities stood in a rough circle, symbol of a rude equality. It was a mutually enforced equality, meaning only that none of their number was willing to concede pride of place to any other. When graybearded Zeus, a laurel wreath embracing his massive head, moved forward majestically as if after all he intended to occupy the center of the circle, a muttering at once began around him. The sound grew louder, and it did not subside until the Graybearded One, with a frown, had converted his forward movement into a mere circular pacing, that soon brought him back to his old place in the large circle. There he stopped. And only when he stopped did the muttering die down completely.

And still with each passing moment the shape of another god or goddess materialized out of the restless air. By now two dozen or more tall forms were in place around the circle. They eyed one another suspiciously, and exchanged cautious nods and signs of greeting. Neighbor to neighbor they muttered in near-whispers through the wind, trading warily in warnings and backbitings about those who were more distant in the circle, or still absent. The more of them that gathered, the more their diversity was evident. They were dark or fair, old-looking or young-looking. Handsome—as gods—or beautiful—as goddesses—or ugly, as only certain gods and goddesses could be.

Twice more Zeus opened his mouth as if he intended to address them all. Twice more he seemed on the verge of stepping forward, taking the center of the circle, and trying to command the meeting. Each time he did so that warning murmur swelled up into the frozen air, through the blasting wind, giving notice that no such attempt was going to be tolerated. Zeus remained silently at his own station in the ring, stamping his feet now and then and scowling his impatience.

At last the individual gossipings around the ring began to fade toward quiet, give way to silent waiting. There was some general agreement, tacitly attained, that now a quorum had been reached. There was no use trying to wait until all the gods and goddesses were here, all of them never attended a meeting at the same time. Never had they been able to agree unanimously on anything at all, not even on a place or an agenda for their arguments.

But now the assembly was large enough.

It was Mars, spear-armed and helmeted, who broke the silence; Mars speaking in a voice that smoldered and rumbled with old anger. The tones of it were like the sounds of displaced boulders rolling down a glacier.

Mars banged his spear upon his shield to get the attention of the assembly. Then he said to them: "There is news now of the Mindsword. The man that other humans call the Dark King has it. He is, of course, going to use it to try to get the whole world into his hands. What effect this will have on our own Game is something that we must evaluate for ourselves, each according to his or her own position."

It was not this news he had just announced to the assembly that was really angering Mars. Rather it was something else, something that he wanted to keep secret in his own thoughts, that made him almost choke on rage. Mars did not conceal his feelings well. As he finished speaking he used a savage gesture, a blow that almost split the air, simply to signify the fact that he was ready now to relinquish the floor to someone else.

Next to speak was Vulcan—Vulcan the Smith with the twisted leg, the armorer and Sword-forger to the gods.

"I am sorry," began Vulcan, slyly, "that my so-worthy colleague is unable to continue at the moment. Perhaps he is brooding too much about a certain setback—one might even call it a defeat—that he suffered at the hands—or should one say the paws—of a certain mortal opponent, some eight or nine years past?"

The response of Mars to this was more sullen, angry rumbling. There also was a murmuring around the circle, some of it laughter at Mars, some a denunciation of Vulcan for this obvious attempt to start an argument.

Aphrodite asked softly, "Is this what we have come here for, to have another quarrel?" Her tall body, all curves, all essence of the female, was wrapped in nothing but a diaphanous veil that seemed always on the verge of blowing away in the fierce wind but never did. She like the other deities was perfectly indifferent to the arctic cold.

Near her, Apollo's taller form appeared emphasized for a moment in a lone ray of light from the newly risen sun. The Sun's bright lance steadily pierced the scudding clouds for just as long as it took the god to speak, and held his body in its light. Apollo demanded, "I take it that we are all agreed upon one thing at least?"

Someone else was cooperative enough to ask Apollo: "What?"

The tall god replied, "That Hermes has not come back from his mission to gather up the Swords again. That he is never going to come back."

"That's two things," another member of the group objected.

Apollo took no notice of such carping. "That our divine Messenger, who no doubt thought himself as secure in his immortality as most of us still think we are in ours, has now been for four years *dead?*"

That word, of all words, had power to jolt them all. Many faced it bravely. Some tried to pretend that it had not been spoken, or if spoken certainly not heard. But there was a long moment in which even the wind was voiceless. No other word, surely, could have brought the same quality and duration of silence to this assembly.

It was the relentless voice of Apollo that entered into this new silence and destroyed it, repeating: *"For four years dead."*

The repetition provoked not more silence, but the beginning of an uproar of protest; still the voice of Apollo overrode the tumult even as it swelled.

"Dead!" he roared. "And if Hermes Messenger can be slain by one of the Swords, why so can we. And what have we done about it, during these past four years? Nothing! Nothing at all! Wrangled among ourselves, as always—no more than that!"

When Apollo paused, Mars seized the chance to speak. "And there is the one who forged those Swords!" The God of War pointed with his long war-spear, and aimed an angry stare at the crippled Smith. "I tell you, we must make him melt them down again. I've said all along that the Swords are going to destroy us all, unless we are able to destroy them first!"

Leaning awkwardly on his lame leg, Vulcan turned at bay. "Don't blame me!" Wind whipped at his fur garments, his ornaments of dragon-scale clashing and fluttering in the gale. But his words ate through the windstorm plainly, suffering no interference from mere physical air. "The blunder, if there was one, was not mine. These very faces that I see all about me now spoke urging me, commanding me, to forge the Swords."

He turned accusingly from one to another of his peers. "We needed the Swords, we had to have them, you all told me, for the Game. The Game was going to be a great delight, something we hadn't tried before. You said the Swords must be distributed among the humans, who in the Game would be our pawns. Now what kind of pawns have they turned into? But no, you all insisted on it, no matter how I warned you—"

Again an uproar of protest was breaking out, and this time it was too loud for any one voice to overcome. Objectors were shouting that, on the contrary, *they* had been the ones against the whole idea of the Swords and the Game from the very start.

Naturally this provoked a strong counterreaction from others present. "What you mean is, you've been against the Game ever since you started losing in it! As long as you thought that you were winning, it was a great idea!"

One of the graybeard elder gods, not Zeus, put in: "Let's get back to our immediate problem. You say that the man they call the Dark King has the Mindsword now. Well, that may be good or bad news for some of us in terms of the Game, but does it matter beyond that? The Game is only a game, and what real difference does it make?"

"You fool! Are you incapable of understanding? This Game, that you're so proud of winning—it got out of hand long ago. Haven't you been listening? Did you hear nothing that Apollo just said about the death of Hermes?"

"All right. All right. Let's talk about Hermes Messenger. He had supposedly gone to collect all the Swords again, to get them out of human hands, because some of us were getting worried. But do you think he would really have destroyed the Swords, once he had them all collected? I don't think so."

That suggestion was greeted by a thoughtful pause, a general silence.

And that silence broken by a slow and thoughtful voice: "Besides, are we *really* sure that Hermes is dead? What solid evidence do we have?"

Now even Apollo the reasoner felt compelled to howl his rage at such thickheadedness. "One of the Swords killed Hermes! Farslayer, hurled from the hands of a mere human!"

Apollo got a venomous retort. "How can we be *sure* that that's what really happened? Has anyone seen the Sword Farslayer since then? Did any one of us see Hermes fall?"

At this moment, Zeus once more stepped forward. He conveyed the impression of one who had been waiting for the exactly proper instant to take action. And it seemed that he had at last timed an attempt correctly, because for once he was not howled down before he could begin to speak.

"Wisdom comes with experience," Zeus intoned, "and experience with age. To learn from the past is the surest way to secure the future. In peace and wisdom there is strength. In strength and wisdom there is peace. In wisdom and—"

No one howled him down this time, but after the first dozen words hardly any of his fellow deities were still listening. Instead they resumed their separate conversations around the circle, taking time out from the general debate while they waited for Zeus to be finished. This treatment was even deadlier than the other. Zeus soon realized what was happening. He retreated again to his own place in the ring, and there withdrew into a total, sulky silence.

Now at another place along the ring there was a stirring and a swirling movement among the snow and rocks. Attention became focused on this spot, just as a new member joined the company there. Rather than coming out of the sky as the others had, this god emerged up out of the Earth. The form of Hades was indistinct, all dimness and darkness, a difficult object even for the faculties of another deity to comprehend.

Hades in his formless voice said that yes, Hermes was certainly dead. No, he, Hades, hadn't actually seen the Messenger fall, or die. But he had been with Hermes shortly before what must have been the moment of that death, when Hermes was engaged in taking some Swords away from some humans. It was Hades' opinion that Hermes had been acting in good faith in his attempt to collect the Blades, though unfortunately they had been lost again.

Now another side discussion was developing. What about that offending human, the one that had apparently thrown Farslayer at Hermes and brought him down? The awful hubris that could strike a god, any god, to earth cried out to heaven for vengeance. What punishment had been dealt to the culprit? Surely someone had already seen to it that some special and eternal retaliation had been inflicted?

The same thought had already occurred, long ago, to certain other members of the group. Alas, they had to report now that when they first heard of the offending human he was already beyond the reach of even divine revenge.

"Then we must exact some sort of retribution from humanity in general."

"Aha, now we come to it! Just which part of humanity do you propose to strike at? Those who are your pawns in the Game, or those I claim as mine?"

Apollo's disgust at this argument was beyond all measure. "How can you fools still talk of pawns, and games? Do you not see—?" But words failed him for the moment.

Hades spoke up again, this time with his own suggestion for the permanent disposal of the Swords. If all those god-forged weapons could somehow be collected, and delivered to him, he would see to their burial. All the other deities present could permanently cease to worry.

"We might cease doing a *lot* of things permanently, once *you* had all the Swords! Of *course* you'd be willing to accept twelve for yourself— and incidentally to win the Game by doing so! Where would that leave us? What kind of fools do you take us for?"

Hades was, or at least pretended to be, affronted by this attitude.

"What do I care now about a game? Now, when our very existence is at stake. Haven't you been listening to Apollo?"

"Our very existence, bah! Tell that stuff to someone who'll believe it. Gods are immortal. We all know that. Hermes is playing dead, hiding out somewhere. It's part of a ploy to win the Game. Well, I don't intend to lose, whatever happens. Not to Hermes, and not to Apollo, and particularly not to you!"

Aphrodite, murmuring softly, announced to all who would listen that she could think up her own ideas for getting back the Swords. Those who had the Swords, or most of them anyway, were only mere men, were they not?

Apollo spoke again. This time he prefaced his remarks by waving his bow, a gesture that gained him notably greater attention. He said that if the Swords could be regathered, they should then be turned over to him, as the most logical and trustworthy of gods. He would then put an end to the threat the weapons posed, by the simple expedient of shooting them, like so many arrows, clean off the Earth.

Before Apollo had finished his short speech most of his audience were ignoring him, bow and all, even as they had ignored Zeus. Meanwhile in the background Mars was rumbling threats against unspecified enemies. Others were laughing, secretly or openly, at Mars.

Vulcan was quietly passing the word around the circle that if others were to gather up the Blades and bring them back to him, and if a majority of his peers were to assure him that that was what they really wanted, he'd do his best to melt all of the Twelve back into harmless iron again.

No one was paying the least attention to Zeus mighty sulking, and he reverted to speech in a last effort to establish some authority. "It seems to me that the Smith here incorporated far too much of humanity into the Swords. Why was it necessary to quench the Blades, when they came from the fire and anvil, in living human blood? And why were so much human sweat and human tears introduced into the process?"

Vulcan bristled defensively at this. "Are you trying to tell me my trade? What do you know about it, anyway?"

Here Mars, gloating to see his rival stung, jumped into the argument. "And then there was that last little trick you played at the forging. Taking off the right arm of the human smith who helped you—what was that all about?"

The Smith's answer—if indeed he gave one—was lost in a new burst of noise. A dozen voices flared up, arguing on several different subjects.

The meeting was giving every sign of breaking up, despite Apollo's best thundering efforts to hold it together a little longer. As usual there had been no general agreement on what their common problems were, much less on any course of action. Already the circle of the gods was thinning as the figures that composed it began to vanish into the air. The wind hummed with their departing powers. Hades, eschewing aerial flight as usual, vanished again straight down into the Earth beneath his feet.

But one voice in the council was still roaring on, bellowing with monotonous urgency. Against all odds, its owner was at last able to achieve something like an attentive silence among the handful of deities who remained.

"Look! Look!" was all that voice was saying. And with one mighty arm the roaring god was pointing steadily downslope, indicating a single, simple line of markings in the snow, tracks that the mundane wind was rapidly effacing.

There could be no doubt about those markings. They were a line of departing footprints, heading straight down the mountainside, disappearing behind snow-buried rocks before they had gone more than a few meters. Though they marked strides too long and impressions too broad and deep to have been made by any human being, there was no doubt that they had been left by mortal feet.

CHAPTER 2

The one-armed man came stumbling along through midnight rain, following a twisted cobblestone alley into the lightless heart of the great city of Tashigang. He was suffering with fresh wounds now—one knife-gash bleeding in his side and another one in his knee—besides the old maiming loss of his right arm. Still he was better off than the man who had just attacked him. That blunderer was some meters back along the twisted alley, face down in a puddle.

Now, just when the one-armed man was about on the point of going down himself, he steered toward a wall and leaned against it. Standing with his broad back in its homespun shirt pressed to the stone wall of somebody's house, he squeezed himself in as far as possible under the thin overhang of roof, until the eaves blocked at least some of the steady rain from hitting him in the face. The man felt frightened by what had happened to his knee. From the way the injured leg felt now when he tried to put his weight on it, he wasn't going to be able to walk much farther.

He hadn't had a chance yet to start worrying about what might have happened when the knife went into his side.

The one-armed man was tall, and strongly built. Still, by definition, he was a cripple, and therefore the robber—if that was all he had been —might have taken it for granted that he'd be easy game. Even had the attacker guessed that his intended victim carried a good oaken cudgel tucked into his belt under his loose shirt, he could hardly have predicted how quickly his quarry would be able to draw that club and with what authority he'd use it.

Now, leaning against the building for support, he had tucked his cudgel away in his belt again, and was pressing his fingers to his side under his shirt. He could feel the blood coming out, a frighteningly fast trickle.

Except for the rain, the city around him was silent. And all the windows he could see through the rain were dark, and most of them were shuttered. No one else in the huge city appeared to have taken the least notice of the brief clash he had just survived.

Or had he survived it, after all? Real walking, he had to admit, was no longer possible on his damaged knee. For the present, at least, he could still stand upright. He thought he must be near his destination now, and it was essential that he reach it. Pushing himself along the wall that he was leaning on, and then the next wall, one stone surface after another, he stumbled on, hobbled on.

He remembered the directions he had been given, and he made progress of a sort. Every time his weight came on the knee at all he had to bite back an outcry of pain. And now dizziness, lightheadedness, came welling up inside his skull. He clenched his will like a fist, gripping the treasure of consciousness, knowing that if that slipped from him now, life itself was likely to drain quickly after it.

His memorized directions told him that at this point he had to cross the alley. Momentarily forsaking the support of walls, divorcing his mind from pain, he somehow managed it.

Leaning on another wall, he rested, and rebuilt his courage. He'd crawl the rest of the way to get there if he had to, or do what crawling he could on one hand and one knee. But once he went down to try crawling he didn't know he'd ever get back up on his feet again.

At last the building that had been described to him as his goal, the House of Courtenay, came into sight, limned by distant lightning. The description had been accurate: four stories tall, flat-roofed, half-timbered construction on the upper levels, stone below. The house occupied its own small block, with streets or alleys on every side. The seeker's first view was of the front of the building, but the back was where he was supposed to go in order to get in. Gritting his teeth, not letting his imagination try to count up how many steps there might be yet to take, he made the necessary detour. He splashed through puddles, out of one alley and into an even narrower one. From that he passed to one so narrow it was a mere paved path, running beside the softly gurgling, stone-channeled Corgo. The surface of the river, innocent now of boats, hissed in the heavier bursts of rain.

The man had almost reached the building he wanted when his hurt knee gave way completely. He broke his fall as best he could with his one arm. Then, painfully, dizzily, he dragged himself along on his one arm and his one functioning leg. He could imagine the trail of blood he must be leaving. No matter, the rain would wash it all away.

Presently his slow progress brought him in out of the rain, under the roof of a short, narrow passage that connected directly with the door he wanted. He crawled on and reached the narrow door. It was of course locked shut. He propped himself up in a sitting position against it, and began to pound on the door with the flat of his large hand. The pounding of his calloused hand seemed to the man to be making no noise at all. At first it felt like he was beating uselessly, noiselessly, on some thick solid treetrunk . . . and then it felt like nothing at all. There was no longer any feeling in his hand.

Maybe no one would hear him. Because he was no longer able to hear anything himself. Not even the rain beating on the flat passage roof. Nor could he see anything through the gathering grayness. Not even his hand before his face. . . .

At a little after midnight Denis the Quick was lying awake, listening to the rain. That usually made him sleepy, as long as he knew that he was securely warm and dry indoors. But tonight he was having trouble sleeping. The images of two attractive women were coming and going like provocative dancers in his imagination. If he tried to concentrate on one, then the other intruded as if jealous. He knew both women in real life, but his real-life problem was not that he had to choose between them. No, he was not so fortunate, he told himself, as to have problems of just that kind.

Denis was well accustomed to the normal night sounds of the house. The sound he began to hear now, distracting him from the pleasant torment of waking dreams, was certainly not one of them. Denis got up quickly, pulled on a pair of trousers, and went out of his small bedchamber to investigate.

His room on the ground floor of the house gave almost directly on the main workshop, which was a large chamber now illumined faintly by a sullen smoldering of coals banked in the central forge. Faint ghost-gleams of firelight touched tools around the forge and weapons racked on the walls. Most of the work down here was on some form of weaponry.

Denis paused for a moment beside the fire, intending to light a taper from its coals. But then he changed his mind, and instead reached up to the high wall niche where the Old World light was kept.

The back door leading into the shop from outside ground level was fitted with a special peephole. This was a smooth little bulge of glass, cleverly shaped so that anyone looking through it from inside saw out at a wide angle. Another lens, set into the door near its very top, was there to let the precious flameless torch shine out. Denis now lifted the antique instrument into position there and turned it on; immediately the narrow passage just outside the door was flooded with clear, brilliant light. And even as Denis did this, the sound that had caught his attention came again, a faint thumping on the door itself. Now through the fish-eye lens he could see the one who made the sound, as a slumped figure somewhat blurred by the imperfect lens. The shape of the fallen figure suggested the absence of an arm.

With the flameless light still glowing in his hand, Denis stepped back from the door. The House of Courtenay generally contained some stock of the goods in which its owners dealt, including the fancy weapons that were the specialty of the house. Also there was usually a considerable supply of coin on hand. The place was a natural target for thieves, and for any member of the household to open any exterior door to anyone, particularly at night, was no trivial matter. The only thing for Denis to do now was to rouse the household steward, Tarim, and get his orders as to what to do next.

Crossing the workshop, Denis approached the door to the ascending stair that led to the next highest level of the house; Tarim slept up there, along with most of the rest of the resident staff. Denis opened the door —and stopped in his tracks.

Looking down at him from the top of the first flight, holding a candle in her small, pale hand, was one of the characters from his recent waking dream, the Lady Sophie herself, mistress of this house. Denis's surprise was at seeing the lady there at all. Family quarters were located on the upper levels of the house, well above the noise and smoke and smell of the shop when it was busy, and of the daytime streets. Her tiny but shapely body was wrapped in a thick white robe, contrasting sharply with her straight black hair. It was hard to believe that any faint sound at the back door could have roused the lady from her bed.

The mistress called down: "Denis? What is it?" He thought she sounded nervous.

Denis stood there hugging his bare chest. "There's someone at the back door, Mistress. I could see only one man. Looked like he was hurt, but I didn't open."

"Hurt, you say?"

It looked and sounded to Denis almost as if the lady had been expecting someone to arrive tonight, had been waiting around in readiness to receive them. Denis had heard nothing in particular in the way of business news to make him expect such a visitor, but such a nocturnal arrival in itself would not be very surprising. As the headquarters of a company of traders, the house was accustomed to the comings and goings of odd people at odd hours.

Denis answered, "Yes, Ma'am, hurt. And it looked like he only had one arm. I was just going to arouse Tarim . . ."

"No." The mistress was immediately decisive. "Just stand by there for a moment, while I go get the master."

"Yes, Ma'am." It was of course the only answer Denis could give, but still it was delayed, delivered only to the lady's already retreating back. Denis was puzzled, and a moment later his puzzlement increased, for here, already fully awake and active too, came Master Courtenay himself. Courtenay was a moving mountain of a man, his great bulk wrapped now in a night robe of a rich blue fabric. With a lightness and quickness remarkable for his size, the master came almost skipping down the stairs, his lady just behind him.

Arriving on the ground floor, the master of the house faced Denis directly. The two were almost of a height, near average, though Courtenay weighed easily twice as much as his lean employee, and was possibly three times as massive as his small wife. Courtenay was not yet thirty, as nearly as Denis could judge, and very little of his bulk was fat, though in his robe he looked that way. Nor could he be described as stupid, as Denis had realized on his own first day here, despite what a first glance at Courtenay's face suggested—of course he could hardly be unintelligent and have prospered as he evidently had.

The master brushed back his almost colorless hair from his uninviting face, a gesture that seemed more one of worry than of sleepiness. In his usual mild voice he said, "We'll let the rest of the household go on sleeping, Denis." Behind the master, his lady was already closing the door to the ascending stair. "The three of us will manage," Courtenay went on. "The man's hurt, you say?"

"Looks like it, sir."

"Still, we'll take no chances more than necessary. Help yourself to a weapon, and stand by."

"Yes sir." In the year and a half that he had been at the House of Courtenay, Denis had learned that there were stretches of time in which life here began to seem dull. But so far those stretches had never extended for any unbearable length of time.

Over on the far side of the shop, the mistress was lighting a couple of oil lamps. And when she brought her hands down from the lamp shelf and faced around again, Denis thought that he saw something trailing from her right hand. He caught only a glimpse of the object before it vanished between folds of her full robe. But, had he not been convinced that Mistress Sophie was only a delicate little thing who loved her luxury, he would have thought that she was holding the leather thongs of a hunter's or a warrior's sling.

The more recent years of Denis's young life had been generally peaceful, first as an acolyte of Ardneh in the White Temple, then here in the House of Courtenay as apprentice trader and general assistant. But he had spent the longer, earlier portion of his existence serving a different kind of apprenticeship. That had been in the slum streets of Tashigang, and it had left him indelibly familiar with the more unpeaceful side of life. So now he was reasonably calm as he moved to the display of decorative weapons that occupied a good part of one side of the large room. There he selected an ornate battle-hatchet, a weapon of antique design but sharp-edged and of a pleasantly balanced weight. With this in hand, Denis nodded that he was ready.

Master Courtenay, already standing by the back door, returned the nod. Then he turned to the door and made use of the peephole and the Old World light. In the next moment Courtenay had unbarred the door and yanked it open. The crumpled body that had been sitting against it on the outside came toppling softly inward.

Denis sprang forward, quickly closed the door and barred it up again. Meanwhile the master of the house had stretched the unconscious man out full length on the floor, and was examining him with the aid of the Old World light.

The mistress, one of the more conventional lamps in her hand, had come forward to look too. Quickly she turned to Denis. "He's bleeding badly. You were a servant of Ardneh, see what you can do for him."

Denis was not usually pleased to be asked to administer medical treatment; he knew too well his own great limitations in the art. But his urge to please his mistress would not let him hesitate. And he knew that his years in Ardneh's service had left him almost certainly better qualified than either of his employers. He nodded and moved forward.

The man stretched out on the floor was not young; his unconscious face was weatherbeaten over its bloodless pallor, and the hair that fanned out in a wild spread on the flat stones was gray. Standing, he would have been tall, with a well-knit, sturdy body marred by the old amputation.

"His right arm *is* gone." That was the mistress, speaking thoughtfully, as if she were only musing to herself.

Denis heard her only absently; the man's fresh wounds were going to demand a healer's full attention. A lot of blood was visible, darker wetness on the rainsoaked clothing.

Quickly Denis began to peel back clothes. He cut them away, when that was easier, with a keen knife that the master handed him. He also tossed aside a mean-looking cudgel that he found tucked into the victim's belt.

"I'll need water, and bandages," he announced over his shoulder. There were two wounds, and both looked bad. "And whatever medicines we have to stop bleeding." He paused to mumble a minor spell for that purpose, learned in his days as Ardneh's servitor. It was about the best that Denis could do in the way of magic, and it was very little. Perhaps it brought some benefit, but it was not going to be enough.

"I'll bring you what I can find," replied the mistress of the house, and turned away with quick efficiency. Again Denis was surprised. He had long ago fixed her image in his mind as someone who existed to be pampered . . . could that really have been a sling he'd seen her holding?

But now the present task demanded his full attention. "We ought to put him on my bed," said Denis. And Courtenay, strong as a loadbeast and disdaining help, scooped up the limp heavy form as if it had been that of a small child, and held it patiently while Denis maneuvered first the door to his room and then the coverings on his bed.

The hurt man's eyelids fluttered just as he was being put down on the bed, and he muttered a few words. Denis heard something like: "Ben of

Purkinje," which certainly sounded like a name. That of the victim himself? No use asking. He was out cold again.

Soon the mistress was back, with such useful items as she had been able to lay her hands on quickly, water and clean cloth. She had also brought along a couple of medicine jars, but nothing that Denis thought was likely to help. While Denis went to work washing and bandaging, the master picked up the sodden clothing that had been stripped away, and went quickly through the pockets. But whatever Courtenay was looking for, he apparently did not find it. With a sigh he threw the garments back on the floor and asked: "Well, Denis, what about him?"

"He's lost a lot of blood, sir. And, where the wounds are, the bleeding's going to be hard to stop. I've packed this hole in his side as best I can." As he spoke Denis was still pressing a bandage into place. "We could use spider webs, but I don't know where to get a bunch of 'em quickly. His knee isn't bleeding so much now, but it looks nasty. If he lives, he won't be walking for a while."

The Old World light had been replaced in its customary wall niche, and the mistress had now brought one of the better ordinary lamps into Denis's room. By the lamplight she and her husband were staring at each other with what struck Denis as curious expressions.

"Knife wounds, I think," said Master Courtenay, shifting his gaze at last back to Denis.

"Yes sir, I would say that's what they are."

"He couldn't have come very far in that condition."

"I'd have to agree with that, sir."

The master nodded, and turned and walked out of Denis's room, leaving the door open behind him. He didn't say where he was going, and nobody asked. The mistress lingered. Denis, observing the direction of her gaze, wondered what it was about the patient's arm-stump that she found so fascinating.

Having been a member of the household for a year and a half now, Denis was—sometimes, almost—treated like one of the family. Now he made bold to ask, "Do you recognize him, Mistress?"

"I've never seen him before," the lady answered, which to Denis sounded like the truth used as an evasion. She added: "Will he live, do you think?"

Before Denis had to try to make a guess sound like an expert opinion, there came again the sounds of someone at the back door of the shop. The sounds were different this time: demanding shouts, accompanied by a strong and determined hammering.

Following his mistress out into the shop's main room, Denis shut the door of his own room behind him. The master, Old World light in hand again, was once more approaching the back door. Even as Courtenay turned on the light and peered out through the spy-lens, the pounding came again. This time it was accompanied by a hoarse voice, somewhat muffled by the door's thickness: "Ho, in the house, open for the Watch! In the Lord Mayor's name, open!"

The master of the house continued to peer out. "Three of 'em," he reported in a low voice. "No lights of their own. Still, it's the real Watch —I think."

"Open!" the smothered roaring voice demanded. "Open or we break it down!" And there came a *thump thump thump*. But they were going to have to thump harder than that before this door would take them seriously.

Quietly the mistress said to her husband: "We don't want to . . ." She let the statement trail off there, but Denis listening had the strong impression that her next words would have been: *arouse suspicion.*

Whatever meaning the master read into her half-voiced thought, he nodded his agreement with it. Looking at Denis, he ordered: "Say nothing to them about our visitor. We've seen no one tonight."

"If they want to search?"

"Leave that to me. But pick up your hatchet again, just in case."

When all three of the people inside were ready, Courtenay undid the bars and opened the door again. In the very next instant he had to demonstrate extraordinary agility for a man of his weight, by jumping back out of the way of a blow from a short sword.

The three men who had come bursting in, dressed though they were in the Lord Mayor's livery of gray and green, were plainly not the Watch. Denis with his hatchet was able to stand off the first rush of one of them, armed with a long knife in each hand. Another of the intruders started toward Lady Sophie. But her right arm rose from her side, drawing into a whirling blur the sling's long leather strands. Whatever missile had been cradled in the leather cup now blasted stone fragments out of the wall beside the man's head, giving him pause, giving her the necessary moment to reload her weapon.

"Ben of Purkinje!" cried out the third invader, hacking again at Master Courtenay with his sword. "Greetings from the Blue Temple!" This attacker was tall, and looked impressively strong.

Master Courtenay, after advising Denis to be armed, had himself been caught embarrassingly unarmed on the side of the room away from the rack of weapons. He had to improvise, and out of the miscellany of tools around the forge grabbed up a long, iron-handled casting ladle. It was a clumsy thing to try to swing against a sword, but the master of the house had awesome strength, and now demonstrated good nerves as well. For the time being he was holding his own, managing to protect himself.

The man who had started after the Lady Sophie now turned back, indecisively, as if to give the swordsman aid. It was an error. In the next instant the second stone from the sling hit him in the back of the head and knocked him down. The sound of the impact and the way he fell showed that for him the fight was over.

Denis was distracted by the lady's achievement—unwisely, for a moment later he felt the point of one of his opponent's long knives catch in the flesh of his forearm. The hatchet fell from Denis's grip to the stone floor. Scrambling away from the knives, clearing a low bench in a somersaulting dive, Denis the Quick lived up to his nickname well enough to keep himself alive.

He heard one of the bigger workbenches go over with a crash, and now he saw that Master Courtenay had somehow managed to catch his own attacker by the swordarm—maybe the fellow had also been distracted, dodging feints of a slung stone. Anyway it was now going to be a wrestling match—but no, it really wasn't. In another instant the swordsman, bellowing his surprise, had been lifted clean off his feet, and in the instant after that Denis saw him slaughtered like a rabbit, his back broken against the angle of the heavy, tilted table.

The knife-wielder who had wounded Denis had now changed his strategy and was scrambling after the lady. Suddenly bereft of friends, he needed a hostage. Denis, reckless of his own safety, and wounded as he was, threw himself in the attacker's way before the man could come within a knife-thrust of the mistress. Denis had one quick glimpse of the lady, her white robe half undone, scooting successfully on hands and knees to get away.

And now Denis was on his back, and the knife was coming down at him instead—but before it reached him, the arm that held it was knocked aside by a giant's blow from the long ladle. The iron weight brushed aside the barrier of an arm to mash into the knifer's cheekbone, delivering most of its energy there with an effect of devastation. Denis rolled aside, paused to look back, and allowed himself to slow to a panting halt. The fight was definitely over.

In the workshop, only three sets of lungs were breathing still.

The lady, pulling her robe around her properly once more (even amid surrounding blood, terror, and danger, that momentary vision of her body was still with Denis; he thought that it would always be.) Now she let herself slide down slowly until she was sitting on the floor with her back against one of the upset benches. Evidently more angered than terrified by the experience, she said to her husband acidly, "You are quite, quite sure, are you, that they represent the Watch?"

Courtenay, still on his feet, looking stupid, breathing heavily, could only mumble something.

Once more there came the sound of pounding on a door, accompanied by urgent voices. But this time the noise was originating within the house. The door that closed off the ascending stair was being rattled and shaken, while from behind it a man's voice shouted: "Mistress! Master! Denis, are you all right? What's going on?"

The master of the house cast down his long iron ladle. He stood for a moment contemplating his own bloodied hands as if he wondered how they might have got that way. Denis saw an unprecedented tremor in those hands. Then Courtenay drew a deep breath, raised his head, and called back, almost calmly, "It's all right, Tarim. A little problem, but we've solved it. Be patient for a moment and I'll explain."

In an aside he added: "Denis, help me get these . . . no, you're hurt yourself. Sit down first and bind that up. Barb, you help me with these visitors. Drag 'em around behind that bench and we'll throw a tarp over 'em."

Denis, in mild shock now with his wound, took a moment to register the unfamiliar name. Barb? Never before had he heard the master, or anyone else, call the lady that . . . it wasn't going to be easy, he realized, to bind up his own arm unaided. Anyway, the wound didn't look like it was going to kill him.

Courtenay, while keeping busy himself, was still giving orders. "Now close the street door." He dropped a dead man where he wanted him, and pulled out a heavy tarpaulin from its storage. "No, wait, let Tarim see it standing open. We'll say some brigands got in somehow, and . . ."

Tarim and the other awakened staff were presently allowed to come crowding in. Whether they fully believed the vague story about brigands or not, they took their cue from their master's manner and were too wise to question it. The outer door was closed and barred. Tarim himself had to be dissuaded from standing watch in the workshop for the rest of the night, and eventually he and all the others were on their way back to bed.

Alone in the workshop again, the three who had done the fighting exchanged looks. Then they got busy.

Courtenay began a preliminary clean-up, while the mistress applied a bandage to Denis's forearm, following his directions. Her small fingers, soft, white, and pampered, did not shrink from bloody contact. They managed the bandaging quite well, using some of the cloth that had been brought for the first patient.

When the job was done, her fingers held his arm a moment more. Her dark eyes, for the first time ever (he thought) looked at him with something more than the wish to be pleasant to a servant. She said, very quietly but very seriously, "You saved my life, Denis. Thank you."

It was almost as if no woman had ever touched him or spoken to him before. Denis muttered something. He could feel the blood flowing back into his face. What foolishness, he told himself. He and this lady could never . . .

A quick look at the stranger now occupying Denis's bed showed that the fight in the next room had not disturbed him. He was still unconscious, breathing shallowly. Denis, looking at him, came round to the opinion that nothing was likely to disturb this man again. With two wounded men now on hand, the mistress announced that she was going upstairs to search more thoroughly for medical materials.

The master said to his lady, "I'll come up with you, we have to talk. Denis can manage here for a few moments."

The two of them climbed in thoughtful silence, past the level where Tarim and other workers slept, past the next floor also. Reaching the topmost level of the house, they passed through another door and entered a domain of elegance. This began with a wood-paneled hall, lit now by the flame of a single candle in a wall sconce. Here the lady turned in one direction, going to rummage in her private stocks for medical materials. The master turned down the hall the other way, heading for a closet where he expected to find a fresh, unbloodied robe.

Before he reached the room that held the closet, he was intercepted by the toddling figure of a kneehigh child, an apparition followed almost immediately by that of an apologetic nurse.

"Oh sir, you're hurt," the nurse protested. She was a buxom girl, almost a grown woman now. And at the same time the child demanded: "Daddy! Tell story now!" At the age of two and a half, the little girl fortunately already showed much more of her mother's than her father's looks. Brazenly wide awake, as if something about this particular night delighted her, she waited in her silken nightdress, small stuffed toy in hand.

The man spoke to the nursemaid first. "I'm all right, Kuan-yin. The blood is nothing. I'll put Beth back to bed; you go see if you can help your mistress find what she's looking for."

The nurse looked at him for a moment. Then, like the other employees, wise enough to be incurious tonight, she moved away.

The huge man, who for the past four years had been trying to establish an identity as Master Courtenay, wiped drying gore from his huge hands onto a robe already stained. With hands now steady, and almost clean, he bent to carefully pick up the living morsel he had discovered he valued more than his own life.

Carrying his daughter back to the nursery, he passed a window. Through genuine glass and rainy night he had a passing view of the high city walls some hundreds of meters distant. The real watch were keeping a fire burning atop the wall. Another light, smaller and steadier, was visible in a slightly different direction; one of the upper windows glowing in the Lord Mayor's palace. It looked as if someone was having a busy night there too; the observer could only hope that there was no connection.

Fortune was smiling on the huge man now, for he was able to remember the particular story that his daughter wanted, and to get through the telling of it with reasonable speed. The child had just gone back to sleep, and the father was just on his way out of the nursery, shutting the door with infinite care behind him, when his wife reappeared, still wearing her stained white robe.

"We have a moment," she whispered, and drew him aside into their own bedroom. When that door too had been softly closed, and they were securely alone, she added: "I've already taken the medicine downstairs to Denis. He thinks that the man is probably going to die . . . there's no doubt, is there, that he's the courier we're expecting?"

"I don't suppose there's much doubt about that, no."

The lady was slipping out of her bloodied robe now, and throwing it aside. In the very dim light that came in through the barred window from those distant watchfires, her husband beheld her shapely body as a curved warmed silver candlestick, a pale ghost hardly thickened at all by having borne one child. Once he had loved this woman hopelessly, and then another love had come to him, and gone again, dissolved in death. Sometimes he still saw in dreams a cascade of bright red hair

. . . his love for his darkhaired wife still existed, but it was very different now.

As she dug into a chest to get another robe, she told him calmly, "One of those we killed tonight cried out, something like: 'Greetings to Ben of Purkinje, from the Blue Temple.' I'm sure that Denis heard it too."

"We're going to have to trust Denis. He's proved tonight he's loyal. I think he saved your life."

"Yes," the lady agreed, in a remote voice. "Either trust him—or else kill him too. Well." She dismissed that thought, though not before taking a moment in which to examine it with deliberate care. Then she looked hard at her husband. "And you called me Barb, too, once, down there in his hearing."

"Did I?" He'd thought he'd broken himself long ago of calling her that. Ben—he never really thought of himself as "of Purkinje"—heaved a great sigh. "So, anyway, the Blue Temple has caught up with me. It probably doesn't matter what Denis overheard."

"And they've caught up with me, too," she reminded him sharply. "And with your daughter, whether they were looking for us or not. It looked like they were ready to wipe out the household if they could." She paused. "I hope they haven't located Mark."

Ben thought that over. "There's no way we can get any word to him quickly. Is there? I'm not sure just where he is."

"No, I don't suppose we can." Barbara, tightening the belt on her clean robe, shook her head thoughtfully. "And they came here right on the heels of the courier—did you notice that? They must have been following him somehow, knowing that he'd lead them to us."

"Too much of a coincidence otherwise."

"Yes. And the alliance still holds, I suppose, between Blue Temple and the Dark King."

"Which means the Dark King's people may know about the courier too. And about what we have in our possession here, that the courier was going to take away, if the rest of the shipment ever arrives." He heaved another sigh.

"What do we do, Ben?" His wife spoke softly now, standing close to him and looking up. At average height he towered over her.

"At the moment, we try to keep the courier alive, and see if he can tell us anything. About Denis—we're just going to have to trust him, as I say. He's a good man."

He was about to open the bedroom door, but his wife's small hand on his arm delayed him. "Your hands," she reminded him. "Your robe."

"Right." He poured water into a basin and quickly washed his hands, then changed his robe. Half his mind was still down in the workshop, reliving the fight. Already in his memory the living bodies he had just broken were taking on the aspects of creatures in some awful dream. He knew they were going to come back later to assail him. Later perhaps his hands would shake again. It was always like this for him after a fight. He had to try to put it out of his mind for now.

While he was getting into his clean robe, Barbara said, "Ben, as soon as I saw that the man had only one arm, you know what I thought of."

"Mark's father. But Mark always told us that his father was dead. He sounded quite sure of it."

"Yes, I remember. That he'd seen his father struck down in their village street. But just suppose—"

"Yes. Well, we've got enough to worry about as it is."

In another moment they were quietly making their way downstairs together. The house around them was as quiet now as if everyone were really sleeping. Ben could picture most of his workers lying awake, holding their breaths, waiting for the next crash.

In Denis's room on the ground floor they found the young man, his face pale under his dark hair, sitting watch over a stranger who still breathed, but barely. The mistress immediately went to work, improving on her first effort at bandaging Denis's arm. Ben thought he could see a little more color coming slowly back into the youth's cheeks.

And now, for the third time since midnight, a noise at the back door. This time a modest tapping.

Something in Ben wanted to react with laughter. "Gods and demons, what a night. My house has turned into the Hermes Gate to the High Road."

And now, for the third time, after making sure that his wife and his assistant were armed and as ready for trouble as they could get, Ben maneuvered light and lenses to look out into the narrow exterior passage. This time, as he reported to the others in a whisper, there were two human figures to be seen outside. Both appeared to be men, and both were robed in white.

"It looks like two of Ardneh's people. One's carrying a big staff that . . ." Ben didn't finish. Barbara caught his meaning.

Those outside, knowing from the light that they were under observation from within, called loudly: "Master Courtenay? We've brought the wooden model that you've been waiting for."

"Ah," said Ben, hearing a code that gave him reassurance. Still he signed to his companions to remain on guard, before he cautiously opened the door once more.

This time the opening admitted neither a toppling body nor an armed rush. There was only the peaceful entry of the two in white, who as Ardneh's priests saluted courteously first the master of the house and then the people with him. Denis, this time holding his hatchet left-handed, was glad to be able to lower it again.

White robes dripped water on a floor already freshly marked by rain and mud and blood. If the newcomers noticed these signs of preceding visitors, they said nothing about them.

Instead, as soon as Ben had barred up the door again, the older of the two whiteclad priests offered him the heavy, ornate wooden staff. It was obviously meant to be a ceremonial object of some kind, too large and unwieldy to be anything but a burden on a march or a hike. Tall as a man, cruciform in its upper part, the staff was beautifully carved out of some light wood that Denis could not identify. The uppermost portion resembled the hilt of a gigantic wooden sword, with the heads and necks of two carved dragons recurving upon themselves to form the outsized crosspiece.

"Beautiful," commented Denis, with a sudden dry suspicion. "But I wonder which of Ardneh's rites requires such an object? I saw nothing at all like it in the time I spent as acolyte."

The two white-garbed men looked at Denis. Then they turned in silent appeal to the man they knew as Master Courtenay. He told them tiredly, "You may show us the inside of the wooden model too. Denis here is fully in my confidence, as of tonight. He's going to have to be."

Denis stared for a moment at his master, who was watching closely what the priests were doing. The younger priest had the staff now, and was pressing carefully with strong fingers on the fancy carving. In a moment, the wood had opened like a shell, revealing a velvet-lined cavity inside. Hidden there, straight iron hilt within wooden crosspiece, was a great Sword. The plain handle, of what Denis took to be some hard black wood, was marked in white with a small symbol, the outline of an open human hand. The Sword was in a leather sheath, that left only a finger's-breadth of the blade visible, but that small portion of metal caught the eye. It displayed a rich mottling, suggesting centimeters of depth in the thin blade, beneath a surface gleam of perfect smoothness. Only the Old World, or a god, thought Denis, could have made a blade like that . . . and Denis had never heard of any Old World swords.

"Behold," the elder priest of Ardneh said, even as the hand of the younger drew forth the blade out of its sheath. "The Sword of Mercy!"

And still Denis needed another moment—but no more than that—to understand fully what he was being allowed to see. When understanding came, he first caught his breath, and then released it in a long sigh. By now almost everyone in the world had heard of the Twelve Swords, though there were probably those who still doubted their reality, and most had never seen one. The Swords had been forged some twenty years ago, the more reliable stories had it; created, all the versions of the legend agreed, to serve some mysterious role in a divine Game that the gods and goddesses who ruled the world were determined to enjoy among themselves.

And if this wonderous weapon were not one of those twelve Swords, thought Denis . . . well, it was hard to imagine what else it could be. In his time at the House of Courtenay he had seen some elegant and valuable blades, but never before anything like this.

There were twelve of them, all of the stories agreed on that much. Most of them had two names, though some had more names than two, and a few had only one. They were called Wayfinder, and Farslayer, and the Tyrant's Blade; there were the Mindsword, and Townsaver, and Stonecutter, called also the Sword of Siege. There were Doom-giver, Sightblinder, Dragonslicer; Coinspinner and Shieldbreaker and the Sword of Love, that last thrice-named, also as Woundhealer and the Sword of Mercy.

And, if any of the tales had truth in them at all, each Sword had its own unique power, capable of overwhelming all lesser magics, bestowing on its owner some chance to rule the world, or at least to speak on equal terms with those who died. . . .

The older priest had carefully accepted the naked Sword from the hands of the younger, and now Denis observed with a start that the old man was now approaching him, Denis, with the heavy weapon held out before him. Half-raised as if in some clumsy system of attack, it wobbled slightly in the elder's hands.

Even in the mild lamplight the steel gleamed breathtakingly. And

Denis thought that a sound was coming from it now, a sound like that of human breath.

Whether he was commanded to hold out his wounded arm, or did so automatically, Denis could not afterwards remember. The room was very quiet, except for the faint slow rhythmic hiss that the Sword made, as if it breathed. The old man's thin arms, that looked as if they might never have held a weapon before in all his life, reached out. The blade, looking keener than any razor that Denis had ever seen, steadied itself suddenly. It moved now as if under some finer control than the visibly tremulous grip of the old priest.

And now the broad point had somehow, without even nicking flesh, inserted itself snugly underneath the tight bandage binding Denis's forearm. The bloodstained white cloth, cut neatly, fell away, and the Sword's point touched the wound directly. Denis, expecting pain, felt instead an intense moment of—something else, a sensation unique and indescribable. And then the Sword withdrew.

Looking down at his arm, Denis saw dried blood, but no fresh flow. The dried, brownish stuff brushed away readily enough when he rubbed at it with his fingers. Where the dried blood had been, he saw now a small, fresh, pink scar. The wound looked healthy, easily a week or ten days healed.

It was at this moment, for some reason, that Denis suddenly remembered something about the man who, the legends said, had been forced to assist Vulcan in the forging of the Swords. The stories said of that human smith that as soon as his work was done he had been deprived of his right arm by the god.

"It is shameful, of course," the elder priest was saying, "that we must keep it hidden so, and sneak through the night with it like criminals with their plunder. But if we did not take precautions, then those who would put Woundhealer to an evil use would soon have it in their possession."

"We will do our best," the lady of the house assured him, "to keep it from them."

"But at the moment," said the master, "we have a problem even more immediate than that. Sirs, if you will, bring the Sword this way with you, and quickly. A man lies dying."

Denis led the way, and quickly opened the door to his own room. The master stepped in past him, and indicated the still figure on the bed. "He arrived here not an hour ago, much as you see him. And I fear he is the courier who was to have carried on what you have brought."

The two priests moved quickly to stand beside the bed. The young one murmured a prayer to Draffut, God of Healing. The first quick touch of the Sword was directly on the wound still bleeding in the side of the unconscious man. Denis, despite his own experience of only moments ago, could not keep from wincing involuntarily. It was hard to imagine that that keen, hard point would not draw more blood, do more harm to human flesh already injured. But the slow red ooze from the wound, instead of increasing, dried up immediately. As the Sword moved away, the packing that Denis had put into the wound pulled out with it. The cloth hung there, stuck by dried blood to the skin.

Feeling a sense of unreality, Denis passed his hand over his eyes.

Now the Sword, still in the hands of Ardneh's elder servant, moved down to touch the wound on the exposed knee. This time when the bare metal touched him, the man on the bed drew in his breath sharply, as if with some extreme and exquisite sensation; a moment later he let out a long sigh, eloquent of relief. But his eyes did not open.

And now the tip of the Sword was being made to pass back and forth over his whole body, not quite touching him. It paused again, briefly, right above the heart. Denis could see how the arms of the old priest continued to tremble, as if it strained them to hold this heavy weapon— not, Denis supposed, that this Sword ought to be called a weapon. He wondered what would happen if you swung it against an enemy.

The tip of the blade paused just once more, when it reached the scarred stump of the long-lost arm. There it touched, and there, to Denis's fresh surprise, it did draw blood at last, a thready red trickle from the scarred flesh. Again a gasp came from the unconscious man.

The bleeding stopped of itself, almost as quickly as it had started. The old priest now slid the blade back into its sheath, and handed it to his assistant, who enclosed it once again within the staff of wood.

The elder's face was pale now, as if the healing might have taken something out of him. But he did not pause to rest, bending instead to examine the man he had been treating. Then he pulled a blanket up to the patient's chin and straightened.

"He will recover," the elder priest announced, "but he must rest for many days; he was nearly dead before the Sword of Mercy reached him. Here you can provide him with the good food he needs; even so his recovery will take some time."

Master Courtenay told the two priests of Ardneh softly, "We thank you in his name—whatever that may be. Now, will you have some food? And then we'll find you a place to sleep."

The elder declined gravely. "Thank you, but we cannot stay, even for food." He shook his head. "If this man was to be the next courier, as you say, I fear you will have to find a replacement for him."

"We will find a way," the lady said.

"Good," said the elder, and paused, frowning. "There is one thing more that I must tell you before we go." He paused again, a longer time, as if what he had to say now required some gathering of forces. "The Mindsword has fallen into the hands of the Dark King."

An exhausted silence fell over the people in the workshop. Denis was trying desperately to recall what the various songs and stories had to say about the weapon called the Mindsword.

There was, of course, the verse that everyone had heard:

> *The Mindsword spun in the dawn's gray light*
> *And men and demons knelt down before*
> *The Mindsword flashed in the midday bright*
> *Gods joined the dance, and the march to war*
> *It spun in the twilight dim as well*
> *And gods and men marched off to—*

"Gods and demons!" Master Courtenay swore loudly. His face was grave and gray, with a look that Denis had never seen on it before.

Moments later, having said their last farewells, the two white-robed men were gone.

Denis closed and barred the door behind them, and turned round. The master of the house was standing in the middle of the workshop, with one hand on the wooden Sword-case that stood leaning there against the chimney. He was looking it over carefully, as if it were something that he might want to buy.

The lady was back in Denis's room already, looking down at the hurt man on the bed. Denis when he came in saw that the man was now sleeping peacefully and his color was a little better already.

Out in the main room of the shop again, Denis approached his master —whose real name, Denis was already certain, was unlikely to be Courtenay. "What are we going to do with the Sword now, sir? Of course it may be none of my business." It obviously had become his business now; his real question was how they were going to deal with that fact.

His master gave him a look that said this point was appreciated. But all he said was: "Even before we worry about the Sword, there's another little job that needs taking care of. How's your arm?"

Denis flexed it. There was a faint residual soreness. "Good enough."

"Good." And the big man walked around behind the big toppled workbench, and lifted the tarpaulin from that which had been concealed from Ardneh's priests.

It was going to be very convenient, Denis thought, that the house was so near the river, and that the night was dark and rainy.

CHAPTER 3

The chase under the blistering sun had been a long one, but the young man who was its quarry foresaw that it was not going to go on much longer.

Since the ambush some twenty kilometers back had killed his three companions and all their riding beasts, he had been scrambling on foot across the rough, barren country, pausing only at intervals to set an ambush of his own, or when necessary to gasp for breath.

The young man wore a light pack on his back, along with his long-bow and quiver. At his belt he carried a small water bottle—it was nearly empty now, one of the reasons why he thought that the chase must soon end in one way or another. His age would have been hard to judge because of his weathered look, but it was actually much closer to twenty than to thirty. His clothes were those of a hunter, or perhaps a guerrilla soldier, and he wore his present trouble as well and fittingly as he wore his clothes. He was a tall and broad-shouldered young man, with blue-gray eyes, and a light, short beard that until a few days ago had been neatly trimmed. The longbow slung across his back looked eminently functional, but at the moment there were only three arrows left in the quiver that rode beside it.

The young man had fallen into a kind of pattern in his movement. This took the form of a trot, a pause to look back over one shoulder, another scramble, a quick walk, and then a look back over the other shoulder without pausing.

According to the best calculation he could make, which he knew might very easily be wrong, he still had one more active enemy behind him than he had arrows. Of course the only way to make absolutely sure of the enemy's numbers would be to let them catch him. They might very well do that anyway. They were still mounted, and would easily have overtaken him long ago, except that his own ambushes set over the past twenty kilometers had instilled some degree of caution in the survivors. These high plains made a good place for ambush, deceptively open-looking but cut by ravines and studded with windcarved hills and giant boulders that looked as if some god had scattered them playfully about.

By this time, having had twenty kilometers in which to think it over, the young man had no real doubt as to who his pursuers were. They had to be agents of the Blue Temple. Any merely military skirmish, he thought, would have been broken off long before this. Any ordinary patrol from the Dark King's army would have been content to return to camp and report a victory, or else proceed with whatever other business they were supposed to be about. They would not have continued to risk their skins in the pursuit of one survivor, not one as demonstrably dangerous as himself, and not through this dangerous terrain.

No, they knew who they were after. They knew what he had done, four years ago. And undoubtedly they were under contract to the Blue Temple to bring back his head.

The young man was finding time in his spare moments, such as they were, to wonder if they were also closing in on Ben, his friend and his companion of four years ago. Or if perhaps they had already found him. But he was not in a position right now to do anything for Ben.

The youth's flight had brought him to the edge of yet another ravine, this one cutting directly across his path. To the left of where the young man halted on the brink, the groove in the earth deepened rapidly, turning into a real canyon that wound its way off to the east, there presumably to join at some point a larger canyon that he had already caught sight of from time to time. In the other direction, to the young man's right, the ravine grew progressively shallower; if he intended to cross it, he should head that way.

From where he was standing now, the country on the other side of the ravine looked if anything flatter than the plain he had been crossing, which of course ought to give a greater advantage to the mounted men. If he did not cross, he would go down into the ravine and follow it along. He could see that as it deepened some shelter appeared along its bottom, provided by rough free-standing rock formations and by the winding walls themselves. If he went that way he would be going downhill, and for that reason might be able to go faster.

It was the need for water that made his choice a certainty. The big canyon ought to be no more than a few kilometers away at most, and very probably it had water at its bottom.

He was down in the bottom of the ravine, making good time along its deepening trench, before one of his over-the-shoulder looks afforded him another glimpse of the men who were coming after him. Three heads were gazing down over the rocky rim, some distance to his rear. It looked as if they had been expecting him to cross the ravine, not follow it, and had therefore angled their own course a little toward its shallower end. He had therefore gained a little distance on them. The question now was, how would they pursue from here? They might all follow him down into the ravine. Or one of them might follow him along the rim, ready to roll down rocks on him when a good chance came. Or, one man might cross completely, so they could follow him along both walls and down the middle too.

He had doubts that they were going to divide their small remaining force.

Time would tell. He was now committed, anyway, to following the ravine. Much depended on what sort of concealment he could find.

So far, things were looking as good as could be expected. What had been a fairly simple trench at the point where he entered it was rapidly widening and deepening into a complex, steep-sided canyon. Presently, coming to a place where the canyon bent sharply, the young man decided to set up another ambush, behind a convenient outcropping of rock. Lying motionless on stovelike rock, watching small lizards watch him through the vibrating air, he had to fight down the all-too-rational fear that this time his enemies had outguessed him, and a couple of them were really following him along on the high rims. At any moment now, the head of one of them ought to appear in his field of vision, just about *there*. From which vantage point it would of course be no trick at all to roll down a deadly barrage of rocks. If they were lucky his head would still be recognizable when they came down to collect it.

Enough of that.

It was a definite relief when the three men came into sight again, all trailing him directly along the bottom of the canyon. They were walking their mounts now, having to watch their footing carefully on the uneven rock. As their quarry had hoped, at this spot they had no more than half their visual attention to spare in looking out for ambush.

The young man waiting for them already had an arrow nocked. And now he started to draw it, slowly taking up the bowstring's tension. He realized that at the last instant, he'd have to raise himself up into full view to get the shot off properly.

The moment came and he lifted his upper body. The bow twanged in his hands, as if the arrow had made its own decision. The shot was good, but the man who was its target, as if warned by some subtle magic, begun to turn his body away just as the shot was made. The arrow missed. The enemy, alarmed, were all ducking for cover.

The marksman did not delay to see what they might be going to do next. Already he was on his feet and running, scrambling, on down the canyon. Only two arrows left in his quiver now, and still he was not absolutely sure that there were no more than three men in pursuit.

He hurdled a small boulder, and kept on running. At least he'd slowed his pursuers down again, made them move more cautiously. And that ought to let him gain a little distance.

And now, suddenly, unexpectedly, he had good luck in sight. As he rounded a new curve of the canyon there sprang into view ahead of him a view into the bigger cross-canyon that this one joined. Ahead he saw a narrow slice of swift gray water, with a luxuriant border of foliage, startlingly green, all framed in stark gray rock.

A little farther, and he would have not only water and concealment, but a choice of ways to turn, upstream or down. The young man urged his tired body into a faster run.

In his imagination he was already tasting the cold water. Then the tree-tall dragon emerged from the fringe of house-high ferns and other growth that marked the entrance to the bigger canyon. As the young man stumbled to a halt the beast was looking directly at him. Its massive jaw was working, but only lightly, tentatively, as if in this heat it might be reluctant to summon up the energy for a hard bite or even a full roar.

The young man was already so close to the dragon when he saw it that he could do nothing but freeze in his tracks. He knew that any attempt at a quick retreat would be virtually certain to bring on a full charge, and he would have no hope of outrunning that.

Nor did he move to unsling his bow. Even his best shot, placed perfectly into the eye, the only even semi-vulnerable target, might do no more than madden a dragon of the size of this one before him. His best hope of survival lay in standing still. If he could manage to do that, there was a bare chance that his earlier rapid movement would be forgotten and he would be ignored.

Then something happened that surprised the young man profoundly, so that now it was astonishment more than either terror or conscious effort that kept him standing like a statue.

The dragon's vast mouth, scarred round the lips with its own quondam flames, opened almost delicately, revealing yellowed and blackened teeth the size of human forearms. From that mouth emerged a voice, a kind of cavernous whisper. It was perfectly intelligible, though so soft that the motionless man could scarcely be sure that he was really hearing it.

"Put down your little knife," the dragon said to him. "I will not hurt you."

The man, who had thought he was remaining perfectly motionless, looked down at his right hand. Without realizing it he had drawn the dagger from his belt. Mechanically he put the useless weapon back into its sheath.

Even as the man did this, the dragon, perhaps three times his height as it stood tall on its hind legs, moved closer to him by one great stride. It reached out for him with one enormous forelimb, armed at the fingertips with what looked like pitchfork tines. But that frightening grip picked up the man so gently that he felt no harm. In a moment he had been lifted, tossed spinning in the air, and softly, safely, caught again. At this moment, that seemed to him certain to be the moment of his death, he felt curiously free from fear.

Death did not come, nor even pain. He was being tossed and mauled quite tenderly. Here he went up again, propelled with a grim playfulness that tended to jolt the breath out of his chest, but did him no real damage. In one of these revolving airborne jaunts, momentarily facing back up the side canyon, he got his clearest look yet at the whole small gang of his surviving human pursuers. They had been even closer behind him than he had thought, but now with every instant they were meters farther away. The three of them, two looking forward and away, one looking back in terror, were astride their riding beasts again, and never mind the chance that a mount might stumble here. All three in panic were galloping at full stretch back up the barren floor of the side canyon.

The dragon roared. The tossed man's own whirling motion whirled the riders away, out of his field of vision. He felt his flying body brush through a fringe of greenery. His landing was almost gentle, on shaded ground soft as a bed with moss and moisture. He lay there on his back, beneath great dancing fronds. This position afforded him a fine view of the dragon's scaly green back just as, roaring like an avalanche, it launched a charge after the three riders.

In another moment the riders were completely out of sight around the first curve of the side canyon. The dragon at once aborted its charge and ceased its noise. It turned, and with an undragonly air of calm purpose came striding back to where the man lay. He just lay there, watching its approach. The creature hadn't killed him yet, and anyway he could never have outrun it even had his lungs been full of breath.

Once more the huge dragon gently picked him up. It carried him carefully for a little distance, deeper into the heavy riverside growth of vegetation. Through the last layer of branches ahead the man could plainly see the swift narrow stream that threaded the canyon's floor.

The dragon spoke above the endless frantic murmur of the water. "They will never," it told the man in its sepulchral voice, "come back and follow a dragon into this thicket. Instead they will return to their masters and report that you are dead, that with their own eyes they saw you crushed and eaten." Saying this, the dragon again deposited the man on soft ground, this time very gently.

Then the dragon took a long step back. Its image in the man's eyes flickered, and for one moment he had the definite impression that the huge creature was wearing a broad leather belt around its scaly, bulging midsection. And there was a second, momentary impression, that from this belt there hung a scabbard, and that the scabbard held a sword.

The belt and Sword were no longer visible. Then they reappeared. The man blinked, he shook his head and rubbed his eyes and looked again. Some kind of enchantment was in operation. It had to be that. If it—

The Swordbelt, now unquestionably real, was now hanging looped from a great furry hand—it was undeniably a hand, and not a dragon's forefoot. The fur covering the hand, and covering the arm and body attached, was basically a silver gray, but it glowed remarkably with its own inner light. As the man watched, the glow shifted, flirting with all the colors of the rainbow.

The enormous hand let the belt drop.

Standing before the youth now was a furred beast on two legs, as tall and large as the dragon had been, but otherwise much transformed. Claws had been replaced by fingers, on hands of human shape. There were still great fangs, but they were bone-white now, and the head in which they were set no longer had anything in the least reptilian about it. Although the figure was standing like a man, the face was not human. It was—unique.

The great dark eyes observed with intelligence the man's reaction to the transformation.

The young man's first outward response was to get back to his feet, slowly and shakily. Then he walked slowly to where the belt and Sword were lying, on shaded moss. Bending over, he observed that the jet-black hilt of the Sword was marked with one small white symbol; but, though the man dropped to his knees to look more closely, he was unable to make out what that symbol was. His eyes for some reason had trouble getting it into clear focus. Then he reached out and put his fingers on that hilt, and with that touch he felt the power he had expected enter into him. Now he was able to see the symbol plainly. It was the simple outline of an observant human eye.

Turning his head to look up at the waiting giant, the young man said: "I am Mark, son of Jord." As he spoke he got to his feet, and as he stood up he drew the Sword. His right hand held up that bright magnificence of steel in a salute.

The giant's answer came in an inhumanly deep bass, quite different from the dragon's voice: "You are Mark of Arin-on-Aldan."

The youth regarded him steadily for a moment. Then he nodded. "That also," he agreed. Then, lowering the Sword, he added, "I have held Sightblinder here once before."

"You have held others of the Swords as well. I know something of you, Mark, though we have not met. I am Draffut, as you must have realized by now. The man called Nestor, who was your friend, was also mine."

Mark did not answer immediately. Now that he was holding the Sword of Stealth, some inward things about the being he was looking at had become apparent to him. Just how they were apparent was something he could not have explained had his life depended on it; but across Draffut's image in Mark's eyes some part of Draffut's history was now written, in symbols that Mark would not be able to see, much less interpret, once he put down the Sword again.

Mark said, "You are the same Draffut who is prayed to as the God of Healing. Who knew Ardneh the Blessed, as your living friend two thousand years ago . . . but still I will not call you a god. Lord of Beasts, as others name you, yes. For certainly you are that, and more." And Mark bowed low. "I thank you for my life."

"You are welcome . . . and Beastlord is a title that I can at least tolerate." Actually the huge being seemed to enjoy it to some extent. "With Sightblinder in your hand I am sure you can see I am no god. But I have just come from an assembly of them."

Mark was startled. "What?"

"I say that I have just come from an assembly of the gods," Draffut repeated patiently. "And I had Sightblinder in my own hand as I stood among them so each of them saw me as one of their own number . . . and I saw that in them which surprised me, as I stood there and listened to them argue."

"Argue . . . about what?"

"In part, about the Swords. As usual they were able to agree on nothing, which I count as good news for humanity. But I heard other news also, that was not good at all. The Dark King, Vilkata, has the Mindsword now. How and when he got it, I do not know."

For a long moment Mark stood silent. Then he muttered softly, "Ardneh's bones! The gods were saying that? Do you believe it?"

"I am glad," said Draffut, "that you understand that what the gods tell us is not always true. But in this case I fear it is the truth. Remember that I held the Sword of Stealth in my own hands then, and I looked at the speakers carefully as they were speaking. They were not telling deliberate lies; nor do I think they were mistaken."

"Then the human race is . . ." Mark made a gesture of futility.

". . . in trouble." Looking down at the blade he was still holding, he swung it lightly, testing how it felt in his grip. "If the question is not too impertinent, how did you come to have this? The last time I saw it, it was embedded in the body of a flying dragon."

"It may have fallen from the creature in flight. I found it in the Great Swamp."

"And—again if you do not mind my asking—how did you come to be spying on the gods?"

Draffut rested one of his enormous hands on a treetrunk that stood beside him. Mark thought he saw the bark change color around that grip. It even moved a little, he thought, achieving a different tempo in its life. Many were the marvelous tales told of Draffut. Now the Beastlord was speaking.

"Once I had this Sword in my hand, I decided that I would never have a better chance to do something that I had long thought about—to find the Emperor, and talk to him face to face."

"You did not go first to find the gods?"

"I had met gods before," Draffut ruminated. In a moment he went on. "The Emperor is not an easy man to locate. But I have some skill in discovering that which is hidden, and I found him. I had been for a long time curious."

Mark had sometimes been curious on the same subject, but only vaguely so. He had grown up accepting the commonly held ideas about the Emperor: a legendary trickster, perhaps invented and unreal. A practical joker, a propounder of riddles, a wearer of masks. A sometime seducer of brides and maidens, and the proverbial father of the poor and the unlucky. Only in recent years, as Mark began to meet people who knew more about the world than the name of the next village, had he come to understand that the Emperor might have a real importance.

Not that his curiosity on the subject had ever occupied much of his time or thought. Still, he now asked Draffut, "What is he like?"

"He is a man," said Draffut firmly, as if there had been some doubt of that. But, having made that point, the Beastlord paused, as if he were at a loss as to what else to say.

At last he went on. "John Ominor, the enemy of Ardneh, was called Emperor too." At this offhand recollection of the events of two thousand years past, Mark could feel his scalp creep faintly. Draffut continued. "And then, a little later, some called Prince Duncan, a good man, by that title."

Draffut fell silent. Mark waited briefly, then pursued the subject. "Has this man now called the Emperor some connection with the Swords? Can he be of any help to us against Vilkata?"

Draffut made a curious two-handed gesture, that in a lesser being would have suggested helplessness. When he let go of the treetrunk its surface at once reverted to ordinary bark. "I think that the Emperor could be an enormous help to us. But how to obtain his help . . . and as for the Swords, I can tell you this: I think that Sightblinder did not deceive him for a moment, though I had it in my hand as I approached."

"It did not deceive him?"

"I think he never saw me as anything but what I am." The Beastlord thought for a moment, then concluded: "Of course it was not my intention to deceive him, unless he should mean me harm—and I do not believe he did."

The speaker's intense, inhuman gaze held Mark's eyes. "It was the Emperor's suggestion that I take this Sword and use it to observe the councils of the gods. And he told me something else: that after I had heard the gods, I should bring Sightblinder on to you."

Mark experienced an inward chill, a feeling like that of sudden fear, but with a spark of exhilaration at the core of it. To him both emotions were equally inexplicable. "To me?" he echoed stupidly.

"To you. Even the Sword of Stealth cannot disguise me well enough to let me pass for human, or for any type of creature of merely human size. At a distance, perhaps. But I cannot enter the dwellings of humans secretly, to listen to their secret councils."

"You say you're able to spy on the gods, though. Isn't that even more important?"

The Beastlord was shaking his head. "The war that is coming is going to jar the world, as it has not been jarred since the time of Ardneh. And the war is going to be won or lost by human beings, though the gods will have a role to play."

"How do you know these things?"

Draffut said nothing.

"What can we do?" Mark asked simply.

"I am going, in my own shape, to try to influence the actions of the gods. As you may know, I am incapable of hurting humans, whatever happens. But against *them* I can fight when necessary. I have done as much before, and won."

Again Mark could feel his scalp creep. He swallowed and nodded. Apparently there was some basis of truth for those legends that told of Draffut's successful combat against the wargod Mars himself.

Draffut added: "I am going to leave the Sword with you."

Again to hear that brought Mark a swift surge of elation, an emotion in this case swiftly dampened by a few memories and a little calculation.

"Sir Andrew, whom I serve, has sent me on a mission to Princess Rimac—or to her General Rostov, if he proves easier to find. I am to tell them certain things . . . of course, I can take the Sword of Stealth along with me. And I suppose I could give it to them when I get there . . . but what did the Emperor have in mind for me to do with it? Do you trust him?" Questions were piling up in his mind faster than he could ask them.

"I have known and dealt with human beings for more than fifty thousand years," said Draffut, "and I trust him. Though he would not explain. He said only that he trusts you with the Sword."

Mark frowned. To be told of such mysterious trust by an apparently powerful figure was somehow more irritating than pleasing. "But why me? What does he know about me?"

"He knows of you," said Draffut immediately, in a tone of unhelpful certainty. "And now, I must be on my way." The giant turned away, then back again to say, "The Princess's land of Tasavalta lies to the east of here, along the coast, as I suppose you know. As to where Rostov and his army might be at the moment, you can probably guess as well as I."

"I'll take the Sword on with me, then, to the Princess." Mark raised his voice, calling after the Beastlord; Draffut, moving at a giant's walk considerably faster than a human run, was already growing distant. Mark sighed, swallowing more questions that were obviously not going to be answered now.

Splashing through the shallow river, Draffut turned once more, for just long enough to wave farewell. Then he began to climb the far wall of the great canyon. He climbed like a mountain goat, going right up the steep rocks. Mark thought he could see the rock itself undergoing temporary change, wherever Draffut touched it, starting to flow with the impulses of life.

Then Draffut was gone, up and over the canyon rim.

Left alone, Mark was suddenly exhausted. He stared for a long moment at the Sword left in his hands. Then he bent to enjoy, at last, the drink he needed from the river, whose name he did not know. He cooled himself with splashing. Then he stretched himself out on a shady moss, with Sightblinder tucked under his head, and slept securely. Any enemy coming upon him now would not see him, but instead some person or thing that they loved or feared, or at any rate would not harm. Of course there might come a sudden thunderstorm upstream, a canyon flood, and he'd be drowned; but he had lived much of his life with greater risks than that.

Mark did not awake until the sun had dropped behind the high stone western wall and it was nearly dark. Before the light had faded entirely, he managed to get a rabbit with one of his two remaining arrows. He even managed to retrieve the arrow undamaged, which convinced him that his luck was definitely improving. After cooking his rabbit on a small fire, he devoured most of it and slept again.

It was deep night when he awoke the second time, and he lay looking up at the stars and wondering about Draffut. The Beastlord was a magnificent and unique being, and it was small wonder that most folk thought he was a god. His life had begun so long ago that even Ardneh's struggle with the demon Orcus was recent by comparison. Mark, holding the Sword of Stealth while he looked at Draffut, had seen that that was true.

The Sword had allowed Mark to see something more wonderful still.

He had seen, very plainly, though only for a moment, and in a mode of seeing impossible to explain, that the Beastlord had begun his long life as a dog. A plain, four-footed dog, and nothing more.

That was a mystery beyond wondering about. Mark slept yet again, and awoke beneath turned stars. Just after his eyes opened he saw a brilliant meteor, as if some power had awakened him to witness it.

He lay awake for some time, pondering.

Who, after all, was the Emperor? And why and how did the Emperor come to be aware of Mark, son of Jord? Of course Mark's late father was himself a minor figure in legends, through his unwilling conscription by Vulcan to help in the forging of the Swords. And Mark had taken part in the celebrated raid of four years ago on the Blue Temple treasury. But why should either of those dubious claims to fame have caused the Emperor to send him a Sword?

All the stories agreed that the Emperor liked jokes.

Mark was no closer to an answer when he once more fell asleep.

In the morning he was up and moving early. Soon he found a side canyon that appeared passable, and led off to the east. He refilled his water bottle before leaving the river, then followed the side canyon's gradually ascending way. When, after some kilometers, the smaller canyon had shallowed enough to let him climb out of it easily, he did so. Now eastern mountains, blue as if with forests, were visible in the distance. Tasavalta, he thought. Or somewhere near to it.

He was a day closer to those mountains when he saw the mounted patrol. He was sure even at a considerable distance that these riders were the Dark King's soldiers. He had fought against such often enough to be able to distinguish them, he thought, by no more than the fold of a distant cloak, the shape of a spearhead carried high. The patrol was between him and his goal, and was heading almost directly toward him, but he did not think that they had seen him yet.

Mark had automatically taken concealment behind a bush at his first sight of the riders, and he continued watching them from hiding. He was planning, almost unthinkingly, how best to remain out of their sight as they passed, when he recalled what Sword it was that now swung at his side. He had used Sightblinder once before, and he trusted its powers fully.

Boldly he stood up. Hand on the hilt of the Sword, feeling a stirring of its power as he approached his enemies, he marched straight toward the oncoming riders. But before the patrol saw him they altered course slightly, perversely turned aside. Mark muttered oaths. If he had been helpless and endeavoring to hide, he thought, they would have stumbled over him without trying.

They were completely out of sight when he reached their trail, but he followed it into the setting sun, blue mountains now at his back. His messages for Princess Rimac were really routine. His soldier's instincts told him that here he might have an excellent target of opportunity.

An hour or so later he found the patrol, a dozen tough-looking men, gathered by their evening fire, which was large enough to show that they had no particular fear of night attack. The hilt of Sightblinder was vibrating smoothly in Mark's hand as he strode into the firelight to stand before them.

They looked up at him, and they all sat still. Hard warriors though they were, he could see that they were instantly afraid. Of what, he did not know, except that it was some image that they saw of him. Looking down at his own body, he saw, as he had known he would, himself unchanged.

Mark left it to them to break the silence. At last one who was probably their sergeant stood up, bowed, and asked him: "Lord, what will you have of us?"

"In what direction do your orders take you?" Mark's voice, to his own ears, sounded no different than before.

"Great Lord, we are bound for the encampment of the Dark King himself. There we are to report to our captain the results of our patrol."

Mark drew in a deep breath. "Then you will take me with you."

CHAPTER 4

Jord scratched delicately at his itching arm-stump, then grimaced at the unaccustomed soreness there. He rubbed at the place, more delicately still, with a rough fingertip. There was some kind of minor swelling, too.

Not that he was complaining. On the contrary. He was lying on a soft couch covered with fine fabric, in morning sunshine. Birds sang pleasantly nearby. Otherwise he was alone on the elegant rooftop terrace, largely a garden of plants and birds, fresh from last night's rain. The terrace covered most of the flat roof of the House of Courtenay. A plate of food, second helpings that Jord had been unable to finish, rested on a small table at his side. He was wearing a fine white nightshirt, of a material strange to him, that felt as what he supposed silk must feel. Well, he'd obviously and very fortunately reached wealthy and powerful friends, so none of these details were really all that surprising.

What did surprise him—what left him in fact almost numb with astonishment—was what had happened to his wounds.

The husky men, obviously some kind of servants, who had carried Jord up here to the terrace this morning had told him that he'd arrived here at the House of Courtenay only last night. Jord hadn't questioned the servants beyond that, becuase he wasn't sure how much they knew about their master's secret affairs, and about who he, Jord, really was, in terms of his business here.

Jord's last memories from last night were of being afraid of bleeding to death, and of trying to pound on the back door of his house, knowing that if he fainted before he got help he'd likely never to wake up. Well, he must have fainted. And he had certainly awakened, feeling almost healthy, ravenously hungry—and with his wounds well on the way to being completely healed.

The sun, rising higher now, would have begun to grow uncomfortably hot, but at just the proper angle a leafy bower now began to shade the couch. The noise of the city's streets was increasing, but it was comfortably far below. Jord had learned enough about cities to live in them when he had to, but he felt really at home only in a village or small town.

The trellises that shaded him, he noticed now, also screened him well from observation from any of the city's other tall buildings nearby. Meanwhile the interstices of latticework and leaves afforded him a pretty good outward view. Slate rooftops, like trees in a forest, stretched away to the uneven horizon formed by the city's formidable walls. Tashigang was built upon a series of hills, with the Corgo, here divided into several branches, flowing between some of them. The House of Courtenay, practically at riverside, was naturally in one of the lowest areas. The effect was that some of the sections of the wall, and the hilltop buildings in the distance, loomed to what seemed magical height, becoming towers out of some story of the Old World.

"Good morning." The words breaking in upon Jord's thoughts came in a female voice that he did not recognize. He quickly turned back from peering through the trellis. She was young and small, really tiny, and black-haired; dressed in white, she was obviously a lady. A young nursemaid and a small child were visible in the background, out of easy earshot along a graveled path that helped make the rooftop look like a country garden.

"Good morning, Lady." In the past ten years or so Jord had been often enough in cosmopolitan society that now he could feel more or less at ease with practically anyone. "The men who brought me up here told me that I was in the house of Mistress and Master Courtenay."

"So you are; I am the mistress of this house. Gods and demons, don't try to get up. And you are Jord."

Jord abandoned his token effort to rise. "I am Jord, as you say. And I thank you for your help."

"Is the food not to your taste?"

"It's very good. Only they gave me more than enough."

The lady was looking at him thoughtfully. There were chairs nearby but just now she evidently preferred standing. "So, the Princess Rimac sent you to us. As courier, to carry two Swords back to her."

Jord tried to flex his wounded knee a little, and grimaced at the sensation. "I seem to have failed in that task before it was fairly started." It was said matter-of-factly. "Well, I'll do as best I can with whatever comes next. It seems I'll need to heal before I can do much at all."

The lady continued to regard him. It appeared that for some reason she was strongly interested. Presently she said, "The servants—all except Denis, who's really more than that—think that you are simply a fellow merchant, who's had an encounter with thieves and is in need of help. Such things are all too common in our business."

"And in mine, unhappily. Again I thank you for saving my life." Jord paused. "But tell me something. Those who carried me up here said that I arrived only last night. But . . ." He gestured in perplexity toward his wounds.

"One of the blades that you were going to take to Princess Rimac is the Sword of Mercy."

"Ah." Jord, who had been supporting himself on his elbow, lay back flat again. "That explains it."

The lady had turned her head away. The little child was babbling somewhere on the other side of the roof. But someone else, a huge man of about the lady's own age, was approaching around a corner of trellis. Birds flew out of his way. "My husband," she explained.

Again Jord raised himself on his elbow. "Master Courtenay. Again my thanks."

The big man smiled, an expression that made his face much more pleasant in appearance. "And you are welcome here, as I expect my wife has already told you."

Jord's hosts seated themselves together on a bench nearby, and asked to hear from him about last night's attack that had left him wounded. Both appeared relieved when he told them he had dispatched his lone assailant before he had collapsed himself.

The master of the house informed him, "A few more of those who were following you arrived a little later. But we managed to dispose of them."

"Following me? More of them?" Jord swore earthily, calling upon various anatomical features of several gods and demons. "I feared as much, but I saw nothing of 'em." He groaned his worry.

Master Courtenay's thick hand made a gesture of dismissal; there was nothing to be done about that now. Then Courtenay glanced at his wife, a look transmitting some kind of signal, and she faced their guest with the air of someone opening a new subject.

"Jord," she asked him, "what village do you come from?"

It had been years since that question had surprised him. "Why, you're quite right, Ma'am, I'm a village man, not of the cities. And I've lived in a good many villages."

"But twenty years ago you were living in Arin-on-Aldan, weren't you? And still there, up to about—ten years ago?"

Jord nodded, and sighed faintly. "Like a lot of other villages, Lady, it's not there any longer. Or so I've heard. Your pardon, gentlefolk, but most who start asking me about my village have an earlier one than that in mind. Treefall, the place that Vulcan took me from to help him forge the Swords. Yes, I'm that Jord. Not too many Jords in the world with the right arm missing. Often I use another name, and I put most people off when they start asking where I'm from. But you of course I'll answer gladly. Whatever you'd like to know."

"We," said the huge, broad man, "are no more gentlefolk than you. The name I was born with is nothing like Courtenay, but simply Ben. That was in a poor village too, where one name was enough. Ben of Purkinje, some call me now. You've heard that somewhere, most likely, within the past four years. I'm the Ben who robbed the Blue Temple, and they're out to hunt me down. I'm pretty sure it was their people who followed you here last night."

"And my name is really Barbara," the lady said simply. She moved one small pale hand in a gesture that took in the luxury of the terrace, her whole house. "This is all Blue Temple wealth, or was. A single handful of their chests and baskets full of jewels."

"Ah." Jord nodded. "I've heard of the man called Ben who robbed those robbers. That story has gone far and wide—"

The lady interrupted him, eagerly. "Since you've heard the stories, you must have heard that a man named Mark was in on the raid with Ben, here." Here Barbara really smiled at Jord for the first time. "And you have a grown son named Mark, don't you?"

"Yes," said the man on the couch. "It's a common enough name. Why?"

"Because it is the same Mark," the lady said. "And we are his good friends, though we have not seen him for a long time. He took no wealth for himself from the Blue Temple. He's still out there soldiering, in Sir Andrew's army. And I'm afraid he thinks that you are dead."

"Ah," said their visitor again. He lay back flat, and closed his eyes, and clenched his fist. His lips moved, as if he might be praying. Then he opened his eyes and once more raised himself a little on his elbow.

He spoke to his hosts now almost as if he were their prisoner and they his judges. "Mark had to run away from the village, that day . . . is it ten years now? Almost. He had to take Townsaver and get away with it. Yes, he saw me struck down. He must have been thinking ever since that I'd been killed. He wasn't able to come back, nor we to find out where he was. So much happened, we had to leave the village. We never had any news . . ."

Jord's voice changed again, happily this time. "Tell me about him. Still soldiering, you say? What—?" He obviously had so many questions that he didn't know where to start.

Again someone was arriving on the rooftop. Jord heard a door close, and footsteps came crunching lightly along the graveled path. A pause, and a few words in what sounded like the nursemaid's voice. Then the footsteps resumed. This time there appeared a slender, dark-haired youth who was introduced to Jord as Denis, nicknamed the Quick. He greeted the older man courteously, and stood there rubbing his forearm through its long sleeve as if it might be sore.

Jord rubbed his arm-stump again. Already it seemed that the swelling, where the Sword had touched him, was a little greater.

Ben asked the new arrival, "What news from the streets?"

"None of the local people on our payroll noticed anything out of the way around midnight. It was a good night to be staying in."

"Denis," said Ben, "sit down." And he indicated an unoccupied chair nearby. Then he turned his head and called: "Kuan-yin? Take the baby downstairs, would you?"

Presently a door closed again. Four people looked solemnly at one another. Ben said to his young employee, "There's one thing we've not told you about Jord yet. His reason for coming here." And at that point Ben paused, seemingly not knowing quite what to say next.

His wife put in, "You must know by now, Denis, where our political sympathies lie."

"The same as mine, Mistress," the young man murmured. "Or, indeed, I wouldn't be here now." But he knew that was not true; he would have stayed anyway, to be near her. Might he have stayed to be near Kuan-yin? That was more problematical.

Ben said to him, "You also know that our guest here is a secret courier, if not the details. And, as you can see, someone else is now going to have to do the job. It can't wait, and Jord can't walk."

Jord was listening silently, frowning but not interfering.

"I can't leave town right now, nor can Barbara. It'll be a well-paid job, Denis, if you'll do it."

"Please do it," the lady of the house urged softly.

Denis could feel his cheeks changing color a little. He indicated agreement, almost violently. "I'll need no special pay, sir, mistress."

Jord was still frowning at Denis intently.

Barbara, correctly interpreting this look, hasted to reassure the older man. "Denis came to us a year and a half ago, on the recommendation of the White Temple. We had gone to them and told them we were looking for a likely, honest prospect to be trained to help us in our business. A lot of people recruit workers there, you know."

Jord asked Denis: "How long were you there, at the White Temple?"

"Three years, a little more."

"And why were you ready to leave?"

Denis shrugged. "They were good people, they saved my life. And it was good to serve Ardneh for a time. But then . . ." He made a gesture, of something fading, falling away.

"You must have been only half grown when you went to them."

"And half dead also. They picked me up out of the street after a gang fight, and brought me back to life. I owed them much, but I think I repaid their help in the time that I was there. We parted on good terms."

"Ah," said Jord. He appeared to have relaxed a little. He looked at Ben, and said, "Well sir, the matter's in your hands, not mine. Maybe sending this lad is the best choice now."

Ben cast a cautious look around, though he must have been already certain that they were secure against being overheard. Then he said quietly to Denis, "You'll be carrying two Swords."

"Two," said Denis, almost inaudibly, and he swallowed.

"Yes. They're both here in the house now, and I think we must get them away as quickly as we can, since we must assume now that the enemy are watching the house. The city authorities are disposed to be friendly to me; but of course the Lord Mayor is ultimately responsible to the Silver Queen as his overlord. And she, as we all know, is at least sometimes an ally of Vilkata, and of the Blue Temple too. So we cannot depend with any certainty on the Lord Mayor's friendship, or even on his looking the other way as we do certain things."

"I'll do my best. I'll get them there safely," said Denis suddenly. He looked at Barbara as he said it. And she, smiling her approval, could see a pulse beating suddenly in his lean throat.

"Good," said Ben. "You're not going to take them to the Princess, though. You'll take them in the other direction, to Sir Andrew. I fear someone's already waiting to waylay you on the road to Princess Rimac. After what happened here last night I can almost feel it."

Jord nodded agreement, slowly and reluctantly. "We must get the Swords into action somewhere. And Sir Andrew's a good man, by all I've heard about him."

"And your son serves him," Barbara reminded her guest.

"Aye, Lady. Still . . . I know that Rostov was counting on the Swords. Well, the responsibility's yours now. I failed early on."

A little later, Denis and Jord were both watching while Ben dug out from its hiding place the second of the two Blades that Denis was to carry. The three men were down on the ground floor of the house now, in a little-traveled area behind the main shop, inside a storeroom that was usually kept closed with a cheap lock. None of the miscellaneous junk readily visible inside the shed appeared to be worth anyone's effort to steal.

Ben was bent over, rummaging in a pile of what looked like scrap metal, consisting mainly of swordblades and knifeblades, bent or broken or rusted, in all cases long disused. Denis could not remember when he had seen any of the metalworkers actually using this stuff.

From near the bottom of this pile of the treacherously sharp edges, Ben carefully brought out, one at a time, two weapons—the blades of both were long, blackened, but unbent. And these two also had hilts, which a majority of the others did not.

Before wiping the two blades clean, Ben held them out to Jord. The older man put out his hand, hesitated, and then touched a hilt, all of its details invisible under carefully applied oil and grime.

"Doomgiver," said the only human who had ever handled all the Twelve. "There's not one of them I'd fail to recognize."

The remainder of the day and much of the night had passed before Denis was ready to depart. He was not allowed one thing he asked for: a private good-bye with young Kuan-yin, the nursemaid—Ben said they would tell her that Denis had had to leave suddenly on a business trip of an indefinite duration. That had happened before, and Kuan-yin should not be too surprised.

Denis got in some sleep also. There were instructions to be memorized, which took a little time. He dressed in white, in imitation of a lone Ardneh-pilgrim, for his departure. Ben gave him some money and some equipment. And Denis also had a private conference with Jord.

When it was time to go, in the hour before dawn, Denis was surprised not to be conducted to the back door, where Jord had come in. Instead the master, Old World light in hand, led Denis down a flight of stairs into a place that Denis knew as nothing more than a cramped basement storeroom. The place smelled thickly of damp. There were the scurrying sounds of rats, evidence that the creatures somehow defied the anti-rodent spells and poisons that were both periodically renewed.

The master used his strength to shift a heavy bale out of position. Then it turned out that one of the massive stones that made up this chamber's floor could be tilted up. Looking down into the cavity thus created, Denis was surprised when the light showed him a steady current of water of unknown depth, scarcely a meter below his feet. Even though he knew how close the house was to the river, he had never suspected.

The man who Denis was now beginning to know as Ben bent down and caught hold of a thin chain within the opening. Then he tugged until the white prow of a well-kept canoe appeared, bobbing with the water's motion.

"I loaded her up this afternoon," Ben grunted, "while you were sleeping. Your cargo's under this floorboard here. The two Swords, wrapped in a blanket so they won't rattle. And sheathed, of course. They may get wet but they won't rust." Ben spoke with the calm authority of experience. "There's a paddle, and I think everything else that you're going to need."

Denis had used canoes a time or two before, on trading missions for the House of Courtenay. He could manage the craft well enough. But it wasn't obvious yet how he was going to get this one back to the river.

Ben gave him directions. You had to crouch down low in the boat at first, to keep from banging your head on the low ceiling of the secret waterway. Then you moved the craft forward through the narrow channel by pushing and tugging on the stonework of the sides. There was not far to go, obviously, to reach the river.

There were no markings on the white canoe, Denis observed as he lowered himself carefully aboard. There was nothing in it, or on Denis, to connect the canoe or him to the House of Courtenay. Once Denis was on his way, the plan called for him to play the role of a simple Ardneh-pilgrim; his White Temple experience would fit him well for that. As a pilgrim, it was relatively unlikely that he'd be bothered by robbers. Everyone had some interest in the availability of medical care, and therefore in the wellbeing of those who could provide it. A second point was that Ardneh's people were less likely than most to be carrying much of value. In the third place, Ardneh was still a respected god, even if the better-educated insisted that he was dead, and a good many people still feared what might happen to them if they offended him.

Last farewells were brief. Only the mistress of the house, to Denis's surprise, appeared at the last moment, to press his hand at parting. The warmth of her fingers stayed with his, like something sealed by magic. He could not savor it now, nor get much of a last look at her, because it was time to crouch down in his canoe, to give his head the necessary clearance. Somebody released the chain for him, and he began to pull the light craft forward, working hand over hand against the rough wall of the narrow subterranean passage. He was propelling himself against the current, and away from the light. Darkness deepened to totality as the floorstone was lowered crunching back into place.

Denis pulled on. Presently a ghost of watery light reached his eyes from somewhere ahead. He managed to see a low stone lintel athwart his course, and to bend his head and body almost completely down under the gunwales to get himself beneath the barrier.

His craft had now emerged into a larger chamber, and one not quite as completely dark. There was room enough for Denis to sit up straight. In a moment he realized that there were timbers about him, rising out of the water in a broad framework, and supporting a flat wooden surface a meter or so above his head. Denis realized that he was now directly underneath a riverside dock.

There were gaps between pilings large enough for the canoe to pass, and leading to the lesser darkness of the open, foggy night. Emerging cautiously from underneath the dock, using his paddle freely now, Denis found himself afloat upon a familiar channel of the river. Right there was the house he had just left, all windows darkened as if everyone inside were fast asleep. If there was other traffic on the river tonight, he could not see or hear it in the fog. At this hour, he doubted that there was.

Denis turned the prow of his canoe upstream, and paddled steadily. The first gleams of daylight were already becoming visible in the eastern sky, and he wanted to reach the gate in the city walls at dawn, when it routinely opened for the day. There would probably be a little incoming traffic, produce barges and such, waiting outside; the watch ought to pass him out promptly, and most likely without paying much attention to him.

This channel of the river took him past familiar sights of the great city. Most people Denis had met said that it was the greatest in the world, but who knew the truth of that? Here on the right bank were the cloth-dyers, as usual starting their work early, already staining the water as they rinsed out the long banners of their product. And on the other bank, one of the fish-markets was opening.

Now through thinning fog there came into Denis's sight the city walls themselves, taller than all but a very few of the buildings they protected, and thick as houses for most of their height. They were built of almost indestructible stone, hardened, the stories had it, by the Old World magic called technology. They were supported at close intervals by formidable towers of the same material. Tested over five hundred years by scores of sieges (so it was said), threatened again and again by ingenious engines of attack, and various attempts at undermining, they still stood guard over a city that since they were built had never fallen to military attack. Kings and Queens and mighty generals had raged impotently outside those walls, and would-be conquerors had died there at the hands of their own rebellious troops. Siege, starvation, massacre, all had been threatened against Tashigang, but all in vain. The Corgo flowed year-round, and was always bountiful with fish. The prudent burghers and Lords Mayor of the city had a tradition of keeping good supplies of other food on hand, and—perhaps most important of all—of choosing their outside enemies and allies with the greatest care.

Now the gate that closed the waterway was going up, opening this channel of the river for passage. The river-gate was a portcullis built on a titanic scale, wrought by the same engineering genius as the city walls. Its movement was assisted by great counterweights that rode on iron chains, supported by pulleys built into the guard-towers of the wall. The raising made a familiar city-morning noise, and took some little time.

There was another huge iron chain spanning the channel underwater, as extra proof against the passage of any sizeable hostile vessel. But

Denis did not have to wait for that to be lowered into the bottom mud. With a wave of his hand that was casually answered by the watch, he headed out, plying his paddle energetically.

He went on up the river, now and again looking back. With the morning mist still mounting, the very towers of Tashigang seemed to be melting into it, like some fabric of enchantment.

CHAPTER 5

In Mark's ears was the endless sound of hard, hooflike footpads beating the earth, of moving animals and men. Day after day in the sun and dust, night after night by firelight, there was not much in the way of human speech. He and the patrol of the Dark King's troops escorting him entered and traversed lands heavily scarred by war and occupation, a region of burned-out villages and wasted fields. With each succeeding day the devastation appeared more recent, and Mark decided that the army that had caused it could no longer be far away. The only human inhabitants of this region clearly visible were the dead, those who had been impaled or hanged for acts of resistance perhaps, or perhaps only on a whim, for a conqueror's sport.

At first Mark had known faint doubts about where he was being taken. These now disappeared. It was his experience that all armies on the march caused destruction, but only the Dark King's forces moved with this kind of relentless savagery. A few of the human victims on display wore clothing that had once been white; evidently not even Ardneh's people were being spared by Vilkata now.

Even animal life was scarce, except for the omnipresent scavenger birds and reptiles. As the patrol passed, these sometimes rose, hooting or cawing, from some hideous feast near roadside. Once a live and healthy-looking goat inspected the men through a gap in a hedge as they went cantering by.

Mark's escort had never questioned his right to give them orders, and they got on briskly with the business of obeying the one real order he had so far issued. Familiar as he was with armies and with war, he considered these to be well-disciplined and incredibly tough-looking troops. They spoke the common language with an accent that Mark found unfamiliar, and they wore Vilkata's black and gold only in the form of small tokens pinned to their hats or vests of curly fur.

One more thing about these men was soon just as apparent as their discipline and toughness: they were for some reason mightily afraid of Mark. In what form they perceived him he could only guess, but whatever it was induced in them quiet terror and scrupulous obedience.

In Mark's immediate presence the men rarely spoke at all, even to each other, but when they were at some distance he saw them talking and gesturing freely among themselves. Occasionally when they thought he was not watching one of them would make a sign in his direction, that Mark interpreted as some kind of charm to ward off danger. Gradually he decided that they must see him as some powerful and dangerous wizard they knew to be in Vilkata's service.

Upon recovering from their first surprise at his approach, they had been quick to offer him food and drink, and his pick of their riding beasts for his own use—they had been traveling with a couple of spare mounts. Each night when they halted, Mark built his own small fire, a little apart from theirs. He had soon decided that they would feel somewhat easier that way, and in truth he felt easier himself.

The country grew higher, and the nights, under a Moon waxing toward full, grew chill. Using the blanket that had been rolled up behind the saddle of his borrowed mount, Mark slept in reasonable comfort. He slept with one hand always on the hilt of Sightblinder, though he felt confident that the mere presence of the Sword in his possession would be enough to maintain his magical disguise. He was vaguely reassured to see that the patrol always posted sentries at night, in a professional manner.

The journey proceeded swiftly. On the afternoon of the fourth day after Mark had joined them, the patrol rode into sight of Vilkata's main encampment.

As the riders topped a small, barren rise of land, the huge bivouac came into view a kilometer ahead, on slightly lower ground. The sprawling camp was constructed around what looked to Mark like a large parade ground of scraped and flattened earth. The camp appeared to be laid out in good order, but it was not surrounded by a palisade or any other defensive works. Rather it sprawled arrogantly exposed, as if on the assumption that no power on earth was going to dare attack it. Mark considered gloomily that the assumption was probably correct.

As he and his escort rode nearer to the camp, he realized that it probably contained not only more human troops than he had ever seen in one place before, but a greater variety of them as well, housed in a wild assortment of tents and other temporary shelters. The outer pickets of the camp, men and women patrolling with leashed warbeasts, made no attempt to challenge Mark and his escort as they approached. And Mark observed that when the human sentries were close enough to get a good look at him, they, like his escort originally, shrank back perceptibly.

He had to wonder again: Who, or what, did they see? And who or what would Vilkata see when Mark entered his presence, if Mark succeeded in pushing matters that far? It was hard for Mark to imagine that there could be anyone the Dark King either feared or loved.

Only now, at last, did Mark clearly consider that he might be headed for a personal encounter with the Dark King. He had first approached the patrol with no more than a vague idea of eavesdropping on the enemy's secret councils, just as Draffut said he had moved unrecognized among the gods. Now for the first time Mark saw that it might be his duty to accomplish something more than that. The thought was vastly intriguing and at the same time deeply frightening, and he did not try now to think it through to any definite conclusion.

He rode on, still surrounded by his escort, until they were somewhere deep inside the vast encampment. There the patrol halted, and its members began an animated discussion among themselves, in some dialect that Mark could not really follow. Judging that the debate might be on how to separate themselves from him as safely and properly as possible, he took the matter into his own hands by dismounting, and then dismissing both his steed and his escort with what he hoped looked like an arrogantly confident wave of his hand.

Turning his back on the patrol then, Mark stalked away on foot, heading for a tall flagpole that was visible above the nearby tents. The pole supported a long banner of black and gold, hanging limp now in the windless air. Mark hoped and expected that this flag marked the location of some central headquarters. As he walked toward it he saw the heads of soldiers and camp-followers turn, their attention following him as he passed; and he saw too that some people either speeded up or slowed their own progress, in order not to cross his path too closely.

Now he had to detour around some warbeasts' pens, the smell and the mewing of the great catlike creatures coming out of them in waves. Now he was in sight of one corner of the vast parade ground. From the farther reaches of its expanse, somewhere out of Mark's sight, there sounded the chant and drumbeat of some hapless infantry unit condemned to drilling in the heat. Looking across the nearest corner of the field, he could now see the tall flagpole at full length. There was a wooden reviewing stand beside the flagpole, and behind the stand a magnificent pavilion. This was a tent larger than most houses, of black and gold cloth.

Mark stalked directly toward the great pavilion, considering that it had to be the Dark King's headquarters. His right hand, riding on the hilt of sheathed Sightblinder, could feel a new hum of power in the Sword; perhaps there were guardian spells here that had to be overcome.

The front of the reviewing stand displayed another copy of Vilkata's flag, this one stretched out to reveal the design, a skull of gold upon a field of black. The eyesockets of the skull stared forth sightlessly, twin windows into night.

Again Mark had to make a small detour, round more low cages that he at first thought held more warbeasts. But the wood-slatted cages looked too small for that. All but one of them were empty, and that one held . . . the naked body confined inside was human.

Abruptly something shimmered in the air above Mark's head, broadcasting torment. As Mark moved instinctively to step aside, this presence moved with him. Only at this moment did he realize that it was sentient.

And only a moment after that did he realize that he was being confronted by a demon.

And the demon was addressing him, demanding something of him, though not in human speech. Whether its communication was meant for his ears or to enter his mind directly he could not tell. Nor could he grasp more than fragments of the meaning. It was basically a challenge: *Why was he here? Why was he here now, when he ought to be somewhere else? Why was he as he was?*

He realized with a shock that he was going to have to answer it, to offer something analogous to a password before it would allow him to pass this point, or even release him. What image it saw when it looked at him evidently did not matter. Here, approaching the pavilion, everyone must be stopped. And he doubted there was anything, or anyone, that this demon feared or loved.

Mark could no more answer the demonic voice intelligently, in its own terms, than he could have held converse with a bee. He knew fear, exploding into terror. He ought to have foreseen that here there might be such formidable guardians, here at the heart of Vilkata's power and control; the Dark King himself was most likely in that huge tent ahead. Here, perhaps, they had even been able to plan defenses against the Sword of Stealth. Here its powers were not going to be enough—

Only moments had passed since the demon had first challenged him, but already Mark could sense the creature's growing suspicion. Now it sent an even more urgent interrogation crashing against Mark's mind. Now it was probing him, searching for evidence of the signs and keys of magic that he did not possess. In a moment it would be certain that he was some imposter, not a wizard after all.

In his desperation Mark grasped at a certain memory, four years old but still vivid. It was the recollection of his only previous close encounter with a demon, in the depths of the buried treasure-vaults of the Blue Temple. Now, in desperate imitation of what another had done then, Mark gasped out a command into the shimmering air:

"In the Emperor's name, depart and let me pass!"

There was a momentary howling in the air. Simultaneously there came a tornado-blast of wind, lasting only for an instant. Mark caught a last shred of communication from the thing that challenged him—it was outraged, it had definitely identified him as an imposter. But that did not matter. The demon could do nothing about it, for in the next instant it was gone, gone instantaneously, as if yanked away on invisible steel cables that extended to infinity.

Now the air above Mark was quiet and clear, but moments passed before his senses, jarred by the encounter, returned to normal. He realized that he had stumbled and almost fallen, and that his body was bent over, hands halfway outstretched in front of him, as if to avoid searing heat or ward off dreadful danger. It had been a very near thing indeed.

Hastily he drew himself erect, looking around carefully. Wherever the demon had gone, there was no sign it was coming back. A few people were standing, idly or in conversation, near the front of the pavilion, and he supposed that at least some of them must have noticed

something of the challenge and his response. But all of them, as far as
Mark could tell, were going on about their business as if nothing at all
out of the ordinary had taken place. Maybe, he thought, that was the
necessary attitude here, in what must be a constant center of intrigue.

Mark walked on. Having now passed the prison cages and the reviewing stand, he was within a few paces of the huge pavilion, by all indications the tent of Vilkata himself. Having come this far, Mark swore that
he was going forward. Two human sentries flanked the central doorway
of the huge tent, but to his relief these only offered him deep bows as he
approached. Without responding he passed between them, and into a
shaded entry.

Cool perfumed air, doubtless provided by some means of magic,
wafted about him. Mark paused, letting his eyes adjust to the relative
gloom, and he had a moment in which to wonder: How could any spell
as simple as the one he had just used, recited by a mundane non-
magician like himself, repel even the weakest demon? And what a repulsion! Repulsion was the wrong word. It had been instant banish-
ment, as if by catapult.

His puzzlement was not new; essentially the same question had been
nagging at him off and on for the past four years, ever since a similar
experience in the Blue Temple treasure vaults. Mark had recounted that
event to several trusted magicians in the meantime, and none had given
him a satisfactory explanation, though they had all found the occur-
rence extremely interesting.

He was not going to have time to ponder the matter now.

From just inside the inner doorway of the tent he could hear voices,
five or six of them perhaps, men's and women's mixed, chanting softly
what Mark took to be words of magic. The voices came wafting out
with the cool air and the perfume, some kind of incense burning. There
was another odor mingled with it now, one not intrinsically unpleasant;
but when Mark thought that he recognized it, the strength seemed to
drain from his arms and legs, making it momentarily impossible to go
on. He thought that he could recognize the smell of burning human
flesh.

Ardneh be with me, Mark prayed mechanically, and wished even
more ardently that living, solid Draffut could be with him also. Then he
put back a heavy curtain with his hand, and made himself walk forward
into the next chamber of the tent. A moment later he wished that he
had not.

The human body fastened to the stone altar-table was not dead, for it still moved within the limits of its bonds, but it had somehow been deprived of the power to cry out. Yesterday it had probably been young; whether it had then been male or female was no longer easy to determine, in the dim light of the smoking lamp that hung above the altar. Around the altar half a dozen magicians of both sexes were gathered, various implements of torture in their hands. There was a lot of blood, most of it neatly confined to the altar itself, where carved troughs and channels drained it away. Near the altar stood a small brazier, with the insulated handles of more torture-tools protruding from the glow of coals.

Mark had seen bad things before, in dungeons and in war; still he had to wait for a moment after entering. He closed his eyes, gripping tightly the hilt of Sightblinder, cursing the Sword for what it had let him see when he looked at the victim. He knew a powerful urge to draw the Sword, and slaughter these villains where they stood. But a second thought assured him that it would not be easy to accomplish that. The air in here was thick with familiars and other powers, so thick that even a mundane could hardly fail to be aware of them. Those powers might now be deceived about Mark, but let him draw a sword and they would take note, and he thought they would not permit their human masters to be slaughtered.

And there was something more important, he was beginning to realize, that he must accomplish here before he died.

The half dozen who were gathered around the altar-table, garbed and hooded in various combinations of gold and black, paid little attention to Mark when he entered. One of their number did glance in the newcomer's direction, taking a moment from the chant between the great slow pulse-beats of its hideous magic in the air.

"Thought you were off somewhere else," a man's voice casually remarked.

"Not just now," said Mark. He exerted a great effort trying to make his own voice equally casual. Whatever the other heard from him was evidently acceptable, for the man with a brief smile under his hood turned back to his foul task.

Mark stood waiting, praying mechanically for a sign from somewhere as to what he ought to do next. He did not want to retreat, and he hesitated to move on into the interior doorway he saw at the other side of the torture chamber. And he continued to wish devoutly that he could somehow get out of sight of what was on this table.

Presently one of the women in the group turned her face toward him. She asked, in a sharp, businesslike voice: "This area is secure?"

Not knowing what else to do, Mark answered affirmatively, with a grave inclination of his head.

The woman frowned at him lightly. "I thought I had detected some possible intrusion, very well masked . . . but you are the expert there. And I thought also that our next subject, the one still in the cage outside, possesses some peculiar protection. But we shall see when we have her in here." Briskly the woman turned back to her work.

Mark, with only a general idea of what she must be talking about, nodded again. And again his answer appeared to be acceptable. Whoever they took him for, none of these people seemed to think it especially odd that he should continue to stand there, watching them or looking away. He continued standing, waiting for he knew not what.

Quite soon another one of the men turned away from the altar, as if his portion of the bloody ritual were now complete. This man left the group and approached a table near Mark, there to deposit his small bloodstained knife in a black bowl of some liquid that splashed musically when the small implement went in.

Then, standing very near Mark and speaking in a low voice, this man asked him, "Come, tell me—why did he really summon you back here?" When there was no immediate reply, the man added, in a voice suddenly filled with injured pride, "All right then, be silent, as befits your office. Only don't expect those you keep in the dark now to be eager to help you later, when—"

The man broke off abruptly at that point. It was as if he had been warned of something, by some signal that Mark totally failed to perceive. The man turned his face away from Mark, and toward the doorway that Mark had supposed must lead into the inner chambers of the pavilion.

Meanwhile one of those still at the altar warned, in a low voice: "The Master comes." All present—except of course the sacrificial victim—fell to their knees, Mark moving a beat behind the rest.

It was Vilkata himself who emerged a moment later through the curtains of sable black. Mark had never laid eyes on the Dark King before, but still he could not doubt for an instant who this was.

The first impression was of angular height, of a man taller than Mark himself, robed in a simple cloth of black and gold. The hood of the garment was pulled back, leaving the wearer's head bare except for a simple golden circlet, binding back long ringlets of white hair. The exposed face and hands of the Dark King were very pale, suggesting that the whiteness of the hair and of the curled beard resulted from some type of albinism rather than from age.

The second impression Mark received was that some of the more horrible tales might be true, for the Dark King was actually, physically blind. Under the golden circlet, the long-lashed lids sagged over what must be empty sockets, spots of softness in a face otherwise all harsh masculine angles. According to the worst of the stories, this man in his youth had put out his own eyes, as part of some dreadful ritual necessary to overpower his enemies' magic and gain some horrible revenge.

Looped around Vilkata's lean waist was a swordbelt of black and gold, and in the dependent sheath there rode a Sword. Even in the dim light Mark could not fail to recognize that plain black hilt, so like the one he was now clasping hard in his own sweaty fist. And Mark, his own vision augmented in some ways by Sightblinder, could not miss the small stylized white symbol of a banner that marked Vilkata's Sword.

It was of course the Mindsword, just as Draffut had warned. Mark was struck with the instant conviction that what he had to do now was to get the Mindsword out of Vilkata's possession, prevent his using it to seize the world. The decision needed no pondering, no consideration of consequences.

Vilkata's blind face turned from left to right and back again, as if he might be somehow scrutinizing his assembled magicians carefully. Mark could read no particular expression on the harsh countenance of the Dark King. Then one large, pale hand extended itself from inside Vilkata's robe, making a lifting gesture, a signal to his counselors that they might stand. Would the King have known, Mark wondered, if they had all been standing instead of kneeling as he entered? But then there would not have been this faint robe-rustle sound of rising.

Mark held his breath as the blind face turned once more toward him, and this time stayed turned in his direction. Behind those eyelashes, white and grotesquely long, the pale collapsed lids were as magnetic as any stare. Something about them was perversely beautiful.

There was a tiny almost inaudible humming, a miniature disturbance in the air near the Dark King's head. Some demonic or familiar power was communicating with him—so Mark perceived, watching with Sightblinder's handle in the grip of his hand.

The Dark King seemed about to speak, but hesitated, as if he were magically aware that something was wrong, that matters here in this innermost seat of his power were not as they should be. Still the blind face confronted Mark, and Vilkata whispered a soft question into the air. A humming answer came. Mark could feel the power of the sheathed Sword at his own side suddenly thrum more strongly.

When Vilkata did speak aloud, Mark was surprised at the sound of his voice, smooth, deep, and pleasant.

"Burslem, I am surprised to see you here. I take it that the task I sent you on has been completed?"

Burslem. To Mark the name meant nothing. "It is indeed, my lord. My head on it."

"Indeed, as you say . . . now all of you, finish quickly what you are about in here. I want you all at the conference table as quickly as possible. The generals are waiting." And Vilkata and his half-visible familiar vanished, behind a sable swirl of draperies.

One wizard, a junior member of the group perhaps, stayed behind briefly to settle whatever still remained to be settled upon their ghastly altar. The others, Mark among them, filed through the doorway where Vilkata had disappeared. They passed through the next chamber, which was filled with what looked like draped furniture, and entered the next beyond that.

The room was larger, and somewhat better lighted. It contained a conference table large enough to accommodate in its surrounding chairs all of the magicians and an approximately equal number of military-looking men and women, who as Vilkata had said were already seated and waiting. The military people wore symbolic scraps of armor, though as Mark noted none of them were visibly armed there in the presence of their King. Vilkata himself, predictably, was seated in a larger chair than the others, at one end of the table. Behind him a map on a large scale, supported on wooden poles, bore many symbols, indicating among other things what appeared to be the positions of several armies. There was Tashigang, near the center of the map, there the winding Corgo making its way northward to the sea. There was the Great Swamp. . . .

Mark was making a hasty effort to memorize the types and positions of the symbols on the map, but the distractions at the moment were overpowering. The magicians were taking their places at the table, and fortunately there seemed to be little ceremony about it. But again Mark had to delay marginally, to be able to make a guess as to what place Burslem ought to take. He was not sure whether to be relieved or not, when he found himself pulling out the last vacant chair, some distance down the table from the King.

As the faint noise of people seated themselves died out, a silence hold upon the room, and stretched. As Vilkata sat on his raised chair, the hilt of the Mindsword at his side was plainly visible to the rest of the assembly. And the humming presence above the King's head came and went, all but imperceptibly to the others in the room.

"I see," the Dark King said at last—and if there was irony in those two words, Mark thought that it was subtly measured—"that none of you are able to tear your eyes away from my new toy here at my side. Doubtless you are wondering where I got it, and how I managed to do so without your help. Well, I'll give you all a close look at it presently. But first there's a report or two I want to hear."

Again the blind face turned back and forth, as if Vilkata were seeking to make sure of something. A faint frown creased the white brow, otherwise youthfully unlined. "Burslem," the Dark King added in his pleasant voice, "I want to hear your report in private, a little later. After you have seen my Sword."

"As you will, Lord," Mark said clearly. In his own ears, his voice still sounded like his own. The others all heard it without noticing anything amiss. But whatever Vilkata heard did not erase his faint suspicious frown.

Now some of the magicians and generals, following an order of precedence that Mark could not identify, began to make reports to the King and his council, each speaker in turn standing up at his or her own place at the table. The unsuspected spy was able to listen, half-comprehending, to lists of military units, to descriptions of problems in levying troops and gathering supplies, to unexpected difficulties with the constructions of a road that would be needed later to facilitate the unexplained movement of some army. It seemed to Mark that invaluable facts, information vital for Sir Andrew and his allies, were marching at a fast pace into his ears and out again. Listen! he demanded of himself in silent anguish. Absorb this, retain it! Yet it seemed that he could not. Then there came a relieving thought. When he saw Dame Yoldi again, she would be able to help him recapture anything that, he heard now; he had seen her do as much for others in the past.

If he ever got to see Dame Yoldi's beautiful face again. If he ever managed to leave this camp alive.

There was the monstrous Sword at Vilkata's side, and here was Vilkata himself, seated within what looked like easy striking distance of Mark's own Sword, or of his bow—Mark still had his two arrows left. More important by far, thought Mark, than any mere information that could be collected, would be to deprive the Dark King of the Mindsword, and, if possible, of his own evil life as well.

Mark knew of no way by which the Mindsword, or any of its eleven peers, could be destroyed. The only way he could deprive the enemy of its use would be by capturing it himself, and getting away with it. There was a chance, he told himself, maybe even a good chance, that Sightblinder could disguise and preserve him against demonic and human fury while he did so. Against demons he had a new hope now, hope in the inexplicable power of a few simple words.

It seemed likely that he would have to kill Vilkata to get the Mindsword from him. And that would be a good deed in itself. Yes, he would kill Vilkata . . . if he could. If the evil magicians in the outer chamber had had magical defenses, how much stronger, if less obvious, would be those of the Dark King himself?

To strike at Vilkata successfully, he would have to choose his moment with great care. Bound into his own thoughts by calculation and fear, Mark lost touch with the discussion that was going on around the table. Presently, with a small shock, he realized that the Dark King was now addressing his assembled aides, and had been speaking for some time. All of them—including Mark himself, half consciously—were answering from time to time with nods and murmurs of agreement. Probably Mark had been roused to full attention by the fact that the voice of the Dark King was now rising to an oratorical conclusion:

"—our plan is war, and our plan goes forward rapidly!"

There was general applause, immediate and loud. The first to respond in a more particular way was a bluff, hearty-looking military man, who wore a scrap or two of armor to indicate his status. This man leaped to his feet with apparently spontaneous enthusiasm, and with a kind of innocence in his face.

There was a tone of hearty virtue in his voice as well. "Who are we going to hit first, sir?"

Vilkata paused before he turned his blind face toward the questioner, as if perhaps the Dark King had found the question none too intelligent. "We are going to hit Yambu. She is the strongest—next to me—and therefore the most dangerous. Besides, I have just received disturbing news about her . . . but of that I will speak a little later."

Here Vilkata paused again. The almost inaudible humming, almost invisible vibration, continued to perturb the air above his head. "I see that most of you are still unable to keep from staring at my plaything here," he said, and put his pale right hand on his Sword's hilt. "Very well. Because I want you, later, to be able to concentrate upon our planning—I will demonstrate it *now!"*

The last word burst in a great shout from the Dark King's throat, and in the same moment he sprang to his feet. And Mark thought that the Mindsword itself, as the King drew and brandished it aloft, made a faint roaring noise, like that of many human voices cheering at a distance.

Even here, in the dim smoky interior of this tent, the flourished steel flashed gloriously, seeming to stab at the eyes with light. Mark had never seen, nor ever imagined that he would see, anything so beautiful. Like all the others round the table he found himself on his feet, and he was only dimly aware of his chair toppling over behind him.

At that moment, Sightblinder, with Mark's hand on its hilt, came leaping by itself halfway out of its own sheath, as if it were springing to accept the challenge of its peer.

But Mark could not tear his eyes free of the Mindsword. The terrible force of it was tugging at him. Wordlessly it demanded that he throw his own Sword down at Vilkata's feet, and himself after it, pledging eternal loyalty to the Dark King. And already, only half realizing what he did, Mark had gone down on his knees again, amid a small crowd of wizards who were doing the same thing.

The cheering roar of the Mindsword drowned all other sound, the glitter of its blade filled every eye.

Mark wondered why he had come here to this camp, why he had entered this tent . . . but whatever the reason, it hardly mattered now. All that mattered now was that instantly, instantly, he should begin a new lifetime of service to Vilkata. That flashing steel thing told him that he must, that glorious Blade that was the most beautiful thing under the heavens or in them. Nothing that it told him could possibly be wrong.

He stood somehow in danger, danger of being left behind, left out, if he did not swear his fealty at once, as the other kneeling shapes around him were doing now. Voices that in the outer chamber had sounded cynical were now hoarse with fervor, gabbling the most extravagant oaths. What was it that made him, Mark, delay? Something must be wrong with him, something about him must be unforgivably different.

He was groveling on the floor with the others, mouthing words along with them, but he knew his oaths meant nothing, they were not sincere. Why was he hesitating? How could he? He must, at once, consecrate himself body and soul to the Dark King. How glorious it would be to fight and conquer in that name! And how perfect would be a death, any form of death, attained in such a cause! There was nothing that a man need fear, as long as that glittering Sword led him. Or, there was but one thing fearful only—the chance that such a glorious opportunity might somehow be missed—that death might come in some merely ordinary way, and so be wasted.

So why, then, did he delay?

Mark's mind swayed under the Mindsword's power, but did not yield to it entirely. A stubborn core of resistance remained in place. He was not carried into action, beyond the meaningless imitative oaths and grovelings. Part of his mind continued to understand that he must resist. His right hand still clutched Sightblinder's hilt, and he thought that he still drew power from it. Inside the core of his mind that was still sane, he could only hope and trust in the existence of some power that might save him—even though he could no longer remember clearly just why he needed saving.

Cowering on his knees like those around him, Mark watched the Mindsword flash on high. From that beautiful arc emanated a droning roar, as of many voices raised in praise, voices that never stopped to breathe. Against the background of that sound, the voice of the Dark King was rising and falling theatrically, like that of some spellcaster in a play. Vilkata was reciting and detailing now all of the malignant and detestable qualities that marked the Queen of Yambu as a creature of special evil. One accusation in particular, that the voice emphasized, caught at and inflamed Mark's imagination, stinging him with the unimaginable foulness that it represented. Even among her other shameless deeds this one stood out: Not only did she possess the Sword called Soulcutter, but she intended to begin to use it soon. And to use it against the blessed Dark King, the savior of the world!

In spite of himself, Mark groaned in rage. He found himself imagining his hands locked on the throat of the Silver Queen, and strangling her. Other groaning, outraged voices joined around him, until the pavilion sounded like the torture chamber that it truly was.

And when the Dark King paused, the voices rose up even louder, crying aloud their heartfelt protest against Yambu. That she should so plot to warp their minds with Soulcutter's foul magic, that she should even for a moment contemplate such a thing, was a sin crying to the gods for her to be wiped out, expunged from the Earth's face, at once and without mercy!

Vilkata had lowered the blade a little now, holding the hilt no higher than his shoulders. But still the steel kept twinkling above them like a star. As far as Mark could tell, there was no resistance at all in any of the audience except himself. And how much was left in him, he did not know.

One of the wizards, he who had whispered conspiratorially to Mark in the outer chamber, now abandoned himself entirely. With a great frenzied howl he sprang up on the conference table, his arms outstretched to gather that glorious Blade to his own bosom. But the Dark King withdrew the weapon out of the wizard's reach, and with a lunge the magician fell on his face among the tipped and scattered chairs.

It seemed a signal for general pandemonium. Men and women rolled back and forth on the tent floor. They scrambled to stand on furniture, they danced and sang in maddened cacophony. Cries and grunts came jolting out of them, until the council chamber looked and sounded like a small battlefield.

The sounds of a more familiar danger helped Mark regain some small additional measure of control. He huddled almost motionless on the floor, trying to remember where he was, and who he had been before that Sword appeared.

Now the Dark King flourished his Sword above his head in a new gesture, like a field commander's signal to advance. And now Vilkata, guided by the humming presence that hovered always near him, was moving in long, sure strides around the conference table, passing through the litter of chairs and humanity that almost filled the room. He was heading for the front entrance of the pavilion.

Mark, caught up in the rush of people following the King, was jostled against the torture-altar when passing through the outer chamber. He felt something sticky on his hand, gazed at it dumbly and saw blood. It was frightening, but he could not understand. . . .

Exiting from the pavilion's front door, Vilkata strode forth into the sun, whose light exploded from the Sword he carried into a thousand piercing lances. His little mob of followers, including Mark, accompanied him out into the glare, leaping and chanting with a look of ecstasy. At once their numbers were augmented by those who happened to be near when the Dark King emerged with glory in his hands. The air above the swelling crowd was wavering, as if with the heat of a great fire; familiar powers and small demons were moving in concert with their magician masters, and sharing their excitement, whether in joy or fear Mark could not tell.

The Mindsword swung in Vilkata's grip. It shattered the bright sun into lightning, whose bolts struck left and right. The hundreds who were near, and then the thousands only a little farther off, gaped in surprise, and then were caught up in the savage enthusiasm.

Vilkata marched on without hesitation, heading for the reviewing stand. The crowd surging around him was growing explosively, and already seemed to number in the thousands. Men and women, caught by curiosity, by the attraction of the growing crowd itself, came running through the camp from all directions, to be captured at close range by the sight of the blinding Blade. Again and again, through the waves of merely human cheering, Mark thought that he could hear the surf like roar of the Sword itself, grown louder in proportion to the crowd it led.

Now, somewhere out on the parade ground, beyond the cages for prisoners and beasts, an enormous drum began to bang. The growling and snarling of the caged warbeasts went up, to challenge in its volume the whole mass of human voices.

Now, across the whole vast reach of the parade ground, humans and trained beasts alike were demonstrating spontaneously at the sight of the Blade that waved above Vilkata's head. The cry of his name went up again and again, each time louder than the last. A thousand weapons were being brandished in salute.

Now the Dark King had reached the reviewing stand, and now he mounted quickly. His closer followers, Mark still with them, swarmed up onto the platform too. Immediately the stand was overcrowded, and people near the edges were jostled off. A small clear space—more magic?—remained around the person of the King. All around the base of the platform and across its surface where they had room, grand military potentates and dreaded wizards were prancing and gesturing like demented children. The aged and dignified abased themselves like dogs at one moment, and in the next leaped howling for the sky. And the very sky was streaked by demons, speeding, whirling in a pyrotechnic ecstasy of worship.

Grimly Mark held on to the small margin of self-awareness and self-control that he had regained in the pavilion. He thought that he would not be able to hold onto it for very long—but perhaps for long enough. He remembered now who he was, and what goal he had determined to accomplish. He still held Sightblinder's hilt in his right hand. But . . . to strike at Vilkata, possessor of the Mindsword . . . how could anyone do that? Or even plan to do it?

To strike at one who held the Mindsword might well be more than any mere human will could manage. If once Mark summoned up the will to try, and failed, he was sure that he could never try again.

Even to work his way through the press of frenzied bodies on the platform, to get himself close enough to the Dark King to strike at him, was going to be difficult. Get close to the Dark King, he ordered himself, forget for the moment why you are trying to get close. He had almost forgotten his bow, still slung in its accustomed place across his back. And there were two arrows left . . . he groped with a trembling hand, and found that there were none. Spilled somehow in the jostling? Or had some enthusiast's hand snatched them away?

He was going to have to strike with Sightblinder, then. Even had his mind been clear, entirely his own, it would not have been easy. Most of the people on the platform were also struggling to get closer to the Dark King, to touch him if possible; the ring of those who were closest, constrained to do all they could to protect the Mindsword's master, were striving to hold the others back. Their task was perhaps made easier by the fact that Vilkata was swinging the Sword more wildly now, inspiring fear as well as ecstasy in those near enough to stand in some danger from the Blade. There was still a cleared space of several meters directly around the king.

Mark elbowed room enough to let him draw Sightblinder—no one, he thought, was able to see that he was holding it, no magical guardians struck at him yet.

The small crowd atop the reviewing stand surged again, chaotically, as more people kept trying to climb on. Inevitably at one edge, more people were pushed off.

Mark forced himself a little closer to Vilkata, but then was stopped, pushed back again. *This is impossible,* he thought. *I cannot fail simply because I can't get through a crowd.* Still he dared not use the Sword to hack bodies out of his path; surely if he did that the magical defenses of the King would be triggered, and he would have no chance to strike the blow that really counted.

He had to get closer without killing. He gritted his teeth and closed his eyes, and blindly bulled his way ahead. His Sword, invisible to the people in his way, he held raised awkwardly above the jostling bodies that would otherwise have carved themselves on it.

But even as Mark scraped up new determination and tried again, the crowd surged against him, and its hundred legs effortlessly bore him even a little farther away. The cause of this last surge was one of Vilkata's sweeps with the Mindsword. Mark exerted one more great effort, and forced his way through, or almost through, but was deflected in the process to a place precariously near the platform's edge.

Now, one more effort . . . but the Blade in the Dark King's hand came swinging heedlessly past, and grazed Mark's forehead. The Dark King was laughing thunderously now, to see his courtiers duck and dodge in terror, and at the same time come pressing helplessly forward all the same.

Those next to Mark in the crush violently shoved back. Tangled with others, he fell over the edge of the platform, others falling with him. The distance to the ground was no more than a man's height, and the ground below was soft. Mark landed with a shock, but without further injury. By some miracle none of those falling with him had impaled themselves on Sightblinder, which lay on the soft earth under his hand.

He had failed, not heroically, but as by some demonic joke. He grabbed up his Sword and got to his feet again. Then he understood that he was hurt more than he had thought at first by Vilkata's accidental stroke. He could see blood, feel it and taste it, his own blood running down from his gashed forehead into his left eye. A centimeter or two closer to the Mindsword's swing and it would have killed him.

The fall had taken him out of reach of the Dark King; but at least it had also broken his direct eye contact with that flashing, hypnotic Blade. Now, with freedom roaring louder than the Mindsword in his mind, Mark looked up to catch a glimpse of Vilkata's back on the high platform. The monarch was turned away from Mark at the moment, facing out over the excited masses of the crowd at its front edge.

He must be struck down, Mark repeated grimly to himself, *And I must do it, do it now, no matter what, and get his Sword.*

He tore himself free of a fresh tangle of frenzied bodies on the ground. Shoving people out of his way with one hand, holding Sightblinder uplifted in the other, he ran along his side of the reviewing stand and then along its front. The pain in his wounded forehead savaged him, made him yearn to strike out at those villainous legs of officers and sorcerers that danced and pushed for advantage on the platform before him at eye level. But he held back his blow, grimly certain that he would be able to strike no more than once.

Blood bothering his eyes, pain nailing his head, Mark looked up trying to locate Vilkata again. It seemed hopeless. The sun was dazzling. The Mindsword flashed in it, and flashed again. Only in surrender to it was there hope. Mark had to look away, bend down his neck to get away from it. He could not let his eyes and soul be caught by it again—

As he turned his gaze away from the platform, there came into his vision the vast expanse of the parade ground and its howling mob of people. Sightblinder made two details stand out in rapid succession, each so strongly that they were able to distract him even now.

The first, astonishingly for Mark, was the prison cage with its lone occupant, even though he could glimpse it only intermittently now through the swirl of ecstatic bodies. He had encountered the sentry demon beside that cage, and he remembered, or almost remembered, something else, something that one of the magicians had said inside about the prisoner—

And then the second distracting detail captured Mark's attention even from the first. He saw a small gray cloud, rolling in a very uncloudlike way down the steep flank of a distant mountain. Inside that cloud Mark's sharpened perception could pick out half a dozen living beings, all apparently of human shape.

Already, as he watched, the cloud reached the comparatively level land at the mountain's foot. Now it rolled closer rapidly, directly approaching the encampment, moving independently of any wind. It was traveling with deceptive speed, outracing wind, traversing kilometers in mere moments.

Some of the people on the platform above Mark had now become aware of the cloud as well. The uproar immediately surrounding the Dark King had abated somewhat. Mark cast a quick look toward Vilkata, and saw that the King was lowering his own Sword, giving the approaching cloud his full attention.

A shrieking in the air passed rapidly overhead. A flight of the airborne demons, acting either on their own or at some direct command from their human masters, had melded themselves into a tight formation and were flying directly at the approaching cloud, intent on investigation and perhaps attack. But just before they reached the cloud their formation recoiled and burst, its members scattering. Mark had the impression that they had been brushed aside like so many insects, by some invisible power.

In a flash understanding came. The gods were coming to take charge. Through his pain and blood and fear Mark gasped out a sob of deep relief. Humanity had hope of being saved, by the beings who had made the Swords, from powers that were too much for it to manage. He had seen gods handle savage and rebellious men before. Vilkata, shrunken to the stature of a noxious insect in their presence, might be crushed before his horror could reach over the whole human world. Mark's own Sword might be taken from him too, but on the scale of these events that would make little difference.

The cloud, no longer serving any purpose of concealment, was being allowed to dissipate, and it vanished quickly. The handful of beings who had ridden it were walking now, already entering the parade ground at its far side, and approaching quickly. The sea of humans occupying the open space parted at the deities' approach. Four gods and one goddess, each tall as Draffut, came striding forward without pause, and Mark got the impression that they would have stepped on people without noticing had any remained in their way.

Towering taller and taller as they drew near, the five advanced, marching straight for the reviewing stand. Mark thought that now he could recognize some of them individually. Four were attired with divine elegance, wearing crowns, tunics, robes ablaze with color, gold, and gems. But one, who limped as he strode forward, was clad in simple furs.

Again Mark glanced back quickly at the platform. Vilkata was out of striking range, and still closely surrounded by his people and his magical attendants.

The Dark King had sheathed the Mindsword now, and was issuing terse orders to certain of his wizards. In the next instant one of these magicians gave a convulsive leap that carried him clear off the platform. He fell more heavily than Mark had fallen, and lay writhing helplessly on the ground. Mark could guess that some protective spell of this man's had somehow impeded the divine progress; and that when the spell was snapped, like some ship's hawser in the docks, he who had been holding it was flattened by the recoil.

Whatever magic had been in their path, spells perhaps triggered automatically by their intrusion, the gods had broken their way through it; they were irritated, Mark thought, looking at them, like adults bothered by some maze of string set up by children.

At last the four gods and one goddess halted their advance. They stood on the parade ground only a score of meters from the platform, their heads still easily overtopping that of the Dark King who faced them from his elevation. Everyone else on the platform was kneeling, Mark realized, or had thrown themselves face down in abject panic, and everyone near him on the ground also. He and the Dark King were the only two humans within a hundred meters still on their feet. How curious, Mark wondered distantly. The only other time in his life when he had seen deities as close as this, why that time too he had been able to remain standing, while around him other humans knelt or huddled in collapse. . . .

The limping god was moving forward. In the silence that lay over the whole camp, his ornaments of dragon-scale could be heard clinking as he lurched to within one great stride of the platform. That is Vulcan the Smith, thought Mark, staring up at the fur-garbed titan—he who took off my father's arm. Vulcan paid no attention to Mark, but was looking at Vilkata. As far as Mark could tell, Vilkata did not flinch, though when the god halted he was close enough to the platform to have reached forth one of his long arms and plucked Vilkata from it.

Wind came keening across the camp, blowing out of the bare, devastated lands surrounding it. Otherwise there was silence.

A silence abruptly broken, by the voice of Vulcan that boomed forth at a volume appropriate for a god. "What madness is this that you fools of humans are about? Do you not realize that the Swordgame is over?"

Vilkata summoned up his best royal voice to answer. "I am the Dark King—" It was no surprise at all to Mark that the King's voice should quaver and falter and quit on him before the sentence ended. The only wonder was that the man could stand and speak at all in such a confrontation.

Vulcan was neither impressed nor pleased. "King, Queen, or whatever, what do I care for all that? You are a human and no more. Hand over that tool of power that you are wearing at your side."

Vilkata did not obey at once; instead he dared to answer once more in words. Mark did not hear the words exactly, for his attention had once more been distracted by something in the distance. This was another cloud, and it looked as unusual as the first.

This cloud was not rolling down a mountainside, only drifting through the air, but its path was at a right angle to those of other clouds and the wind. Now the strange cloud was hovering, hesitating in its slow passage. It appeared to be maintaining a certain cautious distance from the scene on the parade ground. With Sightblinder still in hand, Mark could perceive in this second cloud also the presence of figures of human shape but divine dimensions. There was one, a perfect essence of the female, that he thought could be only Aphrodite. He could see none of the others so clearly as individuals, though all of their faces seemed to be turned his way.

The distraction had been only momentary. Now Vulcan, made impatient by even a moment's temporizing on the part of this mere human king, thundered out some oath, and stretched forth his arm toward Vilkata. With a swift motion the Dark King drew the Mindsword from its sheath—but not to hand it over in surrender. Instead he brandished it aloft.

Vulcan cried out once, a strange, hoarse tone, like masses of metal and rock colliding. The lame god threw up a forearm across his eyes. He reeled backward, and fell to one knee. Mark could feel in the ground under his own feet the impact of that fall.

Just behind the Smith, the four other deities who had come out of the cloud with him were kneeling also.

Once again a long moment of silence held throughout the camp. The distant airborne cloud was moving faster now, departing at accelerated speed. Mark gazed after it numbly for a moment. The gods had failed. The thousands of human beings massed around him were cheering once again.

Now Vilkata was speaking again. After Vulcan's thunder the King's voice sounded puny, but it was triumphant and confident once again as he shouted an order to the kneeling gods, their heads still higher than his own. "Follow me! Obey!"

"We hear." The ragged chorus rolled forth. The wooden stand, the earth, vibrated with it. "We follow, and obey."

The huge wardrum boomed to life again, and from the crowd went up the loudest roar yet. The mad celebration resumed, twice madder than before.

The gods on the parade ground were climbing ponderously back to their feet. "Surely this is Father Zeus!" Vulcan cried out, pointing with a tree-sized arm at the Dark King. "He who has been playing that role among us must be an imposter!"

The Smith's divine companions roared approval of this statement, and launched themselves spontaneously into a dance, that looked at once ponderous and uncontrolled. The ground shook; Mark could see the tall flagpole swaying in front of the King's pavilion. The crowd of humans in the vicinity of the reviewing stand began to thin, with everyone who was anywhere near the dancing gods being eager to move back. Yet they remained under the Mindsword's spell, and many joined the dance.

Mark stood drained, exhausted, leaning on his own Sword. With pain stabbing at his forehead, and blood still trickling into his eye, he watched the maddened gods and had the feeling that he was going mad himself. But surely he ought to have expected something like this. If one of the Swords could kill a god—and with his own eyes Mark had seen Hermes lying dead, the wound made by Farslayer gaping in the middle of the Messenger's back—then why should not another Sword have power to make slaves of other gods?

What power had Vulcan called upon to forge them, that was greater than the gods themselves?

And was he, Mark, the only being here still capable of resistance?

With his pain, with the drip of his own blood that seemed now to burn like poison, he could no longer think. But maybe he could still act.

He gripped Sightblinder in his two hands, and moved for the third time to try to kill Vilkata.

If the crowd on the ground was moving more wildly now, it was thinner, and that helped. But when Mark raised his eyes to the Dark King, who still stood on the platform, the Mindsword dazzled him again, sent splintering shafts of poisoned light into his brain. He was stumbling toward the sun in glory, and it was unthinkable for anyone to try to strike the sun.

Vilkata, the god! Holder of the Mindsword, he who must be adored!

Mark lifted his own Sword in both arms. Then he realized that he was not going to strike, he was going to cast down Sightblinder as an offering. It was all he could do to tear himself free. Still desperately holding onto his own Sword, lurching and stumbling, he fled the platform, his back to the glory that he dared no longer face. It tugged him and tore at him and urged him to turn back. He knew that if he turned for an instant he was lost.

The prisoner's cage loomed up ahead of him. Someone in the crowd jostled Mark, turning him slightly sideways so that he saw the cage and its inmate quite clearly.

With no consciousness of making any plan, acting on impulse, Mark raised the Sword of Stealth high in a two-handed grip, and brought it smashing down against the wooden door and its small lock. The Sword's magic did nothing to aid the blow, but its long weight and keen edge were quite enough. The cage had not been built to sustain any real assault. Mark struck again and the door fell open. Amid the pandemonium of jumping, screaming bodies and brandished weapons, no one paid the least heed to what he was doing. The earth still shook under the tread of the bellowing, dancing gods.

He sheathed his weapon and reached in with both hands to grasp the helpless prisoner. The body he drew forth was that of a young woman, naked, bound with both cords and magic. The cords fell free quickly, at a touch of Sightblinder's perfect edge. But the magic was more durable.

One arm about the prisoner, half carrying and half pulling her through the frenzied crowd, Mark headed straight away from the reviewing stand, still not daring to look back. Whatever the people around saw when they looked at him now, it made them draw back even in their frenzy, leaving his way clear.

There seemed no end to the parade ground, or to Vilkata's maddened army. With each retreating step the pressure of the Mindsword eased, but only infinitesimally. Steps added up, though. Now Mark could begin to think again, enough to begin to plan. There, ahead, a little distance in the crowd, were two mounted men who looked like minor magicians of some kind. Mark set his course for them, dragging the still stupefied young woman along.

The magicians, looking half stupefied themselves with their participation in the Mindsword's glamor, paid no attention as Mark approached. These two, Mark hoped, did not rate guardian demons. He desperately needed transportation.

Sightblinder obtained it for him, quickly and bloodily, working with no more magic than a meataxe. Again, in the general surrounding madness, no one appeared to notice what was happening.

Mark wrapped the girl in a cloak of black and gold that one of the magicians had been wearing, and got her aboard one of the riding beasts, and got himself aboard the other. Once in the saddle, he could only sit swaying for a moment, afraid that he was going to faint, watching his own blood drip on his hands that held the reins.

Somehow he got moving, leading the girl's mount. No one tried to interfere with them as they fled the camp. No one, as far as Mark could tell, even took notice.

The booming of the wardrum and the roaring of the gods followed them for a long time, pursuing them for kilometers of their flight across high barren lands.

CHAPTER 6

A kilometer or two upstream from Tashigang, before the Corgo split itself around the several islands that made parts of the city, the current was slow enough that Denis the Quick could make fairly good time paddling his light canoe against it. Here it was possible to seek out places in the broader stream where the surface current was slower still, with local eddies to make the paddler's task less difficult. This made it easy for Denis to stay clear of the other river traffic, which in early morning was mostly barges of foodstuffs and other commerce coming downstream. There were also some small fishing craft out on the river, and one or two light sailboats that appeared to be out purely for pleasure. Here above the city there were no ships of ocean-going size, such as plied the reaches downstream from Tashigang to the sea.

Two kilometers upstream from the walls, Denis reached the first sharp upstream bend of the Corgo and looked back again, ceasing to paddle as he sought a last glimpse of the high towers. Visible above the morning mist that still rose from the river, the lofty walls and battlements caught rays of the early morning sun. Here and there upon the venerable masses of brown or gray stone, glass or bright metal sparkled, in windows, ornaments, or the weapons of the Watch. On several high places the green and gray of the city's own colors were displayed. Upon the highest pole, over the Lord Mayor's palace, a single pennant of black and silver acknowledged the ultimate sovereignty of Yambu.

As he paddled farther upstream, Denis's canoe passed between shores lined with the villas of those wealthy citizens who felt secure enough about the prospects of long-term peace to choose to live outside the city walls. These were impressive houses, each fortified behind its own minor defenses, capable of holding off an occasional brigands' raid.

Independent villas soon gave way to suburbs of somewhat less impressive houses, built together behind modest walls; and these in turn to farms and vineyards. These lands like Tashigang itself were tributary to the Silver Queen, though enjoying a great measure of independence. Yambu in her years of domination had maintained general peace and order here, and had wisely been content to levy no more than moderate tribute and to allow the people to manage their own affairs for the most part. Tribute flowed in regularly under such a regime, and the Queen built a fund of goodwill for herself. Meanwhile she had been busy venting her aggressive energies elsewhere.

Pausing once to eat and rest, Denis made an uneventful first day's journey up the river. By evening he was far enough from the city's center of population to have no trouble in locating a small island that offered him a good spot to camp. He even succeeded in catching a suitable fish for his dinner, and was rather pleased with this success in outdoor skills.

On the second day he got an early start again. He had a worker's calloused hands and did not mind the constant paddling overmuch; the healed wound in his forearm did not trouble him at all. This day he kept a careful eye out for certain landmarks, as Ben had instructed him. Around noon he was able to identify without any trouble the tributary stream he wanted, a small river that entered the Corgo on a winding course from the northeast. This smaller river, here called the Spode, drained a portion of the Great Swamp—it did not, unfortunately, lead directly to the part where Sir Andrew and his army were likely to be found. To reach that, Denis would have to make a portage later.

The voyager passed three or four more days in similarly pleasant journeying. Each day he saw fewer people, and those he did see usually greeted the acolyte of Ardneh with friendly waves. Some offered him food, some of which he graciously accepted.

Denis spent much of his mental time in wondering about his hidden cargo. He knew something now at first hand about the Sword of Mercy. But what exactly did the Sword of Justice do? Denis had not wanted to ask, lest they believe he was pondering some scheme of running off with it. (The treacherous thought had crossed his mind, in the guise of yet another delicious daydream. So far—so far—his other, fiercer feelings had kept him from being really tempted by it.)

And Ben had not thought it necessary to discuss the qualities of the Sword of Justice with Denis at any length. The master of the House of Courtenay had said only one thing on the subject.

"Denis, if it does come down to your having to fight someone on the way, I'd recommend you get Doomgiver out and use it, if you have the chance. Don't try to fight with Woundhealer, though. Not if your idea is to carve up someone instead of making him feel good."

But so far there had not been the remotest danger of a fight. So far the journey's only physical excitement had been provided by occasional thunderstorms, threatening the traveler with lightning and drenching white robes that had not been waterproofed.

On Denis's fifth day out he passed through calm farm country, in lovely weather. That night he again made camp on a small island.

And dreamed, as he often did, of women. Kuan-yin, the governess he had embraced in real life, and thought of marrying, beckoned to him. And tonight he dreamed also of the mistress of the House of Courtenay, who in real life had never touched him except to bind his wounded arm. Denis dreamed that she who he had known as the Lady Sophie had come to visit him in his room beside the workshop. She sat on his cot there and smiled, and held his hand, and thanked him for something he had done, or was perhaps about to do. Her white robe was in disarray, hanging open, but incredibly she seemed not to notice.

The dream was just approaching its moment of greatest tension, when Denis awoke. He lay in warm moonlight, with the sense that the world to which he had awakened was only a perfected dream. There was a scent in the air—of riverside flowers?—incredibly sweet and beautiful, too subtle to be called perfume.

And there was in the air also—something else. A fearless excitement. Denis's blood throbbed with oneiric anticipation, of he knew not what. Yet he knew that he was wide awake.

He looked along the river, his gaze caught by the path of reflected moonlight. He saw a shadow, as of some drifting boat, enter upon that path. It was some kind of craft—a barge, he thought—speckled with its own small lights, and moving in perfect silence. Almost perfect. A moment more, and Denis could hear the gentle splash and drip of oars.

As the barge drew closer, he could see that it was larger than he had thought at first, so large that he wondered how it managed to navigate the narrower places in this small river. The lights along its low sides were softly glowing amber lamps, as steady as the Old World light that Denis was familiar with, but vastly subtler.

Denis was on his feet now. He still had no doubts that he was awake, and he was conscious of being—more or less—his ordinary self. Whatever was happening to him now was real, but he had no sense of danger, only of thrilling promise. He moved a step closer to the bank, the water murmuring like lovers' laughter at his feet. He stood there leaning on the upended bottom of the canoe that he had prudently pulled out of the river before retiring.

As the barge drew closer still, Denis could see that it bore amidships a small house or pavilion, covered by an awning of some fine cloth. Just forward of this there was a throne-like chair or lounge, all centered between two rows of strangely silent and briefly costumed young women rowers.

A woman was reclining upon the lounge, in the middle of a mass of pillows. With only the Moon behind her, and the dim lamps on her boat, Denis could see her at first only by hints and outlines. At first his heated imagination assured him that she was wearing nothing at all. But presently his eyes were forced to admit the fact of a garment, more shimmering mist and starlight, it seemed, than any kind of cloth. Most of the woman's body was enclosed by this veil, though scarcely any of it was concealed.

Denis's heart lurched within him, and he understood. A name sprang into his mind, and he might have spoken it aloud, but just at that moment he lacked the breath to say anything at all. He had never seen a god or goddess in his life before, and had never really expected to see one before he died.

In response to some command unseen and unheard by Denis, the inhumanly silent rowers stopped, in unison. He was vaguely aware, even without looking directly at them for a moment, of how comely they all were, and how provocatively dressed. With the Goddess of Love herself before his eyes, he could not have looked at any of them if he had tried.

The barge, under a control that had to be more than natural, came drifting very slowly and precisely toward Denis on the island. From inside the cabin—he thought—there came a strain of music, lovely as the perfume, to waft across the small width of water that remained. Every note was framed in perfect silence now that the silvery trickle from the oars had stopped.

With an undulating movement Aphrodite rose from her couch, to stand in a pose of unstrained grace.

"Young man?" she called to Denis softly. The voice of the goddess was everything that her appearance had suggested it might be. "I must speak with you."

Denis started toward her and stumbled. He discovered that it was necessary to make his way around some large and unfamiliar object—oh yes, it was his canoe—that somehow happened to be right in his path.

"Lady," he choked out, "I am yours to command. What would you have of me?" At this point he became aware that he had just fallen on his knees with a loud squelching sound, right in the riverside mud. This would not have mattered in the least, except that it might tend to make the goddess think that he was clumsy; and when he got up, she was sure to see how muddy his white robes had got, and he feared that she might laugh.

So far, thank all the gods and goddesses, she was not laughing at him.

"Young man," said Aphrodite, "I know that you are carrying two Swords with you. I understand that one of them is the one that heals. And the other . . . well, I forget at the moment what they told me about the other. But that doesn't matter just now. I want you to hand both of them over to me at once. If you are quick enough about it I will perhaps allow you to kiss me." The goddess paused for just a moment, and gave Denis a tiny smile. "Who knows what I might allow, on such a romantic night as this?"

"Kiss me," Denis echoed vacantly. Then, giving a mad bound, he was up out of the mud and on his feet, stumbling and splashing about. He had to find the two Swords she was talking about—where were they, anyway?—and give them to her. What else was he going to do with them, anyway?

They were in the canoe . . . where was the canoe?

He tripped over it and almost tumbled himself back into the mud before he really saw it. Then he broke a fingernail getting the craft turned rightside up.

Aphrodite encouraged him in a friendly way. "That's it. They're hidden right in the bottom of your little boat or whatever it is there—

but then I suppose you know that." The goddess sounded mildly impatient with his clumsiness—how could she not be? But she did not yet sound angry; Denis silently offered thanks.

He thought he was going to lose another fingernail getting the trick board pried up. Then he realized that he would do a lot better prying with a knife instead.

Aphrodite slowly approached the near side rail of her luxurious barge. Gracefully she knelt there upon a small mound of silken cushions, between two of her inhumanly beautiful rowers. They paid her no attention.

"Be quick, young man! I need what you are going to give me." The goddess beckoned with one hand, and her voice, melded with her laughter, stretched out in silken double meaning. Her laughter, Denis desperately assured himself, was not really meant to be unkind. Yet still it somehow wounded him.

He pried with his knife, and the small nails holding the board came squeaking out. The hidden compartment lay open, its contents exposed to moonlight.

Aphrodite, to get a better look, gave a pert little kneeling jump, a movement of impossible grace that made the softer portions of her body bounce. What color was her hair? Denis asked himself desperately. And what about her skin? In the moonlight he could not tell, and anyway it did not matter in the least. And was she really tall or short, voluptuous or thin? From moment to moment all those things seemed to change, with only the essence of her sex remaining constant.

Now she was standing at the rail of her craft. The barge continued to drift minutely in toward shore, ignoring the current even though the oars were raised and idle.

"Be quick, young man, be quick." There was a hint of impatience in her voice.

Denis, groping almost sightlessly for his treasure to hand it over, felt his hand fall first upon Woundhealer. Somehow he could identify the Sword from its first touch. Humbly he brought it out, sheathed as it was, and with a kind of genuflection handed it over, hilt-first, to the goddess. She accepted it, with a sprightly one-handed gesture that showed how strong her smooth young-looking arm could be.

She held the Sword of Mercy sheathed, and said: "The other one now. And then I believe that—perhaps—you will have earned a kiss."

He fumbled in the bottom of the canoe again, and brought out Doomgiver.

This Sword he held with one hand supporting its sheathed blade, and the other holding the hilt, and through the hilt he felt a flow of strange and unfamiliar power. It gave him a sense of steady certitude. The sheath seemed to fall free of itself, the Sword was drawn.

Denis straightened up, intending to present this Sword as well to the goddess. But when his eyes fell on her he was shocked to see that she was changed.

Or was the change in him—and not in her?

Aphrodite let fall her arm that had been extended to receive the second Sword. She stepped back, her other hand still holding the sheathed Sword of Mercy.

Again Denis pondered: What does she really look like? But still the moonlight (he thought it was the moonlight) made it quite impossible to tell.

Certainly more lovely than any mortal woman could ever be. Yet now, since he had drawn the second Sword, he thought she was in some way inferior to even the least of human mortals. In some way she was—unreal.

He realized that he did not want her now.

Power was still flowing from the Swordhilt into his hand. In sudden curiosity he looked at what his fingers gripped. He saw in moonlight, without understanding, the simple hollow white circle that marked the black.

Wonder of wonders, the goddess appeared to be fighting some inner struggle with herself.

"Give me—" she began to say, in a voice that still fought to be commanding. But after those first two words her voice faltered and her speech broke off.

She sagged back from the railing of her barge (Denis was shocked to see how graceless the movement was), and stopped half-kneeling on her silken pillows once more. The cloud of her moonlit hair concealed her face.

"No," she contradicted herself, speaking now in yet another voice, much softer. "No, do not give it to me now. I am a goddess, and I could take it from you. But I will not."

Denis's arm that held the Sword of Justice faltered, and the blade sank down slowly at his side. It hung in his hand like a dead weight, though still its power flowed. He felt an overwhelming—*pity*—for the goddess, mixed with a slight disgust.

"Do not give it to me," repeated Aphrodite, in her soft and newly thoughtful voice. "That would cause harm to you." After a pause she went on, marveling to herself. "So, this is love. I have always wondered, and never known what it was like. I see it can be terrible."

She raised her head until her wide-spaced eyes were visible under the cloud of moonlit hair. "I see . . . that your name is Denis, my beloved. And you have known a score of women before now, and dreamed of a thousand more. Yet you have never really known any of them. Nor will you, can you, ever really know a goddess, I suppose." And Aphrodite gave a sigh, her bosom heaving.

Denis could only stand there uncomfortably. He felt more pity for this lovely woman than he could bear, and he wished that she would go away. At the same time he wanted to let go of the Sword in his right hand; he wanted to throw it in the river. It seemed to him that his life had been much more intense and glorious just a few moments ago, before he had drawn Doomgiver. But the Sword would not let him throw it away just now, any more than it would allow the goddess to take it from him.

"I love you, Denis," the goddess Aphrodite said.

He made an incoherent noise of embarrassment, low down in his throat. As speech, he thought, it was inadequate, clumsy, mundane, and mean, like everything else he did. He did not love her, or even want her. He could not, and he wished that she would leave.

She said to him softly, "And the blade that you hold there, my love, is truly called Doomgiver, for I see now that it truly giveth me my doom."

"No!" Denis protested, feeling so sorry for her already, not knowing just what it was he feared.

"Ah yes. I, who have for ages amused myself with the love of men, must now feel what they have felt. And, as I love you now, I cannot take Doomgiver from you. To rob you of the Sword of Justice now, my little mortal darling, would do you much harm. As a goddess I can foresee that. But Woundhealer—it will be better if I take that with me now."

Denis wanted to tell her that he was sorry. The words stuck in his throat.

"How sweet it would be if you could tell me that you loved me too. But do not lie." And here the goddess extended her arm that still held the Sword of Love, across the narrow strip of water that still separated her from the island, and with the sheathed tip of Woundhealer touched Denis over his heart. "I could . . . but I will not. My full embrace would not be good for you—not now, not yet. Someday, perhaps. I love you, Denis, and for your sake I must now say farewell."

And the goddess leaned forward suddenly, and kissed him on the cheek.

"No . . . no." He stumbled forward, into mud. Was it only pity that he felt now?

But the marvelous barge was already shimmering away into the moonlight.

CHAPTER 7

The two riding beasts must have been well rested when Mark seized them, for they bore their riders willingly and swiftly on the first long stage of the flight from Vilkata's encampment. The young woman stayed in her saddle firmly, like an experienced rider, but instinctively, passively, and with no apparent understanding of what was happening to her now. Her blue-green eyes stared steadily out at horror, some horror that was no longer visible to Mark. Her body was thin, almost emaciated. Her face was pale under its mask of grime; her hair, colorless with filth, hung long and matted over the captured cloak that she clutched about her with one hand. Since Mark had pulled her from the cage she had not spoken a single word.

The two of them rode for a long time, side by side, over roadless and gradually rising ground, before Mark stopped the animals for a rest. He had at last been able to convince himself that there was no pursuit. Phantom echoes of Vilkata's demonic celebration had persisted in his exhausted mind and senses long after the real sounds had faded.

He was living now with ceaseless pain, and with the taste and sight and smell of his own blood, for the oozing from his forehead wound would not diminish. And Mark could not shake the feeling that there was something wrong now with his own blood, with the way it smelled and tasted, as if the Mindsword had left a shard of poisoned sunlight embedded in his brain.

Mark dismounted the first time he stopped the animals. He spoke gently to the young woman, but she only continued to sit her mount in silence, staring straight ahead, not responding to him at all. He decided not to press the matter of communication, as long as she remained docile. The all-important thing was to get farther from Vilkata.

Presently they were under way again. Now their course, aimed directly away from Vilkata's camp, took them into a range of low hills. Now the encampment, which had still been intermittently visible in the distance, dropped permanently from sight. Here in the hills the land still showed devastation wrought by the Dark King's foragers. Soon the fugitives came to a stream, and a thicket that offered shelter of a kind. Mark stopped again.

This time he employed gentle force to pry the young woman's hands from the reins, and to get her down from the saddle. Still half-supported by Mark's arm, she stood beside the animal waiting for whatever might happen to her next. Her lips were cracked, hideously dry. Mark had to lead her to the stream, and get her to kneel beside it. Still she did not appear to realize what was in front of her. Only after he had given her the first drink from his own cupped hands did she rouse from her trance enough to bend to the water for herself.

"I can stand," she announced suddenly, in a disused croak of a voice. And stand she did, unaided, a little taller than before. A moment later, her eyes for the first time fastened on Mark with full attention.

In the next instant he was startled to see joyous recognition surge up in her face. In a much clearer voice, she murmured, "Rostov . . . how did you ever manage . . . ?"

The instant after that, she fell unconscious in Mark's arms.

He caught her as well as he could, and stretched her out on the grass. Then he sat down, and, holding his own head, tried to think through his pain. Rostov was a Tasavaltan name, borne by the famed general, and, Mark supposed, by many others as well. He was still wearing Sightblinder, and the young woman had seen him as someone she knew and trusted.

Mark lay down and tried to rest, but his wound made that practically impossible. Presently he decided that they might as well go on, if he could get his companion back into the saddle. She roused herself when he tugged at her, and with his help she got mounted again. Though she appeared now to be asleep, with closed eyes, she sat steadily astride the riding beast, wrapped in the cloak of gold and black. That hateful cloak might be a help, thought Mark, if any of the enemy should see her from a distance. He himself was still protected by Sightblinder, but his companion would not be.

Still his wound throbbed mercilessly. He was sure now that the Mindsword must have had some poisonous effect, but unless he could find help somewhere there was nothing he could do about it. He rode on, side by side with his companion, Mark now and then rousing himself enough to realize that neither of them was more than half conscious. Grimly he concentrated—whenever he was able to concentrate —on maintaining a generally uphill direction; that ought to at least prevent them from riding in a circle right back to Vilkata and his captive gods.

They stopped again only when full night came, and Mark could no longer see where they were going. There was no food. Mark had lost his bow somewhere, after his last arrows were lost, and anyway he was in no condition to try to hunt. His limbs felt weak and he was shaking with chill. When the young woman had dismounted again and stood beside him, he took the cloak off her and clothed her in his own long hunter's shirt; he could feel her body shivering too, with the night's approaching cold. Then he lay down with her and huddled against her, wrapping the cloak around them both. He was too sick to think of wanting anything more from her than warmth. Feverishly he kept thinking that he ought to get up and do something to tend the animals, but he could not.

In pain and blood, Mark did not so much fall asleep as lapse into unconsciousness. He woke up, half delirious, in the middle of the night. Someone's hand had shaken him awake.

The young woman, still wearing his shirt, was sitting upright beside him. There was firelight, somehow, on her face, and under the dirt he could see a new look of alert intelligence.

"You are not Rostov. Where did he go?"

She had to repeat the question several times before Mark was able to grasp the sense of it. Yes, of course, she had seen him as someone else, when he had been wearing the Sword. When he had been—

His hand groped at his side, to find that she had disarmed him. Weakly he managed to raise his head a little. There was Sightblinder, lying just out of his reach. He could see it by the light of the small fire that his companion had somehow managed to start.

"I took it away from you, you were raving and thrashing about. Where is Rostov? Who are you?"

Mark had great difficulty in trying to talk. It crossed his mind that he was probably dying. He could only gesture toward the Sword.

She said, puzzled, "You killed him with—? But no, you can't mean that."

"No. No." He had to rest a little, to gather his strength before he spoke again. Even so the words wouldn't come out clearly. ". . . was never here."

The young woman stared at him. Her face was still haggard and worn and filthy, but inner energies were making a powerful effort to revive it. Now, as if struck by a sudden idea, she turned away to where the Sword lay, and crouched looking at it carefully. Then she extended one hand, with the practiced gesture of a sorceress, to touch the hilt.

She froze there in that position, one finger touching black.

The grimy girl was gone, and in her place Mark saw his mother, Mala, aged a decade since he had seen her last, her dark lustrous hair now broadly streaked with gray. It was Mala who knelt near the little campfire holding one finger against Sightblinder's hilt, wearing not Mark's hunting shirt but her own peasant's trousers and a patterned blouse that her son could still recognize.

Then the figure of Mark's mother blurred and shifted, became that of his sister Marian. Marian was a woman of nearly thirty now, also altered by the years that had passed since Mark had seen her last, on the day that he fled their village.

Marian turned her face to look directly at him, and now in her place Mark beheld a plump girl of the Red Temple, a girl he had encountered once, casually embraced, and then, somehow, never afterward forgotten. The Red Temple girl turned her body more fully toward Mark, letting go the Sword.

It was the young woman he had rescued from Vilkata's camp, her hair matted, her lean body clad in his dirty, tattered hunting shirt, who approached Mark and bent over him again. Above her head, above the firelight, massed clouds of stars made a great arc.

She drew a deep breath. "I should have realized which Sword that was. Though I have never seen one of them before . . . but now I am fully awake, I hope. I begin to understand. My name is Kristin. Who are you?"

"Mark."

"Well, Mark." She touched his wounded head, so gently that it barely added to the pain. When he winced she quickly withdrew her hand again. "Was it you who came into—that place—with Sightblinder, and got me out?"

He managed a nod.

"And did you come alone? Yes, you nod again. Why? But never mind that now. I will never forget what you have done for me. You saved my life, and more . . . have we any water?"

Then she was quick to answer her own question, looking and finding Mark's water bottle. She gave him a drink, first, then took a mouthful for herself. "Ah," she said, and relaxed.

But only for a moment. "Are you expecting to meet help, here, anywhere nearby? . . . No." Again she stretched forth a gentle hand, that this time touched him painlessly and soothed his face. "Whom do you serve?"

"Sir Andrew."

"Ah. A good man, from all I've ever heard about him. We in Tasavalta honor him, though we don't know . . . but never mind. I must try to do something for that cut on your forehead."

Kristin closed her eyes, and muttered spells, and Mark could feel a shivery tugging at the wound, a quasimaterial endeavor to pull out the knife of pain. But then the knife came back, twisting more fiercely than before, and he cried out.

"At least the bleeding has stopped," Kristin muttered, with heartlessly reassuring calm. "But there's more wrong. I can do little for you here." She glanced up for a moment at the stars, evidently trying to judge her position or the time or both. "Have we any food?"

"No."

She began to move around, looking for something. She was inspecting some of the nearby plants when Mark lost consciousness again.

When he awoke again it was still night. He was shivering violently, though he alone was now wrapped twice round in the cloak of black and gold. His head was supported gently in the warmth of Kristin's lap, and her warm magical fingers were trying to soothe his head.

But he hardly noticed any of that. Something that seemed more momentous was happening also. The tall circle of the gods had formed around them both. Once before, when he was a boy in danger of freezing to death in the high Ludus Mountains, he had seen the gods, or dreamt them, surrounding him in such a way. He tried now to call

Kristin's attention to the ring of observing deities, but she was busy with her own efforts, her own spells. She raised her head once to look, and murmured some agreement, and then went back to trying to soothe and heal him.

He could tell she was not really aware of the surrounding presences. But he knew that they were there. And, just as on that other night when he had seen them in a ring about his lonely fire, they were arguing about him. Tonight what they were saying was even less clear than it had been then, nor were the faces of the gods as clearly visible tonight.

Eventually the vision passed.

Kristin's voice had a different tone now, murmuring real words, not incantations. It sounded as if she were angry with him. "I am not going to let you die, do you hear me? I will not let you die." She raised her head. "This much I can do against you, Dark One, for what you did to me. Damn you, I will not let you have this man!"

And back to Mark: "You saved my life . . . saved more than that . . . and I am not going to surrender yours to them. Poisoned wound or not, you'll live. I promise you."

The night passed for him in periods of unconsciousness, in visions and intervals of lucidity, in a struggle to breathe that at last he seemed to have won.

In the morning they moved on. There was no water where they had spent the night, and they were still uncomfortably close to Vilkata's army. Now it was Mark who needed help to get aboard his riding beast, and Kristin who led his animal as they traveled, and she who chose the route, and sometimes kept him from falling out of the saddle in his weakness. He endured the day. He chewed on roots and berries when she put them into his mouth. Again he experienced difficulty in breathing. But he stayed alive, supported by his own grim will and Kristin's magic.

Another night passed, much like the one before, and another day of traveling much like the last. After that day Mark lost count. His whole life had vanished into this hideous trek, it seemed, and often now he no longer cared whether he lived or not.

At night, every night, his fever rose, and sometimes the gods regathered round Kristin's magical little fire to taunt him and to argue among themselves. Each dawn Mark awoke to see them gone, and Kristin slumped beside him in an exhausted sleep.

A night came when his chills were more violent than ever. Kristin bundled herself with him inside the cloak. She slept, he thought, while the usual parade of deities walked through his fevered mind. He awoke again at dawn, his mind feeling clearer, and told himself he had survived another night.

And then he got a sharp shock, jolting his mind into greater clarity. This morning not all the deities were gone. A woman, statuesque, magnificent, as real as any woman he had ever seen, stood across the ashes of the fire, holding in her strong right arm a Sword.

The goddess was looking down at Kristin, who was asleep sitting beside Mark, the hunting shirt half open at her breast.

"I am Aphrodite," the goddess said to Mark. "I was called; I had to come to you, and now I see I must do something. How sweet, the mortal child, to give you everything. She is restoring your life to you, and giving you her entire life as well in the process, and I hope you appreciate it. But men never do, I suppose."

Mark said, "I understand."

"Do you? No, you don't. You really don't. But perhaps one day you will."

And the goddess approached the two of them with long unhurried steps, meanwhile raising the Sword in her right hand. Mark, alarmed, sat bolt upright. Before he could do more, the Sword in Aphrodite's hand was thrusting straight for Kristin's sleeping back.

The Sword in its swift passage made a sound like a gasp of human breath. Mark saw the wide, bright steel vanish into Kristin's back and emerge quite bloodlessly between her breasts, to plunge straight on into his own heart as he sat beside her. He cried out once, with a pang more intense than that of any wound that he had ever felt, and then he fell back dead.

But then he realized that he was only dreaming he was dead.

Actually, he thought now, he was waking up.

He was lying on his back, that much was real and certain. And the endless pain in his head was gone at last. It was too much trouble, his eyelids were much too heavy, to try to open his eyes to discover if he was asleep or dead.

With a sigh of contentment, knowing the inexpressible comfort of pain's cessation, he shifted his position slightly, and quickly fell into a natural sleep.

When Mark awoke again, he thought that daylight was fading. Had it really been dawn before, when the goddess and her Sword appeared? That might have been a dream. But this, Kristin and himself, was real.

The hunting shirt was cast aside now, but she was here, inside the cloak that enfolded both of them.

It was as if her blood flowed now in his veins, giving healing, and his blood crossed into her body too, giving and receiving life.

Into her body. His own life flowing. . . .

It was morning again when he awoke, gently but at last completely, at first accepting without wonder the pressure of the warm smooth body beside his own. Then he began to remember things, and wonder rapidly unfolded.

In an instant he was sitting upright, raising both hands to his head. He was still caked with old, dried blood and dirtier even than he remembered, and he felt thirsty and ravenously hungry, but the pain and fever were entirely gone. Kristin, as grimy and worn-looking as he felt, but alive and safe and warm, was snuggled naked beside him in an exhausted sleep.

The sun was about an hour high. Nearby were the ashes of a long-dead fire. They were camped in a grove, with running water murmuring somewhere just out of sight. Mark could not recognize the place at all or remember their arriving at it.

A little distance away stood the two riding beasts, looking lean and hard-used, but at the moment contentedly munching grass. Someone had taken off their saddles and tethered them for grazing.

Mark stood up, the cape of black and gold that had been his only cover falling back. Again he raised a hand to his forehead. He dared to probe more firmly with a finger. There was no longer any trace of a wound, except for the dried blood.

Kristin stirred at his feet, and he looked down and saw that his movement had awakened her; her eyes were open, marveling at him.

"You have been healed," she said. It was as if she had been half-expecting such an outcome, but still it surprised and almost frightened her.

"Yes." He was almost frightened himself, at his own suddenly restored well-being. He was almost reluctant to move, afraid to break the healing spell. "You did it for me."

"Mark." It was as if she were trying out the name, speaking it for the first time. Then she asked a question that to Mark, at the moment, did not seem in the least incongruous: "Do you love me?"

"Yes." He gave his reply at once, gravely certain without having to think about it. But then he seriously considered the question and his answer. He knelt beside Kristin, and looked at her and touched her with awe, as if she herself were the great, true question that required his best reply.

"Yes," he repeated. "I love you more, I think, than my own life—if this that has happened to us comes from some enchantment, still it is so."

"I love *you* more than life," she said, and took his hand and kissed it, then held it to her breast. "I thought . . ."

"What?"

She shook her head, as if dismissing something, and then sat up beside him. "I feared that my enchantment would not save you—though it was the best that I could do. I thought we were both lost."

They stared at each other. Mark broke the short silence. "I dreamed that Aphrodite was here with us."

Kristin for some reason thought it necessary to consider this statement very solemnly. It struck Mark that they were gazing at each other like two children, just beginning to discover things about the world, and both gravely shocked at what they learned. He had thought he knew something of the world before now, but evidently there was still much he did not know.

Then what Kristin was saying seized his full attention. "I dreamed, too, that *she* was here. And that she was about to kill both of us, with one of the Swords."

Mark stared at her. Then he jumped up out of the nest again, naked in the morning's chill, and went scrambling about to find Sightblinder. The Sword lay nearby, in plain view. In a moment he had it in his hands.

And froze, staring at the hilt. The little white symbol was not an eye. It was an open human hand.

Kristin was beside him, leaning on his shoulder—in a certain way it was as trusting and intimate a contact as any that had gone before. She whispered: "That's Woundhealer, isn't it?"

"Yes."

"She's left it with us."

"And taken Sightblinder in exchange." They stared at each other in wonder, in something like panic. He began a frantic search of the nearby area, but the Sword of Stealth was gone. It was an alarming thought that Woundhealer was going to be useless if Vilkata's troops encountered them.

Kristin was already pulling Mark's deteriorated shirt on over her head. The garment was dirtier than she was, and beginning to show holes. "We've got to get moving. All thanks to Aphrodite, but she's taken our protection with her."

All the dressing and packing they could do took only moments. And moments after that they had got the animals ready and were on their way.

Kristin indicated a course. "Tasavalta lies in this direction. We'll keep our eyes open as we go, and find some fruit. I've been able to gather enough food here and there to keep us going so far."

The country around them and its vegetation were changing as they progressed. The season was advancing too, more wild fruits coming into ripeness. Kristin appeared expert on the subject of what parts of what plants could be eaten; she had more lore in that subject than Mark did, particularly here close to her homeland. He commented on the fact, while marveling silently to himself that it had taken him so long to realize how beautiful she was.

"I have been trained in the white magic. Sorcery and enchantment were to have been my life."

"Were to have been?"

"I have made a different disposition of my life now." And suddenly she rode close beside him, very close, and leaned sideways in her saddle to kiss him fiercely.

He said, "You were a virgin, before last night—yes, you were to have been consecrated to the white magic, weren't you? Or to Ardneh."

Her expression told him that was so.

"I begin to understand. You have given me what was to have gone to Ardneh." Comprehension grew in him slowly. "That was why, how, Aphrodite came to heal me. You summoned her."

"Goddesses go where they will. I could only try. What else could I do? I discovered that I loved you."

Mark put his arm around her as they rode side by side. The embrace at first was only tender. But soon tenderness grew violent in its own way. They stopped the animals beside a thicket and dismounted.

When, after some little time, they were riding on again, solemnity had given way to silliness; again and again they had to reprove themselves for not watching what they were about, warn themselves to stay alert. Love had granted a feeling of invulnerability.

At about midday they came to a decent stream. By now they had got pretty well beyond the worst damage done by Vilkata's foragers, though the countryside was still deserted, the visible houses abandoned as far as could be seen in passing.

The stream, of clean, swift water, was a marvel, and washing at this stage almost as great a relief as being able to drink their fill. Kristin's hair emerged from the worst of its covering of grime to reveal itself as naturally fair. Whatever color had appeared would have been, in Mark's eyes, the only perfect one.

Bathing together soon led to other activities, self-limiting in duration; there was presently a pause for more varied conversation.

Mark asked her, "How did you come to be a prisoner there?"

Kristin's blue-green eyes looked off into the distance. "A group of us were traveling, through country we thought was reasonably safe." She shrugged. "We were attacked by a patrol of the Dark King's army. What happened to the others in our party I do not know; I suppose they were all killed. The enemy had a magician with them. We had a contest, naturally, and he proved too strong for me. Except that I was able to— to hide myself, in a fashion. I knew little of what was happening to me, and my captors were able to tell little about me. They brought me back to their main encampment. What would have happened to me next—"

Mark put out a hand. "It won't happen now. You're safe."

"Thanks to you. But how did you come to be there?"

He explained his mission in broad terms, first as a diplomatic messenger for Sir Andrew, then on his own after his strange encounter with Draffut. That was a well-nigh incredible tale, he realized, but Kristin watched him closely as he spoke and he thought that she believed him. If she had ever heard of Mark, the despoiler of the Blue Temple, she did not appear to connect that person with the man before her. He sometimes thought, hearing his own name in the song of some passing stranger, that he was famous. But actually the name was common enough. And fortunately for his chances of avoiding the Blue Temple assassins, his face was not famous at all.

Before they left the stream, he tried to study his own face in the quietest available pool. "How do I look?" His fingers searched his forehead.

"There's a scar. No more than that. A simple scar, you'll still be handsome." She kissed it for him.

He sat back. "So, as you see, I was on my way to Tasavalta anyway. As a courier."

"How convenient." She kissed him again.

"Yes. What is the Princess like?"

"A few years older than I am." Kristin paused. "I can hardly claim to know her."

"I suppose not. We'd better get moving."

They were dressed, in washed garments, and packed and back on their animals heading east, before Mark resumed the conversation. "I don't know Tasavaltan customs at all well. Should I be asking you who your parents are? I mean, what is the customary way of taking a wife in your land? Who else must I talk to about it, if anyone?"

"My parents are both dead."

"Sorry."

"It was long ago. Yes, there will be people we have to see. Old Karel first, I suppose. He's my uncle, and also my teacher in magic. A rather well-known wizard. You may have heard of him?"

"No. But I've known other magicians, they don't frighten me especially. We'll see your Uncle Karel . . . by the way, will you marry me?"

Kristin appeared vaguely disappointed. "You know I will. But I am glad you thought to ask."

"Ah yes." And again there was an interval in which no thoughtful planning could be accomplished.

The interval over, Mark said, "I gather you're not exactly looking forward to seeing your old uncle. He was intent on consecrating you as a sorceress, is that it?"

"Partly."

He felt somewhat relieved; he could have imagined worse. "Well, not all the women who are good at magic are virgins, I can assure you of that." He paused. "I mean . . ."

They cautiously approached and entered a deserted house, and then another, and helped themselves to a few items of clothing the inhabitants had not bothered to take with them when they fled. Mark wondered whether to leave payment, and decided not—the arrival of Vilkata's looters seemed likely to occur before the return of the proper owners. Feeling a shade more civilized, they rode on.

It struck Mark that Kristin was resisting making plans for their own future. She loved him, they were going to marry, that much was certain between them. But she was reluctant to go into details at all. A sense of mystery, of something withheld, persisted. Mark put it down to exhaustion. Though Woundhealer had restored them marvelously, still the journey was hard and their food meagre.

Yet it was happy, despite continued difficulties and periods of fear.

And as they left the last fringes of the area already devastated by Vilkata's army, their own foraging became correspondingly easier. Farms and houses were even fewer now; this was a region sparsely inhabited in the best of times.

Mark tried to count up the days of their journey. Watching the phases of the Moon, he decided it was now almost a month since he had approached and entered Vilkata's camp.

At last there came the day when they rode into sight of a banner of blue and green, raised on a tall rustic pole. The Tasavaltan flagpole stood atop a crag that overlooked the road, just where the road entered the first pass of mountain foothills. Kristin shed tears at sight of the flag; Mark had to look at her closely to be sure that they were tears of joy.

She assured Mark that what he had been told of Tasavalta was correct, that although it was not a huge land it was certainly spectacular. In any event he could now begin to see that for himself. Kristin explained the topography in a general way: there were two main mountain ranges, one right along the coastline to the east, the other a few kilometers inland, just inside the first long line of sheltered valleys. Both these ranges were really southern extensions of the Ludus Mountains, now many kilometers to the north.

"I grew up in sight of the Ludus," Mark said. "We could see them on a clear day, anyway, from home."

Despite the southern latitude they had now reached, here in late summer there were still traces of ice and snow visible upon the highest Tasavaltan peaks ahead. The coast was deeply cut with fjords here, and cold ocean currents kept this almost tropic land in a state of perpetual spring.

Mark and Kristin pushed on, urging their tired riding beasts past that first frontier marking. Mark kept glancing at his companion. She was more often silent now, and looked more worried the farther they went.

He asked Kristin suddenly, "Still worried about what your teacher in the white arts is going to say?"

"That's not it. Or not altogether."

Still the secrecy, and it annoyed him. "What, then?"

But she would not give him what he considered a straight answer, and his annoyance grew. Something about her family, he supposed. What they were going to say when she brought home an almost penniless foreign soldier as a prospective husband. Mark was sure by now that Kristin's family were no peasants. Well, the two of them had been traveling alone together for a month. If her people were like most of the well-to-do families that Mark had known, that would be a powerful inducement for them to give their consent. In any case he was going to marry her, he would entertain no doubt of that, and he kept reassuring himself that she showed no hesitation on that point either.

She might, he sometimes thought, be withholding information about some complication or obstacle. If she feared he might be influenced by anything like that—well, she didn't yet know him as well as she was going to.

Once they had passed that first flagpole marking the frontier, the road immediately improved. It also began a steeper climb, sometimes requiring long winding switchbacks. For the first time on this journey Mark could glimpse the sea, chewing at the feet of the coastal mountains. It was deep blue in the distance, then the color of Kristin's eyes, then as it met land frothed into white. Now, on either side of the road, there were meadows, presently being harvested of hay by industrious-looking peasants who were not shy about exchanging waves at a distance with shabbily dressed wayfaring strangers. The lifesaving cloak of Vilkata's colors had long since been rolled up into a tight black bundle and lodged behind Mark's saddle.

Now Kristin pointed ahead, to where the sunspark of a heliograph could be seen winking intermittently from the top of a small mountain. "That may be some message about us. In times like these, the lookouts tend to take notice of every traveler."

"Do you know the code?"

"Yes—but that's not aimed in our direction. I can't see enough of it to read."

Now—oddly as it appeared to Mark—Kristin's worry had been replaced by a kind of gaiety. As if whatever had been worrying her had happened now, and all that mattered after that was to make the best of life, moment by moment. Now she was able to relax and enjoy her homecoming, like any other rescued prisoner.

He took what he saw as an opportunity to try to talk seriously to her again. "You're going to marry me, and right away, no matter what your family or anyone else says about it." He stated it as firmly as he could.

"Yes, oh darling, yes. I certainly am." And Kristin was every bit as positive as he was about it. But he could see now that her sadness, though it had been conquered, was not entirely gone.

Things of very great importance to her—whatever all the implications might be exactly—had been set aside, because it was more important to Kristin that she marry him. Mark made, not for the first time on this journey, a silent vow to see that she never regretted that decision.

He was cheered to see that happiness increasingly dominated her mood as they went on. She was coming home, she was going to see a family and friends who must at the very least be badly worried about her now, who might very possibly have given her up for dead.

The road, now well paved, rounded a shoulder of the same small mountain upon whose peak they had seen the heliograph. Then it promptly turned into a cobblestone street, as the travelers found themselves entering the first village of Tasavalta. It was, Mark decided, really a small town. He wondered what it was called. Not far ahead on the right was a small, clean-looking inn, and he suggested that they stop. He had a little money with him still, carried in an inner pocket. "If they will let us in; we do look somewhat ragged." Their scavenging through deserted houses had added to their wardrobe, but only doubtfully improved its quality.

"All right. We can stop anywhere. It makes little difference now." Kristin looked him squarely in the eye, and added warmly: "I love you."

It was something they said to each other, in endless variations, a hundred times a day. Why should the effect, this time, be almost chilling, as if she were telling him goodbye?

"And I love you," he answered softly.

She turned her head away from him, to look toward the inn, and something in her aspect froze. Mark followed her gaze. Now they were close enough to the inn for him to see the white ribbon of mourning that was stretched above the door. And there was another white ribbon, now that he looked for it, wrapped round the arch of the gate leading into the inn's courtyard from the street.

He said to Kristin: "Someone in the innkeeper's family . . ."

She had turned in her saddle again, and was looking wordlessly up and down the street. Now that they were closer to the other doors and gateways they could see the white bands plainly, everywhere. In this town the badge of mourning appeared to be universal.

"What is it, then?" The words burst from Kristin in a scream, a sound that Mark had never heard from her before. He stared at her. They had stopped, just outside the open gateway of the courtyard of the inn.

In response to the outcry an old woman in an apron, the innkeeper's wife by the look of her, appeared just inside the yard. In a cracked voice she admonished, "Where've you been, young woman, that you don't know—"

At that point the old woman halted suddenly. Her face paled as she stared at Kristin, and she seemed to stumble, almost going down on one knee. But Kristin, who had already dismounted, caught her by the arms and held her up.

And shook her, fiercely. "Tell me, old one, tell me, who is the mourning for?"

The eyes of the innkeeper's wife were pale and hopeless. "My lady, it's for the Princess . . . Princess Rimac . . . has been killed."

Again Kristin let out a scream, this one short and wordless. Mark had heard another woman scream just that way as she fell in battle. Kristin swayed but she did not fall.

He jumped off his own mount and went to her and held her. "What is it?"

She clung to him as if an ocean wave were tugging at her, sweeping her away. For just a moment her eyes, flashing with mystery and fright, looked directly into his. "My sister . . ."

She tried to add more words to those two. But Mark heard hardly any of them. He retreated, one backward step after another in the direction of the inn, until directly behind him there was an old bench, that stood close by the white-ribboned doorway. He sat down on the bench, in the partial shade of an old tree, leaning his back against the inn's whitewashed wall. Already half a dozen more townspeople had appeared from somewhere, to make a little knot around Kristin and the old woman in the courtyard, and even as Mark watched another half dozen came running. They were kneeling to Kristin, seizing her hands and kissing them, calling her Princess. Someone leaped on the back of a fresh riding beast in the courtyard and went pounding away down the street, hooves echoing for what seemed like a long time on distant cobblestones.

Mark remained sitting where he was, on the shaded bench near the worn doorway, while people rushed in and out ignoring him. Now and again through the press of bodies his eyes met Kristin's for a moment. The Sword of Love in its sheath weighed heavily at his side.

Among the other things that people were shouting at her were explanations: how Princess Rimac had ridden out carelessly as was her habit; how there had been a sudden, unexpected attack by one of the Dark King's raiding parties; how now there was going to be war. . . .

The crowd grew rapidly, and Mark's glimpses of Kristin became less frequent. At one point dozens of eyes suddenly turned his way, and there was a sudden, comparatively minor fuss that centered about him —she must have said something that identified him as her rescuer. People thronged about him. Men with an attitude between timidity and bravado beat him on the back in congratulation, and tried to press filled beer mugs into his hand. Women asked him if he were hungry, and would not hear anything he answered them, and brought him cake. Girls threw their tender arms about his neck and kissed him, more girls and young women kissing him now in a few moments than had even looked at him for a long time. One girl, pressed against him by the crowd, took his hand and crushed it against her breast. By now he had lost sight of Kristin entirely, and if it were not for the continuing crowd he would have thought that she had left the courtyard.

There was the sound of many riding beasts out in the street. Now the crowd, filling the gateway, blocking Mark's view of the street, had a growing new component. Soldiers, uniformed in green and blue. Mark supposed that the heliograph had been busy.

Someone near him said: "General." Mark recognized Rostov at once, having heard him described so often, though he had never seen the man before.

Round one thick arm in its blue-green sleeve, Rostov like the other soldiers was wearing a band of mourning white. There was one decoration on his barrel chest—Mark had no idea of what it represented. The General was as tall as Mark, and gave Mark the impression of being stronger, though he was twice Mark's age. Rostov's curly black hair was heavily seasoned with gray, and his black face marked on the right cheek by an old sword-slash. A gray beard that looked like steel fiber raggedly trimmed sprouted from cheeks and chin. His facial expression, thought Mark, would have been quite hard enough even without a steel beard.

Kristin was now coming through the crowd, and Mark from only two yards away saw how the General greeted her. He did not kneel— that appeared to be quite optional for anyone—but his eyes lit up with relief and joy, and he bowed and kissed her hand fervently.

She clung to his hand with both of hers. "Rostov, they tell me that Parliament has been divided over the succession? That they have nearly come to blows?"

"They have come very nearly to civil war, Highness." The General's voice was suitably gravelly and deep. "But, thank the gods, all that is over now. All factions can agree on you. It was only the thought that you were missing, too . . . thank all the gods you're here."

"I am here. And well." And at last her eyes turned in Mark's direction.

Now Mark and Rostov were being introduced. The General glowered at him, Mark thought; that was the way of generals everywhere, he had observed, when looking at someone of insignificance who had got in the way. Still Rostov was quick to express his own and his army's formal thanks.

A hundred people were speaking now, but one soft voice at Mark's elbow caught his full attention. It was a woman's, and it said: "They told me that your name was Mark. And so I hurried here to see."

Mark recognized his mother's voice, before he turned to see her face.

CHAPTER 8

The scar on Denis's arm, the last trace of the wound that had been healed by the Sword of Mercy, looked faint and old already. He thought that the second touch of Woundhealer in the hand of Aphrodite had reached his heart, for there were times when he had the feeling of scar tissue forming there as well. The vision of the goddess as she had appeared to him at night on the river-island was with him still. He still felt pity for her whenever he thought of what had happened; and then, each time, fear at what might happen to a man who dared feel pity for divinity.

His emotions whipsawn by his encounter with Aphrodite, Denis sometimes felt as if years had passed in the few days since his departure from Tashigang. In the days that followed, he went on paddling his canoe into the north and east. He toyed no more with the idea of absconding with the remaining Sword; he was still in awe and shock from that demonstration of its powers, and he wanted nothing but to be honorably and safely rid of it.

With that objective in mind, he tried his best to keep his attention concentrated upon practical affairs. It was necessary now to watch for a second set of landmarks, these to tell him where to leave this river and make the small necessary portage. The markers were specially blazed trees, in the midst of a considerable forest through which the little river now ran. Denis paddled upstream through the forest for a full day, looking for them. The stream he was now following grew ever younger and smaller and more lively as he got further from the Corgo, and was here overhung from both banks by great branches.

On the night that Denis left Tashigang, Ben had told him that if he saw any wild-looking people after he had come this far, they were probably Sir Andrew's. The Kind Knight's folk would escort a courier the rest of the way, or at least put him on the right track, once he had convinced them he was bona fide.

. . . and the Goddess of Love had told him, Denis, that she loved him. Even in the midst of trying to make plans he kept coming back to that, coming back to it in a glow of secret and guilty pride, guilty because he knew that it was undeserved. Was ever mortal man so blessed?

Much good had such a blessing done him. Pride came only fitfully. In general he felt scarred and numb.

He did manage to keep his mind on the job, and spot his required landmarks. The blazed trees were not very conspicuous, and it was a good thing that he had been keeping an alert eye open. Once he had found the proper place, he had to beach his canoe on the right bank, then drag it through a trackless thicket—this route was apparently not much used—and next up a clear slope, over ground fortunately too soft to damage the canoe. This brought him into a low pass leading through a line of hills that the stream had now been paralleling for some time.

After dragging his canoe for half a kilometer, lifting and carrying it when absolutely necessary, Denis reached the maximum slight elevation afforded by the pass. From this vantage point he could look ahead, over the treetops of another forest, and see in the distance the beginnings of the Great Swamp, different kinds of trees rearing up out of an ominous flatness. During the last four years that largely uncharted morass had swallowed up the larger portions of a couple of small armies, to the great discomfiture of the Dark King and the Silver Queen respectively. And neither monarch was any closer now than four years ago to their goal of slaughtering Sir Andrew and the impertinent fugitives of his own small military force.

The stream that Denis had to find now was not hard to locate. It was running in the only place nearby that it very well could run, just beyond the line of hills in the bottom of the adjoining gentle valley. After resting a little while on its bank, he launched his canoe again, and resumed paddling, once more going upstream. In this waterway the current was slower, and Denis made correspondingly better time. But this was a more winding stream, taking him back and forth on wide curves through the forest; he was going to have to paddle farther just to get from here to there.

Denis spent an entire day paddling up this stream before he was challenged. This happened at just about the point where he could see that he was entering some portion of the Great Swamp itself.

His challengers were three in number, a man and two women, one of them standing on each bank of the narrow stream and one on an overhanging bough. All three looked quite tough and capable. Their weapons did not menace but they were certainly held ready. Against this display Denis lifted his own hands, empty, in a sign of peace.

He said, "I need to see Sir Andrew, as quickly as I can. I come from a man named Ben, and I have here a cargo that Sir Andrew needs."

The three who had stopped him spoke quickly among themselves, and two of them promptly became Denis's escort. They made no comment on the fact of his empty-looking boat, as contrasted with his claim of valuable cargo. They did take from him his only visible weapon, a short knife. Then the man got into the rear seat of Denis's canoe, and took over the paddling, while one of the women oared another small craft along behind. As they glided deeper into the swamp, under the twisted limbs of giant trees festooned with exotic parasite-plants, Denis saw a small arboreal creature, of a type strange to him, headed in the same direction. It was brachiating itself along through the upper branches at a pace that soon overtook and passed the boats. He surmised it was some species of half-intelligent messenger.

Presently, after about a kilometer of paddling, Denis was delivered to a camouflaged command post, a half-walled structure made of logs and shirt-sized tree fronds, where he repeated his terse message to an officer. Again he was sent on, deeper into the swamp, this time with a different and larger escort.

This leg of the escorted journey took longer. It occupied a fair portion of the remaining daylight hours, and ended with Denis's canoe grounding on the shore of what appeared to be a sizable island of firm land that reared up out of the swamp. There were people on this island already. He estimated a score of them or more, many of them conspicuously wearing Sir Andrew's orange and black. A few tents had been set up, but the place did not have the worn look of a permanent encampment.

The people who were already gathered here appeared to be waiting for something. They were not, as it turned out, anticipating Denis's arrival, which in itself did not cause much of a stir. His canoe was beached for him, and he was at once conducted a short distance inland, toward one particular knot of people who were engaged in some serious discussion. Taking the chance to look about him from the slightly higher vantage point of this firm ground, Denis realized that this was no true island at all, or else it was a much larger island than he had first assumed. From here he could see a double track, what looked like a regular road, though a poor one, approaching through the trees to end in the small clearing where the knot of people were conversing.

The focus of that group's attention was one man, heavily built, gray-haired, and wearing clothing that might once have been fine. This man was standing with his back to Denis, but the black hilt of a Sword visible at his side convinced Denis that this must be Sir Andrew himself, who was known to hold Shieldbreaker.

Sir Andrew turned. The face of the man known as the Kind Knight showed more age than his strong body did. He was holding a book in his left hand, and had been gesturing with it to make some point, when Denis's arrival interrupted the discussion.

Standing at Sir Andrew's right hand was a woman, not young but certainly still attractive. There was much gray now in the lady's black hair, but Denis thought that in youth her face must have been extremely beautiful. He had no idea what her name might be, but at first glance he was certain she was a sorceress. Certain details of her dress gave that indication, but the impression was created chiefly by an impalpable sense of magic that hung about her. Denis could feel that magical aura, and he did not consider himself a sensitive.

Two pairs of brown eyes, the lady's younger and quicker than Sir Andrew's, studied the new arrival. Names were formally exchanged.

"And where," asked the Knight then, in his slow, strong voice, "is this cargo that you say you have for me?"

"In the canoe, sir. There's a false bottom."

"And what is the cargo? Speak freely, I have no secrets from any here."

Denis glanced around. "A Sword, sir. One of the famous Twelve, I mean. Sent from the man called Ben, in Tashigang. There were two Swords, but—something happened to me on the way."

"I can see that," the enchantress murmured. Her eyes were narrowed as she studied Denis. "Show me this remaining Sword."

They moved quickly to the waiting beached canoe. At Denis's direction the concealing board was pried up once more. Dame Yoldi, the graying sorceress, supervised this operation carefully, and gave the exposed cargo a close inspection before she would allow Sir Andrew to approach it.

She also questioned Denis first. "You say that two Swords were sent, and one lost on the way?"

"Yes Ma'am." Denis related in barest outline, and not dwelling on his own feelings, what had happened between him and the goddess. He heard a snicker or two, and scoffing noises, in the background. But he thought the lady perhaps believed him. At least she stepped back to let Sir Andrew approach the canoe.

The Knight's right hand plucked Doomgiver from the secret compartment, and held it, still sheathed, aloft. There was a general murmur, of appreciation this time, not scoffing.

"Do you feel anything from the two Swords, Andrew?" the sorceress asked gently. "You are holding two at one time—you still wear Shieldbreaker."

He huffed and gave her a look. "I've not forgotten what I wear. No, I feel nothing in particular—you once told me that even three Swords at once would not be too many for some folk to handle."

"And I tell you again that two, in certain combinations, might do strange things to other folk. And you are sensitive."

"Sensitive! Me!" He huffed again.

Dame Yoldi smiled, and Denis could see how much she loved him. Denis wondered suddenly if he himself had actually handled the two Swords at the same time at any point. If he had, he couldn't remember feeling anything strange.

Now Sir Andrew turned back to Denis. "We must soon hear your story about the goddess, and Woundhealer, in more detail. Meanwhile we are all grateful to you for what you have brought to us. But at the moment even such a gift as the Sword of Justice must wait to have my full attention, and you must wait to get your proper thanks."

"You're quite welcome, sir."

Already Dame Yoldi had Denis by the arm and was turning him away. "At the moment you are in need of food and rest." She gestured, and a woman came to take Denis in charge.

He resisted momentarily. "Thank you, Ma'am. But there is one bit of news, bad news, that I must tell you first." That certainly got their full attention back. Denis swallowed, then blurted out the words. "The Dark King has the Mindsword in his hands. So we were told in Tashigang, by some of Ardneh's people." The source put a strong flavor of reliability upon the news.

His hearers received his announcement with all the shock that Denis had anticipated. He braced himself for the inevitable burst of questions, which he answered in the only way he could, pleading his own lack of further knowledge.

At last he was dismissed. Led away, he was given bread and wine, then shown to a tent where he stretched out gratefully upon the single cot. His eyes closed, their lids suddenly heavy, and with a swiftness that might have been genuinely magical, he plunged into a deep sleep.

Denis awoke suddenly, and feeling greatly refreshed. He was surprised to see that the pattern of tree shadows on the tent had shifted very little, and no great length of time could have passed. What had awakened him he did not know.

Listening to the silence outside the tent, he thought that there was some unusual tension in it.

He got up and left the tent. Seeing that some people were still gathered at the place where he had left Sir Andrew and Dame Yoldi, he hurried in that direction. Now, as he walked, Denis could see a few more people in orange and black approaching quickly on foot along the landward road. These were turning and gesturing, as if to indicate that someone or something of importance was coming after them. Everyone nearby was looking in that direction.

Denis halted in surprise at sight of the next two figures that appeared down the road. Both were wearing black and silver, the colors of Yambu. Both were mounted, riding freely, not at all like prisoners. Still, neither was visibly armed. One was a burly man, and the other—

With a silent gasp, Denis recognized the Silver Queen herself. He had seen her twice before, both times years ago, both times in the city of Tashigang. She, as the city's formal overlord, had been appearing then in ceremonial processions. He, then no more than a street urchin, had been clinging to precarious perches above the crowds, eager to watch.

In those processions the Queen had ridden her virtually unique mount, a superbly trained and deadly warbeast. Her steed today was less remarkable, though still magnificent, a huge riding beast matching that ridden by her companion. This burly man, her escort, as they approached Sir Andrew and the others waiting, dropped a deferential half-length behind.

The two riders halted, calmly, at a little distance from where the folk in orange and black were waiting to receive them. They dismounted there and approached Sir Andrew's group on foot, the tall Queen a pace ahead in her light silvery ceremonial armor, taking long strides like a man. Denis calculated that she must be now well into her middle thirties, though her tanned face looked younger. Her whole body was strong and lithe, and despite her stride the generously female shape of her body left no doubt at all about her sex. The Queen's nose, Denis noted now in private impertinence, was too big for her ever to be called pretty, by any reasonable usage of the word. And yet, all in all—well, if he were to meet some woman of attainable station who looked just like her, he'd not refuse a chance to know her better.

And have you forgotten me already? The voice of Aphrodite came to Denis only in his imagination. It shook him, though, in a resonance of conflicting feelings.

Sir Andrew was standing with folded arms, waiting for his visitors, as if the last thing in the world he might do would be to make any gesture acknowledging his old enemy's greater rank. But she, approaching, as if she thought he might do so and wished to forestall him, was quick to make the first gesture of greeting, flinging up her right hand in the universal gesture of peace.

"We meet again!" The Silver Queen's voice, hearty and open, neither assumed a royal superiority nor pretended a friendship that did not exist. "My honored enemy! Would that my friends and allies were half as dependable as you. So, will you take my hand? And never mind the fripperies of rank."

And when Dame Yoldi moved between them, Queen Yambu added: "Aye, lady, you may look at my hand first. I bring no poisoning, no tricks; which is not to say that none such were suggested by my magicians."

Dame Yoldi did indeed make a brief inspection of the Queen's hand. Meanwhile Denis was having to use his elbows to keep himself from being crowded back by the small but growing throng of Sir Andrew's people who wanted to observe the meeting closely. There had evidently been more than twenty on the island after all. He managed to remain close enough to see that the Queen's hand looked like a soldier's, being short-nailed, spotted with callouses—the sort that came from gripping weapons—and strong. But, for all that, it was shapely, and not very large.

The Queen's offered hand was briefly engulfed in Sir Andrew's massive paw. And then the Knight stood back again, grim-faced, arms folded, waiting to hear more.

The Queen cast a look around her. Sir Andrew's friends and body-guard, heavily armed, most of them impressive warriors, were hovering suspiciously close to her and her companion, and looking as grim as Sir Andrew did himself.

She said to the Knight: "I do trust you, you see, and your safe-conduct guarantee. In nine years of fighting you, off and on, I've learned to know you well enough for that."

The Knight spoke to her for the first time. "And we have learned something of your character as well, Madam. And of yours, Baron Amintor. Now, what will you have of me? Why this urgent call for a meeting?"

The Baron was as big and solid as Sir Andrew, and with much the same hearty and honest look, though the Silver Queen's companion was probably the younger of the two men by some fifteen years. Both were battle-scarred, Denis observed, evidently real fighters. Amintor's eyes were intelligent, and Denis had heard that he was gifted with a diplomatic tongue when he chose to use it.

And the Queen . . . this Queen had been no more than a half-grown girl when she ascended to the throne of Yambu. Her first act afterward, it was said, had been to put to death the plotters who had murdered both her parents in an abortive coup attempt. Nor had the throne been easy for her to hold, through the twenty years that followed. Many plotters and intriguers during that time had gone the way of that first set. Ever since its shaky beginning, her reign—except in a few lucky places like Tashigang—had not been gentle. It was said that she grew ever more obsessed with the idea that there were plots against her, and that about four years ago she had sold her bastard adolescent daughter into slavery, because of the girl's supposed involvement in one. The girl, Ariane, had been her only child; everyone knew that the Silver Queen had never married formally.

Now the Queen said to Sir Andrew, "I like a man who can come straight to the point. But just one question first: are you aware that the Dark King now has the Mindsword in his possession?"

The Knight answered calmly. "We have been so informed."

Both the Queen and Baron Amintor appeared somewhat taken aback by this calm response. Yambu said, "And I thought that you were existing in a backwater here! My compliments to your intelligence service."

And Amintor chimed in: "You'll agree, I'm sure, Sir Andrew, that the fact does change the strategic situation for us all."

Sir Andrew took just a moment to consider him in silence, before facing back to the Queen. "And just what, Madam, do you expect this change to mean?"

The Silver Queen laughed. It was a pleasant, rueful sound. There was a fallen tree nearby, a twisted log that rested at a convenient height on the stubs of its own branches, and she moved a couple of steps to it and sat down.

"I foresee myself as Vilkata's first victim, unless I do something about it, quickly. I'll speak plainly—if you've begun to know me, as you say, you know that's how I prefer to speak. If Vilkata with the Mindsword in his hand falls on my army now, then unless they can withstand it somehow—and I've no reason to hope they can—then my army will at best melt away. At worst it'll join Vilkata and augment his strength, which is already greater than yours and mine combined.

"You, of course, will applaud my fall and my destruction—but not for very long."

The Knight, his aspect one of unaltered grimness, nodded. "So, Queen of Yambu, what do you propose?"

"No more than what you must have already guessed, Sir Andrew. An alliance, of course, between us two." Yambu turned her head slightly; her noble bearing at the moment could almost turn the fallen log into a throne. "Tell him, good Dame, if you love him—an alliance with me now represents his only chance."

Neither Sir Andrew nor his enchantress gave an immediate answer. But the Knight looked so black that, had he spoken, Denis thought the conference would have ended on the instant.

Dame Yoldi asked the Queen, "Suppose we should join forces against Vilkata—what then? How do you propose to fight the Mindsword, with our help or without it?"

It was the Baron who replied. "To begin with, we mean to avoid battle with Vilkata's troops unless we're sure he's not on the scene himself—he'll never turn the Mindsword over to a subordinate, you may be sure of that. Your people and ours will exchange intelligence regarding the Dark King's movements. Yes, it'll still be damned difficult even if we're allied—but if we're still fighting each other at the same time, it's going to be impossible."

Yoldi had another question. "Supposing for a moment that such an alliance could be made to work, even temporarily—what do you intend doing with the Mindsword, after the Dark King has somehow been defeated?"

Yambu smiled with what looked like genuine amusement. It made her face more attractive than before. "Why, I would leave that up to you."

"You'd turn the Mindsword over to us?" Yoldi asked the question blankly.

The Queen paused very briefly. "Why not? I can agree to that, because I think that your good Knight there is one of the few men in the world who'd never use it."

"And what of my people who are now your slaves, my lands that you have seized?" This was from Sir Andrew. He had now mastered his obvious anger, and was almost calm, as if he were only discussing some theoretical possibility.

"Why, those are yours again, of course, as soon as you and I can reach agreement. As soon after that as I rejoin my own people, I'll send word by flying beasts to all my garrison commanders there, to begin an evacuation at once."

"And in return for that, what do you want of me?"

"First, of course, immediate cessation of hostilities against my forces, everywhere. And then your full support against the Dark King, until he is brought down. Or until he crushes both of us." The Queen paused, giving an almost friendly look to Sir Andrew and his surrounding bodyguard. She added: "You really have no choice, you know."

There was a long pause, during which Sir Andrew studied the Queen even more carefully than before. At last he said, "Tell me something."

"If I can."

"Did you in fact sell your own daughter into Red Temple slavery?"

Denis saw a shadow, he thought of something more complex than simple anger, cross the Queen's face. Her voice when she replied was much less hearty. "Ah," she said. "Ah, and if I tell you the truth of that, will you believe me?"

"Why not? Apparently you expect us to believe your proposal to give us the Mindsword—perhaps at this moment you even believe that yourself. Still, I would like to hear whatever you wish to say about your daughter."

This time the pause was short. Then, with a sudden movement, the Silver Queen got up from her seat on the dead tree.

"Amintor and I will walk apart a little now, while you discuss my offer. Naturally you will want to talk to your close advisers before giving me an answer. I trust they are all here. Unfortunately—or perhaps fortunately—there isn't time for diplomacy as usually conducted. But I'll wait, while you have your discussion."

And the two visitors from Yambu did indeed walk apart, Baron Amintor apparently pointing out some curiosities of the swamp flora to the Queen, as if neither of them had anything more important than wild plants on mind.

Sir Andrew and several others were huddled together, and Denis could imagine what they were saying: About Vilkata and the Mindsword, it must be true, for now we've heard it twice. But, an alliance? With *Yambu?*

But, thought Denis, the Queen was right. He has no real choice but to accept.

CHAPTER 9

Kristin, crowned only hours ago in hurried but joyful ceremony as Princess Regnant of the Lands of Tasavalta, was alone in one of the royal palace's smaller semipublic rooms, sitting on one of her smaller thrones. She had chosen to sit on this throne at this moment because she was tired—exhausted might have been putting it mildly—and the throne was the most convenient place in the room to sit. There were no other chairs. She could willingly have opted for the floor, but the fit of her coronation gown, which had been her sister's, and today had been pressed into service hurriedly, argued against that.

She was waiting for her lover Mark to be brought to her. There were certain things that had to be said to him, and only she could say them, and only when the two of them were alone. And her impending collapse into exhaustion had to be postponed until after they had been said.

The room was quiet now, except for the distant continuing sounds of celebration from outside. But if Kristin thought about it, she could remember other days in this room. Bright days of loud voices and free laughter, in the time when her older sister had been alive and ruling Tasavalta. And days from an earlier time still, when Kristin had been only a small girl, and there were two girls in this room with their father, a living King, who joked with them about this throne. . . .

Across the room in present time a small door was opening, quietly and discreetly. Her Uncle Karel, master of magic and teacher of magicians, looked in, saw she was alone, and gave her an almost imperceptible nod of approval. Karel was enormously fat and somewhat jolly in appearance, red cheeks glowing as usual above gray whiskers, as if he had just come in from an invigorating winter walk. As far as Kristin could tell he had not changed in the slightest from those bright days of her own girlhood. Today of course he was decked out, like herself, in full ceremonial garb, including a blue-green garland on his brow.

He reached behind him now to pull someone forward. It was Mark, dressed now in strange borrowed finery, that he thrust gently into the room where Kristin waited.

Karel said to her, in a voice that somewhat belied his jolly face; "Highness, it will look bad for you to be alone for very long with this—"

She stood up, snapped to her feet as if brought there by a spring, weary muscles energized by outrage, by the tension of all that had happened to her today. "Uncle Karel, I have been alone with him for a month already. Thank the gods! For before that I was alone with Vilkata's torturers, and *you* were not there to bring me out."

That was unfair and Kristin knew it; her voice softened a little. "There are important matters that I must—convey to this man. Before I dispatch him on a mission that will take him out of Tasavalta."

Her uncle had winced at the jab about Vilkata's torturers, but his relief at her last words was evident. He bowed himself out silently, closing the door behind him.

Mark heard the same words from Kristin with muted shock, but no real surprise. It was hours now since he had opened his mouth to say a word of his own to anyone. Many had spoken to him, but for the most part only to give him directions: Bathe here, wait there, put this on and see if it fits. Here is food, here is drink, here is a razor. Stand here, wait. Now come this way. He had been fed, cleaned up, draped with robes and what he supposed were honors, then shunted aside and left to watch from an inconspicuous place during the coronation ceremony.

Now he marveled to himself: it was less than a day ago—hardly more than half a day—that this girl and I were riding alone as lovers, on the edge of the wilderness, both of us still in rags. I could have stopped my mount then, and stopped hers—yes, even in sight of that first flagpole bearing blue and green—and got down from my saddle, and pulled her down from hers, and lain with her on the ground in our rags, or out of them, and she would have loved it, welcomed it. And now. . . .

This audience chamber, in which Mark now found himself alone with Kristin, was like the rest of the palace—like the whole domain of Tasavalta, perhaps—a larger and somehow more important place than it had appeared at first impression. It was a sunlit, cheerful room, beautiful in a high vertical way. The air moving in through the open windows smelled of flowers, of perpetual spring; drifting in with the scents of spring came the music of the dance that was still going on far below the windows, part of the coronation celebration. The dance and the music, like the rest of the day, had become to Mark something like a show to which he need only listen, and watch. As if none of it had anything, really, to do with him.

The windows of this room were equipped with heavy shutters, as was fitting in a castle constructed to withstand assault. But on this upper level of the castle, high above any possible assault by climbing troops, the windows were large, and today all the shutters had been thrown open. Framed in their casement openings, the sea and the rocky hills and the town below all appeared like fine tapestries of afternoon sunlight, thrown by some Old World magic on the walls.

Kristin had risen quickly from the throne when the door opened, and when her uncle had closed it again behind him she had moved a few paces forward, toward Mark. But now the two of them, she and Mark, were still standing a little apart, looking at each other as if they had nothing to say—or perhaps as if neither of them could manage to say anything.

But their eyes drew them together. Suddenly they were embracing, still without a word of speech. Then Kristin tore herself away.

"What is this they've given you to wear?" she asked, as if the sight of the costume they had put on him, some antique ceremonial thing, made her want to laugh and cry at once.

But still he said nothing.

She tried again, not with laughter, but now with an almost distant courtesy. How fine that he had already been reunited with his family. She'd had no idea, of course, that they'd been living here. In recent years a lot of refugees, good people, had come in. Did Mark's mother and sister know him after so long a time? How long had they been living here in Tasavalta? Did he have any trouble recognizing them? It was too bad his father was away.

"Kristin." As he called her by her name, he wondered if it was the last time he would ever be able to do so. "Stop it. Have you nothing real to say to me? Why didn't you *tell* me?"

There was a pause, in which Kristin drew a deep breath, like a woman who wondered if it might be her last.

"Yes," she said then. "I must say something very real to you, Mark. For the sister of a Princess Regnant to have married a—commoner, and a foreigner as well—that would have been very hard. Very nearly impossible. But I would have done it. I wanted to marry you. I wanted it so much I was afraid to tell you who I was. And I was going to marry you, wherever that path led. I hope you will believe that."

"Kristin, Princess . . ."

"Wait! Let me finish, please." She needed another pause to get herself together. "But my sister Rimac is dead. She died childless and unmarried, and I am ruler now. For a Princess Regnant to marry a commoner, let alone a foreign soldier, *is* impossible. Impossible, except—again I hope you will believe me—I would have done it anyway. It would have meant resigning the throne, probably leaving the country; I would have done that for you. But . . ."

"But."

"But you must have heard them! There isn't anyone else to rule! You heard Rostov. If I hadn't come back to take the throne, there would have been a civil war over the succession. Even with attackers threatening us from outside. I know my people. We probably seem to you a happy, peaceful country, but you don't know . . ."

Again Mark was silent.

"I . . . Mark, our land and people . . . we owe you more than we can ever repay. We can give you almost anything. Except the one thing that you want. And that I want . . . oh, darling."

This time the embrace lasted longer. But as before, the Princess broke it off.

Mark was conscious that he still had a duty to perform, and drew himself up. "I am the bearer of certain messages, that Sir Andrew, whom I serve, has charged me to deliver to the ruler of the Lands of Tasavalta."

Kristin, as never before conscious of duty, drew herself up, too, and heard the messages. They were more or less routine, diplomatic preliminaries looking to the establishment of more regular contacts. Sir Andrew had long resisted adopting the diplomatic pretense that he was still actually governing the lands and people that had been stolen from him; but he had recently been persuaded of the value of taking such a pose, even if the facts were otherwise.

Mark concluded the memorized messages. "And now, I am ordered to place myself at Your Majesty's disposal." Again, in the fog of his exhaustion, the feeling came over him that none of this really had anything to do with him; he had stumbled into the middle of a play, there were certain lines that he was required to read, and soon it would all be over.

Kristin said, "I am glad to hear it. You will need a few days in which to rest, and recover from . . ." She had to let that trail away. With a toss of her head she made a new start. "You will be assigned—modest quarters here in the palace." *Quarters far from my own rooms.* So Mark understood the phrase. "Then—you heard what I told Karel. I mean to send you on a special mission. This should not pose any conflict with your orders from Sir Andrew, if they are to place yourself at my disposal. I hope that you will accept the assignment willingly."

He could feel only numbness now. "I am at Your Majesty's disposal, as I said before."

"Good." Kristin heaved an unroyal sigh: part of an ordeal had been passed. "The mission you are to perform for Tasavalta is a result of some magical business of Karel's. In divination . . . you will be given more details later. But according to him, the indications are so urgent that he dared not wait even until tomorrow to confront me with the results.

"You are to go and find the Emperor, and seek an alliance with him for Tasavalta—and an alliance with him for Sir Andrew too, if you feel you are empowered by Sir Andrew to do that. I leave that to your judgement."

"The Emperor. An alliance with him?" Even in Mark's present state of embittered numbness, he had to react somehow to the strangeness of that proposal. An *alliance,* as if the Emperor were a nation, or had an army? Of course the indications were, Mark thought, that the Emperor was, or at least could be when he chose, a wizard of immense power.

Curious in spite of everything, he asked, "Me, negotiate for you in such a matter? I'm not even one of your subjects. Or a diplomat. Why me?"

"Karel says it should be done that way. Though I don't think that he himself knows why. But I've learned over the years that my uncle usually gives his monarch good advice."

"Karel wants to make sure I'm out of the way."

"There is that. But sending you back to Sir Andrew would do that just as well. No. There's something about the Emperor—and about you. I don't know what."

The Emperor, thought Mark. *The man that Draffut, after fifty thousand years of knowing human beings, trusted at first meeting. The man who had said that he, Mark, should be given Sightblinder.*

The man in whose name a simple incantation had twice, in Mark's experience, repelled demons. . . .

The sorcerer Karel—it was, Mark supposed, foolish to think he had not been listening—was back in the room now, as if on cue.

After all that had already happened today, Mark had no real capacity left for surprise, so he felt no more than dull curiosity when he observed that the magician was carrying a sheathed Sword.

Karel in his soft, rich voice said to him: "It is Coinspinner, and it has come to us in a mysterious way. And you are going to take it with you to help you find the Emperor."

Mark's dinner that evening was eaten not in the palace, but in the vastly humbler home of his sister Marian. It had turned out that she was now living in the town, really a small city, not far below.

Mark had by now had a little time in which to savor the great news that his father Jord, who he had thought for ten years was dead, was alive after all. And not only was Jord still alive but well and active at last report, off now on some secret mission for the Tasavaltan intelligence service. Neither Mala nor Marian appeared to know where Jord had been sent or when he might be back, and Mark, with some experience in these matters himself, did not press to find out. For now it was enough to know that he at least had a good chance of someday seeing his living father once again.

At dinner—a good dinner, evoking marvelous memories—Mark heard from his mother and sister how his surviving family had come to Tasavalta years ago, after more years spent in homeless wandering, following the destruction of their old village.

In the nine years or so since then, much had happened to them all, and they had much to talk about. Marian was married now, her husband off somewhere with Rostov's army. Her two small children gaped through dinner at this newly discovered uncle, and warmed up to him gradually.

It was almost midnight, and Mark was having to struggle at every moment to stay awake, before he said goodnight. His "modest quarters" in the palace had no attraction, and he was about to go to sleep on cushions on the floor in the room where they had dined and talked.

Marian had already said goodnight, and had taken the children upstairs to bed.

But Mark's mother lingered. There was a suppressed urgency in her manner. "Walk me home. I stay nearby, here in town, while Jord is gone. It's only a little way."

"Of course."

Once they were outside, Mala clung to her son's arm as if she needed his support to walk, though she was not yet forty and all evening had seemed full of energy, rejoicing in their reunion. But now her mood became suddenly tinged with sadness.

"You've just come back to us," she said. "And before we can begin to know you, you must go off again."

"I must, Mother."

"I know, I know." Mark had yet to encounter anyone at all, in either town or castle, who did not know of his relationship with Kristin, and the potential problems that it raised.

Mother and son walked, slowly. He was very tired. He thought that his mother seemed now to be on the brink of telling him something. She kept asking him, "You'll come back to Tasavalta, though?"

"I'll be here a couple of days yet. I'll see you again, and Marian, before I go."

"Yes, of course. Unless the plan for your departure is changed. In these matters of secrecy, plans can change very quickly, I've learned that. But after this mission, you'll come back?"

"To report on my mission, I suppose, yes, I'll have to. And be sent off again. I can't stay here. The Princess's commoner lover, and a foreigner to boot. If my father had been the Grand Duke Basil, or Prince Something-or-other, things would probably be different."

They were at her door now. It was a modest place, but looked comfortable; probably the government here provided quarters for its secret agents' families.

Mala, her voice quivering as if she were doing something difficult, said: "Mark, come in, there's something I must tell you, while I have the chance. The gods know if I'll ever have the chance again."

It was about an hour later when he emerged from the humble apartment where his parents lived. He stood in the narrow street for a little while, looking up at the stars. They looked the same as always. Beyond tiredness now, Mark remained standing there in the street for what felt to him like a long time. And then he went to his modest quarters in the palace, knowing that he had to get some rest.

Two mornings later, well fed, well dressed, and reasonably rested, armed with the Sword Coinspinner at his side . . . and Woundhealer left safely in Karel's care . . . Mark left the Palace. His departure was quiet, without fanfare official or otherwise. Mounted on a fine riding beast and at the head of a small escort similarly well equipped, he was on his way to seek the Emperor.

Mark looked back only once. He saw a figure that he was sure was Kristin, watching his departure from a distant upper window. But he made no sign that he had seen her.

CHAPTER 10

Over the long decades since his human eyes had gone in sacrifice, and demonic senses had been engrafted magically upon his own, the Dark King had come to be unsure sometimes whether he was awake or dreaming. He saw the Mindsword the same way in either case, as a pillar of billowing flame long as a spear, with his own face glowing amid the perfect whiteness of the flame. He could tell that the eyes on his own face of flame were open and seeing. Whether he was dreaming or awake, that fiery stare for some reason always reminded him that he had never seen with his own natural eyes any of those who were now his closest associates and chief subordinates. The demon showed him his human wizards and warlocks as strange, hunched, wizened figures, and his generals as little more than animated suits of armor; but all of them appeared with exaggerated caricature-faces, that amplified all of their subtleties of expression, so that the Dark King might better try to read them. Whereas demons, in the demonic vision, appeared with noble, lusty, youthful bodies, usually naked and always intensely human, except in their very perfection, their large size, and in the bird-like wings they often sprouted. The Dark King knew of course that they had no real bodies, or wings either, and he did not believe at all in their faces as they were presented to him, shining with kindliness and honor.

Now that the King was in the field with his army, on the march almost daily, the demons sometimes appeared to him on a smaller scale, fluttering in the air inside his tent like monkbirds. Vilkata dwelt now in a tent much smaller than his grand pavilion, because speed was of importance. And he thought that speed was vital now, because of the reports that had recently come in, first announcing and then confirming that Sir Andrew's troops were at last out of the swamp. The army in orange and black was moving in the direction of Sir Andrew's old lands, as if the Kind Knight for some reason thought the time might be ripe to reclaim them.

This news of course made Vilkata wonder what his erstwhile ally, the Silver Queen, might now be planning. As far as he knew she still controlled those lands.

The report of Sir Andrew's movement had also confirmed Vilkata's recent decision that his own strategy had best be altered. Now, he determined to destroy Sir Andrew first, before turning his attention to his other surviving enemies and rivals. Vilkata had arrived at this decision to change his plans largely out of the feeling that his enemies must now know too much about them as they stood.

First of all, the Dark King was now convinced that he had entertained a spurious Burslem, some damned spy, at that memorable council meeting at the main camp, the one where the King had first displayed his Mindsword, and which the gods had so gratifyingly attended later. The real wizard Burslem, Vilkata's head of Security and Defensive Intelligence, had at last returned, and had been positively identified, this time, by careful questioning. How the spy had managed to resist the Mindsword's influence, as he or she evidently had, was something else for the King to worry and wonder about. The Sword Sightblinder was so far the only really convincing explanation to be suggested, and the presence of that in one of his enemies' hands was far from reassuring.

Today, as Vilkata moved about his small field tent in his routine of morning preparations, the small demon that served him as sensory aid presented him as usual with a vision of the tent's interior. Certain things, in accordance with his own long-standing orders, were edited out of the scene as he perceived it. For example, the body of last night's concubine, curled now at the foot of the bed in sleep or a good imitation thereof, was most clearly visible by its shapely torso, the breasts and buttocks particularly emphasized. The irrelevances of hands and feet, and especially the face—who would care about trying to read the innermost thoughts of such a woman?—blurred away into a semi-transparent obscurity. In the case of a bed-partner, better a blur than a face, no matter how well-formed and schooled in smiling. Even such smiles could sometimes be disquieting.

And the Dark King had recently ordered that, when the next battle came, the dead should be edited away too, out of his perception. He had observed frequently, on other battlefields and in other areas where much killing was required, that the dead were a notable distraction. Obstacles when removed ought to disappear, resources once used up were only waste materials. The dead tended to stink, and were in general esthetically unpleasing. He had finally decided to order them filtered out. Someone else could count them up when necessary.

He had decided, too, that many of the wounded, most of them in fact, should also be expunged from his vision. Those remaining should be only the ones still able to play an active part in the day's events, enough to present some possible danger to the Dark King's person, or his cause. This might not always be easy for a busy demon to judge; in doubtful cases the filtering familiar was to let the wounded person remain visible, even if esthetically offensive.

This morning, when Vilkata left his small tent and mounted his warsteed, amid the usual thunderous applause of his troops and officers, his army appeared before him in his demon-sight as neat ranks of polished weapons, the human form attached to each blade or bow not much more than a mere uniformed outline.

A look at the best maps he had available had persuaded him that it ought to be possible to intercept Sir Andrew's force if he moved swiftly, starting at first daylight. The morning's march was hard and long. Scouts, some of them human beings mounted or afoot, some of them winged beasts, kept coming in with reports of what appeared to be the rear guard of Sir Andrew's force not far ahead. They estimated that the enemy army was even a little smaller than earlier intelligence estimates had made it out to be.

But Vilkata, still prudent despite the overwhelming advantage that he thought he held, ordered his infantry forward as against a foe possibly almost their equal in numbers. He also ordered a swift cavalry movement, a reconnaissance in force, to move around Sir Andrew's army, to try to engage the enemy front and if possible prevent successful flight. Meanwhile he maneuvered the main body of his own troops into battle array. Stationing himself just behind the front of this force, near the center, he awaited more reports, and remained ready to draw the Mindsword for what he calculated would be maximum effect upon foe and friend alike.

The first skirmishes broke out ahead. The Dark King drew his weapon of great magic and advanced, mounted, holding overhead what he himself perceived as a spear of fiery glory. He saw the enemy rearguard, in a view tailored by his familiar to his wishes, as mobile though inanimate man-sized obstacles. Still he could see their shapes and their numbers perfectly well, and even note the fact that many of them wore orange and black.

Vilkata saw also, and felt with joy, the terror that he inspired in those men and women ahead when they first saw him, and how swiftly that terror was altered by his Sword's magic into a mad devotion.

He saw with delight how Sir Andrew's soldiers, who at first glance would have formed a rank and fought him, at sight of the Mindsword fell down and worshipped him instead. And how, when he presently roared orders at them, they rose and turned, and went running like berserkers against their former comrades, who must now be just out of sight and trying to get away.

One of the last to bend to the Mindsword's power was a woman, a proud sorceress by the look of her, no longer young and evidently of some considerable rank. One counterspell after another this arrogant female hurled back at the Dark King and his Sword; but they had all failed her, as he knew they must, and as she too must have known; and she too turned at last, snarling with mad joy, like the others, at being able to serve the future ruler of all the Earth.

Denis the Quick had been offered the chance to remain in the swamp, along with a handful of wounded and others who could not travel quickly, when Sir Andrew led his army out. Reports had come in indicating that it would not be wise for Denis to attempt to make his way home alone to Tashigang, and Sir Andrew could afford no escort for him. The situation around the city had deteriorated rapidly since Denis's departure. Strong patrols of the Dark King's forces were in the very suburbs now, challenging the few troops that the Silver Queen had in the region. The wealthy owners of suburban villas had fled, into the city or far away from it. This news offered hope of a kind to Sir Andrew and his people, as it was evidence that the situation between King and Queen was now moving rapidly toward open conflict.

But Denis had declined to stay in the swamp. There was no telling how long he'd be stuck there if he did so, or when a better chance of getting out would come, if ever. He preferred to be out in the great world, to know what great events were happening. He was willing to take his chances on getting back eventually to the city he loved, and to the two women there whose images still stirred his dreams.

On the afternoon of the third day since the army had left the swamp, Denis was walking with some members of Sir Andrew's staff. Sir Andrew himself was on hand at the moment; the Knight had been riding up and down the column of his army, trying to preserve its organization —years of guerrilla tactics in a swamp were not the best practice for a long overland march—and had stopped to talk with Denis about conditions among the people in Tashigang.

They talked of the White Temple, and its hospitals, in some of which Denis had worked during his apprenticeship as Ardneh's acolyte. They began a discussion on how to put Woundhealer to the best possible use; this was of course purely theoretical, as Denis had been unable to deliver it as charged. Sir Andrew still did not appear to blame him, however. Doomgiver was with the column, being carried by an officer of the advance guard, who, as it had seemed to Sir Andrew, had the greater likelihood of encountering the enemy today.

Their conversation was interrupted by the arrival of a small flying scout, with a message from the rear guard.

The true bird, intelligent enough to manage elementary speech, cackled at them: "Black and gold, black and gold. Many many."

"Then Ardneh be with my Dame," Sir Andrew muttered, reining in his mount, and looking behind him fiercely. Dame Yoldi was in the rear. "And with us all."

He cried out then for swift messengers to go ahead, to summon back with all speed the trusted friends who were carrying Doomgiver in the van. Then the Knight tried the movement of his helmet's visor, and with more shouted orders set about turning what few units of his army were in direct range of his voice, and heading them back to the relief of the rear guard. These did not amount to much more than a handful of his own bodyguard and friends.

And Denis heard, even as he saw, Shieldbreaker come out of its sheath now. He heard the legendary pounding sound, not fast or loud as yet but dull and brutal. The matchless magic of the Sword of Force beat out from it into the surrounding air, not with the tone of a drum whose voice might stir the blood, but rather with the sound of some relentless hammer, nailing up an executioner's scaffold.

Now the Knight himself and his close bodyguard, all mounted, set out for the rear of their army, or what had been its rear, at a pace that Denis on foot could not hope to match.

But, as he would be otherwise left virtually alone, he tried to keep up. He might have run in the other direction instead, but he thought the rest of the army would soon be pouring back from there, and he would have to face round again and join them, or appear as a deserter.

Denis was about a hundred meters behind Sir Andrew and his mounted companions, and losing more ground rapidly, when to his surprise he saw at a little distance to his right what looked like the deserted remnants of a carnival, set down for some reason right out here in the middle of nowhere. The booths and counters, the apparatus for the games of skill and chance, were all broken and standing idle. No one was in sight at the deserted amusement place, as Denis halted nearby, panting. The people belonging to the show—and who could blame them?—appeared to have run off even before the tramp of marching armies had drawn near.

Sir Andrew and his bodyguard had not yet got out of Denis's sight, when a cry went up from the same direction and only a short distance ahead of them. Denis, turning his head away from abandoned tents and wagons, saw what had to be Sir Andrew's rear guard, running toward Sir Andrew and his immediate companions, who had just halted on a little knoll. It appeared to be a desperate retreat, though as far as Denis could see the rearguard was not yet panicked totally. They had not thrown their weapons away as yet . . . and then he saw that what he had first taken for a retreat was in fact a charge. The rearguard, running from downhill, and already swinging their weapons like madmen, collided full tilt with Sir Andrew and his little group who had been riding to their rescue. The cry and noise of battle went up at once, and the would-be rescuers, taken by surprise, were many of them already down in their own blood.

"A trick! An enchantment!" Despairing cries went up from those riding with Sir Andrew.

It was no trick as simple as switched uniforms. Denis, dazedly continuing to move nearer, was now close enough to recognize Dame Yoldi's face among those who charged uphill, swinging their weapons, and shrieking mad battlecries. She was headed directly toward the little knoll where Sir Andrew and the surviving handful of his bodyguard and officers were now surrounded and under heavy attack.

Sir Andrew might have tried to turn his mount, break free of his assailants who were on foot, and get away. But he could not or would not try to flee. Instead he kept shouting to his traitorous assailants, calling them by name, trying to command them. He stood his ground, and his bodyguard would not make an effort to break away if he did not.

The hammering sound of Shieldbreaker went up and up, louder and faster now, syncopated into an irregular rhythm. Already it had drawn around its master an arc of gleaming steel and fresh blood. Sir Andrew's mount stumbled and went down, hacked and stabbed by half a dozen weapons, but no attacking point or blade could come far enough within the arc of the Sword of Force to reach his skin.

The Knight, tumbled from the saddle of his dying mount, rolled over on the ground, never losing his two-handed grip on the great Sword. Even when Sir Andrew lay on his back it never faltered in its action. And when he stood upright again, it was as if the Sword itself had pulled him up to fight. Shieldbreaker seemed to drag him after it, spinning his heavy body with its violence, right to left and back again, pulling him forward to the attack when one of his attackers would have faltered and pulled away.

Still, those who an hour ago had been his loyal friends came on against him by the score, shrieking their new hatred, calling on their new god, the Dark King, to strengthen them. Shieldbreaker fought them all. It smashed their weapons and their bones impartially, carved up their armor and their flesh alike.

Denis, hypnotized by what he saw, no longer fully in control of his own actions, crept a little closer still. He had a long knife at his own belt but he did not draw it. It was as if the thought never occurred to him that he might possibly make any difference in the fight that he was watching.

Sir Andrew's bodyguard, greatly outnumbered by berserk fanatics, were all down now, their dead or dying bodies being hacked to pieces by their mad attackers. But Shieldbreaker protected the man who held it. It continued to make its sound, yet faster now and louder. It worked on, its voice still dull despite its blinding speed, its dazzling arc. It worked efficiently, indifferent as to whom or what it struck, indifferent to whatever screams or words went up from those it disarmed or cut apart, indifferent equally to whatever weapons might be plied against it. Denis saw axeheads, knives, swordblades, shafts of spears and arrows, flying everywhere, whole and in a hail of fragments. Human limbs and armor danced bloodily within the hail, and surely that bouncing, rolling object had once been a head.

The mouth of the Kind Knight opened and he screamed, surely a louder and more terrible roar than any coming from the folk he struck. Denis, creeping closer still as if he were unable to help himself, saw that Sir Andrew was now covered with blood from head to foot. It was impossible to tell if any of it might be his own. But if he were wounded, still the mad vigor of his movements, energized by magic, continued unabated.

The Knight roared again, in greater agony than before. Denis saw that Dame Yoldi, possessed, a creature of evil hatred, her face hideously transformed, was closing in on Sir Andrew. Her hands were outspread like claws, as if to rend, and she cried out desperate spells of magic. Even Denis the unmagical could feel the backwash of their deadly, immaterial power.

To the Sword of Force the tools of magic were no more than any other weapons. They were dissolved and broken against that gleaming curve almost invisible with speed, that brutal thudding in the air. Dame Yoldi's hatred propelled her closer, closer, to the man she would destroy, and closer still, until the edge of the bright arc of force touched her, hands first, body an eyeblink later, and wiped her away.

Denis saw no more for the next few seconds. When he looked up again, there was a pause. Sir Andrew stood alone now, knee-deep in a small mound of corpses, all in his own colors of orange and black. The Sword in his hands still thudded dully; for those of his former friends who still survived as maddened enemies were not through with him yet. A small knot of them, the wounded, those who had been slow to charge, the calculating, were gathering at a little distance, scheming some strategy, hatred forced into patient planning.

Denis hurried to Sir Andrew's side. The young man thought, as he approached, that Sir Andrew was trying to hurl Shieldbreaker from him; the Sword was quieter now in the Knight's hands, its sound reduced to a muted tapping. But if he was trying to be rid of it, it would not let him go. Both of his hands still gripped it, fingers interlocked around the hilt, white-knuckled where the knuckles could be seen through blood.

Sir Andrew turned a hideous face to Denis. The Knight's voice was a ghastly whisper, almost inaudible. "Go, catch up with the advance guard. Find the man who is carrying Doomgiver, and order him in my name, and for the love of Ardneh, to return here as fast as he can.''

Denis had hardly got out of sight in one direction before Sir Andrew, looking the opposite way, was able to see the main body of Vilkata's troops in the distance, a black-gold wave advancing toward him. A trumpet sounded from that line. On hearing it, such remnants of Sir Andrew's corrupted troops as were still on the field abandoned their hopeless attack, turning in obedient retreat to join the forces of their new master.

There, in the distance, that man, whitehaired and mounted under a gold-black banner, must be Vilkata himself. In those distant hands a weapon that Sir Andrew knew must be the Mindsword flamed, the sun awakening in it all the fires of glory. To Sir Andrew's eyes, it was not much more than a glass mirror; Shieldbreaker in his own hands protected him from that weapon too. It negated all weapons except itself.

And it was quite enough, he thought; it had quite destroyed him already.

Again a horn sounded, somewhere over there in the army of the Dark King. Next, to the Knight's numbed surprise, Vilkata's hosts that had only just appeared began a measured withdrawal, going back over the rise of land whence they had come. Sir Andrew tried to think that over, his mind working in a newly confused way. He supposed that to Vilkata's calculation the withdrawal was only sense: why order an army to chew itself to tatters, to no purpose, upon Shieldbreaker's unbreakable defense?

Sir Andrew might have pursued that army, he might have run screaming at that central banner bearing the black skull until everyone beneath it had been turned to chopped meat at his hands. But they would not wait for him. Vilkata was mounted and would get away. And anyway he, Sir Andrew, was too weak to run, to pursue and catch up with anyone.

Now that the immediate threat to Sir Andrew himself was over, the strength of magic that had been given him through the Sword was draining rapidly away. The dread sound of Shieldbreaker's hammer thumped more softly, tapping slower, tapping itself down into silence.

He saw himself as if from outside, an old man standing alone on a hill, knee-deep in corpses of those he once had loved. His arms ached, as if they had been pounded by quarterstaffs, from the drill that Shieldbreaker had dragged them through. Careless of the blood, he put the Sword into its sheath.

It was all Sir Andrew could do now to remain on his feet.

It was almost more than he could do, to go and look at what was left of Yoldi.

After that, trying to see his way through tears, he made his legs carry him away. He was not sure where he was going, nor even of where he ought to go. He got no farther than the next small hillock of the field, coming again within sight of the flimsy ruins of the carnival, when the great pain struck him inside his chest. It felt like a spearthrust to the heart.

He collapsed on his back. A fighter's instincts made him draw the great Sword again before he fell. But he faced no weapons now, and the Sword of Force was lifeless.

As Sir Andrew lay in the grass the sky above him looked so peaceful that it surprised him. He considered his pain. It feels, he thought, as if my heart were bursting. As perhaps it is.

He took a look back, quickly and critically, at what he could see at this moment of his own long life. He found the prospect of death, at this moment, not unwelcome.

The pain came again, worse than before.

"Yoldi . . ."

But she did not answer. She was not going to answer him ever again.

When it seemed that the pain was going to let him live yet a little longer, Sir Andrew flung Shieldbreaker away from him, using two hands and all of his remaining strength. He had tried to throw the great Sword away before, tried again and again when he saw Yoldi running at him and realized what must have happened to her, and what was going to happen. But the Sword's magic would not leave him then. This time, now that it was too late, it left his hands as obediently as any stick thrown for a dog. The blade whined faintly, mournfully, turning through the air.

The Knight did not want to die alone. If only there could be a friend nearby—someone.

He closed his eyes, and wondered if he would ever open them on this world's skies again. Would it be Ardneh that he saw when he opened his eyes again, as some folk thought? Or nothingness?

He opened them and saw that he was still in the same world, under the same sky. Something compelled him to make the effort to turn his head. A single figure, that of a man in gray, was walking toward him from the direction of the carnival, the abandoned showplace that Sir Andrew had been perfectly sure was quite deserted. A man, not armed or armored, but . . . wearing a mask?

The gray-clad figure came close, and knelt down beside him like a concerned comrade.

Sir Andrew asked: "Who're you?"

The man raised a hand promptly and pulled off his mask.

"Oh." Sir Andrew's voice was almost disappointed in its reassurance. "You," he said, relieved and calm. "Yes . . . I know who you are."

Denis, returning mounted and at full speed, leading a small flying wedge of armed and armored folk who were desperate to relieve their beloved lord, found the battlefield deserted by the living. Sir Andrew lay dead, at a little distance from the other dead. His body, though covered with others' gore, was unmarked by any serious wound. The expression on the Kind Knight's face was peaceful.

Presently Denis and the others began to look for Shieldbreaker. They looked everywhere among the dead, and then in widening circles outward. But the Sword of Force was gone.

CHAPTER 11

The field cot was wide enough for two—for two, at least, who were on terms of intimate friendship—but tonight, as for many nights past, only one person had slept in it.

Or tried to sleep.

The Silver Queen's field tent was not large, not for a shelter that had to serve sometimes as royal conference room as well as dwelling. According to certain stories she had heard, it would not have made a room in the great pavilion that usually accompanied the Dark King when he traveled with his army.

She felt great scorn for many of the Dark King's ways. But there were other things about him that enforced respect, and—to herself, alone at night, she could admit it—tended to induce fear as well.

The Queen of Yambu was sitting in near-midnight darkness on the edge of her lonely field cot, wearing the light drawers and shirt she usually slept in when in the field with her troops. She could hear rain dripping desultorily upon the tent, and an occasional word or movement of one of the sentries not far outside.

Her gaze was fixed on a dim, inanimate shape, resting only an arm's length away beside the cot. In midnight darkness it was all but impossible to see the thing that she was looking at, but that did not really matter, for she knew the object as well as her own hand. It rested there on a trestle as it always did, beside her when she slept—or tried to sleep. It was a Swordcase of carven wood, its huge wooden hilt formed by chiseled dragons with their long necks recurved, as if they meant to sink their fangs into each other. Just where the case had originated, or when, the Queen of Yambu was not sure, but she thought it beautiful; and after the best specialist magicians in her pay had pronounced it innocent of any harm for her, she had used it to encase her treasure, which she kept near her almost always—her visit to Sir Andrew in the swamp had been one notable exception—as her last dark hope for victory.

A thousand times she had opened the wooden case, but she had never yet drawn Soulcutter from its sheath inside. Never yet had she seen the bare steel of that Blade in what she was sure must be its splendor. She was afraid to do so. But without it in her possession she would not have dared to take her army into the field now, risking combat with the Mindsword and its mighty owner the Dark King.

Some hours ago, near sunset, a winged half-intelligent messenger had brought her word of Vilkata's latest triumph. He had apparently crushed what might have been Sir Andrew's entire army. Then, instead of coming to attack her as she kept expecting he would do, Vilkata had turned his own vast forces in a move in the direction of Tashigang.

Maybe the Dark King's scouts had lost track of where her forces were. But for whatever reason, her own certainty that she would be the first one attacked by Vilkata was proven wrong, and that gave cowardice a chance to whisper in her ear that it might not be too late for her to patch up an alliance with the King. Of course cowardice, as usual, was an idiot. Her intelligence told her that her only real hope lay in attacking the Dark King now, while she might still hope for some real help. Sir Andrew was already gone. When Tashigang too had fallen, then it would certainly be too late.

When the news of Vilkata's most recent triumph had come in, Yambu had first conferred briefly with her commanders, then dismissed them, telling them to let the troops get some rest tonight. But she herself had not been able to sleep since. Nor, though her own necessary course of action was becoming plainer and plainer, had she been able to muster the will to be decisive, to give the orders to break camp and march.

Who, or what, could stand against the Mindsword? Evidently only something that was just as terrible.

And Sir Andrew had been wearing Shieldbreaker, ready at his side. With her own eyes, on her visit to the swamp, she had seen the small white hammer on the black hilt. Vilkata with his Mindsword had evidently won, somehow, even against that weapon. Did Vilkata now have possession of both those Blades? But even if he did, each terrible augmentation of his power only made it all the more essential to march against him without delay.

The Silver Queen stood up and moved forward one short pace in midnight blackness, trusting that the tent floor was there as usual, and no assassin's knife. She put out her hand and touched the wooden case, then opened it.

She stroked with one finger the black hilt of her own Sword. This Sword alone among the Twelve bore no white symbol on its hilt. No sense of power came to her when she touched it. There was no sense of anything, beyond the dull material hilt itself. Of all the Twelve, this one alone had nothing to say to the world about itself.

She glanced back at her solitary cot, barely visible in the dull sky-glow that fell in through the tent's screened window. She visualized Amintor's scarred shoulders as they sometimes appeared there, bulking above the plain rumpled blanket. Amintor was wise, sometimes. Or clever at least. She doubted now that she herself knew what wisdom was, doubted she would recognize wisdom if it came flying at her in the night like some winged attacking reptile.

Quite possibly she had never been able to recognize it, and only of late was she aware of this.

The one adviser whose word she would really have valued now had been gone from her side for years, and he was not coming back. She was never going to see him again, except, possibly, one day across some battlefield. But perhaps when they met in battle he would be wearing a mask again (she had never understood why he did that so often) and he would go unrecognized.

And now, at this point in what had become a familiar cycle of thought, it was time for her to think about Ariane. Ariane her daughter, her only child, and of course his daughter too.

The Silver Queen's intelligence sources had confirmed for her the stories, now four years old, that Ariane was four years dead, had perished with some band of robbers in an attempt to plunder the main hoard of the Blue Temple. Well, the girl was better off that way, most likely, than in Red Temple slavery.

Had that plot, to put Ariane on the throne of Yambu, been a real one? Or had the real plot been to force her, the Silver Queen, to get rid of her daughter, her one potentially trustworthy ally? Even when convinced of the danger, Queen Yambu had been unable to give the orders for her daughter's death. And besides, the auguries had threatened the most horrible consequences for her royal self if she should do so. In the end, as certain of the auguries appeared to advise, she had sold Ariane into Red Temple slavery.

Her own daughter, her only child. She, Queen Yambu, had been lost in her own hate and fear. . . .

Would Amintor, she wondered, if he had been with her then, have had the courage to advise her firmly against destroying her own daughter? Not, she thought, once he knew that she was determined on it.

. . . and now, of course, in this pointless cycle of thought, remembrance, and self-recrimination, it was time for her to recall those days of her love affair with the Emperor, before her triumphant ascension to the throne. Only rarely since that triumph had she felt as fully alive as she did then, in that time of continuous, desperate effort and danger. Then her life had been in peril constantly. She had been in flight day after day, never sleeping twice in the same place, alert always to escape the usurpers' search parties that were frantically scouring the country for her.

That was when she had met him, when the love affair had started, and when it had run its course. She had been an ignorant girl then, only guessing at the Emperor's real power; then, as now, he had had no army of his own to send into the field. But he had saved her more than once, fighting like a demon at her side, inspiring her with predictions of victory, outguessing the enemy on which direction their search parties would take next.

There had been hints, she supposed, in those early days of love, as to what he expected as his ultimate reward. More than hints, if she had been willing to see and hear them. Still she had begun, naive girl as she then was, to think him selfless and unselfish. And then—landless, armyless, brazen, bold-faced opportunist after all!—he had proposed marriage to her. On the very day of her stunning victory, when enough of the powerful folk of Yambu had rallied to her cause to turn the tide. The very day she had been able to ascend the throne, and to order the chief plotters and their families put to a horrible death.

The man who called himself the Emperor must have read her instant refusal in her face. For when she had turned back from giving some urgent order, to deliver her answer to him plainly, he was already gone.

Perhaps he had put on one of his damned masks again; anyway he had vanished in that day's great confusion of unfamiliar figures, new body-guard and new courtiers and foreign dignitaries already on hand to congratulate the winner.

She had refused to order a search, or even to allow one. Let him go. She was well rid of him. From that day forward she would be Queen, and her marriage, when she got around to thinking of marriage, would have to be something planned as carefully and coldly as an army's march.

There had been, naturally enough, other lovers, from that day almost twenty years ago till this. Amintor was, she supposed, the most durable of the bunch. *Lovers* was not really the right word for them though; useful bodies, sometimes entertaining or even useful minds.

But the Emperor—yes, he had been her lover. That fact in some ways seemed to loom larger as it became more distant down the lengthening avenue of years.

But, she thought now (as she usually did when the thought-cycle had reached this point), how could any woman, let alone a Queen, have been expected to live with, to seriously plan a life and a career, with a man like that . . . ?

The Silver Queen's thoughts and feelings, as usual, became jumbled at this point. It was all done with now. It had all been over and done with, a long time ago. The Emperor might have made her immortal, or at least virtually ageless, like himself. Well, as a strong Queen she could hire or persuade other powerful magicians to do the same for her, as they did for themselves, when it began to seem important.

Only after she had refused the Emperor's offer of marriage, and after she had banned that impossible pretender, that joker and seducer, from her thoughts (the banning had been quite successful for a time)—it was only then, of course, that she had realized that she was pregnant.

Her first thought had been to rid herself of the child before it was born. But her second thought—already she was beginning to pick up more hints of the Emperor's latent power—was that the child might possibly represent an asset later. As usual in her new life as Queen, far-sighted caution had prevailed. She had endured the pregnancy and birth.

There was no doubt of who the father was, despite the baby's fair skin and reddish hair, unlike those of either parent. The Emperor had been her only lover at the time. Besides, the Queen could find redheads recorded on both sides of her own ancestry. As for the Emperor's family . . . who knew? Not any of the wizards she had been able to consult.

One thing certain about him; he had been, still was, a consummate magician. The Silver Queen appreciated that more fully now. At the time, as a girl, she had only begun to recognize the fact.

And even now—actually more often now than in those early years of her reign—the idea kept coming tantalizingly back: what if she actually had married him?

That would have been impossible, of course. Quite socially, politically impossible for a Queen to marry one that the world knew as a demented clown. No matter that the wise and well-educated at least suspected there was more to the Emperor than that. But what if she *had* done it, used her new royal power to make it work? There would of course have had to have been a strong concurrent effort to revive her husband's title in its ancient sense, one of well-nigh supreme power, of puissance beyond that of mere Kings and Queens.

Would she have been acclaimed as a genius of statecraft for marrying him and trying to do that? Only, of course, if it had worked. More likely she would have become a laughingstock.

In any case it was nonsense to think about it now. She had been only a girl then, unwise in the ways of ruling, and how could she ever have made such an attempt succeed?

But *he* might have been able to make it work. What if she had let him rule beside her, had let him try . . .

Maybe, she thought, it was the memory of the Emperor's fierce masculinity that was really bothering her tonight. On top of everything else. There had been something stronger about him in that way than any other man she had ever invited to her cot, though physically he was not particularly big.

Enough. There in the dark privacy of her tent, not giving herself time to think about it, she clasped her right hand firmly on Soulcutter's hilt and drew it halfway from its sheath. Still there was no glow, and still no power flowed from it. Rather the reverse. It was as she had feared and expected it would be, but worse; worse than she had thought or feared. Still she could bear it if she must.

Queen Yambu slammed this most terrible of all Swords back into its sheath, and sighed with relief as the midnight around her appeared to brighten instantly. Then she closed the ornate case around Soulcutter, and got up and went to the tent door to cry orders to break camp and march.

CHAPTER 12

Of course the Dark King knew better, when he stopped to think about it. But through the visualization provided him by the demon he had been able to see Shieldbreaker in Sir Andrew's distant hands only as a kind of war-hammer rather than a Sword, a picture matching the sound that reached Vilkata's ears from that distant combat. Soulcutter Vilkata had not yet seen at all, but he knew that it was there now, somewhere behind him, in the hands of the Silver Queen. He knew it by his magically assisted perception of an emptiness, a presence there to which he was truly blind. Any Sword that he did not own could frighten him, and he owned only one out of the Twelve. And now he found himself between two enemies armed with two Swords that seemed to him particularly powerful.

Between the Mindsword in the Dark King's hands behind them and the Dark King's cavalry in front of them, Sir Andrew's little army had certainly been destroyed. That much had been accomplished. Under ordinary conditions a victory of such magnitude would have been enough to make the King feel truly optimistic. But conditions were not ordinary, if they ever were. There were the two Swords Shieldbreaker and Soulcutter, and himself between them.

When the report came in that the Silver Queen was advancing on his rear, Vilkata sent a flying messenger to recall most of his advanced cavalry, and set about turning his entire army to confront her. It was a decision made with some reluctance, because he longed to go instead to search personally on the battlefield for Shieldbreaker. A flying scout had reported seeing from a distance that Sir Andrew hurled the Sword away from him, when the fight at last was over. And what subordinate did the Dark King dare to trust with succeeding in that search?—but at the same time he dared not fail to meet the Silver Queen's advance with the Mindsword in his own hands. He could not be in two places at once.

Anyway Vilkata did not really believe the report about Sir Andrew throwing Shieldbreaker away. Whether the Sword of Force would be dropped and abandoned by any living person on any battlefield was, in his mind, very doubtful to say the least. In the end he ordered certain patrols to the place where Sir Andrew was last seen, to search for the Sword, or to make what other valuable discoveries they could, while he himself turned back to meet the advancing columns of Yambu.

As it turned out, Yambu's main army was not nearly as close as had been reported. The flying, half-intelligent scouts often had trouble estimating horizontal distances; but the King could not take chances. He had not much more than got his army into motion in that direction, when additional disquieting reports came in. These told of gods and goddesses seen in the vicinity of Tashigang, doing extravagant things in the Dark King's name, and proclaiming him their lord and master, the new ruler of the world. That in itself would have been well enough, but the reports also told of the deities offering him human sacrifice, and holocausts of grain and cattle. Besides the waste of valuable resources, it made Vilkata uneasy to realize that the divinities who had pledged loyalty to him were not really under his control. Should he send word to them of his displeasure? But he did not even know where they were right now. Or where they were going to be next, or what they might be intending to do.

The trouble is, he thought, they worship me but I am not a god. Having arrived at that thought, he felt as if he had made some great, vaguely alarming discovery.

Mark and his escort had not been many days out from Tasavalta when they were forced into a skirmish with a strong patrol of the Dark

King's troops. This fight had cost them some casualties. But Coinspinner in Mark's hands, altering the odds of chance in his favor at every turn, saw him and most of his small force through the fighting safely. He had experienced the workings of the Sword of Chance before, and he trusted it—to a degree; it was really the least trustworthy of the Twelve—and felt almost familiar with it. The soldiers of his escort had done neither until now.

When the skirmish was over, the enemy survivors driven into flight, Mark and his troops rested briefly and moved on. He was confident, and the soldiers, who earlier had only grimly obeyed orders, now picked up that attitude from him. Since what he truly wanted now was to locate the Emperor, then to the Emperor Coinspinner's luck would lead him, in one way or another.

As they rode Mark paused periodically to sweep the horizon with the naked tip of the Sword of Chance. When he aimed it in a certain direction, and in that direction only, a quivering seized the blade, and Mark could feel a faint surge of power pass into his hand through the hilt. In that direction was the Emperor. Or, at least, that was the way to go to ultimately reach him.

For several days Mark and his surviving Tasavaltan escort journeyed in safety. Then they began to observe the unmistakable signs of armies near. And then at last there was the noise of a battle close ahead.

From a distance Mark watched an enemy force of overwhelming strength, what he thought had to be the main body of the Dark King's troops, first advance in one direction, then reverse themselves—though not as in defeat, he thought—and trudge in mass formation the other way. The actual fighting had been somewhere beyond them, where he could not see it.

When the enemy had moved out of the way, and almost out of sight, Coinspinner still pointed him toward the place where the battle had been.

When Mark with his small escort reached the battlefield, they found it almost devoid of living things, except for a few scavengers, gathering on wing and afoot. There were a hundred human dead or more, concentrated mostly in one place. Among the fallen Mark could not see a single one in Vilkata's colors. The only livery visible was Sir Andrew's orange and black.

On the field one human figure was still standing. Slightly built, it was garbed in a robe that had once been white, and looked like one of Ardneh's servants who had been through some arduous journey and perhaps a battle or two as well. When Mark first saw it, this figure was bending over one of the dead men who lay a little apart from the others. Then, even as Mark watched, the figure in white began to labor awkwardly at digging—a grave, Mark supposed—using the blade of a long knife.

As Mark and his troops, in the colors of Tasavalta, rode nearer, the figure in white took note of them and stopped what it was doing to await their approach. But it did not try to run.

When Mark got closer, he recognized the isolated dead man as Sir Andrew. In war it was no great surprise, particularly on a field of slaughter like this one, to find a comrade and a leader dead. But still the discovery was no less a shock.

Mark jumped down from his mount and put his hand on the gore-spattered head of the Kind Knight, and remarked his peaceful face. "Ardneh greet you," he muttered, and for a moment at least could feel real hope that it might be so.

Then Mark stood up. Taking Denis for a genuine Ardneh-pilgrim who had probably just wandered onto the scene, Mark asked, "But where are his own people, all slaughtered?" He looked round him at the few score dead. "This can't be his entire army!"

Denis answered. "Many were slaughtered, I fear. The Dark King's cavalry attacked also, ahead, beyond those hills. The officers remaining are trying to rally whatever troops are left. Sir Andrew's close friends wanted to bury him—what I am trying to do—but they decided Sir Andrew would have wanted them to see to the living first. As I am sure he would."

"You knew him, then?"

The youth in ragged white nodded assent. "I had been with him for some days. I think I came to know him, in a way. I am called Denis the Quick, of Tashigang." And Denis's quick eyes flicked around Mark's escort. "I did not know that there were Tasavaltan troops nearby."

"There are not many. My name is Mark."

Nor had Denis failed to notice the large black hilt at Mark's side. "There was a man of that name who had—and still has, for all I know —much to do with the Twelve Swords. Or so all the stories say. But I didn't know that he was Tasavaltan."

"I am not Tasavaltan, really . . . and yes, I have had much to do with them. Much more than I could wish." Mark sighed.

But even as he spoke, Mark was tiredly, dutifully drawing Coinspinner again. While Denis and the Tasavaltan soldiers watched in alert silence, he swept it once more round the horizon. "That way," Mark muttered, as he resheathed the Blade. "And nearby, now, I think. The feeling in the hilt is strong."

The Sword had pointed in the direction of the abandoned carnival, which was just visible over the nearest gentle rise of ground.

Mark began to walk in the direction of the carnival, leading his mount. His escort followed silently, professionally alert for trouble. Denis hesitated for a moment, then abandoned his gravedigging temporarily and came with them too. The ruined show was only about a hundred meters distant.

Standing on the edge of the area of dilapidated tents and flimsy shelters, Mark looked about him with a frown. "This is very much like . . ."

"What?"

"Nothing." But then Mark hesitated. His voice when he replied again was strained. "Like one carnival in particular that I remember seeing once . . . long ago."

It was of course impossible for him to be certain, but he had a feeling that it was really the same one. Something about the tents, or maybe the names of the performers—though he could not remember any of them consciously—on the few worn, faded signs that were visible.

Yes. Nine years ago, or thereabouts, this very carnival—he thought— had been encamped far from here, in front of what had then been Sir Andrew's castle. That had been the night of Mark's second encounter with a Sword, the night on which someone had thrust Sightblinder into his hands. . . .

One of the mounted Tasavaltan troopers sounded a low whistle, a signal meaning that an enemy had been sighted nearby. Mark forgot the past and sprang alertly into his saddle.

There was barely time to grab for weapons before a patrol of the Dark King's cavalry was upon them. Vilkata's troops abandoned stealth when they saw that they were seen, to come shouting and charging between the tents and flimsy shacks.

Mark, with Coinspinner raised, met one mounted attacker, a grizzled veteran who fell back wide-eyed when he saw his opponent brandishing a Sword; the magnificent blade made the god-forged weapons unmistakable even when the black hilt with its identifying symbol was hidden in a fist. Other fighting swirled around them. Mark's riding beast was slightly wounded. He had to struggle to control it, as it carried him some little distance where he found himself almost alone. The Sword of

Good Luck could create certain difficulties for a leader, even when it perhaps simultaneously saved his life. He waved a signal to such of his Tasavaltan people as he could see, then rode to lead them in a counter-attack around a wooden structure a little larger than the rest of the carnival's components.

In a moment he discovered that his troops had evidently missed or misread his hand signal, and he was for the moment completely alone. Swearing by the anatomies of several gods and goddesses, he was wheeling his mount again, to get back to his troops, when his eye fell on the faded legend over the flimsy building's doorway.

It read:

THE HOUSE OF MIRTH

And just outside the House of Mirth, a man was sitting, waiting for Mark. The man, garbed in dull colors, sat there so quietly on a little bench that Mark had ridden past him once without even noticing his presence. Mark was sure at once that the man was waiting for him, because he was looking at Mark as if he had been expecting him and no one else.

The man on the bench was compactly built, of indeterminate age, and wrapped in a gray cloak of quiet but now somewhat dusty elegance. His face, Mark thought, was quite calm and also quite ordinary, and he sat there almost meekly, unarmed but with a long empty scabbard at his belt.

Coinspinner pointed straight at the man. Then the Sword seemed to leap and twist in Mark's hand, and he could not retain his hold upon it. The man on the bench had done nothing at all that Mark could see, but the Sword of Chance was no longer in Mark's grip, and the scabbard at the Emperor's side was no longer empty.

Even apart from Coinspinner's evidence, Mark had not the least doubt of who he was facing. He had heard descriptions. He had heard enough to make him wonder if, in spite of himself, he might be awed when this moment came. But in fact the first emotion that Mark felt was anger, and his first words expressed it. They came in a voice that trembled a little with his resentment, and it was not even the taking of the Sword that made him angry.

"You are my father. So my mother has told me."

The Emperor gave no sign of feeling any anger in response to Mark's. He only looked Mark up and down and smiled a little, as if he were basically pleased with what he saw. Then he said: "She told you truly, Mark. You are my son."

"Return my Sword. I need it, and my troops need me."

"Presently. They are managing without you at the moment."

Mark started to get down from his riding beast, meaning to confront the other even more closely. But at the last moment he decided to hold on to whatever advantage remaining mounted might afford him—even though he suspected that would be none at all.

He accused the seated man again. "It was a long time afterward, my mother said, before she realized who you really were. Not until after I was born. You were masked, when you took her. For a while she thought you were Duke Fraktin, that bastard. Playing tricks, like a . . . why did you do that to her? And to my father?"

Mark heard his own voice quiver on the last word. Somehow the accusation had ended more weakly than it had begun.

The Emperor answered him steadily. "I did it, I took her as you say, because I wanted to bring you into being."

"I . . ." It was difficult to find the right words, properly angry and forceful, to answer that.

The man on the bench added: "You are one of my many children, Mark. The Imperial blood flows in your veins."

Again Mark's injured riding beast began to give him trouble, turning restively this way and that. He worked to control it, and told himself that if only he had his Sword he would have turned his back on this man and ridden away, gone back to join the fight. But his Sword was gone. And now as soon as the animal looked directly at the Emperor it quieted. It stood still, facing the man on the bench and trembling faintly.

And is it going to be the same with me? Will I be pacified so easily? Mark wondered. Already his intended fury at this man was weakening.

Mark said; "I have been thinking about that, too. The Imperial blood. If I have it, what does that mean?"

The Emperor stood up slowly. There was still nothing physically impressive or even distinctive about him. He was neither remarkably tall nor short, and, to Mark's dull senses at least, he radiated no aura of magic. As he walked the few paces to stand beside Mark's trembling mount, he drew Coinspinner and casually handed it up to Mark, hilt first. "You will need this, as you say," he remarked, as if in an aside.

And then, as Mark almost dazedly accepted the Sword, the Emperor answered his question. "It means, for one thing, that you have the ordering of demons. More precisely, the ability to order them away, to cast them out. What words, what particular incantation you employ to do so matters little."

Mark slid Coinspinner back into the sheath at his own side. Now he was free to turn and ride away. But he did not. "The demons, yes . . . tell me. There was a girl named Ariane, who was with me once in the Blue Temple dungeon. Who saved me from a demon there. Was she . . . ?"

"Another of my children. Yes. Did she not once think that she recognized you as a brother?"

"She did. Yes." Now even weak anger was ebbing swiftly, could not be called anger any longer. Now it had departed. Leaving . . . what?

Again the Emperor was smiling at him faintly, proudly. "You are a fit husband, Mark, for any Queen on Earth—or any Princess either. I think you are too good for most of them—but then I may be prejudiced. Fathers tend to be." The man in gray stood holding on to Mark's stirrup now, and squinting up at him. "There's something else, isn't there? What else are you trying to ask me?"

Mark blurted out a jumble of words, more or less connected with the memorized version of Princess Kristin's formal request for an alliance.

"Yes, that's what she sent you after me to do, isn't it? Well, I have a reputation as a prankster, but I can be serious. Tell the Princess, when you see her, that she has an alliance with me as long as she wants it."

There had been another alliance that Mark had meant to ask for. But it was too late now. "Sir Andrew has just been killed."

"I know that."

The calmness in the Emperor's voice seemed inhuman. Suddenly Mark's anger was not dead after all. "He died not half a kilometer from here. If you would be our ally, why aren't you fighting harder on our side? Doing more?"

His father—it was suddenly possible now to think of this man also in those terms—was not surprised by the reproach, or perturbed either. He let go the stirrup, and stroked the riding beast's injured neck. Mark thought he saw, though afterward he was not sure, one of the small wounds there wiped away as if it had been no more than a dead leaf fallen on the skin. Mark's newly acceptable father said, "When you are as old as I am, my son, and able to understand as much, then you can intelligently criticize the way I am behaving now."

The Emperor stretched himself, a weary movement, then moved back a step and looked around. "I think this present skirmish at least is yours. One day you and I will have a long time to talk. But not just now. Now that you have completed your mission for the Princess, I would advise you to get your remaining people to Tashigang, and quickly inside the walls. And warn the people in the city, if they do not already realize it, that an attack is imminent."

"I will." Mark heard himself accepting orders from this man, the same man he had sought for days, meaning to confront in accusation. But this change was not like that brought about by the Mindsword's hideous warping pressure. This inward change, this decision, was his own, for all that it surprised him.

His revitalized mount was already carrying him away. His father waved after him and called: "And you can give them this encouraging news as well—Rostov is bringing the Tasavaltan army to their aid!"

CHAPTER 13

The little column of refugees was composed for the most part of cumbersome carts and loadbeasts, and for several days it had been moving with a nightmarish slowness over the appalling roads. Now and again it left the roads, where a bridge had been destroyed or the only roads ran in the wrong directions, to go trundling off across someone's neglected fields. In this manner the train of carts and wagons had made its way toward Tashigang. The people in the train, all of them villagers or peasants who had been poor even before the war started, were fearful of the Dark King's cavalry, and with good reason. Behind them the land was death and ruin, under a leaden sky hazed at the horizon with the smoke of burning villages. The wooden-wheeled carts groaned with their increasing burden of people who could walk no more, and of the poor belongings that the people were still stubbornly trying to keep. The loadbeasts, in need of food and most of all of rest, uttered their own sounds of protest.

Riding in the second wagon were four people, a man named Birch and his wife Micheline, along with their two small children. The man was driving at the moment, urging on their one loadbeast that pulled the wagon. In general he kept up a running stream of encouraging comments, directed at the animal and at his family indiscriminately. He was not getting too much in the way of answers. His wife had said very little for several days now, and the children were too tired to speak.

Just now the train of wagons was coming to a place where the poor road dipped between hills that had once been wooded, to ford a small, muddy stream. Most of the trees on the hills looked as if they might have been individually hacked at by a hundred axes, then pulled apart by a thousand arms, of people needing firewood or wood for other uses; quite likely someone's army had camped near here not long ago.

The little train of half a dozen wagons and carts now stopped at the ford. All of the travelers wanted to let their animals drink, and the people who were not carrying fresher water with them in their vehicles drank from the stream too. Birch and his family did not get out of their cart. At this point they were not so much thirsty as simply dazed and exhausted.

While the company of refugees was halted thus, a patrol of the Dark King's cavalry did indeed come into sight. Those who were sitting in their wagons or standing beside them held their breath, watching fatalistically. But the patrol was some distance off, and showed little interest in their poor company.

They were greatly relieved. But hardly had the cavalry ridden out of the way when one of the women stood up in her wagon screaming, and pointed in a different direction.

Over one of the nearby hills, studded with its broken trees like stubble on a tough chin, the head and shoulders of a god had just appeared. There was more nearby smoke in the air in that direction, from some farm building on the other side of the hill burning perhaps, or it might have been a haystack or a woodpile smoldering; and the effect of seeing the god's figure through this haziness was somehow to suggest a truly gigantic figure kilometers away, moving about, at the distance of an ordinary horizon.

Birch, the man in the second cart, froze in his position on the driver's seat. His wife, Micheline, who was sitting beside him had clamped a painful grip upon his arm, but he could not have moved in any case. Behind them, peering out from where they had been tucked away amid furniture in the large two-wheeled cart, their two small children were frozen too.

Birch could tell at first glance that the mountainous-looking god coming over the hill was Mars. He could make the identification at once by the great spear and helm and shield of the approaching being's equippage, even though the man had never before seen any deity and had not expected to see one now.

Mars was almost directly ahead of the people in their wagons, advancing toward them from almost the same direction that the train was headed. And the Wargod had certainly taken notice of them already; Birch thought for a moment that those distant eyes were looking directly into his own. Now Mars, marching forward out of the smoke, appeared as no more than three times taller than a man. Now he was lowering his armored helm as if in preparation for battle; and still he tramped thunderously nearer, a moving mountain of a being, kicking stumps and boulders out of his way.

He was descending the near side of the nearest hill now, taller than the treetops of the ruined grove as he moved among them. Before Birch could think of any way he might possibly react, Mars had reached the muddy little ford.

Once there, he raised his arms. Looking preoccupied, as if his divine thoughts were elsewhere, and without preamble or warning, he spitted the man who had been driving the first wagon neatly on his spear, which was as long as a tall tree itself, and only a little thinner. That man's wife and children came spilling around him from their cart, and rolling on the ground as if they could feel the same spear in their own guts.

Mars moved quickly, and came so close that he was hard to see, like a mountain when you were standing on it. Birch felt his own wagon go over next. If that great spear had thrust for him too, it had somehow missed. All Birch could feel was a fall that left him half stunned, and then a growing pain in his leg and hip, and a numbness that threatened to grow into a greater pain still, and the awareness that he could not move. Near him Micheline and the children lay huddled and jumbled in the midst of their spilled belongings. Except for Birch himself they all appeared to be unhurt, but Micheline was gasping and the children whimpering softly in new terror. Still connected to the wagon by the leather straps of the harness, their only loadbeast lay twitching, its whole body crumpled into an impossible position. It had been slaughtered, butchered by a mere gesture from the passing God of War.

Mars' windstorm of a voice roared forth, above the cowering humans' heads: "What's all this talk I hear, these last few years, about twelve special Swords? I've never seen them and I don't want to. What's so great about them, really? Can anyone here answer me that? My war-spear here does the job as neatly as it ever did."

If the god was really talking to the humans he had just trampled, and whether he expected any of his surviving victims to actually enter into a dialogue, Birch never knew. The voice that did rumble an answer back at Mars was deeper and louder by far than any human tones could be. It came rolling down at them from the hillside on the other side of the ford, and it said: "Your spear has failed you before, Wargod. It will again be insufficient."

Birch did not recognize that voice. But Mars did, for Birch saw him turn, with an expression suddenly and almost madly joyful, to face its owner. The God of War cried out: "It is the dog! The great son of a bitch that they call the Lord of Beasts. At last! I have been looking for you for a long time."

Birch was still lying on his back, aware that Micheline and the children were still at his side, and evidently still unhurt; but beyond that he could not think for the moment about himself or his family, nor speak, though his dry lips formed words. Even his own pain and injury were momentarily forgotten. He could only watch. He had never seen a single god in his whole life before, and now here were two at one time.

Lord Draffut came walking downhill, toward the ford and the few crouching, surviving humans, and the poor wreckage that was all that was left of the train of carts. Draffut's towering man-shaped form splashed knee-deep through the small river, now partially dammed by the jumble of wrecked vehicles, murdered loadbeasts and human bodies, all intermingled with the poor useless things that the humans had been trying to carry with them to safety inside the walls of Tashigang. The bloodied water splashed up around those knees of glowing fur, and Birch saw marveling that the elements of water and mud were touched with temporary life wherever the body of Draffut came in contact with them.

"Down on four legs, beast!" the Wargod roared, brandishing his spear at the other god who was as tall as he.

Lord Draffut had nothing more to say to Mars just now. The Beastlord only bared his fangs as he crossed the stream and halted, slightly crouching, almost within reach of the God of War.

The first thrust of the great spear came, too swift and powerful for watching Birch to see it plainly, or for Draffut to ward it in just the way he sought to do. It pierced Draffut's right forearm, but only lightly, in and out near the surface, so that he was still able to catch the spear's shaft in both his hands. A moment later he had wrenched the weapon out of the grasp of Mars completely, and reversed it in his own grip.

Mars had another spear, already magically in hand. The two weapons clashed. Then Draffut thrust again, with such violence that the shield of Mars was transfixed by the blow, and knocked out of the Wargod's grasp, to go rolling away with the spear like some great cartwheel on the end of a broken axle.

Mars cried out, a bellow of rage and fear, thought Birch, not of injury. Even to witness the fear of a god was terrible. In the next moment Mars demonstrated the ability to produce still more spears at will, and had now armed himself with one in each hand.

Draffut lunged at him and closed with him, and locked his massive arms around his great opponent, clamping the arms of Mars against the cuirass protecting the Wargod's body. At the same time Draffut sank his enormous fangs into god-flesh at the base of the thick armored neck. At the touch of the Lord of Beasts, even the magical armor of Mars melted and flowed with life, treacherously exposing the divine flesh that it was meant to guard.

The giants stamped and swayed, the earth quivering beneath their feet; even though his upper arms were pinioned, Mars tried stabbing at his attacker with the spears he held in both his hands. Birch, beyond marveling now, saw how one spearhead was converted by Draffut's life-powers to the giant head of a living serpent, and how the serpent's head struck back at the arm and wrist of the god who held it. Mars shrieked in deafening pain and rage.

Micheline, seeing the fight in her own terms, as an opportunity for human action, demanded of her husband whether he was hurt, whether he could move. Birch, taking his eyes off the contending giants only for a moment, told her that yes, he was hurt, and no, he could not move, and that she should take the children and get on away from here, and come back later when it was safe.

She protested briefly; but when she saw that he really could not move, she did as he had said. The fighting gods were much too busy to notice their departure, or that of any of the other people who could still move.

The spearhead in the right hand of Mars had not been changed by Draffut's touch; it stubbornly refused to flow with life. "You will not melt this weapon down!" Mars cried, and with its bright point and edge he tore open a wound along the shaggy ribs of the Lord of Beasts. And meanwhile Mars had managed to cast the treacherous biting serpent from him.

Now the God of Healing could no longer entirely heal himself. He bled red sparkling blood, from his side and from his wounded arm as well.

Yet he closed with Mars and disarmed him again of his remaining spear. He seized Mars in a wrestler's grip, and lifted him and threw him down on rocks, so that the earth shook with the shock of impact, and the water in the nearby stream leapt up in little spouts.

But as soon as he was free of Draffut's grip, Mars bounced up, a spear once more in each hand, just as before. He was bleeding too, with blood as red as Draffut's, but thicker, and so hot it steamed, rushing out from the place where Draffut's fangs had torn his neck.

Mars said: "You cannot kill a true god, dog-being. We are immortal."

Draffut was approaching him again, closing in slowly and methodically, looking for the best chance to attack. "Hermes died. If I cannot kill you . . . it is not because you are a god. It will be because . . ."

And now again—Birch did not understand, or hope to understand, everything that he was seeing and hearing—it seemed that Mars was capable of fear. "Why?" the Wargod asked.

Draffut answered; "Because there is too much of humanity in you. Human beings are not the gods' creation. You are theirs. You and all your peers who meet in the Ludus Mountains."

This brought on a bluster of roaring and insults from Mars, to which Draffut did not bother to reply. Meanwhile the two giants continued their steady, stealthy circling and stalking of each other.

But, finally, it was as if Draffut's calm statement about humanity had struck deeper than any planned insult. It must have struck so deep as to provoke even the God of War to that ultimate reaction, thought.

Mars rumbled at the other, "What did you mean by that foolishness? That we are their creation?"

"I mean to tell you what I saw, on that day when I stood among you, on the cold mountaintop, with the Sword of Stealth in my hand . . . Sightblinder let me see into the inward nature of the gods, you and the others there. And since then I have known . . . if I could not kill you the last time we fought, and I cannot kill you now, it is because there is in you too much of humanity."

"Bah. That I cannot believe." Mars waved his spears.

Stalking his enemy, bleeding, Draffut said it again. "You did not create them."

"Hah. *That* I can believe. What sort of god would be bothered to do that?"

"They created you."

Mars snorted with divine contempt. "How could such vermin ever create anything?"

"Through their dreams. Their dreams are very powerful."

The two titans closed with each other again, and fought, and again both of them were wounded. And again they both were weakened.

The only human observer left to watch them now was the man named Birch. He would certainly have crept away by now, too, with his wife and children, if he had been able to move. But he could not move. And by now he was no longer even thinking particularly of his own fate. He watched the fight until he fainted, and when he recovered his senses he watched again, for the fight was still in progress. When his thirst became overpowering, he made a great effort and managed to turn and twist himself enough to get a drink from the muddied, bloodied water of the small stream. Then he lay back and kept his mind off his own pain and injury by watching the fight some more.

The sun set on the struggle. It went on, with pauses—Birch supposed that even gods in this kind of agony must rest—through the night. The dark was filled with titanic thrashings and groanings, and splashing in the river where it gurgled gorily and patiently over and around the new dam that had been made out of human disaster.

At least, Birch told himself in his more lucid moments, he was not going to have to worry about predatory animals coming and trying to make a meal of him as he lay wounded. What ordinary beast would dare approach this scene?

When dawn came, Birch found himself still alive, somewhat to his own surprise. In the new daylight he beheld the ground, over the entire area around the ford, littered with broken spearshafts and spearheads, and with monstrous dead or lethargic serpents that had once been spears, all relics of the fight that still went on.

Or did it? This latest interval of silence seemed to be lasting for a longer time than usual—

There was a great, startling, earth-quivering crash, somewhere nearby, just out of Birch's sight, behind some overturned and smashed-up wagons that screened a large part of his field of vision. The ground shook with the renewed fight, which once more seemed to terminate in a final splash. In a moment the watching human was able to see and feel the waves indicating that the two combatants, still locked together, had plunged into the partially dammed pool of the river.

Now for a time Birch could no longer hear them fighting, except for occasional splashes that gradually decreased in violence. But now he could hear the two gods breathing. Ought gods to have to breathe? Birch wondered groggily. Maybe they only did it when they chose, like eating and drinking. Maybe they only did it when they needed extra strength.

Time passed in near silence. Then as the newly risen sun crept higher in the sky, a shadow fell across Birch where he lay. The man opened his eyes, to behold the figure of yet another god. Thank Ardneh, this one had not yet noticed the surviving human either.

Birch knew at once, by the leather-like smith's apron worn by the newcomer, and by the twisted leg, that this was Vulcan. The lame god was wearing at his side two great, blackhilted Swords, looking like mere daggers against the gray bulk of his body. He squatted on his haunches, looking down into the pool where the two fighters had gone out of Birch's field of vision. Now there was a renewed stirring in the pool, at last. A muttering, a splash. A great grin spread across the face of the Smith as he stood up and leisurely approached the combat a little more closely. Before he sat down again, on a rock, he kicked a broken cart out of his way. This incidentally cleared the field of view for the injured man, of whose existence none of the three giants had yet taken the least notice.

"Hail, oh mighty Wargod!" The salutation came from Vulcan in tones of gigantic mockery. "The world awaits your conquering presence. Have you not dallied here long enough? What are you doing down there, exactly—bathing your pet dog in the mud?"

Birch could see now how red the mud and water were around them both. Of the two combatants, Draffut could no longer fight, could hardly move. The God of War was little better off than his bedraggled foe. But now, slowly, terribly, with great gasping efforts, Mars dragged himself free of his opponent's biting, crushing grip, and stood erect, ankle-deep in mud.

When the Wargod tried to speak his voice was half-inaudible, failing altogether on some words. It seemed that he could barely lift the arm that he stretched out to Vulcan. "A spear—a weapon—I have no more spears. Lend me your Sword, Smith. One of them, I see that you have two. This business must be finished."

Vulcan sighed, producing a sound like that of wind rushing through a smoldering forge. He remained where he was, still some twenty meters or so distant from the other two. "Give you a weapon, hey? Well, I suppose I must, since you appear to be the victor in this shabby business after all. How tiresome."

Mars, though tottering on his feet, managed to draw himself a little more fully erect.

"How mannered you suddenly grow, Blacksmith. How fond you suddenly are of trying to appear clever. Why should that be? But never mind. Put steel here in my hand, and I'll finish this dirty job."

"I grant you," said Vulcan, "there is a need that certain things be finished." And the Smith stood up from where he had been sitting, and his ornaments of dragons' scales tinkled as he chose and drew one of his Swords.

" 'For thy heart'," he quoted softly, clasping and hiding the black hilt delicately in his great, gray, hardened blacksmith's hand. He held the Sword up straight, looking at it almost lovingly. " 'For thy heart, who hast wronged me.' "

"Wait," said Mars, staring at him with a suddenly new expression. "What Sword is—?"

His answer did not come in words. Vulcan was moving into a strange revolving dance, his whole body turning ponderously, great sandaled feet stamping rock and mud along the wagon trail, flattening earth that was already trodden and beaten and bloody from the fight, squashing the already dying serpents that had once been spears. The Sword in the Smith's extended arm was glowing now, and it was howling like the bull-roarer of some primitive magician.

Mars, half-dead or not, was suddenly galvanized. He sprang into motion, fleeing, running away. Running as only a god can run, Mars went ducking and twisting his way through the remnants of the hillside grove. He dodged among great splintered treetrunks, and splintering further those trees that got in his way.

Birch saw Vulcan throw the Sword, or rather let it go. After the Smith released it, the power that propelled it came only from within itself. The speed of Mars' flight was great, but the Sword was only a white streak through the air. Virtually instantaneously it followed the curving track of the Wargod's flight.

At the last moment, Mars turned to face doom bravely, and somehow he was able to summon yet one more spear into his hand. But even his magic spear of war availed him nothing against the Sword of Vengeance. The white streak ended abruptly, with the sound of a sharp impact.

Even with Farslayer embedded in his heart, Mars raised his spear, and took one stumbling step toward the god who had destroyed him. But then he could only cry a curse, and fall. He was dead before he struck the earth, and he demolished one more live tree in his falling. That last tree deflected the Wargod's toppling body, so that he turned before his landing shook the earth, and ended sprawling on his back. Only the black hilt and a handsbreadth of Farslayer's bright blade protruded from the armored breastplate on his chest.

CHAPTER 14

At the largest land gate in the walls of Tashigang, which was the Hermes Gate giving onto the great highway called the High Road, one thin stream of worried citizens was trying to get out of the city when Mark and Denis arrived, while another group, this one of country refugees, worked and pleaded to get in. There was obviously no general agreement on the safest place to be during the war that everyone thought was coming. The Watch on duty at the Hermes Gate were implacably forbidding the removal of foodstuffs, or anything that could be construed as military or medical supplies, while at the same time denying entrance to many of the outsiders. To gain entrance to the city it was necessary to show pressing business—other than that of one's own survival, which did not necessarily concern the Watch—or to bring in some substantial material contribution to the city's ability to withstand a siege. Denis, on identifying himself as an agent of the House of Courtenay, was admitted with no further argument. And Mark, along with his escort, was passed as a representative of Tasavalta, as his and his soldiers' blue-green clothing testified.

Mark thought that some of the Watch on duty at the gate recognized

Coinspinner at his side—it was not mentioned, but he suspected that the fact of the Sword's presence was quickly communicated to the Lord Mayor. Mark informed the officer who spoke to him that he too could be reached at the House of Courtenay, and alerted the guardians of the gate to expect the survivors of Sir Andrew's army. That group, two or three hundred strong, was traveling a few hours behind Mark and Denis; it would, they agreed, make a welcome addition to the city's garrison, that Denis said was chronically undermanned.

It was the first time Mark had ever entered a city as large as this one —he had heard some say that there were none larger—and he saw much to wonder at as Denis conducted him and his handful of Tasavaltan troopers through the broad avenues and streets. This was also, of course, the first time that Mark had seen the House of Courtenay, and he was duly impressed by the wealth and luxury in which his old friends Barbara and Ben were living. But he was given little time today in which to be impressed by that. The household, like the rest of the great city around it, was in a state of turmoil and tension. Soon after entering Mark got the impression that none of its members knew as yet whether they were preparing for war and siege, or for evacuation. Packing of certain valuables as if for possible evacuation was being undertaken, by a force of what Mark estimated as at least a dozen servants and other workers, while simultaneously another group barricaded all but a few of the doors and windows as if in expectation that the House must undergo a siege.

Almost immediately on entering the building's ground floor, coming into the clamorous confusion of what must be a workshop, Denis immediately became engaged in conversation with a man he introduced to Mark as the steward of the household, named Tarim.

Denis was already aghast at some of the things Tarim was telling him.

"Evacuation? Tashigang? Don't tell me they're seriously considering such a thing."

"We have heard something of the Mindsword's power," said Tarim worriedly. He turned his aging, troubled eyes toward Mark. "Perhaps you gentlemen who travel out in the great world have heard something of it too."

Denis was impatient. "I think we've some idea about it, yes. But we're not helpless, there are other weapons, other Swords. We've even brought one with us . . . and if they evacuate this city, half a million people or however many there are, where will they all go?"

Tarim shrugged fatalistically. "Flee to the upper hills, I suppose, or the Great Swamp. I didn't say that it made sense to evacuate."

Someone else had just entered the ground floor room. Turning, Mark saw the man who all his life he had thought of as his father. Who was his father, he told himself, in every sense that truly mattered.

And so Mark called him at first sight. For the time being, the Emperor was forgotten.

Mark had been only twelve the last time he saw Jord, then lying apparently dead in their village street. But there was no mistaking Jord, for the older man had changed very little. Except for being dressed now in finer garments than Mark had ever seen him wear before. And except for . . .

The really exceptional transformation was so enormous, and at the same time appeared so right and ordinary, that Mark at first glance came near accepting it as natural, and not a change at all. Then, after their first embrace, he wonderingly held his father at arms' length.

Jord now had two arms.

Mark's father said to him, "What the Swords took from me, they have given back. I'm told that Woundhealer was used to heal me as I lay here injured and unconscious. It did a better job even than those who used it had hoped."

"The Sword of Mercy has touched me too," Mark whispered. And then for a little time he could only stand there marveling at his father's new right arm. Jord explained to Mark how the arm had begun as a mere fleshy swelling, then a bud, and then in a matter of a few months had passed through the normal stages of human growth, being first a limb of baby size, then one to fit a child. It was as large and strong as the left arm now, but the skin of the new limb was still pink and almost unweathered even on the hand, not scarred or worn by age like that on Jord's left fist, visible below the sleeve of his fine new shirt.

Suddenly Mark said, "I've just come from seeing Mother, and Marian. When they hear you have a new arm . . ."

The two of them, father and son, had many things to talk about. Some things that were perhaps of even greater importance than a new arm—and Mark still had one problem to think about that he was never going to mention to this man. But they were allowed little time just now for talk. Ben and Barbara were arriving from somewhere in the upper interior of the house to give Mark a joyful welcome.

Barbara jumped at him, so that he had to catch and swing her. She threw wiry arms around his neck and kissed him powerfully, so that he held her, as he had Jord, at arms' length for a moment, wondering if in her case too there had taken place some change so great as to be invisible at first glance. But then he had to drop her, for Ben, less demonstrative as a rule, came to almost crush Mark in a great hug.

They were followed by a plump nursemaid, introduced to Mark as Kuan-yin who was carrying their small child Beth. The toddler was obviously already a great friend of Jord's, for she went to him at once and asked him how his new arm was.

Kuan-yin, released from immediate duty, at once went a little apart with Denis. Mark could see that the two of them, standing face to face amid the confusion of workers packing and barricading, had their own private greetings to exchange.

"We'd like to get a welcoming party for you started right away," Ben was saying to Mark, "but we can't. It'll have to wait at least until tomorrow. The Lord Mayor has called a council of leading citizens, and Barbara and I are invited. Substantial people now, you know. Master and Lady Courtenay. And the Mayor knows we have some kind of a hoard of weapons, to help defend . . . what's that at your side?"

Ben grabbed the sheath, and looked at the Sword's hilt. "Thank Ardneh, Coinspinner! We've got to go to that meeting, and you've got to come too, and bring this tool along, to see that they don't decide on some damned foolishness like surrendering. You'll be welcome, bringing word from outside as you do. And also as a representative of Tasavalta. And bringing another Sword . . . that'll stiffen up their spines. Townsaver is in town already."

Mark grinned at him. "Doomgiver is on the way."

"Thank all the gods!" Holding Mark by the arm, Ben lowered his voice for a moment. "We can't surrender, and we certainly can't evacuate. Imagine trying to take a three-year-old on that . . . you and I know what it would be like. But if the rest of the city goes, we'll have to try."

The Lord Mayor's palace, like every other part of the city that Mark had seen so far, was a scene of energetic, confused, and doubtfully productive activity. Here as elsewhere the inhabitants appeared to be striving to make ready for some all-out effort, whose nature they had not yet been able to decide upon.

Mark, Ben, and Barbara were admitted readily enough at the main doorway of the Palace. This was a building somewhat similar to the House of Courtenay, though even larger and more sumptuous, and with reception rooms and offices on the ground floor instead of workshop space. Soon they were conducted up a broad curving stair of marble, past workmen descending with newly crated works of art.

On the way, Mark's friends were trying to bring him up to date on the situation that they were about to encounter.

"We're likely," Ben warned, "to run into our old friend Hyrcanus at this meeting."

Mark almost missed his footing on the stair. "Hyrcanus? Is he still Chief Priest at the Blue Temple? But he—"

"He still is," Barbara assured him. "And the Blue Temple is an important faction here in Tashigang."

"I suppose they must be. But I never thought about it until now," Mark murmured. "Hyrcanus. I remember hearing somewhere that he was certain to be deposed. I thought he was gone by now, it's four years since we robbed him. Plundered his deepest rathole, as nobody else has ever done before or since."

"Thank all the gods for that rathole," Barbara murmured. "And send us another like it. A handful of its contents has done well for Ben and me. I hear that the Temple are now considering moving their main hoard of treasure into Tashigang. We just wanted to warn you, Hyrcanus will probably be here, and he won't be happy to see us."

"He thinks I'm dead," Mark murmured. But it was too late now to try to preserve that happy state of affairs.

They had now reached the door of the conference room, a large, well-appointed chamber on an upper floor, and were ushered in without delay. Even after being warned it was a shock for Mark to behold Hyrcanus with his own eyes; it was the first time that he had ever actually seen the man, but there was no doubt in Mark's mind who he was. The Blue Temple's Chairman and High Priest, having survived the efforts that must certainly have been made to depose him after the sacrilegious robbery of the Temple's main hoard four years ago, was still in charge, and had indeed come here today for the Lord Mayor's conference.

Hyrcanus, the High Priest, small, bald, and rubicund, his face as usual jovial, looked up as the three of them entered. His cheerful smile did not exactly disappear, but froze. He must have recognized Ben, at least, by description, at first sight.

The Chairman studied Mark too, and could hardly fail to identify him also, especially as their escort announced his name along with the others in a loud voice. The others who were gathered round the table, a dozen or so men and women, mostly the solid citizens of Tashigang, rose to return greetings and extend a welcome to the new arrivals. Their faces were cheered, Mark thought, at the sight of the Tasavaltan green and blue that he still wore. And their expressions altered still more, with new hope and calculation, at the sight of the black hilt at his side. Mark let his left hand rest upon it, loosely, casually; he did not want Hyrcanus, at least, to be able to read which white symbol marked that hilt.

Mark supposed the fact that he was appearing in Tasavaltan colors might at least give the cheery-looking old bastard pause, and perhaps cause him to at least delay the next assassination attempt.

The Lord Mayor, named Okada, was a clerkish-looking man on whom the robes of his high office looked faintly preposterous. Yet he presided firmly. The arrival of Mark, Ben, and Barbara had interrupted Hyrcanus in the midst of a speech, which he now resumed, at the Mayor's suggestion.

It was soon apparent as Hyrcanus spoke that the Blue Temple Chairman's thoughts were not now on revenge and punishment of past transgressors, but, as usual, were concentrated on how best he could contrive to save the bulk of the Blue Temple's treasure. A siege of the city, a storming of the walls, were to be avoided at all costs—at least at all costs to others outside the Blue Temple. Mark, listening, assumed that Hyrcanus had already made some arrangement, or thought he had, with the Dark King, by which the Blue Temple holdings in Tashigang would be secure, in exchange for co-operation with the conqueror.

Mark could recognize one other face at the council table, though no reminiscences were exchanged in this case either. Baron Amintor was here as the personal representative of the Silver Queen. He recognized Mark also, and gazed at him in a newly friendly way, while Mark looked stonily at this old enemy of Sir Andrew. The Baron, Mark was sure, recognized Ben and Barbara as well.

Hyrcanus continued the speech he had begun, urging that one of two courses be adopted: either outright surrender to the Dark King, or else the declaration of Tashigang as an open city. That last, Mark thought, must amount, in practical terms, to the same thing as surrender.

The speech of the High Priest did not evoke any particular enthusiasm among the citizens of Tashigang who made up the majority of his listeners. But neither were they vocal in immediate objection; rather the burghers seemed to be waiting to hear more. Now and again their eyes strayed toward the black hilt at Mark's side.

Hyrcanus might have gone on and on indefinitely, but Mayor Okada at length firmly reclaimed the floor. Who, he asked, wanted to speak next?

Baron Amintor had been impatiently waiting for his chance. Now he arose, and as representative of the Silver Queen, argued eloquently that the city must be defended to the last fighter. Though he was careful, Mark observed, not to put it in exactly those terms. Rather the Baron was strongly reassuring about the walls, the city's history and tradition of successful resistance to outside attack, and about the commitment of the Silver Queen to their defense.

Hyrcanus interrupted him at one point to object. "What about the Mindsword, though? What are any walls against that?"

Amintor took the objection in stride, and assured the others that Yambu was not without her own supremely powerful weapon. "In her wisdom and reluctance to do harm, she has not employed it as yet. But, faced with the Mindsword . . . I am sure she will do whatever she must do to assure the safety of Tashigang."

One of the burghers rose. "When you mention this weapon that the Queen has, you are speaking of the Sword called Soulcutter, or sometimes the Tyrant's Blade, are you not?"

"I am." If Amintor was offended by the plain use of that second name, he did not show it.

"I know little about it." The questioner looked around the table. "Nor, I suppose, do many of us here. What can it do to protect Tashigang?"

Amintor glanced only for a moment at Hyrcanus. "I would prefer not to go into tactical details regarding any of the Swords just now," the Baron answered smoothly. He almost winked at Mark, who carried Coinspinner, as if they had been old comrades instead of enemies. "Later, under conditions of greater security, if you like. I will say now only that the Queen is wise and compassionate"—for some reason, no one in the room laughed—"and that she will not use such a weapon as Soulcutter carelessly. But neither will she allow this city that she so loves to be taken by its enemies."

Mark had to admit to himself that he had little or no idea what Soulcutter might do. It was the one Sword of the Twelve that he had never seen, let alone had in his possession. Almost all he knew of it was contained in the verse that everyone had heard:

The Tyrant's Blade no blood hath spilled
But doth the spirit carve
Soulcutter hath no body killed
But many left to starve.

Glancing at Ben and Barbara, he read an equal lack of knowledge in their faces.

The Lord Mayor now looked at Mark expectantly. It was time that the meeting heard from the emissary from Tasavalta.

Mark stood up from his chair and leaned his hands on the table in front of him. With faith in what the Emperor had told him, he was able to announce that the Tasavaltan army was on the march, under the direct command of General Rostov, coming to the city's relief. Rostov's was an impressive name, one fit to go with the reputation of the walls of Tashigang itself, and once again most of the faces around the table appeared somewhat cheered. That the Tasavaltan army also was small by comparison with the Dark King's host was not mentioned at the moment, though everybody knew it. Even should the Silver Queen arrive with her army at the same time, Vilkata would still have the advantage of numbers.

"Does anyone else have anything to say?" the Lord Mayor asked. "Anyone else, who has not spoken yet?"

Ben spoke briefly, and Barbara after him. They added nothing really new to the discussion, but reminded everyone again of the city's tradition and promised to help arm the defense from their store of weapons. Before she spoke, Barbara faced Mark momentarily, and her lips formed the one word: *Doomgiver?*

Mark shook his head very slightly. He wanted to keep that news in reserve, to stiffen the council's resolve if they should be swayed toward surrender after all. Right now he judged that was unlikely.

Shortly after Barbara spoke, the Mayor called for a show of hands. "How many are ready to fight for our city?"

Only one hand was not raised. Hyrcanus sent black looks at Ben, and Mark, and Amintor.

Before the Chairman of the Blue Temple could make a final statement and a dramatic exit, an aide to the Mayor entered to announce the arrival of a flying courier with a message for the Lord Mayor. The courier and message container were both marked with the black and silver insignia of Queen Yambu herself.

The beast-courier—Mark recognized it as one of a hybrid species prevented, in the interests of secrecy, from ever acquiring speech—was brought into the room. The message capsule of light metal was opened and the paper inside unfolded.

Okada read through the single sheet alone, in anxious silence; then he raised his head.

"It is indeed from her most puissant Majesty, the Silver Queen herself, and, as the marking on the capsule indicated, addressed personally to me. I will not read the entire message aloud just now; it contains certain matters I do not need to proclaim in council." There followed a look at Hyrcanus, to say wordlessly that important military secrets were not going to be announced in front of him, not in view of the attitude he had just taken. The Mayor continued: "But, there are other parts that I think we all should hear at once."

The Silver Queen's words that the Mayor read were very firm, and could be called inspiring in terms of fear if not otherwise: there was to be no talk of surrendering the city, under penalty of incurring her severe displeasure.

Her message also confirmed that she was already on the march with her army, coming to the relief of this her greatest city—as she put it, indeed the greatest and proudest city in the world. And that she intended to achieve victory by whatever means were necessary.

Hyrcanus walked out. He did it unhurriedly, almost courteously, with considerable dignity, Mark had to admit. The High Priest did not waste time on threats, now that it would have been obviously useless and even dangerous to do so; a behavior somehow, at this stage, thought Mark, more ominous than any threats would be.

The Lord Mayor, looking thoughtfully after the High Priest, was evidently of the same opinion. Okada immediately called in an officer of the Watch from just outside the conference room, and calmly gave the order to arrest the High Priest before he could get out of the Palace; once out, he would easily be able to give some signal to his troops. The Blue Temple Guards in the city, Ben had said, were one of the largest trained fighting forces within the walls.

Now it became at least possible for the council to discuss the city's means of defense in more detail, without the virtual certainty that a potential enemy was listening and taking part in the debate.

Amintor immediately put forward a plan to neutralize the Blue Temple troops by meeting any attempt on their part to rescue Hyrcanus with a countermove against the local Temple and its vaults, whipping up a street mob for the purpose if no regular forces could be spared.

Barbara whispered to Mark that Denis would probably be a good man to see to the organization of such an effort.

In succeeding discussion, it quickly became plain that the key to the regular defense of the city's walls against attack from outside would be the Watch, a small but well-trained body of regular troops loyal to the Lord Mayor. They were only a few hundred strong against Vilkata's thousands, but their numbers could be augmented by calling up the city's militia. Ben whispered to Mark that the quality of the militia was, regrettably, not so high as it might be. But certainly the city's long tradition of defending itself ought to help.

Then there were the fragments of Sir Andrew's army to be considered, the survivors who had followed Denis and Mark to Tashigang, along with the ten or a dozen at most of Mark's surviving Tasavaltan escort. Mark could assure the Lord Mayor that Sir Andrew's people were all good, experienced fighters, though at present somewhat demoralized by the sad death of their noble leader. Given the chance, they would be eager to exact revenge.

Mark revealed now that the Sword he wore at his side was Coinspinner, and he proposed that they consult the Sword of Chance at once to try to determine the best means of obtaining a successful defense of the city. All were agreeable; and all, particularly those who had never seen a Sword before, were impressed by the sight when Mark drew his.

"It points . . . that way. What's there?"

They soon determined that something outside the room was being indicated. They had to leave the council room, and then go up on the roof of the Palace to make sure.

The Sword of Chance was pointing at someone or something outside the city walls, in fact at the very center of Vilkata's advancing army. The Dark King's force had just now come barely into sight, through distant summer haze. It was still, Mark thought, well out of Mindsword range.

And Coinspinner pointed as if to Vilkata himself. Mark looked at Ben, and got back a look of awe and calculation mingled.

CHAPTER 15

The delegation from the palace, two women and one man, arrived at Mala's door very quietly and unexpectedly. It was the afternoon after she heard of Mark's departure from Tasavalta on a mission for the Princess. Her first thought on seeing the strangers at her door was that something terrible had happened to her son or her husband, or to both; but before she could even form the question, one of the women was assuring her that as far as was known, both were well. The three of them had come to conduct Mala to the palace, because the Princess herself wanted to see her.

The Palace was not far above the town, and less than an hour later Mala was there, walking in an elaborate flower garden, open within high walls. The garden had tall flowering trees in it, and strange animals to gape at, hybrid creatures such as the highborn liked to amuse themselves with, climbing and flying amid high branches.

Mala was left alone in the garden, but only for a few moments. Then a certain fat man appeared, well dressed and with an aura of magic about him. He introduced himself as Karel, which name meant nothing to Mala; and he, though obviously a person of some importance, appeared quite content that it should be so. He walked along the garden path with Mala, and asked her about her family, and tried to put her at her ease. That he succeeded as well as he did was a tribute to his skill.

And then he asked her, in his rich, soft voice: "Do you know the Sword of Mercy? Or Sword of Love, as it is sometimes called?"

"I know of it, sir, of course; you must know who my husband is. But if you mean have I ever seen it, no."

"Then have you any idea where it is, at this moment? Hey?" Karel's gaze at her was suddenly much more intense, though he was still trying to appear kind.

"When my son was here, there was a story going about that he—and the Princess—had brought it with them to Tasavalta. But he himself said nothing to me of that, and I did not ask him. I knew better than to be curious about state secrets. Nor could I guess where it is now."

Karel continued to gaze at her with a steady intensity. "He did bring it, and it was here yesterday after he left. That's no state secret." The magician suddenly ceased to stare at her. Shaking his head, he looked away. "And now it's gone, and I don't know where it is either. And whether that ought to be a secret or not . . ." He sighed, letting the words trail off.

Mala felt vaguely frightened. "I don't know either, sir."

"No, of course you don't. I believe you, dear lady, now that I have looked at you closely . . . and there is one other matter that I want to ask you about."

Her frightened look said that she could hardly stop him.

He sighed again. "Here, sit down." And he led her to a nearby marble bench, and sat on it beside her, puffing with relief when his weight came off his feet. "No harm will come to you or Mark for a truthful answer, whatever it may be. I think I know already, but I must be sure . . . who is Mark's real father?"

Under the circumstances the story of more than twenty years ago came out. Mala had thought at the time that the man might be Duke Fraktin. Later she had been convinced that it was not. And later still, slowly and gradually, the truth had dawned.

"But sir, I beg you, my husband . . . Jord . . . he mustn't know. He's never guessed. Mark is his only living son. He . . ."

"Hmmm," said Karel. And then he said: "Jord has served us well. We will do all we can for him. The Princess is waiting to see you. I told her that I wished to speak to you first."

The magician heaved himself up ponderously from the bench, and guided Mala through an ornamental gate, and into another, smaller garden, where there were benches that looked like crystal instead of marble, and paths of what looked like gravel but was too soft for stone; and here the Princess was standing waiting for her.

She looks like a nice girl, was one idea that stood out clearly in the confusion of Mala's thoughts.

Kristin had been hopelessly curious as to what the mother of the man she loved was like; this was largely because she was still curious as to what Mark himself was like, having had little time in which to get to know him. It was all very well to order herself, with royal commands, to forget about him. To insist that Mark was her lover no longer, that if she ever saw him again it would only be in passing, in some remote and official contact; but somehow all these royal commands meant nothing, when the chance arose to talk to Mark's mother in line of duty, in this matter of the Swords.

When the minimum necessary formalities had been got through, the two women were left sitting alone on one of the crystal benches, and Karel had gracefully retired; not, Kristin was sure, that he was not listening. She knew Karel of old, and the fat wizard had more on his mind just now than Swords, or a missing Sword, important though those matters were.

Mala was saying to her: "I had hoped that one day I would get the chance to talk to you, Highness. But I did not want to seem to be a scheming mother, trying to get advantage for her son."

"You are not that, I am sure . . . unless you are scheming for Mark's safety only. Any mother would do that."

Kristin had questions to ask, about Mala, Jord, their family; when she asked about Mark's father, she thought that his mother looked at her strangely; but then how else would the woman look, being brought here suddenly like this, to talk to royalty?

And the questions kept coming back to Mark himself.

More time had passed than Kristin had realized, but still not very much time, when there was an interruption, a twittering from an observant small beast high in a branch above them.

Kristin swore, softly and wearily. "There is now a general who insists on seeing me, if I have learned to interpret these jabbering signals correctly. I have so much to do, and all at once." She seized Mala by the hands. "I want to talk to you again, and soon."

A minute later, Mala was gone, and Kristin was receiving General Rostov.

The General began by reporting, in his gravelly voice, that the man Jord had a good reputation in the Intelligence branch. There was no actual Tasavaltan dossier on the son as yet—rather, one had just been started—but he seemed to have a good reputation with Sir Andrew's people. And a long and strange and intimate connection with the Swords, as Jord did too, of course.

"Nothing to connect either of them, though, Highness, with the disappearance of Woundhealer."

"No, I should think not, General . . . now what are your military plans?"

Rostov drew himself up. "It's like this, Highness. The best place to defend your house is not in your front yard, but down the road as far as you can manage it. *If* you can manage it that way."

"If that is a final . . . what is it, Karel?"

The wizard had reappeared at the ornamental gate. "A matter of state, Highness. You had better hear it before completing any other plans, military or otherwise."

"One moment," said the Princess, and faced back to Rostov. "I believe you, General. And I have decided to go with you. If you are saying that the army must march to Tashigang, because that is where the fate of our people is being decided, then that is the place for me to be also."

Choking in an effort to keep from swearing, General Rostov disputed this idea as firmly as he was able.

"Both of you," said Karel, "had better hear me first. What I have to say is connected with the woman who was just here."

CHAPTER 16

They were kilometers in length, and tall as palaces. They wound uphill and down, in a great tail-swallowing circle, in curves like the back of the legendary Great Worm Yilgarn. They were the walls of Tashigang, and at long last they stood before him.

The taking of the city, even the planning of its capture, were turning out to present considerably greater problems than the Dark King had earlier envisioned. He had once pictured himself simply riding up to the main gate on the Hermes Road, and brandishing the Mindsword in the faces of the garrison, who had been conveniently assembled for him on the battlements. Then, after a delay no longer than the time required for his new slaves in the city to open up the gate, he would enter in triumph, to see to the disposal of his new treasure and the elimination of some of his old enemies.

That last part of the vision had been the first part to turn unreal and unconvincing, which it did almost as soon as Vilkata began to think about it. The Mindsword would seem to rob revenge almost entirely of its satisfaction. If one's old enemies had now become one's loyal slaves, about as faithful as human beings could be, then what was the point of destroying or damaging them?

In any case, Vilkata could see now that Tashigang was not going to fall into his hands as neatly as all that. On the last night of his march toward the city, the night before he first faced the ancient serpentine walls directly, the Dark King had received a warning from his demonic counselors. They had determined, they said, that the Sword Doomgiver had just been carried inside the city's walls, where it was now in the possession of some of the most fanatical defenders. Therefore he, the Dark King, stood in danger of having his most powerful magic—aye, even the power of the Mindsword—turned against him when he tried to use it in an attack.

After receiving this grim caution, Vilkata sat in blind silence for a time, dispensing with the demon's vision the better to concentrate on his own thoughts. Meanwhile those of his human counselors who were attending him waited in their own tremulous silence around him, fearing his wrath, as they imagined that he still listened to the demonic voices that only he could hear.

The Dark King tried to imagine the direst warnings of his inhuman magical counselors coming true. It would mean the devotion of all his own troops would turn to hatred. And also, perhaps, it would mean all of the evil that he had ever worked on anyone now within the walls of Tashigang coming back on himself, suddenly, to strike him down.

And he was warned, too, that the Sword Townsaver might also be within the city. The Sword of Fury in itself ought not to blunt the Mindsword's power. But what Townsaver might do, to any portion of an attacking army that came within a bladelength of its wielder, was enough in itself to give a field commander pause.

The Dark King shuddered, the fear that was never far below the surface of his thoughts suddenly coming near the surface. As he shuddered, the humans watching him thought that he was still listening to the demons' speech.

And then, there was the matter of Farslayer, too. Until he had that particular weapon safely in his hands, he had to be concerned about it. Any monarch, any man, who dealt consistently in such great affairs as King Vilkata did, was bound to make enemies and would have to be concerned. There were always plenty of short-sighted, vengeful little folk about . . . and neither the Dark King's wizards nor his immaterial demons could give him any idea of who possessed the Sword of Vengeance now.

If only he had been able to pick up Shieldbreaker from the field of battle! But no, another distraction, another threat, had intervened to prevent that. And now no one could tell him where that trump of weapons was located either.

Coinspinner was another potential problem. It, too, was now thought by the Dark King's magical advisers to be present inside the walls of Tashigang. And he was sure that the Sword of Chance would bring those damned impertinent rascals good luck, good fortune of some kind, even in the face of the Mindsword's influence. Vilkata kept trying to imagine what kind of good luck that would be. Whatever it was, it would not be good for him.

But despite all of the obstacles and objections, he could be royally stubborn, and he was going forward. None of his fears were great enough to prevent that. In the end he decided to keep his own supernal weapons under wraps for the time being, and to try what he might to induce the city to surrender under threats.

The afternoon he arrived before the walls, he had his great pavilion erected within easy sight of them—though not, of course, within missile range. At the same time Vilkata ordered a complete envelopment of the city, and entrenchment by his troops, as if for a lengthy siege, all along their encircling lines.

Even his great host was thinly spread by such a maneuver, which necessitated occupying a line several kilometers long; but Vilkata intended to concentrate most of his troops in a few places later, if and when it actually became necessary to assault the walls. Meanwhile he wanted to give an impression not only of overwhelming force but of unhurried determination. And still he was not satisfied that things were going well; he kept urging both his scouts and his wizards to provide him with more information.

At dusk on the second day of the siege, the Dark King's vaguely growing sense of some impending doom was suddenly relieved. The last flying messenger to arrive during daylight hours brought in a report saying that the troublesome Beastlord Draffut was finally dead, and the god Mars—who was also troublesome, because he had managed to remain free of the Mindsword's control—was dead with him. And that Vulcan, triumphant over both of them, was headed toward the city of Tashigang, waving the Sword Shieldbreaker and crying his own eternal loyalty to the Dark King.

When the half-intelligent courier was asked to predict the time of the god's arrival, it gave answers interpreted to mean that the progress of the Smith across the countryside was slow and erratic, because he was stopping frequently to offer sacrifice to his god Vilkata, and also because he walked a zig-zag course; but Vulcan continually cried out that he was coming on to Tashigang, where his other Swords were gathering, and where he meant to do honor in person to the King.

His other Swords? Vilkata pondered to himself. Of course the Smith had forged them all, and perhaps that was all that he meant by the use of such an expression. In any case, there was nothing Vilkata could do about the Smith, or any other god, until they came within the Mindsword's range. And the Dark King did not want to appear to be worried by what sounded, on the surface, like very good news indeed. Therefore he gave permission for a celebration of Vulcan's triumph to begin, and sent out trumpeters and criers to make certain that the death of Draffut and the advance of the victorious Vulcan were made known within the walls of Tashigang as well.

Vilkata even took part in the revel himself, at least as far as its middle stages. He retired comparatively early, thinking that in any case he was giving himself time to sleep and recover before Vulcan could possibly arrive. He wearied himself with women, and came near besotting himself with wine, and then tumbled into his private bed to sleep.

His awakening was hours earlier than he had expected, and it came not at the gentle call of his valet, or some officer of his bodyguard. The sound that tore Vilkata out of dreams of victory was the ripping of his pavilion's fabric, not far from his head, by some enemy weapon's edge.

No matter how mad the odds seemed against success, when merely human calculation was applied, Coinspinner had insisted that the defenders of the city organize a sally against Vilkata's camp; a military maneuver involving the sending of what could be at most a few hundred troops, to fight against the Dark King's many thousands. At least this was the only interpretation that could finally be placed on the way that the Sword of Chance, whenever it was consulted, pointed insistently into the heart of the enemy camp.

Mark, Ben, and Barbara, along with the other members of the Lord Mayor's council, discussed the possibility of sending one or two agents or spies, armed with Coinspinner, out into the camp, to try to achieve whatever the Sword was telling them to do there. But Mark had experience of the Dark King's security systems, and without Sightblinder to help he could imagine no way of accomplishing that.

On the other hand, the more carefully the idea of a surprise sally was considered, the less completely mad it seemed. It could, of course, be launched by night, and it certainly ought to take the enemy by surprise. The Mayor drew out secret maps. It was noted that one of the secret tunnels leading out of the city—like most places so elaborately fortified, Tashigang was equipped with several—emerged from a concealed opening under the bank of the Corgo, behind the enemy front line and only about a hundred meters from where Vilkata's pavilion had been set up.

A plan was hastily worked out. Both Ben and Mark would accompany the attacking force, Mark with Coinspinner in his hands. Ben, after speaking strongly against surrender of the city, could not very well avoid the effort now; nor did he want his old friend to go without him. The handful of Tasavaltan troops who had escorted Mark to Tashigang now volunteered, to a man, to go with him again. He was somewhat surprised and gratified by this; either his leadership or his Sword had inspired more confidence than he knew.

The bulk of the raiding force, which was two hundred strong in all, was made up from the survivors of Sir Andrew's slaughtered army. They proved to be as eager for revenge as Mark had expected them to be.

The deployment of the force into the secret, stone-walled tunnel took place in the late hours of the night. The city end of the tunnel was concealed in the basement of an outbuilding of the Mayor's palace.

Waiting in the cramped, dark, and dripping tunnel for some final magical preparations to be made, Mark had some time to talk with his old friend Ben. He told Ben something of his meeting with the Emperor.

When Mark first mentioned the name of Ariane, Ben shook his head, not wanting to hear more; but when he heard that the Emperor had claimed the red-haired girl as his daughter, the huge man turned hopeless eyes to Mark. "But what does it mean? What does that matter now? She's dead."

"I don't know what it means. I know you loved her. I wanted you to hear what he told me."

Ben nodded, slowly. "It's strange . . . that he said that."

"What do you mean?"

"When we were leaving the treasure-dungeon—right after she was killed—I looked up onto that headland, the Emperor's land they said it was, right across the fjord. I thought for a moment I saw—red hair. It doesn't mean anything, I don't suppose."

And now, suddenly, there was no more time for talk.

The Mayor's most expert sorceress was squeezing her way through the narrow tunnel, marking with a sign each man and woman of the raiding party, as she passed them. When her hand touched his own eyes briefly, Mark found that now he could see a dim, ghostly halo behind the head of everyone else in the attacking force. When fighting started in the darkness, they ought to be able to identify each other. At least until the enemy magicians solved the spell, and were able to turn it to their own advantage. Most likely they were more skillful than this woman of the Mayor's. But it was necessary to take what seemed desperate chances. That was what Coinspinner was for.

The party moved out. The tunnel extended for more than a kilometer, and its lower sections were knee-deep in water. An occasional loud splash or oath, the shuffle of feet, the chink of weapons, were for some time the only sounds.

The outer end of the tunnel, in which an advance party had been waiting for some time, was quietly opened. Two by two, moving now as quickly and silently as possible, the raiders launched themselves out of the tunnel into shallow water, and up and out into the open night.

Mark, with Coinspinner in his hands, was the second or third fighter to emerge. Now there could be no mistake about it. The Sword of Chance was directing him, ordering the whole attack, straight to Vilkata's pavilion. The huge tent stood plain in the light of several watchfires near it, its black-gold fabric wrinkling in a chiaroscuro wrought by the night breeze.

The first few of the Dark King's soldiers to blunder innocently into the way of the advancing column were cut down in savage silence. For those few endless-seeming moments, the advantage of surprise held. Then the alarm went up, in a dozen voices at once. The thin column of raiders broke into a charge; still, half or more of their total number had not yet come out of the tunnel.

Now resistance began, weapon against weapon, fierce and growing stronger. But it was still too disorganized to stop the charge. Mark, near the front of the attack, used Coinspinner as a physical weapon. Troops were gathering to oppose the raiders; the alarm was spreading. But now for a moment the pavilion was within reach, the Sword of Chance could touch its fabric. Fine cloth parted with a shriek before its edge.

Men who had been inside burst out with weapons in their hands to bar the way. Already a counterattack was taking form, against both sides of the column and its front. The formation shattered, with its front forced back by opposing swords and shields; the fight became a great melee, a free-for-all.

A different and even deadlier resistance was gathering too. Above the watchfires, over the huge tent itself, the air roiled now with more than rising heat. The demonic guardians of the Dark King and of his chief magicians were readying themselves to pounce upon intruders.

The Lord Mayor's best sorceress, stumbling near Mark's side in the darkness, stopped suddenly and seized Mark by the arm. He could feel the woman's whole body quivering.

"Do what you can," she demanded of him. "And quickly! Else we are all lost. I had hoped they would not be this strong . . ."

Mark himself with his experience had been grimly certain that they would. Still the Sword had brought him here. And he had another power of his own, already tested once.

His faith in it was tested now. Suddenly the Emperor was only one more man, and far away, while the ravening airborne presences that lowered themselves now toward Mark were the most overwhelmingly real things in all the universe.

Mark had rehearsed no incantations beforehand. If he meant to trust the Emperor, he would trust him in that as well, that no special words were needed. The words that came to him now were those of Ariane, uttered in the Blue Temple cave four years ago:

"In the Emperor's name, forsake this game, and let us pass!"

Vilkata, awakened by the sounds of the attack, had just rolled groggily out of bed. The demon that served as his eyes, recalled abruptly to duty, had just begun to send sight-images to the Dark King's brain. Then in a moment the demon was catapulted into a blank distance, and those images were blanked away again.

For a moment the Dark King did not grasp the full import of his full and sudden blindness. Certainly some emergency had arisen, and his first thought was for the Mindsword. He groped for it, but his hands found only a tangled fall of cloth; part of his pavilion was collapsing around him. And the weapon was not where he thought it ought to be. Could he possibly, in last night's drunkenness, have failed to keep the Sword with him, beside his bed as always? He could remember, at some time in the party, using it in sport, trying to drive one of his women mad with devotion to him. But after that . . .

Surrounded by the sounds of fighting, groans, oaths, and the clash of arms, he groped frantically about him on the floor, amid soft pillows and spilled wine. Between the confusion of his awakening and his sudden blindness he was disoriented. No, he had brought the Mindsword with him to his bedchamber, he remembered and was sure. But now he could not find it. Where was it?

The clamor of the fighting continued very near him. The fabric and the supports of the tent must have been assaulted; the bodies of people running and fighting had jostled into it, and more great sheets of loosened cloth were falling, crumpling. They settled and collapsed right on the groping blind man.

The Sword had to be right here, he knew that it was here. But still he could not lay his hands on it. Frantically, sightlessly, he burrowed into the heaps of soft, fine fabric that were coming down and piling up like snow. But his searching fingers were baffled by the cloth, as the eyes of a normally sighted man would be in fog.

And Vilkata was aware by now that not only his vision-demon but all the other demons as well were gone, a great part of his defense dissolved. It was unbelievable, but true. Somehow they had all been hurled away. In the middle distance he could hear the voice of Burslem, screaming incantations, trying to call other, non-demonic, forces of magic into play. What success the magician might be having, Vilkata could not tell. His ears assured him that the physical fight still raged nearby, but the enemy weapons had not yet found his skin. Perhaps, under this baffling cloth, he was invisible as well as blind.

And still, in his confusion, he could not find the Sword. He'd grope his way back to his bed, and start over again from there. If only he knew which way to crawl to find his bed.

Mark was wielding Coinspinner constantly now, as a physical weapon in his own defense. The demons had been satisfactorily expelled, at least for the time being, but minute by minute the Dark King's other defenses were becoming better organized. Confusion still dominated, and because of that fact the bulk of the attacking force still survived. Mark thought that, to the enemy, his attacking force must have seemed to number in the thousands; it would seem inconceivable to the Dark King that any force much smaller than that would dare to attack him in this fashion.

In the outer darkness around the periphery of the struggle, the Dark King's people must often have been fighting one another. Closer to the pavilion, in the light of the watchfires, they prospered better, and began to assert some of the real advantage of their numbers. Mark was wounded lightly in his left arm, when even superb luck ran thin, by a blow that doubtless would have killed him outright but for his possession of the Sword of Chance.

He had lost sight of Ben, and of the sorceress. His Tasavaltan guard were fighting near him. Coinspinner still pointed at the half-collapsed pavilion, but Mark no longer saw how he could get there. The whole invading party was being forced back now, farther away from it.

Only Doomgiver, in the hands of one of Sir Andrew's officers, saved the attacking party from complete annihilation at this point. It repelled blows, missiles, and magic spells, making its holder a center of invulnerable strength, turning each weapon used against him back upon its user. Alone it worked considerable destruction in the ranks of the Dark King's guardians. And, along with the Sword of Chance that Mark still had in his grasp, it allowed a tenacious survival for the attackers even after their hopes of being able to seize the Mindsword had dwindled almost to the vanishing point.

"Back!" Whether Mark was the one who actually voiced the word or not, it was in his throat. "We must retreat. We can't let our two Swords be captured here."

So what had been a forced withdrawal became a calculated one. Now Coinspinner, faithful as always to its users' wishes, also pointed the way back. Mark fought, and moved, and fought again, hampered by his wounded arm, swinging the Sword of Chance as best he could. His Tasavaltan bodyguard was trying to keep close around him, and more than once they saved his life.

"By all the gods, what's that?"

It was not all the gods, but only some of them. No more than three or four, perhaps. They were out near the horizon, kilometers from the walls of Tashigang and the field of human combat. Several large sparks, like burning brands, could be seen out there in the distance, moving back and forth over the earth erratically. Those sparks must be whole burning treetrunks at the least.

Momentarily a near-hush spread across the battlefield, as most of the people on it became aware of that sight in the distance; and in that moment of half-silence, the singing voices of the distant gods were audible. What words they sang were hard to catch, discordant as those far voices were, and whipped about by wind; but enough could be heard to be sure that they sang praise to Vilkata.

And the earth below the moving firebrands, and the sky above them, were no longer fully dark; the greater fire of dawn was on its way.

It was enough, it was more than enough, to turn the retreat into a mere scramble for survival. Even if the gods did not come soon to the Dark King's aid, daylight would; daylight would end the confusion in Vilkata's camp, let his people see how few they really fought against. Whether the scramble for escape was ordered or not, it was already under way.

Many of the city's defenders were able to get back into the tunnel before the tunnel was discovered by Vilkata's people, and a concerted effort made by them to block its entrance. Ben was just a bit too late to be able to use the tunnel, and Mark was later still.

By chance, perhaps, the two things on which the Dark King's hopes depended came back to him almost simultaneously, even as they had been taken: the Mindsword, and his demonic powers of sight. As the first shouts were going up from some of his people near his tent proclaiming victory over the raiders, his hand fell at last on the black hilt. The Sword was still lying where he had left it, undisturbed and unseen, while fighting raged around it. And at the same time the demon, able now to return to duty, brought back Vilkata's sight. His first view was of the Sword in front of him, the column of fire that was his usual vision of the blade now muffled and enfolded within the leather sheath.

The Sword once more in his hand, the Dark King ordered his vision expanded. He got a good look at the partial ruin and still widespread confusion that prevailed around him in his camp. His chief human subordinates were just discovering that he was missing. They were unsure whether he was still alive, and many of them, Vilkata was convinced, were hoping that he was not.

That would change drastically, as soon as he showed them the Blade again. He got to his feet. Now that he could see, it was easy to disentangle himself from fallen fabric. If he had believed in thanking gods, he would have thanked them now.

The Dark King's sense of triumphant survival, of being indestructible, was short lived. Haggard in the early daylight, knowing that he must look weakened and distraught, afraid of trying to seek sleep again, afraid as well of appearing tired or uncertain in front of his subordinates, Vilkata used his private powers of magic to chastise his returning demons. Where they had been, they could not or would not say.

It was different when he demanded to know from them what power had been able to drive them so completely and easily away. Then they responded sullenly that it was the name of the Emperor that had been used against them.

"The Emperor! Are you joking?" But even as he said the words, Vilkata realized that they were not. In his own long study of magic and the world, he had from time to time encountered hints of genuine Imperial power; hints and suggestions and too, of a connection between the present Emperor and the being called Ardneh, the Dead God of two thousand years ago, still worshipped by the ignorant masses. Those hints and suggestions Vilkata had long chosen to ignore.

The Dark King punished his demons, and constrained them as best he could to serve him faithfully from now on. Then he went, exhausted as he was, to confer again with his human wizards, who after the night just passed were quite exhausted too.

The magicians pulled long faces when their lord mentioned the Emperor's name to them. But they had to admit that there might be some truth to the claim of driving demons away by such a means.

Vilkata demanded, "Then why cannot we use it too?"

"We are none of us the Emperor's children, Sire."

"His children? I should hope not. Are you mad?" The term "Emperor's child" was commonly used in a proverbial way, to describe the poor, the orphaned, the unfortunate.

Before the subject could be pursued any farther, there arrived a distraction. It was welcomed heartily, at least at first, by the magicians; and it came in the form of the morning's first flying messenger, bearing news that the Master of the Beasts thought too important to be delayed. It told Vilkata that the Silver Queen's host had now actually been sighted, marching against his rear. This time, Vilkata was assured, the report was genuine.

The observed strength of the army of the Silver Queen was not enough in itself to give the Dark King much real concern. But there was the dread Sword that he knew she carried; and, perhaps equally disquieting, the thought that her timely presence here might well mean that his enemies had worked out some effective plan of co-operation against him.

This last suspicion was strengthened when the Tasavaltan army was also reported to be now on the march, and also approaching Tashigang. Rostov would make a formidable opponent. But it would be a day or two yet, according to report, before his army would be on the scene.

And there was Vulcan—Vulcan was now almost at hand. It struck Vilkata more forcefully now than ever before, that the gods were often stupid, or at least behaved as if they were, which in practice of course came to the same thing.

Holding the Mindsword drawn and ready in his hand, the Dark King rode out to confront this deity who said that he had come to do him honor.

Riding a little ahead of a little group of trembling human aides, his vision provided by a demon now equally tremulous with fear, Vilkata flashed the Mindsword over his head. At the same time he cried out in a loud voice, demanding the Smith's obedience.

Vulcan's first answer was a knowing grin, shattering in its implications. Then the god laughed at the human he had once been forced to worship.

With a wicked gleam in his huge eyes, Vulcan brandished the smoldering tree-trunk that once had been a torch, and announced that he meant to have revenge for that earlier humiliation.

"Did your scouts and spies, little man, take seriously what I shouted to them about my coming here to do you honor? Good! For as soon as I have time, I mean to do you honor in an unprecedented way. Ah, yes.

"I am a god, little man. Remember? And *Shieldbreaker* is now in my hand! Can you understand what that means? I, who forged it, know. It means I am immune to all other weapons, including your Mindsword. There is no power on earth that can oppose me now."

The Dark King, as usual at his bravest when things seemed most desperate, glared right back at the god, and nursed a silent hope that Doomgiver in some human hand might still bring this proud being down. Or Farslayer . . . then he saw another sheath at Vulcan's belt, another black hilt, and he knew a sinking moment of despair.

Vulcan, taking his time, had yet a little more to say. He was going to have his revenge on Vilkata, but not just yet. "First of all, little man, there are more Swords that I must gather. Just to be sure . . . therefore I claim this city and all its contents for my own. And all its people. They will wish that Mars still lived, when my rule begins among them."

And the god turned his back on the King, and marched off to claim his city. However many companions the Smith had had when he came over the horizon, he was now down to just one, a four-armed male god that Vilkata was unable to identify offhand. Not, he supposed, that it much mattered.

As long as Vilkata was actually in Vulcan's presence, he had been able to confront the Smith bravely enough. But when the confrontation was over, the man was left physically shaking. Still, in a way he was almost glad that Vulcan was now openly his enemy. Always, in the past, it had taken a supreme challenge of some kind to rouse Vilkata to his greatest efforts and achievements. When he knew a crisis was approaching, fear gnawed at him maddeningly, and sometimes came near to disabling him. But when the crisis arrived, then he was at his best.

As was the case now. Rejoining the main body of his army, he called his staff together and issued orders firmly. In a new, bold voice, the Dark King commanded them to abandon the siege that they had scarcely yet begun. Once more he set his whole vast host in motion, turning it to meet the Silver Queen and Soulcutter.

Vulcan's turn would come, and soon. There were still certain weapons to which even a god armed with the Sword of Force would not be immune, the tools of boldness and intelligence. Meanwhile, for the time being, Vilkata would abandon the city of Tashigang to the gods.

CHAPTER 17

In the hour before dawn, at a time when two hundred of the loyal defenders of Tashigang were fighting outside the walls, there was treachery in the Lord Mayor's palace. Money changed hands, and weapons flashed, in a corridor on an upper floor, where one room had been made into a cell for holding an important prisoner. Chairman and High Priest Hyrcanus of the Blue Temple was freed, in steps of bribery and violence.

The move to rescue Hyrcanus was planned and executed by his immediate subordinates in the Blue Temple, as part of a general insurrection, in accordance with the High Priest's own previous orders. The intention was to seize control of the city, and welcome in the Dark King and his army.

Attempts by the Blue Temple Guard to seize the walls and gates from inside were unsuccessful. The concurrent try to assassinate the Lord Mayor failed also, nor were the Blue Temple raiders able to capture the palace—not all of the Watch there were easily subverted or taken by surprise. And Hyrcanus was wounded in his escape, so that he had to be half carried, gasping and ashen-faced, back to the Blue Temple's local headquarters on a street not far away.

Once there, propped up on a couch while a surgeon worked on him, the Chairman demanded to be brought up to date on how the situation stood, inside the city and out. When his aides had informed him as best they could, one of his first orders was to dispatch a company of thirty Blue Temple Guardsmen against the House of Courtenay. Their orders were to take or destroy the building, and seize whatever Swords and other useful items they could discover—along with any available gold and other valuables, of course. They were also to take the important inhabitants of the house prisoner if possible, or kill them as second choice; and in general to crush that place as a possible center of resistance.

Then Hyrcanus began to lay his plans to attack the walls and gates once more.

When the first Blue Temple raid struck the palace, in the hour before dawn, Baron Amintor was waiting in a ground floor room for a good chance to see the Mayor privately. When the Baron saw the Guard in its capes of blue and gold come swirling in to the attack, he immediately decided that he could best serve his Queen's interests and his own by remaining alive and active in the city, whatever the outcome of this particular skirmish might prove to be. The fate of the palace and the Mayor still hung in the balance when Amintor prudently retired, and set out through the streets to carry warning to the House of Courtenay. He of course remembered that that was where the young man named Denis lived, who was supposed to be able to set a counterattack of looters in motion against the Blue Temple.

When the Baron reached his destination—not without a minor adventure or two along the way—he found the House already on the alert, its doors and windows sealed. It took him some time and effort, arguing and cajoling, to get himself admitted to speak with someone in authority.

Once inside, he found himself face to face with the tiny woman who had been introduced to him at the palace as the Lady Sophie. Now, surrounded by her own determined-looking retainers, she received his warning with evident suspicion, which he in turn accepted philosophically.

"I can only suggest, Madam, that you wait and see if I am right. Wait not in idleness, of course; order your affairs as if the Blue Temple were indeed leading a revolt. I will await the result with confidence."

"You will await the result in a room by yourself. Jord, Tamir, disarm him and lock him in that closet."

The Baron's capacity for philosophical acceptance became somewhat strained; but at the moment he had no real choice.

The attack by the Blue Temple against the house began presently, just as the Baron had predicted, with fire and sword and axe against the walls and doors and windows. But the attackers met fierce resistance from the start. Brickbats and scalding water were dumped on them from the flat roof, and the first window that they managed to break open immediately sprouted weapons, like teeth in a warbeast's mouth.

Denis was not there to aid in the defense. Barbara had taken the Baron's warning seriously enough to dispatch the young man with orders to put into operation whatever looting counterattack he could. The street connections made in his early life ought to serve him well in the attempt.

And even a feint, or the suggestion of an attack, might serve as well as the real thing. In a city this big, the Blue Temple vaults must hold vast treasure; and Denis had already begun to spread among the city's street people the rumor that the Blue Temple's main hoard, an agglomeration of wealth well beyond the capacity of most people to comprehend, had already been moved into Tashigang for safekeeping. It was unlikely that even a large mob could succeed in looting the Temple here, but even the threat ought to make the misers squirm and roar, and pull in their claws to defend that which they valued more than their own lives and limbs.

As the direct attack on her own house began, Barbara's first act was to see to it that her daughter, with Kuan-yin as caretaker and Jord as personal bodyguard, was put into the safest and strongest room available.

Then Barbara ran upstairs to get Townsaver. If this warning and attack were only part of an elaborate hoax to discover where it was hidden, the Baron was safely locked up now, and would never see. A few days ago the Lord Mayor, perhaps trusting the security of this house as much or more than that of his own palace, had asked Master and Lady Courtenay to keep it here.

She was still climbing stairs when a great crash from below told her that a door had somehow already been broken in. Smoke and the cries and clash of battle rose from below, as Barbara knelt to bring the great Sword out of its hiding place under her bedroom floor.

Fighting nearby, threatening innocent noncombatants in their home, had wakened the Sword of Fury already. The weighty steel arose with magical ease and lightness in her grip, the Sword already making its preliminary faint millsaw whine. For a moment as she held it, there crossed Barbara's mind the thought of Mark's hands, a small boy's hands then, the first time he had held this Sword, his grip no stronger then perhaps than hers was now upon this very hilt . . . she was already hurrying back toward the stairs.

From below there sounded a new crash, a shout of triumph in the invaders' voices.

Their joy would be short lived. In Barbara's hands, Townsaver screamed exultantly, and pulled her running down the stairs.

CHAPTER 18

Ben, caught in Vilkata's camp when the retreat turned into a desperate scramble for survival, bulled his way into the fighting at the mouth of the no-longer-secret tunnel. But it was quickly obvious that the tunnel was now hopelessly blocked as a means of escape. Having no other real choice, he promptly committed himself to the river instead. Many other bodies, alive and dead, were afloat in the Corgo already. All of them, swimming or bobbing, would eventually reach one or another of the great water-gates that pierced the city's walls only a few hundred meters downstream.

Ben splashed and waded and swam his way well out into the current, trying to avoid the hail of missiles, slung stones and arrows, now being launched by enemy troops along the bank. The steadily growing lightness of the eastern sky brightened the water as well. The enemy certainly had the tunnel now. Not that it was going to do them any good as an invasion route; it had been designed for complete and easy blockage at the point where it approached the walls, and also at the inner end, almost below the palace.

The bottom fell off steeply under Ben as he moved out from the shore. And now he had to slip out of his partial armor, and drop his heavier weapons, strong swimmer though he was, if he was going to keep from drowning.

He swam downstream, missiles still pattering like heavy hail upon the water's surface round him. He went under water for a while, still swimming, and came up for air and swam again. The high walls rose up before him swiftly; the river ran fast here, and swept him down upon them. The gray-brown of their hardened granite was brightening in the new daylight. Now Ben could see that this portion of the walls, along with the upstream water-gates, was being manned in force by the Watch in gray-green uniforms. More of the Watch were down at water level, just inside the gate ahead of him, admitting one at a time through a turnstile arrangement the returning survivors of the sally. There was already enough daylight to let them do this with security.

Ben swam a few more strokes, and then could pull himself up, first on rock and then on steel bars, magically protected against rust. Around him a steady trickle of other survivors were doing the same thing; a bedraggled crew, he thought, but not entirely defeated. He did not see Mark anywhere, but that did not necessarily mean anything.

Once he had been let in through the turnstile, Ben's way led upward, into and behind the wall, along a flight of narrow steps. His last glance at the scene outside the city showed him that Vulcan and some other god, a many-armed being Ben did not recognize, were approaching, now no more than a few hundred meters away.

Others soldiers were stopping on the stairs to watch. Ben, for his part, had had more than enough of confrontations and fighting for a time; he was anxious to get home and see what was happening there.

Among the Watch officers who were seeing to the admission of returning fighters, confusion reigned. It was the situation more often than not in any military, Ben had observed. Someone was announcing that the survivors were to stand by for debriefing and then reassignment on the walls. But someone else, not an officer, passed on a rumor that the Blue Temple was in revolt, and the House of Courtenay under attack within the city. Ben on hearing this ducked out and hurried through the streets toward his home. In the confusion no one appeared to notice his departure.

The streets of Tashigang were largely empty, what stores and shops he passed were all of them closed and shuttered. Once he observed, a few streets away, a running group that looked like some detached fragment of a mob. Ben stayed out of their way, whatever they were about.

Tired and generally battered, though essentially unhurt, he stumbled at last into the familiar street. There was his house, at least it was still standing, and his heart leaped up in preliminary joy; this was followed in a moment by new anxiety, when he saw how the building was scorched and still smoking above ground level, and how the windows and doors to the street were battered. Now he could see part of what looked like a bucket brigade of his faithful workers, stretching between the house and the nearby river.

Ben ran panting through the broken front door, into the main room of the ground floor, and stopped. Carnage was everywhere. Amid broken furniture and weapons were piled hewed and mangled bodies, the great majority of them wrapped in cloaks that had once been blue and gold.

Barbara, elated, looking unhurt, came bounding from somewhere to greet him.

"Townsaver," she explained, succinctly, indicating the condition and contents of the room. "They started a fire, and broke in . . . but then some of them were glad to get away."

Then, in sudden new worry, she was looking behind her husband, at the empty street. "Where's Mark?"

"I don't know. We were separated. He may be all right." And from the way the question had been asked, Ben understood that she would have preferred him to be the one still unaccounted for.

Vulcan, standing waist-deep in the swift Corgo, was unhurriedly rending open one of the huge water-gates of steel and iron bars. He might of course have climbed the city wall, or flown over it somehow, but this mode of entry struck him as more appropriate. He had made the city his now, and he was going to enter his city through a door.

Shiva, his recently acquired companion, was squatting nearby on the riverbank and watching. The rivets and other members of the gate were breaking one at a time, parting with loud pops as Vulcan bent his strength upon them, the fragments flying now and then like crossbow bolts.

Vulcan was speaking, but, as often, his words were addressed mainly to himself. "If I were capable of mistakes, that would have been one . . . letting my twelve Blades go so meekly, after I had them forged. Giving them away to Hermes like that, to be dealt out to the human vermin for the Game . . . a mistake, yes. But now I'll make no more."

Now Shiva pitched into the river the smoldering treetrunk that he had still been carrying. The huge spar of wood went into the water with a steamy splash.

As if in reply, there was a swirling in the water, and the nebulous figure of Hades appeared just above its surface. On the high city wall there were a few human screams. The few human watchers who had remained in the immediate area were quickly gone, getting themselves out of sight of that god's face, of which it was said that no man or woman might look on it, and live thereafter.

Hades said, in his formless voice, that he had come to bring a warning to his old comrade Vulcan. It was that anyone who used Farslayer could never triumph thereby in the end.

Vulcan glared at him. "To a true god, there is no end. Was that a warning, troglodyte, or a threat? If you choose to deal in threats, Farslayer is here at my side again, and as you say, I do not hesitate to use it."

The almost shapeless words of Hades' answer came back to him: *Death and darkness are no more than portions of my domain, Fireworker; such threats do not concern me.*

And again there was a stirring of the river and the earth, and Hades was gone.

Vulcan cast aside the remnants of the gate he had now torn down, and waded through the stone arch it had protected, and went on into the city. From the inside, Tashigang looked about as he had expected; he had heard that this was the largest city that the human vermin had ever built. He noted with indifference that the four-armed god Shiva was still following him.

There was a running human figure nearby, caped in blue and gold, and Vulcan bent down and shot out a hand and scooped the creature up, inflicting minimal damage; he wanted some information from it.

"You, tell me—where is the place you call the House of Courtenay? I hear that they are hiding some of my Swords in there."

He got his directions in a piping voice; the man pointed with the arm that had not been broken by Vulcan's grab.

The Smith let the creature fall, and limped away briskly through the streets. But now Apollo's head loomed over a nearby rooftop.

"Beware, Smith. We must meet and think and try to talk about all this. I am calling a council—"

"Beware yourself. We've met and talked enough, for ages, and got nowhere. And think? Who among us can do that? Maybe you. Who else wants to? I don't. I just want what is mine."

He marched on, moving quickly in his uneven gait. A street or two later, there was another interruption. Atop an indented curve of the great city wall, which was here only about as high as Vulcan's head, a human in green and gray was brandishing some unknown Sword, as if daring the gods to attack him. It must be a Sword in which the man had confidence.

Vulcan detoured to confront this man. Shiva, interested, was staying right with him.

The tiny teeth of the man on the wall were chattering. But he got out the words he was trying to say: "This is Doomgiver! Stay back!"

"Doomgiver, hey?" That particular Sword had been, in the back of Vulcan's thoughts, a lingering concern. Wishing to take no chances, he aimed a hard swing with the Sword of Force. Its thudding sound built in a moment to explosive volume. There was a dazzling flash, a thunderclap of sound, as the two Blades came in contact, opposing each other directly.

Vulcan stood there, blinking at ruin and destruction. A chunk of stone as big as his fist had been blasted out of the wall before his eyes. Of the human being who had been standing on the wall, holding the opposing Sword, there was almost nothing left. Although Shieldbreaker appeared the same as ever, there appeared to be no trace of Doomgiver.

"Doomgiver, gone? Just like that? No, there must be some pieces here; I'll find them, and carry them back to my forge, and make it new!"

But that proved to be impossible. Though Vulcan diminished himself to half his previous height, the better to search for tiny scattered objects, he could not turn up even the smallest fragment of the shattered blade. He found only the black hilt, bearing the simple white circle, a line returning on itself. The Sword of Justice was no more.

He told himself that he might still try to recast it, some day, beginning the job from the beginning again; but he was not sure now that he remembered how he had accomplished it the first time. And anyway, what need had he of a Sword of Justice now? Just twenty years ago, things had been simpler; all the gods knew what they were doing then, and what they were supposed to do; and no human being had yet thought of challenging their rule.

Vulcan was angry, as he went limping on toward the House of Courtenay.

Over rooftops he saw the heads of Apollo, Zeus, and Diana, come to chide and challenge him again.

Diana demanded: "Why did you strike down Mars?"

He snarled at them all: "Because he insulted me, and bothered me! Who needed Mars, anyway? What was he good for? And as for the Great Dog, I'm not even sure he's dead. I wasted no time on him, one way or the other."

As soon as Vulcan swelled himself back to his usual height, and waved Shieldbreaker at them, the protestors fell back out of his way, as he had known they would.

"By my forge, I think that this must be the house."

The four-story building, standing close by one of the branches of the river, had already been attacked by someone else, and was still smoking. On the flat roof of the house, amid vines and flowers and garden paths, a human stood. The little creature was strong and bulky for a mere man, and held another Sword in hand.

Shiva pounced forward, meaning to take that weapon for his own. He ignored Vulcan's rumbled warning.

The Sword in the man's hand screamed with its own power. By the shrill note Vulcan recognized it, at once and with satisfaction. Townsaver!

The god of the four arms screamed too, in pain, not triumph, and pulled back a badly mangled hand. The injured god ran reeling, devastating small buildings as he crashed into them. His screams continued without pause, as his bounding, bouncing flight took him away to the city walls again, and over the walls and out of sight.

"Hah, the fool!" Vulcan grumbled to himself in satisfaction. "Now I'll take that Sword too. Or else see it destroyed, like the other."

He stepped close to the man on the roof, and slashed quickly with the Sword of Force, right to left and back again. With the motion of his arm his right fist struck a corner of the building, close to the part of the roof where the man was standing. As the two Swords came in contact, and the Sword of Fury disappeared in another explosive flash, the building opened up under the impact of Vulcan's fist, and the man who had been holding Townsaver dropped down inside the walls, disappearing in a cloud of dust and a small landslide of debris.

"That must have been Townsaver, by its voice . . . but, by the Spear of Mars, it's gone now too! Damnation to all human vermin who destroy my property! But there may be other Swords in this nest. He who told me said more than one."

Vulcan considered the battered structure, its roof terrace gaping at the corner where his fist had struck, its lower floors blackened on the outside and still smoldering where someone had earlier tried an assault by fire. It would be easy enough to pull the house down, but it would be awkward to sift the whole pile of wreckage for his Swords afterward. No.

After taking thought for a few more moments, the Smith shrank himself once more, this time to little more than human size. Now he ought to be able to enter most of their rooms and passages. The shrinkage of course left his strength undiminished, and had the extra advantage of making it easier for him to grip Shieldbreaker's merely man-sized hilt.

He kept the Sword of Force in hand and ready, just in case the building when entered might contain surprises.

There was no need to kick the front door in; someone had already taken care of that. Inside, he encountered first a pile of ugly human dead; nothing that he wanted there. He could tell now that there were some live ones also present in the building, but so far they were all trying to hide from him. It didn't matter what they did. He'd seek out what he wanted.

This was some kind of human workshop here. It was well stocked with weapons, but none of divine manufacture.

The Smith shouted: "You might as well bring them out to me! I forged them, all of them, and they are mine!"

Next he kicked open a wall, behind which, his senses told him, there was some kind of a hidden door—but all he uncovered, all that had been hidden here for safety, were a plump human girl and the small child she was trying to shelter.

"Hah! This is their treasure?" The ways and thoughts of humankind were sometimes small beneath all Vulcan's comprehension.

Now a light weight of some kind fell from somewhere to land on Vulcan's neck, and it took him a moment to realize that it was in fact a living human body. A man had just jumped deliberately upon him, from above and behind. A lone man, whose weaponless arms, locked around Vulcan's mighty neck, were straining in an evident effort to strangle him.

The god laughed at this puny assault; laughed at it, when he got around to noticing it for what it was. At first it did not even distract him fully from his search. The Swords, the Swords . . . there ought to be at least one more of them around here somewhere. . . .

He would have them all, or he would destroy them all, to perfect and insure his ultimate power over the other gods and goddesses. So, they thought the Game had been abandoned, did they? Well, it was over now, or very nearly over. But not abandoned. No. He, the Smith, the cripple, was winning it, he had almost won. . . . and, just to be sure of course, he needed the Swords to perfect his power over men and women too. He wanted at some time to be able to put Shieldbreaker down and rest; but he thought that time would not come while even one of the other eleven remained in other hands than his, or unaccounted for.

He had turned away from the girl and the baby, ignoring them even as he forgot the rag of living human flesh that was a large, strong man still hanging on his neck. He would brush that away the next time that he thought of it.

Now Vulcan's progress was blocked by a strong, closed door, and he grabbed with his free hand at a projecting corner of the doorframe, intending to tear the whole framework loose.

But he met startling resistance. Here was mere wood and stone, and of no heroic dimensions, refusing to yield to him.

Still, such was the Smith's impatience that his first concern was still getting through the door, and not wondering why he could not. Instinctively he used Shieldbreaker on the door, which now gave way quite satisfactorily.

Irritated by the delay, and more so by the fact that the room uncovered this time was empty, Vulcan became more fully aware of another irritation, the man who was still hanging on his back. The god, reaching back with his free hand to peel the annoyance off, achieved a belated recognition.

"What's this, human? Grown back your right arm, have you, since last we met? Well, we can fix that. . . ."

But for some reason the puny human body would not peel free. Applying the best grip that he could one-handed, without setting Shieldbreaker down, Vulcan again had the curious sensation of being almost powerless. The link of those two human arms that held him would not part.

It was almost as if the chronic lameness in his leg was growing worse, spreading to other parts of his body. The Smith did not care in the least for the sensation of being without strength. It was becoming really alarming. Not only a stone wall, a wooden door, but even flesh was able to resist him now.

While all the time, in his right hand which felt stronger than ever, the limitless power of Shieldbreaker tapped out its readiness to be used.

". . . we can fix that like *this* . . ."

And Vulcan, reaching behind himself somewhat awkwardly with the

Sword, moved it to cut loose the clinging human flesh. Awkward, yes. His hands that had worked with divine skill to forge this weapon and its peers felt clumsy now when he tried to use it behind his back.

"Aaahrr!" All he had accomplished was to wound himself slightly in the neck.

He aimed his next blind cut more cautiously—*there.*

That time, Vulcan assured himself, the Sword had, it must have, passed right through the body of the clinging man. The trouble was that the man still clung on as tight as ever, giving no indication of being killed. The muscles of those human arms even tightened a little more. Their force should have been inconsequential in terms of what was needed to choke a god, but Vulcan imagined that his own breathing had become a shade more difficult, enough to be annoying, anyway.

Why was he, a god, worrying about breathing? But suddenly it seemed to matter.

The human's mortal breath, gasping with exertion but still full of life, sawed in Vulcan's ear. "I was there with you when you forged this weapon, God of Fire. My blood is in it, and part of my life. I know it—"

Standing in the middle of a large room, beside a fireless forge, Vulcan braced himself and strained with his left hand again. But still he could not break the other's grip.

"—know it as well as you do, Firegod. Better, maybe. I can feel the truth of Shieldbreaker, now that it has touched me again. You cannot hurt me with it, as long as I have no weapon of my own."

By now Vulcan's search for other Swords had been forgotten. This foolish business of letting a human being attack him had gone too far, he had to end it. He had to rid himself of this clinging *thing,* and do it swiftly.

But even as he strove to do so, another human, approaching unnoticed by the god in his distraction, leaped upon him. This one was a tiny female with dark hair. Vulcan moved just as she jumped at him, so that she almost missed. But still she had him by one ankle now, and she was trying—who would have believed such a thing?—to tip him over.

Vulcan used the Sword on her. Or tried to use it rather. He saw with his own eyes how the blade of Shieldbreaker passed through her body, or gave the illusion of doing so, again and again, without leaving the least trace of damage after it.

With his Sword perversely useless now, against this fragile flesh that grappled with him, the Smith let out a great roar, of mental pain and choking rage. He would have thrown the Sword away now, but it refused to separate from his hand. His fingers would not release their grip upon the hilt.

All right then, he'd use it, in the only way it would still work. He laid about him with the Sword, knocking down furniture and walls, sending bricks and timber and plaster flying. Dragging his two human tormentors helplessly with him, he chewed a passage through the ground floor of their house. He'd bring it all down on their heads, these useless human vermin.

A new idea came to him, and he tried to increase his stature, to swell himself once more to true god-size. Appallingly, he found that he could not. All the powers that had once been his were shrinking, concentrating, being driven minute by minute into the one focus of his perfect Sword, the blade of Shieldbreaker itself and his right arm and hand that held it.

Now, other humans, emboldened by the survival of the first two, were coming to join in the attack. Human hands fastened on Vulcan's left arm, more human hands on his other leg. Someone's hand snatched Farslayer from its sheath at his belt; not that he'd really dreamed of wasting it on any of these puny . . .

More people were coming at him, a grappling swarm of them. Now they were strong and numerous enough to drag him against his will. They were forcing him a step at a time out of the house, going through some of the very openings he'd just created. He lashed out wildly with the Sword, and more wood and dust and tile came crashing down, on Vulcan's head and all around him, not bothering him much but laying one or two of his assailants low. Through the chokehold on his neck he gurgled minor triumph.

Still more and more of the vermin came pouring out of their holes, now daring to attack him. Jord cried a warning to one of these, but too late. The man had leaped at Vulcan, swinging an axe at the Smith's head. Shieldbreaker tapped once and brushed the weapon away, along with the arms of the man who had been holding it.

Another man tried to grab Vulcan by the Swordarm. Still too much power there, too much by far, perhaps more power than ever. The man was flung off like mud from a wheel, to break his body on the wall.

But still the other people held on. Half a dozen of them were gripping the god now, each of the vermin seeming to gain determination from the others, each of them sapping some minute portion of his strength.

Vulcan roared out threats, though he knew that it was now too late for threatening. Words and yells did him no good. He fell, and rolled upon the floor, brushing off some of his assailants, crushing others, damaging them all, savaging those who persisted in clinging on. Yet persist they did, and still more came, out of the wreckage of their house. As soon as he rid himself of one, one or two more jumped on him, coming at him endlessly out of the rooms and ruins.

A crossbow bolt came streaking at him, launched by some concealed and unwise hand. Shieldbreaker tapped once again, unhurriedly, and shattered the missile in midair. Fragments of the bolt drew blood from the people who were wrestling with the god.

Jord, in a weakening voice, cried warning once again: "No weapons! No weapons, and we can win!"

Concentrated now in the one Sword was all of Vulcan's power, and all his hope. He knew that he must win with it, or die. Once more, then, behind his back, carefully and hard—there, that must have cut the pestiferous human leader clean in two!

But it had not. Or if it had, the man had been able to survive such treatment handily. The human's legs and feet still behaved as if they were connected to his brain, and he rode the god as if Vulcan were no more than a riding beast.

And Vulcan could feel a new pain in his back, and more of his own blood; once more he'd done himself some damage with the Sword.

Still he fought on, straining to stab, slice up, destroy, the desperately wrestling human horde. They clung to him and submitted to being battered when he rolled on the ground again. When he was back on his feet, they dragged him about, and would not be shaken off. He slipped and fell, in a patch of his own blood.

And now they picked him up.

Now in their score of hands they bore him, raving, thrashing, screaming, outside the building, and he could no longer try to bring it down upon them. The arc of the Sword of Force flashed at them, passed through their bodies as through phantoms, leaving them unharmed.

The original grip on Vulcan's neck was really choking now. Every muscle of his body was growing weaker and weaker—except those in his right arm. That limb felt more and more powerful, but all that it could do was wield the Sword, and in combat against unarmed flesh the Sword was useless. Meanwhile, Vulcan's blood drained from his self-inflicted wounds.

He relaxed suddenly, playing dead.

In a moment, stunned and battered themselves, the people had all let go of him.

He leaped up, raging, wise enough now to use his first free effort to throw the Sword away from him. But in the presence of his enemies it would not let him go.

A moment later, a huge man, who had just come stumbling out of the half-ruined house, had hurled himself alone at Vulcan, and brought the god down with a tackle.

And then they were all on him again.

Now another group of people, these in white robes, recognizable to the struggling Smith as servants of the Dead God, Ardneh, were running into the street before the house. These, coming late to the scene, were clamoring in protest. From their words Vulcan could tell that they thought they were witnessing a lynching, a mob attack upon some poor helpless man.

The people who were grappling the Smith down tried to explain. "Completely mad, he thinks he's Vulcan." And a kind of exhausted laugh went round among them.

An aged priestess of Ardneh, looking wise and kind, came to take the useless Sword out of the madman's grasp. It came to her easily out of his cramped grip.

"To keep you from hurting yourself, poor fellow, or anyone else . . . my, what a weapon." The priestess blinked at the Sword. "This must be put away, in safety somewhere."

"I'll take it," said Ben.

The old woman looked into the huge man's eyes, and sighed. "Yes, you take it. There is no one better here, I think. Now we must bind this poor fellow for a while, so he does no more harm. How strong he is!— ah, such a waste. But these cords will hold him; carefully, for we must do it out of love."

CHAPTER 19

In all of his fifty thousand and more years of life, the creature named Draffut, the Lord of Beasts, had never been closer to death than he was now. Yet life, his almost inextinguishable life, remained in him. He clung to it, if for no other reason than because there was an injured human being nearby, who cried out from time to time in his own pain. Draffut, still true to his own nature, felt compelled to find a way to help that man.

But he was unable to do anything to help the man, unable even to move enough to help himself. The very stream that laved his wounds seemed to be slowly drawing his life away instead of assisting him to heal.

It was daylight—whether of the last day of the fight, or some day after that, he was not sure—when he became aware that another presence, intelligent but not human, was approaching him.

The Beastlord opened his eyes slowly. A goddess, recognizable to him as Aphrodite, was standing above him at a little distance, looking down at him where he still lay in the mud at the water's edge.

Aphrodite was standing just where Vulcan had stood, and there was a

Sword in her hands too. But Draffut knew at once that this was different than Vulcan's approach, and he felt no fear as she drew near him, and raised the Sword.

It struck at him, and he cried out with a pang of new life, as sharp as pain. "Woundhealer," he said, suddenly strong enough to talk again. "And you are Aphrodite."

"And you are the Healer," she said. "Therefore I think it right that you should have this Sword. Humans quarrel and fight over this one, even as they do with all the others. So I took it back from them. And I am weary of trying to decide what to do with it next—so much love allows but little time for pleasure."

With a motion marked by a slight endearing awkwardness, she dropped the Sword of Mercy on the surface of the mud beside him.

Draffut, able to move again, put out his huge hand, weakly and slowly, and touched the blade. "I thank you, goddess, for your gift of life."

"There are many who have life because of me . . . ah, already I feel better too, to be rid of it. But that Sword suits you, I think. You are not much like me."

"Except in one way. We are both of us creations of humanity. But I only in part. And out of their science, not their dreams. I will still exist, if—when—humanity changes its collective mind about me."

The goddess tossed her perfect hair—and was it pure gold, or raven black? "You say that about us, but I don't believe it. If humanity created us, the gods and goddesses, then who could possibly have created them? But never mind, I am tired of all this philosophy and argument. There seems to be no end to it of late. I think the world is changing."

"Again. It always does." And now Draffut was dragging himself to his feet. The mud that had caked upon his fur when he was dying was falling off now, crumbling and twisting even as it fell, moving in the glow of the renewed life within him.

Painfully, a stooped, slow giant carrying the Sword of Mercy, he began to make his way across the muddy ground toward the injured man.

Rostov listened long and intently to what his latest and best source of information had to tell him about what was going on inside the walls of Tashigang, and what had happened last night during the outrageous, heroic sally against the Dark King's camp.

One of Rostov's patrols had luckily picked up the young man, who was carrying Coinspinner in his right hand, in the garden of one of the abandoned suburban villas along the Corgo.

"Trust a bad copper to turn up," the General had growled at first sight of him; then he had allowed his steel-bearded face to split in a tight grin. "The Princess will be anxious to see you, Mark. No, I shouldn't call you that, should I? What's the proper term of address for an Emperor's son?"

"For . . . who? The Princess, you say?" the wounded youth had answered weakly. "Where is she?"

"Not far away. Not far." Rostov still grinned. He could begin to see now what the Princess had seen all along in this tough young man. Who, as it now turned out, not only had good stuff in him, but Imperial blood. That was evidently, in the rarefied realm of magic and politics where these things were decided, something of acceptable importance. Rostov was glad—it was time that Tasavalta had some sturdy warrior monarchs on the throne again.

On a field not many kilometers from Tashigang, the armies of Yambu and Vilkata confronted each other, in a dawn dimmed almost to midnight by an impending thunderstorm. The Silver Queen was preparing herself to draw Soulcutter. She knew that she would have to do so before the Dark King brought the Mindsword into range; if not, her army would be lost to her, and she herself perhaps maddened into becoming Vilkata's slave.

She had recently received a strange report: first the god Vulcan had been seen inside the city, bound helplessly by the gentle hands of white-robed priestesses and priests; and then he was gone again. Some said that an angry unarmed mob had seized the Smith, and the wooden frame he had been bound to, and had thrown him in the river, and he had floated out of the city through the lower gates.

Queen Yambu thought: and is the world now to belong to us humans, after all? If we can overthrow the gods, and kill them—possibly. Not that they had ever bothered to rule the world when it was theirs. Perhaps it has been ours all along.

Without really being startled, she became aware that a man was standing in the doorway of her tent, and gazing in at her impertinently. She assumed he was one of her officers, and was about to speak sharply to him for staring at her thus, when she realized that he was not one of her own men at all. The words died on her lips.

His face was in shadow, and not until she shifted her own position did she see the mask. "You," she said.

He came in uninvited, pulled the mask off and helped himself to a seat, grinning at her lightly. He had not changed at all. Outside she could still hear the sentries walking their rounds, unaware that anyone had passed them.

The Emperor said to her: "I still have not had my answer."

It took the Queen a moment to understand what he was talking about. "You once asked me to marry you. Can that be what you mean?"

"It can. Didn't you realize that I was going to insist on an answer, sooner or later?"

"No, I really didn't. Not after . . . what happened to our daughter. Have you forgotten about her? Or is this visit just another of your insane jokes?"

"I have not forgotten her. She has been living with me." When Queen Yambu stared at him, he went on calmly: "Ariane was badly hurt, about four years ago, as you know. But she's much better now. She and I have not talked about you much, but I think that she might want to meet you again some day."

The Silver Queen continued to stare at her former lover. At last she said, "My reports, and I have reason to trust them, said that Ariane was killed, in the treasure-dungeon of the Blue Temple."

The Emperor scowled his distaste for that organization. "Many have died, in that . . . place. But Ariane did not die there. Even though the young men with her at the time were also sure that she was dead. One of those young men is my son, did you know that? I like to take care of my children, whenever I can. She is not dead."

And still Queen Yambu stared at him. She could not shake off her suspicion that this was all one of his jokes, perhaps the prelude to a hideous revenge—she had never been sure, even when they had been lovers, whether he was a vengeful man or not.

At last her royal poise abandoned her for the moment, and she stammered out: "I—I sold her to the Red Temple."

The frown was turned at her now, and briefly she understood what ancient Imperial power must have been, that Kings and Queens had quaked before it.

"I might have killed you for that, if I had known about it when it happened. But years have passed, and you are sorry for that selling now. She has survived, and so have I. And so have you."

In anger she regained her strength. "I have survived without you, you impossible . . . and you say you want to marry me, still? How do I know you mean what you are saying now?"

"How do you know when to trust anyone, my dear? You'll have to make a choice."

She wanted to cry out that she did not know when to trust anyone; that was her whole problem. "You madman, suppose I were to answer you and tell you yes. Could you defeat the Mindsword for me then?"

"I'll do all I can to help you, if you will be my bride. We'll see about the Mindsword when it comes."

"It's here now. Oh, you bastard. Impossible as always. Leave now. Get out of here, or I'm going to draw Soulcutter." And she put her hand on the unrelieved blackness of that hilt, that rested as always within reach. "And I suppose you'll go on seducing brides, and fathering more bastards, after we are married?"

He said, softly and soberly, "I will be more faithful to you than you can well imagine. I love you; I always have. Why do you think I fought for you, beside you, when you were a girl?"

"I don't believe it, I tell you. I don't believe any of it. Leave now, or I draw Soulcutter."

"It's your Sword, to do with as you will. But I will leave when you decide to draw it."

She started to draw the Sword, and at the same moment called out in a clear voice for her guards. When they came pushing into the tent a moment later, they found their Queen quite alone, and Soulcutter safely in its sheath, though her hand on the hilt was poised as if for action.

The soldiers found themselves staring half-hypnotized at that hand, both of them hoping that they would be out of the tent again before the Sword was drawn; and already in the air around it, around themselves, they thought they could feel the backwash of a wave of emptiness.

Queen Yambu wasted no more time, but gave the orders necessary to get her troops into the state of final readiness for battle. That done, she ordered an advance.

With Vilkata's ranks still no more than barely in sight, she waited in the middle of her own line, mounted on her famous gray warbeast, ready to draw the Sword of—of what? As far as she knew, this one had only one name.

Now the enemy lines were creeping forward. There, in their center, that would be Vilkata himself, waiting for the perfect moment in which to draw the weapon that he was gambling would be supreme.

The hand of Queen Yambu was on her own Sword's hilt. She urged her mount forward, a little. Not yet.

Now.

The Mindsword and Soulcutter were drawn, virtually simultaneously.

Her own first reaction, to the overwhelming psychic impact of her own Sword, was that she wanted to throw it away—but then she did not. Because she could no longer see how throwing it away would make any difference, would matter in the least.

Nor did anything else matter.

Nothing else in the whole universe.

The Mindsword was a distant, irrelevant twinkle, far across the field, beneath the gloom of thunderclouds. While near at hand, around Queen Yambu herself . . .

Those of her own troops who were closest to her had been looking at her when she drew. After that they were indifferent as to where they looked. Around her a wave of lethargy, of supreme indifference, was spreading out, a slow splash in an ink-black pool.

In the distance, but drawing rapidly nearer, a charge was coming. Vilkata's troops, with maddened yells, the fresh inspiration of the Mindsword driving them.

Some of the Queen's soldiers, more and more of them with each passing second, were actually slumping to the ground now, letting their weapons fall from indifferent hands. It appeared that they would be able to put up no resistance, that the Dark King might now be going to win easily.

But of course that did not matter either.

With berserker cries, the first of the Dark King's newly energized fanatics rushed upon them. The defense put up by the soldiers in black and silver was at best half-hearted, and it was weaker the closer they were stationed to their Queen.

But the attackers, Vilkata's men and women, were now entering the region of Soulcutter's dominance. It was their screams of triumph that faltered first, and then the energy with which they plied their weapons. Next their ranks came to a jostling, stumbling halt.

The Queen of Yambu—not knowing, really, why she bothered—slowly raised her eyes. The Sword she held above her head was so dull that it almost hurt the eyes to look at it.

The Sword of Despair—she had thought of the other name for it now. Not that that mattered, either. Not that or anything else.

Why was she bothering to hold the Sword so high? She let her arms slump with its weight. When her warbeast, puzzled and suffering, wanted to move, she let it go, sliding from its back. She stood almost leaning on the Sword now, its point cutting shallowly into the earth.

Nor did any of that really mean anything, as far as she could tell.

The fighting that had begun, sporadically, was dying out. Soulcutter was winning, all across the field. If neither victory nor survival mattered, to anyone, there would be no battle.

Yambu was aware, though only dimly and indifferently, that so far the Dark King's weapon had been able to shield him, and a small group of his followers around him, from Soulcutter's dark, subtle assault.

That group began to charge toward her now, yelling warcries. But its numbers shrank, and shrank more rapidly the closer it came to Queen Yambu. One by one the people in it turned aside from the charge, to sit or kneel or slump to the ground, giving up the effort in despair.

King Vilkata's demons were the last to desert him. And even before that had happened, he himself had given up the attack and was in full flight from the field.

Rostov, out having a personal look around, turned his scouting squadron back when they came to the edge of the field. Ahead of him the General could see what looked to him like the worst slaughter he had ever beheld, in a lifetime spent largely amid scenes of butchery. There were two armies on the field, and as nearly as he could tell from this distance, both of them had been virtually wiped out. But the General turned back, and ordered his soldiers back, not because of what he saw but because of what he felt, what they had all felt when trespassing upon the fringes of that grim arena. Another few steps in that direction, thought Rostov, and he would have been ready to throw down his weapons and his medals and abandon life.

He was wondering what orders to give next, when he saw a giant figure appear in the distance. With swift, powerful, two-legged strides it drew closer, also approaching the field of despair. It was Draffut, called a god by some; although General Rostov had never seen the Lord of Beasts before, who else could this be?

There was someone else; a man-shape, riding familiarly on Draffut's shoulders.

Draffut did not approach Rostov and his scouting detachment, but instead halted at another point on the rim of that terrible battlefield. There the giant stopped, and set down the man who had been riding on his shoulders; and from that point the man alone, a gray-caped figure bearing a bright Sword in hand, walked on alone into the field of doom and silence.

Rostov, puzzled, tried to make out where the man—was he wearing a mask?—was headed. Then the General realized that there was still one other human figure standing on the battlefield—way out there, at its center.

It was the Silver Queen, leaning on the blade that she was too immobilized to cast down. When Rostov and his soldiers saw the Emperor take it from her hands, and sheath it, they could feel how a change for the better came instantly over the nearby world.

The General turned to his troops, shouting: "They're not all dead out there! Some of the Dark King's hellions are starting to wake up already! What're you waiting for, get out there and disarm them while you can!"

EPILOGUE

When the party of the surviving gods in their retreat had climbed above the snow level of the Ludus Mountains, the blind man they carried with them began to curse and rail at them again. He ranted as if they were still under his command; and Vulcan, listening, began to be sorry that he had picked the man up and brought him along.

The Smith still had other company, present intermittently. Graybearded Zeus, proud Apollo, Aphrodite, Hades. They and some others came and went. Hades was, as always, never far from his true domain, the Earth. Diana had walked with them for a while, but had dropped out of the group early, saying only that she heard another kind of call.

Vilkata, the man they had brought with them, was shivering and in rags. The golden circlet had fallen from his head days ago, and his power to command demons had gone with it. He kept groaning, whining that he'd lost his Sword. He was raving now, demanding that food and slaves and wine be brought to him.

Why did I bring him with me? Vulcan pondered once again. The Smith himself had regained some of his strength since the servants of Ardneh, perceiving him as no longer violent and dangerous, had loosed his bonds and let him go. But he was still far from what he once had been, and sometimes he feared that he was dying.

Apollo had told them all several times in the course of the retreat that they were all dying now, or would be soon, himself included. The world had changed again, Apollo said.

The man they carried with them at least gave them all some connection to humanity. Though Vulcan still did not want to admit they needed that.

He said now to the man perched on his shoulder, as if talking to some half-intelligent pet: "We might find some food for you somewhere. But there is no wine—none that you can drink—and certainly no human slaves."

"But I have you as my slaves," the man rasped back. Today his proud voice was weakening rapidly. "And you are gods, and goddesses. Therefore all the Earth is mine."

From behind, Apollo asked: "You cannot feel it, little man?"

"Feel what?" He who had been the Dark King turned his blind face back and forth. In a more lucid voice he demanded: "Where are we?" Then, a moment later, again: "Feel what?"

Apollo said: "That the humans whose dreams created us, and gave us power, are now dreaming differently? That our power, and our lives as well, have been draining from us, ever since we gave you Swords to use?"

Among the gods there were still some who could persuade themselves to argue with this viewpoint. "It's all part of the Game—"

"The Game is over now."

"Over? But who won?"

That one wasn't answered.

"In the mountains, in the upper air, we'll start to feel strong again."

They trudged on, climbed on. The capability of swift effortless flight had once been theirs. Vulcan thought that none of them were starting to feel stronger. In fact the thin air was beginning to hurt his lungs.

He would not have it, would not *allow* it to be so. Bravely he cried out to Apollo: "You still say that we are their creations? Bah! Then who created them?"

Apollo did not reply.

Occasional volcanic rumbles now shook the Earth beneath their feet; here and there subterranean warmth created bare steaming spots of rock amid the snow.

Their flight, their climb, was becoming slower and slower. But it went on. Now where was Aphrodite? Vulcan looked around for her. It was not as if she had departed, in the old, easy way, for somewhere else, he thought; she was simply and truly gone.

He had not seen Hades for a long time, either.

Vilkata sensed something. "Where are you all going?" the man shouted, or tried to shout. "I command you not to disappear. Turn round instead, take me back down to the world of humanity. I'm going to freeze to death up here!"

Vulcan had no wish to put up with the man's noise any longer, or with his weight that seemed to grow and grow; and the god cast the blind, mewing man aside, down a cliff into frozen oblivion, and moved on.

The Smith summoned up his determination, trying now to regain the purpose with which he had begun this climb, long days ago. He mused aloud: "It was near here—near here somewhere—that I built my forge, to make the Swords. I piled up logs, earth-wood, and lit them from the volcanic fires below. If only I could find my forge again—"

Presently he realized that he was now alone, the man having gone down a cliff somewhere, the last of his divine companions having vanished, as if evaporated upon the wind. The last wrangling voice of them had been chilled down to silence.

But not quite the last.

"Then who created THEM?" the Smith bellowed, hurling forth the question like a challenge to the universe, at the top of his aching, newly perishable lungs.

He looked ahead.

There was something, or someone, lying in wait for him, beyond that last convoluted corner of black rock. Some new power, or ancient one, come to claim the world? Or only the wind?

He was afraid to look.

The whole world was cold now. The Smith could feel the awful cold turning against him, feel it as easily and painfully as the weakest human might.

He wanted to look around the corner of the rock, but he could not. He was afraid. Just in front of him, volcanic heat and gas belched up, turning snow and ice into black slush in a moment.

Vulcan lurched forward, seeking warmth. He fell on his hands and knees. Dying, in what seemed to him the first cold morning of the world, he groped for fire.

THE END